FAMILY FORTUNES

Louis
Auchincloss

FAMILY
FORTUNES

The Rector of Justin
The House of Five Talents
Portrait in Brownstone

Galahad Books • New York

Published in 1993 by
Galahad Books
A division of Budget Book Service, Inc.
386 Park Avenue South
New York, NY 10016

Galahad Books is a registered trademark of Budget Book Service, Inc.
Reprinted by special arrangement with Houghton Mifflin, Inc.

Library of Congress Catalog Card Number: 93-70380
ISBN: 0-88365-825-9
Designed by Hannah Lerner

Printed in the United States of America.

Contents

The Rector of Justin

For Two John Winthrops
My Son and Brother

1

BRIAN'S JOURNAL

SEPTEMBER 10, 1939. I have always wanted to keep a journal, but whenever I am about to start one, I am dissuaded by the idea that it is too late. I lose heart when I think of all the fascinating things I could have described had I only begun earlier. Not that my life has been an exciting one. On the contrary, it has been very dull. But a dull life in itself may be an argument for a journal. The best way for the passive man to overtake his more active brothers is to write them up. Isn't the Sun King himself just another character in Saint-Simon's chronicle?

In Europe a world war has started while in this country Brian Aspinwall is about to go to work in his first job. Surely if I am ever to keep a journal, now is the time. A first job at twenty-seven! I shall be an instructor of English at Justin Martyr, an Episcopal boys' boarding school thirty miles west of Boston. The telegram from a Mr. Ives came in only yesterday. One of the masters wants to go to Canada to enlist in the RCAF which is why I have been taken on without interviews. It makes me feel better about my rejection by the British Army before I left Oxford in July. Naturally, they were not keen about an untrained Yankee student with a heart murmur! Perhaps had I stayed over there, now that war has actually come, they might have lowered their standards, but at least this way I can feel that I am releasing an able-bodied man to fight the antichrist in Berlin.

It is the obvious moment for stock-taking. In the questionnaire that was sent out this year by my class secretary at Columbia, I had nothing to contribute but the meager fact that I had gone abroad to study for a master's degree. And now because I was too sensitive to stay in Oxford out of uniform I will not even get that! I suppose all I have basically done since my seventeenth year has been to seek refuge in literature from the agony of deciding whether or not I am qualified to be a minister. Perhaps life in a church school will help me. Please God it may.

But I must try not to be too hard on myself. That is, after all, another kind of conceit. It is a fact that I suffered all during my boyhood from ill health. It is another fact that as the only child of elderly parents I had to spend a great deal of time with them in their last illnesses. It was a joy—and I write the word sincerely—to be able to help them, but it was still time out of a career. So it is not altogether my fault that I have made so late a start—if it can be said I have even yet started.

With God's grace I shall learn my true capacities at Justin Martyr. It is a good size for a school (450 boys), and its headmaster and founder, the Reverend Francis Prescott, D.D., is probably the greatest name in New England secondary education. He is old now, nearly eighty, but he is a minister, and may have much to teach me. It may even turn out that I have been "called" to Justin.

I am shy and lack force of personality, and my stature is small. I stammer when I am nervous, and my appearance is more boyish than manly. All this will be against me. But I am not afraid to say what I mean, and I think in a real crisis I can be counted on to stand up for the right, if only because I have such a horror of letting God down. Let us hope I add up to a teacher.

September 16. Justin Martyr. I arrived the day before yesterday, a week ahead of the boys, to work up my courses with Mr. Anders of the English department. It is all very rush, but everyone knows I am an emergency replacement and Mr. Anders is kindness itself.

I am not yet entirely sure what I think of the looks of the school. On Monday it depressed me; on Tuesday I felt better about it; today (in glorious weather) I like it. It is fairly consistently in the H. H. Richardson tradition, with masses of dark red brick, Romanesque arches in rock-faced granite, rotundas and long colonnades. A certain leaning to heaviness, suggestive of some medieval monastery in southern France, or, less remotely, of some solid New England summer colony at the turn of the century, is lightened by the profusion of verdurous lawns and hedges and by the glory of elm trees. God, as usual, has done a better job than man.

To be more particular, the school is built around an oval campus at whose northern end stands Lawrence House, the main building, which contains the library, the dining hall and the headmaster's residence. Moving clockwise next comes the schoolhouse, with high Gothic windows in its great assembly hall and an octagonal open bell house from which the "outside" tolls each morning at seven; then the gymnasium, with a Florentine note of large stones and small windows, then the dormitories: Depew, Griscam and Lowell, and finally the brownstone chapel, a relief after so much red and grey, with its square craggy tower rising to dwarf the academic community huddled at its feet.

It is a remarkable tower. The eye travels upward to follow its mighty thrust past the narrow open window slits to the castellated top over which a shingle pyramided roof rises and then climbs yet dizzily further into a pointed round angle turret. Mr. Anders says it is like Dr. Prescott's faith, bold and big, beautiful in its disdain of beauty.

I suppose that many people today would find this architecture ponderous, even banal. They would insist that youth should be educated in modern buildings with plenty of glass to let in God's out-of-doors. Yet I wonder if it is altogether sentimentality that makes me begin to find this campus a heartening place. It seems to me that Dr. Prescott must have recognized from the beginning that boys have no eye for architecture and yet are influenced by it. I imagine that he may have wanted a style that would suggest ruggedness and strength while offering at the same time a certain solid comfortableness, and how better could he attain it than by going back to a Christian tradition of days when the faith was not wholly secure from pagan assault?

For there are aspects of the fortress everywhere: in the machicolated roof of the infirmary, in the grey walls and slit windows of the gymnasium, even in the great tower of the chapel itself. It was this that initially depressed me. Now I see that the sweeping lawns and shady elms make the idea of war retreat into a past of muffled drums. Peace prevails on the campus, and on a brilliant fall day like this one it seems almost a sleepy peace, at least while the boys are still away, and only the hum of an automatic lawnmower breaks the stillness. But it is a peace of dignity, a peace of honor, against the quiet pageant of pinkish red and grey, a peace in which strife has not been forgotten, nor toil neglected, the peace of the Church Militant.

Yes, I think I shall like Justin Martyr.

September 17. Perhaps I have spoken too soon. Yesterday I had not met the headmaster.

He has been here all summer as his wife is very ill, and I ran into him quite by chance as I was passing his front door. I say "ran into him." Let me correct that. One does *not* "run into" Dr. Prescott.

My pen is a poor substitute for the camera to describe a man so magnificently photogenic and so often photographed. He is short for one that dominating, about five feet six, which is accentuated by the great round shoulders, the bull neck, the noble square head, the thick shock of stiff, wavy grey hair. I wonder if he is not a bit vain about his hair, for they say he never wears a hat—even in seasons when it is required of the boys. This afternoon he had on a blue opera cape with a velvet collar fastened by a chain, and he carried a black ebony walking stick, a combination that might have seemed theatrical had it not been so exactly right for him.

His face is remarkably clear for his years, except for deep lines at the corners of his mouth; he has a wide pale brow, thick bushy eyebrows, a straight nose with an almost imperceptible hook at the end, and large eyes, far apart, of a dark brown streaked with yellow. Mr. Anders says that his critics claim that he looks too much like a great man to be one.

I paused when I saw him coming down the steps, not wishing to intrude upon his privacy, but when he paused also, I realized that he was waiting for me to come up to him. He can summon one to his side without a word or a twitch of his great eyebrows.

"You are Aspinwall?" His voice has a deep, velvety melancholy. "We were happy to get you at such short notice. Have you been assigned a football team?"

I assumed that he had mistaken the nature of my duties. "I believe I'm to be in the English department, sir."

His stare was cold. "I'm quite aware of that. But it is our custom at Justin—as you will find it is at other schools—for the younger masters, particularly the unmarried ones, to take part in the athletic program. We might find you a team to coach in one of the lower forms. The Fourth Monongahelas."

"The fourth what, sir?" I dared not confess that I did not even know the rules of football.

"The whole school is divided into two teams for the purpose of intramural sports," he explained in the deliberate, patient tone of one who never repeats. "The Monongahelas and the Shenandoahs." There was not even the hint of a smile as he brought forth these wonderful Indian names. "Of course, the varsity team which plays other schools is made up of both. The Monongahelas wear blue jerseys and the Shenandoahs red. A boy is assigned to one or the other in his first week at the school and remains in that team until his graduation."

When I am nervous I should be silent. I was appalled to hear myself answer: "That's nice." Would he think I was making fun of him? But he took no note of it.

"You were at Oxford?" he inquired.

"Yes, sir. Christ Church."

"I'm a Balliol man myself." He pursed his lips in a way that pulled his cheeks down and turned the square of his countenance into a triangle of speculation. "We must have a talk one of these days. Poor old England, she's in for it now." And he turned away to proceed on his walk.

So this is the famous Rector of Justin! Not a word about the subject that I am hired to teach; only a lecture on intramural sports. I had not realized that the god of football had conquered even the church schools. It is a dim augury.

September 28. The boys have been here now for five days. I did not wish to record my impressions of the school in session before, as I have learned to make allowance for the timid and apprehensive side of my nature which has a way, like a ghostly and mischievous extra brush, quite beyond the painter's control, of dubbing clouds and rain squalls into the sunniest landscape. If I am ever to be a minister, with God's help, I must learn joy. But now, after more than a hundred hours of boys, when my spirits are still in my boots, I begin to wonder if I will ever be able to adjust my trudge to the noisy march of Justin. I had not imagined there could be so much noise. I have a constant sense of being about to be overwhelmed.

The other masters have been kind, but in the way people are kind who expect you to swim after the first plunge. Mr. Ives, the senior master, whose relation to Dr. Prescott is that of an executive officer to a ship's captain, a small, delicate birdlike man with a yellow stare that seems to take in everything, patiently briefed me in my duties the first day, but as he obviously expected me to take it all in the first time, I was seized with panic and could only nod stupidly to the meaningless flow of his perfectly organized sentences. It is a sad feeling to stand on the threshold of the school year and know that one's day of reckoning may be tomorrow.

I have seen almost nothing of Dr. Prescott. Thank God he has forgotten the football team! His poor wife is not expected to live, so he has been spending much of his time with her. However, he conducts the chapel service every morning and presides at assembly in the Schoolhouse. The awe which he inspires among the boys and faculty has to be seen to be credited. The masters are always telling tales of his prodigious memory, his uncanny perspicacity, his terrible temper. To hear them go on one would assume that he still handles every detail of school administration, yet in sober fact I suppose it is the ubiquitous Ives who really runs the school. A headmaster, particularly one so venerable, must be like a constitutional sovereign. He performs his function by being seen.

September 30. Worse and worse. My fourth form dormitory has been sizing me up, and now they have decided they can ride me. There were terrible squeals after lights tonight, and I was in a wretched quandary. How does one cope with forty fifteen-year-olds in the dark? Finally in a panic lest the sounds would come to the all-hearing ears of Mr. Ives, I strode to the door into the dormitory, turned on the overhead lights by the switch and called out in what I fear was a trembling falsetto: "Who is talking in this room?" Someone shouted back: "You are!" and the roar of laughter that followed must have been heard all over Lawrence House. In desperation I cried: "I am going to report the whole dormitory to the headmaster!" and slammed the door. Sitting at my desk again, my hands clasped to my throbbing temples, I took in gradually that the dormitory at last was silent. But what good does it do when in the morning they will all realize I have not carried out my threat?

For I never will. How can I? How can I afford to admit that the boys were out of control? I can only pull out this journal and foolishly wish that I could climb inside of it and pull its covers close over my shamed and ridiculous head. Oh, Journal, if you could only hide me, if I could only turn myself into ink! Dear God, will I ever make a go at teaching? And if I can't handle a few boys, is it feasible that I can ever be a missionary? Or even administer a parish? Perhaps all I am good for is to embrace the Roman Church and join a contemplative order. Please, dear God, keep my dormitory quiet.

October 4. I had my second talk with the headmaster this afternoon. Like the first, it arose from a chance meeting. I was on my way to the river, walking past the athletic fields, when I encountered the stocky figure in the sweeping blue cape. He was crossing the road from the first squad field where he watches the football practice for a daily half hour, leaning silently on his walking stick. When he saw me, his expression was not friendly.

"Good afternoon, Aspinwall. Whither are *you* bound?"

"To the river, sir," And with the instinctive good manners of the non-academic world I inappropriately added: "Would you care to join me? It's such a beautiful day."

His stare dismissed the irrelevance of weather. "Don't you have one of the lower school teams to coach? I thought Mr. Hinkley was going to assign you one."

"He was, sir. But when he found I didn't know the rules, he gave it up as a bad job."

"Then I suggest you come with me and learn them," he said sternly. "Football is more than a game, you know. It's a combination of training body and character. If you want to understand the boys here, you must understand it. Let us see what the second squad is up to."

For forty miserable minutes I stood dumbly by the empty bleachers and watched the play as Dr. Prescott explained it. At first he was gruff and short, but as the forward passes of one fifth former, evidently a rising star, began to arouse his enthusiasm, he became more friendly, and after a particularly long one, successfully completed, he actually hit me on the shoulder. "By Jove, that Craddock can throw like an angel! Do you begin to see what I mean, Aspinwall?"

When he left me at last, he suggested that I should remain and continue to study the play. I thanked him and murmured that I hoped Mrs. Prescott was better. He shook his head, as if it were not my place to ask. "She is doing as well as can be expected," he said gloomily. "I shall see that Mr. Hinkley gives you a football manual. Good day, Aspinwall."

And this is the man with whom I had meant to discuss my hopes for the ministry! This is the spokesman for the Church of Christ at Justin. Who, spotting my one poor rag of consolation, my free hour in the afternoon, strips it off that my whole pelt may be exposed to the pricks of his institution.

October 10. A new low. In my third form English class this morning the five boys in the back bench managed with their feet to move it completely around while I was writing the test questions on the blackboard so that they had their backs to me when I turned. I gave each a black mark, but the three in the middle protested so vigorously that only the two on the ends had perpetrated the revolution of the bench that I cravenly gave in and suspended all five marks. I noticed that the faces of the rest of the class were now frankly contemptuous. Dear God, if I become a pitiable creature, spare me at least from the sin of self-pity. I have a terrible leaning to it.

October 12. I found a dead frog in my bed last night, and the touch of it against my bare foot scared me so that I was sick to my stomach. I wonder if such a trick has ever before been played on a master at Justin. But obviously I'll never know, as I shall never dare admit that it happened. Dear God, will it ever be over?

October 14. Mr. Ives is a small man, with hands and feet that are proportionately even smaller, and he wears shoes without laces or buckles that look like fairies' slippers. He has yellowish-white hair which descends over his high, egglike forehead in a soft, neat triangle and yellow, stary eyes which, with his small hooked nose, might give him the appearance of a sparrow hawk, did not his habit of wearing thick fuzzy suits and of moving his head forward and backward as he walks suggest a less distinguished bird.

In character as well as appearance he seems the opposite of Dr. Prescott, which perhaps a good executive officer should be; his glory is in detail, and he makes no secret of it. To the headmaster is left the field of intangibles: God, a boy's soul and school spirit; Ives reigns over the minutiae of the curriculum and infractions of discipline. The boys credit him with second sight in such matters; he seems to know by instinct who is smoking in the cellar and who has gone canoeing on the Lawrence without leave. Yet for all his deviousness, for all his biting sarcasms, for all his lilting reprimands and snapping fingers, this epicene martinet is extremely popular, and to be asked to play bridge in his study on a Saturday night is deemed the highest social honor that a sixth former can attain.

But for the younger boys and, alas, for the younger masters he is Mephistopheles, and he has been eying me as a coyote might eye a wounded cow. I am sure that nothing has happened that has not been brought instantly to his notice, and I imagine that he must be debating whether to let me go now, with all the trouble of a midterm replacement, or to patch me up so that I'll last the school year. He summoned me this morning to his office in the Schoolhouse and told me that there had been complaints about noises in my dormitory after lights.

"Surely, Mr. Aspinwall, you have not left the boys unsupervised?"

"Oh, no, sir. I'm always there."

"Have you been having any trouble with your hearing?"

"No, sir. I shall try to do better."

"Do so, Mr. Aspinwall." Here he snapped his fingers. As he always spoke in the same mocking tone he must have adopted this mannerism to put his hearer on notice when he was serious. "Do so, I beg of you. You will find that you have my full backing and that of Dr. Prescott in any disciplinary measures that you seek to impose. The law of a boys' school is the law of the jungle. When you're strong, we're behind you, but if you're weak, we throw you to the boys."

As if he had to tell me. As if I didn't know that the whole lot of them, boys and masters, were part of the same pack! But perhaps now reading the despair in my eyes and not wishing to overwhelm me, he added: "What about your prefects? Where have they been?"

"I haven't wanted to interrupt their studies at night. I thought I should be able to handle the dormitory myself."

"Sometimes it's hard to get started," he said more kindly, looking at me as he appeared to debate something. "I shall see that you have one prefect on duty every night for the next two weeks."

And as I am making this entry at my desk tonight, Bobbie Seymour, one of the football team, is seated on the sofa opposite, reading a movie magazine which is supposed to be banned from the school grounds. But never mind. In the ominous black of the dormitory beyond the open door an absolute silence reigns. I may have been humiliated by the calling in of extra police, but it is better to be humiliated than lynched. I shall now be able to read in peace another delightful chapter of *Clarissa*. Escape? Who calls it escape? It's salvation!

October 17. I have at last met Mrs. Prescott. Every Sunday after lunch the faculty and their wives foregather for coffee in the headmaster's study, a large, square, book-lined room added like a box to the back of the Prescotts' house. Today, Mrs. Prescott's nurse wheeled her in in her chair and stationed her in a corner, and we all stood about, in a respectful half-circle, while Dr. Prescott, in what must have been for him the unaccustomed role of court chamberlain, brought people up, one by one, for a half minute's conversation.

The poor woman is terribly emaciated and gaunt; her face seems to have been absorbed into her great aquiline nose so that with her dyed thin hair and half-closed eyes she suggests a turkey buzzard sleeping on a dead limb. Yet there is still something rather magnificent about her, something that suggests the grim character and determined intellectualism of an earlier New England. Or is it just that I happen to know she is a great-niece of Emerson?

I was surprised when the headmaster took me by the elbow to propel me to his wife's corner, having assumed that her brief visiting time would be taken up by my seniors, but he explained that she always wanted to meet the new masters. Harry Ruggles, of the history department, one of those wiry fellows with thick black curly hair who are always smiling, was talking to her as we came up, but he did not have the tact to rise, so I was left standing awkwardly between the wheelchair and the sofa arm on which Ruggles was familiarly perched. He was being tedious on the subject of what he called "labor novels," and I was glad to see that Mrs. Prescott was obviously bored.

"There's a great deal of solid fiction being written today," he was telling her, "by men who understand that the fundamental structure of our society changed with the New Deal. You may not like it, Mrs. Prescott, but I don't see how you can deny it."

"Why do you assume I don't like it?" she asked in a tone that would have warned anybody but Ruggles.

"Well, I thought, ma'am, a lady of your background and generation would be instinctively opposed to F.D.R."

"I'm not a background or a generation, thank you very much. I happen to be a human being, and I was a democrat before you were born, young man."

"Well, fine! Then you will sympathize with my idea of having the boys read some of our more important labor novels. It ought to be fun to see their self-satisfied bubbles pricked."

Mrs. Prescott glanced at me here, and I had a distinct feeling that she had somehow divined my sympathy. "Labor novels?" she demanded. "What are labor novels? I know only good novels and bad novels."

"What do you consider a good novel?"

"*The Egoist*."

"Meredith?" Ruggles' smile just acknowledged him. "He was all very well for his day, I suppose. People had time for him then."

"I have time for him now," Mrs. Prescott insisted. "Don't you, Mr. Aspinwall?"

I do not know if it was the surprise that I felt on her remembering my name or the unexpected tremor of real feeling that I may have imagined in the old woman's flat tone that made me think I might at last have found an ally at Justin Martyr. All I know is that in that minute I fell in love with Mrs. Prescott, and that my love made me bold. "I will always have time for Meredith," I responded warmly. "I will always have time for good novels. And I agree that there are only good ones and bad ones. In art the subject can make no difference."

"There speaks the English department," Ruggles said sneeringly. "I suppose Aspinwall would rate Jane Austen with Tolstoy."

"Higher!"

Dr. Prescott came up now to take us away, but his wife reached out to put her hand on my wrist. "Leave me Mr. Aspinwall, Frank. He and I have something to say to each other." When Ruggles had departed with the headmaster, she shrugged. "What an ass that fellow is. Can you imagine the pricking of *his* self-satisfied bubble? It would be like the explosion of the *Hindenburg*. Why does teaching always seem to attract the intellectually flabby?"

"Perhaps because we want to seem infallible and think that little boys may find us so. How wrong we are."

Mrs. Prescott grunted. "How wrong indeed. The only people Mr. Ruggles could hope to fool would be his contemporaries. But don't worry. He won't last. I can tell by the way Frank holds his elbow that he's seen through him."

I had heard that Mrs. Prescott had become embarrassingly candid with old age, but this still struck me as excessive. After all, I was the most junior of the faculty and she was the headmaster's wife. "I fear he held mine the same way," I ventured.

"No, there was a difference. I can always tell." Her nurse was approaching; it was time to go. "Tell me, Mr. Aspinwall, would you come to see me some afternoon? I'm at my best in the afternoons, though I'm afraid my best isn't much these days. But perhaps we could talk. Or are you a brute, to prefer football to philosophy?"

"Oh, no, I should love to come!"

"Maybe tomorrow then. Any time after three. Only don't tell my husband. He would undoubtedly set you to some violent form of exercise."

At this she was wheeled away, head down, staring at her knees, acknowledging none of the bows or greetings from the faculty on either side. I wonder, when I present myself tomorrow, if she will even remember her invitation. Surely the thread that holds her strong spirit to this world is of gossamer, and I could well sympathize if she identified all other humans with her own body which, decaying, has ceased to be her friend.

October 21. I have had two visits with Mrs. Prescott this week, one on Monday and the second today, each of about forty minutes in length. The second went better than the first because I at last divined what it is she wants of me. She wants to be read to, and by someone whom she doesn't regard as a total simpleton. On my first visit I tried to talk of some of my passions: Balzac, Daudet, George Eliot, Virginia Woolf, but I soon found out that talking tired her. Besides, whereas my education—if it can be called that—is almost entirely in poetry and fiction, hers is vastly broader, encompassing philosophy and history and the visual arts. George Eliot leads her immediately to John Stuart Mill and Virginia Woolf to Bertrand Russell. She smiled tolerantly, her eyes half closed, as I chattered on, interrupting me with an occasional grunt or brief comment, but when I mentioned Henry James she stopped me.

"You know he dictated the later novels," she said. "People think that odd for so accomplished a stylist, but of course it's not odd at all. He always wanted to be read aloud, and how could he know how it would sound unless he thought aloud?" She paused here and seemed to be studying me. "Of course, now that my eyes are so bad it's the only way I can know James."

"Do you have him on records?" There was an old gramophone in the corner of the living room, but it had an air of not having been played in years.

"There are records, of course, for the blind," she muttered, but very little of what I want. Those unfortunates seem to be an uncultivated lot."

"I'd be only too happy to come in and read to you, but I fear I'm not very good at it. The boys get quite restive in the reading period before their bedtime."

"I'm not the boys, Mr. Aspinwall," she said with the ghost of a smile. "I should be grateful. But don't you have athletic duties?"

I thought of the headmaster's injunction and shuddered. "Not really."

It was touching how eagerly she caught me up. "Perhaps we could start next time you come. Do you like *The Ambassadors?*"

"It's my favorite!"

And indeed we did. Today I read for three quarters of an hour before the nurse came in. I thought I did very well, but I had read over the chapter in advance and was prepared. Mrs. Prescott seemed to sleep during part of it, but even that may be good in her present state of health. At least I can hope that I am finally doing something for *somebody* at Justin Martyr.

October 30. It is curious how much my readings to this silent, still old woman mean to me. She offers a contrast to the noisy, active school that is like a little chapel by a thronged highway. Some tiny fragment of her dauntlessness may have shaken off upon my frail shoulders for I actually believe that I am more at ease with my dormitory now and in my classes. Not much, surely, but a little. It helps to know that there is one other soul in this dark male world that cares about beautiful things.

My admiration extends to her surroundings. The big, square parlor in which poor Mrs. Prescott now spends all of her long days is to me everything that a room should be, probably because it *is* everything. By that I mean there seems to be nothing either of the Prescotts or of Justin Martyr missing from it. The school is represented by the number of chairs and small round tables, some of simple porch wicker, used for games on "parlor" night, by the big mahogany chest in the corner that will never quite close, crammed as it is with sets of parchesi, halmar and checkers, by the snapshots everywhere of beloved graduates, by the citations of those gloriously dead in war. The Prescotts are represented by an oval portrait of the three dark-eyed daughters as rather formidable children, inappropriately clad in white silk with big blue ribbons in their hair, by a wonderful sketch of Emerson in profile, by a watercolor of Dr. Prescott's father as an officer of the Union Army, and by Mrs. Prescott's books, in German, French and English, in old bindings, in modern, and in paperbacks, filling the cabinets, piled on tables, even stacked on the floor. True, the room is cluttered and the furniture is of every period, yet over the whole there reigns a certain harmony, a curious dignity, an even more curious simplicity.

One begins to note fine things among the junk; a superb little Boudin under a framed cartoon from *The New Yorker* with a joke about the school, a first edition of Johnson's dictionary looming over the bound volumes of *Punch,* a gleaming Sheraton breakfront full of mediocre China-trade porcelain. But the real reason for my net impression that the room is so innately civilized is in Mrs. Prescott herself. It is not only the inner temple of the school; it is at the same time her refuge from the school. She knows where to lay her fingers at once on even the smallest item, nor is there any object without its function of present utility or fond association. What seems at first a pot-pourri is in fact the perfectly catalogued and constantly functioning collection of her life.

November 1. Mrs. Prescott surprised me today by asking me to skip to the great chapter in Gloriani's studio where Strether warns Little Bilham not to waste his life as he has done. She told me, in the most matter-of-fact of tones, that in her physical condition she had to pick the high spots of a long book. But, of course, I was not prepared, and James is difficult to read at sight. I would rush into the sentences only to find myself caught up by the undertow of an unexpected construction and cast back, breathless, on the sands of my unfamiliarity. On one of these occasions, observing Mrs. Prescott's closed eyes and motionless head, I decided it would be safe to push on without rereading the passage.

"You'd better try that sentence again," she interrupted me, without opening her eyes. "I think you'll find the second 'he' refers to Chad and not Strether."

Not a nuance escapes her. She is one of those rare people who can read James with the whole magnificent forest constantly in mind and yet not miss a single tree. Her husband, apparently, does not share her admiration for the master. One of the takeoffs that he sometimes performs on "parlor night" is called "Mr. James Takes the Shuttle at Grand Central." But then one cannot imagine Dr. Prescott troubling his head over the refinements of moral choice open to James or Strether. Obviously, had *he* been sent to Paris to collect the erring Chad, he would have had the young man back in Woollett by the end of the first chapter!

November 5. The dissension between Dr. Prescott and his wife in their estimates of Henry James resulted in a scene this afternoon that I found embarrassing. Towards the end of my hour with Mrs. Prescott the head-master made an unexpected appearance. Immediately I closed the book. He had never come in at other readings, and I could not but speculate uncomfortably that this visit was more to check up on me than on his wife. Was it not implicit in the whole Justin tradition that a young master should find more vigorous employment on a glorious fall afternoon than sitting in a close room with an old woman reading *The Ambassadors*? Indeed, when I saw the glance with which he took me in, I assumed that a final judgment of my poor case had already been made.

"Let me not interrupt the reading," he rumbled. "Let me slip quietly into a seat over here and enjoy it."

"No, no, nobody could read James in front of you, Frank," Mrs. Prescott said testily. "You'll just sit there and make faces. Go away and leave us be."

"There's a friendly greeting," he replied imperturbably, settling himself on a small straight armless chair. The very bareness of the seat belied the sincerity of his intention to remain. "I promise I shall make no faces. Proceed, Aspinwall. Which of the novels are you reading?" I murmured the title. "Ah, yes, the fine flower of the later style. It has all that is gorgeous in the master, all that is sublime. And all that is ridiculous."

"What do you mean, ridiculous?" Mrs. Prescott demanded at once. "What is ridiculous about *The Ambassadors*?"

"Simply that it has nothing whatever to do with life on this poor planet of ours."

"It has a great deal to do with *my* life."

"Do you see yourself, my dear, as a Lambert Strether?"

"Certainly I do!" his wife exclaimed with sudden violence. "Strether didn't know until he saw Paris that he'd wasted his life. Well, it took more than Paris to teach me that. It took this abominable wheelchair!"

The moment that followed this outburst was almost unbearable. I clenched my fists and stared at the faded old Persian rug and prayed idiotically that it would sweep me up in the air and carry me far away from all the terrible things in Justin Martyr. In that moment I think I learned the real tragedy of living too long. It is not losing one's health or one's memory or even one's mind; it is losing one's dignity. For I am absolutely sure that Mrs. Prescott's outburst was uncharacteristic. The woman who could throw that reproach in her husband's face was a different woman from the proud creature that she had so obviously been all her life.

If I dared not look at her husband's face to see the pain that I had no doubt he was concealing, I could not avoid his voice. He was talking now, in a quiet tone, filling in a pause that had to be filled in, addressing me in the knowledge that after what his wife had just said, any further reading aloud was out of the question.

"My wife, Aspinwall, takes Mr. James too seriously. That is not to say that one should never take him seriously. But I'm a great believer in safety valves, particularly where art is concerned, and one cannot read James properly without bearing in mind that for every three parts genius he is one part ass."

"Oh, Frank! What utter rot you're talking."

"Let Aspinwall be the judge between us, my dear. Take this very novel you're reading. Strether, an elderly, provincial widower, is dazzled out of his senses by the sudden apparition of Paris. Certainly his creator knows how to evoke the city. Oh, I own that! Renoir himself could not have conveyed a more vivid sense of the greens and greys of the boulevards or of the stately stillness of Louis XV interiors. Strether imbibes Paris through every pore. He is revived and rejuvenated. Yet what spoils it all for him? The simple fact that Chad Newsome, the young blade whom he has come to bring home, turns out to have a French mistress. Which everyone under the sun, including the reader, knew from the beginning and which was indeed the very reason for Strether's mission! What in the name of Gallia did he *expect* the young man to be up to? Yet he finds his vision of Paris incompatible with this simplest of biological facts, and all is wrecked for him. Tell me, Aspinwall, is poor old Strether, like poor old James, not a bit of a dunce?"

"But it is *not* all wrecked for him!" Mrs. Prescott exclaimed passionately. "Chad and Strether may both be going back to Woollett, but Strether is going back with his vision, and his vision will sustain him."

"His vision of what?"

"His vision of Paris. Of life!"

"But *is* it life? Isn't it rather, a vision of the bits and pieces of Paris that he didn't find too sordid? Would you recognize any part of it as the Paris of *L'Assomoir*?"

"It's a vision of beauty. And James transmits it. That is art. And therefore it must be life."

"Or dope!"

"What a Philistine you really are, Frank. Scratch a headmaster, and you'll find one every time. And when I think that you complain about the others!"

At this point it was evident that Mrs. Prescott was becoming too excited, and with the smallest motion of his head her husband indicated that it was time for me to go. I rose and murmured my farewell, but he followed me out and closed the door behind us.

"Aspinwall," he said, taking my elbow as he guided me to the front door, "you are very kind to devote so many afternoons to my wife."

"Oh, it's my pleasure, sir. Truly, I love it."

"It can't be very gay for a young man," he pursued, "and I want you to know that I am not ungrateful. Allow me to see that you are compensated with extra time off."

"Oh, sir, that won't be necessary," I exclaimed, shocked. "Mrs. Prescott is the most wonderful woman I've ever known!"

The grip tightened on my elbow. "Bless you, my boy. Bless you for seeing that."

Outside I almost ran back to the main door of Lawrence House, so full of emotion that it was all I could do to keep from skipping. What a man was this! A man who could read the later James and love his wife so tenderly, a man who could appreciate what a silly mite like myself, the reverse of all he expected in a master, could offer her and not hesitate to ask that mite to continue his offering. This was magnanimity on a scale for the gods. Looking up at the formidable dark tower of his chapel I laughed aloud in jubilation at the thought that there *might* at last be a place for me in Dr. Prescott's Justin.

2

BRIAN'S JOURNAL

NOVEMBER 6, 1939. I was reading aloud to my dormitory tonight when I received an unexpected visit. This reading period, incidentally, has not been any more of a success than my other activities. I read too fast and too low, and I tend to become so absorbed in the matter that I hardly notice that I have lost my audience. It is different with Mrs. Prescott where the reading is so much more a shared experience. The boys whisper and giggle and even play games. I know that I should reprimand them, but I cannot help feeling that it is supposed to be their time off and that they should be allowed to do as they choose. Tonight, even in my abstraction, I became gradually aware of a deepening silence about me, the silence of songbirds in the sudden shadow of a hawk, and looking up, I saw the headmaster himself standing in the doorway.

"Go on, please, Mr. Aspinwall," he directed me with a friendly wave of his arm as he came slowly forward to take the nearest seat, from which a boy now jumped. "You must think I have nothing better to do than interrupt your readings. I shall listen a bit, if I may. What is it tonight? Not *The Ambassadors* again?" He smiled as he glanced about the room. "I suppose not for this crowd."

"Oh, no, sir. *The Moonstone.*"

"And a corking good yarn." His approving nod was decisive. "Let us get on with it."

I read for several minutes in a silence which I found as disturbing as it was unusual. Then the rich level voice interrupted me again. "Excuse me please, Mr. Aspinwall, but what do I see there? Over there by the fireplace? Is that a checkerboard? Good gracious me, I believe it is. Were you two boys actually *playing* while Mr. Aspinwall was reading?" I was aware in the silence of two small moons of dismay over the half-concealed board. "Have you lost your tongues, sirs? *Were* you?"

"Yes, sir."

"Then go to bed. Go to bed right away. And mind you make no noise undressing to disturb the reading. Pray proceed, Mr. Aspinwall."

I kept my eyes fixed on the print to avoid stammering, glancing up only once to see if the minute hand of my clock would *ever* reach nine.

"Carstairs!" the dreaded voice boomed out again. I had learned that one could never tell when Dr. Prescott would address a boy by his name or simply as "boy." It apparently had nothing to do with his memory. "Are you chewing *gum*?"

"Well, sir, I—er—"

"Er?" demanded the headmaster. "What does 'er' mean? Don't say 'er.' Keep your mouth closed until you have the words ready that you want to use. Now I repeat. Are you chewing gum?"

"Yes, sir. But I started before you came in."

"What difference does that make? Do you think the rules operate only when I am present? You must know it is not allowed to chew gum inside any building on the campus. Spit it out. Yes, now. Spit it out in your hand, boy." But when poor Carstairs complied with his order, it seemed only to make Dr. Prescott angrier. "Ugh! What a disgusting sight. Go to bed, boy, right away. We don't want to see you any more tonight. All right, Mr. Aspinwall. We may proceed again."

In a trembling tone I continued the now shattered reading session, knowing that I was but marking time before the next outburst. In two more minutes it came.

"I'm afraid you must excuse me once more, Mr. Aspinwall. I can hardly credit my eyes, but it seems to me that the two boys crouching on the other side of your desk have no ties on. Can it be? Stand up you two, Morgan and the boy next to Morgan. Gracious me, these old eyes were right again. But I fear this time being sent to bed will not be enough. No, I fear I shall have to give you each a black mark. See that the black marks are recorded, Mr. Aspinwall."

"I'm sorry, Dr. Prescott, I'm afraid it's my fault. I allowed them to remove their ties." I hadn't at all, but I had known they were doing it, and I could not have them punished for my own laxness in enforcing the rules.

"Have you indeed, sir?" the headmaster queried, with soaring eyebrows. "How very singular. Then I shall, of course, rescind the black marks, but let it be clearly understood by all present that ties are *not* to be removed nor shoes unlaced until it is time to retire. When a gentleman undresses, a gentleman goes to bed. And as I do not wish to continue to gaze at Morgan's bare neck or at the bare neck of Morgan's friend, I suggest that the whole dormitory go to bed right now, even though it is still ten minutes before the hour."

He remained in my study while the boys prepared for bed and then accompanied me on my round of the cubicles as I pulled each curtain and bade good night to each occupant. His mood seemed to have softened for he paused to banter Carstairs about the chewing gum. After lights, however, he became grave again, and in my study he motioned me to close the door to the dormitory as he took a seat by the fireplace and lit his pipe.

"I want to give you a little lecture about discipline, Brian," he began, using my Christian name for the first time. "You are obviously having trouble with it, and the reason is twofold. In the first place you think it's some kind of trick with which you do not happen to be endowed. That is nonsense. If you were a missionary facing a crowd of cannibals or a lone sheriff facing a lynching mob, you would need what the army calls 'command presence.' But a schoolmaster does not need that. Oh, it's a useful thing to have, certainly, but it's not *necessary*. You have the power of the black mark, and that is all you basically need. When the boys begin to get the idea that the least impertinence to Mr. Aspinwall means missing the Saturday afternoon game or the Saturday night movie, they will give up their impertinence. It's as simple as that."

I realized that he was being kind, which gave me the courage to appeal to him. "But I hate being unjust, sir, and sometimes it's difficult to know who's the culprit. If a boy, for example, makes an insulting noise when my back is turned in class, what am I to do?"

"You can give six black marks to the boy you first suspect. If you are wrong, this will often have the effect of making the true culprit confess. Or you can give the whole class a black mark apiece. This will put the innocent against the guilty, and you can be sure the former will make life so miserable for the latter that the episode will not be repeated. The big thing is not to worry too much about guilt or innocence. A class where an impudent noise is made is apt to be an impudent class. Your dormitory is now a bad dormitory. If you gave every boy in it six black marks on the spot, I wager the great majority of them would be deserved."

"You wouldn't have me do that, sir?"

"No. But I would have you establish your authority. A week after that is done, you'll have a good dormitory. Which brings me to the second reason for your trouble. You want to be popular."

"Oh, surely not, sir!"

"Well, then, you're afraid to be unpopular which comes to the same thing. I've watched you, Brian. I have my spies. Now what I want you to do is this. I want you to give out twelve black marks before the end of next week. Don't worry. There will be plenty of occasions if you keep your eyes open. I shall consult the Black Ledger a week from Saturday at noon and see what you have entered. Is that fair?"

He stood up now, his pipe clenched between his teeth, and I stood up after him, trembling in the knees. "I'll try, sir."

"Good boy." He reached out to pat my shoulder. "You will be unpopular, but you will be respected. And in time you will build a more solid kind of popularity on respect. Take my word for it. I'm an old hand at this game, and I know what I'm doing." Here he suddenly raised his voice to a roar. "I know, for example, there's a boy listening on the other side of that door." In the silence that followed we both could make out the patter of rapidly retreating feet. "There you are, Brian," he said grimly. "The whole dormitory will know of our conversation in the morning. But that's fine. Let them know what you're going to do and then *do* it. Good night, my boy." And he left me to the ominous silence of that dark, awake dormitory and to the blessed anodyne of this journal.

November 14. Well, I made up my twelve black marks. It almost killed me, but I did it. I have been so nervous that I couldn't write a word in this journal until it was done. I gave two to a boy whose voice I thought I recognized after lights. He protested bitterly that it had not been he, and I wavered, but then I remembered Dr. Prescott's warning and told him firmly that he would have to accept my verdict and that I was sorry if it was a mistaken one. He accepted this so philosophically that I realized he must be guilty.

I next gave a black mark apiece to two boys whom I caught fighting in the shower. This was clearly fair, and I began to gain confidence. Four out of twelve. But already the dormitory was becoming orderly, and the week was going by. I then gave one each to two boys who took their ties off during my reading period. Unfortunately this touched off a real test of my authority, as the whole dormitory burst into protest, clamoring that the offense called only for a demerit. Again I wavered, sick at heart, fearing an actual riot, and again I remembered the headmaster's reminder that my power was absolute. I picked up a lead paperweight and banged it down on my desk with all my might. There was instant silence.

"Spruance!" I cried at the ringleader. "You started all this, and I'm giving you six black marks. If I hear a single word more from you, I shall send you to Dr. Prescott. And the entire dormitory is going to bed. *Now*."

It was a terrible moment, and I knew that my career in Justin hung in the balance. When the dormitory rose at last and sullenly filed past me to their cubicles, I had to strain every muscle not to let the surging tide of relief flood into my silly face. I might be a monster, but I had won! And dear God, let my journal be witness that I am humbly grateful for all your help in my foolish crises and for sending to my aid the strong arm of Dr. Prescott. Let me not be proud at petty victories, and let me remember that if I *should* ever become respected by the boys, it will be my task to be merciful and gentle and kind. I am here, after all, to serve *them*.

November 16. Dr. Prescott has played a very mean trick on me. He has doubled all my black marks except Spruance's, telling each boy that I am of such a notorious leniency that he is exercising a headmaster's prerogative of bringing my punishments in line with those more generally meted out. My dormitory is sullen, silent and obedient. I am really unpopular now, which I hate, but I have to confess that it is not a disagreeable sensation to give an order and know that it will be carried out. It is like driving a new car after struggling with a stalling jalopy. Am I being corrupted by power? Please, God, forgive and help me if this is so. At least Dr. Prescott has not given me a new stint of black marks to hand out. I do not think I could have borne it if he had.

November 18. Poor Mrs. Prescott is beginning to go downhill rapidly now, and there are signs that her mind is failing. Twice last Monday it was evident that she thought I was reading William and not Henry James, and yesterday afternoon she seemed to have forgotten all about our project and only wanted to talk. She dwells in the past, as I believe is natural in such cases, except that in hers there seems to be a strong drive to reduce isolated incidents to some kind of pattern. It is difficult to make out, but I believe she is trying to give me an oral memoir of memorable events in her life. It is as if, at the end of a long existence of intelligently receiving impressions, by eye and ear and even touch, she wants at last to give something back, to leave some little record of what Harriet Prescott has observed.

It is pathetic, even agonizing, to see this remarkable woman thrash about in her memories for some bit of tangible evidence that she has been, after all, remarkable. And now it is too late. She told me of her visit to Proust's cork-lined chamber with an old bachelor friend of Dr. Prescott's and of a talk she had had with Mrs. Jack Gardner at the time of her purchase of the great Titian "Europa." But as our vivid memories of sights abroad, of Chartres or the Parthenon, merge in time with the most banal of postcards, so have Mrs. Prescott's impressions become more ordinary than she suspects. I wanted to tell her to stop, to talk only about herself; I wanted to convince her that her life itself had been a work of art and that even the memory of her in my puny mind would be a greater memorial than the observation that Proust was a snob or Mrs. Gardner a sensationalist. But what can I do? She is way past my helping.

November 21. There is certainly no question that the headmaster's approbation has made a great change in my campus status. In a word, I am become respectable. So strong is the power of Dr. Prescott's personality in this little world of his creation that his special favors are accepted by all without overt resentment. Mr. Ives himself now asks me to coffee gatherings in his bachelor's wing of Lowell House. I sometimes wonder what is behind those yellow-streaked eyes, but he is certainly pleasant. Best of all, my dormitory seems to have accepted me. When I offered to give up reading in the evening and let them play games instead, the boys actually voted to have me finish *The Moonstone*. Henry James and Wilkie Collins have been my sponsors in Justin! Even the once formidable red and grey stones of the architecture have softened in color, and the dark craggy chapel tower seems occasionally to wink at me. I see what up until now has escaped me: that the common denominator of the heterogeneous faculty is an extraordinary devotion to the headmaster. I am actually happy, however precariously. Have I sold out, and if so, to what? Help me, dear God, not to be puffed up.

November 24. Mrs. Prescott took such a bad turn on Monday that the daughters were summoned, but she has improved again, and they have gone. I saw them all at lunch with Dr. Prescott at the head table and was struck by their resemblance to him. They look much alike, with pale skins and squarish faces and dark hair, and they are all very animated. In fact, there was rather more laughter at the head table than seemed to me quite appropriate under the circumstances. But then in these days the smallest display of grief is considered morbid. I must try to avoid the sin of judging others. Perhaps I wish to denigrate the filial feeling of Mrs. Prescott's daughters so that I may pose to myself as her only true friend. Count on the devil to work overtime!

November 25. I saw Mrs. Prescott this afternoon but only for a minute. She seemed very weak but clearer than before, and she told me that nothing rallied her "old carcass" like a gathering of the clan.

December 1. Mr. Ives fell in with me today, walking after breakfast from Lawrence House to morning chapel. One never feels that anything with him is a coincidence. I am sure that every minute of his day, every colloquy, every walk, every meal is somehow put to the service of Justin. He seems to have no interest in anything beyond the campus and, within the boundaries of the latter, only in matters corporeal. When I confided in him that I had a strong but still unmatured drive towards the ministry, he looked faintly surprised as if I, a nice young man of irreproachable manners, had suddenly told an off-color story. Yet in his narrow field he can be wonderfully illuminating

"I hear that you have become the official reader to the headmistress," he began this morning in his lilting, half-mocking tone. Now that I know him better, I realize that this tone has merely become a habit and does not reflect, as I had first assumed, an attitude of sustained contemptuousness. "In the court of France it was a coveted position."

"It was a career open to humble gentlewomen," I retorted mildly. "I trust I do not seem presumptuous in aspiring to it."

Mr. Ives glanced sidewise at me as he had a way of doing before changing his emphasis. "My dear fellow, we're all very happy indeed that you're able to do anything to amuse poor Mrs. Prescott. We others have tried and failed."

"But I do nothing!" I exclaimed, embarrassed by his novel note of gravity.

"In a sense, of course, there is nothing one can do," he agreed. "But that makes the tiniest thing loom large. Harriet Prescott is dying, and she resents the process. When you reach my age, you'll know how common it is to resent death. At the same time she has come to resent most of her old friends. We can only love her in silence. But to you, a newcomer, has fallen the privilege of amusing her. Some of us may be jealous, but I assure you that all of us are grateful."

"I'm glad that you call it a privilege, for that is certainly the way I look upon it. *If* it is true that I have amused her, which I very much doubt."

"Oh, she likes you. You have not yet become identified with the school. It is natural that as the end draws near, she should have a jaundiced eye for the institution which has been her greatest rival and which will soon have her husband all to itself. You must have noticed how impatient she is with Dr. Prescott."

"I have indeed. And I've found it very painful."

"You needn't. He understands. Few husbands, Brian, can have been loved as that man has been. And yet she must have always known, as *I* have always known, that for every gram of love that comes back from Francis Prescott, a pound goes to the school. That is the way things are." He looked at me now with his hard, birdlike stare, and I had my first sense of how much emotion it might curtain. "That's the way things always are with great men. But sometimes, for aging wives and senior masters, it's a bit hard."

I made no answer, for we had reached the steps of the chapel doors, and I could hear the tumbling notes of the organ in a Bach fugue.

December 5. My heart is low tonight for I fear I have seen the last of my dear new friend. Please, God, make her parting swift and painless. She will indeed be one of thy ministering angels. I received word at three o'clock that she wanted to see me, and I went for the first time to her bedroom where I found her very feeble and gaunt, but still inclined to talk. The nurse told me I must stay only ten minutes, but when my time was up and the warning white figure appeared in the doorway, Mrs. Prescott sent her away, saying sharply: "I have all eternity in which to rest, Miss Mitchell. Leave us be."

I was uncomfortable about this, but it seemed to me that it would probably be worse for her to be frustrated than tired. She was lying back on the pillow with her eyes closed and talking more to herself than to me. Her thoughts seemed to dwell no longer with famous personalities of the past but with her own youth. I made as few comments as possible, just enough to steer her drifting craft down that quiet stream.

"Oh, that was before I was married," she murmured. "That was when I was only twenty and spending the winter in Paris. We had a tiny apartment in an old *hôtel* on the Rue Monsieur, I and my sister and a maiden aunt. I shall never forget the uproar in the family when it was discovered that we had a sofa in the living room."

"A sofa? What was wrong with a sofa?"

"Why, can't you see what unimaginable intimacies it suggested?" Her eyes were still closed, but the hint of a smile passed over her thin white lips. "There had to be only stiff little chairs for our nonexistent callers. And there were rules about these, too. Oh, yes, those were still the days of *maintien*. One could never, for example, offer a guest a chair in which one had been sitting."

"You mean he always had to have a fresh one?"

"If there was one. Of course! Can you think of anything more horrid than a warm seat? *Voilà qui serait dégoutant!*" She was silent after this so long that I thought she might be unconscious. When she spoke again her voice had a trace of thickness. "Ah, those innocent, happy days. How I rebelled and loved rebelling. My daughters have suffered terribly from frustration because they couldn't shock me. How mean of me it was, as I look back. I wonder if it hasn't been the thing that has hurt them most in life, that desperate, unsatisfied need for a convention to hit at." Here she seemed to be trying to catch her breath. "The mealy nothingness of a civilization that has no hates or loves!"

"But should a parent pretend to be stuffy?" I protested. "Should a mother assume a prejudice if she has it not?"

"Perhaps. Perhaps indeed she should." Again she was silent for at least a minute, and when she talked her voice was very low, and her thoughts seemed to linger in the French past already evoked. "It's all so—so hopeless to convey. Like Paris then. Not a Renoir, no. Not a Pissarro." The pauses between her phrases increased. "No, it wasn't that. I see it more brightly. More lighted. It's funny, isn't it? More like a bad academy picture. A Meissonier. A Gérôme. Rose-cheeked girls with dogs. The Bois. A carriage. And all those market scenes." She smiled again. "How funny if the impressionists were wrong. How—how—funny. And Mother would never let me— Mother would never—" Here I could no longer make out her words, and I rose in alarm to get the nurse whom I found just outside the door.

"Go now," Miss Mitchell whispered angrily. "Please go."

But I was beyond Miss Mitchell's anger now. I went to the bed and leaned down to kiss my poor dear friend's bony withered hand.

"Crébillon," she murmured, very distinctly, and I left the room. I had thought she was wandering, and only just now, as I wrote the word, did I remember that he was the author of *Le Sopha*.

December 6. Mr. Ives told me this morning as we were going into breakfast that Mrs. Prescott had died just before midnight. I had to go back to my study because I could not have the boys at my table see my tears. But after a few minutes I was under control, and I came down. Would I have wanted her to live longer? No. Dear God, she is one of thy angels now, and I have no doubt one of the most beautiful. A bell in the chapel tolled a deep note every minute for an hour this morning from eight to nine. In a curious way the notes seemed to accumulate and spread, as in a basin slowly filled by drops, until a rich deep grief overflowed and saturated the campus. It was quite wonderful to me that a sense of death should sit so easily and nobly on a school dedicated to youth. It was as she would have wished it.

December 8. I have seen Dr. Prescott for the first time since her death. I was summoned to his study where I found him at his desk in an attitude of deep contemplation. He did not even look up at me as he asked in a low voice: "It occurs to me, Aspinwall, that you must have been the last person to hear my wife speak. Would you be good enough to tell me what were her last words?"

There was an odd chill in his tone, almost as if he were jealous of this final intimacy. It was noticeable that he did not call me "Brian" as he had before. I had heard something from Mr. Ives of the "hard" period of his life, before the benignity of his old age, and I wondered if his present demeanor might not be a vestige of it. But I was too full of sympathy and love to bear the least resentment. "Crébillon," I murmured. "Crebillon was the last word I heard her utter."

"*What?*"

Stupidly, I repeated the name.

"Surely, you don't mean the French eighteenth century author of salacious novels?"

Haltingly, wretchedly embarrassed, I explained the context while he stared at me with total gravity. When I had finished he was silent.

"How peculiarly unfitting," he said at length in the same solemn tone, "that the last recorded utterance of the woman who contributed more than any other person to this school should be the name of a writer whose books are not even allowed in the library." Then, without smiling, he winked at me. "How like Harriet. How gloriously like her. To go out on such a note of protest. Thank you, my dear Brian. Thank you for telling me that." He rose and reached his hand across the desk to me. I grasped it and then to my horror I began to sob. I covered my face and sobbed. "It's all right, dear boy," I heard him say in the kindest of tones "You loved my wife, and I deeply appreciate it."

"Oh, I did, sir," I murmured, "but what a shocking scene I'm making." I looked up at him, in sudden beseeching despair. "Do you suppose a man with so little control could ever become a minister?"

"Is that what you want to be?"

"Oh, yes!"

Dr. Prescott came around to my side of the desk and put a hand on my shoulder. "It's a good thing to have feeling, Brian. One can't really control it unless one has it, can one? You'll be all right. You have a great deal to give to others, and I think your calling may be a true one. But I don't think you're ready yet. I think maybe a year or two at Justin may be precisely what you need."

I rubbed my eyes, grasped his hand again and hurried from the room. I, who should have been consoling, had asked consolation and had received it munificently! Will a lifetime of good works make up for the blessings I have received? Help me, dear God, to be worthy.

3

BRIAN'S JOURNAL

MARCH 8, 1940. I have made no entries now for three months, not because nothing has happened but because so much has. When I started this journal last September it served no definite purpose, but as time went on it came to serve two. I had a confidant in the first lonely weeks of teaching and a record of my prayers and aspirations from which I hoped to assess my qualifications for the ministry. But now I am not only happy at Justin; I am beginning to be boldly and wonderfully convinced that if God continues willing I shall one day be ready to enter divinity school. And yet I still feel a mysterious compulsion to continue these entries.

I think I know what this compulsion may be, and I am going to write it down now. I am going to make myself do it, no matter how presumptuous it may sound. After all, what is more seemingly presumptuous than the act of becoming a minister? It is robbed of its presumption only by the fact that one is called, and one must learn to distinguish between true and false calls.

What I am trying to say is that I may have a call to keep a record of the life and personality of Francis Prescott.

There, I have said it.

Was it not thus that the gospels and the lives of the saints came to be written? It is not, of course, that there will be any lack of lives written of Dr. Prescott. But since Mrs. Prescott's death I have had opportunities to talk to some of the graduates who have visited the school to offer their sympathies to the headmaster, and it has struck me that they do not see him as I see him. The legend has begun to obliterate the man, and I have the temerity to wonder if the truer vision may not rest with the newer eye, if Dr. Prescott may not be most closely revealed to a non-Justinian.

Mr. Ives, I think, may see him clearly and see him whole, but I wonder if Mr Ives isn't satisfied with his private vision. Somehow I do not see him memorializing it. He strikes me as a man who has no faith in anything *but* Dr. Prescott and hence who would not see the point in writing anything that survived Dr. Prescott. I do not mean by this that I am trying to make this journal a biography of Dr. Prescott. I am simply seeking to capture something that may ultimately save him from the obliteration of the "official" biography.

If again I am not presumptuous. But then I must learn not to be so afraid of presumption. Such fear may be temptation.

To resume: after his wife's funeral there was a great deal of pressure on Dr. Prescott from friends and family to take the winter off. Each of his daughters wanted him to come to her, but he insisted on going on with his duties. Mrs. Turnbull, the youngest, firm of flesh and manner and loud of voice, with a goodly remnant of the dark looks that won her two husbands, and of the temper that must have driven them away, came up from New York to settle in the headmaster's house and cheerfully to patronize us all, but after a month of paternal snubs she departed. Dr. Prescott was finally to be allowed to handle his grief in his own fashion.

It was then that Mr. Ives called me to his study to tell me his proposition.

"The only way we can help Dr. Prescott is to lighten his load, and the only master who can accomplish this is you. Your stock is high at the moment because of your friendship with Harriet. I am therefore creating a new faculty position for you: assistant to the headmaster. You will help him with his mail and correct the themes of his sacred studies classes. You will be available to walk or drive with him in the afternoons. It's a job, of course, that you'll have to play by ear as you go along. If he lets you, there'll be plenty to do."

"But will he let me?"

"I don't know. When I told him about it, he simply grunted. But he didn't refuse. He didn't knock my head off, as I thought he might. All we can do is try. I shall take over your fourth form English, and you will be relieved of study hall periods."

"Oh, sir, that won't be necessary."

"Perhaps not. But in case this plan *does* work, I want you to be free. Don't worry about not carrying your load. If you can be the least help to Dr. Prescott, you'll be doing more for Justin than any other way."

"I will certainly try my hardest."

This conversation took place a month ago, just after the Christmas vacation. The next morning, according to my instructions, I presented myself at the headmaster's office and asked if I could help with his mail. He waved me to a seat and proceeded to read his letters and dictate answers to his secretary, Miss Burns, without paying the least attention to me. I left at eleven, for first form grammar. It was awful.

The next morning, when I again presented myself, he handed me a belligerent letter from a graduate asking how many courses the school gave in "dead languages."

"They're always trying to brand me as a classicist," he grumbled. "Actually, despite my own fondness for Greek poetry, there's less emphasis on the ancient tongues in Justin than in most of the other schools. The older I get the more I realize that the only thing a teacher has to go on is that rare spark in a boy's eye. And when you see *that*, Brian, you're an ass if you worry where it comes from. Whether it's an ode of Horace or an Icelandic saga or something that goes bang in a laboratory."

He made no comment on the answer that I drafted, but he signed it, and thereafter, without further discussion, I found myself in charge of the letters from graduates.

It fascinated me that there were so many of these. At times it seemed to me that Justinians had nothing better to do than write their old headmaster. Some of the letters were childishly boasting. "You will observe from the letterhead that I am now a partner in . . ." or "Did you ever, Dr. P, expect to address me as a fellow doctor?" In others the writers criticized Dr. Prescott bitterly, holding him responsible for unfortunate developments on the national or international scene, even the war itself. There was a shrill note to these, a "Now it can be told," an ultimate twisting, at a safe postal distance, of the old lion's tail. *See* what has come of your emphasis on football, Latin, cold showers, compulsory chapel, grace before meals or stiff collars on Sunday! "Would it interest you to know, Dr. P, how many of my formmates have been swindlers, dope addicts, alcoholics, lechers, pederasts? And whose fault was it, Dr. P?" "Do you know, Dr. P, that I never really felt like a man until I tore up the prayer book you gave me?"

I mention these first because the others, the encomiums, the congratulations, the almost tear-drenched tributes, were in the vast (and ultimately tedious) majority. I concluded that the common denominator of bad and good, favorable and unfavorable, was that in respect to Dr. Prescott most of his graduates had never grown up. They continued to love him or hate him as if they were still at school and to praise or excoriate him as if they were in a "bull session" in the cellar or a canoe on the Lawrence River. He did not seem to dwindle, as childhood figures usually do, and when they came back to visit the school, instead of seeming a sort of quaint Mr. Chips (was *this* what awed me at fourteen, this lovable Meissen granddaddy with his finger athwart his nose?) they saw the same rector, except indeed that he was even more formidable, for the school having dwindled, he suddenly loomed over it, grotesquely large, the manipulator of the puppet show revealed after the final drop of the curtain. The Prescott they had remembered, by Cod, was the *real* Prescott!

His schedule is phenomenal for a man of eighty. He rises at six, in the tradition of the great Victorians, and reads for an hour before breakfast. He claims that a mind continually soaked in small school matters needs this daily airing to preserve any freshness. He reads speedily and broadly, with an emphasis on philosophy and history, and although he keeps abreast of modern fiction, he is happiest with the Greek poets. He then officiates at morning chapel, presides over assembly and spends a busy morning in his office at the Schoolhouse. Lunch at the head table is followed by a half hour of faculty coffee, known as the "time for favors," when he is at his most easy and affable. The afternoon is devoted to the physical inspection of his plant, and in the course of a week he visits every part of the school grounds, some of them many times over: the playing fields, the infirmary, the gymnasium, the locker rooms, the dormitories, even the cellars and lavatories. Dinner is at home, with guests, usually visiting graduates, but after the meal he retires to his study for two more hours of paper work and conferences with boys. At ten o'clock he has a couple of strong whiskeys and the day is over. During prohibition he gave these up, and he tells me that it was a sore denial.

March 15. This afternoon Dr. Prescott and I watched a great snowball fight between the first and second forms, "new kids" against "old kids." Except in a few individual struggles, the latter prevailed; they were bigger and stronger and had been toughened by an additional year of the rigors of Justin Martyr. The scene was like a battle canvas of the Victorian academic school. At a distance it was picturesque, even cheerful, full of red faces and brightly colored jerseys against a white background cut by stark, slaty elms. But on closer inspection the details were more lurid. I saw one little boy with a bleeding lip cut open by a piece of ice and another carried off the field with what turned out later to be a cracked ankle. Dr. Prescott did not seem in the least disturbed.

"You've got to let the boys be animals once in a while," he answered my protest as we walked away. "Social life was more attractive when gentlemen defended their honor with swords and not with lawsuits."

"You don't mean you're in favor of dueling!"

"No, no, of course not," he growled. "I said that life was more attractive, not better. When every sniveling calumniator knew that he ran the chance of being called out. Just the way boys are more attractive when they're allowed to take justice into their own hands and not squeal!"

I was learning, little by little, not to be overwhelmed by him. "Do you suggest that boys are mollycoddled at Justin today, sir?"

The question obviously irritated him, for he stomped ahead of me and did not answer, but after a few moments, when I had caught up with him, he said mildly enough: "Well, of course, there's no hazing now. All the schools have done away with it, and we had to, too. The snowball fight is the last vestigial remnant of it. You have just witnessed a rare survival, my friend."

"It did not make me nostalgic."

"Perhaps you are right." He had resumed now his more reasoning tone. "Perhaps my bias for things English made me see a moral value in hazing where none existed. There was a great deal of cruelty in English public schools in the last century, but it went hand in hand with a certain intensity of friendship between boys—almost a passion, you might say—that gave a kind of golden glow to Victorian youth. Of course in America this sort of thing was understood only at its lowest level, with the result that we took over the hazing and discouraged the friendships. It may have been this that gave our boarding schools their peculiar dryness. Oh, yes, Brian," Here he paused to nod his head affirmatively. "The hazing had to go."

"But you never discouraged close friendships between boys, did you, sir?"

"Did I not?" He grunted loudly. "I was one of the worst!"

"Why, sir?"

"Because, sir," he exclaimed loudly, driving his stick into the snow, "I did not think a hundred examples of David and Jonathan were worth one of sodomy!"

I was too shocked to say more. But I am beginning to glimpse some of the conflicts in his nature. He is an artist as well as a preacher, an intellectual as well as a man of God. He probably adores Swinburne and forces himself not to read him. In this he differs from the famous Dr. Peabody of Groton who preached here last week. Peabody would not see the beauty in Swinburne or be tempted by the Loreleis of art. His is a simpler path.

March 16. I asked Dr. Prescott this afternoon his opinion of Peabody. He gave me one of his foxy, sidelong looks and snapped: "A man who considers that Theodore Roosevelt was America's greatest statesman and *In Memoriam* England's finest poem is well equipped to train young men for the steam room of the Racquet Club."

"That's not where Franklin Roosevelt ended up," I pointed out.

Dr. Prescott threw back his head and roared with laughter. "No, but ninety percent of the Grotties wish he had! And evaporated there!" His laugh ended in a spluttering cough, and he leaned over until he recovered himself, "Of course, I'm being facetious. Cotty Peabody is a great man, in his way.

What I really resent is that my graduates are not more different from his. For all my emphasis on the humanities and his on God, we both turn out stockbrokers!"

"Oh, come, sir. You're not being fair to yourself. Or to Dr. Peabody."

"And yet it may be just what explains our popularity," he continued in a more speculative tone, ignoring my comment. "Most fathers would rather see their sons dead than either cultivated or devout. They commend our efforts, but even more our failures. Yes, the greatness of the private school, Brian, is not that it produces geniuses—they grow anyway, and can't be made—but that it can sometimes turn a third-rate student into a second-rate one. We can't boast publicly of such triumphs, but they are still our glory."

"I wonder if Dr. Peabody would agree with that."

"Dr. Peabody doesn't believe in laughing at sacred things," he said dryly. "And Dr. Peabody is right. A sense of humor is excess baggage in a boys' school. Except to fight snobbishness." He nodded ruefully. "Yes, we need it to fight snobbishness."

"Is there so much snobbishness at Justin?"

"My dear fellow, we're riddled with it! Every private school is. Snobbishness is a cancer in America because we pretend it's not there and let it grow until it's inoperable. In England it's less dangerous because it's out in the open. In fact, they glory in it. But if a boy can only *see* it, there may be one chance in ten that he'll fight it."

"You mean that ninety percent of Justinians are snobs?"

"'I have answered three questions, and that is enough,'" he quoted irritably, "'be off, or I'll kick you downstairs'!"

That was the end of our conversation for that afternoon, and it has taught me a valuable lesson. When he is in one of his destructive moods, it is fatal to try to check him. It is as if on the heath I tried to argue with the raging Lear. My function is to listen, not to console.

April 18. The Reverend Duncan Moore, Rector of St. Jude's Church in New York, was the visiting preacher this morning. I listened with the keenest interest for he is generally regarded as the most likely candidate to succeed Dr. Prescott. I'm afraid I did not like him. He is a big, beaming, smiling, balding, large-nosed man, handsome in an aggressive way and too good a speaker (*I* think) to be truly spiritual. But of course I am horribly prejudiced. I cannot bear to think of anyone succeeding Dr. Prescott.

As a preacher he is drawn to humility like a lemming to the sea. His theme this morning was the war in Europe which he seems to regard as a judgment upon us for the arrogance and materialism of the inter-war decades. Mr. Moore may not actually believe that God sent the war as a scourge, but he seems to think that we should pretend he did, that we should assume a superstition if we have it not.

I walked to Lawrence House after the service with Mr. Ives and found him at his most sarcastic.

"I feel so reassured, don't you, Brian? I have been foolishly worried about the war. Isn't it nice that Mr. Moore has found time to desert his fashionable parish and travel north to give us the good word? To think that all along it has been a blessing in disguise!"

I no longer glanced about to see if any boys were within earshot. I had learned that they never were. Mr. Ives' indiscretions were totally discreet.

"I suppose it's only human to try to make the best out of things," I urged. "Even war."

"Rot, Brian," he retorted sharply. "And you know it, too. Nothing but death and destruction come out of war. England and France are fighting Hitler. If they can put him down, that's all they can expect. The patient after surgery doesn't emerge better than if he'd never had a tumor."

"Even if he has faith that he will?"

"Then it will be the faith that has done it and not the operation."

I shrugged. "I can't argue with you. You know I agree."

"Then will you kindly admit that Duncan Moore is an egregious ass!"

"How can I?" I pleaded in pain. "How can I admit that Dr. Prescott has anointed an ass?"

"Because it's precisely what great men do."

"Moore may improve with responsibility. He will have you to advise him."

"Oh, no, he won't!" Mr. Ives exclaimed in a barklike tone that came closer to expressing fervor than any of his others. "I shall not remain in Justin a minute after Dr. Prescott goes. And I am very much afraid he will go soon."

I stopped to stare in dismay at the small hawklike figure at my side. "What makes you say that?"

"There are signs," he said flatly. "I am very sensitive to signs. There was one, for example, in the sermon today. The new edifice to be erected on the site of the old. The fresh air in stale rooms. Don't you get it? A glittering new Justin Martyr to be fabricated by Duncan Moore out of the rotten timbers of the old."

The calm clear blank sky, the few, almost stationary wispy clouds, the hard pink buds on the dogwood trees by the Schoolhouse, the sudden whoop of a group of boys, the twittering swallows above my head and the deep clang of the Schoolhouse bell that tolled the quarter hour filled me with a sense of sadness at the transiency of good things. My soul seemed to cry out: let me enjoy it, dear God, if this is all there will be to enjoy! The campus of Justin may be a haven from the war, a haven from reality, but when reality is so grim, to be a haven may be a virtuous thing. Soon, only too soon, reality will burst the walls and swell the gutters of the school to boiling livid streams, but the interim is ours and is not the interim as real as reality?

4

BRIAN'S JOURNAL

May 15, 1940. This is my first entry since the catastrophic invasion of the lowlands. Dr. Prescott has great faith in the English and French armies, particularly the English, but I have a sad tendency to identify the "good" side in any conflict with the weak side and to see the war as Brian Aspinwall against a German tank division. It seems curious that I should have such faith in God and so little in man. But then barbarians have prevailed before, have they not? The dark ages *did* exist.

May 18, 1940. The fiend in Europe goes from triumph to triumph. If only I were there. If only I had stayed in Oxford. Surely, even with my heart murmur they would have accepted me now. But there I go again, thinking of the war in terms of what *I* could do in it, even though I'd be a rotten soldier. What would my enlistment amount to but the placation of my own grubby little sense of guilt? Oh, ego, ego, burning like an ember in the conflagration of the world!

May 21. Even Dr. Prescott is beginning to be depressed. "If they get France, it's all over," he told me this morning. "What can England do without a proper army or air force? If she had time, yes, but where is the time coming from? Oh, to be able to fight, Brian, to be able to *fight*. Every useless old man like myself should be given a rifle and rushed to the front." *He,* too!

May 22. The fall of Brussels. It's wonderful how little the boys care. But that must be the hope of the world, indifference. If we cared, how could we live?

May 23. Disaster has sent a peculiar ambassador into our peaceful midst. It is Mr. Horace Havistock, Dr. Prescott's oldest friend, who has lived in Paris for fifty years and who, with rare foresight, decided to repatriate himself only two weeks before the blitzkrieg. He stays shut up in the headmaster's house and has appeared only once in the school dining room, where he sat at Dr. Prescott's right. He seems much older than his host, though they are supposed to be the same age. He is very bent and brown, with thick snowy hair, and he leaned heavily on Dr. Prescott's arm as he hobbled in and out of the dining room. Yet taken as a remnant of the mauve decade he is rather superb. He was wearing a high wing collar, striped trousers, a morning coat and black button boots of lustered polish. Mr. Ives tells me that his valet has to get up every night at two to "turn" him in bed.

May 25. Stories about Mr. Havistock, who remains secluded, continue to enliven the faculty coffee hour. A school is like a small town, and we all need a bit of comic relief in these grim days. Dr. Prescott's houseguest has the function as the porter in the second act of *Macbeth*; he keeps the suspense from becoming unbearable.

Apparently he requires constant service. Breakfast must be on the dot of eight, and when poor old Mrs. Midge, the housekeeper, comes toiling up the stairs with his heavy tray, she is apt to find him waiting on the landing, his eye fixed to his great gold pocket watch, demanding: "Pray tell me, Mrs. Midge, is my watch fast? I have eight-one." A pity he didn't wait in Paris for the Germans. They'd have fixed him!

How on earth did Dr. Prescott ever become intimate with this elegant old dandy? Mr. Ives says it must be a case of opposites attracting.

May 26. Dr. Prescott told me this morning that he was much upset by Mr. Havistock's opinion of the inner state of France. "He says it's rotten right through. That we must anticipate not only defeat but active collaboration with the enemy."

"You don't suppose he's judging it by his own social circle?"

Dr. Prescott looked up with a trace of amusement in his eyes. "What do you know about his social circle?"

"Nothing. But isn't it the same one that Proust wrote about?"

"Or what's left of it," Dr. Prescott conceded with a chuckle. "As a matter of fact, he was a friend of Proust's. He took Harriet to call on him once in the cork-lined chamber. He wouldn't take me; he said I was too noisy. But you mustn't judge Horace's intellect by Horace's social life. He may be a hothouse plant, but he sees a great deal from his hothouse windows. He is wise, Horace. Very wise."

"He is wise, anyway, in his choice of friends," I ventured.

"Oh, Horace only cut his teeth on me," Dr. Prescott said with a laugh. "We were at school together. Since then he has gone way beyond me. But he is loyal. He remembers the old days."

"I shouldn't think a life in the Paris salons was necessarily going so far beyond Justin Martyr."

Dr. Prescott seemed thoroughly amused by my reservations about his friend. "Ah, but Horace did not confine himself to duchesses. He knew your hero, James. He knew Conrad and Hardy. He was intimate with Proust. Redon did the panels in his living room, and Braque the drawings in his study. Horace has an instinctive understanding of the problems of important people. He loves them as our Lord loved little children."

"And how does he feel about little children?"

"Perish the thought!" Dr. Prescott threw up his hands. "I see you have been listening to school tattle about poor Horace. No doubt Justin can make little enough of him. But come and have tea with him this afternoon and judge for yourself."

"What on earth will I talk to him about?" I cried in dismay.

"James! The master," he retorted with mocking emphasis and turned to his mail.

Well, I went. I was nervous all day and my nervousness was not diminished when I came into Mrs. Prescott's old drawing room and found Mr. Havistock seated before her tea tray checking each plate before dismissing the hovering Mrs. Midge. He paid no attention whatever to my entrance.

"Now, let me see. Is my half piece of lime there? Ah, yes, I see it is. And is the toast buttered on *both* sides? It wasn't yesterday." He inspected a piece. "Oh, good. Well, I think that will be all for now, Mrs. Midge. I'll ring if I need anything."

The world in flames and he worries about his toast being buttered on both sides! There must have been five minutes of fussing with the tea things before he finally leaned back in Mrs. Prescott's old chair, touched the tips of his long fingers together before his hawk nose and gazed at me shrewdly.

"Well, Mr. Aspinwall! Frank tells me you were a friend of Harriet's. I can imagine no greater recommendation, for she was a woman of perfect taste. Oh, perhaps not always in clothes . . ." He raised his dark eyebrows which formed a striking contrast to his snowy hair and coughed. "And yet even her clothes, in a wonderful basic Bostonian way, had style."

I looked back now into his small cold grey eyes with a greater sympathy. "It is true. She had great style."

"It is to your credit that you recognize it, young man, for your generation has had little opportunity to observe it. It went out with the last war. Or even before." There was a long pause as he took a sip of his tea and a bite of his doubly buttered toast. "Style," he repeated reflectively. "Odette in the Bois as Proust describes her in *Swann*." He looked up at me now with sudden aggressiveness. "Do you agree there have been no writers since Proust?"

"Not Hemingway?" I protested. "Not Lewis or O'Neill or Fitzgerald?"

"They had talent." His shrug implied that this was to the man what the cravat was to the wardrobe. "I knew Lewis and young Fitzgerald. But they were not presentable. You couldn't depend on what they'd do or say. They bore in their souls the malaise of a dying world. It was art but corrupt art."

I saw there was no purpose in going on with *that*. "Dr. Prescott tells me you knew Henry James."

"My dear fellow, of course I knew him. Don't you know the Lubbock correspondence? There are several letters to me in it."

So he was *that* Havistock, the "dear, dear boy"! Was it possible that this relic before me had once been young? I can quite see Dr. Prescott as a youth, but not Mr. Havistock. Perhaps it was only one of James' hyperbolean compliments.

"Have you ever written your memoirs, sir?"

"Not really. I started a little book that was to be entitled 'The Art of Friendship,' but I never got very far with it, and now I never shall." He smiled complacently. "I'm too old."

"But I would have thought that just the time to write memoirs."

"Also I'm lazy, Mr. Aspinwall." He shook his head solemnly as if he were proclaiming a virtue. "I was born for the oral and not the written word. Some of the pages were all right, but oh, the *work* it took. I have a nice little thing on Réjane and a few good stories about Anatole France. But the only one I completed was the piece on Frank Prescott. About our early days."

My mouth went suddenly dry. "You wouldn't let me see it?"

"Oh, good gracious no. It's highly confidential."

"But if I swore I'd never repeat a word of it?"

He looked up at me, surprised at my eagerness. "Why should you care? When you have Frank in the flesh, what is the fascination of ancient memories?"

"Because I want to know everything about him. How it all started, for example. The whole idea of Justin!"

"You wish to write his life?"

"Oh no, sir. I'm not so ambitious. I simply want to *know*."

"You have no axe to grind?"

"But the very sharpest! I feel . . . how shall I put it? That to know Dr. Prescott is to be enriched. The more I know, the richer I shall be. Oh, yes, I'm quite selfish."

Mr. Havistock smiled almost pleasantly. "But not vulgar. Not yet anyway. You are still uncorrupted. I tell you what, Mr. Aspinwall. When I am settled in Long Island, where I have rented the only Ogden Codman house I could find, I shall go over my papers, and I will consider your request. Yes, I will consider it."

He now tasted a piece of toast from the second tier of the tea stand, one on which marmalade had been spread, and it was evidently not his special brand, for poor Mrs. Midge had to be rung for, and a long discussion ensued. I was disappointed in him. He had taste and perception, no doubt, but the world that he tasted and perceived existed only for his own amusement. He liked marmalade and he liked Proust, which seemed to put them on the same footing. I wonder if the Edwardian era did not contain many such figures in the background, if behind the beauty of James' fiction and of Sargent's portraits there were not a good many limp pieces of toast that had to be buttered on both sides.

May 27. Apparently I passed muster with Dr. Prescott's friend for I was asked to a small dinner tonight at the headmaster's house. It was not a success. Following our host's lead, we all deferred as respectfully to Mr. Havistock as if he had been Walter Lippmann or Dorothy Thompson, but the old boy was in a foul mood (perhaps his valet forgot to "turn" him last night) and answered our questions about the war in grumpy monosyllables. It was obvious that he has no use for any schoolteachers outside of Francis Prescott. He ended by being positively offensive to poor Mr. Ruggles who had the misfortune to suggest the invincibility of a Frenchman "fighting on his own soil."

"As proved, I suppose, in 1815 and in 1870," he snapped. "Unhappily for Europe the clichés of the American tourist will not save the day. The

French peasant may be brave enough; peasants usually are. But in this black century of ours a country is no stronger than its ruling class, and I have known the ruling class of France for forty years."

When the others rose to go, shortly after the silence that followed this outburst, Dr. Prescott winked at me to indicate that I should stay on. Old Horace continued to sit morosely by the fireplace and sip his brandy as he descanted on the horrors of the war.

"Over here you see that things are bad, but you have no conception of how catastrophic they really are. You see that the old world of grace and leisure and art, *my* world if you will, or the remnants of it, is doomed. Obviously. But what *you* don't see, Frank, is that your world is doomed, too."

"What do you call my world, Horace?" the headmaster asked in the milder tone that he used with this old friend.

"The world of the private school," Mr. Havistock answered with a snort. "The world of the gentleman and his ideals. The world of personal honor and a Protestant God. When a civilization crumbles, it crumbles all together. The colors run out, the good with the bad. Roman virtue goes with the Roman arena. Voltaire and Watteau with the *lettre de cachet*. Francis Prescott with Horace Havistock. You can't pick and choose in a flood."

"Please! You make me feel like an old piece of antimacassar."

"You may laugh, my friend, but it's just what you are."

I trembled with indignation to hear Dr. Prescott so slighted. For if he was jesting, Mr. Havistock was not. How did this old fop dare to come up to Justin to taunt the headmaster in his bereavement!

"You'll be telling me I should retire next," Dr. Prescott said in a gloomier tone.

"Of course I will," Mr. Havistock retorted promptly. "It's precisely what I've come up to tell you."

"But if everything is going to pieces," I protested in dismay, too upset now to be silent in the presence of my elders, "why does it matter whether Dr. Prescott retires or not?"

They both looked up at me as if they had forgotten I was there, and I had a sharp sense of intrusion upon an ancient intimacy.

"Because there's such a thing as dignity," Mr. Havistock explained coldly. "And dignity requires one not to hang on."

At this I lost all restraint. "What a cruel thing to say!"

"It's a cruel world."

Dr. Prescott, turning from both of us, had arisen and was staring moodily into the fire. "There must be a limit to what is expected of the old," he said in a grave, melancholy tone. "If we do our job, must our years be thrown in our teeth? Where am I weaker, Horace, than I used to be?"

"You read the service now from the prayer book. The time was when you recited it right through by heart."

Dr. Prescott turned on him, stung. "And *you* claimed it was theatrical. Must I be condemned by my own high standards?"

Mr. Havistock seemed to relent a bit at this. He passed his fingertips over his temples in a brushing gesture that made me suddenly realize that for him, too, the scene might be proving a strain. "Do you remember, Frank, when you used to admire Browning? And 'Pheidippides'? 'Never decline, but, gloriously as he began, so to end gloriously'? Don't decline now."

"But the years have taken me from Browning to Tennyson," Dr. Prescott came back at him. "Like Ulysses, I claim that 'old age hath yet its honor and its toil.' How do you know, Horace, that no 'work of noble note' remains for me to do?"

Mr. Havistock shook his head relentlessly. "The work of noble note is to quit while you're still ahead. I've always given you good advice, Frank. You won't get it from your graduates or your trustees. They're all too scared of you. Believe me, my friend."

Dr. Prescott had turned back to the fire, and his face was drawn down in an expression of bitterness. Suddenly he gripped the mantel with both of his hands and kicked a log viciously. "Nobody's scared of me," he muttered. "Sometimes I wish they were."

"Harriet would have told you the same thing."

"Oh, go to bed, Horace, and stop croaking! You just want everyone else's world to come apart because yours has."

Mr. Havistock did not seem to resent this in the least. He asked me if I would be good enough to fetch his valet, and when I returned from the kitchen with Jules, he and Dr. Prescott were actually laughing!

Of course, I know that at eighty Dr. Prescott cannot go on forever, but I doubt if there is a single master or boy at the school who thinks him inadequate for his job. I had hoped that he might continue a few more years and perhaps have the blessed luck to die in office. But tonight I know there is no such chance. Old Havistock is too practiced a vulture to have come prematurely to the scene of demission. It is perhaps his very undertaker's face that Dr. Prescott has awaited.

June 2. Prize Day, and Mr. Havistock's seed have borne bitter fruit. Dr. Prescott made the announcement of his retirement at the close of the ceremonies. It came as a complete surprise and shock to his audience.

The weather, at least, was perfect. The whole school, in Sunday blue, and the parents sat on benches in the middle of the campus facing the dais for the headmaster and visiting dignitaries. I have never seen so brilliant an azure sky, so emerald a lawn. The awakened earth seemed to burst with promises that had nothing to do with disaster across the seas.

When the last diploma had been handed out and the last prize given, the headmaster stood silent for a long moment before the amplifier, both hands in his pockets, his eyes fixed beyond the crowd at the point where the river path disappeared into the woods.

"I have one more brief statement to make. Since the death of my beloved wife I have felt the moral support of every boy and of every master in the school. I have been buoyed up in a difficult time by close to five hundred pairs of arms. With such a backing I have almost fooled myself that I could go on forever. But time is remorseless, and I have passed by a whole decade the biblical limit of threescore years and ten. I shall remain in office for one more year so that my successor may have time to prepare for the transition. In June of 1941 the Reverend Duncan Moore will become headmaster of Justin Martyr. God bless you all. We will now adjourn for lunch."

There was a stunned, staggered silence and then gasps and then cries of "Oh, no!" Dr. Prescott walked abruptly to the edge of the dais, and we heard the quick click of his heels descending the steps. He strode rapidly down the aisle and was almost out of sight before next year's senior prefect, very red in the face, leaped to his feet and screamed hoarsely: "Let's have a long cheer for Dr. Prescott!"

We all rose and roared that cheer. It echoes in my ears as I write this.

June 3. Dr. Prescott has, of course, been surrounded by people since his great announcement. Graduates, parents and trustees mill about him to try to impress their little pinpricks of sympathy and admiration into his bland, impersonal attention. I have a discreditable feeling of resentment, as if they were taking him away from me and had no right to, as if I alone and not they had any true appreciation of his greatness. Of course this is nonsense and egotism, yet I cannot help feeling that the man I see when we're alone is different from the idol of the crowd.

He sent for me tonight before supper in his study and asked me if I wished to go to divinity school in the fall. He had spoken to the Dean at Harvard about me. He was so gentle, and I was so touched that he should remember my problems that I stammered too badly to be understood.

"Oh, sir," I protested at last, "I only want to stay and help you!"

"But I shan't need you now, Brian. I only needed an assistant while I was trying to conserve my energy. Now that I'm going to retire I can be a spendthrift. I can blow it to the winds."

"Well, if you don't need me, sir," I pleaded, "then I need *you*!"

He coughed with a hint of disapproval. He disliked any demonstration of feeling, particularly with regard to himself. "You don't need *me*, young man, but perhaps you need another year at Justin. Particularly if you want to come back here when you've taken orders. What will you do this summer?"

"I thought I might go to Columbia for a course in Elizabethan drama."

He laughed. "It's better reading than the papers today. Perhaps I may try a bit of it myself."

August 1. New York. Since the last entry France has surrendered, and England has entered her hideous ordeal. I have been unable to write. I sit in my rented room on upper Broadway with windows open on a sultry silent avenue and immerse myself in Beaumont and Fletcher. It has been as if a dark curtain had blessedly been lowered over the agonizing vividness of the past year, over death in Europe and death in Justin Martyr. It has been as if I had died and gone to a seventeenth century spirit kingdom inhabited by jealous sovereigns and crafty nephews, by ambitious cardinals and cynical clowns, by melancholy and madness, bones and diadems.

This morning I received a large brown envelope from Mr. Havistock containing the typescript of his chapters on Dr. Prescott and the following note:

Dear Aspinwall: Here is the "Prescottiana" that you wanted. I make you a present of it. The world is full of asses, but they are particularly abundant among the loyal graduates of New England church schools. Justin Martyr is no exception. Poor Frank is so surrounded that you may be the only chink through which he can be seen. Unless you become an ass, too. Don't.

Your friend from another century,
H.H.

As I read the words I felt again the throb of my ancient faith. God's presence had been suspended, not withdrawn, and I blush for my craven doubts and turn to Mr. Havistock's piece.

5

FROM HORACE HAVISTOCK'S "THE ART OF FRIENDSHIP"

As I LOOK back upon a long and (I hope) non-useful lifetime over decades devoted to cultivating the luxuries and letting the necessities go scrape for their sordid selves, I am perfectly clear that the greatest and most indispensable of the former has been that of my friendships. The art of making these, distrusted of women, has never been much cultivated in America, and I have had largely to pursue it abroad, but I will always remember and will here gratefully record that my first lesson was taken under the ashen sky of a New England winter.

I met Frank Prescott when we were sixteen, at St. Andrew's School in Dublin, New Hampshire, in the fall of 1876. Had he not been in my form, I should certainly not have been able to last out till Christmas. It was bad enough that I was at once a new boy and a fifth former, an incongruous situation, but it was a good deal worse that I had been brought up exclusively by nurses and tutors and kept safe until well past puberty from the savage competition of my contemporaries. How I happened to be suddenly shorn of my curls and stripped of my velvet suits and isolated with members of my own sex—total strangers every shrieking one of them—involves my telling something of my own beginnings.

I am the youngest child of a marriage of June and January, and, alas, I cost June her life. My father, Gridley Havistock, had children of an earlier match who were older than my mother; he was sixty at my birth and survived to my thirtieth year. He was a huge, big-bellied, bulbous-nosed, pig-eyed bewhiskered old-school New York gentleman, magnificent in his authoritarianism, but testy, snappish and accustomed to obedience. A great deal that he said was banal, and all of his aphorisms were platitudes, but he *looked* like a business leader and certainly acted like one, and in his generation appearances counted for more than they counted later when scalawags like Gould and Fiske had taught New Yorkers to be suspicious of everyone.

I doubt if Father would have been president of the Merchants' Bank and a trustee of New York Central a generation later. He was not in the league, financially, mentally or immorally, with the new magnates of steel and rail, but he had the happy good sense to have learned to get on with them and to be able to make them feel that an invitation to 310 Fifth Avenue or "Gridley Court" in Newport was one of the things they had dreamt of in their log cabins or steerage days. This good sense, I may add, he conveyed to his children, and it has proved the most valuable gift of the few with which he endowed us.

My older brothers of the second bed enjoyed Father's rude health, but I was a rheumatic child, subject to constant respiratory complaints, and was turned over at a tender age to the ministrations of the one person who wanted me, a faded, ailing, old maid half-sister who presided timidly over her terrifying father's table and who, because of the difference in age of more than a generation, was addressed by her demi-siblings as "Sister Sue." She, dear creature, was full of recipes and quaint medicinal superstitions; she ventured out of doors in only the balmiest weather and then swathed in furs and scarfs over the black of her perpetual mourning for perpetually dying cousins. My childhood was spent in upstairs parlors before small well-tended fires, reading English and French fiction while Sister Sue worked on her needlepoint, and in the blur of early memories Grant in the Wilderness, Sherman riding to the sea, my brother Archie winning a tennis match or the bray of laughter from downstairs at Number 310 where Father was entertaining the Hone Club, were part and parcel of a men's world, happily no more real and not nearly as exciting as the romances of Dumas or Jane Porter.

I managed to protract this dreamlike existence to my fifteenth year and might have stretched it to my own maturity had poor Sister Sue not died of a breast cancer. Of course, it was not put that way to me. "She was tired and went to sleep," was the Havistock diagnosis. And I was discovered, or perhaps I should say "realized," by my family for the first time, an ungainly, despairing, dressed up doll, abandoned on top of the pathetic little heap of her possessions. Everyone tried to be kind, but their kindness congealed into something more brittle when the great doctor, from whom Sister Sue had guarded me behind the opaque wall of her quacks, pronounced me to be in fully adequate health for boarding school.

My brother Archie, as oldest of the second bed, now "took me in hand," promising Father that he would have me ready in a few months' time for St. Andrew's where all my brothers had gone. He went straight to work, firmly and I think fairly, with lessons and exercises and instruction in sports, but all his preparations were blown to bits by the first crisp blast of an autumnal New England wind and the terrifying shouts from the football field on the day that he delivered me to and abandoned me at my new abode.

It is important briefly to describe St. Andrew's, as it existed in the seventies, because it later became the model of all that Frank Prescott thought a school should not be. Life there, outside of classes, was totally disorganized. The boys played informally at football and baseball, making up their own rules, but they were quite at liberty, if they pleased instead, to roam the New Hampshire countryside and fish or trap in their afternoons. They were equally at liberty to haze the weak and to group themselves into fierce little competing clubs. They bathed but once a week and never changed, even when exercising, from their stiff collars and itchy flannel underwear, so that the evening meal after a hard game of soccer was a trial for the sensitive. I will admit that they seemed to have enjoyed themselves, but to me the school was another Dotheboys Hall.

I was always cold, always dirty and generally disliked. I was mocked and chastised, not only by my peers in the fifth form but by boys much younger who quickly grasped the idea that I was hopeless at fisticuffs. I was called "Frenchy" because of my suits and "Willow" because of my walk. Archie's standards of clothes, however Spartan in contrast to Sister Sue's, seemed grossly luxurious to St. Andrew's. From the morning bell and my pail of icy water to evening prayers and the threat of a turtle in my bed, life was a series of hideous apprehensions.

The faculty lived in a world of their own, as remote from the daily problems of the boys as the quaint Gothic gingerbread buildings which gave to the little campus the air of an English college in a puppet show. In this they followed the example of the headmaster, Dr. Howell, a tall, spare, otherworldly cleric, garbed in rather dirty black, who never used any term of address but a vaguely benevolent "my dear" and who made no secret of his low opinion of boys, or "apes" as he blandly called them. He had the iron will of the temperless religious fanatic, and he exercised absolute authority over the small areas of school life that broke through the icy wall of his spiritual preoccupation. He cared for our souls and only for our souls; he took no interest in games or recreations and used to revile the human body as an "unlovely thing." An uncompromising Episcopalian, he would remind boys whose families were known to be friendly with Unitarians or Baptists that members of these sects would occupy a lower social level in the hereafter, and he was said to have fired a boy who came to his study to confess that he was suffering from doubts as to the apostolic succession.

Yet the extraordinary thing about America in the last century was that Dr. Howell was not only revered by graduates; he was held in respect and awe by the boys. He is a legend in the vastly expanded St. Andrew's School of this day, and to suggest that he was a bigot and a tyrant would be regarded as appalling heresy by a generation which knows him only from the great Chase portrait in the school dining room, a fabulous study in the El Greco manner of zealous faith and asceticism.

I myself looked up to him as a creature happily exempted from my own sordid tribulations. I admired his detachment from problems that I regarded as inevitably, if humiliatingly, my own personal doom. Watching him drive his pony cart about the campus, so blissfully unaware of the cold, the rain, the horrid little boys and all the horrid things in their horrid little minds, like a priest in the Middle Ages who has had the sense to understand that only by the cassock could he escape the armed strife and dominate the armored figures, I could almost persuade myself that I, too, might one day be a free soul.

Frank Prescott at first seemed as remote as the headmaster. He was also a fifth former but, unlike me, he had been in the school for three years, and he led our form, not only in studies but in athletics. His short, thick figure and broad shoulders made him a superb tackle in football, a game which he played with a passion and roughness that was more the way it came to be played in the nineties than it was then. But Frank, however respected and admired, was not as popular as one might have supposed. He cared too little for the opinions of others, and he could be brutally outspoken in his speech. He was a silent, moody boy, and there was an air of truculent, rather un-lovable superiority in his pale square handsome face and in those big calm brooding wide-apart brown eyes.

He was an orphan of small means but of the best Boston connections, a distant cousin of the historian, and even as a boy he had the natural dignity of a New England aristocrat. To me he was a romantic, Byronic figure from the beginning, an impression that was intensified when I learned that he was an orphan, the only child of a father who had died a hero at Chancellors-ville and of a beautiful, grief-stricken mother who had quickly followed him to the grave. Frank never joined the others in making sport of me, but then he never seemed to notice me at all.

The episode that brought us together was an attack launched upon me with iced snowballs by three fourth formers one early December afternoon as I was leaving the library. After pelting me unmercifully, they threw me in the snow and would have jumped upon me had not Frank at that moment appeared down the path. When he shouted at them to leave me alone, two of them ran discreetly off a ways, but one, the smallest, stood his ground.

"What business is it of yours, Prescott?" he cried shrilly. "He's a new boy, isn't he? He's fair game. Who the hell do you think you are? God almighty?"

Frank stepped forward quickly and struck the boy so viciously across the mouth that he fell his length on the snow. When he struggled to his feet I saw that his lips were bleeding.

"What did you do that for?" he shrieked, but for all his outrage he dared not make a move to strike at Frank, nor did his two friends, hovering, take any step to come to his aid.

"To teach you a lesson about upperclassmen."

"But he's a *new* boy!" my persecutor insisted again.

"I don't care. He's a fifth former, and you'd better remember it."

When I was alone with my rescuer, I tried to thank him, but in the suf-focation of my gratitude I stammered so badly that I made no sense. Frank cut me short with words as brutal as his blow to the other boy's cheek.

"I didn't do it for you, Frenchy, don't worry. I did it for the honor of the form. Pick up your ridiculous hat. You're a disgrace to us, allowing yourself to be beat up by fourth formers. Why didn't you even put up a fight?"

"They were three to one!"

He did not deign to answer this, but strode off, leaving me to the shame that he felt I ought to feel. But I have never wasted much time on shame. I have always freely accepted myself and my limitations. What struck me most as I stared after that broad, retreating back was the vision of how different life would be if I could always count on such a protector. Might it not make life even at St. Andrew's bearable?

Now the reader may wonder how one of my lowly position in the school could possibly aspire to a friendship with such a boy as Frank Prescott, particularly after the rebuff which I had just received. There were two reasons: first, that I was quick enough to grasp that the rebuff had really come from Frank's dislike at being thanked for striking a smaller boy, and second, that I was already unconsciously developing the theory of friendship around which I was to build my life. This theory was simply that any man who wants strongly enough to become the friend of another will succeed if there are no unbridgeable class or racial gaps and if he wastes no time in worrying about his own inferior attainments. The unlovable Boswell pursued and captured Paoli, Rousseau and Voltaire before he even started on Johnson. I am known today as a veteran collector of paintings and bibelots, but the collection of which I am proudest is that of my friends. They are a distinguished and variegated lot, beginning with Frank Prescott, and ending (at least to date) with Scott Fitzgerald.

Two days later I walked as boldly as I knew how down the fifth form study corridor to knock on Frank's door. "I know you don't want to see me," I began, "but one good turn deserves another. I've been thinking of what I could do for you in return for what you did for me, and I've decided the only thing I'm any good in is French. I had a real mademoiselle and used to talk it with her. I can help you, if you'll let me try." Frank stared at me with unfeigned astonishment for several moments and then broke into a rude laugh. "Well, I'll be damned," he exclaimed. "If Frenchy doesn't want to teach me to be a frog!"

"Very well, if that's the attitude you want to take," I retorted with what I hoped was a chilling dignity. "But I meant it nicely, Prescott."

I went back to my own study, and fifteen minutes later he knocked at the door. "I'm sorry, Havistock. May I sit down? I'm having the devil of a time with this chapter of *Émilie*."

I discovered that winter that I was a first class tutor. Indeed, I could have made my living at it had my situation in life so required. I even gained a small headway against Frank's Boston accent which must be one of the greatest obstacles the Gallic tongue has ever encountered. But the friendship, for all my assiduousness, developed very slowly. Frank had too little time for human relationships. He studied hard, read a great deal and exercised violently. When he did allow me to accompany him on one of his long Sunday hikes, I would be too exhausted keeping up with his quick stride to have the energy to break his silences.

Yet he tolerated me, that was the great thing. I never had to fight with him the usual adolescent's snobbishness which frowns on the least companionship between a popular and an unpopular boy. Frank may have cared little enough for me, but I was quick to note that he cared as little for anyone else.

Gradually, a more personal note came into our colloquies as we walked together to chapel or as we sat side by side at meals. Frank had an aunt, a Miss Jane Prescott, to whom he was very devoted, and I told him about Sister Sue. It was a bond, if a tenuous one. Others followed. We discovered that we both liked Greek drama and despised Lord Tennyson. That we both liked chess and sneered at checkers. That we both revered the shade of Lincoln and deplored a civilian Grant.

But Frank had terrible prejudices which would sometimes make a clean sweep of all the little ropes and grappling hooks that I kept casting up to his decks. He passionately believed that an age of heroes had died with his father in the red clay of Virginia and that a generation of jackals now gorged itself on the bloated carcass of valor. He completely blew up at me when I suggested that the Civil War might have been avoided had more people, like my own father, tried to compromise the issues.

"You New Yorkers would compromise with the devil himself to save your pocketbooks!" he exclaimed bitterly. "You must have all fainted with relief when you found out, after war *did* come, that you could still make money out of it. We Bostonians, poor idealistic fools, went south to fight while you bought substitutes. The Prescotts died poor while the Havistocks filled their cashboxes!"

He was a strange, proud, bitter boy, and he could be very cruel indeed when he wanted. I did not mind his outbursts against New York or my family which I felt were more or less justified, but I minded very much one night, in front of the whole dormitory, when he volunteered a wicked parody of my early ablutions on a cold winter morning. It was such an unexpected blow, so brutally repudiating to what I was just beginning to look upon as friendship, and he did it with such unexpected and fiendish skill, that I burst into tears and embarrassed everybody. Everybody but Frank himself.

In the spring I made my great bid. Archie had suggested to Father that I be allowed to ask a friend to visit us in Newport, and I invited Frank. I had an unfair advantage in that I already knew that his only alternative to a hot summer in Boston with his Aunt Jane was to tutor a rich brat of a Prescott cousin on the Cape. Perfectly fairly, he expressed no gratitude when I made my offer; he simply informed me that he would have to consult his guardian. The latter, fortunately for me, approved of this solution of his ward's summer and even advanced the funds for an outfit that would not disgrace a Prescott amid the Havistocks, and Frank was delivered to me in early July, bound, so to speak, in summer wrappings. It was a curious reversal of our roles, that he, the athlete and school leader, should become a boy put up, almost as a charity, for the summer to be a playmate for the delicate and difficult Horace. But, needless to say, it did not take him long to put things back in their proper place.

Newport in the seventies was beginning to show signs of turning into the silly jumble of derivative palaces that it later became. The little white hand to which Henry James was to liken the summer colony of his childhood was already filling with gold. But the essence of the old Newport was still there, the Newport of Julia Ward Howe and romantic Gothic and ladies' archery contests on small bright green lawns, the Newport, as James was again to put it, "of a quiet, mild, waterside sense, one in which shores and strands and small coast things played the greater part." It was a Newport that had not yet succumbed to the Vanderbilts and Goelets, and the only Newport I have ever cared for.

Our house, which was grand for those days, stood in the center of a twenty acre plot on Bellevue Avenue surrounded by a huge, beautiful lawn shaded with great elms. It was an Alexander Jackson Davis structure of smooth brown stucco, utterly asymmetrical, with many little balconies and unexpected porches and odd, protruding conservatories. As its arched windows, though multitudinous, were tiny, it was utterly dark within. Father, still magnificent at seventy-seven, with his five young sons, four of whom, at least, were handsome blades, continued to be an impressive figure in the summer colony. His bays were the sleekest, his carriages the most gleaming, and when the six of us, in black coats and striped grey trousers, marched down the aisle to our pew in Trinity Church of a Sunday morning, it must have been a pretty good show.

All of the family were immediately attracted to the silent, handsome boy whose good manners (for Frank's manners with adults were always perfect) never seemed to compromise his rugged independence of thought. He had a bit of a row with Father over the reconstruction of the South, but he won it decisively. Father was one of a small persistent group who, despite the posthumous sanctification of Mr. Lincoln, still regarded the late President in the rail-splitter tradition. He had actively supported McClellan in the 1864 campaign and thought Lincoln "soft" on the South, positions that might seem inconsistent today but which then quite commonly went together. When Frank, one night at dinner, spoke up loudly to condemn the loss by the living of the precious unity for which the dead, including his own father, had been sacrificed, there was no further waving of the bloody shirt.

The summer was a happy one for me. Frank, as a guest, reined in much of his natural sarcasm and took me sailing almost every clear day. He loved to poke about the rocky inlets along the coast and to fish and swim from the boat, and he loved returning in the early evening and watching the spires of old Newport against the setting sun. I was asked to parties now, because all the girls were interested in Frank, and I discovered, not without a pang of adolescent jealousy, that he had a very distinct taste for their company. I wanted to keep him to myself, but I was shrewd enough, even at seventeen, to know that the smallest effort in this direction would be fatal to our still precarious relationship. It had to be my consolation to remember that back at St. Andrew's there would be no silly girls to giggle at his least funny remarks and to lead him on to talk, unbecomingly, of his prowess in sport. I believed then, as I believe today, that men are at their most attractive in the company of other men.

I paid for the entire happiness of that summer in a single incident that occurred after our return to school. I do not know if it happened because of Frank's restlessness under the burden of his imagined duty of gratitude, or because he felt cut off from the other boys at so marked an association with one who was still considered "different," or because he was stifled by the now compulsory blanket of friendship that the summer had seemed to throw over us. At any rate, one night at the sixth form table during a general discussion of our future careers, he answered my innocent question about his own by lashing back at me in a voice for all to hear: "Oh, I'm going to Newport in a red and yellow blazer to court the richest heiress I can find. And when I've married her, I'll lie back in silk sheets like a Havistock and puff at Turkish cigarettes and be so, *so* above the poor old vulgar world."

My eyes filled with tears (I still hadn't learned to repress them), and I abruptly left the table. In my room alone I reviewed the history of my relationship with Frank. I considered each aspect with what I hoped was a minimum of self-pity and decided in the end that the pain outweighed the pleasure. The little bits of kindness that he occasionally tossed me did not compensate for his cruelty. I was not even angry as I came to my sad conclusion. I felt sincerely sorry for him. He would probably go through his life antagonizing everyone who tried to be nice to him, slapping away helping hands and spitting in sympathizing eyes. Well, so it would have to be. It was better to have no friend than the like of him.

I did not speak to Frank for the next two weeks, and he took no notice of it. He was busy with football, and as one of the school prefects he had to act as an assistant to Dr. Howell. But one afternoon, when he had sprained his wrist and was unable to play his favorite game, he appeared at the door of my study and without the least hint of an apology for his past conduct, blandly suggested that we take a walk. When I told him that I did not care to associate with a person who had pretended to be my friend and later made public mock of me, he simply laughed.

"Don't be an ass," he said. "Come along. I thought we might sit in chapel for a bit and then watch the football."

"Why sit in chapel?" I asked in surprise.

"Because it's nice."

He walked down the corridor, and I sat looking after him until it broke in upon me that this was his way of apologizing. I could choose between my pride and Frank, and I have never been one to spite my face by hacking off its features. I hurried after him, and we walked to chapel where we sat for half an hour in adjoining choir seats, absolutely still and silent, while Frank stared up at the big, beautiful altar window that portrayed, in glowing whites and reds, the transfiguration.

I found the experience a bit embarrassing, as if we had happened uninvited into God's house and caught him in his dressing room. Religion to the Havistocks was a formal matter. God and man met only in their Sunday best, and one did not talk about him, any more than one talked about one's hostess at a party, except in terms of perfunctory respect.

I suspected, however, that God meant more than this to Frank, not from anything that he had ever said, but from the way he closed his eyes in prayer. One knew then that he was not thinking of games or girls. In that half hour at chapel he may have been with the father whom he had never known, coughing blood in the mud at Chancellorsville or with the poor little white shadow of a mother, roaming the dark corridors of the Marlborough Street house with crooning moans. Or he may have simply been opening the pores of his soul to the Holy Spirit and passively allowing it to enter. I have never had any faith of my own other than one in that of others, a curious kind of heretical suspicion that God would not abide in such as me but might abide in such as have been my friends. Call it what you will, faith or superstition, it has got me through most of a long life.

Frank nodded to me at last, and we left the chapel. "That was bully, wasn't it?" he asked, and I was embarrassed again by the unexpected adjective.

We walked down to watch the football which bored me but which seemed of unending fascination to Frank. A play had just ended in a violent scrimmage, involving most of the members of both teams, when an odd thing happened. We suddenly saw the headmaster hurrying across the field, waving his umbrella and shouting in a shrill tone. I had never seen him on the athletic field before, much less running. When he reached the scrimmage heap he tried to pull away one of the boys by his legs, and I could now make out his high voice exclaiming: "Don't kill him! Don't kill the boy underneath! What are you doing? Dear God, what are you *doing* to him?"

All the boys stood up now bewildered, and we heard the embarrassed but respectful coach explaining to Dr. Howell that the scrimmage, far from being an organized pogrom, was a natural, indeed an integral part of the game. Dr. Howell, however, did not seem in the least embarrassed by his mistake and proceeded on the spot to draw up a new code of rules. Why was it necessary for the boy carrying the ball to be brought to the ground? Why should it not be sufficient simply to touch him? I was thoroughly enjoying the discomfort of the players when I realized that I was alone, and, turning, saw Frank striding swiftly away towards the Dublin Lake Road. I ran after him and caught his arm, but he shook me impatiently off.

"Don't you want to see how they settle it?" I asked. "Honestly, it's a circus!"

"To you it is. You don't care about football."

"Well, if you care so much, why don't you stay and argue with him?"

"Oh, what the hell, Horace!" he exclaimed impatiently. "We'll be out of here in the spring! Let's go on to the lake. I need a walk and some air. Let that old baboon turn it into a game of tag if he wants."

"You call Dr. Howell a baboon?" I cried, scandalized. "I thought you admired him."

"Admired him!" Frank stopped and looked at me in perplexity as if he would never come to the end of my quixoticism.

"For what do you take me? Admire that bigoted, sanctimonious jackass?"

I remember distinctly that it was then and there that I decided that I would have to establish limits to the domination of Frank Prescott. "You go too far," I retorted. "You always go too far and get violent about things. Dr.

Howell is rather superb, really. He's a kind of symbol, like a sovereign or pope. He's above the vulgar hurly-burly of school competition."

"Above it!" Frank shouted. "What business does he have being above his boys? Football is a tough, hard game, the way life is, except for a few favored souls like the Havistocks. A headmaster ought to be down on that field playing with the boys himself. He ought to be *in* that scrimmage, not whimpering about it!"

"Dr. Howell? Would you want to kill him?"

"Well, he ought to know the rules, then, and what a scrimmage is. You're the most impossible romantic, Horace. You have to visualize him as some kind of Michelangelo prophet with flowing robes and a thunderstorm in the background. You can't bear to see him as a silly, preoccupied old boy in a dirty black suit pulled around the campus in a pony cart because he's too lazy to walk!"

I burst out laughing. "Can you blame me?"

"Oh, to hell with him." Frank gave it up and slapped me painfully on the shoulder. "He's not worth a row. But I can promise you there won't be any Howells in my school."

"In *your* school? Are you going to have one?"

"Maybe some day." He shrugged, but I knew at once by his suddenly averted eyes and the quick set of his jaw that he was entirely serious. "Why not? Don't you think I could manage one?"

"On the contrary, I think you'd manage it very well. Would it be a church school?"

"Certainly."

"But wouldn't you have to be a minister?"

"I'm going to be a minister, Horace." He turned to look at me hard now, and those glittering brown eyes defied me to smirk. "I'm going to be a minister and a schoolmaster. You asked me once what I was going to be, and I put you off. Well, there it is. I'm going to England next year because I think an American schoolmaster should know all there is to know about English schools. My guardian's arranging to get me into Balliol, at Oxford. Would you like to go to Oxford with me?"

"I should love it!" It was all very startling, but I have always made decisions quickly, and this was an easy one. Harvard had loomed before me like an extension of St. Andrew's, and the prospect of a life abroad and shared with Frank seemed almost impossibly glamorous. "Perhaps I could teach at your school, too. You remember I taught *you* French." But a sudden horrid doubt assailed me. "Would I have to play football?"

Frank threw back his head and roared with laughter. "God forbid! No, you could teach French and handle the mothers when they thought I was being too hard on their precious darlings."

I was enchanted that in two minutes' time my entire future, which until then had been such a dreary blank, should now be so cheerfully disposed of. "Where will the money come from?"

"For the school? What about yours?"

"I don't think I have any," I reported ruefully. "Father always tells me

I'll have enough to live on 'decently,' whatever that means, provided I stay a bachelor. If I want to marry, I shall have to work."

Frank seemed to find this enormously funny. In fact, his mood was exuberant now, almost hilarious. "Let's hope that no such terrible sacrifice will be required of you. Don't worry about the money. I have some rich cousins. There's always a bit of money to be had for a worthy cause in Boston. For example, my guardian was able to find a trust fund to pay for the education abroad of any descendant of my great-grandfather."

"So that's why we're going to Oxford!"

Frank winked. "Let's put it that I'm killing two birds with one stone."

I realized that the half bantering, half solemn temper of the conversation had been Frank's way of telling me that my long submitted bid for his friendship had been accepted. There was never anything else said to establish this, but nothing else, to a boy of Frank's reticences, was necessary. I had weathered his coldness, his rebuffs, his actual insults; now they would cease. Once admitted to Frank's intimacy—and I am proud to say that very few have been—one found oneself a life member. He expected to be the dominant partner; he expected me, for example, to attend the college of his choice and to help him in the creation of a school of which *he* would be headmaster. But that was the way I wanted it. I was quite willing to settle for the junior position provided only that I was at liberty to speak my mind.

For the rest of the school year we walked together on Sunday afternoons and made elaborate plans for the future. He lectured me about my triviality and sophistry and tried to interest me in sport, while I mocked him when he took himself too seriously and laughed at his moodiness. The element of the female in my nature matched well with the masculine in his; in many ways our relationship was like that of a strong, singleminded husband and a clever, realistic wife. I quite realize that in the days in which I am writing, it will be impossible for a reader of the last sentence not to jump over a Freudian moon, but I belong to a simpler and less polluted generation. I have always gloried in my conception of friendship, and I will insist to my dying day that it has nothing of sex in it.

For a time it seemed that I had everything in life that I could possibly want: a friend whose approval made me at last a respectable figure on the little campus of St. Andrew's and a European future, just around the corner, that loomed, like the great pack on a Santa Claus' back, with spires of old cathedrals and castle turrets jutting out of its open end. I had, for the first time in my life, everything that I seemed to desire, with everybody's blessing, to boot. And what did I feel? Simply a small, half-recognized, vaguely tickling ennui. It was my first lesson from the gift-bearing Greeks.

The trouble, I found, lay in the very core of my supposed happiness: in my intimacy with Frank. He, too, had never had a confidant before, and once he had overcome his initial reticences, he helped himself, in increasingly liberal doses, to my extravagantly offered attention. He would have listened to me, no doubt, had I had confidences of my own of equal value. But I had little to show for my years of loneliness but my daydreams and fantasies, and he had the whole complicated structure of his school, created in his mind over the adolescent years, course by course, master by master, building by building. No wonder he had been a silent and moody boy. Like Frankenstein, he had been locked away in a mental laboratory, creating his monster.

I call it a monster because I had already begun to fear that it would swallow me. To him it was something far, far different. To him it was nothing less than the source of regeneration of a modern world that had been corrupted by carpetbaggers and venal politicians. Frank believed passionately that the maw of civil strife had swallowed all that had been finest in the generation before us and had ended, fittingly enough for such a holocaust, with the assassination of the sainted Lincoln. Grant was to him the body of the hero which has lost its soul, the plight of a nation of ex-warriors grubbing for gold. And God would work through Francis Prescott, a humble instrument selected to reward his father's sacrifice, to raise up new leaders of men.

"I know it is what my father would have wanted of me," he would tell me somberly, over and over. "It is the only way I can give to God what he gave."

I used to visualize Frank's God with a little shudder as a despondent general, sitting, chin in hand, on a campstool by a tent, like one of those lithographs of Napoleon in Russia, surveying the field of that day's defeat and waiting for a miracle in the morning. Frank's father, his own faith and his projected school were all inextricably intertwined, and my early knowledge of this gave me an insight into some of his later peculiarities as a minister which were to baffle and shock so many. Frank was never to be interested in any souls but those of his boys.

Not only did I have to learn more than I wanted about the administration of Frank's still fictional academy; I had to try to improve my own spiritual qualifications to become a member of his imagined faculty. He sought to discover the state of my religious life and asked me questions about my family with the sometimes brutal frankness of one who had none of his own. I have always been the kind of egotist who likes to talk around, rather than about, myself, and I found his probing painful. Our talks on Sunday used to go something like this:

"I'm afraid you must face the fact, Horace, that your family is a peculiarly worldly one. I doubt if I've ever in my life seen such an emphasis on appearances. Indeed, your father seems to believe in nothing but the *appearance* of believing."

"That's what he calls 'setting an example.'"

"You admit, then, he's a Pharisee?"

"I admit he's a magnificent one! If you're going to be a Pharisee, you may as well do it with style."

Frank would shake his head, whistle and quicken his pace, and I, stumbling after him, would simply pray that the glories and fascinations of old England would soon divert him from his favorite topic. My prayer was to be fully answered in six months' time, and I was again to learn the malevolence of those seeming generous Greeks.

6

FROM HORACE HAVISTOCK'S
"THE ART OF FRIENDSHIP"

Our THREE YEARS at Balliol were a happier time for me than for Frank. I developed my character into the essential shape which it possesses to this day, while he pursued his down a side street that dwindled to a dead end. Yet of the two of us he seemed the more content.

He took immediately to English life and English ways. It was as if he had suddenly discovered his natural environment. He was heartier, louder, funnier, more companionable and far better dressed, for the Prescott trust permitted him to become a bit of a dandy. He loved the solid masculine comfort of the English gentleman's life, the large cold stone houses with their roaring fires, the hunting on foggy moors and the long dinners at long tables glittering with more jewelry and silver than seemed quite decent.

He had many letters of introduction from Boston, some to the highest places, and he was much taken up as a Yankee who could talk back without being rude, who could praise his own country without seeming shrill and who was a first class oar and shot. It seemed to me that he spent rather more time visiting castles than schools and that his talk was more of foxes and of wines than it was of masters and boys, but I supposed that this was all part of his education. That is one of the joys of going to school abroad; whatever one does can be chalked up to the imbibing of atmosphere. If Frank, however, seemed to be neglecting the project of his lifework, he did not neglect his courses, for he ended up with a first in "greats" and was offered a fellowship.

I was more Yankee than he in that my eyes kept straying in the direction of Paris. On vacations in France I was apt to spend my time in the capital glutting myself on theatres and art galleries, while Frank bicycled alone through the countryside from cathedral town to cathedral town. When he did come to Paris, he was taken up with pursuits where my presence would have been only an encumbrance, or at least so I assumed, for unlike most young men even of that era, we rarely discussed girls. He was always extraordinarily tactful (when he was not deliberately being rude), and knowing my nature less earthy than his own, he must have supposed that I did not like to be reminded of my unearthiness. Actually, however, I would have been delighted to hear of his conquests. I had grown up while in Oxford and had learned to apologize to nobody for taking my pleasures primarily through the eye and ear.

The crisis towards which we were heading and that I was too obtuse to anticipate exploded at the end of our second year when Frank lost his faith. This was an experience not unusual to serious young men in the last century and was treated as a very grave event. Today, of course, it couldn't happen because nobody has any faith, or if they do, they find it unfashionable to talk about it. But Frank had a very deep one and had been confirmed at his own request at the age of fourteen. His idea of teaching was inextricably tied up with the Episcopal Church, and the only kind of school that he could contemplate founding had always been a church school. I knew instantly, therefore, what a serious matter it was when, pacing back and forth before the fire in my room one night, and stopping occasionally to take a somehow wrathful sip from the glass of whiskey on the mantel, he announced to me that he doubted the divinity of Christ.

"You've been reading too much Renan," I suggested.

"I've been reading a great deal besides Renan," he said with a snort. "I've been reading the early Christian fathers. But you can't get away from the fact that Renan has one terribly valid point. Jesus obviously believed that the resurrection of the dead would occur within the lifetime of his contemporaries. 'Verily I say unto you, There be some standing here, which shall not taste of death, till they see the Son of man coming in his kingdom.'" He became very dry of tone now, like a lawyer with citations. "Matthew 16:28. And again in 10:23. And again in 24:34. And again in Mark, 9:1. And again in Mark, 13:30. And again in Luke, 9:27. And again in Luke, 21:32."

I couldn't help smiling at this show-off of memory. "But not in John? Hasn't John always been your favorite gospel?"

"I find it trivial of you, Horace, to describe a gospel, like a magazine, as a favorite."

"Well, whatever you want to call it then. The most spiritual?"

Frank seemed even more pained at this. "I think I may have described it once as the most sophisticated. In any case, you are partially right. The prediction is *not* made in the same words in John. But you will remember that Jesus hinted that John might not have to die. Which could only have meant that he would live to see the second coming." Here he paused and shook his head. "Matthew, Mark and Luke must have meant *something* by all those statements. And certainly the early fathers took them literally. It explains so much of the casting away of the world. The church had to be totally reconstructed when Christians finally realized that they were in for the long pull."

His worries must seem absurd to twentieth century readers. The teachings of a protestant Christ have long been watered down to a gentle ripple of aphorisms about the poor and meek, and nobody troubles his head any more about the question of divinity. It is probably the work of thousands of loose thinkers like myself. I had read Renan and found his pastoral idyll of a mortal Jesus struggling under his messianic illusion and finding relief in death from his impossible, self-imposed mission a charming one. I now suggested this to Frank.

"Charming!" he cried in disgust. "Is there nothing more important to you than charm? Is that all the gospels mean to you? Charm?"

"Well, I don't see the point of getting all worked up about them. Maybe the Catholics are right in not encouraging the reading of the Bible. Look at the funk it's got you in!"

"How can a man *not* be in a funk if his whole life depends on it?" Frank paused to take another fierce gulp of his drink. "Don't you see, I want to be a *minister*? How can I preach the gospel of a deluded mystic who traveled about the countryside foretelling the end of a world that never came? And consider, Horace, the presumption of such a man if he was not God. How did he dare threaten the multitudes with damnation? Oh no, my friend, I tell you, he's God or nothing." Frank shook his head again, slowly and gravely, half a dozen times.

"You call the Sermon on the Mount nothing?"

"You can find the same principles among the Essenes. There's nothing in the least original about them." He shrugged impatiently and continued to pace about, his voice rising sharply as his argument became more violent. "What I cannot stomach, at least in the founder of *my* faith, are the miracles. As the work of God, they are awe-inspiring. As the work of a mortal, they reduce themselves to the slickest kind of sleight of hand. 'Go thou to the sea and cast an hook and take up the fish that first cometh up, and when thou hast opened his mouth, thou shalt find a piece of money.' 'Go your way into the village over against you: and as soon as ye be entered into it, ye shall find a colt tied, whereupon never man sat; loose him and bring him.' No, I tell you, Horace, it won't do. Even the miracle of the loaves and fishes becomes a cheap catering trick."

At last he had shocked me. I have always thought it the worst possible taste to depreciate religious values. One certainly did not have to swallow the Bible, but a great many reputable people had, and out of respect for them, if nothing else, one should maintain a discreet silence. When it came to heresy, I found that I could, after all, be a Havistock.

"You should have more respect," I reproved him. "After all, even if he was mortal, might he not have been divinely inspired?"

"Divinely inspired to say he was something he *wasn't*? How could that be?"

We kept reverting to the subject again and again, all that winter and spring, until, alas, I was fearfully bored with the whole topic. I finally suggested that he take his problem to our master at Balliol, the famous Dr. Jowett. Frank was at first reluctant to do so; he did not share in the popular cult of the "Jowler." I pointed out that at least the master was an acknowledged theologian, and I eventually pushed him through that door out of which, like Omar, after "great argument about it and about," he eventually emerged—with the same doubts. But in his case, unlike Omar's, an important practical decision had been taken. He was bright-eyed and feverishly cheerful, and he discussed his faithlessness no more.

Jowett was certainly never Frank's idea of a great man. The Master's plump, soft figure, his silvery white smooth hair, his pink, clear countenance and treble voice, his cerebral, epicene manner and the intellectual (and at times social) snobbishness of his conversation struck the young American athlete as the epitome of all that was worst in English education, of all that *his* school, if he ever founded one, was not going to be.

I, on the other hand, delighted in Jowett's dry wit and worldly anecdotes and in the great names which so frequently adorned his discourse. I knew that I could qualify under none of the three headings to which his intimates were supposedly limited: peers, paupers and scholars, but I was determined that I would nonetheless attract his notice. He liked funny stories and he liked gossip, and the first time that Frank and I were asked to dine at the Master's House I was full of both.

"Havistock is a bit of an ass" Jowett later told a blunt Yorkshire lad who bluntly repeated it to me. "And an American ass at that. But a dinner party is pleasanter for his company, and how many men can you say that about?"

How many indeed? I should like his encomium on my tombstone.

Jowett took Frank more seriously, as an aggressive and possibly danger-ous Red Indian. During that same first dinner Frank actually suggested a correction in our host's famed translation of Plato. Had he been wrong, it would have been the end of their relationship. But he was right, and, as I have said, Jowett liked scholars.

"And to think that such illumination should come to us from the anti-podes!" the Master exclaimed, raising his hands. "The Old World can only bow its head." The tone may have been bantering, but he took out a note-book to record Frank's correction.

Did that wise old man feel a tremor of satisfaction when the brash younger one came to him with his doubts? I think not. Jowett was fundamentally kind. Frank's problems, at least in their initial form, were elementary enough, and the Master was about to suggest a dozen explanations of what Christ had meant by the day of judgment. But he soon discovered that his Yankee pupil had a flare for theological disputation that would have made him at home in the Byzantine Court. Jowett's arguments simply stimulated Frank to deeper research, in Latin, Greek and even Hebrew texts, until he was able to challenge the Master on equal ground.

"If you're the kind of man to lose sleep over whether Jonah was actually swallowed by the whale," Jowett retorted at last, "the church is no place for you. You'd better go back to the fresh breeze of your western prairies."

Of course, they had totally opposite religious temperaments. Jowett admired philosophy; Frank cultivated burning zeal. To one Christianity had been better stated by Plato than by Christ; to the other Christ was all. Frank belonged among the disciples of Phillips Brooks and A. V. G. Allen who gave to Jesus the supreme position in the Trinity which, according to Henry Adams, the thirteenth century had given the Virgin. To Jowett such Christology had a distasteful smack of evangelicism and American exaggera-tion. To him the life and death of Christ was the life and death of Christ in the soul, the imitation of Christ. As a Platonist he saw everything on earth as broken arcs which merely suggested the perfect rounds above. Christ was essentially a larger segment of arc. To insist that he had to be either all God or all man must have struck Jowett as a crudity of youth.

Nonetheless he might have enjoyed indefinitely his theological debates with a mind as keen as Frank's had it not been for bitter memories of the conflict which had torn the Church of England, years before, on the publication of his own views of biblical interpretation. Jowett had come out all right in the end, but the memory of that fuss and feathers over the exercise of a harmless bit of rationalism had given him an abiding distaste for religious controversy. He had little respect for the clergy and barely regarded himself as one of them.

"I wonder if any really great men are ever clergymen," he speculated one afternoon at tea in my rooms. It was his first visit, and I was very proud.

Frank, of course, picked him right up. "Hildebrand? Ximenes? Richelieu?"

"I'm not talking of statesmen in cassocks, Prescott, but of *clergymen*. Why would a great man want to shackle himself with the *gêne* of a creed?"

"Luther was a great man and a clergyman, and *he* did."

"Ah, Luther. I should have anticipated the name of a rebel from the citizen of a separated arm of the Queen's realm."

"But surely, Master," Frank retorted, "a martyr like yourself should sympathize with rebels."

Jowett's face was inscrutable, and I was breathless. I had never heard anyone twit him before with his ancient heresy. But Frank, it seemed, got away with everything. The Master gave him a long, shrewd stare and said: "It's a pity you weren't a young man in 1776, Prescott. I'm sure you would have greatly enjoyed it."

"Would you, Master, have enjoyed the reign of Mary Tudor?"

Jowett grunted. "Perhaps the bar should be your profession. I'm told that lawyers and judges occupy a unique position in your great nation. Can your courts not invalidate laws of congress? Fancy. I propose, then, that you make your fortune at the bar and secure an early appointment to the bench. The judge in this commercial era is the only person who can enjoy the esteem of the worldly with the detachment of the philosopher. Even the proudest burghers dare not yawn when he quotes Latin."

"At home our judgeships are the spoils of politics."

"Be a politician, then!"

"You are full of alternatives, Master."

"They are all the old can offer."

Frank was repelled by this, and though he remained on friendly terms with the Master he did not again seek his advice in personal matters. He had a young man's distaste for compromise; it seemed to him that one must make a clean choice between God and Mammon. At the time it was Mammon, and there was no further talk of his being a minister or a schoolmaster.

What surprised me most was how much *I* minded. One might have thought that the new, more secular Frank would have been closer to the easygoing and worldly Horace. Yet such was not the case. We remained the closest of friends, but something had gone out of the relationship. In my own odd way, if I could get along without God, I could not seem to get on without God in Frank. I felt that he was turning into someone he was not meant to be—a good person, no doubt, but not the person I had visualized. In brief, I suppose I thought myself let down. After all, I, too, had had a stake in that school. I had hitched my modest but well-appointed wagon to a star, and now, looking ahead, I saw it was only another wagon I could have done as well on my own.

7

FROM HORACE HAVISTOCK'S "THE ART OF FRIENDSHIP"

Frank and I came back to America in the fall of 1881, and he visited with my family for several weeks. He had little idea of what to do or where to live and was disconcertingly open to suggestions. My brother Archie, who had always liked him and found unaccountable his intimacy with me, advised him strongly to stay in New York and go into business. He persuaded Father to give him a letter of introduction to Chauncey Depew, and Frank went off to call at the New York Central offices. He came back, dazzled, to tell us that he had been offered a job in his first interview.

"But I daresay it's not very adventurous to start right off in the biggest company," he concluded.

Archie rebutted vigorously what he called the "vulgar" American fallacy that the big fortunes were all made in new ventures. "Stay with the tried and true," he warned Frank. "That's what the big boys understand. The profit is never 'out' of a good business. Central will double again."

So Frank went to work for the Vanderbilts, the "brownstone Medici," as he called them. His heart was certainly never in railroads, but his shrewd intuition and his quick grasp of detail made him a useful assistant to Depew who was later to be the first chairman of the board of trustees of Justin Martyr. Frank's irreverent amusement at the pomp and power of the railway great was manifested in a series of witty monologues that he used to perform for his intimates and, years later, for the boys at school. His best was of William H. Vanderbilt, interviewed by the press on board his Wagner palace car, shifting in his plush chair, coughing, snapping his eyes, playing with his watch fob, mumbling, shy and miserable, and ending finally with a high squeak: "The public be damned!" The companion piece was of the same gentleman in his art gallery bargaining with a dealer for a gory Meissonier battle scene. Frank would stand, his hands behind his back, his nose two inches from the purported canvas, studying the detail of a helmet. But there must have been a dose of admiration in so exact an observance. Frank all his life had a grudging, half-concealed fascination for big business. He used to say that if you sold out to Mammon, you might as well get a seat in the Inner Temple.

In his two years at Central he lived in a small room in a boardinghouse
on lower Madison Avenue and spent his salary on his clothes and pleasures.
He continued the habit that he had acquired in England of being a bit of a
dandy, and on Sundays he hired a horse to ride in Central Park. With his
looks, his name, his confidence, his ease of manner and his amazing general knowledge, he soon became a popular extra man in society. New York
was worldly and Frank was poor, but this is always forgiven a bachelor, and
was he not a Boston Prescott? Even the mothers of heiresses did not frown
at Frank's brown eyes and broad shoulders.

He and I once again played reversed roles in that period, for I found (as
I always have since) New York society distinctly tiresome. There was opulence, but it was a heavy, tawdry opulence, blinking out at one from heavily
laden dinner tables where sour, sleepy-eyed magnates and their stertorous,
big-busted wives overate. There were no artists, no philosophers, no men
of science in that bourgeois world. And worst of all, there were none of
those wonderful, worldly-wise, sympathetic older women, in whom London and Paris abounded, former beauties or demimondaines, who could talk
to a young man of love and art and politics and give him a sense of the
continuity of charm in the history of civilized men and women.

My health was bad again; I had constant colds and was beginning already
to show symptoms of the arthritis that has nagged me all my life. I spent
my days in the comfortable fire-warmed third floor sitting room in which I
had lived as a child with Sister Sue at 310 Fifth Avenue. All my brothers
were married and had moved away, and Father, turning senile, thought only
of dinner invitations which were becoming so rare that I had the mortification of having to solicit them from his old friends. There was little to tempt
me away from the manuscript of a novel that I was writing about Newport
in the Revolutionary War. It was not a good novel, and it was never published, but it was better than many of the novels that were published in those
days.

Inevitably, with my sedentary life and Frank's active one, we saw less of
each other. He never let a week go by without calling at the house, but the
daily intimacy of our English years was gone, and I found that I wanted
another confidant, perhaps even a confidant who was more interested in me
and in the things I cared about than Frank, for all his kindness, ever could
be. Even in his Mammon days, he always leaned to the general while I
tumbled head over heels into the particular; he loved ideas and I personalities; he was all for argument and I yearned for gossip. Neither of us, obviously, could be all in all to the other.

It came as a bit of a shock to me, as it undoubtedly will to the reader of
these pages, that my new friend should have materialized at last in the shape
of a beautiful and popular young woman, a scant year older then myself. I
met Eliza Dean at a small dinner given by Ward McAllister, a foolish fellow
but a very kind one, who, when not pursuing the old and grand, like Mrs.
Astor, could give charming parties where, over the best of food and wine,
something not too far from conversation was occasionally born.

Eliza was a bit in advance of the Gibson girl, but to some extent she
anticipated her. She had thick rich auburn hair, a high ivory forehead, hazel

eyes that gazed at one unflinchingly, the straightest of noses and a chin that would have been almost too resolute had it not suggested the proud princess of fairy tale. Eliza moved, too, like a princess, but I think she may have done so to offer an effective contrast to her free candor of manner and a laugh that was as hearty as the West from which she came. She was the only child of a widowered father, a gnarled old leathery 'forty-niner who had once purchased a senate seat and who had now come to New York to retire on Fifth Avenue and launch his beautiful daughter in society. People suspected the most terrible things about his past and something worse about his present, namely that his reputed fortune was largely fictional, but it helped that he, a morose old bird, did not want to go out, and everyone was charmed by his daughter.

Eliza was far too clever to try to compete with New York girls in their own specialties; she knew that the out-of-the-ordinary, properly handled, could be an asset, and she introduced into her conversation a directness, a forthrightness, a kind of high honesty that seemed designed to fill the stuffy interiors of Manhattan with a fresh wind from over the Rockies. Instead of playing the mincing little thing who wanted to be shielded—from nothing—by a masculine arm, she appeared to offer herself as a brave, free companion to a man, the kind of woman who could fire her rifle alongside him in the Indian-besieged stockade, an Elizabeth Zane with an apron full of gunpowder.

But there was a pointed difference. Elizabeth Zane had not been playing a role, and Eliza Dean most decidedly was. Nobody smelled the paint or saw that the cardboard fortress trembled in the breeze but Horace Havistock, and nobody guessed that he smelled or saw such things but Eliza Dean. It was our recognition of each other's skill that formed the rock, albeit a slippery one, on which our friendship was based.

Like myself, she needed a friend and confidant, and he had to be not only a man, for she was one of those women who had little use for her own sex, but a man who would not spoil their special intimacy by falling in love with her. Had it not been for this latter qualification, so firmly set forth at the beginning, I think I might have. Certainly I came as near to falling in love with Eliza as I ever came to falling in love. But I knew that I would have repelled her, awkward reedy creature that I was, and I was glad to settle for friendship and to content myself with being fussed over, like a doll in the hands of a very determined little girl.

Eliza had a pale blue open Landau with red leather upholstery and a coachman in red livery. She used to pick me up twice a week at Number 310 and take me driving in Central Park as far north as the terrace and the Bethesda Fountain and sometimes all the way to Cleopatra's Needle. If it was a good day, we would get out at the Mall and stroll. It was part of her act of independence to be always unchaperoned.

"You shouldn't be writing a novel about the Revolution," she told me on one of those excursions. "What's happening today is far more exciting, right here in Manhattan. Why, you could fit all of revolutionary New York into five or six blocks of the city today!"

"I'll take those five or six blocks, thank you. And I'll leave you that." I pointed down to the Angel on the Bethesda Fountain that we were passing. "In fact I'll make you a present of everything north of Union Square."

"You'd make me the richest and most powerful woman on earth!"

"Why do you care so much about power, Eliza? Is it so important to be able to order your fellow men about? Of course, they're all your slaves, anyway."

"Not Horace Havistock. He's safe." There was a tiny glint in her eyes as she folded her hands in her muff. "You see, we're utterly different, you and I. You can be perfectly happy just watching the pageant of power. And occasionally sneering at it. But I have to be involved. Oh, don't think that I have a mere vulgar craving for money and preferment." Her hazel eyes were turned on me now, full of a fine scorn at such a concept. "When I speak of power, I mean involvement in all the wonderful things that are going to happen here. Politically and artistically and scientifically. Big business is only a precursor. A herald of the Athenian age. And I want to be in the center of that age!"

"I wonder if the only difference between being 'involved,' as you see yourself, and being a spectator, as you see me, isn't in the choice of seats. You want a box."

She considered this carefully, in all fairness to me. "All right, I want a box," she agreed. "Boxholders, after all, can at least be decorative. They're part of the show."

"Like a queen, you mean? In a royal box?"

"Well, you put it very crudely. But, all right, if you must. Let's say a queen."

"And will it just be you there? Will you be a virgin queen, all alone, or will there be a William for your Mary?"

"Oh, there'll be a William," she answered, with a nod. "There will indeed be a William. I think I even visualize him."

"'Divinely tall and most divinely fair'?"

"He need be neither tall nor fair. It will be quite sufficient if his face shows character. I shall want him, of course, to have brains and imagination, and ambition, of a noble sort. He need not have money, but he should be able to make it if necessary. I have no wish for a dreamer or for a dry academic type. I want a man of intellect who is also a man of action."

"In other words," I suggested with a smile, "a man who is capable of enjoying the success you expect him to achieve?"

"Precisely. Am I presumptuous?"

"Let's say you're optimistic. What fascinates me, Eliza, is that all the things you want are noble things, yet the mere fact of your wanting them is enough to make you . . . well, may I say the most charming of materialists?"

"You may say a materialist. I make no bones about being a materialist." Indeed, it occurred to me, glancing at that fine profile between the chinchilla hat and the chinchilla neckpiece that she was the portrait of what she professed to be. "But it's only fair to myself to add that I consider us all materialists. What do we have to choose from but material? The question is: do we pick the good or the shoddy?"

"Who are your candidates?"

Eliza laughed her loud, smooth clear laugh. It was a remarkable laugh for a woman, so assured and resonant, so chuckling, with just a hint of scorn that was somehow not in the least wounding. I think it was her laugh that made me almost love her. It seemed to warn you that its owner could take you over, but that you might be better off taken over. "You don't expect me to tell you that, do you?" she demanded. "Who are yours? Do you have a man to meet my high requirements?"

"As a matter of fact, I do. You seemed just now to be sketching his likeness."

"Fancy! Do I know him?"

"You've never mentioned him, so I assume you don't."

"Oh, Horace, *who*?"

"I don't think I'm going to tell you. You'd simply grab him, and I may want to keep him for myself."

"Dog in the manger! *You* can't marry him."

"True. Perhaps the woman has the greater right. But I'm a very selfish person. I don't always regard greater rights."

"What an odious pig you are, if I may change my metaphor. You'd better hide your friend very carefully, then, because I warn you, I shall now be on the watch!"

And she was. Nothing could have whetted her curiosity more than my refusal to give her Frank's name. It was comic to watch her maneuvers and machinations, and the pleasure of it came near to compensating me for the realization—one might almost say the prognostication—that she would, of course, meet Frank and capture him. It was much more likely in the smaller New York society of that time than it would have been today. In fact, it was almost inevitable that two young people who dined out as frequently as Frank and Eliza did should ultimately meet. When Eliza discovered one night that her handsome dinner partner was a Balliol man and a friend of Horace Havistock's, the fat was in the fire. As I learned later from Frank himself, she had burst into her vigorous laugh and exclaimed, to his astonishment and mystification: "So it *is* you, at last! Could Horace have *planned* it this way?"

With him it was a case of love at first sight; with her, of love at first foresight. I assumed uncomfortably that my poor personality had been the kindling to set off the torrid blaze of their initial conversations, but I daresay I was soon consumed. I do not mean that they tore me to pieces, but I am sure that they laughed over my foibles and agreed that I was as spoiled as a pampered kitten. And worse, far worse, whether the idea was ever actually articulated or not, there must have been in the air between them the contrast between the puny baby of friendship that I offered to each and the full grown, wonderful glory of the kind of thing that they offered each other. Oh, yes, they made a beautiful couple, Frank and Eliza, Gibson boy and Gibson girl, standing like newlyweds in an insurance poster to represent all the brave new things that life *seemed* to offer. I could not help but be a bit disgruntled; the sexual happiness of others has always an excluding effect.

Frank had first called at Number 310 in an agony of embarrassment, stomping about my third-floor sitting room with darkened countenance, until he had finally managed to stop and blurt out: "Do you care for her?" When he had been assured that I did not, at least not in the sense that he meant, I had been royally and painfully thumped on the back and hugged. Poor fellow, he had been planning to leave New York to get out of my way if he had found that I was courting Eliza, and I believe he would have done so.

But touched as I was by the loyalty and integrity of my friend, I did not find his companionship in the months that followed very stimulating. He was a greater bore on the subject of Eliza than he had ever been on his school, for he assumed that I, as her friend and intimate, was as interested as he in her greater glorification. Did I know that she had the good taste to prefer German to Italian opera? Was I aware that she was an expert horse-woman? Had I ever encountered such a natural generosity of heart or a mind so cultivated and yet so unspoiled? Was she not head and shoulders above the simpering ninnies who cowered behind their growling mammas and waited for some ass of a moneybag to propose?

"It's uncanny, Horace," he would always end. "I never dreamed that I would meet a girl so close to my ideal. Do you realize that she's simply— *perfect?*"

It was even harder on me to be subjected to the same kind of confidences from Eliza. Never have I known a couple who seemed so uncritically enthusiastic about each other, and the remarkable thing was that their enthusiasm seemed to wax with better acquaintance. I understood it with Frank, for at this period of his life, or rather just prior to his meeting Eliza, he had been showing an increasing taste for extremes. He had talked about giving up his job for the Fiji Islands; he had written reams of florid poetry that made very little sense, and he had filled a sketchbook with pictures of the most grotesque monsters. I discovered that he even spent his Sundays at the city hospitals, reading to patients. It was all perfectly all right, but a bit quixotic, a bit bizarre. Eliza, on the other hand, for all her capacity for excitement, had a very level head. I suspected her of puffing her feelings and demonstrations a bit, and this irritated me.

"It's all very well to deify Frank," I told her one afternoon in the Park, "but sooner or later we have to let him drift back down to earth. Granted that he has brilliant gifts, but what has he done with them? What is he so far but a young man at Central who isn't even engaged to a Vanderbilt?"

"He's engaged to me."

"*Is* he? Since when?"

"Since yesterday."

"Well, congratulations! Has your father consented?"

"Oh, I haven't even asked Father. I'm my own mistress, you know. Father's living on an annuity. When he gave me what little I have, he said: 'Here it is, Liza. There ain't going to be no more. You're on your own now, my gal, and make the most of it.'"

"I trust he gave you enough."

"How much do you think?"

I calculated rapidly for a minute and then made a shrewd guess. Eliza burst into her high laugh. "Really, Horace, you old New Yorkers are beyond anything! Where do you get that financial sixth sense?"

"You mean I was right?"

"A bull's-eye! But how did you *know*? I thought I was supposed to be rich." She shrugged her disdain of such things. "Anyway, we won't starve. Frank's going to get ahead in Central. Mr. Depew told me so himself. And he can go from there to anything. The state legislature, congress, an ambassadorship. Oh, you'll see, Horace. Frank may need a little pushing, but look who he's got to push him!"

"He's an unpredictable man," I said grudgingly.

"That's exactly the excitement! But don't you see, with the talents he has, where can he go but up?"

"Do you know he once wanted to be a minister?"

"Of course. And a schoolteacher. And what a good one he'd have been. But he's left all that behind."

"Yes," I said with a little sigh. "He seems to have left it all a good ways behind."

I believed it when I said it. Afterwards, Eliza always thought that I must have suspected something, and she never forgave me for not giving her an earlier warning. But I could not have. I had reconciled myself completely to the idea of Frank as a railroad man. I had fully accepted the notion that the aspirations of his days at St. Andrew's had been mere adolescent religiosity. Frank, to my mind, had simply reverted to the tradition of his family, as I was reverting to that of mine.

But, indeed, his exhilaration of that period was by no means all love. Love seemed to have been rather the catalytic agent that had started the vibrations of every emotional chord in his being, vibrations that boded to be powerful enough to survive even the removal of the agent itself. I made this all-important discovery one night after a dinner meeting of the Hone Club at our house, where Frank and I were guests. After the last of the old boys had left and I had escorted Father to his bedroom, I was very tired, but Frank, who was never tired himself and did not understand the condition in others, suggested that we have a drink of whiskey before he left. I told him flatly that I wanted to go to bed, but he did not even hear me. He was standing by the long table where Father kept his newspapers, turning the pages of one in sheer nervous activity. This was unlike him, as was the odd little feverish glitter in his eye, and I was suddenly attentive.

"Have you something to tell me?"

He did not turn. "Yes."

"About Eliza?"

"No. I mean yes. Yes, in the sense that nothing happens to me that doesn't concern Eliza."

"Something nice?"

"Something that you would call 'charming.'" He turned around with a smile that I can only describe as radiant. No other adjective would fit it.

"I've found my old faith again. I'm going to Boston to see Phillips Brooks on Saturday. He thinks he can get me into divinity school in a month's time."

At this I went to the sideboard to pour myself a generous helping of whiskey. It would mean a terrible headache in the morning, but that no longer mattered. I sat on the sofa, tucked my feet under me, and simply murmured: "Tell."

Frank walked about the room as he told me of his reconversion, his voice jagged with a tense excitement, his hands straying over the surface of tables, tapping books and bronzes, his shiny eyes roving and not seeming quite to take me in when they rested on me. I did not move, except when I took a discreet sip of my drink, nor did I speak, even when he paused for a possible comment. His monologue went something like this:

"I've even had a vision, a visitation, whatever you want to call it. I know that sounds like the most incredible arrogance or the most incredible naïveté—perhaps both—but I don't care. I'm way beyond caring! It didn't happen to me without preparation, as it happened to Paul on the road to Damascus. Oh, no, I was prepared. Only the stubbornest kind of ass could have resisted so much preparation for so long. For, you see, Horace, there's something you don't know about me, something I haven't told a soul. Not even Eliza, at least till the other day. And that is that even after I lost my faith in Oxford, I've never stopped reading the New Testament and the early fathers. In the past year I've read the gospels every night when I came in for two or three hours, in Latin, in Greek, even in French, trying to approach them freshly. Do you know, I can recite Matthew right through? Don't worry, I shan't.

"All I'm really trying to tell you is that the figure of Christ became consistent to me. He *is* the same in all the gospels. Indeed, he is the only thing that is. Verses began to ring in my ears at odd times during the day at the office. 'Why callest thou me good? None is good, save one, that is God.' 'The Son can do nothing of himself, but what he seeth the Father do.' 'For I came down from heaven, not to do mine own will, but the will of him that sent me.'

"Oh, yes, Horace, it is divinely assured selflessness. The selflessness that comes from an absolute knowledge that the praise or scorn of the world is a total irrelevance. The mortal part of Jesus, the assumed shell of the Godhead, hardly exists in the gospels, except for a few twinges, the agony in the garden, the cry from the cross. And even here, in Christ's passion, it is the pain of the Father over what men are doing to his son and hence to themselves. It is the rejection, not the torture that concerns him. And I began to see that the discrepancies and oddities of the gospels are the discrepancies and oddities of mortal writers, mortal witnesses."

He paused here so long that I thought I had to say something. "Was that your vision?"

"Oh, no." He became even graver now. "My vision came a month ago, one night when I had not been able to sleep. I had lain awake, thinking about the passion, until almost dawn. I suppose you will say that I fell asleep, exhausted at last, and dreamed my vision. It doesn't matter. It was equally real, awake or asleep. It was the sudden appearance by my bed of my father.

No, not by my bed. He was somehow everywhere in the room, I can't explain. He did not look like the daguerrotypes that I have seen or like Aunt Jane's miniature, yet I knew that it was he. He was very pale, haggard, perhaps unshaven, in uniform, and for some reason he had his left arm in a sling. He shook his head slowly at me and said in a reproachful voice—but, oh, the kindest, Horace, you ever heard, the very kindest!—'Frank, my poor boy, how many times must you be told before you *see*?'"

Here Frank, overwrought, dropped suddenly into a chair and covered his face with his hands. "To think I had to have a sign! To think I had to disturb my poor father's spirit before I believed! To think I was worse than Saint Thomas!" His voice rose now to a pitch that made me apprehensive of hysteria. "Unless I could see the print of the nails and put my fingers into the print of the nails and thrust my hand into his side, I would not believe. And Christ was as good to me as he was good to Thomas, his own apostle, and took my fingers and made me feel the print of the nails in his flesh and took my hand and thrust it into his side. Oh, Horace, if only I am spared long enough to make *some* return for that!"

I felt at last that I had to pull him up. "Is there any reason to think that you won't be? Do you interpret your vision as implying an early demise?"

He looked startled for a minute, as if at hearing me talk at all. Then he smiled, his old smile, and he was Frank again. "No, of course not. And forgive me, old fellow, for running so off at the mouth. I've given you a dose of it, haven't I? But that's what friends are for. I had to tell somebody."

"Haven't you told Eliza?"

"Oh, yes. But not in quite such detail. Women hate the abstract, you know. The point she went straight to was my giving up Central to become a minister."

"I can imagine. And how did she take it?"

"She was a brick, Horace. A perfect brick. Which I'm sure comes as no surprise to you." He rose now, looking tired himself at last, and came over to put his hand on my shoulder. "It was a shock to her, of course. She hadn't planned on being a minister's wife, much less a schoolteacher's. She broke down at first and actually wept. Oh, it was hard, I can tell you. But the next day she was much calmer. She said she'd have to think it over while I was in Boston. But I have an instinct that she's going to stick."

"No doubt she is readjusting *her* vision to include an arch-episcopal palace."

"Now, Horace, don't be mean. Go to bed and pray that she'll stick. Can you imagine a more magnificent headmaster's wife? And you know she'd love it when she really got into it!"

"Yes," I said bitterly. "I can see it all. *Jo's Boys*."

At that he left me, good-natured enough to laugh, and I finished my drink, deriving a sour satisfaction by contemplating how wretchedly I was bound to feel in the morning.

Eliza was cool and quiet the next time that she took me driving. She was as beautiful as ever, and everything she did, even pouting, she did with a natural grace, but it was evident that she was thwarted, terribly thwarted, and frustration is the hardest thing in the world for a woman to make attractive. When she did begin to talk, it was to question me closely on how long I had known of Frank's state of mind.

"Well, does it matter," I finally put to her, with some impatience in my tone, "how much I guessed and when? I tell you it came as a complete surprise to me, and you won't accept that. But the important thing is that Frank has found his faith again and is happy. Personally, I'm delighted."

"It's all very well for you to say that. It doesn't affect your future."

"On the contrary. If Frank ever starts his school, he may renew his old offer to me to be a master. It could change my whole life."

"*You?* A master?"

"Well, why not?" I demanded, stung by her tone. "Do you think all masters have to be athletes? Do you think there are no sensitive boys who might profit by a cultivated teacher who cares more about art and literature than football? I know I might have been much less miserable at St. Andrew's had there been a Horace Havistock on the faculty."

"I'm sure you would have," she said placatingly, retreating before my sharpened tone. "You must remember that as an only child I've had very little to do with boys. However," she continued with a sigh, looking pensively across the Mall, "it appears that yawning gap is going to be amply filled."

I glanced around. "You mean you're going through with it?"

Her answering look was aloof and steady. "I thought that I had told you. Frank and I are engaged."

"But it hasn't been announced. I should think you were both still free to withdraw."

"What makes you think I want to?"

What indeed? And what made me so sure that she ought to? When I look back upon my decision of that afternoon, it strikes me as sufficiently uncanny. How did I, who had never interfered to the smallest degree in the affairs of others, who had confined myself to chatter over the past and passive speculation as to the future, have the courage, or perhaps I should say the nerve, to betray my best friend by plunging into the troubled tub of his engagement and pulling out the stopper? And how, furthermore, did I manage to do it without any qualms of conscience (besides the shivering from my natural tension at the idea of any action at all) when I knew that my soul was full of a complicated jealousy that Eliza and Frank should each be taking the other from me? Yet I seemed to have had no doubt at all that I was doing the right thing. Could the angel or imp that had sent Frank's father to him have intervened again through me?

"Don't marry him," I said flatly. "Don't marry him, I beg of you."

Eliza did not even blink as she stared at me. Yet she seemed to sense that such impudence must have sprung from a strong conviction, based on something she had yet to learn. "Why should I not?"

"Because you'd make each other miserable."

She drew a quick breath. "I think you underestimate me, Horace."

"Oh, no, I don't! You'd be superb. You'd handle them all magnificently, the little boys, the mothers, the masters and their wives. You'd be beautiful and gracious and decorative and brave. Oh, you'd do it to the queen's taste. And the better you did it, the worse it would be for both of you. Frank would see that he had taken you from the great world where your talents were meant to shine and squandered them in a New England backwater. And you would see it, too. Oh, you would, Eliza! No matter how desperately you tried to hide it from him. You would both always know that you had been sacrificed."

Eliza ran the tips of her forefingers gently across her eyelashes. I wondered if she was catching a stray, rebel tear. If so, her gesture had made the others retreat. It was difficult to tell such things with Eliza. "Perhaps I should be subtler than you think."

"Impossible."

"Why impossible?" she asked, annoyed. "There's one thing that you discount. That *you*, of course, would have to discount. It so happens that I love Frank."

"Oh, love."

"Yes, love!" she exclaimed angrily. "Don't smile at me in that cool, cynical way. If you could see how immature you looked! Only little boys and old men sneer at love. I happen to love Frank Prescott, and he happens to love me."

"Great lovers have made great sacrifices."

She opened her lips to retort and then closed them. Something about my persistence evidently frightened her. "How *can* you go on that way?" she cried in exasperation. "How can you be so sure about what other people should do and not do?"

"Because I know you, Eliza. I know what we have in common. Something that has nothing to do with Frank. We're hopeless egoists, you and I. We want the nicest things, oh, the very nicest things, for ourselves and others, but the best thing about those nice things is always going to be the little personal touch that *we* can give them. You'd never see Frank's school in any other light than as a backdrop for a beautiful headmistress. An inadequate backdrop, at that. And ultimately it would become a backdrop for the pageant of the splendid good sportsmanship of Mrs. Prescott who has given up the world for her husband. I can see you, Eliza, in maturer years, grey and slim and still so lovely, confiding to some soft, admiring long-haired sixth form Horace Havistock, over tea and crumpets, the secret chagrin of your sacrifice."

Eliza's eyes really blazed at this. "Stop, Tom!" she called to her coachman. "Mr. Havistock is getting out."

"Really, Eliza!" I protested. "In the middle of the Park!"

"Then I'll get out!" she retorted, and in another moment she was out of the carriage and walking at a rapid pace eastward along the sidewalk. "Take Mr. Havistock home!" she called back over her shoulder. "I'll walk."

I told Tom to trail her at a discreet distance, and although she must have known we were there, she never turned her head as she strode resolutely forward. At first I was amused, but as I continued to watch her straight, fast-moving figure from the slowly joggling carriage I became uneasy. Could I have been wrong? Had I underestimated that strong, beautiful creature who swept along ahead of me, causing every passerby to turn and stare? For fully half an hour we must have continued our strange procession, while I shifted back and forth between conviction and doubt, until I noticed that she had stopped and was waiting, still without turning, for us to catch up. As Tom brought the carriage slowly abreast of her, she turned abruptly and got in. "Home now," she said and sat in silence, her head averted from me, her brooding eyes taking in the brown sky line to the south.

"I tell you what I've decided," she said at last, still without looking at me. "If I do give Frank up, I shall expect you to do the same."

"You mean, give him up as a friend?"

"No. I mean, give up the idea of being a schoolteacher. In *his* school, at least."

"I doubt if I'd be asked in any other."

"Then there it is. You won't be a schoolteacher."

I had not really thought I had much wanted to be, but now, in the perverse way of humans, I felt that I might be giving up the one occupation for which I was suited. "But why?" I demanded in bewilderment. "Why should you care? Is it just spite?"

"You should know me better," she retorted scornfully. "I don't do things out of spite. I may, as you say, be an egoist, but I hope I'm not a petty one. No, if I give Frank up, it will be because I want him to be free and untrammeled in his new life. If you can sense the corruption in me, it is, by your own admission, because there's a dose of it in you. Let there be none of it at all in Frank's school."

It is odd, but I think I was flattered. I had always been considered such a nonentity where human relations were concerned that the idea that I might have an influence, even a corrupting influence, on one as strong as Frank penetrated my heart with a fierce little sting of pleasure. To be allied with this magnificent girl in a team that might detract Parsifal from his quest of the Grail was to be given at last, was it not, a role in the opera? And wasn't Eliza correct? Had I not felt in my own heart that things were most right with Frank when he had been most alone with his God? I made up my mind in a moment.

"I give you my word," I told her solemnly, "that I will never be a schoolteacher."

"Even if *I should* marry Frank?"

"Oh, particularly not then!" I exclaimed. "I couldn't bear to see a chapter of the gospel turned into a chapter of Trollope." After this, we finished our drive in silence, for I understood, with absolute clarity and for the first time in my life, what a woman was like. I knew then and there that Eliza would never forgive me.

I did not see Frank for several days, but when he called next at the house I was at once aware from his somber face that Eliza must have communicated her decision. Walking about my room as I sat by the fire, he told me about it in harsh, clipped phrases. A life in the church, he said dryly, was evidently not the life for Eliza. He then excoriated New York, its society, its money, its worldliness. We lived in the vilest of ages. By my silence I agreed.

"Oh, what a bloody ass I am!" he cried suddenly, turning on me with a violence that made me jump. "As if a girl like that would want to tie herself up with a shaveling priest who hasn't even taken his orders! I wooed her under false pretenses, Horace. It is *I* who am vile!"

Then he came and sat by the fire and stared into it moodily for five good minutes. When he spoke his voice had a curious softness that I did not remember having heard before, like a sigh after the passage of some terrible pain.

"I thought I was not going to have anything to give up, Horace. I thought I was to have no test. I knew that I could leave the Central and all its rails and the fortune that glittered at the end of them with joy. With *joy!* But I dreamed that I would step forward into the service of God with a strong, beautiful woman on my arm, a helpmate, like an illustration for the last chapter of a Thackeray novel. O God, what fatuousness!" He leaned his head suddenly down in his hands and actually sobbed. "Of course, *she* was the sacrifice you wanted, Lord. So be it. Thy will. *Thy* will. I should be happy to be able to give up something so dear!"

After this outburst, which left me in a rigid shock of embarrassment, he played backgammon with me in morose silence for a full hour and then went home. Never again would he discuss Eliza with me. In fact, he reverted to the fifth former at St. Andrew's who had had no need to communicate his inner discomforts. But then why should he have? Presumably he had discovered a higher source of consolation

He resigned from Central the following week with the full approval of Mr. Depew who was much impressed that a call to the ministry should have been heard above the worldly bustle of his office. Frank even received a handwritten letter of good wishes from Mr. Vanderbilt which went far to allay Archie's violent objections to his step. He then departed for Cambridge to commence his divinity studies, which were apparently to be paid for by another of the mysterious Prescott trusts, and for the first time in seven years I ceased to see him regularly. It was a great light out of my life, but I had learned that one had to have spare luminaries.

I visited Frank in Boston on several occasions in the next two years. I stayed with his dear old aunt in Marlborough Street, and he came over from Cambridge to spend the evenings with me. He seemed in good spirits, but preoccupied with his work, and it was no surprise to any of us when he graduated first in his class. He spoke in a kindly tone of his classmates, but I knew him well enough to sense that he was discouraged by the quality of their intellects. He was to struggle all his life to avoid condescension to his fellow clergymen. "If the church," he once told me, "appealed to the kind of young men who went into New York Central, it would soon conquer the world." But, of course, it didn't so appeal. It didn't, if the truth be told, fundamentally appeal to Frank. He took orders only because he wanted to found a church school, and he sought to get his studies and ordination behind him as quickly as possible.

He had one diversion, however, and that was Harriet Winslow. She was totally different from all the girls in whom I had ever observed him to take an interest, but in her own way she was quite as individual and quite as remarkable as Eliza Dean.

She was plain, but magnificently plain, with a high, intellectual brow, a large, thin, very white aquiline nose and green eyes that seemed to look through the toughest barricade of one's own complacency. A grand-niece of Emerson, she could read Latin and speak German, but she had the reticence of a lady about pushing herself forward. She was neat, efficient, quiet, firm and, to my mind, charming. She belonged to the inner circle of Boston society, the only society in America that Frank ever really enjoyed, being like its English counterpart, unpretentious, self-assured, eccentric and, in parts, genuinely intellectual.

Harriet won my everlasting loyalty by understanding from the beginning that, different though we were, Frank had no better friend than I. She proceeded promptly to establish her own independent relationship with me and on two occasions invited me to lunch at her family's without Frank. It was evident to me that in her quiet but unyielding fashion she was determined to marry him and had accepted as entirely natural that his feeling for her was never going to be what hers was for him. I applauded her resolution in my heart (needless to say, we never discussed it), for it seemed to me that she had everything Frank needed in his chosen life, and so indeed it has proven. I think she even had money, but how does one tell with Bostonians?

I have never known how much she knew about Eliza Dean, but, if she did, she always had the heart and the intelligence neither to resent nor to apologize for the fact that she was second best. When, standing at the side of the newly ordained Francis Prescott, I watched his bride approach us down the aisle, I knew that on that afternoon in Central Park by the Bethesda Fountain I had done the best job in my life.

Nor was it only for him. It was for Eliza, too. She gave up the false start of Manhattan and returned to the West when her father died where she married the man who had bought his mines. He was much older and left her hugely rich. Thereafter she married Byram Shaw, of Wilson's cabinet, and had a splendid career in Paris when he was ambassador. She lives today in a Genoese palazzo on Du Pont Circle in Washington and gives those great diplomatic-political receptions of which everybody knows. She has aged gracefully, but she has become even more Western in tone and manner than she was in the early days in New York. In fact, it has become her distinctive mark.

She has always been cordial to me, but our intimacy has never been resumed. When David Griscam was making his big fund drive for Justin Martyr and asked me for the names of possible donors, I gave him Eliza's. He wrote to her twice, but received neither acknowledgment nor contribution. She must have felt that she had done enough for the school.

8

BRIAN'S JOURNAL

NOVEMBER 15, 1940. Here I have been back at Justin for two months without a single entry, but the purpose of my journal is Dr. Prescott, and I have not seen him alone more than twice since the term started. However superior I run the risk of sounding, I cannot feel that it is my mission to record what everybody could record and what, it now seems, everybody *is* recording. Poor Dr. Prescott has become a public event.

I am no longer his assistant because Mr. Ives, who is also retiring in the spring, has turned over his own executive duties to Mr. Anders and now has time himself to help the headmaster. But worse than this, it is difficult even to get near Dr. Prescott. The whole world of Justin's graduates and friends is awake to the fact that it is his final year, and all want a last glimpse of him in office. Every week that goes by contains a "last" something that must be duly commemorated: the headmaster's speech on the school birthday dinner, his "fight talk" before the Chelton game, his halloween monologue on parlor night.

Graduates come up for a look, a handshake, a snapshot, a bit of talk. Dr. Prescott lives as publicly as a monarch at Versailles. But whereas Louis XIV had only one Saint-Simon among his courtiers, the Rector of Justin seems to have as many as he has graduates. I sometimes feel that I'm the only person on the campus who's not actively engaged in "writing him up," and I've only stopped because I want to be the only one.

There is a professional cameraman here now to make a film, commissioned by the trustees, of a typical day in the headmaster's life. A recording has already been made of one of his sermons. And there is a big easel up in his study in the Schoolhouse where an artist paints him as he works at his desk. I feel that if I so much as stop by to bid him good morning, I run the risk of seeming to be trying to encroach my little ego on the glorious illuminated page of his personal history.

Yet he himself has never been more wonderful. He seems totally resigned to the circus of these final months; he is more than philosophic—he is benign. He smiles with unfailing charm at the gaping world about him. The agony of decision is over, and he appears to be reconciled to the prospect leaving his creation in inferior hands. Perhaps he has reflected that those hands, after all, are also in God's. Nothing in his headmastership becomes him more than the leaving it.

January 21, 1941. He sent for me last Monday and suggested that I attend one of his sacred studies classes.

"If you do become a minister and if you decide to go on with teaching, you will have to face the fact that you'll always be stuck with sacred studies. It might not do you any harm to see how I do it. After all, I've been at it half a century."

This morning I sat in the back of the classroom hung with maps of the Holy Land and the Roman Empire which adjoins his office and watched him with the second division of the fifth form. Like all great plans, his is basically a simple one. Fifth formers have had their biblical and church history, and Dr. Prescott tries to tie the church into their other courses. He calls on a boy and asks what he is studying that day in Latin, history or mathematics and takes the discussion from this.

Today he chose history, and Jimmie Abercrombie answered on the day's assignment.

"The Thirty Years' War, sir."

"Dear me, *all* of it?"

"Well, I think, sir, today Mr. Evans was planning to discuss the role of Richelieu."

"Ah. The role of Cardinal Richelieu. Do you know, Abercrombie, what the Pope is supposed to have said when Cardinal Richelieu died?"

"No, sir. I don't believe it was in the lesson."

"Must we limit ourselves to the lesson, Abercrombie? May we not talk, you and I? May we not seek a bit of truth, hand in hand, so to speak?"

"Oh, yes, sir. I suppose so, sir."

"Thank you, Abercrombie. The Pope is supposed to have said: 'If there be a God, the cardinal will have much to answer for. If not . . .'" Here Dr. Prescott gave a monumental shrug. "'Well, if not, he led a successful life.' Have you any comment on that, Abercrombie?"

"Well, of course, *I* believe in God, sir. It seems strange that a pope should say a thing like that."

"Popes in the seventeenth century were in some ways very broad-minded. As to what things popes were allowed to say. Then you would agree that the cardinal had much to answer for?"

"I suppose he did his best, sir."

"For mankind? Or for France?"

"Oh for France, sir. That was his duty, wasn't it? To his king?"

The headmaster's deep brown eyes here fixed on Abercrombie for a moment of silent reverie. "Evidently *he* thought so. Do you know what he said on his deathbed?"

"No, sir, it wasn't . . ."

"In the lesson. I am aware of that. But I will tell you. He was asked if he had forgiven his enemies. 'I have none,' came the serene reply, 'but those of France.' The man who has been called the architect of modern Europe was evidently satisfied with his handiwork. Think of that, Abercrombie!"

"Shouldn't he have been, sir?"

"I see, Abercrombie, that you are not in a speculative mood. Let us return to the letter of the lesson where you may feel more at ease. What *was* Richelieu's policy in the Thirty Years' War?"

"To support the Protestant cause, sir."

"You astound me, Abercrombie. I had thought he was a prince of the Roman Church."

"He was, sir. That's why he had to do it secretly. Sometimes he helped the Catholics, too. He had to keep the civil war going in Germany as long as he could."

"*Had* to, Abercrombie?"

"Yes, sir. To weaken the power of the Hapsburg alliance."

"Do you think that was ethical, Abercrombie?"

"It worked, sir!"

Dr. Prescott laughed cheerfully now. "What a pragmatist we have in our midst! Does it mean nothing to you, Abercrombie, that millions may have died to effectuate that policy?"

"But not millions of Frenchmen, sir. Richelieu made France the first power in Europe. It wasn't *his* fault if people in other countries were stupid enough to fight about religion."

"And would it have been the duty of the British government during our own civil war to support both sides to prolong the conflict?"

"Perhaps that was different, sir."

"Why? We were stupid enough to fight about slavery, weren't we?"

"Very well then, sir, perhaps it *might* have been Britain's duty. From Britain's point of view."

"Bravo, Abercrombie! You have the courage to be consistent. I don't know that I agree with your ethics, but I concede they might have been those of my old master at Balliol, a most esteemed scholar. They are certainly those of the political world. But let me put you one more question. A general question, Abercrombie, having nothing to do with marks or lessons.

As you look abroad today at a Europe in flames, created by just such policies as Richelieu's, does it not occur to you that the cardinal's inspiration may have been something less than divine?"

"Perhaps, sir. Yes, sir."

"Thank you, Abercrombie. I guess I made it sufficiently clear what answer I wanted."

April 2, 1941. I had an experience today which may have been a reminder of my "call." It has certainly added to the little store of material in this folder and restimulated my zeal as a recorder. But before relating what happened I must briefly describe Mr. David Griscam, chairman of the Justin trustees. He has not appeared in these pages before as I had not thought him of such significance in Dr. Prescott's life. His appearance is deceptive.

He is reputed to be a very good friend of the school. He was taken into Justin early in its history as the penniless child of an absconded financier and has ever since rather lavishly demonstrated his gratitude. Despite a brilliant career at the New York bar, a wealthy marriage and two minor ambassadorships, Justin, according to the all-knowing Ives, has always remained his primary interest. But he does not believe that a trustee's function is simply to raise money, nor does he always behave with the subservience that Dr. Prescott has come to expect from his board. Or rather, according to Mr. Ives, he may behave with subservience at Justin but acts otherwise when he gets back to New York. He has distinct ideas of his own, and they are not always the headmaster's.

Certainly, at least, he *looks* acquiescent. That is what first put me off. He makes a great fuss over Dr. Prescott, who doesn't like to be made a fuss over. I suspect Mr. Griscam of being one of those outwardly deferring, inwardly resisting men who care more about the fuss they're making than how it is received. He is of middling stature, with a good head of smooth grey hair, tranquil grey eyes and what he must consider, from the way he keeps turning his profile to the viewer, an aristocratic Roman nose. Everything about him, however, suggests to me the small man who would like to seem larger, the guest who is trying to look like one of the portraits in the club. I do not mean to be uncharitable, but Mr. Griscam is a most enigmatic character.

This afternoon I met him and Dr. Prescott walking back from the river. I nodded respectfully as they were about to pass, but the headmaster reached out and caught my arm.

"Come, Brian, and join two old men who are bored with each other's company. We'll have a look at the baseball and then have some tea."

His firm grip admitted of no refusal, and I obediently joined them. The headmaster was in a curious mood. He was joking, but his jokes were very dry, like his inclusion of Mr. Griscam, who must have been fifteen years his junior, in the term "two old men."

"I have never much cared for baseball," Dr. Prescott continued as we walked, "but that's my generation. I detest all the chatter. Football is my sport, a clean, silent game." As we crossed to a little summit overlooking the diamond, we passed two boys with tennis rackets coming from the courts in back. "Oh, yes, I allow the fifth and sixth forms to elect tennis now," he said, noting Mr. Griscam's stare, "so long as some of them feel they cannot stomach baseball or crew. You see, David, there is no end to my broadmindedness! Despite my great age and imminent retirement I continue, as they say in magazine fiction, to 'grow.'"

"Who persuaded you of that? You used to call tennis a game for mollycoddles."

"This young man here."

"Aspinwall?" I felt the prick of Mr. Griscam's quick suspicious stare.

"None other. Oh, he is quite transforming me. He is my Father Joseph or my Colonel House. Or my John Brown, depending on the point of view."

Mr. Griscam smiled at the picture of me as Queen Victoria's gilly. "Does he spike your tea with whiskey?" he asked.

"No, Brian is too pure. In fact, I may have to spike his." Dr. Prescott paused for a moment as we watched the baseball. "He made a persuasive argument that it might be as developing to a boy's character to stand out against organized sports as to play them. That it takes courage to be a mollycoddle!" He turned on me now in a sudden quixotic reaction against the very argument by which he had allowed himself to be persuaded. "Perhaps we *have* reached the point where we must talk of courage in such terms. Perhaps it *does* take guts to face a frown, a sneer, a clatter of teacups. There was a time when it took courage to have one's tongue branded or one's ears shorn off or to be broken on a wheel. Don't tell me physical courage isn't the greatest!" He walked away abruptly from the diamond, and as we followed him, I heard him mutter: "The war will teach our young men that. Oh, yes, alas, it will."

Mr. Griscam asked where we were going.

"To tea, of course. Or whiskey. Whichever you want. I can see you have no eye for baseball. There's only *one* subject on your mind. Prize Day."

We had tea in a corner of the square study from whose wide west window one could see across the campus to the chapel. The twelve Caesars occupied niches in three walls covered from floor to ceiling with books. Since his wife's death Dr. Prescott never uses the living room or parlor except for large occasions. Mr. Griscam began talking of plans for Prize Day. He said it should be celebrated as a jubilee and not a leave-taking.

"I'd like to see it as a day of thanksgiving, Frank," he explained earnestly, "with as many graduates coming back as can be accommodated. A thanksgiving for Francis Prescott. We could run buses down from Boston. I know all the trustees feel it should be an ovation to your fifty-five years in office."

"You see what they're trying to do to me, Brian?" Dr. Prescott demanded with a wry smile. "They're trying to bury me with praise. To mummify me with laudation. In the next months, or years if I am spared, I shall be choked with testimonials. I'll become like a bad marble statue in a public park with puckered brow and those wrinkled trousers that the Victorian sculptors used to carve so lovingly. Ugh! If I live to be ninety I may catch a whiff of the same kind of horror that Wendell Holmes went through. I may even get to like it. That's the worst of it."

"But it won't be like that, Frank. It will be a simple ceremony, deeply felt."

"Don't tell me what those things are like, David. I've spent my life attending them. I do not wish this Prize Day to be different from any other Prize Day. When I go, I go. That's all there is to it. Is that understood?"

Poor Mr. Griscam looked crestfallen. "But we've made such plans, Frank. You mean it's really no?"

"I mean it's really no." Dr. Prescott allowed his lips to crease into the briefest smile. "I've always said that if a headmaster's vocabulary were limited to a single word, he might still get by with 'no.'" And then he added, as if with a sense at last that he might have been too rough: "Besides, I'm not really leaving Justin. I've rented the Andrews cottage just down the road."

"Oh, *have* you?" Mr. Griscam asked. "I didn't know that."

"I suppose I am entitled to select my own place of abode," Dr. Prescott said dryly. "*After* my retirement, of course."

"I wasn't suggesting the contrary."

"But you don't approve?"

"Did you expect I would? Is it fair to Duncan Moore?"

"Well, he must learn to put up with it!" Dr. Prescott rose now and paced heavily across the room. "There's got to be some limit to what's demanded of the old. We have to step down when we still feel able to go on. We have to keep out of the way of our children. We have to avoid embarrassing youth with the reminder of what it will come to."

"Don't I know!"

"Pshaw, you're a child, David. Sixty-five, isn't that it? Besides, you have a pot full of money. That's the only way to be respected by the young in this country."

"It isn't a question of age," Mr. Griscam insisted. "It's a question of *you*. You don't realize the force of your personality. How can Duncan Moore be anything while you're still here?"

The headmaster seemed now to regret that he had mentioned the matter. There was almost a coaxing note in his voice. "You'll see, David. In my little house I'll be no more trouble than if it were my grave. Anyway, I've already signed the lease. And all three girls approve. I shan't, at any rate, be inflicting myself on them. With or without my hundred knights."

Mr. Griscam obviously saw that further argument would be vain. "Well I didn't come to advise you about your retirement, Frank. I didn't even come, despite what you say, to praise you. I came to . . ."

"Bury me?" Dr. Prescott sat down again at the table and, raising his cup to his lips, drank off half of it rather noisily. "Have the trustees asked you to commission a fitting mausoleum?"

"Nobody has asked me to do anything. This is entirely my own project." Mr. Griscam paused, and my heart jumped when he proceeded to say exactly what I had divined that he was going to say. "I want to write your life."

"Great Scott, man!" Dr. Prescott exclaimed, putting down his cup with a clatter. "Is Griscam on *Inter-Vivos Trusts* to become Griscam on Prescott?"

"I've known you since I was a child," the chairman continued stubbornly. "I'm one of your earliest graduates, and I've been a trustee of the school longer than anyone. Who else is more qualified? Can't I have a try at it?"

"A try? How on earth can I stop you?"

"By asking me to stop."

The headmaster shook his head impatiently. "I should not dream of giving so small a matter the dignity of a refusal. You may do as you choose."

"But would you cooperate?"

"How?"

"By talking to me about your life with some degree of candor?"

"Never!"

"Then how am I to do it?"

"That's *your* problem. Do you think I will voluntarily assist at my own Stracheyfication?" Dr. Prescott's tone was sharply mocking again. "Do you think I want posterity to know all my foibles through the probing lawyer's eye of David Griscam? No, if you must write a book about me, why not do it in the great Victorian tradition of the two-volume life and letters? With plates of bad portraits covered with onion skin and an index listing my characteristics, such as courage, magnanimity, foresight, judgment, prudence, and so forth?"

"Who would read it?"

"*I* would! If I have lived only to be your subject, David, and you only to be my biographer, why shouldn't we both get some fun out of it?"

"Let's talk of something else," Mr. Griscam said with a sigh. "You're obviously not in a mood for this today."

"No doubt you'll find Duncan Moore an easier headmaster to handle."

I was suddenly sorry for Mr. Griscam. Dr. Prescott's gibes glanced off me as they drove home into his poor trustee who now said in a voice that trembled: "You know how much of my life you've been, Frank. It's bad taste to pretend I won't regret you."

But he should have known that Dr. Prescott was an old hand in dousing sentiment. "That's just why I'm staying!" he cried remorselessly. "That's why I'm taking the Andrews house."

I got up as I heard the "outside" tolling the end of afternoon sports and excused myself to get ready for the Lawrence House study period. Not since my first month at Justin Martyr had I been happy to leave the headmaster's presence. I would not have believed that he could be cruel.

I had not, however, heard the end of it. Tonight, as I was walking down my darkened dormitory after bidding the boys good night and switching off the overhead lights, I saw ahead through the open door to my study that I had no less a visitor than Mr. Griscam himself. He was standing with his back to the doorway, studying the little portrait of Samuel Richardson which hangs over the mantel. This is my one great treasure, given me on my twenty-first birthday by Mother and Father. Painted on copper, it depicts the father of the English novel at the height of his glory, with a seraphic smile oh his serene, round face and a black velvet cap on his bald head, holding a manuscript on a board stiffly out before him.

"Which one do you suppose he's writing?" Mt. Griscam asked, without turning, when he heard my step. A frequent visitor, he is at home anywhere in the school.

"Oh, *Clarissa*," I exclaimed. "At least, that's what I like to think."

"He doesn't seem to be undergoing many of the pangs of creation."

"But should he? Shouldn't the man who's writing the greatest of English novels *beam*?"

"*Clarissa!*" He turned to me now, and his smile, if disbelieving, was kindly. "Is it really that?"

"Well, to me it is. I don't think anyone else could have written so wonderfully about a villain without, deep down, admiring him. The way Milton admires Satan. But I feel Richardson *detests* Lovelace."

"You don't think he envies him a bit?"

"Oh, no!" But now at last I pulled myself together. "What am I thinking of, Mr. Ambassador? Won't you sit down?"

"Please don't call me 'Mr. Ambassador,'" he replied as he settled himself in the armchair by my desk and pulled out his pipe. "I no longer am one, and, besides, Panama is a very small country. I hope you don't mind my popping in on you?"

"I'm most honored." As he filled his pipe, I continued, a bit constrainedly: "But you read Richardson? You like him?"

"I know that note of surprise," he answered with a chuckle. "English teachers are always shocked to find that Wall Street can be literate. You think of us as bullying sparrows who peck canaries to death because we cannot sing. As men who may collect but who never read."

"I'm sure you must do both."

"Oh, I've picked up a few nice things. Especially in the Elizabethans whom Dr. Prescott tells me you admire. To me they're all gold and ebony. They light up the sky of our grey world. Don't you find it so?"

I think it was at this point that I began to have a glimmer of sympathy for Dr. Prescott's disputatiousness with the chairman of his board. There is something about Mr. Griscam that makes one want to take issue with him. It may be the implication in his tone that it is a higher thing for him, a busy man of affairs, to have discovered literature than for a poor teacher. Yet his words imply humility. "I find I don't believe in the things they believed in," I replied. "I don't see it's so vitally important for women to be chaste. I mean so much more important than anything else. And I don't think it's so terrible to die. Why were they so obsessed with symbols of transiency: grinning skulls and graveyards? I *know* we have only a few petty moments of mortal time, and I think it's quite enough."

Mr. Griscam nodded his head slowly as he seemed to consider this, as I am sure he always considered everything. "Don't you think Frank Prescott is a bit of an Elizabethan?" he asked. "Not, of course, that Harriet was not chaste." He smiled, and I objected to his smile, even while I speculated that he might be one of those unfortunate persons who always say the wrong thing when they mean to be kind. It would not be so much that he lacked heart as that he feared that he lacked it. "Frank has a bitter sense of mortality," he continued. "He can be as gloomy as Hamlet when the mood seizes him."

"Yet he has faith," I protested.

"Oh, yes, he has faith. It's his keel. No matter how much rumbling and tossing about he does, you can be sure he'll always straighten up in the end. Sometimes I wonder if he doesn't put on the show just to give us a scare."

I shivered suddenly with resentment. Who was this lawyer to condescend to Francis Prescott? Did he think we were his puppets, playing with little crucifixes and ideals up here in Justin Martyr?

"You don't like Dr. Prescott!"

I could hardly believe that I had uttered the words, even while they were ringing in my astonished ears. Mr. Griscam, however, did not blink. He is too practiced an advocate not to take immediate advantage of a witness's emotionalism.

"It's hard to tell, isn't it?" he answered calmly. "All I know is that I worship him. I suppose it's quite possible to dislike one's god."

"I'm sorry," I muttered, raising my fingers to my now burning cheeks. "I spoke too hastily. I had no right."

"You had every right, my dear fellow. Every right in the world. My trouble may be that having done a good many things for the school, I subconsciously expect more consideration than I get. And what is anything I've done compared to what Frank has done? Nothing. Frank *is* Justin Martyr." He stared into the empty grate of my fireplace and nodded sadly. "Yes, I suppose it's only too possible that I should resent Frank. Just as it's only too painfully evident that he resents me."

"For the same reasons?"

"Oh, there are many reasons for his resenting me. I won't tell you all of them, but I'll tell you one. Frank doesn't like to face the fact that it takes diplomats as well as soldiers to win wars. Even holy wars. Talleyrands as well as Napoleons."

"And you're his Talleyrand?"

"In some ways. Of course, the world loves soldiers and hates diplomats." He shrugged and then looked around at me with that curious little flare of defiance that I had noticed before. "But I'd like to see it get on without us! Frank knows that. Frank, of course, knows everything. But he wants his board of trustees to be like the scaffolding around an edifice under construction and to come off when the building is finished." He suddenly spread his arms wide. "And there is Justin Martyr, bright, inviolate, a shining Valhalla in the sky! Well, I agree with him, that's the funny thing. I make no bid for personal praise or glory. At least not consciously. I realize that the greatest diplomat, by definition, must be the one of whom nobody has heard. And that's the way I would have written Frank's life."

"Tell him so!"

"He'd never believe it." For the first time I heard the naked bitterness in his tone. "He's too afraid that I'd make myself the real hero. But I wouldn't have, Aspinwall. I swear I wouldn't. I wanted to write that book. I wanted to write it more than I've wanted anything in years."

"You can still write it."

"Without his blessing? Would *you*?"

"No. But you might wait until . . . until . . ."

"Until he's dead? He'll never be dead for me. No, Aspinwall, I give it up. I give it up once and for all. It is *you* who must write the book."

"I?" My voice was a whisper. "But I'm not even a Justinian."

"That may be all to the good. There are those who would say: why should a young man who has known Prescott only as an octogenarian be the person to do his life? Yet I can see that maybe only such a person *could* do it. In any event, I don't want to talk about it." He rose from his chair and knocked the ashes out of the pipe that he had only so recently lit. "The whole subject is very painful, and I'm not going to keep you up talking about it. You will note that I have put an envelope on your desk. It contains my notes for the first two chapters of my life of Frank. It is yours to do with as you wish."

"But, Mr. Griscam," I protested in distress, "what reason do you have to think I even contemplate such a project?"

"Only that Horace Havistock told me he had given you *his* papers. I was terribly jealous for a bit. I had gone to see him in Westbury with the express purpose of raiding his desk. Ah, well." He smiled and held out his hand. "It's a job, anyway, for youth. For youth and faith."

No sooner had I taken his hand than he pulled it away and was gone. Obviously he did not trust to the durability of his own magnanimity. Had I had only myself to consider I would have hurried down the corridor after him and stuffed his manuscript into his pocket. But I had to consider that I might be only an agent. That I might not have the right to refuse.

9

DAVID GRISCAM'S NOTES

A BIOGRAPHER SHOULD commence by stating his prejudices, if he knows of any, and I will undoubtedly antagonize my reader at the outset by affirming that I have none. "But you're a lawyer!" he may object, to which I answer: "Exactly. But a *good* lawyer, such as I claim to be, must be without prejudice."

It seems hard to irritate one's audience at the outset, but as I am bound to do it sooner or later I may as well have it over with. People don't like my type. They resent the fact that I never raise my voice, that I am always reasonable, always willing to hear both sides. Because I am everybody's trustee or on everybody's board, because I have the gift of being able to get any old chestnut out of any old fire, people take for granted that I'm dull.

I, in turn, resent this. I have tried all my life not to be narrow and stuffy. I believe I know as much about Elizabethan drama as any man living, short of the great scholars, and my collection, which I am leaving to Justin Martyr, is full of treasures. I have always been a staunch democrat in the very heart of republicanism, and under Franklin Roosevelt I served as assistant secretary of the Treasury and later as ambassador to Panama. I was enthusiastic for the New Deal when most of my friends were for *laissez-faire,* and as Chairman of the Board of Trustees of Justin Martyr I consistently backed Dr. Prescott in every one of his great forward-looking steps. Yet my son Sylvester, a conservative bank vice-president, and my daughter Amy, who cast her first vote for Herbert Hoover, both regard me complacently as an old fogy. Emmaline, my wife, who has devoted her life to good works, is nearer the mark. She simply regards me as a hopeless materialist, which all of us, except Emmaline, basically are.

I must stop before my introduction dwindles into an old man's querulousness and state the essential prefatory things. I was the only child of a wretched marriage, born to the memory of wealth and the prospect of poverty. I cannot remember my father, Jules Griscam, but I have always been told that he was a dark, flamboyant, charming man, full of wit and brassy impudence, the contemporary picture of a villain and the opposite of myself. He dazzled the Joneses (Mother's family and old New York) during the brief period of his success and dazzled my mother, who had never been dazzled before and never was to be again. After the collapse of his insurance company and the discovery of his peculations he fled to Argentina where, a few years later, he died, leaving to his widow and son a pile of debts which in those days it was considered a sacred duty to pay, so that I started life with a price on my head. Grandpa Jones took us into his old brownstone, full of black walnut and stained glass, paid for my upbringing and supported Mother, and to this day I have never been able to figure out how he was able to make us feel so keenly the load of our obligation without ever even hinting at it. It was a trick peculiar to the family, and I think in time I may have mastered it myself.

Mother was that most irritating of females: the kind who believes implicitly and forever in her male progenitor. No wonder Father told her nothing of his business troubles! She minded the shock of his disaster mostly because of its jarring effect on Grandpa, and she lived thereafter a life of muted apology, acting more as a plain, submissive paid companion to the old man than as a daughter. Even as a child I resented her deference to Grandpa in his testy senility and to my uncles in their youthful arrogance. I wanted to be her champion and take her away from the eternally superior Joneses. I wanted to make a fortune and put her back on top of their world. But my dreams dissolved into slush before the hum of her constant admonitions: "Be sure to tiptoe when you go by Uncle Andrew's room in the morning"; "Be careful not to interrupt your Uncle Timothy when he's reading his paper," and "There's a good boy, fetch your grandfather's shawl." How I hated it all! And the cruelest thing they did was to give me no excuse to hate them.

I went to day school until I was fifteen when I was entered in the fourth form of Justin Martyr. I was sent there because it was a new school and cheaper than the others, and because the headmaster, Francis Prescott, had been a good friend of my Uncle Timothy Jones when they had worked together in New York Central. He often called at the house in those days, and, unlike other family visitors, always took notice of the lonely little boy hiding on a landing, behind a chair or under a table. Prescott would reach out suddenly in passing to grab and haul me forth, tousle my hair or pick me up and swing me about his head. Sometimes he would even bring me a present or take me into the backyard to play at catch. I was dazzled, a bit uncomfortably, to find myself so tossed about by this hearty young man. I suppose I appealed to his sympathy because the shame of my father's disgrace attached itself to my woebegone appearance. When he departed for divinity school, acting on a decision that to me seemed as quick as it was quixotic, I felt sadly abandoned.

Justin Martyr in 1891 was only five years old, with forty boys, six masters
and one big yellow barn of a building that stood up barely in the midst of
a large field near the village of New Paisley, thirty miles west of Boston.
People were already beginning to say it had a great future, but to the
hardworking headmaster who combined the functions of minister, teacher,
coach, tutor and superintendent, that future must have still seemed a good
way off.

For me, anyway, coming from the gloom of the old Jones house on lower
Madison Avenue, the first months there were a kind of paradise. The atmosphere seemed more that of a large happy family than of an academy. The
masters, including Prescott, were all young and played football with the boys;
everybody ate together at three round tables, and the Prescotts entertained
the whole school at parlor games and singing on Saturday nights. Discipline
was handled by simple reprimand or occasional extra chores, and sick boys
were put up in the headmaster's wing and looked after, when a trained nurse
was not required, by Mrs. Prescott, who also taught the German classes.
But above all there was a comradeship between the boys, even between those
of different forms, which inevitably disappeared as the school increased in
size. Dawn must give way to morning, but it was still bliss to have lived in
that one.

Prescott himself, who later became a somewhat austere figure to the
multitudes of students who passed under his all-encompassing brown stare,
was then on easy, even bantering terms with the older boys. He had a natural
authority and could check the least familiarity with a glance, and he could
be terrible in his tempers, but the occasions for them were rare. I was a
modest boy and tended to keep myself out of his way in fear that he might
think I was presuming on our old intimacy. I determined that I would win
his respect independently of the family connection, and to do this I worked
hard at my books, paid an almost fierce attention to his sermons in the little
church in New Paisley where the school worshiped and flung myself recklessly at the biggest boys on the football field. As I was a rather small fifteen,
I got badly battered a few times, and once the headmaster himself picked
me up, patted me on the back and said with a laugh: "You're a tough little
fellow Davey, but try to remember it's only a game." How I thrilled at those
words!

Human beings, however, cannot be happy together for long; the compulsion to mar a scene of content is, in my now long experience with my
fellow men, sooner or later irresistible to the average observer. You may think
you're going your own way, inoffensively enough, modestly enough, not
even whistling under your breath, but make no mistake. Someone is watching you and watching you with hate. How could it be otherwise? Animals
live to kill and be killed, and if our food is supplied at table, the hunting
instinct must still be satisfied. Every garden has a snake, and every boys'
school a Hal Leigh. Need I describe him? Surely the reader can see him,
big and brash and sneering, popular with the boys who preferred the dirty
story in the cellar to the clean play of the football field, feared by the weak,
suspected by the strong, a brute, a bully and a toady. How I hate him still!

It was he, one morning at recess time, when we were eating our crackers and discussing a test in mathematics, who brayed out: "Ask Griscam. His old man was a wizard at all that. He could multiply by a million, divide by himself and come out with zero."

I flew at him with a wild confidence that the wrath of the insane would make up for the difference in weight. It did not. My schooldays were not to be those of Tom Brown. I did not even manage to blacken one of Leigh's eyes before he had knocked me over and kicked me down a stone stairway where I sprained both a wrist and ankle and cut an ugly gash in my head. While I was in the dispensary afterwards, having the cut treated by Mrs. Prescott, her husband came in and asked me how the fight had started. I imagined that he suspected the truth and would have gladly punished Leigh for his cruelty, but I refused to tell him a thing about it. No gentleman could have been more staunchly mute in concealing the indiscreet presence of a lady in his bachelor apartment than was I in shielding the hated Leigh. It was my code of honor, and I gloried in it because I thought it was the headmaster's. I did not realize until years later that he was first of all an eminently practical man.

The glory that I felt, however, was no match for my rancor against the unchastised Leigh. He made no further remarks about my father, it was true, but was his silence the equivalent of my limp or the pain in my wrist? I brooded over my injuries, both to my honor and to my person, until it seemed to me that I could not endure another week at school without some kind of retaliation. For all the power of Prescott's personality and the weakness of Leigh's, it was the latter which now discolored for me the light green of the woods and leered over a pale spring sky. I dared not assault Leigh again, for a second beating would have made me ridiculous and might have exposed me to the headmaster's anger. I could not even complain to my friends about his viciousness without repeating his remark about my father. If I were to have my revenge, it would have to be underhanded, and how then was I ever to look Mr. Prescott in the face again?

Unhappily for me, on a half holiday, the perfect opportunity presented itself. Several boys, including Leigh, had gone canoeing on the river, leaving their schoolbooks and papers in piles just inside the boathouse. I noted that Leigh had carelessly left on top of his pile the paper about the Punic Wars on which he had been working all term. It took only a minute to stuff his thesis in my pocket, all but the last page, and leave the door ajar so that the strong wind scattered the copybooks and notes over the dock and into the water. I then hurried off, unseen, to burn the Punic Wars, knowing that it would all seem an accident, as the discovery of that final page with the rest of the litter would confirm.

And so in fact it turned out, but loud as were the howls of Hal Leigh at the loss of his masterpiece, instead of joy in my heart I felt only a sick depression. Even after the headmaster had agreed to give Leigh a mark for the lost paper higher than the original would have probably received, so that my act of vengeance had actually benefited my foe, I felt no relief. I had proved to myself that I had inherited my father's character, and it could now be only a matter of time before I made this manifest to the world. I could visualize already the nodding heads and deep shrugs of my maternal uncles.

As the spring deepened and the spirits of the boys rose, my own continued to decline until, morose and moody, my marks became affected. I caught a severe cold and in my state of dejection a fever followed, and for some days I was seriously ill in the Prescotts' house with a day and a night nurse. But however much I may have romantically wanted to die, the melancholy spirit could not erode the vigor of my sixteen years, and I soon found myself on the road to a vulgar recovery. It may have been my need for a compensating drama that made me confess to the headmaster at my bedside the whole sorry tale of Hal Leigh.

He was wonderful in that he accepted it with the same gravity in which it was offered. "Of course, you did a very wrong thing, Davey, and one that I would not have expected of you. But on the other hand, I would not have expected you to have received such provocation." He shook his head sadly. "And right here in Justin Martyr, too. Yet perhaps it is all for the good. You have to learn, my boy, to live with your father's reputation. You need not be ashamed of it. Indeed, it would be very foolish of you to be ashamed of it. But you must accept it, because it is a fact."

"It's hard to be the only boy with a father like mine."

"Very hard. I don't minimize it."

"*Your* father was a hero."

"And that has its problems, too, Davey. The good Lord deals us our different hands to play, but don't you suppose he keeps score according to how we play them? I find a hero in mine. Played one way he can set me. Played another he gives me rubber. Your father may seem a liability to you, but he can also be a challenge."

"To what?"

"To a grand slam! Look, my boy: you have a name that is temporarily discredited. So be it. You have had a lonely childhood with uncles who are too afraid of being demonstrative to be properly kind. Oh, I know them." He nodded slowly as I stared, fascinated by this new candor. "You have a mother who has been overburdened with disappointment." I did not know then, but, of course, he did, that Grandpa Jones was at last dying and that Mother had refused to leave his bedside to come to mine. "But look now for your trumps. You have a first-class mind, a well-made body, an aptitude for friendship, high ideals and honesty. Are you to be put out of the game in the first rubber with all that?"

"You really think I'm honest, sir? After what I've just told you about tearing up Leigh's paper?"

"Your telling me proves it. It was wrong, to be sure. But you had great provocation, and now you have made confession. It would be maudlin to dwell on it further."

"And *you* believe in me?"

He smiled, for the first time, at the intensity of my tone. "I do believe in you, my boy," he said and patted me on the head. "Now get some rest."

During the three weeks of my convalescence Prescott tutored me for an hour a day, and when I rejoined my classes I was actually ahead of the others. Even at that age I had some dim appreciation of the remarkable keenness and scope of his mind which could reduce anything, an eclogue by Virgil or the War of the Spanish Succession, to a few vivid terms that would glue the material in all but the stupidest mind at least until whatever test was pending. But Prescott was being far more than a brilliant tutor; he was nursing a sick soul. His kindness was overwhelming, without ever being in the least sentimental, without even, perhaps, being personal. He raised the great beaker of his hope to my lips like a communion cup and watched with grave countenance as I drank, and when he took it away, I knew that it was because I had had enough. There was no question of turning my convalescence into a party.

He talked to me of God and of his early doubts and of the loneliness of his own childhood. He talked of the futility of any action in life that was not service to others. He explained to me and made me believe that happiness had nothing to do with one's outward circumstances, but could be created only within. And then he made me laugh, too, by talking of the past and poking fun at the Joneses and persuading me not only that they were less formidable than they appeared but that they might even be human. When he came to my room with the telegram announcing poor old Grandpa's death we knelt together in prayer by my bed, and I found that I was actually weeping.

I was too clever, and also at this point too well acquainted with the headmaster's character, to make the smallest effort, after my return to a normal schedule, to trade upon convalescent days. I adored Mr. Prescott as I had never adored another human being, but it was a worshipful kind of emotion, and I was able to sublimate it into violent activities and studies. I rose to be second in my form, and in my last year I was one of the school prefects. I was not big enough to be very effective at football, but I played it hard, and I edited the school paper, *The Justinian.* The best part of sixth form year was that the prefects were in constant contact with the headmaster, and we could feel that we ran the school in a sort of partnership. Mr. Prescott treated us almost as equals and even allowed me to share in one of his melancholy moments. We had been out together on a cold winter afternoon, snowshoeing on the crisp surface, and as we came back, it was already dark, and we paused for a moment on the crest of the hill overlooking the school and stared down at the lighted building so far below. My heart was so full that I exclaimed: "I can't bear to have spring come!"

"Why not, Davey? Are you so fond of the winter of our discontent?"

"I'm so fond of Justin, sir. I can't bear the thought of graduation."

"But Justin is only a prelude," he protested. "It is nothing but a simple first course. If I thought I had made it the whole banquet of life for any boy, I should know I had failed indeed."

"But it's the whole banquet of life for *you*, sir."

"It is that, Davey." His smile was grave as he stared down at his school. "It is that indeed."

"And how happy it must make you!"

"Very happy," he agreed in a rather somber tone. "I am most blessed. I have what I wanted. I have what I prayed for. And do you know what I pray for now, Davey?"

"What, sir?"

"That the sin of boredom shall never fall upon me."

I said nothing, awed, for I knew that in that moment we were as intimate as we ever again should be.

Graduation was a sad time for me, although Mother came up for it, urged, no doubt, by Mr. Prescott. My friends thought me very emotional, for there were tears in my eyes, but in those days such emotion was still respectable. I felt that I was emerging from a Garden of Eden that might be artificial by the standards of a world that had first applauded and later persecuted my father, but I was armed with the faith that that garden had nonetheless prepared me for that world.

I went to Harvard and made a good record there, but I was never as happy as I had been at school. Harvard was already the world, and although I could cope with it I had not learned to cope with it joyfully. I went back to Justin, now rapidly expanding, on so many weekends that at length Mr. Prescott had to warn me in a friendly fashion that I might be neglecting the social duties of a college man. It was then that I asked him if he would consider me for the faculty of Justin when I graduated. We were walking to the river, and he grasped my elbow as he debated, too long for my comfort, the answer.

"Are you so sure you want to teach, Davey?"

"If I could teach here, sir."

"No, that won't do. You'd have to want to teach anywhere to be able to teach here."

"Then I want to teach anywhere!"

"It might work out." He removed his hand and strode on. "But not until several years after your graduation. You must see more of the world first, Davey, if you're to teach boys to deal with it. And I can't help but wonder if a life at Justin would be the happiest life for you. Your father's name received its blemish in New York. Isn't it there that you must seek to remove it?"

"Is that so important?"

"Not to my thinking. But I thought it was to yours."

"You mean I should pay his debts?" My question, I fear, was belligerent.

"No, Davey," he said patiently. "I mean you should bury his old reputation under the monument of your new one."

Of course he was being reasonable and kind, and who but I had given him the notion of the importance of my father's crime to me? Of course he saw instantly that Justin was a haven for me, a refuge from a world that I deemed cold, if not actually sneering. He wanted no escapists in his school, and he was right. But at the time I refused to discuss the matter any further, and we reached the river in silence. I had been rejected by too many people in my life to be a good sport about being rejected by Francis Prescott.

10

DAVID GRISCAM'S NOTES

ONCE I HAD squarely turned my back on schoolteaching and resolved to become a lawyer, I never wavered again. My poor mother died only a year after Grandpa Jones, and my inheritance was just sufficient to put me through Harvard and Harvard Law. After that I got a job with Prime & Ballard, a small but lucrative "family" law firm, which is now Prime & Griscam and one of the last of its kind on Wall Street. We get our clients everything from theatre tickets to divorces; we file their birth certificates and we bury them. I started as Mr. Prime's law clerk and became in turn his son-in-law, his partner and his executor. It was an old-fashioned success story.

I discovered not only that I enjoyed my law practice, but that I was admirably adapted to it. I am by nature reserved, patient, of even temper and a good listener, and I love the challenge of domestic puzzles. I became a specialist in the multiple prejudices under which Americans suffer in the spending of their money, according to whether it has been earned, married or handed down, and I learned to stay within the framework of the sacred mores surrounding these categories while putting the dollars to work to the greatest advantage of the whole family. I even found that it was occasionally possible to persuade old New Yorkers that money could be used for pleasure.

Once Mr. Prime had made me his partner everything seemed to go my way. I was even assisted by the kind of windfall that is usually the lot only of fictional heroes. I bought from my father's creditors some supposedly worthless gold-mining stock at the price for which he had pledged it, and it turned into a very good thing. What happier ending could there be to the grim saga of the paternal obligations? Was it not what ought to have happened to the conscientious, debt-assuming Victorian son? Paradise was on this earth, where it belonged, and I thrilled with my first sense of the Midas touch.

But the greatest reward of my successful professional life came with a letter that I received from Mr. Prescott on the occasion of my twenty-ninth birthday. He wrote that he had for some time wanted a younger point of view represented on the school board and that he was suggesting my name to Mr. Depew as the first graduate trustee of Justin! It was like him not even to ask my permission. He knew only too well that I would jump at the chance.

From the very beginning, except for my diplomatic years, I never missed a meeting of the board. These were always held at the school, and it would have been worthwhile to attend them if only to watch Frank Prescott handle my fellow members. He would stare hard at the one who was putting the question, not a muscle moving, his big brown gaze seeming to encompass not only the question but the motive behind it. He would nod briefly, express his satisfaction that the point had been raised, immediately associate himself with the complaint, if any, contained, sometimes even rephrasing the question to give it a sharper lunge, and then proceed to defend his administration, then to counterattack, then to defend it again. It was Prescott against Prescott in a duel whose brilliance distracted the attention of the audience from the fact that Prescott was also the referee. I asked few questions myself for I found it more instructive to gather knowledge on my own.

My great project, which I nursed for a year before I even began to sound out the other trustees, was to double the size of the school. Justin in 1906 had reached an enrollment of two hundred where Prescott had arbitrarily cut it short as the maximum number of boys that a headmaster could get to know personally. I doubted that he could get to know even that many. It seemed to me that the attractive intimacy of the school's early days had been lost forever when the roll call had passed fifty and that having lost that, we might as well push on to four or five hundred. If we went too far, of course, the essential character of the school would be lost. The point was to find the greatest number of boys on whom Prescott's genius could still successfully operate. Otherwise we were wasting him. Could any other conclusion follow?

The trustees, on the whole, were responsive, particularly when I made it clear that I would take charge of the necessary fund raising. I had already discussed this with Mr. Prime who had promptly offered me a leave of absence.

"It's precisely the little push that your career needs at precisely this moment!" he exclaimed, briskly rubbing his hands. "You should see every big man in New York, Philadelphia and Boston. They'll all have heard of the great job that Prescott is doing at Justin, and they'll be glad to see you, even if they don't give you a cent. You'll be identified with a great cause. We lawyers have to take advantage of these things, you know. After all, we can't advertise. Go to it, my boy, with all my blessing!"

"I wasn't thinking so much of what it would do for *me*," I protested, taken aback by such crassness. "I was thinking of Prescott and the school and perhaps a little bit of the rehabilitation of my father's name."

"Well, that's fine, dear boy, that's fine," Mr. Prime said soothingly. "There's no reason you shouldn't knock off several birds with a stone as round and smooth as this one."

It was agreed among the trustees, after the project had been reduced to a simple outline listing the proposed new buildings and masterships, that I should be the one to approach Prescott, and with the paper in my pocket and their blessing on my head, I journeyed apprehensively up to Justin for the first conference.

In his study, leaning over the surface of his large uncluttered desk, a fist in each cheek, Prescott moved only his eyes as I talked: to my face, to the blotter, back to my face again. There was not even a hint of surprise in his own and certainly none of gratification. Obviously, he had been forewarned. I began to feel as if I were making a too lengthy confession of a misdeed that was more unattractive than criminal. When I leaned down to pull the outline from my briefcase he finally raised a hand.

"Whoa, David, whoa!"

"Don't you even want to see it?"

"I don't want to see anything for just a minute, thank you," he said in a cool, gruff tone as he stared, seemingly through me, at the window behind my back that looked out at the chapel. "I need a little time to pull myself together now that your proposition has finally come." As he sighed, some of the frostiness went out of his tone. "I always knew it would, you know. From you or another. No matter how much the conception of a school may be one's own, sooner or later, if it has any use, any currency, it is bound to pass into the public domain. We can keep only our failures. Obviously, I cannot keep Justin."

"But it seems to me, sir," I suggested, for I now called him "sir" and "Frank" alternately, "that with two hundred boys you're already pretty well in that domain."

"I had hoped not, David." He shifted his gaze to me from that imaginary audience that he so often seemed to be addressing. "I have tried to preserve some remnant of family atmosphere."

"And you have succeeded!" I exclaimed. "My point is precisely that what is left of it is still compatible with a larger school. You have to recognize, sir, that not only has Justin quadrupled since its beginning, but you yourself have changed.

You can't expect to be as intimate with the boys as when you were a younger man. You have become a rather awe-inspiring figure, like Arnold of Rugby. But the advantage of being on a pedestal is that more people can see you."

Of course, I was an idiot to have used such an image, but I was excited and nervous, and now that it was out, I could only bow my head to the angry storm.

"Then why not expand the school to a thousand or more?" he demanded, spreading his arms mockingly. "Why not build auditoriums throughout New England so that all the world may see me?"

"I doubt we could raise the money."

Prescott turned sullenly to the outline that I now placed on his desk. "But you think you could for this," he muttered. I must have sat for fifteen minutes in silence while he studied it. "Is this supposed to be final?" he asked at last.

"Oh, no, sir. It's simply a draft. A suggestion."

"A draft." His mood seemed to deepen dismally. "It would have to be changed, of course. But that's not the point. It *could* be changed. The point is that so could the headmaster. And I think that you may well need a new headmaster for this magnificent new academy of yours."

This struck me at last as a false note, and for the first time in my term as trustee I showed impatience. After all, I had worked for months on the project, and he had not even suggested that I might, however mistakenly, have the school's welfare in mind. "If you don't like the plan, Frank, the plan will be scrapped. The idea was not so much to sell Justin Martyr as it was to sell Francis Prescott. I'm sorry if you find the admiration of your board so offensive."

He looked up at me quizzically, taking in my change of mood and reflecting, perhaps, that there might be grounds for it. "I'm not acting, David, or putting on airs. You don't know what you ask of me. It's hard on the personality to be a headmaster."

He tightened his lips into the thin line that always marked his moments of peculiar candor. "It's particularly hard on mine. It develops all my tendencies to strut and bully. Here I am, covered with mud from the bottom of my own little puddle, and you want to pitch me into a larger one!"

"It wouldn't be like you, Frank, to deflate the school because you were afraid it might inflate your own ego."

He gave me a shrewd look, grunted and returned to the outline. After another long silence I realized that the conversation was over, at least for that day, and I left his study without even an interchange of farewells.

The following weekend I returned to the school, but Frank hardly spoke to me, and when he did, he was barely civil. At tea on Sunday afternoon, before leaving for my train, in Harriet Prescott's living room, which for all its clutter of books and family photographs and heavy, dark boy-proof furniture still managed to suggest some of its mistress's early New England austerity, I watched her fill my cup from the fine old silver urn that I remembered from "parlor night" in my own school days. Harriet was the bony kind of woman who begins to look old at thirty-five but after fifty seems younger than her contemporaries and more distinguished. At this point she had just started to dye her hair the chestnut color that it was always to remain. She did it, I am sure, not to seem young but to seem ageless, which, with her pale skin, her big, Emerson nose and dull brown dresses, she always succeeded in seeming. I told her that I feared Frank was put out with me.

"Oh, he is that," she agreed readily. "You should hear the catalogue of your iniquities. But don't worry. It will pass."

"Do you think I should not have brought the matter up?"

She considered this a moment, putting down the cup that she had half filled. "It's hard to say. If I thought that nobody else ever would have, I might say yes. You see, I like the school as it is. But now it can never be as it is again. If your plan is rejected, we'll always be a small school that *could* have been a big one. We'll always be justifying ourselves."

"You make me feel very badly."

"You shouldn't. You're probably quite right. If one goes in for education, one might as well educate as many as one can. It's up to Frank and myself to live up to your plan."

"You're laughing at me!"

"Far from it," she said very seriously. "One should never laugh at growth. It's like laughing at life."

"You resent me, anyway," I said gloomily. "Of course you do. Frank will never forgive me for interfering with his school."

"If he doesn't, it will be because he can't forgive himself for wanting what you want."

I stared in astonishment at those cool green eyes in which a glimmer of amusement was just discernible. "He wants a *bigger* Justin?"

"Oh, yes. Frank is ambitious, you know. For himself *and* the school, though they're sometimes confused. But don't imagine he'll admit it. On the contrary, he'll growl and grumble. He'll blame the whole thing on you. He'll talk about the vulgarity of size. Only he'll go along. At the last moment. He'll go along, fighting you every inch of the way. Don't fool yourself, David. It's going to be a bumpy road!"

Harriet was right. Prescott ultimately announced to the trustees his willingness to entertain the "Griscam" project, but only on condition that the plan be entirely revised and that the proposed fund for new masters' salaries be doubled. If Justin was going to increase in quantity, he argued, it would have to increase as well in quality. It would have to achieve the highest academic rating in all of New England. Similarly, the spiritual side of school life would have to be re-emphasized, and the project was again conditioned on funds to be raised for a new chapel designed by an architect of the headmaster's choosing. And finally he stipulated that the committee to go to the public for money under my chairmanship was to operate under his own constant review. It was the most dictatorial program ever presented to my knowledge by a headmaster to a board of trustees, yet the latter acceded to it without a protest or a dissenting vote. It established definitively the master-servant relationship which was to last for the remainder of his long tenure of office.

The principal burden of working under his conditions fell, of course, upon my shoulders. Prescott proved to be a remarkable, indeed an indispensable fund raiser, but I could never be sure that he would not undo six months' good work with a single burst of temper. When I organized dinners for friends of the school and asked him to speak, he would always comply so eloquently, so humorously, so winningly that I believe no tongue could have opened more purses. Yet behind the scenes no Italian tenor of the Metropolitan could have behaved more outrageously. He would fuss and fret over what he called the "Hippodrome" that I had prepared for him and demand in clipped, biting tones if his performance had been up to expectations, if his words had been converted into coin at as favorable an exchange as at the previous dinner. He would describe himself pathetically to friends as David Griscam's dancing bear, led by a ring through its nose from laughing village to smirking town.

Had it not been for Harriet I wonder if I might not have given the whole thing up. She preserved at all times her extraordinary equilibrium and helped me to understand the suffering even of the ambitious artist when he finds his work marketed on a national scale, and to see that Frank was having to learn to share his life's dream with every starched shirtfront that I had gathered in a dozen gilded halls. It must have sometimes seemed to him that the very soul of Justin Martyr would dissolve into the smoky air over the soiled plates and stained napkins and fade away with the waves of stale laughter evoked by his own jokes.

Far worse, however, than the private scenes between us, which had no effect on the fund raising, were his violent reactions to any gifts to which he chanced to see conditions, expressed or implied, attached. Sometimes he was perfectly right, as when he ushered to the door without further ceremony a man who had offered him fifty thousand dollars to admit his delinquent son to the school. At others he was too suspicious of interference, and I would have the devil's own time persuading him that a graduate's offer to build handball courts was not necessarily an improper attempt to add a new sport to the curriculum. But the episode that made him angriest of all was that of the two new dormitories. The donor of one had modestly left its naming to the headmaster, while the donor of the other, in order not to seem a lone egotist, had stipulated that *both* buildings be named for their contributors. Prescott's indignation at such meanness threatened to cost us not one but two dormitories, and only by the greatest diplomacy was I able to persuade the modest donor to allow his name to be used and to restrain the headmaster from mortally insulting the other. Yet for all our difficulties, the money poured in.

We had almost reached our goal, except for the chapel, and I thought I was close to a pledge for that from Shelley Tanager, a Chicago meat-packer who had a boy in the fifth form, when the episode occurred that was to detonate the mounting tension between Prescott and myself and nearly bring our whole project to the ground.

I was spending a week at Justin, where an office and secretary had now been assigned to me, and breakfasting with the Prescotts when Frank explained the troublesome business of the "trots." Apparently translations of Latin and Greek texts had been circulating among the boys, and the masters had been complaining of a growing uniformity in recitations. The sixth form had made raids on desks and studies and confiscated a number of trots, and severe penalties had been meted out, but the practice had stubbornly continued. It was particularly galling to Prescott, himself an accomplished classicist, to be faced with so widespread a resistance to a proper study of the ancient tongues at just the moment when he was determined to raise academic standards in proportion to the contemplated new enrollment.

"It's the kind of thing one expects of little boys," he grumbled, "but it's most offensive to find it in the upper forms. I'm told it's particularly rank in the fifth. And here we are, almost at the end of the school year. Next fall those are the boys on whom I must lean to run the school!"

"Let us hope for good things of the summer."

"It's nothing to be facetious about, David. It's the kind of rot that can bring a school down."

"But, surely, all schools have trouble with trots," his wife put in. "I remember distinctly using one at Miss Yarnell's, in French class."

Prescott glared down the table while Harriet imperturbably continued to pour coffee. "I have announced to the fifth form," he continued, "that any member who is hereafter caught using a trot will not be welcome back next year."

"Isn't that rather stiff?" I asked.

"Perhaps it is. But I have given fair warning. It seems to be the only way to impress upon them that as sixth formers they will share with me and the masters the responsibility of administering the school."

I was faintly bored by the subject and said nothing more. I could not see that the use of a trot would necessarily disqualify a boy from being a good administrator, but I assumed that Prescott's warning, however fierce, would at least accomplish its purpose. I did not dream that any fifth former would be such a fool as to risk his school career for a dozen lines of Ovid.

Yet as early as the third day of my visit, when I was following the boys after morning chapel over the path, soft with spring mud, to the Schoolhouse, Prescott came up beside me with the bad news.

"You'll be sorry to hear, David, that a fifth former has not seen fit to heed my admonition. You'll be even sorrier to hear who it is."

The hope of spring vanished from that day, and the light blue of the sky faded to a dead winter's whiteness. "Shelley Tanager's boy?"

Prescott nodded and then shook his head roughly as if to confound the boy and his father and perhaps myself as troublemakers in an otherwise serene Justin. There was even a hint of something akin to triumph in his eye, almost of downright malevolence, which ended by exasperating me. When I thought back in later years on this scene I wondered if I could not date from it the first appearance of a new trait of hardness in Prescott, a hardness that was to grow, along with his great fame, in the coming decade and a half, culminating at last in the terrible episode of my own son, Jules. No one could write Prescott's biography without considering this side of him. It was a spasmodic, inconsistent hardness; a boy might spend six years at Justin without once encountering it, and I think most did. But those few who ran afoul of the headmaster in this period were apt to remember him for life with bitterness.

"Is there no doubt about it?"

"Well, he denies it." Prescott shrugged contemptuously. "He says the trot was put in his desk by his roommate, Max Totten. It seems sufficiently curious that Totten, a poor orphan whose tuition Tanager's father pays, should find it worth his while to 'frame' his benefactor."

"But not impossible."

"Ah, yes, wouldn't it be nice, David? And then we should not find ourselves in the uncomfortable position of having to expel the son of our potential benefactor, should we?" Prescott's voice rose in a cascade of sarcasm. We had reached the Schoolhouse and were standing outside the big windows of the assembly hall where some of the boys could see, but not hear us. "You must not be so anxious to save the hides of those who can be useful to us. Let us not gain the world and lose our souls!"

"Has it occurred to you," I demanded sharply, "that you may be condemning this boy for the glory of spitting in his rich father's eye?"

For once I saw that I had the upper hand; for once Frank Prescott was taken by surprise. It was part of his charm that he should not have made the smallest effort to conceal it. "Do you suppose that could be?" he asked soberly, raising his eyebrows. "That would be a very terrible thing, David."

"I'm only suggesting that you should not leap to conclusions."

"Would you care to be present when I see the boy? He and Mr. Mygatt, the master who made the charge, will be in my office after assembly."

"I should indeed be interested."

"You may act as his counsel if you wish," he said, and as he turned to go into the Schoolhouse, he gave me one of his slow, unsmiling winks. "I'm sure that Shelley Tanager's father can afford even the charges of a partner of Prime and Griscam."

I sat in a corner of Prescott's office, unintroduced and almost unnoticed, during the arraignment. The master, a rather oily, olive-complexioned fellow, told his story while Shelley Tanager, Junior, a tall, slight boy with curly blond hair and the pouting face, even at sixteen, of a spoiled child, sullenly listened.

The master had suspected Tanager of continuing to use a trot, although punished for it once already, and had been on the watch. He had searched the study which Tanager and Max Totten shared the night before while the school was at supper, and had found nothing. Half an hour later, during study period, he had knocked on their door, sent both boys on contrived errands and had then discovered the trot, open and face downward, as if hastily concealed, in the first drawer of Tanager's desk. Nobody but Tanager and his roommate had entered the study between the two searches.

"And you deny, Tanager, that you placed it there?" Prescott asked in the dry, melancholy tone that he used for such inquests.

"I do, sir."

"If you did not, I take it there's only one other person who could have."

"Only one, sir. That's correct." The boy's expression was certainly unendearing. He seemed totally unconcerned with the improbabilities of his accusation, as if his own malevolence should somehow be taken as ample evidence.

"Why should Totten have had a trot?" Prescott continued in a sterner voice. "He was a first-rate Latin scholar long before the first of these wretched books appeared on the campus."

"How do you know, sir, when the first one appeared?"

Prescott had to nod to acknowledge the unexpected justice of this. "But when do you suggest that he could have concealed the trot in your desk? When did he have time?"

"How should I know? It was *his* trot."

"His, you say. Yet you were caught with one yourself three weeks back, is that not so?"

"Yes, sir."

"And phrases from this trot, the one Mr. Mygatt discovered in your desk last night, have been found in your written exercises."

"If that's so, I got them from Totten. He sometimes helped me with my work."

"Surely, you know, Tanager, that's improper!"

"Yes, sir, but it's not using a trot."

And so it went, for a quarter of an hour, Prescott's questions, like those of a cross-examining lawyer, rising in vigor and hostility. He mercilessly pointed up the contrast between Max Totten the able student, brilliant athlete and natural leader and Shelley Tanager the dunce, the fumbler and lone wolf. Was it likely that the former would resort to a trot that he did not need and then use it to compromise a roommate for whom he had never shown anything but kindness and whose father was his own sole support? Was it not more likely that Tanager, jealous of the superiority of his friend both at home and at school, should have sought to cast his own blame on those stronger shoulders? But Tanager would concede nothing, even if he could explain nothing, and when he had been dismissed, I protested to Prescott against his roughness.

"But the boy not only obviously had the trot," he retorted angrily; "he's trying to get his friend expelled!"

"Aren't you begging the question?"

"Well, what more do you need to convince you, David? Do you have to eat the whole apple to tell it's rotten?"

"Perhaps you would allow me to ask Mr. Mygatt a few questions."

"'Sir, a whole history,'" Prescott quoted impatiently and turned away in his swivel chair as I addressed myself to the master who had been listening with awe to our testy exchange. He had probably never heard the head-master contradicted before.

"Tell me, Mr. Mygatt, when you asked Tanager to go on that fabricated errand, where exactly were you standing?"

"In the doorway to his study."

"How was he able to leave?"

"Why, I stepped aside, naturally."

"Did you step back, or did you step forward into the study?"

Mygatt, perplexed, considered this. "I stepped back into the corridor. Yes, I remember that because I saw Jimmie Dunn across the way reading a magazine, and I made a mental note to speak to him later about it."

"And when you returned to the study occupied by Totten and Tanager, Tanager was gone?"

"Gone? Oh, yes. He had gone to the library, as I told him."

"But Totten was still there?"

"Well, only for a second. I sent him off, too."

"How long had you been in the corridor?"

"Oh, two seconds maybe."

"Not more? Even in the exercise of your inspection of young Dunn's reading habits?"

Mygatt flushed. "No, sir. A few seconds at the most."

"But long enough for Totten to have placed that trot in Tanager's drawer?"

"Oh, not possibly, sir. Besides, I should have seen him."

"How? Through an eye in back of your head?"

"Please remember, David, that you're not in a courtroom," Prescott interrupted. "You happen to be in my office, addressing a member of my faculty."

"I'm very well aware of that, sir. I suggest that I am using no stronger language than you used to Tanager. A boy's whole life may be at stake here."

Prescott faced my stare for a moment and then nodded. "Proceed."

"I meant, sir," Mygatt volunteered, "that I would have been aware of the boy's movements. I was standing so close."

"But has the headmaster not just described Totten as a brilliant athlete?" I pursued. "And does not that imply physical coordination? What would be simpler for an agile boy, while your back was turned, to have crossed a small study, opened a drawer and pushed a book in?"

"But I would have heard him, Mr. Griscam!"

"If he did it stealthily? Come, Mr. Mygatt, all I'm asking you to concede is that it's not impossible."

Mygatt glanced at the headmaster in appeal, but the latter only scowled and grumbled: "Answer the question, Mygatt. It's a fair one."

"Very well, then, sir. I suppose it wasn't actually impossible. Only I can't see . . ."

"Thank you, Mr. Mygatt," I interrupted firmly. "And now to the matter of the trot itself. Where is it?"

"In the faculty room. The Latin masters have been examining it to see what phrases they can pick up in their exercises."

"You mean they've been handling it?"

"How do you mean, handling it?"

"I mean *touching* it. Putting their fingers on it."

"Well, inevitably."

I groaned aloud. "I suppose a print test would show half the fingers of the faculty."

"You don't mean you'd go in for fingerprinting *here?*" Prescott asked, shocked.

"I'd go in for anything to prove a boy's innocence!" I exclaimed. "Let me ask you, Mr. Mygatt, to lock the trot up until this investigation is over." I turned to Prescott. "Will you allow me to see Totten alone?"

He shrugged. "Most certainly. I shall see that he's sent directly to your office."

"Not for an hour, please. I'd like to study his file first."

At my own desk, with the door closed, I studied the contents of the manila folder marked "Totten, Max, Form of 1908." There was a passport-size snapshot of him, full face, showing a high forehead, a big jaw and nose, every feature giving the impression of strength and candor except for the small dark eyes. I learned that his father had been an impoverished cousin of Mr. Tanager's and that he had grown up an orphan in the millionaire's household, earning his keep by bolstering, morally and intellectually, his feebler cousin. He appeared to have the same facility for success that young Tanager had for failure, but despite what were evidently engaging manners he was not popular with his formmates. He was considered "political," according to one master's report and "insincere" according to another's. In each case, I noted, the reporting master disagreed with the boys whom he quoted. Max Totten was evidently a student who knew how to ingratiate himself with the faculty.

When he came in, he struck me as even bigger, darker and more attractive than I had visualized. Unlike his cousin and roommate, he was already a man.

"What can I do for you, Mr. Griscam?" he began, politely enough.

I explained, slowly and carefully, the accusation made against Shelley Tanager and the damning nature of the evidence. All this he knew already and shook his head with a very proper commiseration. I then proceeded to relate Mr. Mygatt's story, beginning with the search of the study during supper and taking it step by step to the discovery of the trot. Totten listened to me with close attention, but betrayed nothing. I was watching for the least reaction to his discovery from my recitation that if he *had* planted the trot in Tanager's desk, Tanager, and later Tanager's father, would necessarily know of it. For Mr. Mygatt's first search, of which Totten could not have previously known, had established that the trot had *not* been in the study before the boys had come in after supper. He did not so much as blink.

"Mr. Mygatt might have put it there himself," he suggested blandly when I asked for his comments.

"Why on earth would he do that?"

"To curry favor with the Rector. He's like that, you know."

"I can't believe it, Totten!"

He shrugged. "It was only an idea. I'd do anything to see poor Shelley cleared. He's the oldest friend I have in the world."

I had to pause here to reflect. The only thing I had not considered was that Totten might not have heard of Tanager's accusation. "That's not what Tanager seems to think."

His eyebrows rose. "It's not, sir? What does Shelley think?"

"He told Dr. Prescott that *you* had put that trot in his desk."

Totten looked at me steadily for a moment, but his expression struck me not so much as alarmed or shocked or even as very much surprised, but simply as interested, intensely interested.

"It must have been you or he," I pursued.

"Or Mr. Mygatt," Totten retorted with a smile that struck me suddenly as impudent. With a familiarity in marked contrast to his former deference, he rose from his chair and went to the window where he stood looking out, casually twirling the shade cord. He must have remained there in total silence for almost three minutes while I stared at his back. I assumed that he was concocting an alibi, and I was too interested in what it might be to interrupt him. "Or dear little mincing Mygatt," he said at last, repeating his obviously insincere accusation.

"Please remember, Totten, that Mr. Mygatt is a member of the faculty of this school and that I am a trustee."

"Oh, keep your shirt on, Griscam," he retorted with a cool, shocking insolence, turning back to me with a now brazen smile. "You and I don't have to kid ourselves, do we? You're scared shitless this little affair will do you out of old Tanager's dough, aren't you?"

"*Totten!* I shall have to report you to the headmaster."

"What the hell, lay off it, will you!" His barking tone startled me with its authority. "I knew when they put a shyster like you on my trail, the game was up. All right, so I put the goddam trot in little Shelley's desk. Is that enough for you? Can I go now? Or shall I give old Prescott other grounds to throw me out by kicking you first in the tail?"

As I stared, my dignity shattered, at that grinning, insinuating, oddly unhostile countenance, I found that for all my years at the bar, I had no idea what to do next. It was he who solved it. He walked slowly up to me, still smiling, and suddenly stuck out his hand. Hypnotized, I took it, at which he laughed aloud, winked and left the room. Certainly he had a kind of disgusting animal charm. There was an uncomfortable democracy in his total cynicism. I sighed, shuddered, shook my head and prepared to make my report to the headmaster.

Prescott took my news like a gentleman. He put his arm about my shoulders and gave me a hug. "You've saved me from an act of brutal injustice, David. I must learn a proper humility with regard to your profession. I confess to the ancient and unworthy prejudice against lawyers. I have always accused them of not seeing the forest for the trees. Yet *I* was the one who couldn't see those trees." He shook his head ruefully. "I would have torn up young Tanager, a tender sapling, roots and all. Yes, *there* was prejudice. Because the poor boy was unattractive and unathletic, I would have had him vicious, too. While the one who was clever enough to cast himself in the image that I set up was the real rotter. Oh, it's a lesson for me, David!"

Harriet Prescott, however, professed to find the whole thing incredible. "I'm not going to say it to anyone else," she told me as I circled the campus with her and her dogs before lunch. "Obviously, if Max Totten has confessed, I'm bound by it. But I will say to you, David, that it baffles me. I've watched that boy carefully. He always came to my parlor nights. I feel that I know him and that I like what I know. The boys may not, but I do. He's more mature than the others. He's had a bitter and humiliating childhood, and he's going to make up for it in life. Oh, yes, he's devious and sly and intriguing. He'd use a thousand trots and swear on the Bible he hadn't. But I can't believe that he'd have placed that trot in Shelley Tanager's desk. His one virtue is loyalty!"

I was greatly troubled, for I knew Harriet to be a shrewd judge of character, considerably shrewder, even, than her husband. Also, it occurred to me that it was odd that Totten, even if guilty, should have confessed to an action that would forever embroil him with his patron, Mr. Tanager. Why would he not have brazened it out? Might he not have convinced the father that the son was lying, or at least mistaken? And, after all, he had nothing to lose by trying, for this way he was both expelled from Justin and damned with the Tanagers. After our walk I went to the chapel, so soon, as I hoped, to be replaced by a new and greater one, and prayed earnestly for guidance, but I received none. I have never thought that the good Lord, like his servant, Frank Prescott, took a proper interest in lawyers.

That afternoon I made my way to Max Totten's dormitory in Lowell House. At the end of the long empty corridor between the varnished cubicles, each sheltered by a green curtain, I saw a trunk and standing before it, putting shirts in a drawer, was Max. His back was to me, and I could hear him humming "After the Ball." To my astonishment I saw that he was smoking a cigarette which he made no effort to conceal as he turned and saw me.

"Hello, Mr. Griscam," he called with the same cheerful impudence. "Is this the official farewell?"

I walked down the corridor and stood watching him as he continued his packing. "I came to tell you that you could drop the bluff. I know you didn't do it."

Totten looked up at me cagily but with his same smile. "Know? How do you *know*?"

"You wouldn't have had time to wipe your fingerprints off the trot."

His smile became fixed as he continued to stare at me. "What makes you think they weren't on it?"

"Because I sent it into Boston this morning, with prints of Tanager's and Mygatt's fingers. They were the only ones found on the cover. The detective just called me."

"And have you told the Rector?"

"As a matter of fact, I haven't told anybody. I thought I'd better come straight to you first. Why did you confess to something you hadn't done?"

I was a bit ashamed, watching those darkening eyes, of my own pleasure at outbluffing a mere boy, but the scene that morning still rankled. My pleasure, however, was not to be of any duration. Totten was a master at table turning.

"Look, Mr. Griscam, you strike me as a realistic guy. Can't you and I make a deal? We each have a hell of a lot at stake in this business. You want old Tanager's money for a greater Justin, isn't that it? In fact, your whole wagon cart may fall in if you don't get it, and you sure as hell won't get it if little Shelley is bounced. I, on the other hand, have my own deal with old Tanager. He knows all about Shelley and what poor stuff the kid is. He'll know who had that trot, never fear. But he's crazy to have the boy graduate, and it's my job to see that he does. If you will be kind enough to let me go through with my little plan, I'll see that you get through with yours."

I gaped at the boy, more stupefied than I had been that morning. "But you'll have given yourself a bad character!" I protested.

"For using a trot? Come off it. That's in the category of boyish pranks. And I'll have Mr. Tanager where I want him for life. Oh, I have great plans there. *Great* plans. Shelley's never going to be any use to his old man in the business. But *I* am. And his old man, deep down, prefers me to Shelley. He and I are the same type."

"Do you honestly expect me to make such a deal with you?"

"Why not? Isn't it for the glory of God? He gets his chapel, and you get your big school, and I get my benefactor. And otherwise we all get nothing."

I hesitated, which of course was fatal. "But you're too young to be allowed to take that responsibility on your own shoulders."

"Do you really believe that?"

I looked into those small glinting eyes, so full of premature worldly wisdom, and decided sadly that I did not. I imagined that the understanding between this boy and his patron was complete, and I felt a sudden certainty that the future would work out exactly as he saw it. I even wondered if he might not be a closer relation to Mr. Tanager than cousin. He had all the jauntiness, guile and charm of a papal bastard in the Renaissance.

"You won't mind leaving school?"

"*This* dump? Are you kidding?"

"Of course," I murmured sadly as I turned away, "it's just what I am doing. Kidding myself as well as others. God forgive me, Totten, but I'll go along with you."

"It's a deal then?" For a second time that day he held out his hand, and for a second time I took it.

"It's a deal." I walked back down the dormitory corridor and turned back at the end. "By the way," I called to him, "that business about the fingerprints was a bluff. The trot has never left the school grounds."

His roar of laughter filled the big empty chamber. "What a tricky old shyster you are, Griscam! When my ship comes in, I'll hire you for my lawyer."

I may as well put in here that as president of the Tanager Yards he remains to this day one of my most valued clients. But then, sick at heart with my own duplicity, I went to Prescott and pleaded with him to commute Totten's sentence to a month's suspension.

"How can I, my dear David?" he protested. "If it were simply the business of the trot, I might reconsider. But how do we get around the business of his trying to throw the blame on Shelley Tanager? That destroys all my sympathy. Doesn't it yours?"

What could I say? I had sealed my bargain with Max Totten in a handshake, and for all his scant sixteen years I knew that I had been dealing with my peer. I suddenly felt very tired, and I decided that I would return to New York that night. There was no telling of what indiscretion I might be guilty if I remained another day at Justin.

Mr. Tanager's pledge came in the following month for exactly double the amount I had requested, and the great job of fund raising was at last completed. In the next two years the new dormitories, the chapel, the gymnasium, the handball courts, the wings to the Schoolhouse, the infirmary and six new masters' houses were erected, and by 1910 Justin Martyr had assumed very much the external appearance that it wears today. The enrollment and the faculty were doubled, and Francis Prescott took a long stride towards the deanship of New England headmasters.

The new, larger school was more democratic than the old. Justin Martyr has never had the aura of snobbishness under which Groton and St. Mark's have suffered. Well endowed with scholarships, it has many boys of humble background as well as sons of the old and new rich. My own work in interesting some of the greatest of our new industrialists in the school has swollen its treasury beyond that of any other comparable private school. Justin's reputation is an aggressive one, both in sports and studies. It is known not to suffer fools gladly. Perhaps it has been a bit severe, but one can't have everything. The school was named for the early martyr and scholar who tried to reconcile the thinking of the Greek philosophers with the doctrines of Christ. Not for Prescott were the humble fishermen who had their faith and faith alone.

Shelley Tanager graduated the year after Max Totten's expulsion, but only by the blond hair of his head. He then proceeded to drink his way through Harvard to an early grave. But in his more drunken bouts before the end he was inclined to tell strange stories, and there was one in particular that came to my tensely listening ears about a self-sacrificing friend. It had two versions. In the first the friend was a sort of Sydney Carton who repaid his debt to his roommate's father by assuming his roommate's misdeed. In the other he was a sinister creature who used a seeming sacrifice to replace his roommate in the affections of a millionaire parent. I confess that my first reaction to the news of Tanager's death was one of relief that the source of these rumors was now dry.

I never got up the courage to ask Prescott if he had heard them, but I did once ask Harriet, on one of our walks after a trustees' meeting.

"Of course he heard them," she replied. "Frank hears everything. People say he's so formidable, but it doesn't seem to keep them from blabbing their secrets to him. It's unbelievable what they tell that man! Perhaps they want to shock him."

"But did he believe it? I mean, that Max Totten let himself be expelled to protect Tanager?"

She gave me the briefest glance. Oh, the briefest! Harriet knew how to do that. "Do you?"

"Not in the least!"

She nodded, apparently accepting it. "Well, I don't know what Frank thought. I suspect that he didn't really face it. In fact, I wonder if he didn't turn his back on it."

"That doesn't sound like him."

"It doesn't, does it? But, you know, David, every man has his moments of evasion. He wouldn't be human if he didn't. And you know how he cares about *that*." She turned and pointed with her umbrella to the great dark craggy tower of the new chapel that dominated the campus and even the countryside, the tower which had become already, on platters and seals and postcards, the very symbol of the school and of Frank Prescott's bold thrust into the infinity of ignorance. "How do you think," she demanded, facing me with her challenging stare, "he could live with it if he thought it had been built on a lie?"

11

BRIAN'S JOURNAL

NOVEMBER 15, 1941. On opening this neglected journal I find that there have been no entries since April. My only excuse is that when Dr. Prescott retired in June, the bottom fell out of my life. Before he left for the Cape to visit his daughter, Mrs. Homans, he arranged for my scholarship at Harvard Divinity in the fall and offered me the hospitality of Justin in July and August to do my preparatory reading. Nothing could have been more kindly meant, and nobody could have been more unworthy of his kindness. During the long hot summer in the deserted school, with too many books and too few people, my nerves went back on me.

Everything on the campus from the graceful elms to the great beetling chapel tower reminded me of Dr. Prescott and seemed to point up the contrast between us. Did I dare aspire to ordination in a church where such men as he were priests? As the turgid days wore on, his absence and his retirement combined to create in my fantasies the hallucination of his demise, and the heavy red and grey of the school's architecture seemed to enclose me in a granite mausoleum. Within the campus and all around me was the death of dignified and mighty things and without, borne in by black head-lines, was the death of barbarians in the ghastly Russian struggle. I did not lose my faith—not quite—but I lost everything else. By September I was in no possible state to enter divinity school.

It was in this condition that Mr. Griscam found me when he stopped at the school on his way down from Northeast Harbor. He took me out for dinner at the New Paisley Inn, forced me to drink two strong cocktails and elicited the dreary story of my summer. He guessed at once that what most appalled me was the prospect of telling Dr. Prescott the small advantage I had taken of his goodwill.

"My dear fellow, leave that to me," he said blandly. "Frank will under-stand. He's the last person to push anyone into the ministry. Why, he had to go into the railroad business before he could make up his own mind. The only thing to do with a doubt, to paraphrase Oscar Wilde, is to give in to it. But afterwards one mustn't just mope. What are you going to do?"

I told him that my heart classified me as 4F, but that I hoped to get a Red Cross job that would send me overseas.

"So like a young man," he said with his tolerant smile, "to think first of his conscience and last of his utility. You'd all rather clean latrines than be

Secretary of War, so long as you can get into something that looks like a uniform. But you should be above that, Brian. You should come and work in my 'Freedom First' Committee."

He explained that this had been organized to combat the "America First" movement and spread propaganda for immediate intervention in the war. If I believed, he argued, what I professed to believe: that every man and woman in the free world should join the fight against Hitler, then I ought to help to persuade them. When I protested in dismay that I would be urging other young men to shoulder arms in a struggle where I could take no active part, he pointed out that the moral comfort which I would thus be giving up might be precisely the sacrifice which the war demanded of me. When I insisted that I could never accept a salary for such work and could hardly live in New York without one, he offered me room and board in his own house and a chance to earn pocket money by cataloguing his Elizabethan collection.

I was no match, certainly in my nervous state, for the arguments of so persuasive a lawyer and diplomat. The very next day he bore me off, with my few chattels and the little portrait of Richardson, in the back seat of his big black Cadillac, and before I quite realized what had happened, I found myself in a long row of desks in a big office overlooking Fifth Avenue whose walls were covered with the banners of occupied nations, writing releases on what it was like to live under the Nazi boot. It has all been a bit of a nightmare, but I keep reminding myself of Mr. Griscam's injunction that I am sacrificing the only thing I could sacrifice: my own isolation and ease of conscience. It has been a consolation to think that in all likelihood we will soon be in the war, and then the offices of "Freedom Now" can be shut for good.

Life with the Griscams in Sixty-eighth Street is as comfortable, I'm sure, as money, servants and good management can make it, and it is only my self-consciousness that makes me suffer. I cannot convince myself that the maid who does my room in the morning does not regard my presence as an imposition and that the grave old butler in the dining hall below does not resent having to set an extra place at table. Yet their demeanor, I hasten to record, is perfect. Everything, in fact about this big yellow sandstone house is perfect. Perhaps that is just my trouble.

It is not, however unbecoming it may be in a guest to say so, that the "things" are good. Mr. Griscam himself is under no illusions about them. The mural of shepherds and shepherdesses in the yellow and pink "Louis XVI" parlor, he tells me, are copies of Hubert Robert, and the refectory table in the medieval dining room was manufactured to his measurements. Indeed, the oldest things in the house (outside of the folios in the library) are the big academic paintings of mountainous landscapes and rather fierce animals collected by Mrs. Griscam's late father. But what makes it all different, what makes it unique, is the "mint condition" (to borrow one of Mr. Griscam's bibliophilic terms) in which everything is kept, which ends by giving to the mansion a kind of museum glow that awes and dominates.

It is also noteworthy that Mr. Griscam does everything himself. It is to him that the servants look, and it is his eye that they fear if an ashtray goes more than five minutes unemptied. Mrs. Griscam seems to be above such matters. She is a "saint" who gives her time and energies to the Army of the Holy Word, an evangelical organization devoted to the intenser religious life. Some of the benignity of her cause seems to have washed over her person. She is tall, pale, lovely, with a high brow, soft grey hair and mild, undistinguishing blue eyes. I cannot help feeling that her love for the masses must have somewhat diluted her feeling for individuals and that her family may find her a bit impersonal as a wife and mother. But one's heart goes out to her when she walks. Nature meant her to be regal, and she limps awkwardly on a leg withered by childhood polio.

She was slightly put off the first night at dinner when Mr. Griscam told her of my abortive clerical career. Evidently she regards the church as inclined to be critical of evangelical movements. But when I turned the conversation to what I thought would be the more congenial subject of Dr. Prescott, I was surprised to discover that I would have done better to stay with her "army." Indeed, she was almost crisp.

"Frankly, Mr. Aspinwall, I have never entirely approved of Dr. Prescott's influence on my husband. It has always seemed to me that a private church school is a contradiction in terms. How can religion be packaged for the privileged and sold to the select?"

I was taken aback that *she*, in such "private" surroundings and the mother of two Justin boys, should take so sharp an attitude, but I reflected that the family as well as the household decisions were probably left to her husband. Mrs. Griscam seems to live as a kind of guest, however critical a one, in her own home.

"I suppose Dr. Prescott might answer that he would gladly build enough Justins to educate all America. He does what he can."

"Which I'm afraid is not enough," Mrs. Griscam rejoined with a touch of asperity. "I'm prepared to admit that Frank Prescott believes in God, but he's very fussy about how God is retailed. In my organization we believe in distributing God wholesale."

I sighed. "I wonder if that's not easier."

"Perhaps you would like to come to one of our meetings," she suggested with a flicker of interest, and when I told her that I would be glad to and when she saw that I meant it, we achieved a mild friendliness.

Yet if Dr. Prescott was not always a name enthusiastically received in Sixty-eighth Street, I discovered that it invariably hit some kind of nerve, in the children as well as the parents. There had been three of the former, two of whom, Sylvester and Amy, survive and live at home. I knew from Mr. Ives that the other son, Jules, had committed suicide after a disastrous career at Justin and Harvard. Sylvester, a long, gangling man with yellow-grey hair and Mrs. Griscam's blue eyes (except that his are watery) has recently been estranged from his second wife and has moved home, as he tells me frankly, because it's cheaper than his club. He professes a devotion to Dr. Prescott, but I wonder if the latter might not prefer his mother's more caustic attitude.

"I'm sorry my little son Davey won't have the old man when he goes to Justin," he told me one morning at breakfast. "You can say what you want about his being too rigid and behind the times, but you can't get away from the fact that he's a magnificent example."

"Of what?" I asked, in sincere curiosity.

"Why of anything!" Sylvester exclaimed in surprise. "Of the Christian ethic, if you like. I remember Sam Lovell at his Fly Club initiation getting up on a table and shouting: 'Dr. Prescott is the nearest man to God on earth!' and Jim Copperly shouting back: 'God damn it, man, he *is* God!' No, you can't get away from it, Brian, it was a great thing to have been exposed to him."

I noted the repetition of the idea that I couldn't "get away" from such an allowance. It is one that I have heard before from Justin graduates, the concept that it is somehow desirable to be "exposed" to Dr. Prescott, as if he were a childhood malady like measles. Few of the old Justinians seem to have any feeling that his principles should have a continuing validity in their lives. I find it upsetting.

I could listen to Amy on the subject with less apprehension, for Amy did not represent any possible failure on Dr. Prescott's part. Amy lives for horses and horse shows. Thirty-seven and unwed, she is fair and bulky, with big, handsome features and a voice that carries to the furthest corners of the large stone house. She sets herself up to be her father's champion, but the bluntness of her partisanship must at times embarrass him.

"How do *you* feel about Dr. Prescott, Miss Griscam?" I made bold to ask her that same morning when Sylvester had left the table. "Do you like him, as your brother does, or do you feel, like your mother, that his influence on the Griscams is not altogether for the good?"

"It's never been a question of my liking him. I didn't have to like or dislike him. I wasn't a boy. But I certainly resented him."

"Because your father admired him?"

"No. Because he dwarfed Daddy. You know what they used to say of Teddy Roosevelt? That he was like a magnificent plane tree. That nothing grew in his shade. Well, Dr. Prescott is that way. Like a great Broadway star whom the people out front applaud. But as a child I was always in the wings. I could see the other people: the director, the stage manager, the electricians." Here she paused significantly. "I could even see the author of the play."

"But surely Dr. Prescott is the author of Justin Martyr," I protested.

"Only in the beginning. He had the initial idea, I grant. But who raised the endowment fund? Who doubled the enrollment? Who instituted the exchange masterships and brought the finest minds to the school? Who established the pension plan? Who bought the big neighboring estate and saved the school from finding itself in the center of a housing development? And, finally, who discovered Duncan Moore?"

"Your father, of course. Yet I imagine most people think of Justin as Dr. Prescott's school. The two names are almost synonymous."

"And who made them so?" she exclaimed triumphantly. "Whose idea was it that the school needed a prophet? Why, the legend of Frank Prescott is simply the pinnacle of Daddy's masterwork!"

I decided that it would be idle to press the point further and asked about her hunters in Westbury.

Mr. Griscam himself dwelt continually on the subject of the biography which he had now persuaded himself that I was actually writing. It was in vain that I kept telling him that I was not even positive that I would ever do so. He was determined that if he was not going to write the book himself, he would at least have a hand in its preparation. In similar fashion, as I knew from his notebooks, when he had seen that he would never teach at Justin, he had concentrated on being a trustee. Now he wanted me to interview graduates, and he was quite prepared to make all the necessary appointments. In desperation, I finally had to refuse point-blank.

"I must do things my own way, Mr. Griscam," I pleaded. "Please try to understand that."

"I would try to understand it if I could see that you were doing anything," he said in his patient, remorseless tone. "If you're too shy to talk to the Justin men, what about the women? Cordelia Turnbull lives right around the corner. She'd adore to see you any time. She *loves* to talk about her father!"

"If I'm going to talk to Dr. Prescott's daughters," I said evasively, "shouldn't I start with the oldest?"

"With Harriet Kidder?" He shook his head firmly. "You wouldn't get anywhere. I've tried. Harriet is that executive type of Manhattan matron to whom 'sweet charity' is synonymous with the speakers' dais at the Waldorf Astoria. Of course, she's very much admired—that sort of woman always is. 'Isn't Harriet wonderful?' people keep asking me. But when you've sat on as many committees with as many Harriets as I have, you know that their real genius lies in passing the buck."

"She wasn't interested in the book?"

"Oh, she was interested, all right. She considers herself 'Pa's favorite.' But every time she condescended to open the purse of her reminiscences out would tumble some tired old bit of folklore that any first former at Justin might know. You'll find that's apt to be so with the children of famous persons. Marie Antoinette's daughter will always tell you how her mother let the poor eat cake."

"What about the second daughter?" All that I knew about her was that she wasn't in New York, but that made me prefer her to Mrs. Turnbull.

"Evelyn Homans? She's worse; She married back into old Boston and believes that a man belongs exclusively to his descendants. She presumed to dictate to me what facts I could and could not use, even when they were facts that *I* knew at first hand and she didn't. She doesn't want a life of her father. She wants a floral tribute."

"But Mrs. Turnbull is different?"

"Oh, Cordelia is different from everyone. Cordelia is a 'character.' After she divorced Guy Turnbull and got her big settlement, she had the sense to convert herself from a bad artist to a good collector. You should go just to see the paintings in that duplex. Room after room full of Picassos, Braques and Kandinskys!"

"I'm sure she'd scare me to death."

"No, no. I tell you, there's nothing she likes so much as talking about herself and her family. I'll call and find out when she can see you."

Protest was futile, and I had to sit wretchedly by while he made the call. Of course he was right. Mrs. Turnbull was only too delighted to see me.

That afternoon, when I was ushered into the great white room, high above Park Avenue, I found her, dark-haired, pale-skinned, with square, stubborn face and luminous brown eyes, reclining in brilliant pink, with an amber necklace and ruby earrings, on a low, backless couch. It was as if Theda Bara were playing Madame Butterfly, or as if Dr. Prescott, in some fantastic masquerade, were playing Theda Bara. "I like your coming straight to me," she said with a half-mocking smile, not unlike her father's. "I like your not going first to Harriet or Evelyn. But, of course, that was David's tip."

I decided in my nervousness that the only way to cope with her tone was to he utterly serious. "You mean they wouldn't be able to help me?"

She shrugged. "I mean that their childhood resentments are too shallow a stream for a biographer to splash about in."

I took a breath. After all, what was I really afraid of? "But yours are deeper?"

"Well, let's put it this way, Mr. Aspinwall. *I* know they're resentments."

"And what do Mrs. Kidder and Mrs. Homans think that theirs are?"

"Why, true pictures of Pa, of course! They *seethe* with hate. They spend their lives trying to reconcile it with the love that 'nice' daughters are supposed to feel for their fathers."

"And to what do you owe your special insight?"

"Psychoanalysis. What else? Four long years of it. It's the only way left to grow up. Weren't you ever analyzed, Mr. Aspinwall?"

"No."

"A pity. You might have learned some interesting things. Why you're so obsessed with Pa, for example. Perhaps you have what Dr. Klaus calls 'Peter Panic.' You want to be a schoolboy again." As she exhaled blue smoke from her cigarette, she studied me carefully. "And why you fiddle with the Phi Beta Kappa key on your watch chain. Isn't that a form of psychic masturbation?"

I flushed crimson as I moved my hands to the black steel arms of the chair. Seeing she had now thoroughly shocked me, she was ready to turn to business. "What do you want to know about Pa?"

What indeed? After a few bewildered moments I found that my mind was empty of all subjects but her own terrible ones. "Would *he* have profited by analysis?" I asked.

"Not in the least." Her headshake seemed to dispose of this and of me. "If a man's lucky enough to be born a great artist, why should he seek to find out what made him that? The duds, like myself, have to, because otherwise they'd never have the sense to stop. But let the Leonardos just go on painting! No, if you want to learn about Pa, you can expect no help from analysts. You have to do the job yourself."

"Well, that lets me out," I said in relief. "I lack the equipment."

"Can't you even make a stab at it?" she demanded indignantly. "It shouldn't be *that* hard. Let's begin at the beginning. You're writing about a schoolmaster. Does he teach boys or girls? Boys. Very well, there's your first question. When did he begin to be attracted to his own sex?"

I hesitated. "I wonder if I'd put it quite that way."

"How else?"

"Surely you don't mean to imply . . . !"

"Oh, you non-analyzed," she interrupted impatiently. "You're so afraid of words. You're shocked to death for fear I'm going to call Pa a homosexual. I tell you, we're *all* homosexual! To one degree or another."

"I should think your father's degree was a very small one indeed," I protested, appalled.

"But still a degree," she insisted. "And if you want to understand human beings, you must jettison all that middle-class squeamishness about technical terms. There are certain very striking facts about Pa. As a handsome, popular young man, he married an exceedingly plain woman."

"But there were ladies before your mother," I pointed out, beginning, despite my agonized embarrassment, to wax hot. "Very beautiful ladies, too."

"Oh, yes. Before *and* after. That's still another story. But he married the plain one. Another striking fact is his horror of the very subject we're talking about. He was always suspicious of any more than casual friendship between two boys."

"But a headmaster, Mrs. Turnbull, . . ."

"Let me finish, dearie. Everyone knows that Pa had a bee in his bonnet about perversion. And naturally, we all know that a completely normal man does not fear that sort of thing. We only fear what *threatens*."

"I thought there were no normal men. I thought we were all homosexuals."

Seeing she had at last made me angry, she smiled and proceeded to wax philosophic. "I'll tell you *my* theory about Pa. Actually, it's not Freudian, it's Jungian. I believe that Pa is an archaic type. A throwback to the ancient Greeks. He has always looked down on women. You have to have been his daughter to know how much. They don't really exist for him, except to satisfy a man's physical needs, bear his children and keep his house. Hence beauty in women is not essential, any more than it is essential to animals. Sex is divorced from love. Only men are worthy of love, platonic love, and this love among men is stimulated by beauty of mind, beauty of soul, even beauty of body. Do you see?"

I was dangerously close now to calling her a silly ass. It was too irritating to hear this cocksure woman, who had made a mess of two marriages, sneer at her parents', which had lasted half a century. But Mrs. Turnbull, if an ass, was no fool, and she was obviously dying to talk. I began to understand that Mr. Griscam might be right and that perhaps it was my duty to take it down. "Would you be willing to tell me more about it?" I asked. "I mean about you and your father?"

"Right now? On the couch? By free association?"

"Any way you want to."

"Let's have a drink and start!"

Actually, it took us only two sessions. Or rather two was all *I* could take. I have a suspicion that she would have been glad to prolong them indefinitely. I took no notes while she was talking, but each evening I confided my recollections to the typewriter as soon as I got back to Sixty-eighth Street. What follows is thus not a transcript of Cordelia's actual words, but my memory of them. Yet I venture to think that I have caught some of her flavor.

12

CORDELIA'S STORY

I WAS BORN in 1895, the baby of the family, the third of three girls, and because of complications attending my Caesarian birth it was decided that Mother should not be allowed to try again for the son whom she and Pa had so desperately wanted. Poor little fellow, I may have cost him his life, but when I think of the problems that any son of Pa would have had to face, it occurs to me that a wise providence may have known what it was about. Pa took his revenge on me by a gleeful exercise of his sardonic sense of humor in the choice of my name. Imagine the lifetime of bad jokes that I have had to endure, as a third daughter, with the name Cordelia!

But Shakespeare was a game that two could play, and there have been times, I'm sure, when poor Pa would have carried me across the stage, hanged and dead, with only mirth in his heart as he cried: "Howl, howl." I cannot imagine why Mother ever put up with such nonsense except that she had a rich aunt who was also named Cordelia. The aunt, incidentally, left me nothing.

Mother was acutely aware from the beginning of the difficulties of bringing up her daughters in the center of a boys' school. She was determined that we should not be petted and spoiled and grow up with silly notions of standing, like musical comedy princesses, on balconies while choruses of hussars sang our praises, and saw to it instead that we received instruction even tougher than that meted out to the boys. But however well she was able to teach me to read Greek at twelve and to understand Darwin at fourteen, she was less successful in coping with the strong strain of romantic melancholy that I inherited from Pa.

Mother was as rational as she was plain, as sensible as she was unimpressable. I think of her now as she was in her later years, tall, gaunt, a bit bent, with dyed brown hair and a great hook nose and small, darting eyes, walking around and around the campus, even on the wettest afternoons, dressed in brown tweed with a small brown ridiculous beret pulled tightly about her oval head. I am sure the boys called her a witch, but I hope they thought her a friendly one. She was sometimes formidable and sometimes almost scaringly detached as a parent, but she always tried to make her girls feel that they were as important as Pa's sacred boys.

I don't know how good a headmaster's wife she was, by ordinary standards. She wasn't gracious; she wasn't stately, and she made a poor enough show on the dais on Prize Day squinting nearsightedly at the titles of the volumes that she handed out. But she never forgot a boy's name, and she would argue with them over games of chance and in debates on "parlor night" as hotly as if they had been contemporaries. She was absolutely democratic, in an early Boston transcendentalist way, and she helped Pa to keep faculty feuds over precedence to a minimum. Above all, she could maintain Pa on an even keel when everyone else had failed. I think it must have been clear to all their intimates that she adored him (how that man was adored!) but she was never in the least a submissive wife.

I remember one summer at the Cape when Pa had been paying too much attention to a pretty neighbor (oh, yes, Mr. Aspinwall, that happened—you needn't look so shocked—maybe not actual infidelities, but cozy chats in windowseats and long, *long* walks on the beach) that Mother simply disappeared for three days. It turned out later that she had been in a hotel in Boston. When she came back, as seemingly cool and detached as ever, without offering the smallest excuse or explanation of where she had been, Pa, who had been frenzied by her absence, was a chastened man. He might have endured being left alone with his boys, but never with his girls.

We children grew up without ever feeling that we belonged to any particular group or class. Pa and Mother, of course, were supreme at Justin, but from the beginning we knew that Justin was not the real world. The real world was a summer world, seen on trips to Europe or at the Cape, and although it treated Pa and Mother with respect, it was the kind of respect that people might pay to the sovereigns of a small Pacific Island kingdom, more exotic than powerful, not quite to be taken seriously, perhaps even a bit ridiculous. I thought I could sense as a child among the graduates and the parents of the boys that curious half paternal, half protective, almost at times half contemptuous, attitude of men of affairs for academics, and I was determined that I should lead my own life in such a way as to be able ultimately to bid a plague on both kinds of houses. I would be neither sneered upon nor a sneerer. I would be an actress, a poet, a great artist and return to Justin only when Pa begged me, as a special treat, to come back and perform to the dazzled boys.

I should like to skip as quickly as possible over my first big mistake. Green as I then was, I still blush for it. I eloped with a young man whom I met at a tea dance given for me in Boston when I was seventeen by my great-aunt, Cordelia Hooper. His name was Cabell Willetts; he came of an old, devout Catholic family, and he had never in his life been away from his bigoted old mother, even to go to boarding school. He was mild and sweet and weak and ultimately stubborn. It's easy to see what he represented to me: he was the reverse in every respect of what Pa would have wanted a graduate of Justin to be.

I had hoped that my family would be shocked and by like token, impressed, by a daughter who had found her consolation in an older faith and in an older God, married to a husband who had always been above the juvenilities of football and "school spirit." I should have known better. The eloping couple were greeted back with smiles and open arms, and Pa told me, in a private conference, shaking his head in his gravest manner, that he, too, had had his doubts over the historic break with Rome. If I, like Cardinal Newman, had been losing my sleep over the idea of a church founded on a king's lust for Anne Boleyn, who was Frank Prescott, a simple, groping parson, to say I was a foolish worrier?

Really! Anyone who hadn't known Pa would have thought he was making fun of me. What was I to Anne Boleyn or she to me? The only queen who entered my mind in the wretched three years of my married life was Eleanor of Guienne who said of Louis VII that she had married a monk. But she, at least, got her divorce. Willetts and his mother adamantly refused me mine, and when I finally left the house in Dedham, with all its stucco virgins and gold crosses and jewel-studded missals, I felt lucky to be able to take the clothes on my back.

I could have established a residence in a state with easy divorce laws, but at that point I could not be bothered. I went to New York and to Greenwich Village and rented a studio and tried to paint. It was what I call my "Edna St. Vincent Millay period," and the less questions you ask about it, the better. What? You have none? How disappointing. But, of course, I must remember that you are interested only in Pa and that I exist simply in the biological fact that he sired me. It is a point of view to which I have become *very* accustomed.

I don't pride myself that my bohemian life scandalized Pa. I doubt if he wasted a serious thought upon it. Mother occasionally came to New York and insisted on staying at the studio and sleeping on a daybed; she shut her eyes to my men and opened them to my paintings. I think she was honest when she said that she liked them, and I have a suspicion that she envied me my independence. When we entered the war in 1917, I went abroad with the Red Cross, relieved and exalted to see the chaos of the world, and Pa, thoroughly approving of my adventurousness and jealous that I should be so near the Front and he so far, wrote me long, introspective letters to the effect that a lifetime's education was not the equivalent of a minute of Armageddon.

No, alas, I don't have those letters. I always destroy letters. It's a leftover from the days when they might have proved embarrassing. And, of course, I knew that Pa was not really writing to me; he was simply soliloquizing. We did not communicate, in the sense of his truly thinking of *me* and I of him, until more than a year after the war, in Paris where I had remained, an appropriate addition to the riffraff of Americans who could not face a return to a normalcy for which they tried to believe that the war had disabled them.

Oh, Aspinwall, don't shake your head; I know they weren't *all* riffraff. But *I* was. And I was well aware that Charley Strong was not. It was over Charley that my first real bout with Pa began.

He was one of Pa's golden boys, Justin' 11, senior prefect and football captain, a kind of American Rupert Brooke, at least in romantic appearance, blond, with sleepy grey eyes, a bit on the short side, but muscular and stocky, terribly serious and sincere, a savage tackle but gentle as a mother with children, honorable, naïve, charming, the kind of man who would protect his lady fair from a hundred wild Indians but whom *she* would have to protect from a swindling salesman—in short a magazine-cover hero, a Parsifal, Pa's ideal because the opposite of Pa.

What, you may ask, was such a man doing with such a gal as me? Was not the chrism upon his head, on mine the dew? They were, indeed, but Mrs. Browning's next line applied also, for death *did* dig the level where these agreed. Poor Charley was a shrapnel victim in 1919, one of his lungs torn to shreds, and he had stayed on in Paris, because, as he put it, there wasn't enough of him to be worth taking home. He was condemned, but still beautiful in his decline, and the puzzled hurt look in those now desperately searching grey eyes was enough to turn to soapsuds a much harder heart than mine.

We had met, of course, at Justin in the early days, but he had been one of those athletic adolescents who will not so much as look at the other sex until complete maturity. And if he had been interested earlier, he would not have looked at me, a snappish, pigtailed, awkward girl who tried to conceal her sticks of legs in blue-stockings. "Billy Budd," I called him, in revenge for his indifference, but he was too unlettered to know what I meant. In Paris after the war, however, our physical positions had been reversed. I had "filled out," and Charley, poor darling, was a coughing shadow of the former football captain. He was dumfounded by the apparition in a city that symbolized to him the snatching of the day of a daughter of Francis Prescott.

We met at Horace Havistock's, that mean old friend of Pa's whose final decadence, after a lifetime of sipping tea in Walter Gay interiors, cackling gossip and collecting the most banal kind of impressionist canvases, was to assemble in his chaste halls the forlornly aging youth of the lost generation. You smile. Do you know him? Well, that's the way he is, isn't it? He wanted, the old vulture, to console himself for his own wasted life by surrounding himself with wasted youth.

Charley and I sat on his terrace till early morning, talking about what was real and what was sham. Charley had become very intense and passionate about finding what he called "some clean little rag of truth in the dirty laundry of the world."

What he wanted to know of me was whether or not the prewar Cordelia Prescott had been real. Had we actually existed, I and my sisters, in those quaint far-off Justin days? For if we had existed, then perhaps Justin had existed, and, of course, Pa, too, and how could he reconcile Pa and God (for Pa *was* God, I suppose) with what he had seen in the trenches?

He wanted dogma, whether from heaven or hell, and he certainly got it, for I was then at my most dogmatic. I told him that reality consisted of intensity of emotional experience and that we lived solely in our feelings. We had only the present, and very little of that; most people, in fact, never lived at all. The past existed only in remembered emotion: therefore the retained horror of the trenches was more real than the vague, sweet pastoral idyll that had been Justin. Charley listened to me carefully. I don't believe that anyone had ever spoken to him with such authority since the days when he had been under the spell of another Prescott. It was like a road company performance of *Tannhauser,* where the same soprano doubles for Elizabeth and Venus. Charley must have felt that he had heard that voice before.

"There is sensation," he kept muttering, "and there is Paris."

"And they're one and the same. Let's make the most of it!"

We became lovers, but not as soon as you might have thought in those easy days. I had first to overcome his scruples about Pa. It took me three months to erode the paralyzing vision of his old headmaster in the pulpit, a hand and forefinger outstretched. Poor Charley wanted to marry me, but I was still undivorced, and the absurdity of my legal position, shackled to a monk, was my trump card in persuading him that Pa himself would not wish me denied all sexual gratification. Yet for all my chatter, for all my efforts to liberalize his thinking, after our first night together Charley solemnly took my hand in his and told me that in the eyes of God, if there was a God, we were now man and wife.

We lived as such, anyway. Charley rented a beautiful studio in the Place des Vosges, embarrassingly grand for my inadequate oils but ideal for parties, and we soon became well-known hosts to the floating expatriate world that made a fetish of disillusionment. One begins to find references to us now in the journals and letters of the period that are being published. There is a tendency to sentimentalize the "lost generation" and its Paris refuge, and I suppose that it did include some important writers and painters. But for every man of talent in our group, there were three drunks, and a drunk is a drunk the world over.

One thing I will admit about old Havistock is that he was the first to recognize this. He early became disenchanted with the disillusioned. My liaison with Charley may have hastened the process. For all his vaunted freedom from prejudice he was shocked to the core and dropped us both. Perhaps he was afraid that Pa would hold him responsible. Or perhaps he simply made the old distinction of a nasty Victorian bachelor between the monde and the demimonde. A lady, at least one who had been born one, could not exist in both. Horace Havistock was a malevolent survival from an early Bourget novel.

You mustn't get the notion that Charley and I did nothing but carouse. He would have died even earlier had that been the case. On weekdays we led a very regular life. I painted in the mornings, and Charley wrote, and in the afternoons we went for a drive, for he tired too easily for walking. We went to bed early, as he woke up continually in the night, and sometimes I would find him at dawn, sitting by the big studio window, a pad in his hand, usually blank, for he wrote very sparingly. He was working, he told me, on a semi-fictional journal about his childhood and the war, a kind of literary free association. Charley had read with passionate interest the first of Proust's novels and had been taken by Mr. Havistock to visit the author in his cork-lined room. I suppose the journal was his own *recherche du temps perdu*.

I would not read it, at least then. I was too sure that it would be bad, and I did not want to discourage him in any enterprise that gave him an interest in living. Also, I was afraid of the effect of what I then imagined would be a turgid, childish prose on my image of the doomed Keatsian hero. I was sophisticated enough to know that the written word is no mirror of the writer's character, that the amateur, though a selfless angel, may show himself a pompous ass, while the professional, a monster of ego, can convince you in a phrase that he has the innocence of a child. I had in my mind's eye a likeness of Charley that, for all my would-be realism, might have been sketched by Rossetti or Burne-Jones. I did not want it blurred.

As I look back, I realize that I must have known him very little. Perhaps I talked too much. I always have. I thought he was conventionally neurotic, a standard case of postwar despair. I did not appreciate the difference between one like himself, who had lost a real faith, and one like me who had never had one. I wore the mood of Yankee Paris in 1920 as if it had been a new hat; he wore it in his soul. Charley was not content, like the rest of us, to bask picturesquely in the cemetery of his hopes, a shaker of martinis on one headstone, a pipe of hasheesh on another. He was desperately and earnestly fighting the chaos which I wanted to cut up into colorful strips to use for studio decorations. If he resented me, he was too much of a gentleman ever to say so. Besides, he needed a friend, a companion and, increasingly, a nurse. In the latter capacity my war training stood me in good stead. It gives me a bit of consolation now, in view of how often I failed him, to remind myself that at least I ministered to his physical comfort.

One late June day at noon, while I was working on a still life, a glass of red wine on a table by my easel, and while Charley, still in a kimono and pajamas, was lounging on a sofa, pad in lap, gazing moodily out the window, there was a loud rap at our door. As I went to open it, I heard Pa's unmistakable deep basso, singing, in perfect key, the theme of the students from the first act of *Bohême*. For one horror-stricken moment I debated not opening. Then I turned to warn Charley who fled to our bedroom. When Pa stepped over the threshold, his arms loaded with packages, he was at his most ebullient, his most awful.

"Cordelia, my dear child! May the mild bright sky that shone on Vigée-le-Brun and Rosa Bonheur shine upon your palette! Give me a hug! Your mother and I docked last night at Le Havre. She's unpacking at the Vendôme."

Once he had embraced me, he went straight to my canvas, taking in the wineglass with a flicker of the eye, as hard to miss as it was ostensibly tactful, that would have done credit to a veteran performer at the Française. "And is this what the French call a dead nature?" He nodded slowly as he gazed at my poor effort. "Ah yes, my child, I can see that you have made strides, and with seven-league boots! Only I wonder if that lemon couldn't do with a little perking up."

It was just what it did need, damn him. "Look, Pa," I said sourly, "if you and Mother have sprung this surprise visit to make an honest woman of me, you can save your breath. Charley and I are quite happy with things as they are."

"Can't an old couple come to Europe on their vacation without being accused of interfering?" Pa rolled his eyes in a graphic parody of reproach. "Do you realize we haven't crossed the Atlantic since 1912? Do you and Charley *own* Paris? Should I have gone to you for a visa?"

"You know perfectly well what I mean."

"I'm blessed if I do. How *is* poor Charley?"

"Why don't you ask him?"

Pa turned to face Charley who had just emerged from our bedroom, in grey flannels and a red sweater. He was pale as I had never seen him, and his eyes had a dull glitter.

"Charley, my boy!" Pa approached him with outstretched arms, but Charley stepped quickly back.

"No, Dr. Prescott," he said in a strangled voice, "I cannot take your hand until I know that you respect me."

"Respect you? Of course I respect you! What on earth are you thinking of?"

"I mean, respect Cordelia and me as man and wife."

Pa's pursed lips and soaring eyebrows, his immediate grave headshake and the suppressed whistle that one could almost hear would again have been worthy of French classical comedy. "But, my dear fellow, isn't that precisely what you're not? Isn't it, so to speak, the point?"

"The point of what?"

"Why, the point of your being so prickly and defensive. The point of your not taking my hand." Here Pa turned suddenly and shrewdly back to me. "Do *you*, Cordie, consider that you and Charley are married?"

"Legally, no, of course not."

"Religiously, then?"

"I don't happen to be religious."

"Alas, poor child, you have suffered from an overdose of Rome." He returned his full attention to Charley. "But of course I see what you mean. You mean that your relationship with Cordelia is a serious one. That neither of you would be unfaithful to the other. That you *would*, indeed, be married were it not for Cabell Willetts' arbitrary refusal to give Cordelia a divorce. But I must still insist, all that does not make a marriage. It does not even make what is called a common-law marriage. Now, wait, wait, Charley, before you blow up."

Pa placed two heavy hands on Charley's trembling shoulders and shook him gently. "I haven't come to call down anathemas on you and Cordie. I'm not the old blood and thunder type of parson. It's a wonder those old men didn't drive their flocks straight back to the Pope. Perhaps some of them did. Try to remember that I, too, was young once and that there was a Paris even then."

"Oh, young," Charley muttered with a searing bitterness. "You'll never be as old as I am now, sir." And he pulled himself free of Pa's grip and sat down morosely on the sofa, plunging his face in his hands.

Pa interpreted his action as at least accepting his own continued presence. He took a seat by the sofa and continued to address himself exclusively to Charley. "I'm not pretending that I'm pleased to have you and Cordie living as you are. You wouldn't believe it if I said I was. But I love you both, and I want to help you. Don't throw me out, Charley. Don't hurt me. I've tried not to hurt you."

"Oh, Dr. P.," Charley moaned, his face still covered. "It's too crazy to have you in Paris like this. Don't you see my position? It's impossible, utterly impossible!"

"Don't you see mine? Nothing is impossible if we both try."

"But I'd ceased to believe you existed!" Charley exclaimed, half hysterically now, looking up at Pa in agony. "Cordie had persuaded me that you weren't real!"

Pa shot a glance in my direction. Just a glance, but it would have convinced a total stranger which of the two of us he had come to save. "Really, Charley," I protested, annoyed, "I didn't mean Pa personally. I meant Justin, or rather what Justin stood for in your mind."

"Cordie has her motives for not wanting me to be real," Pa said with a hint of grimness. "Every child has. But parents are not that easily destroyed. We continue to exist, if for no other reason than that we may be able to help our children's friends."

It was evident at this point that Pa was going to stay and that he and Charley wanted to be alone, but I had no intention of leaving them. Unfortunately, as it was our cook's day off, I had eventually to go to the kitchen to fix lunch, and brief as I was when I returned with a tray of lettuce salad and cold chicken, they were on intimate terms again.

"No, you're wrong, Charley," Pa was saying earnestly. "I *can* see that death might become the only reality. Of course, I've never been in a war. I've never been wounded or hungry or even particularly uncomfortable. But I have always been acutely conscious that such things existed. My father, you may remember, was killed in the Civil War when I was an infant, and I grew up in a world from which I thought all valor had departed. You would be astonished if you knew how many times in my life I have longed for the test of battle. How else could I know that I was a man? Or 'real,' as you would put it?"

"You wouldn't have longed for a war if you'd ever seen one," Charley muttered.

"Don't be too sure. Have we not all imaginations? Can one not visualize, at least to some degree, how it would feel to be cold and wet and hungry, smelling a mountain of rotting flesh, and knowing that any moment one might be added to it?"

"Please, Pa," I protested, "you'll only upset Charley."

"Don't interrupt, Cordie!" Charlie barked at me with a rudeness that he had never shown before, and I flushed angrily that Pa should be the witness of my humiliation.

"Oh, yes, my boy," Pa went on, heedless of the interruption, "we, too, have our nightmares, we who are left at home, haunted by never knowing how we would have measured up. They say that if the old men who made the wars had to fight them, we'd have eternal peace. I am not so sure. They might rush into battle! Here is reality, at last, at last. When I think of the nights that I have lain awake, imagining myself with limbs blown off in a trench, or burnt alive in the engine room of a sinking battleship or starving in a freezing prison camp, I sometimes wonder if I have not suffered as much from fancy in peace as I might have from reality in war. If so, it has served me right, for morbidness is a kind of vanity. My final punishment will probably be to die painlessly in bed."

Charley looked at him with wondering eyes. "Is courage so important? I should have thought courage mattered very little."

"That's because you have it. And *know* you have it."

Charley was too interested now to waste time in modesty. "And it is *that* you envy me? How curious. I should not give it a pin's fee alongside your faith. What can courage do? As Falstaff said of honor, can it set an arm? Can it take away the grief of a wound? But one *can* eat faith. One can live on faith." He stared at Pa for a moment and then, with a curious gesture of appeal, a faltering extension of his right arm, he asked: "*You* do, don't you?"

Pa's eyes glittered as he shook his head sadly. "If I had real faith, Charley, I should not worry about courage. For my fear would be cast out, would it not? And without fear, there would be no need of courage."

"But you *have* faith, do you not?" Charley persisted, with a stubborn, childish literalness. "You must have. For, after all, you do have courage, everyone knows that. It's just that you *think* you may not. You had the faith on which you built Justin. You did build it, didn't you?" He glanced now at me with what was beginning to seem like actual hostility. "I mean Cordie isn't right, is she? There is a school there, isn't there?"

"If I can convince you of that, then I haven't come to Paris in vain!" Pa exclaimed, slapping the little table on which I had lain his plate. "I don't care how you rate Justin. I don't care if you call it, as one graduate did, 'a motley derivative pile of red brick, shrouded in the fog of its headmaster's platitudes.' All I care is that you should admit it exists. Exists at least as much as that slithery rat that tried to eat your rations at Chateau-Thierry!"

Charley rose to his feet, trembling. "What do you know about that rat?" he cried hoarsely. "How could you know about that rat?"

"My dear fellow, don't look at me as if I were a magician. You wrote me about it."

"*I did*? And you got my letter?"

"Why should I not have got it?"

"Oh, I don't know." Charley collapsed again into the sofa. "I suppose because I doubted there was a world beyond the trenches."

"But I wrote you, too. Didn't you get my letters?"

"Yes, I suppose I did." Charley had a fit of coughing now which lasted until tears appeared in his eyes. "Yes, of course, I got your letters, Dr. P. Bless you for them. A fine return I've made for your kindness."

I rose at this, too suffocated by the sentiment in the room to remain there longer, and went to our bedroom to await Pa's leaving. Later that afternoon, alone with Charley, I tried to reason with him. I told him that he was not well enough to subject himself to the strain of further visits and that we both knew all that Pa would have to say. That under whatever guise of tolerance Pa chose to travel, his only purpose could be to separate us. That he was a wily old fox working subtly for the forces of superstition and bigotry. I suggested that I should make an appropriate number of filial visits to the Vendôme and leave Charley out of it.

"But you don't understand!" he shouted at me. "Your father doesn't care about *us*. He's trying to save my soul!"

"And he's given up on mine?"

"Of course not. But he has time for yours!"

"Really, Charley," I protested, "this isn't like you. I want you to have peace and quiet—"

"Peace and quiet!" he retorted brutally. "What do you know of peace and quiet? A woman like you can kid herself into believing that simple distraction is a philosophy of life. But I can't! I tell you, Cordie, stay out of this!"

I was so hurt that for a moment I was almost frightened. I would not have dreamed that Charley could have been so rough. I stood in the middle of the studio, a hand over my lips, staring at him like a little girl who has been unexpectedly and viciously slapped in the face. But he would not even look at me; he went to his post by the window and stared gloomily down into the street. I think I would have left him on the spot had I not known that he was dying. Even I was not such an egotist as to abandon a dying man.

Pa called every day at the studio in a rented touring car with a chauffeur and took Charley for a drive. They usually ended up sitting on a bench by the Seine where they had long religious discussions. At home Charley grew more and more taciturn. Sometimes he would hardly speak to me at all. He looked grey and haggard, and his coughing was much worse. Twice I found blood on his pillow in the morning, but when I begged him to go to the doctor he simply stared at me and shrugged. He was like a dope addict for whom the real world has ceased to exist. Pa, of course, was feeding him the dope, and I found myself as much ignored as some old ranting peasant mother whose boy had discovered urban amusements. If I dined at the Vendôme with Pa and Mother, Charley would refuse to accompany me. He had reached the point where he could no longer share my father. He had to have him all to himself.

I suppose it was jealousy, as well as frustration, that made me read the manuscript of Charley's book. He had often offered it to me, and I had always refused to look at it. Now, as I dipped surreptitiously into its pages while he was out with Pa, sitting by the window so that I would see him if he should come home early, I felt horribly guilty. For I wanted to find something in the book that would shock Pa if I should ever show it to him. Not that I had any intention of showing it—I had not dropped that low. But I wanted to feel that there was a part of Charley that would never belong to Pa, even if it never belonged to me. Alas, if there was such a part, I did not find it. The book was as pure as its author. Charley was that rarest of creatures: an innocent who was able to convey a sense of his own innocence.

Certainly it was a curious manuscript. A chapter might start with a list of the things that Charley had observed from the studio window, described in the plainest, flattest terms. This list would continue until his mind took off, like an airplane on a runway, and then there might follow panoramic pictures of Justin days, boating on the river and football and then more intimate ones, of Pa in chapel, of myself in Paris at a restaurant, or painting, or even in bed. The manuscript was candid without being in the least salacious. It had some of the quality of an amateur film. At times the characters seemed to be moving at a frenzied pace, jumping up and down and jabbering; at others the inaction and repetition became cloying. The most unusual aspect of the book was its jumbling of dates, so that a walk with me and a lyric description of rowing at Justin and the death of a sergeant in the trenches seemed simultaneous. And not only simultaneous but of equal value. Charley was intent on breaking down his experience into units of the same size, a procedure that enabled him to introduce a dreary, at times a rather frightening order into his chaos.

It embarrasses me to confess, even at this late date, that my first reaction was one of pique. Charley, whom, in matters of art, I had treated with such condescension, had produced a more interesting work than any of my *natures mortes!* The shallow artist is apt to make the best critic, and I was a shallow artist. My second reaction was equally egotistical, but less painful—I imagined that I saw the manuscript already published and heard my name on every tongue. I saw it printed on thick parchment by a private Paris press (the kind that Harry and Caresse Crosby later started) with heavy black script and drawings by Derain or Picasso. If Pa was taking Charley away from me, he at least had left me his book.

He had also left me Mother, with whom I spent my afternoons. She adored Paris and was trying to make up for the lost years of summer travel which the war has cost her. She could spend hours at the book counters along the Quai Conti where bargains were still to be had, and she was indefatigable at poking into back alleys in search of some surviving fragment of a medieval wall or keep. As her Paris seemed to end with Louis XI while mine began with Degas, it was all sufficiently boring for me, but I had not the heart to begrudge her the obvious pleasure of these peregrinations.

It would have been difficult to imagine a more un-Gallic figure than she cut, with her dull Boston clothes, her big nose and long unpowdered face, her total indifference to the preoccupations of Paris women, even to food and drink, yet at the same time I had to admit that she fitted into the city quite as easily as I did. There was a distinction about her, made up of her total honesty, her probing curiosity and her wonderfully good manners, to which the French immediately responded.

"The thing about your mother," a young French novelist told me, "is that the Atlantic doesn't exist for her. Most of you Americans are either absurdly proud or absurdly ashamed of living on the wrong side of it. But your ma's a genuine internationalist."

Of course, I took this to mean that *I* wasn't. Mother not only was making me feel a Philistine in the Paris to which I thought I had fled for Art's sake; now she was taking over my friends. At a party of painters and writers, she became the storm center of a discussion that raged over Henry Adams' study of Mont St. Michel and Chartres. She attacked him as a staunch medievalist for sentimentalizing, if not actually inventing, the cult of the virgin, and her loud driving syllables seemed to lay flat every distinction of age and class in the room so that we were all students together.

I decided that I would have to get out of Paris. The midsummer heat was becoming unbearable, and Mother made matters worse, the old lizard, by showing no effects of it while I unbecomingly sweated. I suggested that she and I go to Venice while Pa and Charley worked on the latter's soul and then down the Dalmatian coast to Spalato where I knew she would want to see the noble remnants of Diocletian's palace. The idea intrigued her, and we went off; we spent two weeks in Venice and two in Spalato. In the middle of our visit to the latter, where conditions were primitive, we changed hotels, and Mother made a mistake in forwarding our new address to Paris. A total suspension of communications resulted, and when we finally got Pa's telegram, Charley had been dead two days.

We went straight from the train to the American Cathedral where Pa was to conduct the funeral, and we had no chance to speak to him before the service began. Never had I heard him read the comfortable words in a more beautiful or resonant tone, but in my numbed state, where feelings of bitter grief and abandonment loomed like dead monsters under the dark ice of my despair, he might have been declaiming a paean of triumph.

We sat in a pew behind Charley's widowed mother and spinster sister who lived on the Riviera and whom I had never met. After the service Pa walked with them to a waiting limousine to drive to the Protestant cemetery, and Mother persuaded me to return with her to the hotel. Only later did I learn that this had been at the request of Mrs. Strong. She had been afraid that if we met at the edge of the grave, an introduction would have been unavoidable, and she would have had to touch the hand of the woman who had debauched her dying boy.

I shall never forget my last glimpse of those two ladies sitting primly on either side of Pa as their car drove away from the cathedral. He did not, of course, have his arms around their shoulders, but I felt that he might as well have. He had an air of having taken them, as well as Charley, under his big wings, of hugging to his benevolent chest all creatures but his own Cordelia. King Lear had not been content to deny me my share of his kingdom; he had seized the little principality that I had gained on my own. Obviously he felt that he had little to fear from filial ingratitude.

13

CORDELIA'S STORY

I can see from your face, Brian, that I must sound very cold and unfeeling. I assure you I did not sound so at the time. Charley's death turned me inside out, and I could not get through a day without at least one fit of tears bordering on hysteria. I had to close the studio, as I could not possibly spend a night there alone, and move to the Vendôme, in a room next to my parents, where I plagued them by calling Mother at least twice during each night to come and sit by my bed and hold my hand.

All that, however, was a long time ago, and I have since been psychoanalyzed, so that if I sound detached today it is because I have faced up to the fact that I was really more detached then. What I fundamentally minded about Charley's death, as I now more honestly see it, was that he had departed in peace, owing none of that peace to me. Or to put it more baldly, he had owed it to my absence. On my analyst's couch I plumbed the humiliating depths of the egotism and possessiveness of love. But at the time I thought myself an inconsolable widow, which must have been hard for my parents to bear.

Pa, in fact, did not bear it. Two weeks after Charley's death we had our first big row when he told me that he had destroyed the manuscript of Charley's book. He insisted that he had done so in obedience to Charley's dying instructions, but I denied that this was an excuse.

"It was a work of art!" I kept shouting at him. "No one has the right to destroy a work of art, not even the artist. Supposing Lavinia Dickinson had burnt all her sister Emily's poems? Think of the loss to civilization!"

"Charley's manuscript was hardly the equivalent," Pa said dryly. "He had read parts of it aloud to me. But even if it had been, I should have felt constrained to do as he had asked. I cannot admit that works of art, any more than artists themselves, are outside the moral law."

"We don't have so much beauty in the world that we can afford to go about destroying it!"

"The beautiful thing about Charley was the way he met his death," Pa said gravely. "His little book was simply one of the steps that led to it. Of course, *you're* all excited about it, because it was a book. Communication is everything to you artists. You can't look at a landscape or a bowl of fruit without thinking how you will put it on a canvas so that somebody else will see it as *your* landscape or *your* bowl of fruit. That is the inescapable vulgarity of art."

"And why I'm proud to be an artist!"

"What you are, my dear girl, is not in question. It's what Charley was. He used his pen to try to see God. When he had seen him, his papers were no more use than autumn leaves."

"Might they not help someone else?"

Pa shook his head firmly. "They were too personal. Besides, they contained references to living people which would have been very painful."

"You mean references to *me*," I cried, aflame now with indignation. "References to me that in print would have been painful to *you*. You couldn't face the idea of letting the world see that I was Charley's mistress!"

"It would be nearer the point to say that I couldn't face your pride in letting the world see it," Pa retorted.

"That's a vile thing to say. Just because I wanted the one beautiful unique thing that Charley created in his short, unhappy life to survive as his memorial!"

"Ah, uniqueness," Pa muttered with a gesture of impatience. "There it is again. That's all you care about. To stand out. To have people say: look, look, look. See me with my little pen or paint brush or chisel. I did it all myself!"

"What else is there but death and annihilation?" I cried desperately. "Can't you let us poor mortals live a bit first? *Your* trouble, Pa, is that you hate what happened to Charley in Paris. You had to tear up the record of his accomplishment and turn him back to an adolescent robot on the playing fields of Justin! You and his old bitch of a mother had to burn up everything but your own juvenile image of him." I was now completely out of control. "I believe you killed Charley! Killed him with the dope of your nihilistic religion. And if he came to life, I believe you'd happily do it again!"

Never shall I forget the look that Pa gave me then! Those great brown eyes glowered at me for what must have been half a minute, and then I saw a strange glint of yellow in their irises. I had the sudden terrible feeling that Pa was looking at me as a magistrate might have looked at a screaming, muddy street urchin caught in a bestial act and dragged before his bench.

"You use the word 'bitch' very easily, Cordelia," he said icily, as he turned away. "Take care you don't give others cause to."

At this I had my first attack of real hysterics, and Mother had to sit up with me all night as I sobbed and screamed. By morning an equally violent reaction had set in, and my anger melted down with exhaustion to a murky cesspool of remorse. I insisted now that I was indeed a bitch and that a lifetime of penance and good works would hardly suffice to redeem me. I acknowledged, over and over again that I had sinned in distracting Charley from his one true path to consolation. And finally I announced solemnly that I would go home with my parents and assist them in their duties at Justin Martyr.

Mother, who distrusted the durability of my mood, advised against it, but Pa, who for all his scorn of artists was inclined to see penitence in the light of a colorful drama of oils by Veronese or Tintoretto, insisted that I be taken at my word. When we sailed from Cherbourg I brought only three dresses from all my Paris stock. The rest I gave away, determined to select a new kind of wardrobe in Boston. I might have been taking the veil.

Oh, that winter at Justin! Even my own powers of self-dramatization were barely enough to get me through it. I helped Mother with "parlor night," Tuesdays and Fridays, when boys having the required grades were invited to our house from eight o'clock until nine to play games. Mother had a large and venerable collection of parlor games and puzzles, in all of which she used to participate with a passionate interest and competitiveness. I can still see her wonderful old witch's profile over the parcheesi board and those glassy eyes intent upon a little boy counting out the steps for his disks. But I was bored by the games and played them badly and could never keep order at my table which was always in an uproar, to Pa's extreme disapproval. In the mornings I earned a little money by tutoring boys in French, and in the afternoons I walked with Mother or trudged around the slushy campus by myself. As part of my penance I had given up painting; it was also the perfect way out of an artistic career for which I had little aptitude. I never went out to meals, and on the evenings when there was no parlor I would sullenly read Proust and Joyce by the fire and dream of the lives I had given up and of the lives I had never had. By early spring I was on the edge of a full nervous collapse.

Mother, however, had been watching me. She knew well my habits of self-mortification and understood that to try to rescue me from my own stubbornness too early would only make matters worse. She also knew that when she did move, it would have to be decisively. One morning at breakfast she announced that I was to spend the spring vacation with my sister Harriet in New York.

"Your father's going to the ecclesiastical council at Hartford, and I'm going to stay with your Aunt Maud at Pride's. The whole house is going to be painted, and I want everyone out. Harriet feels you've neglected her, so I took it upon myself to tell her you'd go."

I pretended to be angry and sulked for a day, but actually I appreciated Mother's tact in getting me out of my own prison. I had had my fill of Justin and self-pity, for a while anyway. It is always a tricky business for a grown-up child to live with parents, particularly at her own request. She is in no position to throw bricks. Pa was little interested in advice as to how to run his school from anyone, let alone a daughter, and I had before me, night and day, the frustrating image of that educating machine that I could not even criticize. I do not mean to imply that Pa was not kind to me, for he was. We walked together at least one afternoon a week, and we breakfasted together every morning. But he took it painfully for granted that I had nothing better in which to interest myself than his school. He even expected me to know the names of the sixth formers and who were the prefects.

Pa had the advantage over me in that he had been able to create a monster to which he could transfer an egotism that must in his youth have been even worse than mine, a monster of red brick and Romanesque arches, of varnished, carpetless halls and dreary stained glass windows, a monster that howled with the carnivorous howl of its four hundred and fifty cubs. I knew that if I did not get away, it would ultimately break me, as it had broken the plain, smiling, creeping, softly speaking wives of the masters.

My sister, Harriet Kidder, "Goneril" as we called her in the family, had married to advantage in New York and lived in considerable state. She was ten years my senior, fifty pounds heavier and hundreds of times richer, but for all her disapproval of my bohemianism, she has too many of the basic Prescott doubts to enjoy a really comfortable sense of superiority. In fact, Harriet's insecurity has often manifested itself in the crudest kind of boasting about the Kidder possessions, so that people meeting her for the first time are often surprised to discover that she was born a Boston Prescott.

She and Evelyn and I seem to have in common a fatal incapacity ever to put anything quite behind us. In the library we tend to gaze out the window at the garden party which we have passed up and deplore an afternoon wasted on mere musty books, but the moment we have changed our minds and joined the garden party we turn from its trivia to stare back in at those abandoned tomes that now seem to contain the only true richness. We have the minds of scholars (oh, yes, we're as bright as Pa, each one of us!) and the hearts of Pompadours. We would have done much better had we favored Mother.

It was at Harriet's that I met Guy Turnbull. Of course, it was not a co-incidence. I was still married to Cabell Willetts, but Harriet insisted that getting a divorce was simply a matter of getting the right lawyer and that she would get him for me when the time came. Guy, a widower some fifteen years older than myself, was a great friend and business associate of my brother-in-law and constantly at the house. It was really very generous of Harriet to offer him to her erring sister. He was big and stout and loud and still blond, but he could have regained what must have been strikingly good looks by taking off sixty pounds—which he never did. He had that odd, almost ladylike fastidiousness in taste and speech which so often goes with strong, self-made men and which whets the appetite of jaded creatures like myself who are titillated by a sense of the crudeness that must be so concealed.

Guy wore silk shirts with jeweled cuff links and ordered his suits and boots from London; at restaurants he was always sending back dishes and examining the silverware for spots. Yet he thrilled me when he shouted at a taxi driver or snarled at an offensive drunk. He could be terrifying in his sudden animal loudness and his obvious hankering for a fight. And his laugh was frankly vulgar; he seemed in his hilarity to be recklessly trying to rip down all the illusions that one supposed him to have been at such pains to build up. Had Guy been less of a sentimentalist, had he not talked quite so much about his poor dear dead wife, I might have fallen seriously in love with him.

As it was, there was only one place where Guy and I really belonged, and we soon got to it. Do you guess where that was? Really, Brian, don't try so hard not to look shocked. Be natural. Of course you disapprove of my having gone to bed with Guy. He disapproved of it himself. There has always been something about me that has made my lovers want to keep me straight.

With Charley it was the image of Pa, pursuing us to the most intimate recesses, but Guy had never met Pa, nor had his background been one to bring him under the shadow of the Prescott legend. Guy lumped Mother and Pa in a group that he loosely described as "society," a term that he by no means used slightingly. On the contrary, he thought that "society," like the Philharmonic and the opera, was something which ought to receive every self-made man's support. And he was not at all sure that he was properly supporting it by making me his mistress.

Harriet was furious. She accused me of a neurotic compulsion to become *déclassée*. She pointed out that it was just as easy to marry a man as to seduce him, and that, after all, I owed *something* to our parents. She explained at length her subtle maneuvers in convincing Guy that a wife of Prescott lineage was the one jewel missing in the crown of his material triumph. When I simply laughed at her, she sent me packing back to Justin and dispatched a long letter to Mother in which she suggested that Pa should summon up his heaviest battalions to combat my moral delinquency. I went back north, very pleased with myself. Guy and I had arranged to meet in Boston on the weekends to carry on what Harriet called our "intrigue." Fortunately, it was convenient for him as he had to make periodic inspections of one of his textile mills in Lowell.

Pa and Mother said nothing on my return, and I was divided between relief at being let alone and resentment at the idea that they had given me up. I consoled myself with the prospect of my weekends, and on early spring afternoons, circling the campus behind Mother and her two old beagles, I would look up defiantly at the great craggy oversized chapel tower, as ugly as Pa's deity, and think that I, at least, enjoyed a real relation with a real man, that Guy and I gave each other the pleasure of our bodies without the cant of religious fantasy. And what was Justin Martyr to a man like Guy? Had he gone to such a school? Had he needed to? Could he have made any more money if he had? Might it not even have paralyzed some of his initiative? Schools like Justin, I decided, were endowed with the excess funds of patrons like Guy, and headmasters, like the big-hatted, black-robed tutors and pedants of seventeenth century comedy, had to perform grotesque antics in their benefactors' audience chambers.

But, indeed, I had not been given up. The coils of Justin had actually been tightening around me. One evening after supper in the school dining room Pa asked me to come to his study, and there, as I faced him across the huge square desk, like a boy about to be disciplined, he told me that he had finally persuaded Cabell Willetts to seek an ecclesiastical annulment of our marriage. I was so surprised that for a moment I could only stare.

"It appears that he desires another union," Pa added dryly.

"With a nun?"

"With a widow who shares his own deep faith." Pa was not one to spoil his sarcasm with even a glint of the eye. His gravity was perfect. "Those of the Roman persuasion will not admit that a marriage has existed when there has been no matrimonial intent. If you will testify to a priest from the Rota that you never intended to be bound by your oath or to have children . . ."

"But I did!"

Pa surveyed me for a moment. Then without twitching a muscle in his face, without in the least compromising his solemn mien, he slowly lowered and retracted his left eyelid in a wink uncannily like that of a chicken. I was not amused.

"A Catholic priest doesn't count, is that it?" I demanded scornfully. "It's all right to tell a lie to a Hottentot? Well, having no church, I can't afford to dispense with my few principles so sweepingly. We agnostics, thank you very much, *do* have principles. If Cabell wants his annulment, let him tell his own lies. Even a Jesuit is entitled to the truth!"

Pa nodded, but sighed. "It seems a pity. I have thought deeply in the matter, and I could not help wondering if it *was* a real marriage. You were so young and so determined to shock the old folks."

"I wasn't as young as all that! And I had every intention of having a child. Thank God I failed!"

"Amen," Pa replied, with a sincerity that annoyed me. "Very well, my child, that is all there is to it. I thought it my duty to put the matter before you. But, of course, I shall never counsel you to go against your conscience."

When Mother heard about my stand, she was angrier than I had ever seen her. She could be terrible in her tempers, cold, articulate and biting. She seemed to lose all sense of her relationship with the person at whom she was angry, and she would strike at her own flesh and blood as if we were thieves in the night. The occasions were rare, but feared by all, even by Pa, or perhaps I should say particularly by Pa.

"Even from you such gall astounds me!" she exclaimed. "To give your poor father a cheap sermon on intellectual honesty. After all he's done for you. Do you think it was easy for him to go to the Willetts? Do you think it was pleasant for him to have to stick his arms into the mud of a Catholic annulment? Do you think he *enjoyed* having to root out all the facts of Cabell's sanctimonious little love affair? I tell you it made him sick! But he did it because he thought that his daughter, who's made such a stinking mess of her life, was entitled to another chance. And he did it, too, against his own conscience, after days of prayer and tortured reflections, to keep *you* from turning into the complete tramp that you show every sign of wanting to be. Well I tell you here and now, my girl, if you don't go through with this annulment, you've seen the last of me. And I mean it!"

As in Paris I had collapsed before Pa, so now did I collapse before Mother. None of us girls had anything like the force of personality of our parents. I could sneer at Pa and sulk with Mother, but I was no match for them in their real tempers. Without even talking to Pa I went to Boston and saw Cabell's lawyer and prepared my testimony. The Willetts had great connections in the church, and in three months the annulment was procured. During the following summer I went to Reno and obtained my civil divorce. I then did a thing of which I am still ashamed. I wrote Cabell a letter in which I told him that my testimony was perjured and that the annulment was void in the eyes of God. He never answered, but I have often speculated about the effect of my message on his marital relations with the holy widow. Oh, yes, it was a bitchy thing to do, but you must remember that if he had given me my divorce when I had first wanted it, I could have married Charley and brought peace to the last months of his life.

Everybody was pleased with the new, compliant Cordelia, even Guy, who after formally proposing to me at lunch in the Boston Ritz, announced that our other relationship would have to be suspended until marriage. Evidently the future Mrs. Turnbull—and he took it for granted, quite correctly, that despite my refusal to commit myself, I would ultimately become such—had to be beyond suspicion, even if it was a whitewash job. Guy was much more at his ease in the status of fiancé to a Prescott than of lover. I suspected that he had another mistress, on a lower social level, to take care of his physical needs, and that this explained his preference to have me chaste. Guy was enough of a bull to be fairly indiscriminate about his cows. I was a "lady," and, to change the simile, he liked his pigeons to stay in their pigeonholes.

Of course, he was enchanted with Pa. On the weekend when he was first invited to Justin, Pa took him over every nook and cranny of the school, and Guy thoroughly berated me afterwards for my past irreverence.

"I realize, Cordie," he told me, "that it must have been hard for a girl to be brought up in a boys' school. But the fact remains that you're prejudiced. Your father has created an extraordinary thing in Justin. He'd have made a tremendous businessman!"

This was actually an idea that had often occurred to Pa himself. He had his moments, not so much when he regretted the fortune that he had not made as when he begrudged fortunes to those who had made them with less than his own capabilities. I remember a rich visitor to the school, who arrived in a long yellow Hispano-Suiza with glittering accessories, saying to Pa after lunch: "I'd give up all my corporations to have been the founder of Justin," and Pa snapping back at him without a grin or a wink: "I'd give up Justin for your car."

But if nothing made Pa more scornful than wealthy men who sighed after the spiritual life, wealthy men who gloried in the bitter competition of the marketplace and in a creed that put the profit motive ahead of all intrigued him. Perhaps, he felt that like soldiers, they were nearer the basic male than himself. For all Pa's faith and for all his accomplishments there was a side of him that tended to identify the priest's cassock with a woman's skirt and to sneer at the world of education as an ivory tower. He was in it himself, to be sure, but he had the vanity to want you to know that, unlike most of the inmates, he had not fled to it for refuge. He *could* have survived on the ringing plain. And he liked Guy for promptly recognizing this.

"He's a natural, that fellow Turnbull," he told me. "Hang on to him, Cordie. I sometimes wonder if we don't send forth our graduates to a holocaust in which they must try their tinfoil swords against the steel of men like that. I wonder if he'd consider teaching a seminar course to the sixth form in business competition?"

"He'd crave it!"

And do you know, he did? He taught every Saturday morning during the fall term. Guy and Pa became the most devoted friends. They inspected Guy's big mill at Lowell together as carefully as they had inspected the school, and Pa put me in mind of Boswell's description of Dr. Johnson at the sale of the deceased Mr. Thrale's brewery, bustling about amid the boilers and vats like an excise man, with an inkhorn and pen in his buttonhole, and talking pompously of the duties of his executorial office. Back at school he diverted the prefects' table with an account of his excursion, including a graphic description of the chairman's office.

"I paused at the threshold, dazzled by the scene in front of me. As far as the eye could reach stretched grey sofas, mahogany tables, murals, shining appurtenances. I took a step forward; I lost my foothold; I cried out." Here Pa stretched his arms wide. "Gentlemen, I solemnly assure you, I had sunk knee-deep in carpet!"

Perhaps you can see what he was doing already, the old rascal. It was soon to become a pattern. He was undermining Guy with ridicule. Oh, yes, I realize that I sound inconsistent, and I repeat that he admired Guy. But he was also jealous of him. He envied Guy his business success, as he had envied Charley his war career. The only way that he had been able to reassure himself that he was as much of a man as Charley had been by asserting his religious leadership. He was smart enough to see that this would never work with Guy. For Guy he had to put into action his own superior intellect and erode with little sarcasms the uncomfortable image of the tycoon who could build a dozen Justins by signing detachable pieces of paper from a little black book that had nothing to do with hymns or prayers.

I don't want to sound too Freudian, but I was certainly in basic competition with Pa. My two men were men, after all, and they had looked to me for something that Pa could not offer. But Pa, the old magician, had ways of recovering distracted attention. He could prove to them that he, too, was a man, that he was more than a man; he could show them a heavenly kingdom where women and wars and moneymaking did not exist. And when Pa decided to be a prophet, he did so on a Cecil B. De Mille scale. He ended by making even Guy suspect that business was not all.

My second marriage lasted seven years, but it was a failure from the start. Guy was carnal to a degree that even I had not believed possible. I learned to be glad every time he took a new mistress. He had some disgusting practices with which I need not shock you, and the foulness of his language in our bedroom was an education in vice. When he realized at last that there were certain things to which I was never going to submit, that I was not titillated but genuinely revolted, he began to hate me and to humiliate me whenever he could. Fortunately his large means and multiple business trips made it easy for us to live apart, and when we finally agreed upon a divorce he surprised everybody by the big alimony that he allowed me. I suppose he wanted even an ex-Mrs. Turnbull to live grandly and be a credit to him, for he provided that the payments would cease on my remarriage. However, I have fooled him, for I have arranged my life quite satisfactorily without marrying again. He should have remembered that I had learned the trick before.

During the years of our marriage and despite its deterioration, Guy's relations with Pa and Mother went from good to perfect. He frequently stayed with them at Justin without me. I would have thought that some of the crudity of the man would have repelled Mother, but she seemed immune to it. There was a worshiping little-boy quality about Guy as a son-in-law that was apparently irresistible. The line that he drew in his own mind between me and my parents was the line between the flesh and the spirit. All his reverence for the Prescotts as a symbol of what he called "distinguished living" went to Pa and Mother, while I became increasingly a mere physical convenience to him, and when I ceased to be convenient, I became nothing. Basically he must have always regarded me as a tramp with a lineage that was detachable and could be acquired by himself. Even after our divorce he continued to be on as good terms at Justin as ever.

I resented it, of course. I resented Pa's and Mother's whole attitude about my marital troubles. It was only too obvious that they believed that any nice reasonable girl could have got along with Guy. When in desperation I told Pa a few of the true facts, he listened with an interest that I was sure did not stem entirely from sympathy with his daughter. Part of it was the natural lubricity that exists in even the holiest mortals and part was perhaps his feeling that such activity as I described was characteristic, however unfortunately, of any real male. Or perhaps he simply thought that I was making it up, and his attention was a mask for the horror that he felt at having sired so morbid and malevolent a daughter. In all events he never referred to it, but continued to see Guy as before.

I fumed at such disloyalty, but I fumed in vain. Pa stimulated Guy's interest in the school to the point where he did something that was in direct contradiction to every principle in his self-aggrandizing nature. He made an anonymous gift. Yes, I see how big your eyes are, Brian. You can't believe that the man I have described would forego the glory of a public presentation. But do you know why? Because his money was allocated to the erection of that grey sweeping temple dedicated to the god of sport and named for the dead hero whose beautiful statue by Malvina Hoffman, so radiantly evocative of golden youth cut short, stands before its portals. Charley Strong and Guy Turnbull had more in common at last than the physical possession of Cordelia Prescott.

14

BRIAN'S JOURNAL

APRIL 3, 1942. It seems like a miracle (and how do I know it's not?) that I can open this journal and record that I am living in Cambridge, enrolled at last in divinity school!

I can hardly take in that only four months have elapsed since my last entry. It has been, anyway, a period long enough to go to hell and back, and I say this fully and humbly recognizing that during every minute of it I have been safe and sound while American boys were dying in the Pacific. But I have learned that safety and soundness can have their own hellish twist.

It started with Pearl Harbor, which was greeted by the Griscams with the hysteria that children might show to a premature Santa Claus. War seemed the extra dimension that had been needed in their lives. To Mrs. Griscam it was the ultimate opportunity for her "army," through military recreation centers, to reach American youth; to Amy it was escape into glamour through the Red Cross; to Sylvester it was the dignity, after domestic scandal, of a naval officer's uniform and a desk in Church Street where his father could not check up on him, as opposed to one in Wall, where he could. And to Mr. Griscam, happiest of all, it meant secret trips to the State Department, even the White House, and the rumor of a diplomatic post to the governments in exile. In the bustle of those days it seemed to my saddened eyes that nobody over five and thirty could possibly want peace.

Not that I was left out in the division of spoils. Mr. Griscam spoke of taking me abroad as his private secretary. "Freedom First" had been officially closed, and I was helping to liquidate the office. But I felt a violent and unreasonable aversion to clambering on the Griscam band wagon. I wanted *my* war to be a grimmer, obscurer business. As I could not continue to accept Mr. Griscam's bread and shelter under the circumstances, I quietly decamped during one of his absences in Washington, leaving four polite and grateful letters to my hosts, and moved to a boardinghouse on West 90th Street. I then took a volunteer job, suggested by one of my fellow workers at "Freedom First," from midnight to eight in the dispatcher's office of the Fire Department at Central Park. I figured that I could just subsist on my own small income and make this token contribution to the defense of the city.

I moved through the cold, dreary winter like a man who has been drugged. I performed my almost mechanical tasks at the dispatcher's office with adequate efficiency; I enrolled as an air raid warden, and I contributed my services as a dishwasher to a stage door canteen. There still remained a goodly number of hours in each week when I would sit on the bed in my little room and read Trollope. Only after I had done everything for the war that I could think of doing did I permit this escape to the world of Plantaganet Palliser and Lady Glencora.

I would have seen nobody at all had it not been for Mrs. Turnbull. She tracked me down through the Griscams and insisted that I dine with her on my night off from the Fire Department. When I went there, unable to think of an excuse, I found a large party of artists and dealers who did much drinking and talking. Nobody but my hostess, who insisted that I call her "Cordelia," paid the least attention to me, but I found it diverting for a change to hear talk that was not about the war, and I went again on several occasions.

I suppose I should have suspected that Cordelia had her own plans for me. After all, it was obvious that I was not being asked because I could

paint or talk, and she was very put out once when I refused to linger after
the others had risen to go. But she must have been fifteen years my senior,
and I have suffered all my life from a feeling that I am unattractive to women,
a feeling which has survived (I may say at least to my journal without fatuity) a certain amount of evidence to the contrary.

My naïveté in this case let me in for an appalling scene. One night I went
to the duplex to find myself the only guest. Cordelia, reclining in a pink
negligee before a pitcher of martinis in which she had obviously been imbibing prior to my arrival, might have scared me to instant flight had not
her voice been so gruff and matter-of-fact.

"Yes, sweetie, we're all alone," she said as she took in my apprehensive
glance at the table set cozily for two by the window. "After dinner I'll play
soft music and show you my etchings. Don't look so scared. It won't hurt.
Here, give yourself a drink." But when she abruptly changed the subject, I
decided in a flutter of relief that she must be joking. "This damn war," she
continued. "I'm sick of it already. The last one was bad enough, but at least
there was all that Wilsonian idealism. Oh, I grant you, it nauseated me at
the time, but now I find it's worse without it. All you young people are so
terrified that anyone will think *you* think you're making the world safe for
democracy that of course you won't. Not a chance of it."

She continued morosely in this vein all during a lengthy cocktail period
and a much shorter dinner. I wondered hopefully if the amount of gin that
she was consuming might not end by disposing of my problem, but her
capacity seemed unlimited. Only her temper was affected, for it grew shorter
and shorter. After the meal she blew up at me for suggesting that we listen
to *The Magic Flute*.

"Everyone likes Mozart now," she grumbled. "Tinkle, tinkle, tinkle, that's
all you youngsters want. Give me Beethoven. He's obvious, but God knows,
so am I. At least, he was a *man*."

We listened to the Seventh, I constrainedly, she moodily. I noted that
she had shifted to bourbon.

"I said I was obvious, honey," she repeated in a more ominous tone.
"What did you think I meant by that?"

"Simply that you liked loud, emphatic music."

"And not loud, emphatic men?"

"Perhaps them, too." I managed a shrug. "What a pity they're all away."

"Isn't it just?" she took me up sarcastically. "Isn't it hard on poor Cordelia?
But it luckily happens that she also has a taste for quiet little boys of milder
emphasis. Like you, bunny. Yes, dear, I fancy *you*. Can you bear it?"

"I'm glad you like me."

"Oh, come off it, bunny!" she exclaimed sharply. "I didn't say I liked
you. I'm not at all sure I do. I said I *fancied* you. Don't pretend you don't
know what that means. Don't you think you could fancy me for a bit?" Her
tone was of mock cajolery. "Just for a wee bit, bunny?"

"I'm sorry, Mrs. Turnbull . . ." I began in an agony of embarrassment.

"Cordelia!"

"I'm sorry, Cordelia, but I don't think I could ever . . . well, I don't

think I could ever feel that way about you. I respect you very much, but
I'm not . . ." I braced myself. "Well, I'm not in love with you."

Her shriek of laughter was shocking. "I should hope not! I'm not in love
with you. But you have a scared littly bunny look that I find intriguing.
Don't you think it might be fun to pretend we were in love just for tonight?"
She looked at me with bold, penetrating, still laughing eyes. "Are you a
virgin, bunny? I'll bet you are."

"Please, Cordelia!"

"Well, why be ashamed of it? All would-be ministers should be virgins
till they marry, shouldn't they? I *like* the idea of your being a virgin!"

I rose, trembling with embarrassment and indignation. "I think I'd better go now."

She reached out and caught my arm and pulled me down on the sofa
beside her. "Is it Pa you're worried about? Forget him. He understands a
lot more things than you think. Come on, bunny, relax. It's a great big lonely
war, and Cordelia's all warm and nice and huggy."

"No!" I tore myself away and jumped up.

"Oh, but yes, bunny." She rose and threw her strong left arm about my
neck and implanted a sticky, whiskeyed kiss on my shrinking lips while with
her free hand . . . !

I cannot write what she did with her free hand.

Again I ripped myself from her embrace and made a frantic dash for the
hall. In the foyer I kept my finger on the elevator bell as if I were escaping
a fiend. As the doors swung open and I plunged into the car I could hear
through the open front door behind me, her mocking farewell: "Good night,
Joseph Andrews!"

All that night in my rented room that cry sounded in my ears. Joseph
Andrews! Did that shameless hussy know that poor Joseph Andrews who
saves his virtue from the brazen Lady Booby, naked under her sheet, was a
caricature of my adored Mr. Richardson's Pamela? Was it not enough that
Cordelia had confused the image of her sainted father in my mind with that
of a leering vamp? Did she have as well to make the father of the English
novel, whose little portrait by my bed had been a consolation in war and
peace, ridiculous? It seemed to me as I lay tossing that Cordelia had fouled
not only her nest but the universe, that the very war was hardly worth winning if *she* was what our boys would come home to.

Things went from bad to worse. I could not recapture in the days that
followed even the flitting sense of utility that my frenzied war activities had
briefly given me. It seemed to me now that I was only a fool and, like all
fools, thinking only of myself. Had I not allowed an unchristian prejudice
against Mr. Griscam to keep me from assisting him in what was perhaps an
important diplomatic post? Wasn't my whole attitude about the war simply
a demonstration of my need to appease the ego? I found I could not even
read Trollope and took to going to the movies in the afternoon.

One night, going to work, I had a distressing experience in the subway.
It was raining, and the car was very crowded and stuffy. When the doors
opened at Seventy-second Street a group of rather rowdy Negro boys, in

red and yellow jackets, shoved their way in, jostling and pushing the other passengers, laughing loudly and using rough language. This in itself was nothing, and the passengers hardly noticed the intrusion. The boys, after all, if rude were not bad-tempered. They were even in a rather pleasant mood. But what distressed me was that in the heat and closeness, listening to the high laughs and the crude remarks, I momentarily lost my faith.

I thought: how could God want all the creatures in that car, including myself (oh, yes, including myself) to enter into eternal life? It was not that those cackling boys were wicked, but whatever they were, good or bad, the point struck at me that a mortal lifetime seemed quite as long as one could want for them. A long happy lifetime—to be sure, one wished them that— but *immortality*? Were they up to it? I thought of Calvin and his answer to my problem in the doctrine of elected souls, but wasn't it worse to have *some* saved than none? That was the horror of Calvin, like the horror of the Inquisition and the horror of Hitler, and where these horrors did not exist, I faced the horror of the empty grins and silly laughs in the underground of Manhattan.

I suppose it was inevitable that in this mood and with my odd hours of work I should have sickened and that a feverish cold should have turned into pneumonia. My landlady behaved with the greatest consideration, and the doctor whom she called pulled me through, but for a day I was delirious. It seemed to my darkened mind that the only thing to dread was recovery.

And then, just as I passed the crisis, he came. I heard the rich, deep voice from far away:

"I am going to take care of you, Brian. As soon as you're feeling better I shall move you to my daughter Harriet's apartment. She and her husband have gone to Washington. It will be a good place for your recuperation."

"But how . . . how . . . ?"

"How did I know? You put my name down as the person to notify in emergency on the form that you filled out at the Fire Department. It touched me very much, dear boy."

Had I? It all seemed a dream but a wonderful one. If I had died, I had gone to heaven, and wasn't that just the place I would expect to meet Dr. Prescott?

But I had not died. Sitting in Mrs. Kidder's beautiful Georgian living room overlooking the East River, we spent our mornings with books and games and puzzles, and often just gazing down at the tugs and naval vessels and the big squawking gulls that flew low over the thick grey eddying fullness of that rapid water. I would not have believed it possible to be so relaxed with him. When I started once to make a murmuring effort to articulate my gratitude, he pulled me firmly up:

"Let us settle the question of thanks once and for all, Brian, and then it needn't bother us again. I am an old man, and I have nothing else to do. I like you, and I want to help you. You may show your gratitude, if you must, by allowing me to finish up the job I've started."

In a week's time we were taking little walks in Carl Schurz Park to take advantage of the brief new sunshine. I was feeling now the beginnings of a restoration not only of my body but of my mind. I still had the sense that I had had since Pearl Harbor of suspended animation—of existing in an echoing void—but the sense had ceased to be disagreeable. The echoes were softer, almost at times consolatory. As soon as Dr. Prescott felt that I was strong enough, he began to talk to me about the ministry.

"I see now that I made a mistake when David Griscam told me about your decision not to go to Harvard. I should have left the Cape and gone to you at once. But I hesitated to use any pressure. I thought that if your call was not clear enough, that might be a warning that the church was not your true vocation. What I failed to see was that you are the exception to an otherwise valid rule. I am now confident, my boy, that your call is a true one and that the impediments in your way have been simple nervous afflictions that will disappear once you have learned to face them. That is why I want you to go to divinity school as soon as you are well. I do not even want you to wait until next fall. The sooner you are actually taking courses the better."

"But won't I have to wait for the beginning of the school year?" I protested, drawing back instinctively from the prospect of decision.

"For credit, yes. But I have arranged with the Dean that you may be admitted now as an auditor."

"I'm afraid, sir, I'm not ready!"

"You never will be if you wait. With you and me faith will always be a matter of exercise. But the faith that you work for is just as fine as the faith that is conferred. Perhaps finer!"

I told him now of my dismal experience with the Negro boys in the subway and asked him if one of such visceral reactions had any right to become a minister.

"We all have such reactions," he replied. "I am besieged with them myself. Moments of vacuum, I call them. I'm sorry to say they do not disappear with age. Nobody can believe in a life hereafter *all* the time. What you must do is accept your moods of doubt, as you have just accepted your illness. You must say to yourself: 'Here I am, a believer who is doubting.' Then you will find that, although alone with yourself in that terrible vacuum, you still can see yourself. See yourself doubting. Instead of self-revilement, there may be calm. Instead of blame, there may be sadness. And if you will wait quietly enough and long enough, that vacuum may suddenly and thrillingly begin to throb again with your awareness of the presence of God."

"But isn't it a terrible thing to think so little of one's fellow humans? I had no *right* to be put off by those colored boys."

"No right, of course. But you were. You have to accept the fact that there is that in you. But why does it matter?" Here he stopped and turned on me and smote his fist into the palm of his other hand. "You *know* God exists, and you *know* those boys have immortal souls! That you didn't believe it for a time is simply a fact. A little fact that, like so many others, is of little importance."

"I pray that may be so, sir."

"It is so, Brian, believe me." He pricked his brows and became sunk in reverie. "We can overcome a great many things by the simple expedient of accepting them. I used to worry that I did not sufficiently love my daughters. You see, dear boy, I am taking you into my deepest confidence. But now I see that loving them inadequately was part of me and part of the condition into which they were born. God did not expect me to love them more. I couldn't. He expected me to tend them devotedly. Ah, love." He grunted suddenly. "Those who merely love get too much credit from a world of geese. It isn't love children need. It is devotion."

As I came gradually to accept his theory that I should stop fretting about faith, a wonderful peace began to creep over me. One by one he disposed of my remaining objections.

"You've tried to fight, and they wouldn't have you," he retorted to my protest that I should do war work. "That's all that can be expected of a man. Now your place is back in the church. Do you think God's work must stop in wartime? Do you think ministers won't be needed when peace comes?"

I asked him if it was fair to take up a place in divinity school, particularly on a scholarship, when I still had doubts if I would ever be ordained.

"But ordained or not ordained *you* are always going to be a minister," he insisted. "Personally, I think you will come back to Justin and teach. There is no real distinction between the pulpit and the classroom. I tried to put God into every book and sport in Justin. That was my ideal, to spread a sense of his presence so that it would not be confined to prayers and sacred studies and to spread it in such a way as to make the school *joyful*." He shook his head ruefully. "Oh, if I could have done *that*, Brian, Justin would have been a perfect thing. It would have been the model for all preparatory schools!"

"It is, sir."

"It is *not*, my boy, but I'm counting on you to help make it so."

There was no resisting this. Besides, I no longer wanted to. I had a new conviction now that I would be able to stick it at Cambridge. I even wondered if I might not like it. And I have. Of course, I know that he is only thirty miles away at the Andrews cottage at Justin, and that thought helps to sustain me. But I do not run to his side every time I feel giddy. It has been agreed between us that I must learn to stand on my own feet.

Before we left New York he discovered something that I had not dreamed he would ever discover. On our last day he suggested that I come and lunch at Cordelia's, and I declined, saying that I did not wish to intrude on a family party. When he insisted, and I continued to refuse, flushing deeply, he grunted.

"She told me you wouldn't come. What's it all about? Has something happened between you and Cordie?"

"Oh, no!" I cried in dismay. "Nothing, I assure you!"

"Nothing, eh?" He gave me a shrewd stare. "Well, I daresay it wasn't her fault. But I see she must have given you a scare. You've got to learn not to worry about women like Cordie. They're basically simple creatures.

She says she told you about her marriages." His smile was faintly grim. "Poor Cordie. Harriet used to say it was all our fault. That we didn't cuddle her enough when she was little. I'm afraid she's made up for that since. Did she tell you about Charley Strong?"

"A bit."

"I loved Charley, and it was my sad duty to have to rescue him from Cordie. Of course, she could never forgive that."

"She says you destroyed his book."

"Yes, I told her so. At the time she was very distraught, and I thought the truth would upset her more. Actually, Charley destroyed it himself for fear she would publish it. All but one chapter which he gave to me. I still have it." He stared for a minute down at the river, and when he looked up at me there was a gleam of amusement in his eyes. It was a sarcastic, an almost impish gleam. "I'll send it to you, if you like. When you're safely ensconced in Harvard. It mightn't be a bad thing for you to read. You'll see the terrible consequences of sex. Or, perhaps I should say, the consequences of brooding about sex."

He took no chances with me as he did last summer, but accompanied me, when the doctor pronounced me recovered, to Boston, where his daughter Evelyn put us both up in Arlington Street. There we stayed until Dr. Prescott had introduced me to the faculty at the divinity school, enrolled me as an auditor in the courses and even helped to find me a room in Cambridge. I was thoroughly settled, almost, one might say, hammered down, by the time he returned to Justin. It has been an awesome experience to have found myself the beneficiary of all the energies of the ex-headmaster, but my ultimate reaction has been one of bursting pride. The uneasy feeling that I *must* make good has been ameliorated by the growing suspicion that I really may.

Two weeks after his departure he sent me the surviving chapter of Charley Strong's book. I happened to read it just after attending Dr. Vane's famous lecture on gnosticism, and the comparison was stimulating. Certainly poor Charley must have been a curious study in heresy. It is a pity that he could not have written the final chapter of his story and told how Dr. Prescott, in their talks by the Seine, had lifted his eyes from the mortal headmaster to the God in and behind them both. But at least the few pages that he did not destroy show that this ending was possible.

15

CHARLEY STRONG'S MANUSCRIPT
(1921)

IT HAPPENED IN Southampton in the summer after my fifth form year. Claude is a cousin of Mummy's, halfway between our ages, a giddy, discontented old maid who is always trying to put her hands on me and stares in provoking, smiling silence during family meals. When she asked me to come to her bedroom to tell me a "secret," I went, to find her naked and still smiling. She was shameless and shrill, and the white puffy flesh on her buttocks gave way under my groping fingers as if it had been cotton on sticks. I took it for granted that she would be pregnant and that I would get syphilis. Neither event occurred, but when war came, and mud, they seemed a natural consequence.

There is very little purity in Paris, and yet the air is pure. There is very little cleanliness about the French, and yet their minds are clean. How the visiting Sunday preachers at Justin dwelt on purity: clean young men land clean young women offering each other unstained bodies in a marriage of true sacrament! Harry Nolan tells me that he and Libby wake up sometimes at night and find themselves consummating the act. I think that in the greenish light of the chapel I must have visualized the wedding night like that. A love that transcends embarrassment, an orgasm that explodes as the Grail is raised to the altar, a naked odorless copulation, passionate but unsweating, before a white surpliced choir, witnessing without concupiscence and bursting into song. Is it not thus that Henry Esmond would copulate? And Prince Albert and the Chevalier Bayard? And even the preachers themselves, old as they are, if they still do it, and my Latin master, Mr. Van Wormser, sitting in the back with his big bony wife in the little straw hat with the silly peonies? Imagine how much of it there is and how blessed!

People always think me innocent, naïve, good. They whisper things they think I shouldn't hear. Oh, Charley, sweetie, no, she's not for you, I'm not for you, you need a nice girl. I am cream chicken and green peas at a children's party; I am spun sugar and ice cream; I am the peck of a kiss after a subscription dance at the Plaza on a spring vacation. I am confusion and hot, slow tears after a wet dream. Little do they know, giggling by the shoe lockers in the cellar of Lowell House or hiding under the beds while the old women clean the cubicles to look under their skirts, that Charley, who blushes at their stories, Charley whom they delight to shock,

pretending to be doing things that even *they* wouldn't really do in the showers, Charley who falls asleep at nights and dreams of sports and Mother,
this same Charley has no bottom to his voluptuousness. Nay, your wives,
your daughters, your matrons and your maids could not fill up the cistern
of my lust.

Hope for redemption can lie only in casting myself at the feet of him
whom I have betrayed. For it is he, I know, who made me senior prefect;
the upper school's election is merely advisory, and it is by no means clear
that I had a majority. I enjoy the transient popularity of looks and football
prowess, and I have no avowed enemies. But I am deemed too much a
Christer to be a real leader, and when he told me of my appointment, I
trembled and wept at such an act of trust. He it was who baptized and
confirmed me, he who talked to me of my doubts and miseries, he who
gave me a love that made the shallow, prattling love of shallow, prattling
parents seem like the spray on one's face in a speedboat at sea.

Yes, hope is only in him. Redemption is only in him. He prefers Saint
Augustine to Saint Francis, the Magdalene to Saint Cecilia. He knows that
purity is not to be confused with inexperience. Those also are saved who
flee from Alexandria to the desert and raise long grey El Greco arms and
roll wide white El Greco eyes to a God who glares fiercely over their heads
at the flickering light of the about-to-be consumed city revels which they
have shrewdly abandoned. I must go to the Cape and leave Southampton;
I must abandon Father, Mother and Cousin Claude; I must flee to the Cape
to confess and kiss his feet, wash his feet, sit at his feet.

Daddy cannot understand my leaving in the middle of the season. When
I tell him that the Rugby fifth esteemed it the greatest of honors to be asked
to Dr. Arnold's in the summer holidays, he says it is nonsense. Daddy thinks
everything is nonsense. There is something eternal about people who think
this, and I find it hard to believe when I visualize the gay striped summer
waistcoat over the round little belly, the shivering pince-nez, the coughs as
he taps his egg at breakfast, a Dickensian Yankee, that Daddy is as dead as
ever I shall be, that Mother is a widow on the Riviera and that my sister
Alice is an older maid than Claude.

Daddy concedes that Dr. Prescott may be a great headmaster, but doubts
that he is quite a gentleman. Old Boston family? What has that to do with
it? King Edward is not a gentleman. The Kaiser is not a gentleman. Very
few royalties, indeed, are gentlemen. But Delancey Parker is a gentleman;
so is Emlen Rutherford. It takes Harvard on top of Justin to make a gentleman. A club on top of God. Never forget that, my boy.

At Lola's last week on the Rue de Peur, under a window through which
I could see at dawn the flèche of the Sainte-Chapelle, two young men in
red silk shirts huddled side by side, arms about each other's necks. Lola, in
one of her moods, had gone to an inner room with a Russian who had parked
his taxi below, and outside the door Leo, cigarette dangling, dispassionately
waited. These are the innocents. What do they know of the flickering sky
over El Greco's deserts? What do they know of damnation? They were not
taught by a master.

"I am sorry, Charley, for what transpired, particularly that it should have happened in your home, but I suspect there was an element of seduction. Stay up here, my boy, until your cousin has left Southampton. And do not think that life is over because of this. *I* was not pure when I married. You see how I honor you with my confidence. You could make a good tale of this next term, but you won't. No, boy, don't weep. Get up and go out. Walk down the beach and breathe in the Atlantic. Recite *Dover Beach* if you must. It will go well with your present sentiments. But don't be late for dinner. Mr. Depew is coming, and I want my senior prefect to entertain him."

Had I fornicated only that I might be forgiven?

When Madame de Genlis returned to Paris after an exile that had lasted a quarter of a century, a period which had encompassed the revolution, the directorate, the consulate and the empire, what struck her most was that ladies who received their callers on the chaise-longue no longer covered their ankles. The *couvre-pied* had fled with democracy; France had wanted neither one nor the other, and are there grades of importance in the junk pile? Seduction by Claude, forgiveness for seduction by Claude, the love of Prescott and shrapnel in the Argonne.

Sixth form year! With the sixth behind him Dr. Arnold wouldn't have traded his job for any in England. I see the blond senior prefect standing on the dais with eye on wristwatch and finger pressing the assembly bell; I see him dashing down the football field, one arm stiffly out, for an eighty-yard gain; I see him singing loudest in the song fest, laughing loudest at the headmaster's reading of Leacock. He keeps exhorting the lower forms to a greater showing of school spirit and the upper to a greater cooperation with the prefects, until at last he fades through innumerable examples of example giving into a kind of cinema poster of Tom Brown, a puppet to jig about the stage and prattle in a disguised voice, manipulated by five strong fingers behind the curtain, a Faust who has sold his soul to God.

In the whole process of non-living it is the least lived year, waiting for the emerald green of June with the creamy white parchment and prize books rebound in morocco leather, thinking of graduation first as a day to be dreaded, then as a release and finally as an extinction, not because there is no life after school (though that may be) but because school has sucked out one's life, and the holy vampire with the arching eyebrows who loves to read Lucretius and Epictetus has taken one's blood and bones for the cause (as of course one had begged him to!) and spread upon his green, green campus a fragment of one's translucent skin, a lock of yellow damp hair.

That was the life one made love to, was it not; that was the sacrifice one sought, to let the middle-aged god return to his earth and his boys in the guise of one of them, to rejuvenate and redeem his school through the medium of a captive senior prefect? What does it matter that there is nothing left of one when the great spirit moves out of one's body? Is the process not ecstasy? Or as near it as one would ever come?

When I think of early communion I always think of it as being in the spring, and I feel the sweet sad tug of a pointless melancholy and the light, exhilarating caress of a warm zephyr against my cheeks as I cross an empty campus to what I hope will be an almost empty chapel. And then I remember the sting of the sour cheap wine on its passage to my empty stomach and the wonderful rumble of the comfortable words. How he could say that word "comfortable"! It seemed to have more syllables than four and to be filled with the biggest of pillows; it suggested a great dark cool leathery gentlemen's club with discreet silent attendants, visible only because of their white raiment, passing between the half-sleeping members with delectables. And I would close my eyes, kneeling at the altar rail, so tightly that I would see explosions of light and spots of blue, and when the service was over would go back, faithful hound, to help him with his disrobing and listen mutely to the flow of the day's instruction.

"I have noticed, Charley, that Mr. Taylor's dormitory is habitually late for morning roll call. I have noticed that there are more books overdue in the library, that the back row in the schoolroom was giggling last night at prayers, that there was a fight with tin basins in Mr. Dugdale's lavatory, that shoes are not always shined, that tongues are not always clean, that minds are spotted and flesh is vile (at least as second formers may conceive it), that virtue has departed from the campus and the great veil in the temple is rent in twain. Do you know who rent it?"

How could I think I would survive being his boy, his son, his victim? My formmates keep their respectful distance; the faculty step gingerly by me. The Rector's hound is safe only when the Rector is present, to allay with a finger's touch the bristling hair on his neck. But if I give him youth, he gives me redemption. I enter into him and become but a pulse of a mighty being. With what dawdling sentiment do I see myself as an aide-de-camp standing on a hilltop over the battle, absorbed in my general's tactics and mindless of the shells and bullets over my head! But there will be other battles in which such things may receive their due consideration.

The war has been a godsend for people who like to blame things on things. My virgin sister Alice and my virgin-in-heart mother at Cannes, on terrace after terrace, nibbling macaroons under a macaroon sun, tell of me and my vices in subdued tones that throb with pride. A total wreck, so much promise, such a tragedy, such a loss. Oh, yes, it might have been better had he been killed outright. There are worse things than death, far worse, and it is I, his mother, who tell you that. I hope when I go, I go quickly, like dear Mr. Popley, at eighty-eight, on his tennis court at Hyères last Sunday. I should never wish to survive my faculties or live to be a burden to Alice. I want to live just so long as I'm useful, not a minute longer. Well, it's kind of you to say so, but if I *do* look young for my years, it's because I try to take an interest in what the young people do and say. After all, the future depends on them. And that's what I mind about Charley. He doesn't seem to care what's happening in the world today outside of that woman (I won't mention her name!) and her trashy crowd. Well, of course, I can't imagine *what* Dr. Prescott thinks about it! When Alice was last in Paris, she ran into her right smack in the Rue de la Paix. Naturally, she cut her. Oh, yes, she cut her dead. Alice is one of the few of her generation who remembers how to do that. It's another of the arts that was lost in the war.

I can hear the rumble of Dr. Prescott's laugh in the rustle of autumn leaves on the Champs Elysées as I sip my cointreau. I can hear it in taxi horns. I heard it in the exchange of artillery in the Argonne; I heard it in the slush of boots through the oozing mud of the terrible spring of 1918. He was always bigger or smaller than life, louder or softer than any sound. At times he was as silly as a letter from Mother; at times he seemed to bear as little relation to my present as the memory of one of Alice's big marquise dolls. And at times he loomed over the war-lit battlefield like a leering caricature of the Kaiser, exulting in Armageddon, or exulting that he had predicted it, flitting back and forth across the beam streaked firmament with Cardinal Richelieu in a grotesque game of tag, now the pursued, now the pursuer, like a dog and cat in a jerky animated cartoon.

Ridiculous? The only faith of Marlowe and Webster was that the grinning skull was less ridiculous than the jeweled crown that it wore askew. But can naught be funnier than zero?

16

BRIAN'S JOURNAL

DECEMBER 7, 1942. I am a bit shamefaced to enter in this journal, on the first anniversary of Pearl Harbor, that I am happier than ever before in my life, but I am beginning to understand that happiness is a state of which God approves. A man who has attained spiritual union with him could be happy in the Roman arena; indeed, we read of saints who were. Dr. Prescott used to quote Phillips Brooks who, when asked if he was happy, would reply: "Yes, perfectly." Well, I have not achieved any such state of grace, but I think I can safely say I have attained peace of mind. I believe that I am doing what I ought to be doing and that if I live and graduate I will be ordained in the spring of 1945.

I would go every weekend to visit Dr. Prescott, to whom 1 owe it all, if he would allow me, but he says that it is unpatriotic to take up train space. Actually, the train to New Paisley is never full, and what he really wants is to have me learn to stand on my own feet. He realizes the effect of his personality on mine. There are those who say that his continued presence so near the school is evidence that he doesn't realize its effect on Mr. Moore's, but they are wrong. There is no such effect. Duncan Moore is totally independent of Dr. Prescott, and Dr. Prescott is well aware of it.

Which does not, of course, mean that Dr. Prescott likes it. That is another story.

Last weekend he let me come to Justin because he was preaching in chapel. I arrived at the start of morning service and slipped into a back pew as the choir was passing down the aisle singing "Ten Thousand Times Ten Thousand," followed by the two headmasters, acting and emeritus, Moore towering over his predecessor, his firm bass voice clearly distinguishable above the sopranos and tenors, and Dr. Prescott, very grave and majestic, his lips moving but emitting no audible note, his eyes fixed on the great altar window of St. Justin before Rusticus. For all Moore's height and noisiness he might have been a schoolboy walking beside his principal.

Divinity school has made me more aware of Dr. Prescott as a clergyman. Mr. Griscam told me once, in his half denigrating way, that as long as the headmaster had to be a minister only an hour a week, his conscience required him to put on a good show for at least those sixty minutes. There was a small degree of truth in this, for Dr. Prescott at times felt guilty, not at having no parish duties (for, obviously, he had no time for them), but at never having wanted them. His principal reason, however, for giving so much care and devotion to the chapel service was that he regarded it as the keystone of his educational plan. God might indeed be everywhere, but he was particularly in chapel when masters and boys worshiped together.

As Mr. Havistock had once pointed out, there might have been a touch of the theatrical in Dr. Prescott's one-time practice of reciting the service by heart, but I think almost everyone agrees that he is a great preacher. Mood follows rapidly upon mood; pathos, humor; the rich, resonant tones soar into serenity and dip into raking sarcasm. He can be funny; he can be awesome; he can be sublime. Only the envious could begrudge him the pleasure that it so obviously gives him. It is the pleasure, after all, of a great artist.

That morning he took his text from the parable of the laborers in the vineyard, and he described amusingly the natural exasperation of those who had borne the heat and burden of the day only to receive the same wage as the Johnny-come-latelies of the afternoon. But then suddenly the note of levity fell away; a pucker appeared in his brow and the tone deepened.

"What then in all seriousness, my boys, should be our attitude to the blessed of this earth? To those who have better looks, better bank accounts, better health? Or even better character, or better faith in God? Should we not pray (and this can be hard!) that they may be as happy as they *seem*? And should we not confess to ourselves that the ease of their circumstances does not necessarily mean that God loves them less? Indeed, he may love them more. For the blessed of this earth can be very lovable indeed. And none of us is a Christian until he has accepted the parable of the laborer in the vineyard. Until he is willing to share the kingdom of God equally with those who have toiled but a fraction of his working day. Until he has recognized that it would not be the kingdom of God if there were any differences in it."

After chapel, as I was greeting Dr. Prescott on the steps, Mr. Moore came up to ask me very cordially to lunch at the head table. To my surprise Dr. Prescott intervened impatiently.

"No, no, Duncan, I'm taking him to lunch at my house. I want to find out how he's doing at school."

"Perhaps then you will both come over afterwards?"

"He has to get back to Cambridge. I'm going to put him on an early train."

I had known nothing about either lunch or my train, but obviously my role was silence. It occurred to me that Dr. Prescott was treating his successor with much the same testiness that he had used to show Mr. Griscam. Was it the treatment that he meted out to those who disputed his absolute control of Justin? Feeling sorry for a headmaster who had to operate under such a handicap, I felt impelled to observe, when we had left Mr. Moore: "Everyone tells me he's doing a splendid job."

Dr. Prescott stopped short and plunged his walking stick into the earth. "Are you trying to bait me, Aspinwall?"

"No, sir!"

"Well, you're behaving as if you were. Every Tom, Dick and Harry makes a point of seeking me out to tell me what a great job Moore's doing. They want to see if the old lion can still roar. They're trying to goad me into breaking the sacred rule that condemns the retired to silence."

"Surely, sir, you can't think that of *me?*"

He gave me a sharp, hard look, pulled up his stick, grunted and continued his way across the grass. "Well, I grant that you've always seemed a particularly fulsome admirer of mine. Keep it up, my boy, keep it up. If it's not sincere, tell me it is. The old live on flattery, you know."

Happily I knew him well enough now to discount some of the seeming malevolence of his mood. "Wherein has Moore been so deficient?" I asked as I caught up with him.

He stopped again abruptly and once more stuck his walking stick in the ground. "Have you noticed how the boys go into the dining room? Always in my day they were dismissed by forms from assembly and passed to their places at table in a double line. Now they all push in together in a crush that jams up in the doorway like a New Year's Eve crowd in Times Square!"

I was too surprised for a minute to say anything. Was this the man who twenty minutes before had transported me to a vineyard in Palestine, who had given me fresh insight into what could be accomplished from the pulpit? Could one descend from so spiritual a sublime to so earthy a ridiculous?

"I suppose they still manage to get into the dining room," I said wonderingly.

"Of course they get *in*. But does appearance mean nothing to you? When you've been a schoolteacher as long as I have you'll know that appearances are three-quarters of the battle." He pulled his stick up. "No, nine-tenths!"

"I am surprised to hear it from one so steeped in fundamentals."

"Oh, I know, you think I'm an old fusspot," he muttered crossly as he walked on. "But that's just because I happen to *be* old. If I were twenty years younger and said the same thing, people would say I was profound. That's the hell of old age. You'll find out, Brian!"

"I doubt it, sir. With my heart I shall not make old bones."

He gave me a swift appraising glance. "You seem very accepting."

"Oh, but I am. I don't mind at all. I shall probably have much more time than I need to make the small contribution that I'm likely to make."

We talked now of more cheerful things, of the beautiful clear winter weather and the prospect of snow. I had spoken designedly of my heart because I had wanted to interrupt his own inclinations to self-pity. We went to the little cottage that he had rented and ate Mrs. Midge's good roast beef. He lives very simply, waited on by his devoted housekeeper and one maid. I have heard that Mrs. Prescott's trust went to the daughters on her death and that he has refused any contribution from them. But he has no interest in worldly things. All he wants is a seat from which to watch the continuation of his school. I am only sorry that he watches it quite so closely.

April 6, 1943. The Dean preached at Justin this morning, and knowing that I always like to go back to the school he very kindly asked me to drive over and back with him. I was surprised not to see Dr. Prescott in chapel, but Mr. Moore explained at lunch that he had a slight cold and had been told to stay in.

"Go see him if you have a minute," he admonished me, as if such a visit were a charity and not a privilege. "He's all cut up about the news we got yesterday of Martin Day. You remember Martin, don't you? He was senior prefect in '37. Shot down in the Pacific. A wonderful boy. But tragedy's all we hear these days, isn't it?"

The Dean said he would not be leaving for Cambridge for an hour, and as soon as the meal was over I hurried to Dr. Prescott's house. I found him alone in the living room by a fire, very morose and rather remote, but obviously glad to have someone to talk to. I sat in the chair opposite and occasionally poked the fire, allowing him to ramble on at will about Martin Day.

"He was the kind of boy you couldn't fault, Brian. Straight as they come, hardworking, hard-playing, devoted to a widowed mother, the inspiration of younger brothers and sisters. Yet he seemed to look at life with an impassive resignation, a kind of contained bitterness, as if he were saying: 'Oh, yes, I'll do my best; I'll even make it a good best, spit on me though you may.' He was the best senior prefect I ever had; he took infinite burdens off my shoulders—and yet, do you know, Brian? I never warmed to him as I should have. He was charmless. Totally charmless. Can you imagine a priest of God caring about such a trifle as charm?" In disgust he smashed his fist down on the table beside him and made the lamp and ashtrays jump. "Can you imagine a supposedly serious headmaster caring about a smile, a trick of expression, a way of joking? Yet *I* did. Charley Strong, whom you know all about, had extraordinary charm. But he was no finer than Martin Day. Less so. Oh, yes, less so." He sighed and shook his head regretfully. "And poor Day *wanted* my affection and knew he wasn't getting it, and he accepted this just as he accepted everything else. Just as I'm sure he accepted that last horrible dive into the blue of the Pacific!"

"Oh, come, sir," I interrupted at last. "Surely you're making things worse than they are. I was with you once when Day joined us for a walk, down on a visit from Harvard. You were exceedingly nice to him. I remember it distinctly."

"If I was, it was because I was making up for what I didn't feel. A man who sets himself up to be a headmaster should distribute his affections equally."

"You mean he should *appear* to," I corrected him. "Even our Lord preferred John to the other disciples."

He gave me a testy stare. "Will you tell me why you are always so bent on excusing me, Brian?" he demanded. "Is it because of that work of hagiography on which you are embarked? Do you object to my departing an inch from the role of saint to which you have so ruthlessly condemned me?"

I remembered how he had torn into Mr. Griscam for his proposed biography and could only suppose that it was my turn now. He had never before mentioned my habit of making notes about him, but I had known, of course, that he must be aware of it. Cordelia, if no one else, would have told him.

"I wouldn't really call it a work of anything," I answered humbly. "It is true that I collect stories about you. Would you care to see what I've got? I'll burn them all if you wish."

I had not expected that so little oil would settle such troubled waters. Dr. Prescott looked suddenly almost sheepish. "No, no, dear boy, you're very welcome to what you've got. If anyone is going to 'collect' me, I had as soon it be you." He looked again into the fire for several silent moments. "As a matter of fact I have a prize bit of 'Prescottiana' for you that I was looking over this morning. When one is past eighty one doesn't wish to have papers in one's possession that one would not be willing to have anyone see in case of a sudden demise. This document must decidedly be either burned or placed in trusted hands. Would you take it subject to two conditions?"

"What would they be?"

"To be sure that David Griscam never sees it. It was written by his son, Jules, who died twenty years ago, and it would pain him."

"I promise."

"Wait. That's not all. You will also promise me that if you ever publish anything about me, you will incorporate the gist of this document. Of course, you need mention no names."

I hesitated. "May I ask why?"

"Because it is the record of my greatest failure. That's why I got it out yesterday when the news came about Martin Day. Martin was not so great a failure of mine as Jules. The Japs killed Martin, but I killed Jules. Or, not to be melodramatic, I sent him down the path that ended in his death."

It was my turn now to stare into the dying fire as I debated my next remark. "I thought he committed suicide."

"I have always dreaded to think so, for if it was suicide, it was also murder. Jules' car, a Bugatti sports model, left the highway between Nice and Cannes and crashed into a rock pile. It was traveling at eighty miles an hour, and Jules, as usual, had been drinking. But Jules was not the only person killed. There was a girl in the car. Why should he have made that poor little Riviera tart pay the price of his own mad follies?"

"Maybe she wanted to die with him."

"And maybe somebody has a taste for cheap cinema," Dr. Prescott retorted crisply. "Two months before his death he sent me—out of the blue, for we hadn't met in three years—an extraordinary document. So far as I know, nobody but myself has ever seen it—except, of course, the French psychoanalyst for whom it was apparently written. He must have been trying to get Jules to exorcise me by writing me up. I have heard of such therapies. One dredges up the old guilty incidents and reduces them to impotence by simple articulation. I suppose Jules was so proud of the finished composition that he wanted to show it to his old headmaster." His smile was very wry. "Or maybe he just wanted revenge."

"Did he get it?"

"He got it when he died."

He rose and went slowly to his desk from which he took a thick pile of white papers held together by a rubber band. When he handed it to me I saw that the top page bore the letterhead Hotel du Parc and was closely covered by a thin, spidery handwriting.

"You accept my conditions?" he pursued.

Again I hesitated. But, after all, I had only not to publish. "Without reservation."

"Then it's yours. Along with whatever you got from poor old Horace Havistock. He died, you know."

"Oh, no, I—didn't."

"Yes. Two weeks ago." He nodded gloomily. "High time, too. His mind was going. And I believe David Griscam gave you something?"

"He did."

"We're always in David's debt, aren't we?" He continued to nod, but more in distraction now. "It's amazing how many people are and how much they mind it. Yet David doesn't rattle the keys of his prison. I have never figured out if he has deserved much more of life or if he has got all that he had coming to him. But tell me, Brian. You think you'll stick it now? You think you'll be ordained?"

"God willing, sir."

"Good boy." He put a hand on my shoulder. "I'm sure of it. Work hard, and don't come back here. I may go to Florida, anyway, next winter. The point is that I don't want you to see me. Or rather I don't want you to see what I'm turning into. I hate old age, and I'm becoming a nasty, cantankerous old man. No, I mean it! I'm put off by the merest trifles. I can still see that they're trifles, but the time may be coming when I won't. I want you to remember me as I was."

"But, sir," I pleaded, "don't you see that I need you?"

"I do not," he said firmly. "I see that you're on the verge of becoming a man and that you must go the rest of the way alone. There, isn't that the Dean's car calling for you now?"

I tried to console myself on the ride back to Cambridge with the thought that he did not really mean his interdict, and I was mortified to discover that the weight of the unread manuscript in my lap helped to soften my depression. Is it possible that the acquisitiveness of the collector has reached such a pitch in me that I would rather have the relic than the saint? It has happened before to those who have tried too hard to persuade themselves that they are divinely inspired. Help me, dear Lord, to be moderate.

17

JULES GRISCAM'S MEMOIR

WHEN FATHER NAMED me Jules, after my grandfather Griscam, the black sheep whose evil doings had blotted our escutcheon, he must have felt that he could close the books at last on the dreary tale of the performance of his filial duties. I suppose he had reason to pride himself on having been a good son, but there was no reason for his being so tiresome about it. If I heard the story of those paid debts once, I must have heard it a hundred times! I naturally felt sorry for poor old Grandpa Griscam, whose magnificently delinquent obligations should have been so ignominiously satisfied, and modeled myself from boyhood on a romantic misconception of him. For all the mess I have since made of things I am still glad that I did not do as my brother Sylvester. He modeled himself on Grandpa Prime and became a prize stuffed shirt.

I have never been in the least congenial with Father. Our philosophies, if either can really be said to have one, are at opposite poles. Yet I will admit that he is a hard man to dislike steadily. He is so damnably reasonable. He has an infinite faith that there is no problem in the world that can't be solved by sitting down and talking it out. Oh, those talks! He would have talked the heart out of Keats and the sublime gaiety out of Mozart.

Some basic instinct of self-preservation always made me resist him, as country dwellers resist the intrusion of signposts and hot dog stands into the beauty of the landscape. It is true that he professed to care about art and beauty, but if they ever got through to him at all, it could have been only by the written word. He had no real response to his physical surroundings, in painting or sculpture or even in natural scenery (though he did keep a bird list) and in music he was deaf to all but the noisiest Verdi choruses. Indeed, his worst danger as a Philistine consisted in his efforts not to be one. He was so determined that culture, like calisthenics and tennis lessons, should have its proper place in our lives. The epicurean had to keep step with the puritan down the long aisle to the altar of the well-adjusted God.

But what Father could never comprehend and what ultimately destroyed his system was that if you put things in pairs, the cruder twin is bound to predominate. I think that he and Mother must have had a subconscious belief that it was all right to be grand if you were uncomfortable, all right to be social if your parties were dull, all right to be extravagant if you bought the second-best. And so we lived in large, drafty stone houses, filled with dubious period furniture, and did a great deal of pointless entertaining of ostensibly "important" citizens.

The fear that we children would be spoiled was a constant obsession. Sylvester and I slept in a cold gymnasium on top of the city house, and in Northeast Harbor summers, while all our friends were sailing or playing tennis, we had to work on Father's mainland farm, purchased for the sole purpose of keeping us occupied. Amy, even in her coming-out year, could not dance after midnight on Saturday because Father, an agnostic, saw fit to borrow from the church its disciplines if not its consolations. Similarly, although an active opponent of the Eighteenth Amendment, he welcomed the excuse of its passage to ban all liquor from the house.

As a family we were un-American to the extent that Father ruled the roost. There was no aspect of our education too trivial for his interminable planning. Mother accepted it all passively, not because she was weak but because she was not interested. She was a terrible disappointment to me, for she would not even pretend to need my passionately professed championship. She was beautiful (or so I thought), stately, remote and lame, the perfect combination for a fanciful boy who wanted to be a knight-errant to a princess in distress. On the rare occasions when Father was unable to control his temper, and it exploded at Mother with a force all the greater for its long suppression, how gladly would I have leaped to her defense had I thought she was in the least affected by the ranting little man at the end of the table!

But Mother needed nobody's help; she had her causes: woman suffrage, birth control, the Army of the Holy Word, and she knew that in the period of abject apology that inevitably followed Father's outbursts she would be offered a large and useful check for her current favorite. She loved humanity, but she looked with a misty, faintly bored benignity towards its individual specimens, even when that specimen happened to be her oldest son. Father was officious and irritating, but at least he cared.

The romance of his life—and this may explain some of Mother's domestic apathy—was Dr. Prescott. I am not well enough versed in the new theories of Freud to be able to determine how much of this attraction was sexual; all I know is that his worship of the headmaster was of a jealous, proprietary kind and that it provided him with the only emotional excitement and quickening of the heart that I suspect his dry nature was ever to know. At least, I am sure he did not find such things with his wife and children. I imagine that in his subconscious he must have played at every possible relationship with Prescott: as son, as brother, as lover, as wife. We children naturally resented Father's hero, not only for the affection lavished upon him at what we felt was our own expense, but for the smallness of its return.

For it was obvious that however indebted Prescott was to Father, however even fond of him he might be, Father was still not a "man" as Prescott conceived of one. Sylvester and I as boys in Northeast Harbor, on the great man's summer visits, shifting restlessly under his deep brown stare and whimsical, rhetorical questions (he was uneasy with children, for like a dictator visiting a free country, he knew that his power was suspended), brooded with a dark foreboding of the great disciplinary factory to which our infatuated father had irrevocably destined us. Dr. Prescott had only to bide his hour, and we would be his.

Nor was there anything about Justin Martyr, when the hour came, to falsify my apprehension. A handy case of tonsilitis delayed my going for one year, and jaundice for another, cutting my prison term from six to four, but in the fall of 1918 I was duly entered as a third former, and my long duel with Dr. Prescott began. To an egotist of fourteen the mighty events across the Atlantic hardly existed. The holocaust that was ending in Europe was dwarfed by the difficulties of adjusting to the school hierarchy. I was the only "new kid" in my form and ranked socially with those in the two below. What was the agony of the trenches, sublimated as it must have been, according to my wishfully thinking mother, by the wonderful comradeship engendered by shared dangers, to one of my Byronic pride who had to endure alone the indignities of hazing? The ultimate humiliation was my family's assumption that I was homesick. There was surely a difference between homesickness, to which morbid malady I was always a stranger, and a natural, healthy detestation of Justin Martyr!

My first important discovery was that Dr. Prescott was a master and my father a mere amateur in the great nineteenth century art of making life uncomfortable. "Fun" was defined in terms of group activity, such as football or singing or even praying; the devil lay in wait for the boy alone, or worse, for two boys alone. The headmaster believed that adolescence should be passed in an organized crowd, that authority should never avert its eyes unless the boys were engaged in fighting or hazing or some other activity savage enough to be classified as "manly." Life beyond the campus was universally suspect: the drugstores, with their sodas and lurid magazines, the slatternly country girls, the very woods and streams that encouraged boys to take long walks and wax sentimental about nature and perhaps each other.

Where Prescott excelled above all was in his intuition as to where temptation lay. As a young man and an Oxford dandy, he had strolled by the Thames reading Baudelaire and Rossetti. He was widely, and I think justly, reputed to have a perfect ear for music and a fine tongue for wine, and he could actually speak Greek and Latin. Had it not been for the perverted violence of his puritan conscience, he might have been a great artist or at least a great voluptuary. But he had crushed the joy in his own nature, and so far as he could, in those of others, pleading with his angry God to help him, his hands tightly clasped, his eyes squeezed tightly shut, waiting as much as thirty seconds between the prayer that he recited at the end of chapel, and his own thundering "Amen," knowing, the old ham, that the congregation was reverently watching his silent communion. He would have been a glorious repertory actor of the Henry Irving school, playing Iago one night and Tamburlaine the next.

Yet he got away with it. My own father is proof of that. If you want to be taken seriously in this life, you must start by taking yourself seriously. Prescott was surrounded with an atmosphere of almost incredible awe, to which the parents, trustees and faculty all contributed. I do not think that many of the boys liked him, but they respected and feared him, which was much more fun, both for them and for him. At least a quarter of the student body, like myself, were sons of graduates and had grown up in his legend. They were proud of his fame, excited by the rumble of his leadership and diverted by his wit, his inconsistencies, even by his sermons. As I have said, he was basically a ham actor, and the school was a captured but still admiring audience.

I got off to an immediately bad start with everybody by resisting the hazing. The rules of hazing, like those of all activities not protected by law, were exact. One was meant to fight back, but not too hard. One had to resist just the right amount (immediate surrender would have been "flabby") and then submit, and then, after a fixed period, the hazing ceased. Violent resistance, like violent hazing, was bad form because it brought the masters into an unconstitutional area which by tacit consent had been left to the boys. But I failed to appreciate such delicacies. I fought like a cat with nails and teeth and was so badly beaten up that I had to spend two days in the infirmary. Dr. Prescott, who had hitherto ignored me—afraid, perhaps, that I would presume on his friendship with Father—came to see me and was gruffly sympathetic, but I suspect that he had already spotted me as one of those who would never fit in. Had I deliberately incited my formmates to mayhem to give his school a bad reputation? Perhaps Father had warned him that I was capable of it.

The hazing came ultimately to an end, burnt out by its very intensity, and I found myself suddenly and blessedly left alone, ignored now by boys who believed that the silent treatment was the hardest of all to endure. They did not comprehend that they had left me a New England sky and ultimately a New England spring, a library with all the poetry I could want, woods to hike in and occasionally another maverick to befriend. It was thus that I came to know Chanler Winslow, a strange, blond, lazy, quiet boy who, although handsome and athletically competent, was shunned by the others as "crazy." Chanler was very slow and had abominable grades; he was surly and unsociable, and he had a murderous temper that, unlike my own, was widely feared. He would not, for example, have hesitated to use a knife if attacked. He liked me because I asked nothing of him and because we shared a passion for the out-of-doors.

It was still the era when boys were allowed to have huts in the woods, and there were a number of these along the Lawrence River, two miles from the school, made of timber and old shingles and used on Sunday afternoons and holidays. The privilege dated from one of Dr. Prescott's rare sabbatical leaves in the tenure of an indulgent substitute, and it was known that the headmaster was waiting for the first infringement of his many regulations of the huts to abolish them. For what were they but a challenge to his theory of moral protection in crowded living, a defiant community of independent Thoreaus camped on the very border of his village of robots? Chanler and I built the biggest hut of all and furnished it with an old rug and some wicker chairs purchased from a local junk shop. Had we been allowed to keep it I think I might have finished my career at Justin Martyr without ignominy.

For the hut was helping me to become a man by absorbing and dignifying my resentment of the school. When Chanler and I sat on the banks of the turgid Lawrence, chewing grass and watching the kingfishers plunge for their prey, or when we fished ourselves or climbed trees looking for eggs, or even when we lay on our backs and watched the clouds and the triangles of ducks and geese, far from the nervous atmosphere of ringing bells and hurrying feet, I could pity rather than despise the old man who thought that boys went to the woods only to smoke or drink or masturbate.

But that old man and I were not to be allowed to pass each other like ships in the night. An officious young master, the kind of twisted sadist that is the bane of secondary school education, hoping to curry favor with the Rector, spent a week-day afternoon searching the empty huts and discovered three cigarette butts. It was flimsy evidence of illicit smoking, for there were always tramps in the neighborhood, but Dr. Prescott had waited a long time, and he must have decided that it was as good as he was likely to get. The next morning at roll call he announced that the huts were to be dismantled before the end of the week.

For the first and last time in my life I tried honestly to reason with him. That night after supper I asked for an interview and was told to go to his study at nine. When I knocked at the appointed hour and heard his deep, weary "Come in, boy," and, coming in, saw him leaning over the great square desk so that the one burning light illuminated his broad gleaming forehead and rich crop of gray hair, I knew that the stage had been set on which only his victories could be played. Was it a coincidence that the corners of the room and the big busts of the Roman emperors in the surrounding book cases were shrouded in darkness, so that Prescott was the center of what dim light there was? Was it chance that the stillness was in such dramatic contrast to the noises of the school? Was it unintentional that the few objects on that expanse of mahogany surface should have been of heavy gold: a cross, a fish, a miter and a paperweight that was a crude replica of Trinity Church in Boston?

I told him, as he gravely listened, that I thought it unjust that all the huts should have to pay for the sin, if sin it was, of one. I insisted that our activities had been innocent. I protested that even my father encouraged us to stay out-of-doors.

"Out-of-doors, exactly," Dr. Prescott interrupted with a whimsical smile. "I am not interfering with the out-of-doors. In fact, by removing the roof of your hut I am removing a bar between you and heaven."

I returned at this to the safer ground of the injustice of making many pay the fault of one.

"But, my dear boy, that is exactly the injustice of life," he pointed out. "All the German people are now paying for the fault of the Kaiser and his advisers. All members of a football team are penalized if one is offside. But more fundamentally—yes, Jules, much more fundamentally—we all share in original sin. And why not? Why should we pay only for our own little crimes? Isn't there something petty and avaricious in such a plea?" Here Dr. Prescott looked up and seemingly through me, in the pose of one alone, struggling with his despised mortality. "Why should another man be hanged for a murder that *I* was never tempted to commit? Is it anything but coincidence that I am not a thief? Or a perjurer? I sometimes think it would be impossible for any of us to suffer injustice. That our greatest blessing lies in the sins we have *not* been led to commit."

"But, surely, sir, you would not walk into the schoolroom and give a black mark to the first boy you saw on the ground that he might smoke if he had the opportunity!"

Dr. Prescott smiled, and his smile, I admit, was charming. "No. But I might remove the opportunity. And that is why the huts must go."

"You mean Winslow and I must really tear down our hut? Ourselves?"

The smile faded, and the brown eyes searched me gravely. He had taken in my note of desperation, and he knew that he could either allow me a dignified retreat or provoke me to a stand that would involve my expulsion from the school. Did he wish to lance the ulcer that I represented? Or let it naturally disappear? His eyes became for a moment quizzical, and then he glanced away.

"I understand, Jules, that you and Winslow have exercised much industry and imagination in the adornment of your hut. I appreciate that it would be distressing for you to carry out the work of demolition personally. I am not, whatever you boys may think, totally devoid of delicate feeling. I will make arrangements for your hut to be taken down by others. Good night, Jules. Please remember me to your parents when next you write. They are well, I trust?"

"Perfectly well, sir."

It was not until I was out of his study that I realized how cleverly I had been handled. By accepting my complaint about the method of demolition, he had obliged me to accept its fact. It was a formidable matter for a schoolboy to be up against a diplomat as well as a general.

In the year that followed this incident I brooded much over my wrongs, but my overt resistance was confined to sniping in sacred studies class. This was Dr. Prescott's one vulnerable period, for if there was anything sincere in his vaudeville nature it was his belief in his mission to persuade boys to join the company of Jesus Christ. He would, no doubt, have liked to have ordered them to sign up and to have damned the recalcitrant, but he knew that his God was as mean as himself and would never let him get away with anything as easy as that. He could order a boy to play football or to take a cold shower or to destroy a hut, but he could not order a boy to love God. This was a matter of propaganda, and sacred studies was its allotted time. He and I would have dialogues in class such as the following:

"Please, sir, we always seem to take for granted that monotheism is superior to polytheism. But is it so? Why should it not be just as good to have many gods as to have one?"

"That is a good question, Griscam. I'm glad you asked it. It seems to me that a faith diffused in many gods must lose much of its efficacy. Which one, for example, do you pray to? And after you have chosen, can you be sure that your god will not be thwarted by the jealousy of another god? That is why, in great cultures that have practiced polytheism, like the Roman and Greek, there is always a high degree of fatalism. The believing man tends to regard himself as a mere plaything of gods absorbed in their own internecine conflicts. There is nothing like the magnificent strength and consolation of knowing that there is *one* God, here and everywhere, in you and in every particle of nature."

"That may be, sir. But the fact that it might be nicer if there were only one God doesn't mean that there is, does it?"

There was an ominous blink of those brown eyes, a twitch of those shaggy eyebrows. The word "nicer" had been a dangerous touch. "Of course, it doesn't, Griscam. That is a matter of faith. And in this school, which is a church school, we are dedicated to the sustenance of that faith. We hope that every graduate will know the joy of believing, but it is only a hope."

In church history I was always ready with questions about the mercenary motives of the Crusades, the jealous destruction of pagan literature by priests, the burning of heretics, the religious wars. Dr. Prescott would shake his head heavily and agree that terrible things had been done in the sign of the cross, but when I suggested that we at Justin Martyr could avoid the guilt of these associations by dating our religion from the ordainment of Phillips Brooks, whom he was always quoting, I had finally gone too far.

"You are not sincere, Griscam," he told me wrathfully after class. "You are making mock of sacred things. Doubt I allow. Intellectual curiosity I encourage. But there is no place in this classroom for cheap cynicism."

"But I only want to learn, sir," I protested in a tone so earnest that I almost convinced myself. "I only want to be sure that the church has not done more harm than good. How can I be confirmed until I have answered that question?"

"I am sorry to say that I doubt you."

"Oh, sir, I mean it!"

"If you do, then I have made an error to speak to you so. Perhaps a grave one." He sighed heavily. "But I make them. Oh, yes, I make them. You will be excused from sacred studies for the rest of the term, Griscam. You may spend that hour with extra lines of Virgil. We may as well derive *some* benefit from your preference for the pagan authors."

Once again I was worsted by the old charlatan, but this time with more dramatic consequences. It was apparently unique in school history for a boy to be suspended from sacred studies, and I was made to feel like a Lutheran priest imprisoned in the somber courtyards of the Escorial. The absorbent powers of the school were strong and could in time embrace most mavericks, but there were limits to the permissible period of dissent, and Chanler

Winslow and I had let ours expire. We came to be permanently regarded as "outsiders," and my only answer (for Chanler was far too inert and indifferent to have one) was to win an occasional recruit to our isolated fraternity.

The picking was not good. By fifth form year our group consisted of only two besides Chanler and myself: Gus Crane, a snippety, effeminate, crabby old maid of a boy who had at last given up a fawning cultivation of the form leaders, and Sandy McKim, a small, dull, gentle, inarticulate lad who worshiped Chanler because the latter, traditional for once, had pulled him out of the Lawrence on a school holiday when his canoe had capsized. They all followed my lead, not because of the strength of my personality but because I alone had the will and imagination to clothe our mere unpopularity in the robes of a creed.

For I gloried in standing for art and the individual against football and the mass. I did not realize that my revolt was as hackneyed as the conformity of the majority. I had not then read the dreary heap of English and American fiction that deals with unhappy boyhoods. I thought my independence wonderfully unique, my hate fresh and pure. When I walked by the river on glorious October Saturday afternoons, I reveled less in the golden brown of the foliage and in the cold melancholy of the fall breeze than in the smug knowledge that I was *not* attending the football game and that I would attend none for the entire season, not even the final one with Chelton that marked the climax of the athletic year, the great patriotic event of the school calendar. I realized my project, but the sixth form decided that I should be "pumped."

Pumping was a penalty that fell in a semi-official zone between the boys and faculty. It was given for "bad school spirit," a crime that subjected the offender to no official penalty, but that was particularly odious to the headmaster. On a pumping day the whole school was assembled for roll call by the senior prefect, and no master was present. The sixth form stood about, their arms tightly folded, glaring at us and frowning. "Wipe it off, Jones!" one of them would bark if Jones dared, in his tension, to let his lip crease into a nervous smile. It was well done, on the whole. It was a bit of a nightmare even to me. But on the terrible day of my ordeal I was borne up by the ecstasy of my passionate sense of wrong and the idea that, like the Count of Monte Cristo, I might have a lifetime for my revenge.

I had decided in advance how I would act. When the senior prefect shouted: "Griscam, go to the cellar! On the double!" I would not jump up like a scared rabbit and scamper from the room followed by a line of six executioners, ponderously, ridiculously, pacing in step. This would be no Mexican sacrificial ballet with a cooperating victim, decked in flowers, swaying up the steps of the altar to bare his throat to the obsidian knife. No, if they wanted me, they could come and get me.

When I heard, through the haze of my brave resolution, as if from another, meaner world, the rasp of my name and the well-known order, I simply folded my arms, in mocking parody of the sixth formers, and remained at my desk. They had to come and lift me and carry me out, and when in retaliation they nearly drowned me, ducking me in the big sink of the laundry below, as I gasped for my breath, I made myself remember the laughter that had broken out in the schoolroom over my act, the laughter that could blow away the sixth form like chaff.

They had at last gone too far. The old man had gone too far. There was a deep reaction in my favor, and in the days that followed I felt surrounded by nods of sympathy. Never again was it suggested that I attend an athletic event. If I had lost one hut, I had gained another, built with the bricks of rebellion on the very grass of the campus, and I was to be allowed to occupy it thenceforth unmolested. The sixth form and the faculty might surround it by a *cordon sanitaire*, but they would not again try to level it.

My own sixth form year, when it came, was something of a triumph. I made independence almost the fashion. By submitting a poem which had been rejected by the *Justinian* to Frank Crowninshield and having it published in *Vanity Fair* I won a glory that even Dr. Prescott could not ignore.

"You have put us on the map, Griscam," he told me gruffly one morning after chapel. "There may be a question in some minds if that is where we wish to be, but nobody can belittle the feat of getting us there."

So it seemed that my school career might be ending on an actually pleasant note, that my long duel with the headmaster might conclude in the banality of exchanged salutes. And so it might have had I not, by the simple act of turning a small piece of metal in a three hundred and sixty degree arc, brought about a series of catastrophic events that were to shake the school to its very foundations. Nothing could illustrate more graphically the shifting sands on which the whole absurd structure had been jerry-built than the fact that my act was the simple physical one just described, that it hurt nobody and that it had not been designed to hurt anybody. But Prescott, like all the great idiots of history, was always willing to burn the world for a toy, a prayer, a cross, a thimble.

18

JULES GRISCAM'S MEMOIR

IT HAPPENED, LIKE all bad things at school, at the end of the winter term. Spring was coy that year, and the cold season had a long and fretful death. We blotted out the days, one by one, with elaborate inkings on the calendars in our sixth form studies and talked interminably of girls and Easter dances. And beyond the lagging spring loomed graduation and the unbelievable prospect of liberty. The once formidable school was shrinking around us to the dimensions of a small provincial village, as quaint as Cranford, and poor boys on scholarships, who had once scorned me as a nonconformist, began to show unlovable signs of awakening to the values of a world beyond the campus where the friendship of families like mine might count more than the silver plate trophies of the athletic field. Only the figure of Dr. Prescott remained the same, and it may have been his failure to fade, along with an institution that was proving less durable than himself, into the backyard of discarded childhood things that made me try to push him there.

One morning after classes, just before the bell announcing the roll call that preceded lunch, I was standing with Chanler Winslow, Gus Crane and Sandy McKim in the Audubon Corridor by the main schoolroom where all the forms were about to assemble. The headmaster's study, from which he would shortly emerge, after the bell had ceased ringing, to proceed to the schoolroom for the midday announcements, was just adjacent, and the door was closed. I happened to notice that the key was in the lock. The study was never locked from the inside, only from the out when it was unoccupied.

"Do you know what would be fun?"

The other three glanced at me curiously, for my tone had been sharp. I suddenly remembered the windmill on Granny Prime's place in Long Island. It had a shaky wooden ladder leading up to the platform under the vanes, and Sylvester used to dare me to climb it. I always did, hating it, because anything was better than to be afraid.

"What would be fun?" Gus demanded suspiciously.

"To turn the key and lock the old bastard in!"

Three pair of eyes followed mine to the door, and in a sudden tense exchange of looks, I understood that my friends had seized the feasability of the project. There must have been forty boys moving up and down the corridor, talking or reading their mail which had just been distributed. Detection would be almost impossible.

"Shall I?" I asked.

It was the terrible moment of the first rung in the windmill ladder. I read assent in their eyes, even in Gus's, and I walked quickly past Prescott's door, pausing just long enough to turn the key and pull it out. In three steps I was back, smiling at the horror in Gus's eyes as they took in that key.

"Jesus God!" he whispered. "Put it back, you fool!"

"Put it back?" I sneered. "When all I need do is this?" I rubbed it quickly with my handkerchief and dropped it out the open window. "Now move on, all of you. Move quietly. Be natural."

Twenty seconds later the bell for assembly shrieked through the building, and we walked to our places on the back benches for the upper school behind the desks of the lower. Mr. Coogan, the master in charge, stood on the dais until all were seated and then nodded to the prefect at the door who took his hand from the bell. He then turned to the other door through which Dr. Prescott always emerged and waited.

He waited for a full minute. I stared at him, careful not to look to either side to catch the eyes of my friends. Then he scurried down the steps from the dais, crossed the floor to the hall and stood before the headmaster's door. We heard first the rap and then the sound of a knob being violently turned. "Are you all right, sir?" Mr. Coogan shouted, and we heard a muffled angry, indistinguishable sound from the other side of the door. "Did you say it was locked, sir?" Coogan inquired. "No, there is no key on this side. Are you sure it's not on the floor in there, sir?" There was another incoherent rumbling from behind the door, implying both a negative and an angry reproach for the question. "Shall I get a ladder to the window?" The answer to this put Mr. Coogan in a real flurry, for he hurried off, and a little group of masters began to gather about the door, until they, too, were dispersed by another muffled roar.

At last Mr. Ives, the senior master, appeared. He ignored the commotion about the headmaster's door, sauntered to the schoolroom dais, read out the announcements with his usual imperturbability and dismissed the school to Lawrence House for lunch. As I looked back across the campus ten minutes later I saw a ladder by the headmaster's window supported by a group of prefects with heads raised. Then I saw the large familiar figure, like a great beetle, move slowly out the window and slowly down. When Gus Crane poked me, I gave him an aloof stare and passed before him into the washroom.

I had figured that no boy could have seen me except my comates, and I had figured correctly. But there was someone whom *I* had not seen. That amateur sleuth, Mr. Ives, a man who always looked at his watch if he heard an unusual sound to be prepared, if necessary, to testify in court as to the exact time of its occurrence, had left Dr. Prescott's study just four minutes before the assembly bell, closing the door behind him. He had observed— for he observed everything—the proximity of my group to the headmaster's threshold. At four o'clock that afternoon he had found the key under the window near which we had been standing. This, plus our bad reputation, was all he needed. We were summoned to Dr. Prescott's study after supper, where Ives, in his passionless, singsong tone, recited his findings and his deadly conclusion. One of us four must have done it.

Dr. Prescott glanced up from his brooding pose as his junior finished. We were standing in a row before his desk. "Which?" he asked, in a weary, seemingly bored tone.

We were silent. We exchanged no glances.

"Let me tell you something," he went on somberly. "You are sixth formers. As such you are officers of the school. You are, or should be, above the code of little boys who will not 'snitch.' To tell on a fellow officer who has tried publicly to humiliate his commander-in-chief is a simple duty. If that fellow officer is too cowardly to confess, seeking to implicate you in his contemptible conduct, why should you protect him? I ask you again: which did it? Was it you, Griscam?"

"No, sir."

"Was it one of you?"

"I couldn't say, sir."

"You couldn't or you wouldn't?"

"I couldn't, sir. I didn't see it."

He turned to Chanler. "And you, Winslow? Was it one of you?"

"I didn't see, sir."

"And you, McKim?"

"I didn't see, sir."

"And you, Crane?"

"I saw who did it, sir, but I don't think I should be asked to tell. It wasn't me."

How I despised Gus Crane! Until then the old man had evidence, good evidence, but no proof. We could have bluffed it out. But now!

"It wasn't 'I,'" the headmaster corrected him without a smile. "If you will not tell me who it was, you must share in his punishment."

"But that's most unfair, sir!"

"It would be, if you were not a sixth former." Prescott now stared slowly from one to the other of us. "Very well, gentlemen. I will give you twenty-four hours. If within that time one of you has not given me the name of the culprit, I shall not consider that any of you has the right to protest whatever penalty I may see fit to impose." He paused again, for he was a master of dramatic emphasis. "No matter how heavy that penalty may be. You are all excused from classes tomorrow morning. I wish you to have full time to reflect. Or to telephone your families for their advice."

It was a curious twenty-four hours that ensued. In the morning the four of us trudged through the mud to the river and sat on the crew dock, chewing grass and watching the sluggish, eddying Lawrence. Dirty patches of melting snow under the stark trees and the bleak sunlight emphasized the belt of void that surrounded the little shrill idealism of the marooned school. I had stepped to the perimeter and was ready and willing to fall into that void. So was Chanler, whose truculent defiance of the universe I tried to interpret as loyalty to myself. So was Sandy McKim, whose loyalty to Chanler was impervious to any test that a mere Prescott might impose. Only Gus showed any inclination to consider the value of what we might be turning our backs upon, and as the morning drew on he became strident and vindictive.

"Why should we all be punished for what you did, Jules?"

"We all did it," Chanler retorted. "We all agreed."

"I *never* agreed!" Gus spouted. "Jules said it would be fun, and before I knew what he was talking about, he went over and turned that key. Nobody could say it was my fault."

"Why don't you go and tell, then?" Chanler jeered. "Why don't you go to Dr. P, like a good little girl, and tell him what a naughty boy Jules was?"

"Because I don't want to be a snitcher, of course! Who wants to be a snitcher and have the whole school know? That's why Jules has got us so neatly on the spot. I'd be as infamous as Benedict Arnold. But why doesn't Jules confess? Why, if he's going to be kicked out anyway, does it do him any good to have the rest of us kicked out with him?"

"Because we're in this thing together," Sandy McKim answered unexpectedly. "We've been in everything together. If Jules confesses, I'll say we put him up to it."

I was touched, for I would not have anticipated such fineness of feeling from one as passive as Sandy. "Look," I pointed out. "Nobody's going to be kicked out. The old boy wouldn't dare. Four sixth formers, three months before graduation, because none of them would snitch? Think of it! The trustees, all the graduates would be up in arms. No, mark my words, the old boy's bluffing, and it's up to us to call his bluff. Besides, what a triumph!"

"But supposing he's not bluffing?" Gus insisted.

"Then if he's not, I can always confess. That much I promise. He certainly can't expel you after he has his culprit."

Gus had to be satisfied with this or shoulder the terrible onus of snitching, and he gloomily elected silence. He refused to speak any more to any of us, and when we filed into Dr. Prescott's study that night, he stood sullenly to the side. The headmaster looked grey and grim; his lips were a pale thin line. But his eyes were tired, and there was something faintly quizzical in their expression, as if he wondered where we had come from, four imps whose very existence seemed designed to plague him.

"Well, this is your last chance," he announced quietly. "Will one of you tell me now who turned that key?" There was a silence in which we all listened to Gus's panting. "Will you, Crane?" Gus caught his breath, and I clenched my fists. "No? I will count out a minute." He pulled out his thin gold watch, a gift, as I remembered, from my father, and waited while the second hand spun a circle. "Very well, gentlemen," he said in a voice now of infinite sadness, putting the watch away. "You have given me no recourse. You will proceed to your dormitories to pack your clothes. You will spend this night in the infirmary annex. I will telegraph your families to make arrangements for your departure tomorrow. For I must inform you that you are no longer members of our school community and that you will not graduate from Justin Martyr. That will be all, gentlemen."

So great was the lingering spell of his authority that I had dumbly followed the file of the other three to the door before I recollected what it was I had to do. Quickly I closed the door after them and returned to stand alone before the headmaster's desk.

"Of course you know it was I who did it."

There was no flicker of the lids over those great gravely staring brown eyes. "I had my suspicions, yes. What a grief this will be for your poor father."

"Shall I call the others back now?"

"What for?"

"So you can tell them they're not expelled."

"But they are." The rich voice had become metallic. "I see no cause for revision."

"You mean you'll make them pay for what *I've* done?"

"No. For what they have done. By their deliberate silence they have associated themselves with your deed. Now they may associate themselves with your punishment."

Had it not been for my despair I would have laughed aloud at such hypocrisy. As it was I uttered a kind of strangled groan. "Do you think I don't see through your game?"

"You forget yourself, Griscam."

"Forget myself! When have I seen myself more clearly? Or you, sir? Why it's as open as daylight. By rejecting my confession, you brand me for life as the boy who got his pals fired to save his own hide! Oh, it's beautiful. It's diabolic. To think that *I*, who thought I was so smart, should have heaped up my own faggots and handed you the torch!"

Dr. Prescott leaned back in his chair and folded his arms magisterially across his chest. He raised his eyes to the ceiling and did not shift his gaze for several seconds. He might have been seeking in that dirty plaster some hole through which his deity might vouchsafe him an explanation of my conduct. He was no longer angry or even reproachful. He pursed his lips as he looked back at me as though he and I together had a theological problem to unravel.

"Tell me, Jules," he said at last in a milder tone. "Why do you ascribe to me so violent an animosity? Why should I wish to apply a torch to your faggots, as you put it?"

"Because my will was stronger than yours! Because you asked those three to tell on me, and I asked them not to! And they obeyed *me*, at the cost of being expelled."

In my exultation I was not in the least put off by the sudden concern in his eyes. Obviously, he would have to take the position that I was deranged. What alternative had I left him?

"I think you've been under a great strain, Jules," he began. "I think I had better talk to your father . . ."

"Never mind about Father." I cried. "Everyone knows that he's your rubber stamp. You've hated me from the beginning because you were shrewd enough to know that I saw through you. You had to get me before I got you!"

"And when you saw through me, what did you see?"

I was not taken in by his almost conversational tone of curiosity. I paused, but only to spit out the words more offensively. "I saw you weren't God. I saw that you don't even believe in God. Even in yourself as God. I saw you were only a cardboard dragon."

"I will pray for you, Jules," he said in a very soft tone, almost a whisper. "And for your father."

"And I, dear Doctor Prescott, will pray for you. Till we meet in hell!"

This time his eyes really sparkled, and I knew it was my moment to turn about and march from the room. If he had won, I had had the last word. And a pretty magnificent last word, at that.

Two days later Father and I walked on the banks of the Lawrence in the damp exhilarating air of what seemed at last to be spring. From time to time he paused to identify a bird, and once he expressed surprise at seeing a chewink so early in the season. There were no sermons or recriminations.

Father knew when milk had been spilt, and he was not one to try to scoop it back in the bottle. Even I had a dim appreciation of what it must have meant to him to have a son expelled from Justin, and for once in my life I made an effort to be diplomatic. I told him that I was sorry for what had happened and that I accepted my punishment, but that I hoped he would be able to use his good offices to obtain a pardon for the unoffending three.

"I have already tried that, Jules," he told me in his dry, matter-of-fact tone. "I first made it clear to Dr. Prescott that I was not asking for any reconsideration of your own case. That would have been hopeless. But I begged him only to suspend your friends and allow them to return for graduation. Unfortunately, their parents have already organized a group of graduates into a noisy campaign of telegrams. This, of course, will be fatal to their case. However, they didn't consult me."

He shrugged in that way I knew so well, the shrug of the foreign minister who moves disdainfully aside when militarists or radicals take over the government. Father had only contempt for stupidity. I think he believed that the stupid deserved to suffer, unless they had the inspiration to take their problems to David Griscam.

"You mean there's no chance he'll change his mind?"

"Not *now*," Father emphasized. "Dr. Prescott was never a man to be stampeded."

"But can't the trustees overrule him?"

"And have him resign?" Father gave me a pitying glance. "Do you really think they'd be willing to lose the greatest figure in American secondary education to save the scalps of your three little friends? You don't know the world, my boy."

"I don't want to know the world," I said bitterly, "if the world admires a man like Dr. Prescott."

"You're not to criticize him to me," Father retorted with sudden sharpness. "It comes most ungraciously from you, who have caused this whole sorry mess. I have not reproved you, Jules, because I feel you have suffered enough and, alas, that you are going to suffer more. Our job, yours and mine, is to work out a future for you."

"How can we? The old man's done me in. I'll always be known as the boy who wouldn't own up to save his buddies."

"For 'always' read 'six months,'" Father said with a brisk little headshake. "You won't believe how soon this will pass. No, you won't," he repeated sternly, raising his hand as I was about to protest. "Don't let's discuss it. Youth is hopelessly astigmatic. All I ask is that you cooperate with me in getting yourself and your friends into Harvard."

Harvard! I had not dreamed that such a horror was still possible. Was there to be *no* end of the New England experiment? Had I climbed the windmill ladder only to have to do it again and again? "Father," I pleaded in sudden desperation, "I don't think Harvard is the place for me. Couldn't I go abroad for a year? With Chanler? Or off somewhere on a tramp steamer? Please, Father," I went on, even more earnestly, as I saw him stiffen, "I think it might be the making of me. I think it might be the only way!"

"I thought you would have something like that in mind, Jules. But don't you see, that to run off to Europe would be to stamp yourself forever with this wretched business? No, my boy, you must make a go of Harvard and then it will be forgotten. Or if remembered at all, it will seem a boyhood prank."

I knew from his tone that the case was hopeless. I was being "handled," and there was no appeal from that. "It's one thing to get me into Harvard," I said sullenly. "It's another thing to make me go."

"I think you will make yourself go," Father retorted blandly. "For the simple reason that if you don't, I shall not speak to President Lowell about your three friends. You have been instrumental in their losing their Justin degrees. Will you wish to be involved in the loss of their Harvard ones?"

"But that's blackmail!"

"It is no such thing. It is a fair exchange. I do something for you, and you do something for me. You're a difficult young man to bring up, Jules. One has to fight you for your own good all the way." He stepped suddenly to the side of the path and peered down the slope into a clearing. Then he snapped his fingers. "Dammit all!" he exclaimed, forgetting the proximity of the Justin campus. "I should have brought my field glasses. I could swear that was a great northern shrike."

19

JULES GRISCAM'S MEMOIR

FATHER, IN HIS usual fashion, did an efficient job, and it was arranged that all four of us would be admitted to Harvard, provided that we passed the entrance examinations. Unhappily, he could not take these for us, and Sandy McKim failed. Gus Crane, who now hated me with all the vindictive force of his womanly nature, told everybody that Sandy had failed because of a nervous crackup brought on by our expulsion from Justin. It may have been partly true, and it was certainly widely believed, and I found that the smudge of that black eye which Dr. Prescott had dealt me, for all of Father's patient scrubbing, was never entirely going to come off.

Father was good to his word and did not give me any formal punishment, as I had "suffered enough," but he suggested that it might be more "appropriate" that summer if, instead of joining the family on their stately tour of first-class hotels in European capitals, I should work as a counselor in a camp for city boys of which he was a trustee. I agreed to do this, seeing in it the opportunity to square my accounts with him, and when I entered Harvard in the fall I felt no longer under the least obligation for what he had done—

or tried to do—for my fellow delinquents. It was a curious thing, considering how little Father expected to be thanked, that nobody could ever bear to be indebted to him.

The only thing that Harvard seemed to offer me was freedom: freedom from home and freedom from Justin Martyr, and Chanler and I, as roommates, determined to drink as deeply of it as we could. We avoided our old school classmates and spent our evenings and our money in the areas of Boston from which it had been a goodly part of Dr. Prescott's ambition to exclude his graduates. Chanler was really interested only in low women and I in booze, and we made a gloomy enough couple for two young men who wanted to revel in their new-found liberty.

Father had given me a very large allowance on which, in accordance with his usual "responsibility" theories, I was expected to support myself and two indigent old maid Griscam cousins, and I reduced the poor dears to a lamentable state of need, promising them golden things in the future. I knew that they would ultimately complain to Father, but the moment was mine, and the moment was all I wanted. I did not really believe in Harvard or in Father or in his dreary theories. Reality was gin and whiskey and poetry and fast driving and the evil memory of Justin Martyr.

For the maddening thing about Dr. Prescott was that he still refused to shrink into the past. It sometimes seemed to me that his shadow was actually broader at Harvard than it had been at school and that we had not so much gained our freedom as he had enlarged his jurisdiction. My faculty counselor was always asking about him. He prided himself on being a liberal and opposed to private schools, but he liked to describe Prescott as the only intellectual who had ever been a New England head-master. Men whom I met in classes, on the campus, on Boston evenings, when they heard I'd been to Justin would immediately identify it with Prescott and make some inquiry such as: "Is the old boy the ogre they say he is?" But there was usually a note of respect in the question. Even Chanler's tarts had heard of him. And certainly the evidences of his whip were still around me, in the proximity of poor Sandy McKim working unhappily in a Boston insurance company, in the bitter glances of his older brother, Bert, a sophomore, in the dozen little weekly reminders, by chance allusions or semi-snubs, of my own still fetid reputation.

It was as if Dr. Prescott had challenged me to a game of proving which of us was real and was now laughing in his triumph. "You thought you'd find *your* world after Justin, didn't you? But, my dear boy, you woefully underestimated your old prestidigitator. See where the universe has become a school!" Of course, it hadn't—I knew that. He knew it, too, the old devil. But he could make it *look* that way. He knew that if men cared little about faith, they still yearned to be hypocrites. The single lunatic in a world of timid sanity, he made his fellow beings pretend they were in an asylum.

I think it was my feeling of helplessness in defeat that made me drink. I doubt that I was ever really alcoholic. For after I had conceived my great idea, after I had felt with loving fingers in the pocket of my soul the long sharp secret weapon that I was going to use, I lived more on exhilaration than on gin, reverting to the latter only when my weapon seemed dull or in the desperate moments when my clutching hand could not find it at all.

My idea was born in the unlikely delivery room of a party that Chanler Winslow and I gave after the Yale game. Half the people who came we did not know. Some of them had simply happened upon the wrong party. Chanler's tart friends from Boston did not improve the tone, and after a couple of hours I retired to a window seat, in fuzzy isolation, with a glass and a bottle of whiskey, to consider sardonically the scene before me as it might appear to my solicitous father's eye.

"Well if it isn't our Jules! The spunky little guy who wouldn't squeal—on himself."

I contemplated thoughtfully the tall rangy figure of Sandy's brother, Bert McKim, that sprouted into a small, spotty head with small features and sticky blond hair. "How charming," I replied. "In the stuffy old days people used to feel they shouldn't go to parties of people they disapproved of. Now, with their inhibitions removed by their host's liquor, they feel free to vent their spleen on him."

Bert stared down at me with troubled irresolution. "Party? Whose party? Not *yours*."

"Oh, but it is, my dear fellow. And please don't misunderstand me. You are very welcome. You hate me, because of Sandy. I hate the world, because of Sandy. We have more in common than you think."

"Sandy's as good as they make 'em," Bert said in a slow, sullen suspicious tone, "and what happened to him shouldn't have happened to a dog."

"I quite agree. But you seem very solicitous for an older brother. I cannot pride myself that I would share a similar concern over my brother Sylvester. Though I hope, at least, I would have the decency to show it."

"Sandy and I have always done things together." Bert sat down unsteadily on the window seat, and I was astonished to see what appeared to be tears in his eyes. Was he simply drunk and maudlin? Acting on a sudden prick of inspiration, I began piecing together what I knew of him. I knew that he and Sandy were the children of their father's first marriage and that they had the bond of a lost mother and an unsympathetic successor. Bert had not gone to Justin because of a sinus condition, since cured, but he had frequently visited the school with his father and certainly knew the grounds. As I caught the first glimmer of my idea I was so dazzled by its beauty that I threw back my head and laughed.

"Laertes," I exclaimed, in jubilant paraphrase, "was your brother dear to you? 'Or are you like the painting of a sorrow, a face without a heart?'"

"What are you talking about?"

"About Sandy. About what really happened to Sandy. About you and me. And what we can do about it."

"Don't you think you've done enough?"

"Bless you, my boy, I haven't even started!"

"Oh?"

Bert seemed totally confused, and I saw it was the moment to take a firm position. "I care for Sandy as much as you do, Bert. Make no mistake over that. But I don't propose just to moan. I propose to act. If I can find the right partner."

"Act?"

"I want to get back at the mean old man who did him in," I said bluntly. "But now is not the time to discuss it. You and I must meet alone, if you're interested. I will let you know when. And where. What I want you to do now is leave the party in a big huff, telling people you didn't know I was giving it and that you won't stay another minute. Lay it on thick. Do you want me to help you?"

As he stared at me blankly I arose and cried out for all to hear: "Well, if you feel that way, why don't you get the hell out?"

Bert rose slowly. "I'll get out all right," he said sullenly. "I'd never have come if I'd known whose room it was." He was so convincing that I thought my plan was ruined until, as he turned to go, I noticed that the eye away from the room was closed in a long wink.

Two nights later I sat in Bert McKim's room and watched his small, glittering eyes as I told him the story, or rather *a* story, of what had happened to Sandy. I started with the episode of the overturned canoe on the Lawrence River when Chanler Winslow had swum out to rescue Sandy, and I made much of the docile devotion with which Sandy had affixed himself thereafter to the bumpy course of Chanler's school career. But the beautiful little twist that I added and that made Bert's sullen breathing come suddenly in gasps was to suggest that Dr. Prescott, who had a notorious aversion to "sentimentality," had diagnosed Sandy's affection for Chanler as being of that nature and had surveyed them from afar with brooding eyes.

What under this interpretation had been the whole ridiculous episode of the turned key in the door but the old man's long awaited chance to get rid of Sandy and Chanler on the shallow pretext of a failure in their duties as sixth formers? Had not the indignation of the parents and trustees, nay, of the whole graduate body, sufficiently testified that the official story was too flimsy? And now that I was giving to Bert, and only to Bert, this more convincing explanation, I could reflect with exhilaration that he would never be able to check on it without the danger of starting up the very rumor whose accuracy he was testing. Oh, how it fitted. How it all fitted.

The effect on Bert was almost too great. He could hardly speak for several minutes. "And is such a man to get away with that?" he finally stuttered. "Is the old fiend to go on from glory to glory? With his praises sung by every idiot in Massachusetts? Is he to croak without knowing what I think of him?"

I stared at him sternly until he was calmer. Then I smiled and crossed my legs. "I have given the matter the most careful thought, and I think I have found a way to get at Prescott. I believe I have discovered the chink in his armor through which we can jab the burning needle."

"Where? Tell me."

"Patience, my friend." I held up a restraining hand. "And listen. To comprehend requires a bit of philosophy. The old man is wily and quick and crooked as a corkscrew. He can persuade you and even himself that Christ came down to earth to found a boys' academy under the tuition of Francis Prescott. But one thing he *must* believe, and that is the 'mystique' of his school."

"What are you leading to?"

"You will see. To strike Dr. Prescott where he can be hurt one must commit an act of desecration on the school grounds.

The act must be clearly that of a Justinian, and it must be anonymous, so the old man will never know again, in shaking a graduate's hand, whether or not he is shaking the hand of the desecrator."

Bert nodded slowly as my idea settled in his mind. "You think that would really hurt him?"

"I think it might even destroy him."

"How would you perform this . . . this desecration?"

"Ah, that is the crux. After much thought, I have decided on three things. The face must be cut out of the portrait of Phillips Brooks in the school dining room." I smiled grimly as I heard the click of Bert's closed teeth. "The manuscript of the school hymn by Richard Watson Gilder in the library must be torn to shreds. And a hole must be poked through the figure of Justin Martyr in the altar window in chapel."

"Oh, no!" Bert protested, shocked. "What do the saints have to do with Prescott? Can't we leave the chapel out of it?"

I shook my head very firmly. "There is a mystical significance in these three things. Any one or two is useless. All *three* must be perpetrated. If it makes you feel any better, my father gave that window, so I have a quasi right to its disposition."

Bert looked at me suspiciously, but a bit in awe. "When would we do this?"

"You mean when would *you* do it, my dear Bert."

"Me? Me alone?"

"I'm afraid so. I will plan the operation in such a way as to be practically devoid of all risk. But I cannot go myself. In fact, I must have an airtight alibi the night it's done, for I will obviously be the first suspected. Nobody, on the other hand, would ever think of you. You didn't even go to the school, so how would you know its symbolism?"

Bert was silent and motionless for at least two minutes. Then he got up to get a bottle of whiskey out of his desk. "Tell me your plan," he said tersely.

"You will hire a car in Boston. I have the place and the money. The school is forty minutes' drive. I have a map that will show you just where to park. The buildings are open at night. You can enter the dining hall easily and cut the portrait. The library, as you know, is in the adjoining wing, and the key to the glass manuscript case hangs on a hook by the librarian's desk. Finally the chapel. I will give you a bamboo pole with a steel head that will reach to the window. This is the only act that will make any noise, but it need make very little, and the chapel is far enough from the nearest dormitory so that it shouldn't be heard."

"Is there no watchman?"

"There's old Pete, but he reads newspapers and drinks coffee in the housekeeper's kitchen. He makes a tour of the campus every hour on the hour. You can start at a quarter past, and you should be finished in twenty minutes."

"How do you know some of these things haven't changed? You haven't been at the school since last year."

"Nothing changes at Justin. At least nothing sacred does."

"We hope! Supposing I'm caught? Do I take the rap alone?"

"I will give you a letter setting forth our scheme. All you will have to do to inculpate me is deliver it to the authorities."

Bert was silent again and then nodded. "I'll think it over," he conceded grimly. "I admit it doesn't sound so bad."

Only two days later I received a laconic note in the mail saying "Okay" and fixing our next appointment in Bert's room. From then on our plan raced ahead, for Bert wanted it executed while his enthusiasm was at its peak. He studied my map that showed the exact locations of the picture and manuscript and selected a night of half-moon. We agreed not to meet the next day which would be a Wednesday, but that on Thursday, when we both had a class in Adams Hall, we would meet briefly in the washroom at eleven.

I decided that I would spend the night of the great deed with Chanler in the flat of two of his tart friends. When the detectives reported to the headmaster and to my distinguished father the whereabouts of Jules Griscam, they would have an added shock to the one already inflicted. Yet in point of fact I was too excited to do anything but drink and sit up late, reciting poetry and talking wildly about school days to the disgust of Chanler and the boredom of the girls. All the next day I kept looking in the faces of my classmates, of my professors, of people in the street for some indication that the deed was done. I even kept turning my eyes in the direction of the distant school as if I expected to see a red glow in that portion of the sky. But nothing, of course, occurred to distinguish the day from other days.

On Thursday at eleven I waited tensely in the Adams washroom until Bert, astonishingly self-possessed, swung the door open. He glanced about to be sure that we were alone and then took a brown manila envelope from under his jacket.

"Here's the portrait face. Do you want to see it before I burn it?"

"Yes! And the poem?"

"That's destroyed."

"Oh, Bert! My Achilles! And the window?"

He shook his head curtly. "I couldn't do it. At the last moment. After all, God damn it, it's a church. This is enough."

I winced as if he had drawn a razor across my cheek. "Let me see the portrait, anyway," I hissed.

He pulled a piece of canvas out of the envelope and flashed it before my unbelieving eye. What I saw was a part of the cheek, oddly cream-colored, the hooked nose, oddly red, and one great eye and one great, fatally familiar, bushy eyebrow.

"But that's not Brooks," I gasped in horror. "That's Prescott. It's the Laszlo portrait!"

"Yes, I thought it would be better to cut up the old bastard himself than Bishop What's-his-name. I thought perhaps you hadn't remembered that his portrait was there. Sst! Someone's coming." And Bert snatched back the bit of canvas and left me to the explosion of the heavens and the downpour of despair.

I don't remember how I got back to my room. My next memory is of lying on my bed and biting my pillow between angry sobs. Macbeth was no more frustrated by the escape of Fleance than I by this grisly chance that had turned the beautifully conceived eagle of my revenge into a croaking blackbird. For what would Prescott care about such petty vandalism? That some embittered Justin boy should have attacked *his* likeness—how small, how puerile, how like a cashiered servant, a disgruntled janitor! And, indeed, if suspicion were to fall on me, either as principal or agent in the deed, how easily could he not shrug his shoulders and say: "After all, what more could one expect from a boy who got his friends fired in an effort to save his own skin?" It was too much, after everything, too much for my hate, for my pride, for my love of self to bear. I sat up and drank from a bottle of gin until I was full of fire.

Somehow I was not killed in my wild drive in Chanler's car to the school. Somehow I stumbled from the road to the shadowy hulk of the chapel, clutching a rock that I had carried all the way from Cambridge, and made my way to the back where I could see by the moonlight the high, black arched panes of the great Justin Martyr window over the altar. And somehow, even more miraculously, I was able to spot the two figures scurrying towards me from each side and was able to heave the rock and hear that soul-satisfying crash of glass before I was pinioned and hurled to the ground by detectives.

I had plenty of time the next morning, lying on the cot in my cell at the New Paisley jail and feeling the long, shuddering throbs of my hangover, to contemplate the nadir of my short and unhappy career. Here I was at last, sin incarnate. At least I could hope that the rock through the altar window had elevated me to the dignity of sin. Sin, the real sin, in the eyes of our society is almost always a symbolic act. For what, after all, had I done? Had I killed anybody? Had I even hurt anybody? Did a single mortal ache in any joint or go thirsty or hungry because of me?

All I had done from the beginning was to turn a piece of metal in a full circle and toss that piece of metal out a window to the grass where it had ultimately been recovered. Then I had caused the destruction of a piece of paper on which were traced the lines of a very bad poem, of which, unfortunately, thousands of other copies existed. More seriously, perhaps, my agent had slashed a painting and I had broken a window, both inferior artifacts and one of which was easily reparable. Had all my little damages been accidents, nobody would have been in the least concerned. It was my intent that made the sole difference, my contempt for the little jumble of lares and penates, in short, my desecration of the holy things of our superstitious Christian society. Could I hope, in a lifetime, to do a fraction of the more real harm to others that was accomplished by "good" men like Prescott and approved by "good" men like Father? If Satan was not a headmaster, he was at least a parent. Where in the world was there room for anyone as wicked and harmless as myself?

Dr. Prescott came to my cell late that afternoon in the guise of the weary philosopher who has tried all, lost all and accepted all. It was a superb performance, enhanced by his beautiful, rumpled, cashmere grey suit and black vest and by the melancholy modulations of his address.

"When I leave, Jules, you will be free to go yourself," he told me. "The school will press no charges. Unhappily, Harvard has been less forgiving. You may not return there. But it may perhaps interest you to hear that I interceded on your behalf with President Lowell. Alas, to no avail. He is quite adamant. One night's bad work might have been forgiven. Not two."

"Two?" I demanded sharply. "What do you mean by two?"

"A copy of your letter to Bert McKim was found in your rooms this morning," he replied dryly. "It cleared up the mystery of your having been with Winslow at a place of ill repute last Tuesday night. Once again, Jules, you have managed to implicate another. I am glad to tell you, however, that President Lowell may reconsider McKim's case."

I shrugged. I cared very little about Bert McKim. Perhaps I had hardened since my sixth form year. Perhaps I was simply disgusted at the way he had bungled the job. "Where am I to go when I go?" I asked. "Does Father know?"

"Your father is here. I asked him to let me see you first. He is talking now with Mr. Ives about the possibility of your continuing your education abroad."

"Good old Father!" I exclaimed with a mocking laugh. "Always at work over a piece of broken crockery. If he can put this one together, he should be in line for a commission on Humpty-Dumpty."

The dark line down the center of Dr. Prescott's forehead deepened as he sighed windily. "Tell me, Jules, have you no remorse?"

"Remorse? For what you've done to *me*?"

"There was a time when people were considered as being possessed. Possessed by the devil." He shook his head to and fro vigorously. "I sometimes wonder if we have not too easily flung it away as superstition. How else can I explain the extraordinary malevolence that you have evinced against the school and myself from the very beginning?"

"Mightn't we *both* be possessed? Mightn't our devils have recognized each other?"

As he stared back, it seemed to me that I could make out in those big eyes a mixture of apprehension, curiosity and something like awe. "Tell me what you mean by that."

"Don't people with devils feel them early?" I exclaimed. "I'm sure I've always been aware of mine. Like a lazy tapeworm, all warm and comfortable, feeding on the jumble of my cerebrations. But yours, I suspect, had a harder time. For when you first became aware of his coiled presence, you saw instantly all the possibility of staging a great drama about your conflict with him. You built the school as your amphitheatre where through the decades generations of wondering boys could watch your Laocoon act. Oh, it was something! Until the devil peered out and saw his supposed victim strutting about on the rostrum, praying and preaching and exhorting, and realized that a new Barnum had put him on the boards and was making a fortune as a snake charmer!"

"And then what did he do?" Prescott's question came almost in a whisper.

"Well, devils have a way of having the last word, you know," I said, looking at him hard, "particularly with those who are making a peepshow of God's mercy. Who are using God's things as props in vaudeville. And so it was that your beautiful academy, your palace of lies, should have at last a graduate—a moral graduate, shall we say—who carries your act to its ultimate degree and shatters for a gaping multitude the great glass window of your idolatry."

Prescott dropped his big head into his hands and groaned: "Jules, Jules, my boy, what have I done to you?"

When he looked up and gazed at me wretchedly there were actually tears in those great brown eyes! Tears, while mine were dry! The tears of his defeat, of his collapse, tears that would fall and splash until the very tower of the school with its clanging bell would crack and be submerged. He wept, ah, yes he wept at last, but what was there left for me in a world of water?

20

BRIAN'S JOURNAL

October 8, 1945. It seems unbelievable to be back at a Justin Martyr of which Dr. Prescott is no longer head. Of course I have come here, since his retirement, as a visitor, but it doesn't really hit you until you return, as I do now, once more a master. Not that Mr. Moore is doing such a bad job. Far from it. He is big and cheerful and forceful and probably more popular with the boys than Dr. Prescott ever was. But what one cannot imagine is how he can have the courage (perhaps some would say the nerve) to move so jauntily along paths hallowed by his great predecessor, particularly when that predecessor is watching from so close at hand. For every brick of Justin, every fountain and porch, every structure from the glorious dark struggling chapel, a drama in stone of the Protestant soul, to the old green bleachers by the football field are impregnated with the Prescott personality. It is as if God had paused and withdrawn to a misty mountain-top to see how man will manage his creation.

Only in the afternoons now does the familiar figure with the long blue coat and stick appear, on the still daily round of the campus and grounds: once about the lawn, thence to the garth for ten minutes' meditation on a memorial bench, thence to the football practice, thence to the river and back. It is quite a stint for one of eighty-five. He stops to speak to boys and masters; he smiles and sometimes laughs his high-pitched laugh. He seems with his every gesture and syllable to defer to the new order, but how I would hate to be that new order under that glassy eye!

October 12. As a clergyman, I have been relieved of even the most formal athletic duties, and I have taken to walking of an afternoon. I watch from my study window until Dr. Prescott has passed before going out and taking the opposite direction. I do not wish to intrude upon him, for I still feel constraint about working for his successor. It is not, God knows, any feeling that I am being disloyal, for Dr. Prescott was the person who championed my return to Justin, but as a minister I am more identified with the new order than others of the old faculty. I assist the headmaster in chapel, and I mark his term papers in sacred studies. No doubt I am unduly sensitive, but I will wait for Dr. Prescott to make the first move in resuming our old intimacy. So far he has not done so.

My clerical status does not seem to have improved my disciplinary powers. In fact, I am almost back where I was when I first started. I fear that my reversed collar (unlike Mr. Moore's or Dr. Prescott's—oh, so unlike!) is taken for a symbol of weakness. I am again aware of whisperings and giggles in the back row of my classroom and odd noises in my dormitory after lights. The boys know that it is painful for me to give black marks and, all too naturally, they take advantage of this. Yet I have qualms about penalizing them for my own failure to be obeyed. If I were interesting, my classroom would be silent, and if I had a shadow of "command presence" (instead of its opposite) there would be no moving between the cubicles at night.

My fourth form English class (for I am to teach that as well as sacred studies) is reading *Persuasion,* and I am disheartened by my utter incapacity to make them see what an exquisite thing it is. I feel woefully inadequate when I contemplate all the delights which Jane Austen might offer them if only *I* had the ability to get her across. I know that Mr. Dahlgren, the head of mathematics, would call me absurdly naïve. He believes that only a tiny number can be expected to see the light. But to me this is Calvinism. Why should only a few, arbitrarily chosen, be saved?

October 21. Dr. Prescott came up behind me this afternoon as I was leaving the garth and grabbed me by the arm. "Won't you walk with me, Brian? Have you been avoiding me, dear fellow? We seem to be the sole pedestrians in an autumn world prostrate before the idol of football. Can we not unite our forces?" I stammered that I had thought he might wish to be alone. "Alone? Wait till you're an octogenarian widower. You'll find you have your fill of solitude." And holding my arm he walked beside me, asking me questions about my classes and the boys and whether I was satisfied at having become a minister. There was a warmth and a kindness and an interest that made me tremble like an idiot and want to fall down on my knees and kiss his hand. How the richness of his loving nature fills in the crannies of the somber buildings and acts as a great red Romanesque arch over the bleak fall sky! One cannot understand the architecture of Justin without its necessary complement in Dr. Prescott's personality. And what bliss to have back our old friendship again!

I told him of my troubles, of my worries in English class, and he nodded gravely. "If you could transmit some of the beauty of Jane Austen, you would be transmitting a small vision of God. But don't blame yourself too much. It is desperately hard work. Perhaps with that particular novel and those particular boys, it is impossible. I wonder you don't try Melville. I sometimes wish we didn't divide our curriculum into subjects. An equation, a Keats ode, a Gothic Cathedral, a Mozart aria, the explosion of gases in a laboratory, they should be seen by boys as related—and divine. I tried in this campus to convey a sense of oneness and Godliness. Now *that*, for example, is plural and non-God." He pointed with a frown to a white refrigerator truck passing the Schoolhouse to park by the football field.

"I would never have allowed it in my day," he continued more somberly. "You may ask, can soda pop be sinful, if consumed in moderation? Perhaps not. But that truck is sinful *here*." And watching the truck as it passed the chapel, white against dark, a flash of absurdity against the seeming permanence of our place of worship, it appeared in the instant of its silhouette to symbolize the transiency of our commercial mores. I could only agree with Dr. Prescott that so discordant a note was somehow meretricious. Perhaps, as he said, even sinful. As it would be sinful to insert a chapter of John O'Hara into the chaste pages of *Persuasion*.

November 2. I was having a particularly bad time with fourth form English this morning when Dr. Prescott appeared suddenly in the doorway, put his hand to his lips in a gesture that indicated the class was not to be disturbed and noiselessly took a seat in the back. None of the boys who were facing me saw him, so their bad behavior continued. The poem under discussion was Browning's "Meeting at Night: Parting at Morning," and the little devils were pretending that they did not understand what had happened during the night to make the narrator need "a world of men" the next day. Of course, they knew that I blushed easily. Sloane, a dreadful, tall, thin, slick New Yorker was the ringleader.

"But tell me, sir, if he had been with a woman and yearned for a world of men, mustn't there have been something unsatisfactory about the woman?"

"Not necessarily, Sloane." I dared not glance in Dr. Prescott's direction. "He simply needed action after so much emotion. That's understandable, isn't it?"

"You mean there had been no action during the night?" The class tittered, and I felt my cheeks burning. "You don't think, sir," Sloane continued in a false tone of intellectual curiosity, "that he was what is known as a 'queer'?"

"You may leave the room, Sloane."

"But, sir, I was only asking a question!"

"Leave the room, please."

"But, my God, sir, it's not fair when I've just asked a question . . ."

"Sloane!" Dr. Prescott's deep voice filled every cubic inch of the room, and the whole class jumped. Though he had retired before any of them had come to Justin, he was still an awesome campus figure. "Stand up, Sloane, and turn around!"

Sloane leaped to his feet and spun about. "I'm sorry, Dr. Prescott, sir, I didn't see you."

"That is neither here nor there. Your language should not be regulated according to who is present."

"But, sir, it was a word I've heard my own father use. I did not know it was so bad."

"It is not a bad word, Sloane. It was your use of it that was bad."

Sloane looked utterly at a loss. "Queer?" he mumbled.

"No, not *that* word!" Dr. Prescott thundered, rising now himself, and the class rose with him. "I admit, I never expected to hear such a term used in a classroom in this school, but that's a relatively minor matter. The important thing, and the one that you do not even seem to recognize, is that you used the name of God in vain!"

Sloane's face cleared as he recognized at last what must have struck him as a minor misdeed. "Oh, that's true, sir. I did, didn't I? It must have slipped out. I'm very sorry, sir."

"Slipped out? And you're merely sorry? We'll see what the headmaster has to say. You will proceed, Sloane, to Mr. Moore's study where you will report to him exactly what you said. If he is not there, you will wait till he comes."

Sloane hastily left the room, and Dr. Prescott nodded to me. "You may proceed with your class, Mr. Aspinwall. Pray forgive my intrusion."

When he had gone, and the class was seated I enjoyed for the first time the undivided attention of the boys as we turned with subdued monotones to a discussion of "My Last Duchess."

After school, as I was walking to Lawrence House for lunch, I was touched on the shoulder, and Mr. Moore, holding a black velvet bag with the Justin arms on it, where he kept his papers, adjusted his long legs in step with mine.

"Tell me, Brian," he began in his vigorous, amiable fashion, "how did Dr. Prescott happen to be in your classroom today?"

"He just dropped in, sir."

"You had suggested that he pay you a visit?"

"No, sir. Except that I had confided in him some of my teaching problems. I think he wished to help me."

"I see. It's unfortunate that he should have been there when Sloane said what he did. Obviously, we cannot allow swearing on the campus, but neither can we treat it as quite so grave an offense as Dr. Prescott would wish. The boys simply use the expressions they pick up from their fathers, and I fear, even their mothers."

"It was my fault, sir, for allowing the discussion to get out of hand."

"Well, we won't worry about it," Mr. Moore said with a rather forced smile. "These little hitches are bound to occur with the old gentleman being around so much. But if you have teaching problems, Brian, you can always confide them in me, you know. I am never too busy to talk to one of my masters."

"Thank you, sir," I said in a voice chastened enough to acknowledge the mild rebuke in his tone. "I happened to mention them to Dr. Prescott because we walk together."

"Naturally, naturally. And an enviable experience to know the great man. I wish I had more time to see him. I do, indeed."

When I joined Dr. Prescott that afternoon, I found him silent and moody. I dared not apologize or even mention the lamentable scene of that morning, and we walked without exchanging a word. Yet Dr. Prescott's silences, like those of royalty, are not embarrassing. One simply understands that his mind is closed to audiences. On our way back from watching the football practice we passed the headmaster's house and saw Sloane under the porte-cochere washing Mr. Moore's Buick. Dr. Prescott paused.

"We meet again, Sloane," he said gravely.

"Yes, sir," Sloane replied ruefully. "I guess I've learned my lesson this time. I had to miss football practice which means I won't be able to play in the game on Saturday."

"Is your punishment confined to these ablutions?"

"You mean to washing this car? Oh, no, sir, I have to do Mr. Langborne's as well."

"Indeed? We live under a stern regime, Sloane."

"You can say that again, sir!"

Dr. Prescott moved on, and I accompanied him to the door of his house. As I took my leave, he stared down at the flagstone path, and I lingered, unsure whether or not I had been dismissed. At last he muttered sadly: "To have to wash two cars, Brian. For taking God's name in vain. Think of it! In my day he'd have been lucky not to be suspended for the rest of the term!"

November 4. Pierre Dahlgren has taken a fancy to me, which improves my position a bit, not only in the faculty but with the boys. For Pierre, as head of the mathematics department and master of Lowell House, is number three, after the head and senior masters. Indeed, he should by rights have become senior master when Mr. Ives retired, but it was felt that a younger man was needed. No doubt he resents this.

Pierre, at fifty-three, is a tubby, white-haired, mincing, round-eyed, baby-faced bachelor who loves to sit up late and gossip in his beautiful study hung with eighteenth century French and Italian drawings (Pierre is rich, at least for a Justin master). He is a perfect example of what unlikely material Justin can assimilate and turn to its own profit. For all his silliness, he has a lucid, beautiful mind which enables him to teach mathematics as I would love to teach poetry, and his stentorian dignity counteracts his plump softness, so the boys know he is not one to be trifled with. And then he has a passion for the school which for twenty-five years has been his entire life. Dr. Prescott (whom he worships) must have seen from the beginning that there was a place on his faculty for at least one Pierre.

My dormitory is near Pierre's bedroom and study, and he has taken to asking me in after lights for coffee. This is his best time, enthroned in a great armchair covered in blue velvet, before a silver tray and coffee urn, a cigarette always dangling from his lips, an ash always on his silk tie, his eyes snapping as he chews up the juiciest bits of gossip of the school day. Nothing is sacred to Pierre: neither the boys, nor their demanding parents, nor the poor faculty wives who try so hard to look well at lunch, nor even Mr. and Mrs. Moore. He will burst into dry gusts of laughter and then hold his fat hands to his thin lips as the coughing overcomes him. Sometimes he even serves brandy, which is against the rules, but he has a dispensation because of a weak heart.

I told him of the Sloane episode and of Dr. Prescott's reaction to the punishment.

"Well, at least there's one boon," he commented with a wicked chuckle, "and that is we've finally got that jalopy of Mr. Moore's cleaned. I had been on the verge of paying the local garage to do it. Only if I were Moore and had the disposition of Sloane's services I would employ them indoors." Here he smiled nastily. "My maid Ida tells me the girls at the headmaster's house sweep everything under the rugs." Here Pierre went through a pantomime of glancing to his left and right and then leaned forward to hiss at me: "And she says their kitchen's a *sight*."

It seemed to me that we had got a long way from blasphemy. "I'm afraid Dr. Prescott was very upset. Of course, to him swearing is as bad as lying."

"And he's quite right, the poor old superseded darling." Pierre startled me with his sudden stem tone which meant that no sarcasm was intended. It was remarkable how quickly that magistrate could emerge from the dotted garb of the clown. "Dr. Prescott has forgotten more about running a school than Moore will ever learn! He knows that everything is interrelated: the clean collar, the shined shoes, the hard-played game, the deeply felt prayer." Pierre might now have been Dr. Prescott himself; I quailed before his flashing eye. "It is reverence that must be taught, day and night, if boys are not to be apes. When I think what a beautiful thing a disciplined boy can be, I feel a positive hatred for those who allow him to wallow in his native grossness. It's as if some thug had wandered through a gallery of Caravaggios and smeared the faces of his charming youths with brown paint!"

"Perhaps it would be better if Dr. Prescott moved away," I suggested, a bit embarrassed by this outbreak.

"Perhaps it would be better if Dr. Prescott had never retired. He can do a lot more going downhill before he meets Moore coming up."

Even such an admirer of Dr. Prescott as myself was taken aback by the idea that he should still be in office at eighty-five.

"He keeps complaining that his memory is going," was all I could think to say.

"He only *thinks* his memory is going. Because he's old. You, for example, Brian, are presumably not worried about yours. Yet you forgot to read out the detention list before dismissing schoolroom yesterday, and you left your term papers on the desk in faculty hall."

I reflected that it was small wonder that Pierre could control the boys. "I'm sorry. How stupid of me."

"It's quite all right, I put them in your locker," he continued, brushing the ashes from his waistcoat and tie. "You had neglected to lock it."

November 7. Eric Langborne was at Pierre's last night after lights. He is Pierre's age, or a bit younger, and also a bachelor, but in other respects they are opposites. He is skinny and bald, with a long oblong face and white perfect teeth that he likes to show as he articulates his syllables in a dry, superior tone. He is head of the Latin department, and being English born and a Rugby graduate, he obviously considers himself Justin's leading intellectual. Listening to him and Pierre hold forth gravely on such "dangerous" innovations as Moore's suspension of the requirement of blue suits for Sunday wear, one begins to wonder if Dr. Prescott's faculty was not an orchestra that only Dr. Prescott could conduct.

November 10. Eric was particularly lugubrious last night. After a silence of some moments he announced: "Obviously neither of you has heard."

"What?" I asked.

"You haven't heard what he's done today?"

"No, what?"

"Latin is to be made optional after the fourth form!"

Pierre and I exchanged glances. We knew what a blow this must be to Eric's pride. "And what is to be put in its place?" Pierre demanded. "Jujitsu? The history of vaudeville? Or needlepoint?"

"Art appreciation," Eric answered grimly. "The mother of languages must veil her eyes in a darkened room where smirking boys will gape at slides of Dufy and Matisse."

"But they can still *choose* Latin," I murmured consolingly.

"Few boys will choose a difficult subject," Eric retorted. "They will choose you, Brian, where they can read *Jane Eyre* and *Lorna Doone.*"

"Eric, the time has come!" Pierre announced abruptly.

"What?"

"The time has come," he repeated solemnly.

Eric now nodded, but as I continued to stare, Pierre explained: "The time has come to ask Dr. Prescott to join our little meetings. He has wanted to come, I know, but he has been restrained by delicacy of feeling. Now we must tell him that it is his duty. His duty to save the school!"

I had not realized that our "little meetings" had such significance or that we constituted a nucleus of organized dissent. I see now that I must have been cultivated by Pierre because of my intimacy with Dr. Prescott. I have a horror of disloyalty, but it still does not seem possible to me that any gathering could be stained with that quality at which Dr. Prescott is present.

Pierre, for a soft man, talks a great deal about the softness of our age. Dr. Prescott may convince him that it did not all originate with Duncan Moore.

November 15. Dr. Prescott came to Pierre's last night, but the meeting did not go off very well. In the first place the great man was in an obviously sour and despondent mood, and in the second Pierre, very foolishly, had placed four brandy glasses on the silver tray by the decanter. Dr. Prescott glared at these before sitting down and pursed his lips disapprovingly.

"I was aware that *you* had a dispensation, Dahlgren, from the rule about liquor on school premises," he began in the dry, bleak, weary tone that he used to school offenders. "I was not aware that it had been extended to your visitors. Or is that another of the new regulations?"

"Indeed not, sir," Pierre replied heartily, whisking away the offending tray. "I think my poor old Ida must have set them out in your honor."

Dr. Prescott chose to ignore this transparent falsehood. "I shall certainly not break Mr. Moore's rules while I am criticizing his administration."

The discussion went very slowly after this. Dr. Prescott held forth in a melancholy voice about the importance of Latin in the curriculum. It seemed to me that he stressed it much more than he had in the past, and he was obviously tired. Pierre spoke of the importance of daily calisthenics at noon, and Eric deplored the fact that the boys no longer had to wear stiff collars at supper. I had nothing to add and was surprised, when we broke up, to hear Dr. Prescott suggest that we meet again the following week. I had thought he would be through with the Dahlgren circle. I hope to be myself, but so long as Dr. Prescott goes, I will go with him.

December 1. I have not made an entry now for two weeks. I have been troubled, and my mind has not been clear as to which of two is the real reason. Is it that I feel that our Wednesday night sessions are dangerous to the welfare of the school or is it that I feel they are not? In other words, am I worried for the school or for us? Wouldn't I rather see Dr. Prescott, if he *must* play an active role, howl like the anguished Lear in the tempest and ultimately bring ruin to all, so that the usurpers and the dethroned perish in a single fifth act cataclysm? Wouldn't that be better than to have him preside, like an addled old field marshal, over a council of disgruntled roy-alists who have dragged him from retirement to envelop their shabby plans in the musty glory of his ribbons and banners? Yes, in the last analysis, do I not care for Dr. Prescott far more than for his school? Would I not rather have him lethal than absurd? I cannot bear the picture of his gravely nod-ding head as Pierre discusses the iniquities of Mr. Moore's new project of having the boys wait on table.

Yet what can I do? I tried on one of our walks to hint that Pierre and Eric were carping critics. "Oh, yes, of course," he muttered impatiently, "but their hearts are in the right place. That's the great thing."

He would not go on with the topic, and when I left him, he remarked dryly that I did not have to come to Pierre's unless I chose to. I assured him that I did so choose, and that is true. For I love Dr. Prescott, if that is not too presumptuous a term, more than anyone in the world. I cannot bear to be away from his side in time of trouble, even if I can only observe. All my life I have been an observer, and now, when I crave to act, to interfere, to *stop* something, it is ironical that I am compelled to go on in my old role.

December 3. Mr. Moore came up behind me on our way from morning chapel to the Schoolhouse and put his long arm around my shoulders. He is always very friendly, but one feels that he is constantly having to overcome a naturally cold nature. Still he tries, and I believe that he tries sincerely.

"I hear you've been having some interesting sessions at Pierre's," he said cheerily. "I bet I wouldn't have been a very happy fly had I found myself on *that* wall!"

I was so mortified that I could only stammer something completely inarticulate, and Mr. Moore's smile became tighter as did his grasp on my shoulder. "Don't get mixed up in something you're going to regret, Brian," he warned me in a lower voice. "I'm hoping you'll go far at Justin. Leave campus politics alone, my boy. Believe me, that's good advice."

I was paralyzed by his kindness. What could I possibly say? That our little meetings were not conspiratorial? That I attended them only with reluctance? I was too embroiled in disloyalty to be able to affirm my allegiance without seeming to betray my cohorts. And how could I betray Dr. Prescott?

It was an impossible situation, and on our walk that afternoon I was almost able to tell Dr. Prescott so. I finally found the courage to suggest that he did not fully assess the effect of his own personality on others and that he might be pushing Pierre and Eric into an overt opposition of the headmaster. He was very upset and paused to pound the earth with his walking stick.

"I tell you, Brian, you're a fusspot!" he exclaimed. "We're only trying to devise a way to save what is best in Justin. This is not disloyalty. If I make a report, it will be to the trustees of the school, of whom, as ex-headmaster, I am one."

"But your prestige is such that a report might ruin Mr. Moore," I protested. "The trustees and the graduates would be behind you. Too much behind you."

"I don't know about that," Dr. Prescott said gloomily. "The old are soon forgotten. But even if it were so, I must take my chances. What you must learn, Brian, if you are to be an effective priest, is that you belong to the church militant and that means you have to fight! I think I could have put up with anything from Mr. Moore but the depreciation of Justin Martyr as a church school. Do you know, there are six Roman Catholic boys in the present first form? And that they are excused from chapel!"

"They go to mass in the village."

"But we're a *church* school, Brian, that's what you forget. That's what all of you forget today."

"Yet you took Catholic boys yourself, sir."

"Reluctantly. And only on strict conditions." Dr. Prescott set his jaw in a new way to which I was beginning to become accustomed. "When some infatuated graduate, forgetting his manhood, signed away the right to bring up his sons in his own faith and then in sober afterthought came to beg me with tears in his eyes—yes, tears, Brian—to take his boy in Justin . . . well, I relented and took the boy. I let the graduate have his cake and eat it. But the boy had to attend every chapel service and every sacred studies class!"

"And Jewish boys?"

"They were offered the same conditions. But I'll say this for *them*. The conditions were never accepted."

"Then all your Jewish boys were converts?"

"They were *Christians,* Brian!" Dr. Prescott thundered. "I have never admitted the word 'Jew' as any but a religious term. Of course, you'll ask me about Negroes next. That, I admit, is a tougher problem. But I can tell you this. If I found Negro boys who could really profit from Justin and Justin from them, I'd take them. But I'd never take just one, or maybe two, to wear as feathers in my liberal cap!"

It was known on the campus that Mr. Moore was considering a Negro boy for next year's first form. I was afraid of provoking Dr. Prescott into an even more open denunciation of his successor and drew his attention hastily to the fact that it was beginning to snow. He shook his head moodily and plodded on ahead of me towards his house.

December 10. I have had a vicious flu and been a week in the infirmary. Everyone has been very nice about it, though it plays havoc with the curriculum. But what has set me back much more than my own sense of physical unworthiness was a visit that I received from Pierre Dahlgren. He sat by my bed and gave me the gossip of the week, filling the stuffy air of my room with smoke and chuckles, and I lay back on my pillows, my eyes half closed, murmuring positives or negatives as required until he said something that made me sit up.

He was discussing the great plans for the school's diamond jubilee that is to be celebrated in the early spring, an event that is expected to bring to the campus a great troup of graduates. Dr. Prescott, of course, is to be the last speaker at the principal banquet, and of his speech Pierre had the following to say, after leaning forward to see that no one was listening in the corridor:

"I wish you could have been at our last Wednesday meeting. I think that Dr. Prescott's address will come as a bit of a bombshell."

"A bombshell? Oh, Pierre, *should* it be?"

Pierre placed his fingers on his lips as we heard the sound of the nurse's heels in the corridor. "It is the perfect, perhaps the last chance," he whispered gravely, "for the affirmation of our ancient faith!"

It was a relief to have the nurse come in and stick the thermometer abruptly between my lips so I did not have to answer. All that I can do now is to go to Mr. Griscam. For he, thank God, is my opposite. He knows when and how to act.

21

BRIAN'S JOURNAL

JANUARY 22, 1946. I have told Mr. Griscam everything, and he has promised, as I knew he would, to take the needed steps to head off Pierre Dahlgren's little plot. But my visit to the Griscams in the Christmas holidays has produced another and much more extraordinary result: I have been instrumental in raising a great sum of money for Justin Martyr. Among the various small services that I have hoped to do for the school I never dreamed of a financial one. Life is certainly bizarre.

My visit has also had a private significance, being the first time that I have felt accepted by adults as a minister. I had gone straight from divinity school back to Justin where I had to do only with the boys, who made little distinction between ministers and masters, and with the faculty, who continued to see me as the same old Brian Aspinwall with a quixotically reversed collar. But in Sixty-eighth Street the Griscams treated me as a figure of more stature, and I hope I did not let them down too badly. I have a terrible tendency to think of myself as a minister in a play. Please, God, help me to lower that curtain!

They were much the same as in 1941 and greeted me with much the same enthusiasm. Mrs. Griscam was deeper than ever in the affairs of her "army" and was now giving it (I gathered from one of her husband's dry asides) every dollar that he had not hidden away in trust. Amy was still vociferous and firm in her opinions; Sylvester, still separated but undivorced from his second wife. And their father was still wearing the same patient air of the man who has to unravel the knotted affairs of an ungrateful universe. Only, like the gods of Valhalla after the abduction of Freia, they all seemed a bit graver and older. I am afraid that the war must have provided their spirit of youth.

Sylvester was particularly friendly and made me, early in my visit, the embarrassed confidant of his matrimonial troubles.

"When I married Faith—that was my first wife—I was really only a kid. You won't believe me, Brian, but I'd never even kissed another girl."

"Why shouldn't I believe you?"

Sylvester's pause was only momentary. "Well, I suppose you were always religious, even as a boy. Not that it isn't a very fine thing to be. But as a minister you'll have to hear all kinds of things. We may as well start making you a man of the world." He laughed in his loud, cheerful, rather forced fashion. "Take it from me, my friend, it's extremely unusual for a lad of twenty to have kissed only one girl. You see, I'd been engaged to Faith since I was fourteen."

"But you were only a child! Surely, your parents didn't countenance such a thing?"

"Oh, they thought it was cute. Faith's parents were their best friends and all that kind of thing. We were trapped in a family valentine. Not really trapped, of course. But that's how kids are. We thought it was expected of us. Dad and Mother didn't see that I needed anything more than Faith. They've never had any interest in sex themselves."

"That's what we tend to think about our parents," I cautioned him. "But it's not always true."

"Oh, I suppose they were normal for their generation." Sylvester shrugged and poured himself more brandy. We were sitting in the dining room alone after a long Sunday lunch. Mrs. Griscam had retired to the parlor, and Mr. Griscam and Amy were playing backgammon in the library. "Though how normal was Dad, I sometimes wonder, when he proposed to a lame girl who happened to be the boss's daughter?"

"Sylvester," I protested, "please remember I'm his guest!"

Sylvester smiled complacently into his brandy glass and sniffed its contents with a heavy sniff. He was obviously delighted to have shocked me. People, I am learning, like to shock ministers. "A little realism implies no lack of respect, Brian. I still obey the fifth commandment. All I'm saying is that Dad and Mother have sublimated their sexual urges to higher things. Dad has Justin Martyr. Mother has the Army of the Holy Word. Fine. But poor little Sylvester didn't have either, and he had some pretty basic needs. After fifteen years of tepid wedlock, when he suddenly met a secretary at the bank called Estelle . . . I" Sylvester leaned over to put a hand on my shoulder and whisper in my shrinking ear: "Brian, my boy, I tell you I woke up to sex like a giggling freshman on his first visit to a whorehouse!"

"I suppose that's the trouble with young marriages," I murmured uncomfortably.

Sylvester nodded his solemn agreement as he sat back to continue his brandy. "Well, I admit Dad was a trump about it. He didn't like Estelle. Nobody liked Estelle. Only I was blind enough not to see what a bitch she was. Yes, Brian," he repeated gravely as he saw me wince, "my second wife was a bitch. But Dad put up my alimony and made it possible for me to marry her. It wasn't a year before I had to walk out."

"*Had* to?"

"If I wanted to preserve my sanity, that is. You could never conceive in your wildest dreams, Brian, what things went on."

"You mean she was . . . unfaithful to you?"

"A word like 'unfaithful' is a cataclysmic understatement to describe the activities of a woman like Estelle." Sylvester almost smacked his lips as he said this. I couldn't help wishing that it wasn't quite so much fun to impress the innocent. "But don't think I can prove it—not a single act! She's as smart as Satan and can smell a detective ten miles off. No, she's still

Mrs. Sylvester Griscam, five years later, and will be until I ante up a million bucks."

"A million!" I gasped. I had read of such settlements, but only in the tabloids.

"Don't worry, she won't get it. She's got herself a shyster lawyer who likes the sound of big sums. She'll settle for a quarter of that amount. But the point is: where do I get the quarter?"

I could not imagine that Sylvester had come to me for financial advice, but as he continued to stare at me expectantly, I finally asked him why he needed a divorce at all.

"Because I want to marry Doris Drinker!" he exclaimed, as if it were the most obvious thing in the world.

"Perhaps you'd better tell me about Doris Drinker," I suggested with a sigh. "That is, if I'm to be any help. Though I don't see how I can."

"You'll see." Once again his hand was on my shoulder, and once again his voice sank confidentially. "Brian, this little Doris of mine is the wonder of wonders. She was a Wave at Fifty Church Street where I did my stint in the war and the brightest one in the whole office. She didn't know a thing about the Griscams or Dad being an ambassador or any of that rot. To her I was just plain Lieutenant Commander Griscam, another guy in the service. And there hasn't been any rinky-dink, either. No sirree. One good-night kiss on the doorstep has been my ration from the beginning."

Looking at poor Sylvester, so thin and plain and lanky, so heavy of breath and emphasis, so clumsily sincere, I thought of Mr. Griscam's passion for perfection and felt sorry for both of them.

"Maybe when your father understands about Doris, he'll be willing to put up Estelle's settlement."

"Not a chance. He put up for Faith, and he's sworn he won't do it again. The only hope is Mother. There's a way she can get at her trust with my consent. I'm the trustee, you see. She always wants money for her holy army. Very well, then." Here he suddenly gave me a conspiratorial wink. "Do you sniff a way that I can give the old girl what she wants if I get what I need?"

"But, Sylvester, is that honest?"

"Oh, it's honest enough. As trustee I have what is called a power to invade principal for her benefit. But Dad will regard any exercise of that power as highway robbery. He thinks that to let principal out of the family is to be . . . well . . ."

"Unprincipled," I finished for him. "Yes, I'm sure he'll be angry, but what can he do?"

"Oh, there's always something *he* can do. That's why I want you to talk to him." Sylvester's tone became eager again. "Please do it, Brian. You have a way with him. He'll take anything from you."

"Me?"

"Yes. Why he even gave up his plan of writing a life of Dr. Prescott because he saw you'd do it better! What more proof do you need?"

"But, Sylvester, there were other reasons for that."

"Come and talk to Mother, then."

We found Mrs. Griscam in the parlor, sitting straight and apparently serene on a pink bergère against a tapestry of blues and greens that depicted an eighteenth century French hunting scene. But there was something about her straightness, even in the flowing silks that enveloped her (she dressed exquisitely, but as women who dress for a cause) that seemed to repudiate, to shoo away as idle and silly any suggestion of a Pompadour or even of a Lespinasse. As she talked I noted for the first time a slight tremor in her tone.

"I don't want you to think, Brian, that we'd be doing anything wrong. It was my money that went into that trust, and it will be my money that comes out. Sylvester's father can have no just cause for complaint."

"I suppose he cares very deeply that you should be well provided for."

"But I *am* well provided for, that's just the point! My husband has very grand standards. We could all live on a fraction of what he's got. Do you think I need this big house? Why, I'd be happier in three rooms."

Yes, I saw them, those three little rooms, dusky and elegant, polished and neat and efficient, with a small residue of the best bibelots, and Mrs. Griscam writing checks on the cash saved at her slender-legged escritoire. And I saw Sylvester and Doris, happy in a Tudor cottage in Rye and Amy traveling from horse show to horse show. They needed money—oh, yes, they needed plenty of money, more money than I could even visualize—but they didn't need the heavy minted coin in which Mr. Griscam sought to entomb them. They didn't need, or in the least want, the big solid stone house, the shiny town car with the spoked wheels, the thick glass-grilled doors, the pompous porte-cochere, all the external paraphernalia of wealth without which men of Mr. Griscam's generation couldn't quite believe it existed. Poor Mr. Griscam, he had provided all the things that nobody wanted because, as the child of a bankrupt, he couldn't even take in the fact that everybody did not need, like himself, the constant consolation of marble pillars!

The only thing I could do for them, I concluded, was to bring the inevitable to a head. I had to find in my pity the courage for that. "Let me talk to him, then."

"Tell him it is God's will."

What sort of lives were these? Yet over their dryness and desolation Mrs. Griscam's fanaticism (if I can call it that) seemed to rise with the pale radiance of a Ryder moon.

Sylvester, like a little boy, had to bring any projected act to immediate fruition. As I had been dragged to the parlor, so now was I dragged to the library. Amy was induced to leave the backgammon table as she finished a game on the excuse that her mother wanted her, and Sylvester hurried out of the room on her heels.

"What on earth is Sylvester up to?" Mr. Griscam grumbled. "Can't he let me enjoy a game of backgammon? Do you play?" I confessed I did not. "What is it, Brian? You look as guilty as if you'd smashed my best Lowestoft."

"It's not what I *have* smashed. It's what I may be going to. I came to New York to ask your help, and here I am meddling already in your family affairs." I paused uncomfortably. "Sylvester asked me to talk to you about this girl he wants to marry."

Mr. Griscam's expression became impatient. "The Wave? Fine. I'm not stopping him."

"No, sir, but it seems he needs a divorce from his second wife."

"Why doesn't he get it, then? I shan't stand in his way. I never could abide Estelle."

"But it's the settlement he wants."

"Let me ask you something, Brian." Mr. Griscam's tone was very sharp. "If you were a father in my position, would you allow a substantial block of capital to go out of the family to a woman whom your own son describes as a bitch?"

But his very sharpness gave me the spirit I needed. "Yes, sir, I would. If my son's happiness depended on it."

"His happiness! Even if his happiness depended on a *third* marriage? How many times would you make it possible for him to marry? *You*, a minister of God?"

"Three times, sir."

He paused and laughed dryly. "A good answer. But I tell you, I won't do it. No, I won't, Brian. You probably think a father will always weaken, but not I. As I feel at the moment, the only way of having a satisfactory son is to adopt one fully grown, like the Romans!"

"Do you stop to consider that you may be sending him to other sources?"

"What other sources?" he demanded contemptuously, and then as, staring at me with a narrowing fixity, he took in my continued silence and gravity, he slowly reddened. "The trust!" he suddenly shouted. "Emmaline's trust! I knew it! *That's* what he's after, is it?" When I continued silent he seized me by the wrist and shook my arm. "Is it?"

"Mrs. Griscam needs money for her cause . . ."

"Oh, the crook!" He let me go abruptly and hurried out of the room. When I followed him to the parlor, I found the whole family in a state of great agitation. Sylvester had jumped to his feet, and his mother was very pale. Amy, watching her livid father, gave a low whistle.

"Hey, there, take it easy, old man. Do you want to have a stroke?"

Mr. Griscam ignored her as he faced his wife. "Emmaline, is it true? Is it your trust he's after?"

"I believe, David, that is a matter that concerns only Sylvester and myself," Mrs. Griscam retorted firmly. "Isn't that so, Sylvester?"

"Most assuredly." But Sylvester's grey cheeks and shifting eyes belied the confidence of his words.

"It concerns the head of the family, I think," his father said furiously. "Even in today's matriarchy I suppose a husband has something to say when his wife proposes to dump her money in the river!"

"Oh, Father," Amy protested, "must we talk business even on Sunday?"

"If you will let me speak, Amy, I think I can guarantee that even you won't regret it. Some years ago your mother and I agreed to make Sylvester the trustee of her trust. It was a delicate position as the trustee has power to give her principal. However, your brother in those days seemed the exemplification of all my hopes and theories. But love has come to erode the standards of that stern fiduciary." Here he looked with a scowl at Sylvester who continued to stare stubbornly at the Aubusson carpet. "In short, my dear Amy, your loving brother, finding that his sainted mother wants money for her cause, has made a deal with her. He will invade the trust for God, if God will divvy up with Venus."

"You mean, Sylvester," Amy called harshly across the room, "that you're going to blow Mother's money so you can marry that little Wave of yours?"

"She's no longer a Wave, Amy," he retorted bitingly. "If you'd read the papers, you'd know the war was over. But at least she served her nation while it was on."

"I'm sure you'd rather have me call her a Wave than what I'm really thinking!"

"Amy, my *dear!*" cautioned her mother, "Your father has not explained things fully. The money coming out of my trust will be divided three ways. One part will go to me, one to Sylvester and one to you."

"What's so terrible about that, then, Father?" Amy demanded immediately. "Why shouldn't Sylvester have his share so long as I get mine?"

Mr. Griscam turned impatiently from her to his son. "Have you considered, Sylvester, that I may take you to court for looting your trust?"

"What's the use, Dad?" Sylvester, still nervous but with the resolve of desperation, folded his hands on his stomach and peered down at them. "If you go to court, you'll lose. You drew that trust deed yourself, and you know my discretion is absolute."

"Sylvester!" his father exhorted him suddenly. "Leave your mother's trust alone. I'll give you the money you need!"

"I'm sorry, Dad. It's too late. I've given Mother my word."

Mr. Griscam looked from one to the other of his family helplessly. "Emmaline," he appealed to his wife, "tell me you won't give all that money to your ridiculous organization."

"I shall do as I am called to do, David."

"If you'd earned it yourself, if you'd saved it, if you'd even so much as watered it and let it grow as I have, you might have some right to fling it away. But how can you justify taking money that your father made and that I salvaged and increased, money that you've never lifted a finger about, and leave it away from your posterity?"

"If I give it to God," she answered in her stately tone, "God will give it back to them in his own way."

Her husband raised his hands to his temples with a moan of despair. "You ought to be committed!"

Mrs. Griscam and the children exchanged glances.

"I wonder if Mother's the one who should be committed," Amy murmured.

"David, dear, do take it easy."

"Oh, go away, all of you, please go!" Mr. Griscam groaned, leaning forward, his face covered with his hands. "Throw away your money, do anything you like. Nothing ever makes a dent on you. You take everything for granted. That I should spend a lifetime nursing you all, making you rich, why of course. Why not? What else am I good for? Nothing will teach you anything but starvation, and then it will be too late. May the god of money treat you as you have treated me!"

It was a highly embarrassing scene, and when the others had silently left the room I remained alone with my host. It was now that my real job began.

That afternoon Mr. Griscam and I went to Central Park and slowly circled the Reservoir. It was a cold, damp melancholy day, very much like his mood, and even the sea gulls on the ice in the middle of the water seemed to huddle together. The oblong of distant buildings which surrounded us and the circle whose circumference we were traversing seemed to reduce the great city under the starkness of a pale winter sky to two of the simplest geometric forms and Mr. Griscam's life to the simplest of failures.

The burden of his monologue was disillusionment. It seemed to him now, he related, that he had lived for no use, that every person whose life he had thought to have influenced would have done as well without him, that all of his supposed good deeds had been hidden from others, not by what he had proudly regarded as his diplomatic camouflage but by their own innate unimportance. The money that he had made and saved, who wanted it, except for foolish purposes? The clients and relatives whose bad tempers and destructive tendencies he had controlled, the school whose headmaster and board he had kept in harmony, the lawsuits he had settled, even the crisis in Panamanian-American relations that he had smoothed over, what did it all add up to but the fact that he had stood between his fellow beings and the dogfights for which they spoiled? Who cared for the peacemaker, the conservator? To spend, to throw away, to fight, to avenge—wasn't that what they called living? "Well, they'll get enough living one of these days," he concluded bitterly. "They'll all be blown up in a nuclear war, and good enough for them."

For the first time I found myself really liking Mr. Griscam. His mood of self-pity was more genuine than the old role of the vigilant fiduciary. As soon as he turned petulantly on life for what it had done to David Griscam, as soon as he had allowed the gates of his self-sufficiency to be forced, one's compassion could at last come in.

"I had a son, Jules, who died many years ago," he continued. "You've heard of him at Justin. He left a bad enough name there. Poor Jules was one of those tragic souls who make a mess of everything they touch, who bring unhappiness to everyone they meet. And yet he is still talked of with fascination by his friends. Almost with admiration. Why is it, Brian? Why is the world that way?"

At just that moment I had my inspiration. The idea and its articulation were almost simultaneous. "Why have you never put up a memorial for Jules in Justin Martyr?"

"Don't you know what he did there?"

"Of course I know. But it was so long ago. Time harmonizes the most disparate things. You and Jules and Dr. Prescott are all parts of the essential legend of the school. Why should only the happy boys be memorialized? Why not the failures, too? If I were you, I would build a library there and name it after him?"

Mr. Griscam gave me a quick look. "You're pretty free with other people's money, young man. It must be Sylvester's influence. Have you the smallest conception of what a library would cost these days?"

The biting cold suddenly pierced my coat, and I took a few quick steps in advance of him, hugging myself and breathing hard. I think the idea that now irradiated my mind must have chilled me as much as the weather. It was a brilliant idea, perhaps even an inspired one, but I was not used to such things, and I trembled. Had it been heresy to think of Mrs. Griscam as a fanatic? Might she not have been called to give away her money? And might not her husband be similarly called? Why should Justin Martyr which had provided the only home for his unhappy boyhood, which had been the lifelong outlet for his emotional needs, not give him the consolation that he needed in his old age? Oh, how it came to me!

"What does it matter how much it costs?" I asked in an ultimate burst of courage, turning back to him. "Haven't you just been telling me that nobody wants your money except for foolish purposes? Haven't your family already got more than they need? Why shouldn't you take some of the fortune that you've earned by your own sweat and toil and spend it on the things you care about? Why should you build just a library? Why not a new infirmary, too? They need one."

"Whoa, there, young man! Who do you think you're talking to? A Rockefeller?"

"Yes! At least to me you are. Is it so terrible to suggest that you spend your own money in your own lifetime on your own projects? I know one's not supposed to talk to rich men about their fortunes—or even to describe them to their faces as rich—but you have confided in me and I care about you. I want to help!"

Mr. Griscam stood still. We were facing west, and he was staring intently at the great yellow towers of the Beresford that rose into the bare sky with the heavy placidity of an Aztec temple. His breath, I noticed, was short. "I can see why people like you, Brian," he said at last. "You speak straight to the heart. Go on, young man, go on."

In the excited dialogue that followed, his spirits seemed to soar. It must have been true that Justin Martyr supplied the fuel to his being, the very blood to his veins, for his color returned and with it his normal confidence. I even suspected that I had stumbled upon—or been guided to—a project that he had long kept buried in his own mind, but that he had hardly dared mention even to himself. Oh, of course, he had given things to the school before, a window, a fountain, a dormitory wing, but not on *this* scale. As he talked on, I had a dazzling vision of the gleaming glass edifice that might be the Jules Griscam Library and of the sober grey one that might be the Infirmary. When we had completed our tour of the Reservoir, he paused again to look over the grey water. His dark mood was completely gone.

"No, I'm not just an old man yet, Brian. Not yet for a bit. And think of what a glorious moment to announce a big grant. On the diamond anniversary dinner!" He pinned my arm under his as we walked forward in the rapidly chilling air of the darkening afternoon. "It will be a good substitute, will it not, for the naughty speech that poor old Frank is plotting? My God, will it not!"

22

BRIAN'S JOURNAL

APRIL 1, 1946. The great diamond jubilee has exploded and gone, and I sit, so to speak, in a litter of paper hats and cigar butts and reach for my pen to describe its high events.

I have entered nothing since Christmas, for it has been a dull winter term, and Dr. Prescott has been in Florida for most of it. He came back only two weeks before the jubilee, and when I went over to call on him I found there was still constraint between us. He was very critical about everything, even the news of Mr. Griscam's proposed grant.

"But surely," I protested, "it's a princely gesture for a man to offer a new library and a new infirmary at one swoop."

"Princely?" he grumbled. "Why do you call it princely? Princes don't make gifts. David Griscam has always tried to turn Justin Martyr into a thing of his own. He couldn't do it by policy, so now he's trying to do it by bricks and mortar, that's all."

I thought this was pretty grudging, but I said nothing. The only thing that worried me about the Griscam gift was that it threatened to rob Dr. Prescott of some of the glory of a jubilee which I felt should be exclusively his. But, of course, I should not have worried about anyone stealing a show from Dr. Prescott. When the great anniversary came and the graduates descended upon the school at the beginning of the spring vacation, filling up the empty dormitories and giving to the place a comic atmosphere of middle-aged men, cigars in mouth and flasks in pockets, playing at schoolboys, the whole occasion, without its having been in the least so planned, moved about the short, broad-shouldered, plodding figure of the ex-headmaster. He seemed the constant center of revolving circles, a piece of cork helpless on the surface of an eddying stream. For the tide of the jubilee was a rough one for the staid school; it swamped it and covered it with an affection as violent as it was ultimately undiscriminating. Justin over that weekend began to seem to me like Paris occupied by German soldiers. Could the City of Light survive it?

Mr. Griscam asked me to lunch with him at the inn in New Paisley on his arrival and drove me back to the school afterwards. As his car turned in the school gates and started up the drive that wound around the campus, we saw Dr. Prescott coming across the grass followed by a crowd of some thirty graduates. He seemed to be leading them on an inspection tour of recent improvements, but the group conveyed a distinct sense of hilarity, and I was put in mind of the celebrating procession that traditionally followed a victory over Chelton, when the whole school would parade around the campus, following the headmaster in a chair strapped to two poles and borne on the shoulders of eight prefects, stopping to cheer each object or person encountered: the Schoolhouse, the aged oak tree, a master's wife, the fives courts, a dump truck.

Mr. Griscam told his chauffeur to stop, and we got out of the car as the group approached. For just a moment I had the irrational feeling that Mr. Griscam was a threatened symbol of authority about to take his chances with an unruly mob. Dr. Prescott had never struck me before as a revolutionary, but now he might have been a wily old Danton, ready, for the mere excitement of the gesture, to consign the chairman of the board and his limousine to the fury of his followers. Was it my imagination that made me wonder, as he came closer, if he had cast a mocking glance through the open door of the car at the tumbled fur rug upon the floor?

"David, my boy!" he exclaimed, clasping Mr. Griscam's hand. "Now that you're here the jubilee can begin! It's a superb thing you're doing. The gesture of a Medici prince." Was that dry eye upon me? I could not tell. "I trust your family will not be impoverished by this unexampled generosity?"

"Oh, no, Frank. In these days, you know, taxes are everything. They'll hardly feel it."

"Pray don't tell me about taxes," Dr. Prescott protested warmly. "Everything gets so twisted up that there's danger the very concept of gratitude may be lost. I *want* to be grateful. I want to be grateful to David Griscam for his princeliness to his school."

Certainly nobody could turn on the charm better than the old man when he wanted to.

That night the dinner was informal, with only one brief speech of welcome from Duncan Moore, and afterwards we all watched a movie of school activities in the assembly hall. When this was over, I accompanied Dr. Prescott to Mr. Griscam's suite at the Parents' House for a drink with some of the trustees. Mr. Griscam had asked me to this little party at lunch and had told me that he had a particular reason for wanting me to be present. He had a fire going, for it was a cold spring night, and a silver tray with an assortment of whiskeys and liqueurs. After ninety minutes of boys on the screen it was a cheerful sight.

The group was small and, I assumed, carefully selected, for Mr. Griscam always had a purpose for the things he did. Besides our host, there were only three trustees. I knew them all fairly well, for they were frequent visitors to the school. There was Sam Storey, president of Boston City Investors' Trust, a round red shrewd cotton-haired financier, whose mammoth, puffy build contained somewhere the muscular embryo that had made him one of Harvard's greatest quarterbacks. There was Gavin Glenway, like Mr.

Griscam a New York attorney, the senior partner of a great corporation law firm, a dry, caustic, brilliant man, as gaunt as Storey was stout, with all the biting conservatism of a representative of industry and the high temper of a litigator. And finally there was Ira Hitt, a younger man, in his early forties, who had been a scholarship boy at Justin and who had made a fortune during the war, the type of new speculator, dry, bone-headed, sharp-eyed, prematurely balding, with a remarkably strong personality for one of such thin shoulders and unprepossessing appearance. They were all good drinkers, and they had all started early in the festive atmosphere of the day. Dr. Prescott himself had had a few cocktails in the long period before dinner. He was by no means a regular drinker, hut he had a great capacity, whenever he chose to use it. The only effect of liquor was to make him at once gentler and more sardonic.

Mr. Griscam led the discussion into the question of what sort of boys the future Justin Martyr should seek to educate, thus placing in issue Duncan Moore's policy of "broadening the base." Dr. Prescott asked if this was compatible with his concept of the school as a family.

"It's a curious sort of family that can turn down Jack Gregg's grandson," Gavin Glenway suggested, with his deep lawyer's throat-clearing, as he packed his pipe.

"*Has* he been turned down?" Dr. Prescott asked in concern. "Has he indeed?"

"Perhaps we shouldn't be too shocked," Glenway continued, in a tone of weighted sarcasm. "Perhaps we should endeavor to take the modern view. What if Jack Gregg raised a half million dollars for the pension plan? What if no fewer than ten Greggs have graduated from Justin? What if Jack's father was one of the first trustees? What is all that against simple merit? Let Justin Martyr be as stern as Justice!"

"But, Gavin," Dr. Prescott protested, "to admit Jack Gregg's grandson, would we have to consider what he has *given* the school? Is it not enough that he is an old *friend* of the school? And what is so wrong with making an exception for the grandson of an old friend? Would it have to mean that one was truckling to wealth?"

"I'm afraid it would, Dr. P. Because it's hard for a man to become a well-known friend of the school unless he gives to the school. And it's the wealthy who give. However, I am not so scrupulous as you. I most assuredly would manage to find room for any grandson of Jack Gregg who wasn't a Mongolian idiot."

"You mean *because* of his wealth?" Dr. Prescott persisted, shocked.

"I'd never answer that question. Why should I? I'm a practical man."

"And I'm not?" Here Dr. Prescott rose slowly to return to the drink tray, and Mr. Griscam moved to help him. "No, no, sit down, David," he grumbled. "I'm just putting another drop of whiskey in this. You made it too light. Sit down," he repeated irritably, "you're getting old yourself. A practical man!" he exclaimed, his back to the rest of us as he poured his drink. "How many times a schoolmaster has to hear that term! All you graduates like to believe that you have been buffeted by hard realities whereas we

at Justin have lived unspotted by the world. You return here lovingly perhaps, but certainly condescendingly. There's dear little old quaint Dr. P.
Was he the demon who scared us so as boys? Why, he's as soft as sawdust!"
He turned now to face the trustees as they protested and raised his hand to
check them. "Now, stop it, all of you. You know it's true. It's one of the
functions of a school to make even the softest graduate feel hard-boiled."

As we laughed, he sat down again, stirring his drink slowly and gazing
into it as if unsure whether it were friend or foe. "You want to protect me,
so be it. We agree, anyway, about taking the Gregg boy, if for different
reasons. You, Gavin, because of your experience in the law, believe that the
most discreditable reason must be the governing one. I am not so sure of
that. I believe that we could make an exception for Gregg boys simply because we like them and because they belong at Justin."

"Well, we can all agree that there's room in life for exceptions," Gavin
Glenway said placatingly. "I'm sure David will agree with me that a lifetime in the law makes one suspicious of rules."

"Perhaps the exception should *be* the rule," Dr. Prescott said so mildly
that Glenway did not realize that he was being laughed at. "Perhaps that
would be a lawyer's paradise."

"Of course, if Jack Gregg had changed the boy's name to Kowalski, he'd
have gotten in fast enough," Sam Storey intervened explosively. He had
followed Dr. Prescott's example in fortifying his drink. "Next year's first
form might have been garnered at Ellis Island. Now I like to think I'm as
democratic as the next guy, but where do we stop? Do we want to jettison
altogether the principle of a Protestant school for boys of Anglo-Saxon
descent?"

"But there was never any such principle!" Dr. Prescott protested, shocked
again.

"Not in your eyes, sir, I admit. But in the eyes of most of the country
Justin, along with the other New England prep schools, has that reputation. And why should we be ashamed of it? Haven't our boys come of the
families that made America great? Isn't there something in traditions of
honor and responsibility handed down from generation to generation? Look
at the aristocratic tradition in England!"

"I know a bit about that, Sam," Dr. Prescott replied, still, I thought, with
astonishing mildness. "Don't forget that I went to Oxford. But in England
the upper classes used to give something in return for their privileges. They
went into government and into the army and the church. It was a tradition
of public service."

"Well, Groton produced Franklin Roosevelt," I volunteered. I had been
silent so far, respecting the presence of my elders and betters, but I could
not resist this opportunity. The reaction was immediate.

"Ugh!"

"Groton should be ashamed of it."

"Groton *is* ashamed of it!"

"Gentlemen, gentlemen!" Dr. Prescott exclaimed, raising both hands now,
a glimmer of amusement in his eye. "You forget that David Griscam was

one of our late president's diplomatic appointees." There was a murmur of perfunctory apology. "It has always been my chief regret," he continued in a sadder tone, "that Justin has sent so few men into public service. When the English nobility began to turn to the stock market, it seemed to me there was no further justification for an upper house."

"Yet it's just what saved it!" protested Ira Hitt. "That's the only way any of your old families survive. By adapting themselves to the new. Ask Dave here." I had never heard anyone call Mr. Griscam "Dave" before, but no doubt excitement made him intimate. "He's the expert. Would families like the Griscams occupy the position they occupy today if they'd gone into the army or navy or wasted their time in politics? Hell, no! I beg your pardon, Dr. Prescott."

"It's quite all right, dear boy," the old man replied blandly, waving his arm. "Hell no, as you say. Pray go on about the Griscams." He cocked a mocking eye in Mr. Griscam's direction. "I find it most instructive."

"They stayed in the market. They put their money where the new people were putting their money. They even married the new people. Isn't it so, Dave?" He pressed on, ignoring Mr. Griscam's irritated shrug. "Because business is our aristocracy. Finance is our aristocracy. Even after thirteen years of creeping socialism! You should be proud, Dr. Prescott, that you have sent your boys to take their places in the front ranks of American progress. And until the day we go Commy—which may not be far off— business will continue to be the front ranks. I believe Justin Martyr *should* educate the sons of our business and banking leaders. And, of course, a certain percentage of the new people, too. *I* was a new person. I made my way, but I got my start at Justin!"

We were all a bit embarrassed by this outburst, but Dr. Prescott knew just how to deal with it. "That's very gratifying to hear, Ira," he said smoothly. "I remember when you were a third former and wanted to put the school store on a paying basis. You even had a plan to issue stock. We suspected then that you would go far." The rest of us laughed, and Ira flushed with pleasure. "I take it, then, that in broadening our base you would select, in addition to the Cabots and Lowells, boys who look as if they might grow up into Cabots and Lowells?"

"Well . . . yes. As a matter of fact, I rather like that way of putting it."

"I am glad that my phrase was so felicitous. I think I begin to put together the opposition that you gentlemen feel to my successor's program. Gavin would favor the sons of the rich, and Sam, more in the tradition of John Adams, would lean to the well-born."

"Now, Dr. P, it's not that simple."

"Ah, but it's an old man's privilege to oversimplify. And Ira would lean to both while keeping a wary eye on the hordes from which new recruits for the Social Register must be periodically selected. I must say, gentlemen, you make me feel like the patron saint of the Chamber of Commerce. Or should it be the Society of the Cincinnati? My likeness should be raised upon a pedestal at the foot of Wall Street."

"You may laugh at us, Dr. P," Gavin Glenway rejoined, "but in sober truth you should be proud. It is the moral tone of the business community that sets the moral tone of the nation. And you have done your share of elevating it."

"Good, good," the old man muttered.

"Of course, I don't say Mr. Moore is entirely off base," Ira Hitt conceded. "In these days a school must keep an eye on its tax exemption. The time may be coming when it will be politic to have a couple of coons to show the Revenue boys. Just to keep the record straight."

Dr. Prescott's face was drawn to an expression of the tightest fascination. "Coons?" he asked softly.

"Negroes. We may come to that. Oh, a couple would do the trick. And some of them, you know, could pass for whites."

"So?" Dr. Prescott pursued. "Is there an agency that supplies them? Can we write and ask for a Negro with a white face and a Jew with a straight nose and a Japanese who's hardly yellow at all? Ah, the wonders of your liberal world, Ira!"

"I didn't make the world, sir," Ira said sulkily. "You can make fun of me, of course, if you like."

The pause that followed this was a bit weighted with constraint, and Gavin Glenway ended it by asking: "What does David think? He hasn't expressed an opinion."

"Oh, David believes in everything," Dr. Prescott answered in a strong voice tinged with bitterness. "David would have the old families and the new, the bright and the stupid. The Jew and the Gentile. And somehow, when David was through with them, they'd all be the same. They'd all be Davids. Isn't that the American dream?"

As he rose to bring his drink again to the bar table, the trustees exchanged uneasy glances.

"I wonder if it isn't my bedtime," Gavin Glenway suggested.

"I think perhaps it's everybody's," Sam Storey agreed, and we all rose.

"Can I see you home, sir?" Glenway asked Dr. Prescott.

"No, no, I'm going to stay and have a nightcap with David and Brian," Dr. Prescott said without turning from the bottle that he was carefully pouring. "Don't worry about me. I shall be fine. Good night, gentlemen. And thank you for your ideas."

As I watched the departing trustees one by one take Dr. Prescott's hand to bid him good night, adding further stories and opinions to what had already been said, a great light flashed on in the attic of my mind, illuminating suddenly what had been only a dusky doubt. I had been disturbed about something obscurely but unpleasantly at hand in our meeting, a something that seemed to amount to a small sense of surprise that trustees of Justin could be so ordinary, so angular, so predictable. But if predictable, whence the surprise? It was just the answer to this that I now saw: if they seemed predictable it was because they had been predicted, because Mr. Griscam had picked them out and turned them on. He had stacked his hand with the men on whom he could count to persuade Dr. Prescott that Duncan Moore, with all his faults, was an idealist compared to the average graduate. To warn him that if he ever *did* unseat Moore, his successor might be worse!

I saw Mr. Griscam nod to the others as he shut them out, to reassure them, perhaps, that he would take care of the old man, and then return to his seat. Dr. Prescott took his drink back to his armchair. He sat for several minutes staring moodily into the fire, and when he spoke it was clear that he had been thinking my thoughts.

"Did you plan it that way, David?" he asked, and when Mr. Griscam did not answer at once, he pursued: "Did you plan that little discussion to open my long-sealed eyes?"

"I thought you might find it interesting."

"Then you must answer me something. Truthfully."

"When have I not?"

"Oh, many times, David. You are like a Jesuit with truth. You believe in meting it out according to the recipient's capacity to take it. Mine you have always rated very low. But I am learning—oh, yes, I am making strides. I sometimes think my education began with my retirement. I can take most anything now. Tell me truthfully." Here he paused and held up a finger to warn Mr. Griscam that he was in earnest. "Are those three men—Sam and Gavin and Ira—representative of graduate opinion?"

As I opened my lips to protest, I saw Mr. Griscam's eyes fixed upon me in what, surprisingly enough, seemed a rather mild stare. "All right," he appeared to be telling me, "rush in and break things up, go on, impetuous youth. But, remember who came whining down to New York last Christmas for help and tell me afterwards who will keep the old man from making a fool of himself tomorrow night." He continued so to look at me, perfectly patient, ignoring Dr. Prescott's question, throwing me, so to speak, the ball, until in silence and confusion I could only bow my head.

"I believe they *are* typical, Frank," he answered gravely.

"I see." Dr. Prescott gave one of his deep sighs. "I don't, but does it matter? If even *some* are that way! Of course, none of them is actually young."

"The young don't make the decisions. You know that, Frank."

"No. They simply die for those who do. So be it." He was silent again, and there was no sound but the crackling of the fire and the sipping of his drink.

"Don't finish that, Frank," Mr. Griscam suggested softly. "You have a long day tomorrow."

"Don't be impertinent to your elders, David. I know exactly what I can drink, and I have every intention of finishing this one."

We sat for a few minutes more until suddenly Dr. Prescott started talking, in a low, somber tone, gazing into the fire. "I took my daughter Evelyn's youngest child to the circus in Boston last week. There was a clown in it who kept trying to escape from a round bright spotlight trained on him from the top of the house. He ran all about; he tried to escape into the audience. Everywhere the bright circle remorselessly pursued him. Now I see that I was that clown. And the spotlight was the effort of all the rest of you to keep the truth from me."

"The truth?" I burst out in dismay. "What truth?"

Dr. Prescott looked at me as if he had forgotten my presence. But his tone was perfectly kind. "The truth about Justin Martyr, Brian. I was to see only the bright light of the circle in which *I* was to perform. Beyond it was the darkness which was no affair of mine. Oh yes, *you* saw it, David, you and the others. You were used to the darkness. But it was not for clowns. Clowns had to keep clowning so that the rest of you could forget the darkness in which you sat."

"But now you see it," Mr. Griscam said impassively.

"As if it were light."

"And what exactly do you see?"

Dr. Prescott jerked his head around to give his interrogator a cold stare. "I see that Justin Martyr is like the other schools. Only *I*, of course, ever thought it was different. Only I failed to see that snobbishness and materialism were intrinsic in its make-up. Only I was naïve enough to think I could play with that kind of fire and not get my hands burnt. But you, David, of course, understood all that. You even saw how to make a selling point out of my naïveté. You persuaded the world that the gospel of Prescott of Justin was the passport to good society. And the world believed it! When I urged the boys to go into politics or the ministry, they accepted it as Prescottism, so many lines of a lesson to be learned that had no relation to the real world at home. They learned their lines, yes. Some of them even enjoyed learning them. They had been told by their parents that to be a graduate of Justin would be a material aid in that real world. Ah, yes, reality." He grunted here and paused. "Reality was the brokerage house, the corporation law firm, the place on Long Island, the yacht, the right people. The obvious things. One can't be too obvious about them. I was simply added to their list."

"Why, Frank," Mr. Griscam demanded, "must you assume that nobody but you has any idealism?"

"I assume there was no idealism in this room tonight!" Dr. Prescott exclaimed in a loud barking tone. "I listened to those men. I listened carefully. Your unhappy boy Jules thought I was a devil. Had he lived, he would have learned that I was only a fool. Perhaps Jules and I had more in common than either of us suspected. Perhaps we were both clowns imprisoned in our spotlights."

"But you've always been a realist," Mr. Griscam protested, "ever since I've known you. A rather bitter realist, too. There are those who've even called you a cynic. You've professed to understand the worldly motive, the power of snobbery, the dollar. Why suddenly is it so appalling to face those things in Justin?"

"Because I created Justin!" Dr. Prescott cried out. "And I created it precisely because I saw the world as you say. Because of the carpetbaggers who sold out the victory in my boyhood! And now I see that Justin is only another tap for the world's materialism. For *you*, David. Oh, rot!" He rose suddenly and disgustedly to go. "I may be a maudlin old man, but I'm not a complete idiot. I see your game. You've had wind of my speech tomorrow night, and you're trying to head it off. Well, sleep well, old boy. You've succeeded. As you've always succeeded in everything you've tried to do here."

"Please, Frank." Mr. Griscam followed him to the door. "It breaks my heart to hear you talk that way."

"You should know how to mend hearts, David. Isn't it your trade?"

"That's not fair!" Mr. Griscam was suddenly angry himself, "Do you think you're the only one who's ever been disillusioned? Do you think the rest of us have experienced nothing in life? How do you think I felt when Jules pitched that rock through the chapel window that *I* had given?"

Dr. Prescott turned at once and placed his hand sympathetically on the other's arm. "Poor Davey."

"You haven't called me 'Davey' since I was a schoolboy!"

"Then it's time I did. Good night, my friend."

I picked up Dr. Prescott's cloak and put it over his shoulders. "Let me see you home, sir," I murmured.

"Thank you, Brian, I will. These old eyes aren't what they used to be in the dark." He turned now to shake hands with Mr. Griscam. "We've put young Brian through quite a scene tonight, haven't we?"

Mr. Griscam glanced at me in his old, half-suspicious fashion and shrugged. "Oh, Brian is used to them by now, I guess," he said as he closed the door behind us.

The following night, at the big dinner, Dr. Prescott sat at the head table on the dais between Duncan Moore and the Bishop of Massachusetts, looking down over four hundred men in evening jackets at long tables decorated with silver candelabra and red candlesticks. It was a good show. The big portraits were lit, and I happened to be facing the magnificent canvas that Ellen Emmet Rand had painted of the former headmaster under Mr. Griscam's commission to replace the Laszlo portrait which his son Jules had destroyed. Gavin Glenway had already announced Mr. Griscam's proposed gift, and he had received, as anticipated, a standing ovation. Duncan Moore was now concluding his speech with a eulogy to his predecessor.

"Whatever we do at Justin Martyr, whatever we keep of the past, whatever we change, whatever our mistakes and whatever our strivings, in happy moments and in times of discouragement, we are always in the tradition of Dr. Prescott, for the simple reason that there is no other tradition that we can be in. No matter how good a job I may be lucky enough to accomplish, and no matter how brilliant my successors, we will always be the disciples of Francis Prescott. Justin Martyr is his school, his child, his ideal. And whatever he may think of our fumbling, I hope that he will always have his renowned tolerance for those whose best, after all, is only of his own creating."

The whole room arose again in a spontaneous roar of applause, and when they were seated I noticed that Dr. Prescott had remained on his feet. He stood for several seconds until the room was silent. Never had he looked more sage, more beautiful, and only the twitching of the muscles of his left cheek betrayed his conflicting emotions.

"Bishop, Mr. Moore, fellow trustees and Justinians," he began in his grave, slow, carrying tone, and then he paused again.

I could not bear to look at him. I decided it would be less painful to watch the drama that must ensue in the theatre of Pierre Dahlgren's round face, and I fixed my eyes on him and saw his lips open and close.

"You have all heard much fine oratory this evening, much moving oratory. I had hoped that I could add to it, but I find that I cannot. When I think of sixty years of school my heart is too full for comment. Let an old man say one thing and then step back into the shadows where he belongs. May all of you know the joy one day that *I* have now, the greatest joy that can befall a man of my years, the joy of knowing that his work is carried on. To you, Duncan Moore, my more than worthy successor, I lift my glass." Solemnly, slowly, he did this and turned back to his audience. "God bless you, gentlemen."

We all rose for the third ovation of that evening, but this one was far greater than its predecessors. We must have stood clapping and cheering for five full minutes. Poor Pierre Dahlgren! He clapped the hardest of anybody and looked as ashy as if he had had a stroke.

I did not see Dr. Prescott again that weekend. When I called at his house the following afternoon, Mrs. Midge met me at the door and told me with obvious apprehension that he was very tired after the celebrations and was resting in bed. Over her shoulder I saw Duncan Moore coming down the stairs, and *I* turned away, ashamed of the sudden prick of childish jealousy. I went to Parents' House to bid farewell to Mr. Griscam and found him on the porch. The chauffeur was already putting his bags in the car.

"Frank is tired, I hear," he said as I came up.

"Yes, last night took a lot out of him."

"Heroic deeds are apt to."

"What I don't see, sir, is how you could have been so sure that everything would work out as it did."

"I wasn't sure. I took my chances. A lawyer learns that."

"And if I hadn't come to visit you last Christmas you wouldn't have done anything?"

"Naturally not. How would I have known?"

"I see." I nodded stupidly. "I suppose you had to do it. Only somehow I didn't anticipate that you would disillusion him so."

"You must learn, as a minister, Brian," Mr. Griscam reminded me severely, "to bear the consequences of conduct that you believe to be right."

"Yes, of course." I plunged my hands in my pockets and continued to stare at the floor. "Only if I'd known that you would find it necessary to hurt him so deeply, I wonder if I wouldn't have let the whole thing alone. That's always been my trouble. I care more for him than for the school. You don't. You're right, of course."

"Hurt him so deeply?" he queried, and I knew by the exasperation in his tone that he was fighting to stem his own concern. "But surely that's nonsense. Frank has great resilience. You'll see. In a day or two he'll be smiling at the whole thing."

I shook my head. "He's old now, sir. Suddenly very old. That's the difference. And he thinks his life has been a failure."

"But that's absurd!" In his sudden impatience I thought Mr. Griscam was going to shake me. "One doesn't decide one's life has been a failure because one happens to disapprove of the point of view of a handful of trustees!"

"Let's hope not, sir."

"Well, *does* one?"

"I'm sure you wouldn't."

He stood there, biting his lip, frustrated by his inability to convince me. Or to convince himself. "Is there anything I can do?"

I tried not to show in my tone how much more than enough I thought he had already done. "No, I don't think so, sir."

He saw that it was hopeless and shrugged. "Just remember, young man, that you can't make an omelet without breaking eggs." He went briskly down the steps to his car and turned before getting in. "Keep me posted. You know how much I care."

I waved mechanically as the big limousine drove off, remembering my fantasy of its seeming the threatened symbol of authority. I continued to wave, as foolishly as a child, until it was out of sight.

23

BRIAN'S JOURNAL

OCTOBER 10, 1946. Shortly after commencement last spring I was asked by the Bishop of Massachusetts to take a six months' leave of absence to prepare a report on church schools and church education in the diocese, and Mr. Moore thought it advisable that I should accept. I have been living in Boston since June, and only yesterday on my first visit back to school, did I receive the bad news.

I had driven down for the day, as I now have a car for my researches, and after Sunday chapel Mr. Moore came up to me and led me aside from the throng.

"Have you seen Dr. Prescott?" he asked gravely.

"No, I'm just on my way now."

"Good. But you must expect to find him much weaker. We had the diagnosis yesterday."

The bell in the tower above us struck the quarter hour, and the air throbbed with its note and my apprehension. "I didn't even know he was ill!"

"None of us did, though he's been looking poorly and didn't make his usual trip to the Cape this summer. Evelyn Homans finally took him into Boston for a complete test at Massachusetts General."

"What is it, for God's sake?"

Mr. Moore put his hand firmly on my shoulder. "Take it easy, old boy," he said as I shivered. "It's what you'd want at his age. It's what he wants himself. Cancer of the lung. Dr. Larkin says it will be very fast and almost painless." His grip tightened as I suddenly sobbed. "Try to remember, Brian, that he's had a very long and a very happy life."

I nodded, but I couldn't look at him. "Does he know?"

"Oh, yes. You'll find him actually cheerful about it."

"And how long does he have? I mean, is it weeks or months?"

"Weeks, probably. But one never knows. He's so strong. I'm glad you've come, Brian. Go to him now."

I stumbled like a drunkard across the garth to Dr. Prescott's house and found him as cheerful as Moore had said.

"I see you've heard my news," he exclaimed in the tone he might have used to tell me of another honorary degree. "I must say it's not kind of you to look so downcast. A speedy, efficient little killer, isn't that what we all want?" We were sitting on the tiny front porch from which we looked out at the back of the school chapel and up at its great rambling dark tower. Dr. Prescott's little house seemed to squat happily in its shadow like a reverend toad stool. "Think of it. Could any old fogy of eighty-six ask for more? I used to have a dim little hope that my seeming immunity from pain would run out and that one day I would suffer a bit of what other humans have suffered. Well, that hope is apparently going to be a vain one, and it's just as well. Only vanity asks for a test when none is offered."

When he saw the tears start to my eyes and that I was about to blurt something out, he raised a warning hand. "I don't want to talk about it any more. It is very awkward. I have always deplored the selfishness of old people who embarrass the young with unnecessary references to their demises. I have told my daughters and Moore, and I told him to tell you. You are a minister and you must learn to take death in your stride. It is another fact to a professional, that is all."

He then had the kindness to send me away until I should have collected myself. "Go for a walk, dear boy. Go to the river and back. Consider my years and that my career is over. Consider that Harriet has gone before me. Consider what a gentle exit, laced with dope, awaits me. And then ask yourself how much more time you would want for an old man who wants none for himself. You see? It's not so bad. Then come back, and we'll talk about other things."

I did as I was told, and when we had tea together, later that afternoon, I was under control. When I left, I asked him if I could make a habit of driving down to see him every Saturday afternoon, and he consented provided only it did not interfere with my church report. And then in a burst of gratitude and because I had been overwrought by his news, I subjected him to one of my silly fits of conscience. Oh, the egotism of the neurotic!

"Unless you think I'm only coming to collect your last words!" I exclaimed. "Perhaps I am. Perhaps, God help me, I am!"

"Coming to see me is a good deed, Brian," Dr. Prescott replied gently. "It gives me pleasure, therefore it is good. You worry too much about motives. Suppose your motive *is* selfish. Very well. But now suppose yourself an inquisitor of the Middle Ages who would burn my living body to save my soul. The *motive* might be good. But what about poor me at the stake! Do you imagine the good Lord will reward the inquisitor more than you? Of course not. Some of the intrinsic goodness of a good deed must seep into the motive, and some of the bad of a bad deed. Keep doing good deeds long enough, and you'll probably turn out a good man. In spite of yourself."

October 17. I was much ashamed of my outburst of last week, and I resolved not to daub my sick little worries again on the serene canvas of his departure. When I went down yesterday I was able to behave more like a man. I stayed the night in Dr. Prescott's guest room, and the next morning we went to chapel together. The disease is as rapid as he hoped, and his strength is failing fast. He had to pause to rest every few steps of the brief distance.

"I made a foolish resolution last spring," he told me. "I wanted to teach myself a lesson for having interfered with Duncan Moore's administration, and I made a vow that I would never set foot on the campus again. But that, of course, was making poor Moore pay for my mistake. That was sulking in my tent! When I understood this, I decided to make certain regular appearances at the school. On Sunday chapel. At Sunday lunch. At football games with visiting teams. On Prize Day, and so forth. Now I am obliged to cut it down to Sunday chapel, but I shall continue that as long as I am able."

October 24. Alas, he was not long able, for when I arrived this afternoon, I found him in bed and in a very despondent state of mind. He was sitting, hunched up on three big pillows, looking unexpectedly forlorn in a rather ragged old dressing gown. He seemed hardly to mind what I was saying, shaking his head gloomily. As I was about to leave, he told me a story that seemed relevant to nothing but his mood.

"When I was a little boy I used to visit my maternal grandmother in Dedham, and I attended a Sunday school there. The minister, a long, lanky, dour-looking fellow, opened each class by making us hold out our hands with the index fingers pointed upwards. 'Consider, children,' he would tell us in a sepulchral tone, 'the pain of touching the tip of your finger to your mother's stove, even for a fraction of a second. That is an experience which most of you must have suffered. Now try to imagine that pain, not simply on a fingertip but spread over the whole surface of your body, and not for a mere second, but everlastingly. *That*, children, is hellfire."

I shuddered. "And did you believe it?"

"At seven? Of course I believed it!"

"But you don't believe it now?"

"Oh, now." He shrugged. "I suppose not. But I think of it sometimes when I lie awake in the early morning!"

October 31. Today, thank God, he was in an easier mood. I found him sitting in an armchair in his bedroom, dressed in a beautiful blue silk kimono that Cordelia Turnbull had sent him. It looked a bit curious on him, but one forgot about it as soon as he began to talk. I have never heard his voice softer or more melodious.

"Do you know, Brian, that retirement was the making of me? It taught me some elementary lessons in humility. It taught me, for example, that I should have retired ten years ago. For my own good, as well as the school's."

"Surely not for the school's, sir."

"Well, you know what people are saying. 'Old Prescott, he was picturesque, in his way—of his generation, you know. A bit theatrical, a bit violent, but he got away with it. Now, however, one needs a different type. A more accommodating head. One like Moore who knows how to get on with the parents and trustees.'" He turned on me suddenly with some of his old presence. "Do you *dare* deny, Brian, that they're saying that?"

"Some say it, I suppose, sir."

"And they're right, too," he said emphatically. "The crowd has a way of being right, of flaring the ego under the noble ambition. Who was I to think I could change the face of American education?"

"But why, sir, must you always be looking to the high goal you haven't totally achieved? Could anyone have come any closer to it? Why can't you ever consider instead the smaller goals that you *have* reached? The individual boys you've helped?"

"That's all a man should look to, isn't it?" His smile was melancholy. "Yes, Brian, I have asked too much. I have been greedy. I *have* helped a few boys, and I should be grateful for that." He closed his eyes as he cast his mind back. "I think I helped Charley Strong a bit. At the end, anyway. And Gates Appleton, when his parents had that terrible divorce. And Christian Villard when he lost his arm." Then he opened his eyes and shook his head wistfully. "But think of the others, Brian. The ones I hurt. Or killed, even. Like Jules Griscam."

"You didn't mean to. God will know."

"God will know I hated that boy!" he exclaimed violently. "A headmaster should have no hates. Poor Jules. He has had his revenge in my remorse." He shuddered. "Yes, it was terrible, my remorse. For I had allowed him to bring me down to his level, and he *knew* it. When his father tore the scales off my eyes last spring and made me see my lifework for the poor thing it was, I wondered if I couldn't hear Jules' high, screeching laugh. How he would have crowed!"

"Jules was only one of thousands of boys, sir. How could you succeed with them all?"

"I couldn't," he said abruptly. "I'm getting maudlin. You'd better go."

November 8. Today he told me not to come again. He is in bed and likely never to leave it. For the first time he seemed like a dying man. He was lying on his back, staring up at the ceiling.

"There comes a time when the doors should be closed," he said, "when the family takes over. My daughters are coming. Harriet, in fact, is here. It is a rather pleasant atavism, the priority that blood takes over friendship in the end. It is a ceremony in which each participant knows just what to do. I shall say goodbye, Brian. You must be a fine minister and cast out fear. I love you, my boy." He turned now, and the dark eyes seemed to stare through me. "Do you know what my old master at Balliol, Jowett, said at the end? 'I bless God for my life.' It's all one can say. Bless God for my life, Brian. And for yours."

In tears I fell to my knees and kissed his hand, as I kissed his wife's seven years ago. I then remained by the bedside praying. I do not know how long, until I felt a touch on my shoulder. It was Mrs. Kidder, who with a brief but friendly smile indicated that I was to go. I took my last look at my dear old friend, whose eyes were closed, and tiptoed out of the room.

December 10. Duncan Moore telephoned to say that Dr. Prescott died in his sleep this morning. God was merciful to the very end in sparing him the pain he had sometimes wanted and that I have no doubt he would have borne like a hero. He died in peace, and I believe that we should be in peace. But the very sky looks darker to me, and the Boston streets where I walked today seemed dreary and woebegone. He would have scoffed at me and told me not to be a fool. And, God helping, tomorrow I shan't be. But today all is dust within me, and I can write no more.

24

BRIAN'S JOURNAL

APRIL 2, 1947. I returned to my post at Justin in January, and the winter term has been crowded with catching up. I determined, however, that I would spend the two weeks of the spring vacation alone at school and review my thoughts and notes on Dr. Prescott. Ten precious days have now gone by, and I am still in a quandary.

What do I do with these papers?

How can I use them so as to convey the smallest hint of his greatness, bound as I am to include the essence of Jules Griscam's story? Not that I regard Dr. Prescott's condition as a wholly unreasonable one. I agree with him that his failure with Jules was an important part of his record as a headmaster, and with Mr. Griscam that there was a "hard" period in Dr. Prescott's life.

But my trouble is precisely that I am not interested in writing a biography. I am interested only in *inspiring* my reader, and I am much at odds with my century in believing that to demonstrate the best by itself is more inspiring than the best with the worst. I want to reveal Dr. Prescott resplendent in the pulpit with his arms, so to speak, outstretched and his great eyebrows arched. I want the little figures like myself who might turn up on preliminary drafts washed out of the final picture. I know that we live in an age where the homely or psychological detail is considered all-important. We like heroes in shirtsleeves, or, in other words, we don't like heroes. But things were not always that way, and today is not forever.

The Francis Prescott who was Charley Strong's boyhood hero certainly existed, and existed more vividly, to my thinking, than the Francis Prescott who failed to sympathize with Jules Griscam. I say more "vividly" because Charley Strong's vision of God coincided, at least at moments, with Dr. Prescott's own, and it was this kind of bridge, this kind of communication of the ideal, that seems to me the only part of the Justin story worth memorializing. To tell it otherwise is to record a failure, and why do that? Something remarkable happened on that campus, and there is no profit in dwelling on the unremarkable.

Of course, nobody knows better than I that in the end Dr. Prescott deemed himself a failure, but a contrary view seemed to be overwhelmingly borne out when the great coffin, draped in the school colors of red and gold, was carried by the prefects from the packed chapel through a double row of hundreds of graduates, for whom there had been no room inside, all singing at the top of their lungs: "The Son of God goes forth to war." Behind came the Governor, the Bishop, four senators, eight judges and the headmasters of every boys' school in New England. Was it simply, as he himself might have put it, that the survivors of his organization, now that he was dead and harmless, wanted to build a bonfire of glory in which they could warm their trembling fingers and forget their relief?

I think not. I think the demonstration came from the depth of many hearts. For I believe that Dr. Prescott's true greatness lay less in his school than in his impact on individual boys. I even believe that he knew this himself, for he knew himself thoroughly, good and bad. He knew his capacity to be petty, vain, tyrannical, vindictive, even cruel. He fully recognized his propensity to self-dramatization and his habit of sacrificing individuals to the imagined good of his school. Yet he also saw at all times and with perfect clarity that his own peculiar genius was for persuading his fellow men that life could be exciting and that God wanted them to find it so. And having once seen and understood the good that he was thus destined to accomplish, how could he ever stop? How could he ever, even in moments of doubt, switch off his genius and leave his audience before a darkened stage?

Justin Martyr remains to us, as does the legend of Francis Prescott. In this early spring the awakening elms seem more glorious than ever and the brown craggy chapel tower more massive against a white sky streaked with blue. I walked through the empty dining room this morning to look at the

Rand portrait. His hands folded uncharacteristically in his lap, Dr. Prescott gazed serenely over my head at the campus, which appeared in its entirety through the wide south windows. Listening to the purr of the lawnmower outside I had a funny feeling in that silent chamber that he might have been dead a hundred years.

Perhaps that is because I am less concerned now with the man than with the legend. Dr. Prescott was greater than the school which he created and by which he was ultimately disillusioned, and it is my ambition to distill for future generations of Justin boys some bit of the essence of that greatness. To those who would claim that I am contemplating a novel and not a history, I can only respond that the stories of all great men have been in some part works of fiction.

But I must stop rambling. I must cease my everlasting speculations. If I am ever to write anything, even if I give it my whole lifetime, I must still make a beginning. I must still make a mark on the acres of white paper that seem to unroll before me like arctic snows. And I must shut with a man's firmness a journal which seems the softest of self-indulgences in contrast to the austerely empty notebook that now I open.

The House
of Five Talents

In loving memory of Adèle's grandmother,
Florence Adèle Tobin,
who conveyed to me her vivid and colorful
sense of the past in our long, happy talks
at Woodside Acres, where so many of these
chapters were written.

PART ONE

1

Every New Yorker who knows Fifth Avenue knows Grandpa Millinder's houses, or rather what is left of them. When they were built, one after the other in rapid succession in 1873 and 1874, three great solemn placid Renaissance cubes in brownstone, they inaugurated a trend that was to spread two miles up the avenue and make it the most fantastic concourse in the world. It was as if a new Manhattan, vigorously rich and vigorously vulgar, eschewing the aristocratic restraint of ante bellum days and recovered at last from the blood and fever of strife, wanted to parade in all its finery up and down the skinny island. Why Grandpa, after more than six decades of frugal living, should have suddenly decided to splurge, I have never known. Perhaps the building fever of the day simply overcame him. His trio of Roman palaces occupied a whole block front: the center one, where he and Granny lived, faced the avenue across a paved court and a high grilled fence; the other two, parallel with the side streets, flanked it as wings. These in turn were subdivided, so that each of Grandpa's four married children, Papa, Uncle Fred, Aunt Polly Herron and Aunt Euphemia Hoyt, could have a city dwelling under the watchful parental eye. I can remember Mamma, who was ahead of her time in deploring the slavish aping of European styles, remarking bitterly that the only respect in which the Millinders were Roman was that they all lived in the same house.

What is surprising in New York is not what is gone, which we take for granted, but what is left. It is surprising that even one of Grandpa's three houses should survive to this day. And it will continue to survive, too, if I have to pay out my last penny in taxes, so long as I last. The two others and the courtyard have long since gone; in their place stands a great grey dull bank which peers gloomily down on my roof as if it would like to push me, an antiquated relic, into the street below. I will admit the house is far too big for a single woman: Mamma bought Aunt Euphemia's half of the north wing when Uncle Josiah failed in business and converted the whole into a single dwelling. But I have many visitors, and I love the old brown moldering front that seems to snarl defiantly, like a senile bulldog that has lost its temper with its other powers, at the surrounding shopping area. It belongs with me to a past that neither of us very much enjoyed but which has now become our most distinguishing characteristic. The newspapermen love Miss Augusta Millinder; I can always serve to fill out a vacant paragraph. They don't even have to look me up. A rich old maid and a brownstone mansion in a district that has ceased to be residential? The column writes itself. Does not one immediately visualize the pearl choker, the antiquated car, the faithful servants, the opera box, the rigid punctuality and the respectful visits of subdued relatives? For readers of a sentimental bent, one can add a kind heart to the old girl's brusque manner and fill in the picture with glimpses of her presiding benignly over a love tribunal for the romantic problems of beautiful grandnieces. Or if one is writing for mystery lovers, one can embroider on the Wendel theme: the locked safe, the eerie, long-kept secrets, the hint of murder, even of incest, enshrouded behind those dusty curtains. My one fear in old age is that I may slip into the folly of trying to look like one of the roles in which people are always casting me.

Of course, none of the rest of the family live the way I do. They would be ashamed. It is the fashion now for wealth to be inconspicuous, and even my sister-in-law, Julia, conceals her grandeur in a duplex apartment high over Park Avenue. But I have noticed that the further they dwell from the multitude, the more ostentation they allow themselves. The sons of my cousin, George Millinder, who have the bulk of what is left of the family fortune, have built beautiful and impressive modern houses on Maine lakes and Caribbean islands, but in the suburbs of New York they are still sheltered by modest hedges and conventional red brick. And when they do branch out in the city, it's always for a "worthy" reason. Young Alfred has what I call a "mansion" on Ninetieth Street, but he insists that he bought it only to house his collection of modern art. It seems to me that a cellar would have done as well for that. But then Alfred loves to be described in picture magazines as a "daring collector" and to be photographed in his shirt sleeves, pipe in hand, squinting at some practical joke by Picasso that he has just bought for a higher price than my mother paid for her great Holbein. It's all part and parcel of his silly campaign to identify the family name with something he calls "public responsibility." I'm afraid I was a bit snappish when he explained this to me. I think he actually wanted me to move out of my conspicuous old brownstone shell to help his campaign.

"Why should we care what the name stands for?" I demanded. "Unless you're going into politics? *Are* you?"

Alfred was too used now to this question to blush. The determined, sturdy smile on that determined, sturdy face became even sturdier. "But don't you hate to see the name confused entirely with the Social Register?"

"You forget how far I go back," I grumbled. "You forget that I grew up in the days when your grandmother and my mother were breaking their necks to establish that very confusion!"

Alfred smiled his tolerant smile as he forgave his grandmother and great-aunt. "I suppose we shouldn't blame them," he said. "I suppose it was the great indoor game of their day."

God knows I hated the social game as Mamma and Aunt Daisy had used to play it, but I was disposed that afternoon to defend anything that Alfred looked down on. "That's it. A game," I agreed tartly. "Like this little game you're playing with public relations."

Of course he smiled again, but I hoped that his smile was just a bit tighter. "You don't really equate the two, do you, Cousin Gussie?"

"I have reached the point in my old age," I retorted, "when I equate most things people do with their money. You, for example, have to satisfy your need to feel worthy and civic. So you and your brothers buy modern art and create foundations with long, pompous charters. Your grandmother had to satisfy her need for respectability, so she invited the world to her parties. Basically, what's the difference?"

"Oh, come now, Cousin Gussie! Surely Grandma never had any need for respectability. Can you imagine anyone who had more?"

"Nobody. At the end. But you have no idea what it was like for her and Mamma to have to start out under the shadow of their father-in-law's reputation. It was the kind of handicap that made social climbing a real sport!"

Alfred looked at last distinctly annoyed. "I don't know what you call Great-grandpa Millinder's 'reputation.' But I don't imagine he was any worse than the others. It was pretty much a day of dog-eat-dog, you know."

How he said that! With all the smugness of his moral superiority and an added dash of pride in having "pirate blood!" How often today one sees a sleek, well-fed young man, safe in brokerage or insurance, point to the whiskered gentleman over the sideboard and boast: "The old boy? My great-grandfather Jones. A terrible old robber, you know. Made his pile selling paper shoes to both armies in the Civil War."

"You miss the point, Alfred," I said gruffly. "Grandpa had a bad reputation in his *own* day."

"Oh, I don't know about that."

"Of course you don't know about that," I said with a snort. "You hadn't even been born!"

Alfred had risen now to take his leave. Obviously he was afraid that if he stayed any longer he might say something rude to his venerable, old maid cousin. And no child of George Millinder was ever rude. The art in that branch of the family had died with Aunt Daisy. "Well, I suppose at least you'll admit the old boy himself never cared for New York society," he said as he took my hand. "I suppose you'll go that far?"

"Oh, I'll go that far!" I conceded readily. Now that he was going, I was glad enough to make a small concession. "It's a disinclination I've inherited myself!"

I couldn't help feeling a bit uncomfortable after Alfred had gone. I had been brought up, like the rest of the family, in a tradition of gratitude to Grandpa Millinder for making the money that I had never wanted. Even my mother used to speak of him respectfully, at least to us children. Had I been disloyal, or even unfair, in saying that he had a bad reputation? Surely not. Surely it's a matter of history. Was it deserved? Probably not. According to Lucius Hoyt, who wrote his life, Grandpa was morally no worse than his contemporaries. But he was a foreigner, a German immigrant and, I suppose, partly Jewish. How much, if any, we'll never know, for his family papers were destroyed by Aunt Polly Herron. Granny's people were Connecticut Yankees who ran the general store in Fairfield where Grandpa got his start, but no amount of association with them was ever ably wholly to remove that alien look, suggestive of tight, shady deals in overcrowded European cities, that was to remain with him for life and to make the Jewish skeleton in our family closet rattle so much louder than that of other New York families. Julius Millinder could be many things, but he could never be "one of the boys." He always went too far. If Commodore Vanderbilt tried to buy the state legislature, Grandpa tried to buy the Republican Party. There may have been a certain bleak logic in his attitude of "why stop here?" but it was not appreciated by his fellow businessmen who had just defined the border line between honesty and crime at the point where they themselves had stopped. And then, too, in an age that justified its means by its end, an age that was forever pointing to the successful industrialization of a nation as the complete rebuttal of those who carped at the moral cost, Grandpa was never identified with any particular commodity or means of transportation. He was not, therefore, "creative." You could not identify his fortune with coal or steel or railways or even gold. He was a piecer-together of bits and scraps of businesses, a raider, a cornerer, in for the quick profit, a trader who would risk his whole fortune in steamships one year and real estate the next. But his activities were enough like those of his contemporaries to hold an unwelcome mirror before their posturing, and it was agreed in New York society that Julius Millinder was "impossible."

If society had hoped, however, that the three great houses on Fifth Avenue were to constitute Julius' ultimate bid for social recognition, a bid that could have been roundly snubbed, society must have been disappointed. That bid, indeed, was to be made by Millinders, and with a shout and a flurry, but not until after Grandpa's death. He cared nothing for society in the large or the small sense of the word, and I doubt if he and Granny ever gave a single party in rooms whose dimensions seemed to cry out for entertaining. Like so many financiers of the last century, he was a bundle of contradictions. I remember him as a small bearded man, always dressed in a rather dirty black, whose mild, watery eyes and meek, quiet tone gave no hint of the absolute autocracy that he exercised in his family. He was better educated than his business competitors, but he had even worse taste in art. He wanted his sons to be leaders, but he kept them on allowance into middle age and checked their every expenditure. He shook his head sadly over the condition of the poor and gave nothing to charity. As a young and romantically minded girl my predominant reaction to him was disappointment. Here was my grandfather, one of the wizards of the century, a hundred times a millionaire, a man who had outwitted the sharpest brains of his time, a man to whom presidents had appealed in moments of national financial crisis, yet what was this paragon to me but a mumbling old gentleman who scolded me about school marks and gave presents only from the inexhaustible supply of his clichés? Grandpa was the most impersonal man I have ever known. It was impossible to tell by his tone or the subject of his discourse whether he was addressing a child of ten or the president of a railway which he had just acquired.

I am not wandering in as senile a fashion as the reader may expect, because it was Alfred's need to dress us up for his own political ambition that finally induced me to do what no one in the family has been able to persuade me to do: to write these memoirs. I simply cannot bear to have the Millinders survive to posterity pickled in Alfred's formaldehyde. And only the strongest feeling on the subject could have brought me to this labor, for I detest the hollow cant of the usual social story, the kind of thing produced by addled old women to satisfy such appeals as I get from my sister Cora's granddaughters on their visits to this country.

"You *must* write your memoirs, Tante Gussie!" they are always chirping. "Just think of all the things this old house has seen! The famous people! The parties!"

"The scandals!"

"The love affairs!"

Everyone wants to do something to the poor old past. The girls want to dramatize it. Alfred wants to dry-clean it. My nephew Oswald, who's been having such trouble recently with senate committees, wants to vilify it. Cora, who has forgotten her old resentments, wants to sentimentalize it. Leila Hoyt fills it with lovers, real and imagined, and her brother Lucius with his petty business triumphs. Perhaps Aunt Polly at ninety-six is the clearest of all; she doesn't know that it *is* the past. But they all have one thing in common; they are all agreed that the story of the Millinders is the story of a family. It isn't. It's the story of a fortune.

I do not mean this as cynically as it sounds. I think we had between us as much talent and beauty and capacity for living as most other families. But as in most other families no one of us had enough of any of such attributes to make him famous in his own right. No one of us would have really stood out from the crowd without the money. By which I do not mean in the least to imply that the Millinders were inferior people. Decidedly, they were not. I simply mean to recognize the obvious fact that what stands out in retrospect is the gleam of their gold.

At most points in my long life—and I am now in my seventy-fifth year—the people would have been considered the more important part of the story, both by those who consider the possession of wealth as a medal pinned to one's lapel by an approving providence and by those who hold it to be a social leprosy treatable only by a firing squad. Some of my dearest friends have been from the academic and social welfare world, but I have always been aware, from the days of my first courses at Columbia, of a tendency on their part to regard me as a bit of a rarity, a social phenomenon, a sort of duck-billed platypus. There has always been the theory, embraced alike by Tory and Red, that there is something actually different about the rich. But I wonder if this theory still exists. I have learned something of the young today through the friends of Lydig, Junior, my great-nephew and ward. They seem to take it for granted that people are all basically alike, and although they observe every detail of my antiquated and rather showy way of living, they are not in the least impressed, nor do they treat me as a freak. I sometimes suspect that the democracy of their thinking springs more from a belief that all men are the same than that all men are equal. They are slow to kindle, these sturdy, realistic young men of limited ambition; they are hard to inspire. At the risk of seeming a grizzled old war horse, put out to pasture and neighing for cannons and smoke, I may say that I would like to see more adventure in them and less caution. But at least they don't regard young Lydig as a marked man. And that, in view of all that has happened, is what I care about more than everything.

I must, of course, recognize that if I avoid the Scylla of praising my family for reputations that have been largely purchased, I may fall into the Charybdis of blaming the money for all their misfortunes. It's so simplifying. Why shouldn't I blame the money for making Cora a princess and keeping me an old maid, for sapping Papa's ambition while it swelled Mamma's, for killing Lydig in his youth and for preserving Aunt Polly to the century mark, for making Aunt Daisy the idol of conservatives and for turning Oswald into a red? Who ever defends the poor money? In optimistic moods I try to think of all the beautiful things into which it has been converted: the long, clean, humming research laboratories of George Millinder's foundation and the still glass museum cases filled with the yellow and cream and *sang de boeuf* of Mamma's porcelains. But there are other moods when I see the tawdry decay of the great swaggering family palaces along the Ocean Drive in Newport and the endless photographs in my albums of large groups assembled ostensibly for pleasure; groups on porches, on lawns, on the decks of yachts, in fields with guns, on horseback, in fancy dress or even clowning on the beach in billowing black bathing dress. Oh, the pleasure, the relentless pleasure and the grimness of our resolution not to admit that it might have eluded us! No, anything but that.

I have tried, at all events, to be impartial and to give the money its due but no more then that, in composing this chronicle. Now I can sit back, at the end of this year nineteen forty-eight, like the old monk in *Boris Godunov*, with the final page before my weary eyes. It is a comfort to know that when this work is read by other eyes, it will be beyond my powers of correction. For the only possible publication of serious autobiography must be posthumous. It is difficult enough to catch and isolate even the faintest aroma of past events without being confused by the advice and the pasts of others.

2

WE ALWAYS SAT for an hour after Sunday lunch in the gallery, which is the room that comes first to my mind when I think of my childhood. It was Grandpa's particular pride and to me the awesome symbol of adult authority. For I was never supposed to speak in the gallery. Even Mamma and Papa spoke very little in it. There seemed to be a tacit agreement among the family that the gallery on Sunday was the place and time for Grandpa's stories of his business adventures. I should not really say that these stories were dry, for I never listened to them, nor did it occur to me that anyone else did or that Grandpa even expected it. The need to engage in an unheeded flow of discourse was one of those mysterious adult needs that I took for granted. Papa and Mamma and my uncles and aunts formed a circle about Grandpa who always sat with Granny on a sofa by the fire. My brothers and young George Millinder usually managed to play some kind of game, with matches or marbles, unobserved behind the ottoman love seat, and my sister Cora would whisper with our cousin Gwendolyn in a corner, but there was no cousin just my age, and I could only sit and stare at the pictures. Oh, those pictures! How I loved them! When I close my eyes now I can see every detail of them again. They covered the walls from floor to ceiling, with their great gilded frames; others stood about on easels and even on the carpet, resting against the furniture. The room was always dusky, and they were hard to see, but I had that Sunday hour every week to make them out. There was the German general, bearded and arrogant, condemning a spy while having his boots cleaned in a French inn; there was Napoleon, grim and pale, riding at the head of a group of dejected marshals over Russian snows; there was Macbeth, haggard and ghastly before the approach of Birnam Wood. There was nature, too, in vast panoramas, sudden storms over Western plains, giant waves at sea, buffalo in flight from Indians over Western prairies. Perhaps they ruined my taste for modern art, but I wonder if children today have half the fun that I had, with the abstracts that they're obliged to look at. Grandpa's pictures transported me out of that solemn chamber with its nodding circle of grownups into a shimmering world of fantasy and imagination. *I* was that condemned spy; *I* was Marie Antoinette in the Conciergerie writing that letter before my execution; I was even one of those harrassed, fleeing buffalo. If life could be dangerous, might it not also be magnificent? When I stared up at the huge, murky canvas that depicted the murder of Giuliano de' Medici by the Pazzi at the Easter Mass, I thrilled at the idea of the Millinders as the Medici of New York, with crowds under our windows calling: "Palle, Palle!" If Grandpa was Cosimo *Pater Patriae,* Papa could be Lorenzo the Magnificent. But Mamma had a way of catching my eye and signaling to me to bring my knees together and not to slouch. She knew all about my daydreaming and what she called my "silly land." That was the eternal weapon of the other world, Mamma's world, ridicule, as shame was the Achilles' heel of mine. For I would feel as bare and exposed under Mamma's stare as the marble statue that stood on the rounded back rest of the ottoman in the center of the room. Nearly life size, it was called "White Captive" and represented a naked girl, not yet nubile, her hands tied to a post, her eyes raised to her enemies in a proud defiance that could not wholly conceal her bewilderment and fear. It was a popular subject of the period, for it was considered great virtuosity in a sculptor to be able to combine the fear of a child with the courage of an adult, to catch a moment of transition, to suggest the ripened woman in the bare boyish figure of the girl. And then, too, a boyish nude was less embarrassing to a prurient generation, while its very undevelopment and air of innocence had a titillation for the older men. I would think of myself as standing up there, stripped and bound before the assembled family, exposed to their bleak, denigrating stare. But if I was as helpless as the white captive, I could also be as defiant. The world from which we both had been torn was still a better world than Mamma's.

My first real crisis with Mamma came in the blistering summer of 1886 when Grandpa Millinder had his second and final stroke. I was thirteen, just of an age to enjoy most keenly the atmosphere of muffled drama which so mighty an event was bound to create. My brothers were in Canada with a tutor; Cora was abroad with Aunt Polly Herron, and so I was the only child at home in Fairfield with Mamma and Papa. It was a great piece of luck, for otherwise they would never have taken me into town where Grandpa was dying. I know this sounds shockingly heartless, but children *are* heartless. Death is not real to them. When they weep, as I did later, they enjoy that, too. I remember vividly the big closed house with its shrouded furniture and dim cool air and pushing open the window in my bedroom to gaze across the courtyard at the gloomy brown face of Grandpa's house that seemed already to be wearing a woebegone look. Beyond the closed gates which faced Fifth Avenue was a small group of loiterers, perhaps reporters, and I was thrilled to see that a policeman had been stationed there. When through the stifling evening air I heard the shrill cry of a distant newsboy singing out: "Extra! Eeeex-tra! Julius Millinder dy-eeng! Financeer dy—eeng!" I felt that at last it really was Florence and I a Medici princess looking down at a city prostrated by Cosimo's imminent demise. It took not only the magnitude of Grandpa's fortune but all the glory of the past to disguise from my own vision the messy, perspiring, pigtailed girl with the flushed cheeks of a perfervid imagination.

When Miss Page, my governess, found me at the window she pulled me abruptly away. What I was doing was not, as usual, ladylike. I could not be bothered to explain to her the difference between a lady and a princess, but I swept out without a word and went to Mamma's room. I found her in a dressing gown with architect's blueprints spread over a table by her bed. She was intent, as always, on what she was doing and barely glanced at me.

"What are those?" I asked.

"Designs for the house in Newport."

"Are we going to live in Newport?"

"In the summer, yes."

"Why?"

"Because the people there are nicer."

"Nicer than in Fairfield?"

"Much nicer."

"Will I think so?"

"We'll hope so."

Mamma was evidently not disposed to conversation, and I took a blueprint marked "Tea House" and, spreading it out on the floor, lay down on my stomach behind her Japanese screen. But the drawing did not interest me, and after a moment I propped my chin on my hands to watch Mamma.

She was then in her early forties and had lost much of the prettiness that twenty years before had drawn Papa across the East River on Sunday afternoons to call at Brooklyn Heights. If she regretted her youthful looks, she never showed it. Like many of her generation, she had little use for looks, once they had fulfilled their mating function. Mamma was never a very feminine woman. She was short and black-haired and had a tendency to squareness in feature and figure. Her eyes were as black as her hair and very penetrating, her lips thin, and she was very quiet when she stared. And yet withal there was something curiously attractive about her. Her laugh was gruff and candid; it seemed to say: "Don't think I don't see through you." She had quantities of energy and determination and was very brisk when she was not very still, and she loved to wear big jewelry on her pretty white plump hands. If she was selfish, she was also scrupulously fair; she always kept her promises. She was never a very affectionate wife or mother, but she never expected others to be affectionate to her. She was totally devoid of self-pity. The thing that preserved the attention, the curiosity and even the good will of her children was her way of treating them as equals and as equals with whom she was somehow in competition. If I showed Mamma a drawing of mine that had won a star at school, she would as like as not proceed to draw one herself on the same subject. She was like a cat with kittens; if one of them annoyed her, she sometimes cuffed it too hard. I often wonder if I would have cared half as much for her had she cared more for me.

"Eliza?" came Papa's voice from the doorway.

She looked up. "How is he?"

"About the same."

Mamma looked back at the drawings without a word, though he came in and walked to the other side of the bed. From where he stood he could not see me, and with a child's tendency to secrecy I lay absolutely still. Papa, unlike Grandpa, was tall and lean, but he had Grandpa's curly dark hair and arched eyebrows. His nose was long and straight and his big grey eyes had an air of benign distinction. He dressed well, rode well and rarely lost his temper. Usually, if a scene threatened, Papa managed to be at his club. He would provide money and a pat on the back and the most charming smile I have ever seen. He would give you anything in the world but his time.

"It's funny how much one cares when the end really comes," he mused, strolling to the window. "I thought I'd been prepared for Father's death by that first stroke last winter. But I almost broke down when he said in that thin little voice: 'I'm so proud of my two boys.'"

"How's your mother?"

"Living on nerve. Insists on doing everything herself in spite of the three nurses. She says he wouldn't want anyone else to touch him."

"Well, if it helps her, that's the great thing. I'm sure she's wonderful."

The way Mamma said that! Even at that age, it made me shudder. It was not that her tone was cynical or sarcastic. It was really only perfunctory. But there was somehow latent in it the assumption that a greater show of feeling in anybody would be simple hypocrisy.

Papa's tone showed that he recognized this. "I wish you'd help her, Eliza. It's the one time we can do something."

"Help her? When she has three nurses and insists on doing everything herself?"

"I mean by spending a little more time with her."

"But she's always with your father!"

"Well, what of it?"

"Your father and I understand each other, Cyrus," Mamma said in a clipped tone. "I think we even respect each other. But let's not pretend at this late date that we've ever liked each other."

"Eliza, he's dying!"

"That's just the point. I wouldn't want him at my deathbed, and I shan't intrude on his. Don't be sloppy about death, Cyrus. It's another thing that happens to us, that's all."

"I wish I had your philosophy," Papa answered with a note of bitterness. He had turned from the window to look at her reproachfully. "I wish I could sit there so calmly, with all that's going on next door, and study blueprints. What *are* those blueprints?"

"Mr. White's plans for the house in Newport."

"Eliza! How can you think of spending money at a time like this?"

"Spending money fiddlesticks! I had these plans drawn up two years ago."

I lay very still now, scarcely daring to breathe. I knew that I should not be there. It may have occurred to the reader that I shouldn't have been there from the beginning. But Mamma never cared in the least what we overheard. As a matter of fact, I am sure that she had already forgotten that I was in the room. Papa had crossed over to the table, out of my line of vision, and I knew by the crackle of paper that he had picked up one of the blueprints.

"Why, this thing is a castle!" he exclaimed. "What makes you think we could ever afford it?"

"It's no bigger than the one Daisy's planning. And it shows twice the imagination."

"You mean to say Daisy's in this too!"

"You always think Fred and Daisy are such sweet, simple souls," Mamma said scornfully. "Of course Daisy's making her plans. She's been making them for twenty years!"

Uncle Fred Millinder was the plain, plodding member of the family, prematurely bald and dry as a thistle, who assisted Grandpa in everything, a pencil, figuratively speaking, behind his ear. He was the bookkeeper, the conserver, the caretaker of the fortune, who made up in accuracy and good judgment what he lacked in brilliance. Mamma saw him as an obvious Uriah Heep and Aunt Daisy, his small, solemn, humorless wife, as a relentless schemer. I doubt if it ever occurred to her that she might be subject to the same charge. Had she not been a Marston from Brooklyn?

"Well, maybe Fred and Daisy can afford that sort of thing," Papa muttered. I heard the slap of the blueprint as he threw it down on the table and saw his back by the window as he came into view.

"Why they and not us?"

"How should I know? Maybe they're expecting a windfall."

"Has some family secret been kept from me all these years?" Mamma asked sarcastically. "Is it going to turn out that Fred is the older brother, after all?"

"What difference does my being the oldest make? Really, Eliza, you talk as if Father were a kind of king!"

"I only talk the way *he* does. Hasn't he told me a hundred times that he believes in keeping his fortune intact? How is he going to do that if he splits it among the children?"

"By *not* splitting it among the children. By leaving it all to Fred."

"And bypass his oldest son? His favorite? Dream on, my dear!"

"If you had ever listened to Father on Sunday afternoons," Papa retorted, "you might not be so sure I was dreaming. Only a few months ago I remember his glancing up at you while he was talking about pre-feudal German law. But of course you were a thousand miles away!"

Mamma's voice now showed attentiveness for the first time. "What did he say?"

"That in some German states it was the *youngest* son who took all."

In the silence that followed I heard Mamma catch her breath. "Cyrus! You don't mean to tell me there's a serious possibility he's left everything to Fred!"

"A possibility, yes."

I heard the rustle of her dress as Mamma rose. "My God, and you stand there! What are you going to *do* about it?"

"What *can* I do about it?"

"You'll allow your children to be stripped of their rightful inheritance without raising a finger?"

"Nobody's going to be stripped of anything, Eliza." Papa turned now to face her with a show of firmness and patience. "Father would always be fair. Whatever he has done with his money, you can be sure he has made adequate provision for Polly and Euphemia and myself. Probably, if anything, too much. All I'm implying is that he may have left the residuary to Fred. It would seem entirely natural. Fred has always known how to handle business things. He has been invaluable to Father while . . ."

"While you've loafed!" Mamma interrupted heatedly. "I know all that! But still, you're the favorite. You're the one he *likes*! And he likes Willie and Bertie, too, more than George, *much* more. He wouldn't do this to them!"

Even Papa could not face that glare. "Well, then perhaps he hasn't," he muttered, turning back to the window.

Mamma's next question was addressed to his back in a tone that was ominously soft. "Did you *tell* your father this?"

"That I would understand anything he did for Fred? Yes."

"And he changed his will?" Her voice was almost a whisper now.

"I have no reason to believe a change was necessary. Father simply nodded. I think he understood."

"But if you went to him now and told him you'd changed your mind, it wouldn't be too late, would it?" I was startled by Mamma's sudden eager, pleading tone. "If you told him you'd seen it was your duty to go halves with Fred, he could sign a codicil, couldn't he? Just a short one?"

"My dear Eliza, my father's dying!"

"Even so! For your children's sake!" Through the interstices of the screen I saw Mamma clench her fists. "Your father knows what he's doing. He can still sign his name!"

Papa laughed, but it was a dry, embarrassed laugh. "You're priceless, Eliza, you really are. You expect me to wring from a dying man a bequest that I do not want, either for myself or for my children. What could we do with all that money? We'll have more than enough to buy anything in the world we want!"

"So Fred and Daisy will have it!" Mamma uttered a low groan and covered her face with her hands. "What could I ever want after such a humiliation? How could I ever hold my head up again? After all these years!" I was appalled at her look of fury when she dropped her hands. "Because, of course, you did it to spite me! You did it because you thought I wanted the money! It's your revenge!"

I shall never forget the horror of that moment. However dull I may have thought my parents, however unglamorous, I knew now that I wanted them to be that way. Anything was better than having them behave like the painted people on Grandpa's walls. For if they were violent, too, what protection was there for me? When Mamma took a sudden step, I had a fantasy that she was going to strike Papa. I screamed and jumped up, pushing the screen over with a crash. They both stared at me in astonishment. Papa was the first to recover.

"Gussie!" he cried in dismay. "What are *you* doing here?" He turned wrathfully on Mamma. "Great Scott, Eliza, she's heard the whole thing! And you knew she was here, too!"

"Why shouldn't she hear it?" Mamma shouted back at him. "Why shouldn't she know who it is that's destroyed her future? Who it is that's stripped her of her natural rights?"

"Gussie, dear," Papa said in a voice that he tried hard to control, "you must try not to be too excited by what you've just heard. Your mother and I are very upset by Grandpa's illness. But remember this, my dearest child. *Nobody* has deprived you of any natural rights. Nobody has destroyed your future, which is going to be a very happy one."

"Nobody but your own father!" Mamma retorted. "Like the man in the Bible who took his talent and buried it in the sand!"

"Come, Gussie," Papa said firmly, "shall we go back to your room?"

"You think you're strong, don't you?" Mamma continued furiously. "You think I'm crass and material and that you're above it all? But you're *not*! You're simply weak! Too weak to reach out and grasp what is your own due!"

Even in my presence Papa could not resist a retort to this. "There will always be those who confuse vulgarity with strength," he said quietly, and he led me out into the corridor and shut the door between us and Mamma. When we reached my room, I was afraid that he would embarrass me by trying to explain. But he was far too wise. He simply smiled, as easily as if nothing had happened, and left me alone to dream fitfully through the night of him and me, hand in hand, racing over dark fields to escape from some unseen, pursuing fiend. But the fields which our flying feet barely skimmed were fields of blueprints, and like Alice and the Red Queen, we accelerated our speed only to remain in the same position.

The next morning I saw him as soon as I awakened, for he was standing by my bed. He looked oddly worn and tired for one who was usually so fresh. "Get up now, Gussie," he said in a gentle voice. "I want you to get dressed and have your breakfast and then go over to be with your grandmother. Grandpa died last night. It was all very quick at the end, and he hardly suffered at all."

I sat up in bed and threw my arms around him. When I felt the bristles of his unshaven cheek against mine, I realized with a shock that he had lost his *father*. He was like me, a child, but a child who had lost his father.

"Oh, Papa!" I cried, sobbing. "You loved him!"

"I did, Gussie. I really did."

Grandpa's house was full of subdued commotion, but Papa led me quickly upstairs to Granny's sitting room and left me alone with her. I had the same shock on seeing her that I had had on seeing Papa. Granny, usually so neat and staid and formal, who was wont to dole out her smiles and little pecks of kisses to her grandchildren with a rather chilling impartiality, was suddenly an old frightened woman in a dressing robe who treated me as another grownup. She made me sit down beside her while she talked about Grandpa in a flurried, rapid tone and stared at me with eyes that did not seem to take me in.

"He never said a hard thing to me in all these years. Not one! How many women can say that of their husbands? How many, I should like to know? Can my daughters? Can my daughters-in-law? Could my own mother, of beloved memory? No. Not one of them! Not *one*! Even when my father told him he had no right, poor as he was and not yet a citizen, to ask me to be his wife, he said not a word about it to me. All he said was: 'Miss Cox, if you'll have me, I'll take every care off your shoulders that a man can take.' And he was good to his word. He was always good to his word. I don't know what Jacob and I will do without him. Never a hard word in fifty-two years of married life!"

Uncle Jacob was Granny's baby and had a defective intellect. I tried to murmur something consoling to her, but she did not seem to listen to me, and finally I went downstairs and crossed the courtyard back to our house. I found Mamma, already in black, adjusting her veil before a mirror in the hall.

"Where have *you* been?" she demanded.

"To Granny's."

"Oh? How is she?"

I felt suddenly proprietary about my father's family. "Of course, she's had a terrible shock," I said in the tone I had heard so many grownups use. "But I think she's bearing up very well."

"Oh, I'm sure she's wonderful."

It was the same phrase that she had used the day before and the same flat tone. It suddenly seemed very important to me to disassociate myself from that tone. It was as if there might be a kinship between the sadness of those, like Papa and Granny, who truly mourned for Grandpa and the surging emotion that I had felt about the pictures in the gallery. In my sudden passionate need to array myself on the side of those who could weep for Grandpa, I cried out: "You don't care that Grandpa's dead! You pretend to, but you don't!"

Mamma glanced quickly around to see if Osborn, the butler, had heard. He had.

"Go up to your room!" she cried angrily. "And if you come down one minute before I tell you, you'll be a sorry girl! A *very* sorry girl! I'll teach you to play-act in front of me!"

I ran upstairs, burning with shame and anger. I threw myself on the bed and sobbed for an hour. When I was tired of this I lay on the floor and when this grew uncomfortable I paced up and down, working myself to a pitch of near hysteria. When my lunch tray came, I threw it on the floor. I shouted that I wouldn't eat a thing until Mamma came up to see me. *She* would find out if I was "play acting." Poor Miss Page could do nothing with me, and I finally screamed so loud that she became frightened and hurried down to find Mamma. I waited, my heart thumping rapidly, my stomach aching with hunger. Everything seemed at stake between me and my sneering parent.

The door opened at last, but it was only Miss Page.

"Won't she come?" I wailed.

Miss Page put her arm about me and murmured in a voice that suddenly shook. "Dear Gussie, your mother isn't going to come. You must face that. If you wait for her, you'll starve, my child. Your mother is not like other people."

I remember that I took this in, very slowly and very quietly, and that, nodding, I finally dried my eyes. Then, with an air of almost regal dignity, I asked Miss Page if she would bring me a boiled egg. I had learned once and for all that there was no point in playing rough games with Mamma. She never knew when to stop.

Two days later Miss Page and I watched from a balcony the long procession of black carriages that made up Grandpa's funeral cortege as it headed down Fifth Avenue past his three houses. I had not been allowed to go with my parents because Mamma had said I might make another scene. Papa, to whom I had vainly appealed, had simply kissed me and told me gravely to do as I was told. Perhaps he was trying to rebuild the image of parental solidarity that I had seen so rudely shattered. As the last of the carriages disappeared down the avenue, I reflected wistfully that Grandpa had at least gone to his final service in as handsome a manner as the artists who had painted the pictures in his gallery could have wished. If the dull dignified curtain of a grown-up world had been slit down the middle to show me only a terrifying extension of nursery years, how could I face the future except by seizing firmly upon some fantasy, some identification of myself with a princess, a queen, a bluebird, and hold it aloft as the soldiers did their branches of Birnam Wood in Grandpa's painting of "Macbeth"? And when death came, could one not carry the fantasy on, like Grandpa, and be buried with the pomp of an ancient sovereign?

Miss Page had a deep reverence for matters financial, and it was through her that I learned the terms of Grandpa's will. It was published in full in the newspapers, and on the morning it appeared, which happened to be a Saturday so I was not at school, she was unable to get away from me to scan its terms. When I suggested that we read it together, she balked for a moment at such an impropriety, and then, giving in with a quick nod that signified the urgency of her curiosity, she spread the *Times* on a table, and we both leaned forward to devour it. Miss Page kept gasping at the sums, whispering them as if she were reciting a creed, dipping her head at the mention of each million. There was a million dollars to each grandson; there were five millions in trust and five outright for Aunt Euphemia Hoyt, the same for Aunt Polly Herron; there was a trust of ten millions for Granny and Uncle Jacob, and then—

"But is there nothing for Papa?" I cried.

"Bless your soul he's got the whole works! He and your Uncle Fred! Think of it, all that great fortune and not one penny to charity!"

I deduced from the awe in Miss Page's tone that there must have been something splendid in a testament that disposed of so much property without having recourse to anything as vulgar as charity. It was like Grandpa to do things in a splendid way, and I felt proud of him. But when I ran downstairs to congratulate Mamma that Papa had not been left out, I received only a sharp reproof. It was "common," I was told, to discuss people's wills. What struck me, more than this, for I was accustomed to Mamma's inconsistencies and changes of mood, was that she seemed actually angry and disappointed about something. Similarly, I found Papa, when I went to his study, aloof and vexed. He simply dispatched me about my business. Was this the way the great fortune, so long awaited, was to be greeted? And was it only "common" to speak of wills *after* death?

Such, anyway, was my impression of the advent of the Millinder fortune into the lives of Grandpa's descendants and where my chronicle properly begins. I was later to make out the reasons for my parents' disgruntlement. Papa had been quite sincere about not wanting that much money. He knew that once he had actually inherited it, he would never be able to do anything as crude as give it away or anything as petty as deny it to his wife. His one chance had been to avoid having it at all. Mamma's disappointment was less reasonable. She had everything she had ever dreamed of, but someone else had more. For Miss Page had not read the will correctly. The residuary estate was divided, it was true, between Papa and Uncle Fred, but it was not divided equally. Uncle Fred received two thirds and Papa but one. In this way Grandpa had reconciled his devotion to his oldest son with his respect for his second. In a fortune so huge there was no practical difference to their families in the discrepancy between the two shares; we could no more have spent the income of our third than the Fred Millinders could have spent the income of their two. But it was enough to ruin Mamma's pleasure in her new affluence to know that the despised Aunt Daisy was exactly twice as rich. There were things even then that she cared about more than money.

3

LOOKING BACK ON Newport of the nineties, we see it through a haze of clichés. There have been too many memoirs telling us of those dinners that lasted for three hours at tables covered with gold service and hundreds of pink and mauve orchids. My sister-in-law's book, I hasten to admit, is one of the worst. Ione assured me, while she was writing *My Newport, Its Rise and Fall,* that her object in doing so was to "draw the old place from a fresh viewpoint," but had she hired a ghost writer, she could not have filled her pages with a staler collection of banalities. Every ball is "brilliant," every bachelor "eligible" and every woman over fifty a "dowager." And yet Ione's own conversation is never stale. Is it the vulgarizing effect of the social historian's pen, or do we all ultimately see our own pasts in the light of what others have written? I have often noticed that the children of great men are apt to describe their fathers in the same commonplaces that the journalists use. They are the first, perhaps, to believe the legend. And by the same token I must always concentrate when I think of the Parthenon, until my own image of it comes to mind. If I do not, what I naturally see is a photograph or even a picture postcard. And yet how knowing we are apt to feel compared to those whose eyeballs have not been stamped with the image of the thing itself! The thing to remember about Newport in its prime was that it *looked* well. It was all tidied up. When one sees today, through rusting grillwork on Bellevue Avenue, the peeling façade of a Florentine villa surrounded by an overgrown lawn, the effect is not only dismal but somehow meretricious. The derivative seems even more emptily derivative in decay. But if you can imagine the grillwork black where it was meant to be black and gold where it was meant to be gold, if you can see the grass as a surface of green jade and every shutter gleaming with fresh paint, not only on one house but all up and down the avenue, you begin to have a picture of what it was like. There is a charm, even for homely things, in perfect maintenance. And then there were lovely things, too, the sea and the rocks and the golden air. The picture that most comes back to me today is that of ladies in Irish lace with big, feathery hats, drawn in open victorias down leafy avenues. I see Papa in his spider phaeton with a pair of glossy, high-stepping strawberry roans and my sister, Cora, in a white piqué skirt with a sailor hat, driven in a surrey by a coachman in white breeches and a top hat with the green Millinder cockade. It might have been painted by Renoir or Gainsborough. If I romanticize it, remember that its whole purpose was to be romanticized.

There was a childlike atmosphere in the crowded, colorful beach under a bright sun, in the parading up and down, in the stately leaving of calling cards. And there was a particular childishness in the feuds and jealousies, in the long rivalry, for example, between Mamma and Aunt Daisy. Mamma could never understand that she was bound to lose out to her sister-in-law's simple formula of never budging an inch from the sure path of a splendid and moralizing dullness. For it was pre-eminently Aunt Daisy's era. She was short and plump and plain and pompous, but she carried herself with a regal dignity. Receiving in her great marble hall, a small, dark figure with odd clumps of diamonds pinned to her shapeless velvet, she seemed a complacent anachronism—as if, in ancient Rome, at the baths of Caracalla, one had run across her in a black bathing suit with long black stockings. It was commonly said that she had some of the air of Queen Victoria, and I am sure that she did all in her power to accentuate the resemblance.

She and Mamma even expressed their differences in the houses which they built on the Ocean Drive. Aunt Daisy's was rigidly conventional. She and Uncle Fred had commissioned Richard Morris Hunt to build them a late Gothic French château of dull, featureless limestone. It sat up on a high point, a big, bold placid product of the Beaux Arts, absurdly dominating four small acres of lawn and an ocean which it should never have crossed. Mamma, on the advice of Stanford White, built more indigenously of shingle. Her great rambling house seemed to climb out of the very sea and rocks to a tumble of different levels with a sweeping view from every room. A shingled arch surmounted by two floors spanned the entrance drive to form the biggest portecochere in Newport. With its myriad piazzas and machicolated towers and its dark, secret look the house had some of the romance of a castle in a drawing by Howard Pyle. Its fortified appearance emphasized how little place there was for laughter in the serious business of a social life.

Ione, in her book, takes no account of the infantile quality of this struggle between Mamma and Aunt Daisy. She sees it as *they* saw it, in heroic dimensions, as a mortal in a petty age might gaze wistfully back at the conflict of titans. Of course, she was not a member of our family in those days, and if it amuses her to fancy things in that light, I daresay it is a harmless pastime. But I did have to object to the chapter in which she describes my sister Cora as a pathetic and beautiful pawn in the struggle, forced into marriage with Antoine de Conti because Aunt Daisy had got the Earl of Myol for Gwen. When I lunched with Ione to discuss her book I pointed out to her that Mamma had not even been present at Cora's wedding. I must say, she did stare.

"But surely it was your mother who brought Antoine to Newport!" she exclaimed. "Bertie always told me that!"

"Oh, she wanted him originally. But not later. Later she wanted Cora to marry Lancey Bell."

"Lancey Bell!" Ione's surprise was tempered by a mild pity. At seventy she was still a beautiful woman. "But, my dear Gussie, I thought it was a question of him for *you*!"

"Oh, Lancey was a question for everybody!"

"Was he so attractive?"

"Well, yes. But that wasn't all. He was Mrs. Bell's son."

"And who, pray, was Mrs. Bell?"

Nothing could illustrate more graphically the tenuous make-up of that intangible thing called "social position" than Ione's ignorance of the very existence of Mrs. Bell. It is natural to assume about the past that the biggest fortune or the greatest title must have enjoyed the highest place, because the actual minutiae of social distinctions are too gossamer to survive the age of their application. But it is still true that when we first came to Newport, the Millinders were nothing and the Bells everything. It hardly seems to me that Mrs. Bell could even be described as a "member" of the summer colony; it was rather as if she and the colony constituted in themselves a pair, two objects that complemented and defined each other. Or to put it in more human terms, I could project Newport as a huge, pale, pursy sovereign, gorgeously bedizened and nervously giggling, and Mrs. Bell, as the sallow, unpleasantly grinning jester to whom and only to whom an unimaginable latitude of mockery had been allowed. Yet it was always implicit in the situation that the jester might go too far and the nervous giggle might stop and a fat, beringed hand might be sharply raised to summon the halberdier at the door. It might have been her very sense of halberds that made Mrs. Bell so defiant, for, except for her lineage and her wit, she was handicapped with respect to the other hostesses of Newport. She was, comparatively speaking, "poor"; I doubt if Mr. Bell, who spent his time in an old manor house on the Hudson and rarely came to Newport, was worth more than a million dollars. She had no looks to speak of, except for a bearing of great dignity: she was tall and plain with a long horsy face and an oval chin, a small crooked mouth and rather beady green eyes. She dressed elaborately, almost in a parody of the other ladies, and lived in a ramshackle shingle cottage, with two big rooms for entertaining, which she always maintained was the only kind of summer house for a watering place. ("One doesn't build Azay-le-Rideau in Brighton!") Yet she was careful to use what money she did have in the right places; she made a point of having the best chef and the best wines in Newport. For the rest, her precarious but undoubted sway over the social world depended on the inclination of a passive majority, like all passive majorities, to accept her at her own valuation. She was an expert bully; she flung in their faces that she was a Verplanck and descended from three signers while making them feel at the same time that their admiration for this kind of thing was the final puerility. She made fun of them all without mercy, and they scurried about to quote her quips. It was their happy theory—and one that annoyed her intensely—that her sharpness of tongue and abruptness of manner masked an inexhaustible kindness of heart. None of them, so far as I knew, ever bothered to speculate why she insisted on passing her summers away from a family who were known to adore her and at a cost that she could ill afford, in a community that she professed to despise. It probably seemed no more absurd to them than it did to persons of the old regime in France that a duke should happily desert his splendid château to hole up in a small, smelly room at Versailles.

Mamma made an early and fatal mistake with Mrs. Bell. She approached her at a garden party and introduced herself, presuming on a distant connection between the Marstons and the Verplancks. Almost any other approach might have worked. Had she walked up to the tall, expressionless lady with the waving plumes and said boldly: "I'm Eliza Millinder—you can't *afford* not to know me!" she might have received a rasping laugh and a hearty handshake. But to put her own family on a level with the Verplancks was to remove at the first stroke Mrs. Bell's one ground for condescension, and condescension was her stock in trade.

"Well, for pity's sake don't expect me to tell you what relation we are!" Mrs. Bell had exclaimed in a raucous voice that too many people could hear. "I never know *who's* a cousin and who's not. You might be my great-aunt, for all I know. This once, twice and three times removed business is way beyond my poor mental aptitudes. But if we *are* cousins, Mrs. Millinder, you know we can't talk *here*. Weren't you brought up, *comme nous autres* Verplancks, never to talk to the family at parties?"

And she had turned away abruptly without another word. All of which would have been quite bad enough was not worse to follow. She actually took up Aunt Daisy! It was just like her to do so, quite in keeping with her contrary nature, when a cautious, investigating Newport was beginning to say that if Mrs. Frederick Millinder was pompous and pretentious, Mrs. Cyrus at least had wit, to rebut it with:

"Ah, but *no*, you miss the whole point! The one who claims to be everyone's cousin is the bore. The little dry one with the hideous palace who asks you how many laundresses you keep—now she's my type. She purses her little red lips and mumbles phrases like 'fine old families, like yours and mine.' But at least she doesn't put me in *hers*. I daresay I'm not good enough!"

Aunt Daisy may have been laughed at, but Mrs. Bell took her friends there. Mamma suffered in silence, but she was not one to suffer long, and like a good general she might well have cut her losses and tried afresh in Southampton or Bar Harbor had not an odd thing happened. The oddest thing about it was that it should have happened to me, a big, earnest, emotional, gushing girl, immature for sixteen, with flushed cheeks, a pigtail and a tendency either to laugh too loud or to burst into unexpected storms of tears. I was coming out of the Redwood Library one morning with a bundle of sentimental novels when a lady waved to me from a parked landau. I went over and saw to my astonishment that it was none other than the terrible Mrs. Bell.

"Hello, Augusta Millinder," she said in a deep voice, putting both hands on the handle of her umbrella and leaning her head back so that her green, staring eyes could take me in. We had never spoken, but in the smaller

Newport of that day everyone knew who everyone else was. "Who are you clutching there to your bosom?"

"Ouida," I confessed, dropping my eyes.

"Isn't she heaven?"

I looked up in surprise. "Oh, *isn't* she?"

"*Moths* is the best."

"Mamma won't let me read it."

"Mamma's quite right. But I'll lend it to you. In a Henry James jacket. She'll never peek into *that*."

"Oh, would you?" I clasped my hands in excitement. My impulses were so sudden that it already seemed natural to me that this formidable woman and I should be talking about Ouida. "I should *adore* that!"

"If you'd *like* it, that's quite enough," she reproved me. "We don't 'adore' things."

"When can I get it?"

For just a moment she stared. "Oh, *Moths*," she recalled. "I'll give it to you Sunday if you'll come to lunch. My boy, Lancey, is visiting me. He's an architectural student and far too old for you, but he's very clever and good-looking and what I think you girls call 'divine.' Will you come?"

It was my turn to stare. Ladies of Mamma's age never asked girls of mine to lunch. And certainly not to meet "'divine'" young men! "I don't know!" I exclaimed in distress. "I'd have to ask Mamma." And then with a sudden, unexpected burst of confidence in this strange new friend who liked Ouida, I looked into those hard green eyes and added: "Besides, I'd be scared to death."

"Then bring your sister. She'll protect you."

"Oh, really? Can I ask her?"

"One o'clock," Mrs. Bell said with a firm little nod and told her coachman to drive home.

When I told Mamma of our invitation, her face became instantly serious. She never made the least effort to conceal her preoccupations from her children. My news once delivered, I was as lost to her mind as the aide who hands the general a dispatch on the battlefield.

"It's just what I've heard," she speculated, staring right through me. "She takes up the children. When she feels she's gone too far."

"Too far for what?"

"Too far to retreat," she said impatiently. "She knows she shouldn't have snubbed me. She knows we're the coming thing. But if she takes us up now, you see, because you and Cora are friends of Lancey's, she won't lose face."

"But why should she take us up?"

Mamma's eyes continued to rest on me, and for just a moment they seemed to focus. The snap of the eyelids and the twitch of her shoulders might have been to brush me off.

"Because she wants Cora, of course."

"But why should she want Cora?"

"Because Cora's the best thing we've got!"

Cora, indeed, was the fine flower of our family. The thin, high, black arched eyebrows of Grandpa Millinder, the milky-white skin of a Sargent, the tiny hook of the nose and the high, raven hair of a Gibson girl all contributed to make her the very portrait of a beauty of the era. What was lacking was the faintest spark of animation. Cora was devoid of enthusiasms. She accepted everything, but she accepted listlessly. It might have been a reaction to the great store Mamma set on her, or it might have been simply her inheritance from Granny Millinder. Yet her inertness was by no means without its charm. There were few men who did not regard it as a test of their power to attract and who did not make at least one effort to bring a flicker of awareness into those pale features. There was something that fascinated people about Cora's reluctance to participate, as if she were attuned to a sphere remote from vulgar things, and if it was difficult sometimes for a younger sister to distinguish between remoteness and indifference, the difficulty did not make the task of distinguishing a dull one. Cora loved a placid routine, but the slowness of her tempo did not seem to make for discontent. I used to think that she must have found an inner peace, but I wondered occasionally if it was not the peace of an anesthetic. Cora would sometimes look at me across the dining room table for several moments of uninterrupted scrutiny and then give a short, disconcerting laugh which she would never explain.

When Mamma told her that she and I were to lunch with Mrs. Bell on Sunday she simply asked, as Ione was to ask decades later: "And who, pray, is Mrs. Bell?"

"I never can make out, Cora, whether you're putting it on or not. Is it conceivable you don't know who Mrs. Bell is?"

"I suppose she's some great social figure."

"She's the mother of an extremely attractive young man whom you and Gussie will probably both fall madly in love with."

"Then I'd much better not go. I'll leave him for Gussie."

"Oh, please, Cora, let's go!" I cried. "If you don't, I can't. And I *want* to!"

Cora looked at me in mild surprise. "Why? Do you want to fall in love?"

"Doesn't everybody?"

And so, to obtain a copy of *Moths*, which Mamma wouldn't let me take out of the library, I induced my sister to attend that fateful lunch at the Bells. It turned out to be a party of twenty persons, all of Cora's age, but I was spared the discomfort of having to talk to. any of them as we sat at little tables on a glassed-in porch, and Mrs. Bell, her son, Cora and I were all together at one. Mrs. Bell explained this rather curious arrangement by saying that she and I, like January and June, being too old and too young for the others, had to talk to each other. I observed that Lancey Bell was a tall, nervous, loquacious young man; his head, his hands, his long arms seemed constantly on the move with his tongue. Of course, he had eyes only for Cora. I smiled to myself as I heard him open the conversation with a showy quotation from Ruskin, wondering why men were such asses. Couldn't he *see* that she didn't understand? But Mrs. Bell was telling me about the Newport of her childhood.

"It really had charm then," she was saying. "My family lived in a dear old stucco, bracketed thing designed by Upjohn that the Herron woman has just pulled down to make way for her monstrosity. We used to have archery contests on the lawn. Everyone painted or scribbled or sculpted instead of dressing up like peacocks and hurling bits of pasteboard at each other. You'd have liked it, Augusta."

No one ever talked to me this way at home, and I was delighted. What did I care that the "Herron woman" was my Aunt Polly? "It sounds like Fairfield!" I exclaimed. "I like Fairfield ever so much more than Newport. I wish we had stayed there with Granny Millinder."

"Does your grandmother ever come to Newport?"

"Oh no. She says she's too old to start playing the social game. She's always telling us what was good enough for Grandpa is good enough for her. Mamma says it is, too. But then Papa says a man's mother and his wife never understand each other."

"Or understand each other too well," Mrs. Bell amended. "I like the sound of your grandmother. I think she and I might hit it off."

I had drunk a whole glass of white wine by now and felt disposed to be confidential. "Of course, you don't like Mamma," I said. "We all know that. And she's terribly cross about it."

"My dear child, I don't even know your mamma!"

"I know. But you will." I nodded twice to emphasize this. "She says you'll have to."

"Why in heavens name will I 'have' to?"

"Because we're the coming thing."

Mrs. Bell burst into a hearty laugh. "Bless me, child, you make your family sound like the yellow peril. Must we all band together to resist you?"

"I think you'd better!"

At this we both became quite hilarious. I decided that I was a great social success and saw my future as a twentieth century Madame de Staël. By the time Lancey turned to me, the last vestige of my shyness was gone.

"I don't seem to have made much of an impression on your sister," he said, smiling. "I hope I shall do better with you."

I thought it very likely. At first impression he seemed angular and uncoordinated, and he had a rather shrill laugh, but when he focused those intense green eyes on me and I became aware of his pale skin and thick black curly hair, my impression was almost of a Byron.

"I'm much more easily satisfied than Cora," I assured him.

"With men, do you mean?"

"Well, in your case I'm predisposed," I said, feeling more and more like Madame de Staël. "For example, I'm crazy about your mother."

"Ah, but liking one's mother . . ." He shrugged.

"Don't you think it helps?"

"Not always. If I were to make a hit with you, I shouldn't want it to be the same kind Mother made."

"Why not?"

"Why indeed?" He surveyed me for a minute with a faintly mocking smile. "Tell me more about your enchanting sister."

"You find her enchanting?"

"Doesn't everyone?"

"Men do, but men don't know anything."

"What don't they know?" he demanded.

"Well, they think if a girl is pretty, she must be an angel. Cora is pretty, I admit, and in some ways she's very sweet. Of course, she's my sister, and I adore her. But she loves to lock herself up in her room and look out the window or read silly magazines. And her room's always in the most ghastly mess, too."

He laughed as loudly as his mother. "How can you tell?"

"Tell?" I stared. "Why, I see it!"

"But I thought your family had dozens of slaves who plumped up the pillows every time you got out of a chair. What else is money for?"

I began to wonder at this point if he was laughing at me. "My mother says it's very poor form to talk about money," I reproved him. "When you go out, that is."

"Then your mother must be very provincial."

I stared at such rudeness, but even as I stared I considered it. I was more of a Bell than a Millinder already. "Perhaps it's just what she is!" I conceded, but Lancey was no longer listening. He was staring quite openly at Cora. When she turned around and saw us both looking at her, she asked, a bit crossly: "What's the matter?"

"We're spellbound," Lancey said soberly.

"Oh, shush!" Cora retorted and turned back to her hostess.

She was cooler and dryer than usual in the carriage going home. "You certainly were a rattle today."

"I was 'keeping up my end of the conversation,'" I said with dignity. "Just what Mamma says you *never* do."

"Well, I doubt if she'd have liked your keeping it up at the expense of the whole family. I heard you. All that business about Granny and the social game!"

"But it's true! You know it's true!"

"That doesn't mean you have to tell it to someone like Mrs. Bell," Cora retorted. "Couldn't you see she was pumping you? Don't you know what she thinks of people like us? Everything you said will be all over Newport tomorrow!"

"Well, whatever Mrs. Bell may think of us, there's no question of what her son does," I pointed out with an arch smile. "*He* couldn't talk about anything but a certain Cora Millinder!"

Cora flushed. "A lot of bosh, I'm sure."

"He was greatly impressed," I said firmly.

"He's greatly impressed with himself, I guess. He thinks he's pretty smart."

"He *is* smart."

Cora just glanced at me. "How do you know?"

"Mrs. Bell says so."

"Oh, Mrs. Bell," Cora said with a shrug and lapsed into her usual silence.

I went to bed that afternoon with a headache from the unaccustomed white wine, but Mamma, who never had the least sympathy with ailments, came into my room for a full report on the lunch. I stared resentfully at the dark head that loomed over my recumbent figure.

"Did he like her?" she demanded.

"Do you mean Mr. Lancey Bell?" I retorted feebly. "He liked us both, I believe."

"Oh, come how, Gussie, you know what I mean. Was he *struck* by her?"

"Well, he said he was," I conceded with a touch of jealousy. "But he's very joky."

"That doesn't mean he wasn't serious. They all start that way. The next thing is for us to ask him here."

"But Cora doesn't like him!"

Mamma gave me her bleak look. "Cora doesn't like anyone," she retorted as she left the room.

My brother Willie, who was the oldest and the most like Papa, was worked upon to ask Lancey to a family lunch later in the week. He had known him at Chelton School and sometimes played tennis with him at the Casino. Lancey accepted promptly and held forth at our family board with a noisy exuberance that caused Willie and Bertie to exchange amused glances with Papa. But he made a great hit with Mamma, who couldn't seem to take her eyes off him. If any of us spoke to her, she ignored us. She was like a frog on a lily pad watching a butterfly that is hovering nearby. It may seem hard to say that Mamma looked like a frog, for she could still pass for a good-looking woman, but in middle age her face had broadened, her chin had squared and her eyes, I am afraid, had become more staring. When she was smiling or talking and her face was animated, she was still possessed of a certain charm, but when she was still and watching, she exuded an aura that was faintly sinister. It would have been foolish of her to go leaping from pad to pad to follow the butterfly. It was only a question of time before he would come close enough to be caught without effort. But could Mamma wait?

Lancey treated her with more respect than he did the rest of us, but he made fun of her, too, as much as he dared. They discussed houses in Newport, and he told her how his generation of architects meant to change the whole face of summer resorts.

"You will have to build what your clients want," Mamma objected.

"We'll show them what to want."

"They may have their own ideas."

"Then they may have to change them!"

"You're very sure of yourself!"

"Is there any point not being?" Lancey demanded.

"But all through history artists have worked under patrons. You can't get away from the power of the purse, you know."

"Oh, I see what *you'd* have been like, Mrs. Millinder, in the Renaissance!" Lancey exclaimed with his impudent, but infectious laugh. "You'd have been like one of the old popes and locked me up in a damp cellar of the Vatican till I'd designed a tomb the way you wanted it!"

After lunch Lancey walked with Cora in the rock garden, and I watched them from the conservatory. His head was constantly turned towards her, while hers was turned to the water. I supposed that he was doing all the talking while Cora concealed her ignorance behind her usual tapestry of stately silence. Sighing despondently at the quixotic taste of the other sex, I then immersed myself in *Moths* and was not even aware, a half hour later, that the strolling couple had come in until I felt my novel suddenly taken from my hands by Lancey himself.

"What is Miss Gussie improving her mind with?" he demanded. "Ah, dear Ouida!" I made an agonized clutch for my book, but he held it over his head. "Why don't you improve your mind, Cora, like your sister here? Why don't you fill it up with English houseparties, and dashing guardsmen and daring duchesses? There's nothing like culture, is there, Miss Gussie?"

"Give it to me!" I cried, hot with shame, and I caught it from him at last and fled upstairs from his high laughter.

I need not, as it turned out, have felt embarrassed before Cora, because she placed a different construction on Lancey's mockery. The very next morning I ran into her in a most unexpected place. It was at the desk in the Redwood Library, and she was actually taking out a book. In fact she was taking out two! She started visibly when. she saw me and made a gesture as if to conceal the volumes, but when I continued to stare, she recovered herself and extended a defiant hand to show me the titles.

"Ouida?" I asked in surprise. "Since when did you take up Ouida?"

"Isn't that the author you were reading yesterday? The one Lancey said wrote about English houseparties?"

"Yes, but he didn't mean you to read *her*."

"Her? Is it a 'she'?" Cora seemed thoroughly bewildered now. "Why didn't he mean me to? Isn't she supposed to be good?"

"Oh, Cora, she's trash!" I cried. "That was all a joke!"

She turned away quickly, a flush on her cheeks. Cora had always been impervious to my taunts, which was why I was so careless about them. But now I saw that I had hurt her, and I was sorry.

"Oh, *some* of Ouida is all right," I conceded. "*A Village Commune*, for example. That's almost up to Trollope."

"Well, how is one to tell?" Cora asked fretfully. "How is one to tell when he's joking and when he's not?"

"You mean Lancey? Oh, the Bells are always joking."

It was the best thing I could have said, though I had not intended it that way. It gave Cora the chance to regain her shattered superiority. "You say 'the Bells' as if you really knew them," she retorted. "Who do you think you are? Aunt Daisy?"

4

Even Cora could not pretend, in the days and weeks that followed, that Lancey was not a "beau." He played the role almost as if he were playing it on the stage. When I think back now on his tilted straw hat and the bicycle guards strapped around his white flannels and the jaunty way in which he carried his daily tribute of camellias, I seem to picture the swain of the nineties as he would appear today in a musical revue. I see him as tall and lanky, in a red blazer and long yellow scarf, sauntering across the grass courts at the Casino, carrying two racquets, swinging his long legs forward, calling to friends on the veranda, emitting the high, sharp, half-insulting laugh of the Bell family. Lancey had his mother's long oval face and small, green, intelligent eyes, but his lips were thick and sensuous and his hair a mass of black, shiny ringlets. He was always laughing, except when he was being mockingly serious, and Cora's friends were as afraid of his tongue as our parents' friends were of his mother's. Why then should Lancey, with his exotic tastes, his genealogical vanity, his compulsion to cap every story, every boast, his interminable tales of hunting grizzly bears, of climbing Alps, his cult of Baudelaire, have seemed to all of us so dazzlingly attractive? Because for all his irritating qualities, he was so vitally alive, and for all his affectations, so intensely male. Lancey deferred to no one, and deference was the order of the day. In a Newport where everyone was impressed with everyone else's wealth, the Bells were impressed only with themselves. It was exhilarating.

Mamma kept telling the rest of us, with the greatest satisfaction, that Cora was at last sticking her nose out of the thick fog that had enshrouded her since birth and was scenting "life" for the first time. But I was not altogether sure that Cora didn't find her old fog preferable. She had always seemed to derive a quaint satisfaction out of her lonely routines. In Fairfield she had been perfectly happy to propel herself around the shallow edges of a pond, hour after hour, standing on a small raft and using a pole. This outlet was denied her in Newport, but she could spend the same amount of time strumming sentimental tunes on the piano in the conservatory or playing with her three black poodles. These slept in her room and were fed, clipped and brushed by her loving hands alone. She also liked to practice archery against a target on the lawn and to take long walks by the sea. I was the one who was most aware of her passion for solitude, because I was always seeking her company and being rebuffed. It was hard, because Willie and Bertie paid no attention to me and I needed a friend. It was a need, however, that seemed to have been left out of Cora's nature. She got no

pleasure that any of us could see in the tremendous impression she made at
the parties that Mamma obliged her to attend. She took no interest even in
clothes, though she wore them with a natural grace and allowed Mamma
to pick them for her. Cora's tall, straight figure, clad in white lace, crossing
the lawn at a Newport garden party, was a beautiful sight to behold. But it
was also her trouble. She looked to perfection a part that she had no wish
or capacity to play.

I think that Lancey was the first human being whom she had ever wanted
to please. Certainly he was the first man. It must have been because she
had no idea how to go about this that she now sought my company at just
the time when most older sisters would have wished to dispense with it: on
the afternoons when Lancey called. It was a sad commentary on her lack of
friends as well as on her relationship with Mamma that she had no one to
turn to but her giddy and romantic younger sister.

Lancey on several occasions drove us out in his tandem, the three of us a
bit squeezed on the driver's seat. If he objected to my presence, and he
must have terribly, he was too kind to show it. For Lancey was kind, under
his malicious humor and high spirits. He entertained us entrancingly on those
drives with fantastic, imagined tales, insisting that we help him as he made
them up. He populated the houses that we passed with caricatures of types,
"Mrs. Gorham Gothic" and "Mrs. Timely Tudor" and invented feuds and
scandals and romances. Even Cora was induced to make an occasional contribution, and if I blushed at the flatness of her hesitant offerings, it was
never noticed in the explosion of Lancey's congratulations.

"On the nose, my girl, right on the nose! Gussie, this sister of yours makes
the two of us look like a couple of louts!"

Cora would blush and bite her lips and appear to concentrate on some
object in the distance. She was embarrassed by such effusion. But I was too
excited to notice this danger signal. It was a traditional part of the picture
that the beau should treat the gawky young sister with an affectation of
gallantry and that she should fall in love with him, and Lancey and I were
faithful to our roles. If anything, we overdid them. When he spied me from
the driveway on my little porch and shouted up: "It is the East, and Juliet
is the sun!" when he sank on his knees on the lawn, to the destruction of
white flannels, shielding his eyes with his arms as from the glare of my beauty,
when he told Cora it was well for her he had not seen *me* first, I was struck
first into dumbness, then amazement and finally into a fluttery state of
delightful agitation. Until then my only outlet for such emotion had been
in two rather steamy "crushes" on older girls at Miss Dixon's Classes. Now,
in the rocketing course of a single summer, the male image, armed and
visored, had sprung up violently to scatter lesser fantasies.

It was therefore quite as much for the interruption of my own good time
as anyone else's that I resented what now occurred. I was reading one
afternoon in the library when I heard Lancey's high, cheerful voice addressing Osborn, our butler, in the hall, and I bounded up the stairs to Cora's
room to announce him. I found her lying on her stomach on her chaise
lounge, peering over the edge to watch the poodles who were having their

lunch. She did not even look up when I cried out that Lancey was downstairs.

"Tell him I can't see him."

I gaped. "What?"

"Tell him I can't see him," she repeated irritably. "Must I see everyone who comes to the house?"

"Shall I tell him to come tomorrow?"

"You'll do nothing of the sort!" Cora sat up indignantly. "I'm going to Fairfield tomorrow. To stay with Granny."

"For how long?"

"For the rest of the summer."

"I guess Mamma will have something to say about that," I retorted grimly.

"Oh, Gussie, do try to understand for once, will you?" There was a note of smothered tension in Cora's voice. She got up and walked rapidly across the room, the debutante's room, elegant, feminine, alive with flower chintzes, that Mamma had had decorated for her, and stood by the open door to her porch.

"It's just what I am trying to do," I protested.

"I can't keep it up, that's all," she said flatly, her back to me. "I can't keep up this make-believe of knowing things I don't know. You and Lancey are always sneering at houses. Well, *I* don't see why Aunt Daisy's is so ugly. And I don't care, that's the thing. They're all just houses to me. Lancey's full of all sorts of crazy ideas about me. If he knew the real me, he'd be bored to tears. It's easier to get out now, before I'm in too deep."

I immediately resented her tone. It was as if she were trying to turn the whole glittering summer into a child's fantasy of mine. "Oh, well, if that's all you care," I said irritably.

"It's not a question of my caring."

"I only thought it might amuse you to have the most attractive young man in Newport at your beck and call."

"I tell you, Gussie, I can't keep it up!"

And she actually stamped her foot. I stared for a moment at her back and suddenly realized that the reason it was presented to me was that Cora was weeping! In a quick rush of sympathy for this perverted sufferer I cried out:

"But Lancey *cares* so!"

"No, he doesn't!" she retorted, with a new hint of desperation in her tone. "He doesn't care a fig about me. He only cares about running after what the papers call 'a beautiful heiress'!"

I was deeply shocked. "You mean you think he's after . . . the *money?*"

The world had always been divided between the family and friends, the trusted familiars, and the great, grey, clutching, dirty masses who were "after the money," strangers who spoke to one in the street on the specious excuse of asking the time or who smiled at one across the aisle in a theater or sidled up to one's chair on the deck of a Cunarder. It appalled me to think that Lancey could belong to this category, but I had been brought up in the belief that anyone, even the most unlikely person imaginable, could be made to qualify.

"Oh no, not that," Cora said hastily. "I only mean that he's competitive. Fiercely competitive, like his horrid old mother. You know all those stories of his. If he climbs a mountain, it has to be the highest mountain. If he goes to Alaska, he has to shoot the biggest brown bear. And if he spends the summer in Newport . . ." Cora shrugged.

"He has to court the most beautiful heiress!" I finished for her.

"Exactly. I'm in season, that's all."

It occurred to me suddenly that Cora's intuition was keen. There *was* something about Lancey . . . but what was intuition to a girl, any normal girl, against the fact of Lancey? I felt frustrated and helpless, knowing that Cora would not listen to me. Leaving her room, I ran downstairs to face Lancey.

"She can't see you," I said glumly. "She's got a headache."

He stared. "A headache? Since when?"

"Since just now."

"Look here, Gussie, I'm not the kind of fellow who can be brushed off with a headache. You'll have to do better than that."

For answer I could only burst into tears and run out of the hall. Behind me I could hear Lancey's loud whistle and his: "Well, I'll be a son of a gun!"

There was a storm that night when Cora announced her intention of going to Fairfield. Mamma, who was taken completely by surprise, was violent in her disappointment and anger. She described poor Cora as a "lazy, selfish cow" and said that enough had been done for her, that so far as she, Mamma, was concerned, Cora could live and die a dried up old maid who cared for nothing but a few small, smelly animals. Cora simply retorted that she could ask for nothing better. Papa, who was finally aroused from his native inertia by the racket, announced that he would take Cora to Fairfield when he went to see Granny at the end of the week, but that she would have to wait until then. The hot evening air in the Jacobean dining hall was electric with tension.

In the days that followed, Cora refused to go off the place. When she was not sulking in her room, she was walking the dogs by the ocean. She sat silently through meals with eyes that were suspiciously red. As Bertie said, anyone would have thought that *she* was the one who had been jilted. I saw Lancey at the Casino and at Bailey's Beach, but he always seemed occupied with a noisy group who were usually laughing at his jokes. One morning, however, as I was making my gingerly way after swimming, in a long, dripping black suit and stockings, across the sand to the bathhouses, I found myself brought up before the waiting figure of Lancey. He must have been playing tennis, for he had two long scarfs wound about his neck and seemed flushed.

"Aren't you even going to say Hello?" he demanded.

"I don't know," I said judiciously "You haven't been very nice to us recently."

"*I* haven't been nice to *you!*" he cried indignantly.

"Well, you haven't been to see us."

"When the door was slammed in my face?"

"I don't think you're very persistent," I said coyly.

"What do you mean by that?"

"Oh . . . things."

I started to walk on, but to my astonishment, he caught my arm and jerked me roughly back. It was very exciting, but I knew what was expected of a lady.

"How dare you!" I cried. "Do you want me to call my mother?"

"Do you want me to call mine?" he retorted and burst into his shattering laugh. When I tried to proceed, however, my arm was grabbed again, this time even more roughly. "I want to know what you mean," he insisted.

"Well, I hardly think you're much of a beau," I said peevishly. "One little headache, and you run off and sulk like a spoiled child."

"One little headache!" His eyes narrowed. "Did Cora tell you to say that?"

"No—not exactly."

"Then what sort of mischief do you think you're up to?"

"I just don't think you should take on so about a headache, that's all!" I cried, upset by his anger.

"Your sister wrote me a letter," Lancey explained, speaking with a bitter distinctness. "She said she didn't want to see me any more. She said she didn't agree with any of my opinions. She ended her little note, with her own inimitable grace, by saying that she only wanted to be left alone. What redblooded man would come mooning around with a bunch of camellias after *that*?"

I considered this carefully. I had to admit that it had a terse, final ring. "What do you suppose has got into her?"

"I don't have to suppose," he said morosely. "I only have to listen to the chatter at the Casino. Your sister turns out to be a good little Newport girl, that's all. She'll do exactly what Mamma wants."

I looked at him open-mouthed. "And what does Mamma want?"

"Why what all good mothers want these days. A coronet perhaps. Or at least another fortune. You don't suppose she's put on her best bonnet and come to Newport to hand her precious daughter over to an architectural student without so much as a railroad to his name?"

I felt positively giddy at so mammoth a misconception of the true facts. "Is *that* what you think?"

"That's what I *know*!" he retorted. "Imagine what an ass I felt to have pictured Cora as something I had no right to expect her to be. As a free soul." He laughed sneeringly. "As someone who lived in a world apart! Why should I be surprised to find out that she's simply what she ought to be? That she's just another good girl who says 'Yes, Mamma' and 'No, Mamma'? That her idea of a perfect husband is one who has a castle where Mamma might like to visit?"

"Oh, you're right!" I cried, stifling my laughter. "You're indubitably right!" And I ran off happily to join Mamma.

I knew that I would only have to wait for Mamma's questions in the victoria, and when they came, I gave her a full and complete response. She took in my every word and then nodded abruptly.

"Good for you, Gussie," she said. "I know exactly what to do. I shall send a note to Mrs. Bell this very afternoon. I shall ask her to call."

"But I thought that's just what she wouldn't do!" I exclaimed. "Don't you have to call first?"

"Oh, she'll come *this* time," Mamma said with assurance and thereupon dropped the subject.

Mrs. Bell indeed did come. She came the next day. I waited in the front hall while she visited with Mamma in the living room and I was able to see her when she came out alone. She paused for a moment to take in the whitewashed walls and the Gothic windows, and she even raised a lorgnette to examine one of the armored figures. It was extraordinary what skepticism she managed to insert into that gesture.

"How's Ouida?" she demanded, and I jumped, for I hadn't thought that she had even seen me.

"I'm almost through *The Princess Napraxine.*"

"I had thought she lived in a fancy world. But that, my dear, was before I met your mother."

"Are you friends now?" I asked eagerly.

"Oh, I think we understand each other. The 'high contracting parties,' as we say in the law, seem to be in perfect accord!"

I clapped my hands to hear this, and Mrs. Bell passed on, with an enigmatic nod, to her carriage. But, alas, the accord was only on the high contracting level. When Lancey came to the house the next day, as I had anticipated, Cora did see him, alone in the conservatory. I could not control my curiosity, and I am ashamed to admit that I hovered outside that closed door. Hearing no sound from within, I decided that they must have gone out on the porch and thence to stroll on the lawn, so I pushed the door quietly open to observe them from one of the windows. To my mortification I discovered my mistake. Cora was sitting in a wicker chair, staring at the floor, and Lancey was pacing up and down the room. Obviously, neither had spoken for several minutes. They both looked up at my entrance, Lancey with exasperation, but Cora, I felt, with relief.

"I'm so sorry," I murmured stupidly. "I thought I might have left my copy of *Folle-Farine* in here." I looked vaguely about and did not find it. Then, instead of retreating, I stared like an idiot from one to the other. Lancey finally paused in his pacing and turned to me impatiently.

"Gussie, do you *mind*?" he asked, pointing to the door.

"No, Gussie, stay," Cora said abruptly in a tone that was not meant for trifling. "I want you to stay."

Bewildered, I sank onto a wicker stool and looked anxiously from one to the other. Cora simply stared out across the lawn, and Lancey continued to pace back and forth. Suddenly he stopped and turned on her.

"Very well, I'll say what I have to say in front of Gussie!"

"You may do as you please," Cora said with a shrug.

"Your mother has made me a magnificent offer, Gussie!" he continued in a high, shrill tone, turning the full glare of his attention on me. I might have been a shrinking Guildenstern before his ranting Hamlet. "Before I have so much as asked your sister's hand in marriage, she has let me know that it will be crammed with gold! As the son-in-law of Mr. and Mrs. Cyrus Millinder I shall have a house in town and a house in the country, a shoot in the Carolinas and even a yacht! And do you know what I am asked to give in return? Or give up? What, I ask you?"

"What?" I echoed.

"Nothing!" he cried. "Absolutely nothing!" He spread his arms in the air to indicate the void of his, responsibilities, and his tone soared dramatically. He was working himself into a pitch that seemed half hysterical. "Can you conceive of a more idyllic fairyland? Where the princess and all her castles are surrendered to the amorous goatherd without the three tricky questions to be answered at the risk of his head? Without even a cardboard dragon to tilt with? Without so much as a moat to span or a gate to batter down?"

"But you were angry with Mamma yesterday for wanting a fortune!" I cried with sudden penetration. "And now you're angry with her for giving one away!"

Lancey was taken aback. He stared at me in baffled consternation. "I'm angry with her for giving it to me," he retorted at last. "I don't want her money! I'm not a pauper. I have a perfectly respectable competence, and I expect to earn a lot more. It will be quite enough for two." He turned again to Cora. "What about it, Cora? Will you share it with me?" His tone would have been more impressively grave had he not been trying so hard to make it just that. "Will you turn your back on all the gold and tinsel and be just plain Mrs. Lancey Bell? With no yachts or hunters?"

Cora did not even turn her head to look at him, nor did she answer. He continued to stare at her fixedly, and his eyes slowly filled with anger. It seemed to me an unbearable length of time. Finally, I broke in.

"Cora, did you hear him?"

"Of course I heard him."

"Well, what do you say?"

"Does all that oratory require an answer?" She turned now and looked coolly at Lancey. "Very well then. I won't go away with you, Lancey. I don't want to be 'just plain Mrs. Bell.' I don't see why I should give up anything."

His face broke into a magnificent sneer. "You *like* your gilded cage!" he cried in bitter triumph. "The voiceless nightingale doesn't dare leave her gilded cage!"

"That's right," she said in the same flat tone. "I like my gilded cage."

For a moment he stared at her in blank irresolution. I am sure now that he had not expected the scene to end in this way. Lancey was quite capable of acting on his own enthusiasms. He would have eloped with Cora that night and braved the anger of her parents. Whatever he said at the moment, he always meant—at the moment. But now the cold spray of her answer flushed out the fine little flame of his proposal, and I could see in his eyes the sudden sparkle of disdain. It was as if the lights had been turned on in the middle of a scene, and Hamlet, checked in his soliloquy, faced an indifferent audience bent on putting on their wraps and finding rubbers and umbrellas under their seats. But was such an audience worthy of such a play?

"It's what I deserve!" he cried savagely. "It's what I get for being so gullible as to think the kitten could be any better than the cat!"

He turned and marched into the hall, letting the door bang noisily behind him.

"Cora!" I cried in distress. "Don't let him go!" When she said nothing, I ran over to her and fell on my knees, putting my head in her lap. "He loves you!" There was a long silence, but when I tried to look up at her I felt her hand on the back of my head. "He loves you!" I repeated, and the pressure of that hand increased. Then I was still, for I knew with sudden awe that she was weeping again. "Oh, Cora," I murmured wretchedly, "why did you send him away?" She took her hand away, but when I turned, she had covered her eyes. "Cora, please speak to me," I begged. "Please let me help you!"

"There's nothing you can do."

"I can tell him the truth! I can tell him you love him!"

"But I can't marry a man like that!" she cried in a tone of panic. "I can't marry anyone!"

"Oh, Cora!"

"I can't, Gussie." She shook her head violently several times in quick succession. "I'm not fit to be a wife. That's the truth of it. Why does everyone keep shouting at me? It's all they've done all summer, shout at me!"

"Lancey doesn't shout at you."

"But he's the worst of all!" she exclaimed. "He seems to think he has some kind of right to keep waking me up. Maybe I'm better off asleep!"

"But all he wants to do is help you and be proud of you and . . ."

"No!" Cora turned around suddenly, her fists raised to her temples in a gesture of despair. "He wouldn't be proud of me! Don't talk like that! He'd be disgusted and ashamed! He'd want this and that and the other thing."

"Cora, he loves you!"

"He doesn't!" she almost screamed at me. "He doesn't even know what I'm like. He's in love with some idea he has of me. Some idea he's attached to the wax doll Mamma's made of me! Gussie, believe me, I know what I can do and what I can't. I've *got* to be myself!"

In a sudden unbearable burst of guilt at what I had done to her by telling Mamma, I hurried over to throw my arms around her. But demonstrations never worked with Cora. She immediately disengaged herself from my clutching arms.

"I'm sorry," I murmured, mortified.

"I don't want your sympathy," she retorted, staring out the window again. "Everyone in Newport has their little game to play. And they all love it so!" She put her hands suddenly to her eyes. "Dear God, I'm so sick of you all!"

"Cora!" I cried stricken. "Not of *me!*"

"Everyone! You're all so—*blind!*"

When I left her, bitterly hurt, I ran down the lawn to the cliff path and walked past the great houses that loomed up, bare and new, to frown at strolling sailors and parlormaids. I was filled with indignant wrath at Mamma. It struck me for the first time that there was something abnormal in her compulsion to make everyone around her, the young as well as the old, concede the power of her gold, even at the cost of the son-in-law whom she had wanted to buy with it. Mamma had a perfectly clear and logical mind, but with the Bells she had seemed resolved to use no weapon but money. Perhaps she had been too deeply humiliated by Mrs. Bell to be content with anything less than an equal humiliation of her adversary. It would not have been enough if, after Cora's and Lancey's engagement, Mrs. Bell should have been allowed to admit to a mere error of judgment, to tell her friends: "You know, Eliza Millinder really *has* wit," or charm, or good taste, or good blood or whatever. If she gave Mrs. Bell no peg to hang her hat on but a peg of gold, would not the latter have been forced to admit that she had bowed to naked wealth, and wasn't naked wealth the one thing that Mrs. Bell herself so conspicuously lacked? It appalled me, not so much that Mamma was devoid of ideals, but that she so readily let it be seen that her front of appearing to have them was, in fact, a front. She simply took it for granted that nobody else had a whit more of them than she. Life to Mamma was a fancy dress ball where everyone knew that everyone else was wearing a costume, and it was consequently not a tragedy if, from time to time, one's wig fell off. When she insisted on the importance of money, it was less the vulgarity of a parvenu than the erupting impatience of the agnostic who finds unbearably cloying the believer's chant of a heaven of angels and harps. Lancey must have actually wondered if she did not *want* to marry Cora to a fortune hunter! I had stopped as this struck me, and I stamped my foot on the path. At least, I could learn! When my turn came, I, too, could refuse to be led dumbly to the sacrificial altar, a passive Iphigenia, by a mother capable of sweeping Agamemnon aside to seize the knife herself!

Decades later, when Mamma and Aunt Daisy were both dead, I remembered that day on the Cliff Walk. I had returned to Newport to empty Mamma's house which Bertie and I had finally sold to a Catholic order. It had been opened to the public for its final summer, for the benefit of a local charity, and I paid my dollar to go through it with the crowd. I was fascinated by the hushed awe of our group as they were conducted by a guide through the great dark rooms. It was amazing how rotted they appeared, how tawdry the grandeur, as if the house had died with its owner. But my fellow visitors seemed to find it beautiful, and they listened with respectful interest as the guide intoned his memorized lecture: "In this room Mrs. Millinder had tea every afternoon at five. In that corner you will see a marble figure of a poodle that belonged to the Princesse de Conti. The painting over the mantel depicts Julius Millinder receiving President Arthur on board the *Western Star*." The family, it seemed, were treated more royally dead than alive. Afterwards I made my slow way to a point on the Cliff Walk from which I could see both Mamma's house and Aunt Daisy's. As I contemplated their vast, woebegone, peeling façades I wondered for one last time what it was that Mamma had found so different about hers. For time had stripped them both of everything except what they had in common, and what was that but swagger? And, again, even in their decay they seemed to sneer down at me and say in Mamma's old tone: "Oh, very well, that's all we are, but what, in the name of the universe, are *you?*"

5

MAMMA, AS I have indicated, had more imagination than her contemporaries, but not enough more to build a life on the difference, particularly as this difference was not recognized in her world. Her great shingle mansion may have shown more inspiration than Aunt Daisy's French château, but to Newporters of that day limestone was more impressive than wood and an old foreign design superior to a modern native one. And if they enjoyed period costume parties at Mamma's, "a soirée chez Madame Recamier" and Réjane to recite, they were more relaxed at Aunt Daisy's, dressed up as Genghis Khan or Mary Stuart, and listening to Lulu Frolic sing "She may have known better days." Taste did not count for much more then than it does today.

When it came to foreign titles, however, Mamma's greater subtlety was a positive disadvantage. All Newport applauded the engagement of my cousin, Gwen Millinder, Aunt Daisy's only daughter, to the Earl of Myol. An English title, a castle, and ermine for coronations—these were things everyone understood and appreciated. But nobody was particularly impressed to hear Mamma boast that Prince Antoine de Bourbon-Conti, her candidate for Cora, was descended in the male line, through an uncle of Henry IV, from Saint Louis himself and was entitled to wear the lilies of France on his shield. And there was something rather bogus and *opéra bouffe* to the good burghers of the summer colony about his title of Altesse *Sérénissime*. Still, he was French and a prince, and Cora was two seasons out and becoming, if possible, even more inert, and people were inclined to think it might be as good as the Cyrus Millinders were likely to do.

I should say immediately, in defense of the people who were thus casually disposing of my sister in marriage, that Antoine himself was a most agreeable person, delighted with everyone he met, including Cora, though she treated him exactly as she treated everyone else. He was short, which was a pity, as she was tall, and his was a Gallic, bristling heel-clicking shortness which drew attention to itself. But he had dark, limpid, kindly eyes, a fine aquiline nose and long, thick black hair with distinguished if premature grey streaks. When he moved, he moved quickly, like a bird, and when he was still, he was very still. His hands seemed perennially uplifted in astonishment and admiration of all that he saw in America. He was infinitely polite and infinitely cordial; he seemed to defer to everyone without losing an inch of his natural dignity. He wanted to travel and see factories; he delighted

the gentlemen after dinner with his interest in the "miracle" of American
industrial development. It was remarkable that he seemed not to feel the
slightest discrepancy between the restoration of the Bourbons and the age
of mechanization; it evidently never occurred to him that he might be an
anachronism. Like the bland Maximilian of Mexico, he took for granted that
the New World and the *Almanac de Gotha* had equal benefits to confer on
each other.

It was perhaps his sense of tradition that made him so impervious to Cora's
listlessness. They were not yet engaged, it was true, but Antoine was staying in the house, and it was known in the family that he had made formal
application to Papa for her hand. Cora was supposed to be "considering,"
but I had my doubts if she was doing even this. I had taken a considerable
liking to poor, patient Antoine and was privately mortified that she should
treat him so. I could only suppose that, as the product of a thousand years
of arranged marriages, he had the delicacy to understand that the future
brides in his family had often to subdue their personal inclinations. If it was
embarrassing for a house guest who was also a professed suitor to be so
ignored by the object of his admiration, he never showed it. He even had
the good taste to take himself off my family's hands by allowing me to show
him Newport.

It must have been hard, for I was at my most trying period. I was old
enough to claim the privileges of an adult without forfeiting the self-indulgence of a child. I wanted to be left alone and to have my independence
respected and at the same time to be the object of ceaseless family attention. I was prone to sudden tantrums and violent storms of tears, and I would
fling off to my room, lock myself in and sulk for hours at a time. Yet I was
seventeen and due to come out the next season! I don't know whether I
was more the victim of a lazy family tendency to treat me as "Baby" or of
Mamma's preoccupation with Cora's more interesting career. I was not
nearly as unattractive as I pitied myself for being, but I was big and inclined
to be stout and had moist palms. Worst of all, in reaction to the applause
that always accompanied Cora's beauty, I tended defiantly to emphasize an
immature clumsiness of gait, an abruptness of manner and a general disar-
ray of hair and clothes. It was unfortunate, because I had naturally good
features and healthy color, and with an erect posture and a neat simplicity
of dress I could have been passable. But, oh no, I had to glory in my moods
and temperament. I had to refuse to go to any parties given by girls my
own age, with the result that I knew no boys at all. I was not even popular
with my own sex. At Miss Dixon's Classes the girls found me aggressive
and show-off and too interested in books, and whenever I did form a friendship, I always managed to destroy it by my possessiveness. I was in many
ways a very unhappy young woman, yet I had all the conceit and egotism
that are so often the refuge of the unpopular, and I imagined that my
romantic emotions raised me far above my silly, superficial contemporaries.
My poor family had to put up with the scenes that I would have inflicted
on my friends had I had any, and they were only too willing to allow Antoine
to bear the brunt of these. Of course I was delighted to have a companion

of my own who was not only older but a prince, and I drove him all over Newport, from the shipyards to the old Viking tower, and talked his head off. I must say, he was an angel of patience. Only when I aired my genealogical knowledge of the royal family of France, would he occasionally, very gently, submit a correction. I wanted him entirely to myself, and at family meals I insisted on sitting next to him and carrying on the conversation in a loud whisper that greatly exasperated Mamma.

"What are you telling Antoine? Speak up, please! I'm sure you must be boring him terribly."

"We're talking about his mother," I retorted, with injured dignity. "Did you know she's a first cousin of the Empress of Austria?"

"Oh, my dear Miss Gussie, *please!*" Antoine protested, embarrassed. "No one cares about that sort of thing in your great democracy! Excuse me, Madame Millinder, but your younger daughter has a way of *digging* things out!"

"But that's most interesting," Mamma replied, forgetting all about me. "Tell us, is it true what they say about the poor empress, that she's—well, a bit eccentric?"

Antoine flung his hands up expressively. "Mad as a March hare, dear madame! All that family are."

"Are you mad, Antoine?" Cora put in suddenly.

"Cora!" cried Mamma.

"Oh, please, *chère madame*, don't scold her. If I am mad, she knows only too well where to lay the fault!"

"You're mad if you see anything in *her*," Mamma retorted, glowering at Cora.

Lancey Bell had been in Alaska that summer, but he came to stay with his mother late in August, and of course she must have told him all about Antoine. He did not come to see us, but he came to a large dinner that Aunt Daisy gave for Cora. It was almost, Mamma said peevishly, as if Aunt Daisy had been trying to save her the trouble of announcing her own daughter's engagement. We must have been fifty at table, seated in great carved, gilded Venetian chairs before the splendor of a full gold service. The original concept of the dining hall had evidently been to evoke the spirit of the Italian eighteenth century, of masks and dominoes and Goldoni, but the idea had been lost in drafty space and frowned out of existence by the massive grey empty fireplace with its soaring hood and frieze of men in armor.

Probably because he was in general disfavor with the family, Lancey was seated by me. Needless to say, I was in ecstasy, though he was even more restless and sarcastic than before. He made no effort to conceal that he was bored with everyone at the party and kept staring down the table at Antoine, who was seated on Aunt Daisy's right, as if to catch him in some absurd Gallic mannerism. But Antoine was faultless, as restrained and grave as the most magnificent of Lancey's Porcellian Club friends. There was nothing Lancey could do but turn his malice on the decor of the dining room.

"Isn't it gloriously typical of an architect like Mr. Hunt," he sneered to me, "to put what is probably the biggest fireplace of Rhode Island in a house that is only occupied in July and August!"

"But you must admit it's beautiful."

"Beauty, my dear Gussie, can never be divorced from function. At least not in architecture. Cellini himself could not have designed a beautiful ice-box for an igloo."

"I don't agree with you at all," I retorted. "That mantel has a function. Its function is to take me away from here into beautiful thoughts and old places. When I look at it, I think of cold, damp evenings on the Loire and Louis XI plotting as he paces up and down, fingering a rag of ermine around his old gnarled neck." I was suddenly carried away by my own powers of evocation. "Why should you want to tie me down to Newport? When I look up at the ceiling, I can imagine myself . . ." But I stopped as both our gazes turned upward. I had forgotten that the painting there represented the rape of Europa. Lancey laughed in delight at my blushes.

"Is that what you want, Gussie? To escape from Newport on the back of a bull?"

"Please, Lancey!" I begged him, for I was terrified that his upward gaze and high voice would attract the general attention of the table. "Oh, please!" I repeated when I saw Aunt Daisy glance our way.

Lancey looked back at me with a pleased smile. "You see what dreams are stirred by the sentimental and the irrelevant! That is why architecture should harmonize with the age."

"Very well," I assented, recovering my nerve as Aunt Daisy turned back to her guest of honor. "What would you put on the ceiling?"

"I'd put heroic scenes of the rise of the House of Millinder! I'd put old Julius on the steps of the State House, buying the legislature. Or better yet, the apotheosis of Aunt Daisy. I see her in a chariot drawn by porpoises, a trident in one hand, a lorgnette in the other!"

But I was impervious to his sneers, for it was obvious to me that his anger was directed only at the general deference to Antoine.

"How about our guest of honor restored to his lineal rights?" I asked mischievously. "How about Antoine being crowned at Reims?"

Lancey looked at me blankly. "What are you talking about?"

"Well, after all, he has the first claim to the French throne if you leave out the Orléans, who were only usurpers, anyway!"

"And if you leave out the Third Republic," Lancey retorted with a sniff. "But tell me, Gussie. When King Antoine and Queen Cora are seated in triumph in the Salle des Glaces, will Mamma be set up in the Grand Trianon?"

"Stranger things have happened," I said primly.

At this his expression changed. "You, too, Gussie?" he snapped at me suddenly. "Don't tell me that *you* go along with this crazy snobbism of throwing Cora at an airy little Frenchman who has nothing to sell but a bad title to a nonexistent throne!"

"I?" I was taken aback by his tone. "I have nothing to do with it. You don't think anyone consults me, do you?"

"But you don't approve of it?"

I hesitated. "I don't know. As far as airiness is concerned, I can think of others with that quality. Do you think Cora should prefer a man who slanders her grandfather and makes fun of her aunt?"

"A million times!"

When I turned, startled by his violence, and made out the vivid indignation in his eyes, I realized that our joking time was over. This man was still in love with Cora! Was it not the purest Verdi that the tenor should have to watch, at a great, glittering banquet, the sacrifice of his pale, despairing soprano to the triumphant bass? All that was romantic in me thrilled at the idea of Cora's and Lancey's love and at the even more titillating prospect that I might be the agent to bring them together again. It struck me with an odd, sudden force that I had never before acted as a real influence in anybody's life. It was still true, of course, that I liked to think of myself as being in love with Lancey, but this was not in the least a deterrent. If I could not play Juliet, I might at least play the nurse.

"Of course, it would be a terrible *mésalliance* for Antoine," I said pensively. "There wouldn't have been anything as bad in his family since Catherine de' Medici."

Lancey stared. "You mean Cora uses poison and oubliettes?"

"Oh, no. I was simply referring to her birth " I paid no attention to his explosion of laughter, for I was thinking hard about Antoine. After all, I was very fond of Antoine, and I was not so blinded by romanticism as to ignore that I might be doing him an ill turn. But was there any *real* sympathy between him and Cora? Did she even know the difference between a Bourbon and a Bonaparte? No, it would never do. It would be a kindness to both of them to put every obstacle in their way. I leaned closer to Lancey than a lady should at a dinner party and hissed suddenly in his ear: "Save her!"

Lancey really stared now. "Save her? Me?"

"Who else will?"

But even while we looked at each other, he in astonishment and I in flushed pride at my own boldness, I was aware of a grey head lowered discreetly but inexorably between us, and I heard the admonitory whisper from Aunt Daisy's butler that the conversation had changed and that our hostess wished us to talk to our other neighbors. I turned away abruptly as Lancey's high giggle rang in my ear, and I blushed as I heard him ask the uncomprehending man, whose air of high gravity was not proof against the Bell sarcasm, if Mrs. Millinder would not supply a topic with which he could open a discussion with the lady on his left?

Other guests came in after dinner, and there was dancing in the great gilded marble hall that occupied the center of the house, a kind of roofed cortile that rose three stories with encircling balconies over which maids with little white caps furtively peeped. I sat with Aunt Daisy as she worked on her needlepoint. It was a party, of course, for the young, and none of her friends were there. I knew nobody, as usual, except my own relatives, and they were preoccupied. My brother Bertie, it is true, asked me to waltz, but not in a manner that tempted me to accept.

"You should be dancing, my dear," Aunt Daisy observed in her grave, measured tone. "It's not right for a girl your age to be sitting the whole evening."

"But I'm not out yet!" I protested. "Isn't it all right till I'm out?"

"Not at a family party. I'll tell Gwen to find a partner for you."

"Oh, please, Aunt Daisy! I'd so much rather stay here with you. If I were dancing, I might feel that my partner wanted to be with someone else. Or that he was tired or bored. Or that *I* was tired or bored. You see how chancy it is? While this way I can sit here comfortably and have the whole ballroom to myself. In my imagination!"

"I see you're quite a philosopher," Aunt Daisy said with a little shrug and returned her attention to her needlepoint. It was a relief that Aunt Daisy did not, like so many older people, deprecate the idea of the young dedicating their time to her. I was able to give all my attention to Lancey and Cora who were dancing together. He was talking with great animation, and Cora seemed less impassive than usual. Once she looked actually distressed and sent a short, dark glance in my direction. I could hardly contain my excitement. Something was happening between them on that dance floor that *I* had brought about! In the course of a single evening it seemed that I had graduated from the status of Cupid to that of Venus herself! I was clapping vociferously at the end of the waltz when I perceived Antoine at my side. He bowed, gravely and asked me to dance.

"Oh, I'm so sorry!" I cried guiltily. "I have a headache!"

Aunt Daisy looked up from her work as he moved silently off, and I asked her if she did not find him charming. She conceded that he might be that, but her tone implied that Cora would do well, if like herself, she did not look for any such quality in marriage.

"And, of course, he's only a prince," she added. "I understand that on the Continent that's almost as common as 'Mr.'"

"Oh, but he's a royal prince!" I protested, shocked that she should have learned so little from Mamma's boasting. "You can find him in the first part of *Gotha*!"

Aunt Daisy, however, knew nothing of *Gotha*. Her knowledge of royal genealogies was limited to the big chart, beribboned and emblazoned, that hung in the library to prove her own descent from Charlemagne. "But, of course, it's not like being an earl," she said, as if to conclude the discussion. "A real English earl."

"Oh, but there's no comparison! An earl is only a count, really, and Antoine is several times a count. He's even a duke!"

"Why doesn't he use his real title, then?" Aunt Daisy demanded with a sniff. "No wonder I've never understood the French!"

I saw Cora talking to Antoine, but she turned away from him suddenly and came over to us. She looked very proud and beautiful as she crossed the floor.

"It's been a lovely party, Aunt Daisy," she said. "But Antoine says Gussie has a headache. I'd better take her home."

"I can send her, my dear. You needn't go."

"I don't have a headache!" I protested. "I just don't want to dance!"

"Well, *I* have one then," Cora retorted. "You can take me home."

"But Cora," Aunt Daisy objected, "there are still several girls who haven't danced with the prince."

"Oh, I'm leaving *him*! Gussie and I will just slip quietly away."

It was Aunt Daisy's way to accept such things easily, and in a few minutes Cora and I were seated in the carriage under the porte-cochere. Just as we began to move, however, Lancey ran down the steps and stopped us.

"Why are you going?" he demanded, both hands on the door, his eyes staring in the window.

"Please, Lancey, I'm tired to death," Cora said in a low voice.

"Can I see you tomorrow?"

"No, please."

"Send me word at the Casino tomorrow morning!"

"No!"

"Send Gussie!"

"Good night, Lancey!"

He released his hold, and the carriage moved out into the moonlit night. Cora stared out the window for several minutes, motionless, while I watched her closely. When she finally spoke, she did not turn.

"You were talking about me all during dinner, weren't you?"

"Not all. We talked about Antoine, too."

"I thought you were so fond of Antoine."

"I'm fond of all your beaux."

At this Cora turned an expressionless face on me. "Hadn't you better be getting some of your own?"

My first impulse was to try to scramble out of the carriage. The pain was so sharp that I wanted to escape to the open air, to run into a field. I felt Cora's clutch on my arm as I reached for the door. "Let me go!" I screamed. "Stop the carriage! Let me out! I'll walk home!"

"Don't be an idiot!"

"It's all very well for you to say that! You're beautiful, and everyone loves you. I'm sick and tired of hearing about lovely, beautiful Cora. Suppose you were like me?"

But Cora held me firmly till I gave up struggling and sat back sullenly in the seat. "I wish I did look like you, you goose!" she hissed. "I'd give you every scrap of my famous 'beauty,' for all the good it's done me!"

"You would not!"

"You want to be pitied," she said harshly. "Well, I don't pity you at all!" She looked at me sharply to see if I was under control, and reassured, turned again to the window. "You're having the time of your life, sitting up there with the others, watching *me* perform! Jeering every time I forget my lines! And sobbing with sentiment whenever a young man appears in the wings! Well, I'd like to see you up there for a change!"

I had never seen Cora so passionate, and it filled me with sudden awe. "So you could jeer at me?"

"No!" she retorted brusquely. "So you could see what nonsense it all was. What make-believe."

"What?"

"The whole thing! Mamma and Aunt Daisy. Everything that goes on up here!"

"Oh, that!" I laughed in sudden sophistication at the idea of poor Cora, in her pensive, plodding way, having only just now arrived at this conclusion. Was *this* what she had been pondering on her long listless walks by the sea? "Don't you think I know that? But just because that's all nonsense doesn't mean Lancey's all nonsense."

"He's part and parcel of the whole thing!" she cried indignantly. "He and his silly, scheming old mother! Who only comes to Newport to sneer at people who made their money five minutes after her family. Why, she's the worst of the lot. She's the kind of person who *starts* the whole thing!"

"But you can't hold her against Lancey!"

"Can't I? Isn't he just like her? Never wanting anything until he sees somebody else about to get it?"

"Somebody like Antoine?"

"Somebody like Antoine!" Cora's tone was bleak. "Antoine's the only person I've met in Newport who isn't a complete fake. Antoine doesn't talk about democracy while he's building a summer cottage to look like the Villa d'Este. Antoine doesn't mix things up. It's his *duty* to marry an heiress, and he knows it. That's what gives him a dignity the others don't have!"

I was struck by her reasoning. There was even a small disappointment in having Cora proved deeper than I had thought. For if I admired her beauty and detachment, if I was content to be an acolyte at the altar of what I stubbornly insisted to be her heart, I nonetheless nursed a small, hidden sense of intellectual superiority to her. I suppose I must have feared that if I lost *that* advantage, I would lose everything and perhaps disappear altogether from my precarious perch in the make-believe of Newport. It may have been to re-establish whatever degree of influence I still had on her that I caught at the idea, as sudden as it was vivid, that Cora would not be taking quite so high a tone, if she felt about Lancey only what she professed to feel.

"Antoine has no more dignity than Lancey!" I pointed out firmly. "Lancey always hated Papa's money. You two would have been married long ago if it hadn't been for that!"

We had turned down our own drive now, and the trees obscured the moonlight, but I heard her catch her breath. She did not answer me, but in the darkness she suddenly clutched my hand, an unprecedented intimacy for her. I kept talking, a bit wildly, about Lancey and his love for her, and I noticed exultantly that she did not take her hand away. When she kissed me good night at the door to her bedroom, she nodded quickly to my breathless question if I could tell Lancey at the Casino that she would go riding with him.

The following morning I was down early for breakfast, and there was no one at table but Antoine. I felt so guilty about my embassy to Lancey that I could hardly say a word. I then drove my donkey cart to the Casino where I had a tennis lesson, but I had finished long before Lancey appeared. I waited on the veranda until almost eleven when I heard his high laugh and

saw him sauntering across the lawn in his red blazer with Julia Lydig. I will
have more to say about Julia in other places, because she later became my
sister-in-law and played a great role in my life, but suffice it to say here that
she was then to the young women of Newport what Lancey's mother was
to the older ones. She was tall and angular and brilliant and had red hair
and a laugh even shriller than Lancey's. It was she who first spotted me
lurking on the veranda, and I heard her murmur something and point me
out to Lancey. But he, to my embarrassment and relief, came immediately
over to stand below the railing and smile up at me. I mumbled my message
quickly.

"Tell her I'll be there!" he responded cheerfully, unconscious, apparently,
of Julia's figure behind him, hovering curiously just out of earshot. "And
give her this." Quite boldly he handed me up a note. "Now fly, Mercury!
On your way!"

Clutching the envelope, I hurried off to get home and hug the memory
of Lancey's smile. I reached the gate of the Casino and was proceeding to
the post where I had tied my cart when I perceived to my dismay that it
was gone. Where it should have been stood Thomas, one of our footmen,
looking very solemn.

"Greaves has taken your cart home, Miss Augusta. Your mother says you're
to come with her."

With a sinking heart I followed him around the corner to find Mamma
waiting in her victoria. Like myself she was entirely in white except for a
large shiny black hat with a purple veil tucked up under its brim. She looked
hot and cross and even rather stout; her small lips were tightly pursed, and
her square jaw was stuck forward. Yet when she turned to stare at me, she
hardly seemed to see me. It was always that way with Mamma. Her irritation was cosmic; in her abstracted moods she would focus on me just enough
to disapprove.

"Get in," was all she said, and later, as we were driving down Bellevue
Avenue at a smart pace: "Give me that paper you're hiding."

"No!"

"Don't be an idiot, child. I know all about it."

"It's my business!"

Mamma turned to look at me again. She must have realized from my shrill
new tone that something had happened to me. "What a little goose you
are," she said. "You're probably in love with him yourself."

"No!"

She was still looking at me. "Then you're in love with Antoine. It comes
to the same thing. How would you like to be a princess and live in a beautiful old house on the Rue de Varenne?"

"What do you mean?"

"Just what I say." Mamma bowed suddenly to Mrs. Oelrichs whose carriage was passing. "Antoine and Cora aren't engaged. How would anyone
know he hasn't been courting you all this time?"

My head reeled. If she only were joking, if only Mamma ever joked!

"But he's in love with Cora!" I cried.

Mamma seemed about to say something sharp, but she restrained herself. It was not, I am sure, that she cared in the least for my feelings. She had a strong, impatient belief in the salutory effect of facts. But that morning she needed my alliance. "Men get over these things."

"You think a man like that would ever look at *me*?" I asked, incredulous. "After caring about Cora?"

"Why not?" Mamma shrugged. "Your father will do as much for you as for Cora. You know lots of French history. And you have a livelier disposition."

"Oh, Mamma!" I know now that I was terrified that she might be right. How could a thing as fragile as love be expected to survive the equipages of Bellevue Avenue, the miles of grilled fence work, the Irish lace, the glimpses down blue gravel drives of the birthday cake houses and Mamma nodding to Mrs. Oelrichs with a little shake of her parasol? I suddenly saw what Cora had meant the night before. She had been trying to tell me that all my life it was *she* who had been my shield against Mamma. And now I had my first searing vision of what it was I had been protected from! "You can't just treat human beings as pawns!" I cried. "There's such a thing as love!"

"Love!" Mamma closed her parasol abruptly and struck the tip against the floor of the carriage. "This is what comes of letting you sit in the library all morning and read Ouida and Marie Corelli."

"You don't believe in love, do you?" I asked, suddenly excited. It was love, I thought desperately, that would make me Mamma's equal!

"Don't be impertinent, Gussie."

"Is it impertinent to say a person doesn't believe in love?"

"Of course it is. All nice people believe in love."

From soaring wings I gazed down, half in contempt, at my cross, preoccupied parent. "Are you a nice person, Mamma?"

In the silence that followed I waited for her to call upon Thomas to stop while I was evicted from the carriage. But Mamma's set, stony look at last relaxed into a rather ominous smile. "I'm as nice as Cora," she retorted. "And I shouldn't be surprised if I were as nice as you. That's why I'm telling you that if Cora's in love with Lancey Bell she can marry him tomorrow if she wants!"

I was too stunned to say another word for the rest of our drive. As we pulled up under the porte-cochere, however, and Mamma rose, I murmured breathlessly: "And what about Antoine?"

She did not even glance at me as she descended from the carriage. "I told you," she said sharply. "*You* can have him!"

I ran upstairs to Cora's room and found her stretched on a chaise longue, recovering, as I afterwards discovered, from an earlier conversation with our same parent. When I told her about Mamma and Antoine, she covered her face with her hands.

"Go away!" she moaned. "Why can't you leave me alone? *All* of you!"

Which was exactly, in the next few days; what nobody would do. I was treated to the bewildering spectacle of the grown-up world boldly and without apology reversing its position. I didn't like it. I didn't like it at all. It was as if they had hammered against the doors of my fantasies, a motley crowd with horns and streamers, and pushed rudely past me when I had opened just a crack, to parade about, blowing and yelling, in ugly parody of myself. If the interior citadel fell, what was left? I sat at the family board as silent as Antoine, and much more miserable, opposite to Lancey who was now asked to every meal and carried on loud, violent, laughing conversations with Mamma. I blushed at the high frenzy with which she patched up burnt bridges and restuffed her eggs in the discarded single basket. For how could even the cousin-german of an empress be as useful to Mamma as the intransigent Mrs. Bell? Had not the latter called, with all ostrich feathers, and was she not proclaiming everywhere, at Bailey's Beach, at the Casino and within the very earshot of Aunt Daisy, that Eliza Millinder was the most amusing woman in Newport? Could anyone in the Summer colony, much less a battered and impecunious French nobleman of unproved pretensions, stand up to an alliance between two such women? Could Cora? T no longer knew what Cora intended, for she confided nothing to me now. But I could see that she never looked at Antoine, though he gazed at her long and sadly at mealtimes, and I knew that she rode in the afternoons with Lancey.

Antoine behaved perfectly. After three days of this treatment he announced that he had had a telegram that required his immediate appearance in New York on business. Before he left he had an interview with Mamma and Papa in the library. I hovered outside in the conservatory, but I could hear nothing through the stout oak doors. When Antoine emerged, very pale and set, I rushed up to him.

"Antoine!"

"Why, good morning, Miss Gussie." He always called me that.

"Antoine!" I repeated, seizing his hand. "I had nothing to do with it! Nothing!"

For a moment he looked baffled. "Ah, my dear," he then said earnestly. "I trust you have no idea what it is you have nothing to do with!"

"Oh, I don't mean about Cora. I mean about me."

He stared at me, shocked. "Surely—" he murmured.

"They threw me at you, didn't they?" I cried. "They offered me as a consolation prize!"

"Oh, my dear, my dear." He shook his head sadly several times. "I see it is all far worse than I thought. We had better walk out on the lawn. In my country one would not discuss such things with a young lady. But as long as you're in so deep!" We went out by the porch and down the lawn to the Japanese garden. "My dear Miss Gussie," he began gravely, "it is perhaps very terrible of me to criticize your parents. I have been their guest. But I am leaving their house today, and you and I have been friends. Perhaps it is better to speak out."

"It isn't really Papa," I protested, awed by his tone. "It's Mamma, you know who decides."

I did not infer, from his momentarily lowered lids, that I had made things any better. "Even so," he continued, "he stands by, he ratifies. And neither of them seems to know where they are headed. Your mother moves forward with a great deal of steam and resolution, but her sea is uncharted. That is why, if you are to be her passenger, you should be sure to keep a careful log."

"So I can get back?"

"So you can get *them* back. In the long run, Miss Gussie, they may depend on you."

I paused to consider this. It was certainly a topsy-turvy world. The prospect of my ever directing Mamma was rather a scaring one. But it was no worse than my knowledge that I deserved equally with my parents the condemnation from which Antoine exempted me. I could never abide false colors.

"No!" I cried in a sudden burst of confession. "You don't understand! You overrate me horribly! I was the one who started the whole thing! I was the one who persuaded Cora to see Lancey again!" I saw the astonishment spread slowly over those fine Gallic features; I read the retreat in those clear grey eyes, a retreat that seemed to imply an abandonment, with me, of the very continent itself, with its milling till of stridently angry women. I felt giddy with the loss of all predictability in events. "Oh, Antoine, forgive me!" I beseeched him and fell on my knees before him on the grass. "Antoine!" I cried, looking up desperately at his expression of stricken embarrassment. "Take Mamma up! Marry me! You'll never have to see me. Never! I'll stay quietly out in the country in some old château, and you can have all the money and as many mistresses as Louis XIV! Oh, please, Antoine! If you'll only forgive me!"

He suddenly threw back his head and laughed. It was a strange, shrill, rather gasping laugh, and I covered my face, as if to protect myself from the cold shower of his ridicule. Then I felt his hands under my elbows, and I was pulled to my feet.

"My dear child, come now," he murmured in a kinder voice, "this will never do. Suppose one of the maids should see us? Wouldn't she send it to a newspaper? Isn't that what they do here?"

"I don't care!" I cried, stamping my foot in anger as the tears welled up in my eyes. "I don't care who sees me! Mamma owes you a dowry, and you shall have one!"

"Sit down, Miss Gussie," he said firmly and led me to a bench under a wood stand covered with vines. He continued to hold my hand as he talked, but in a paternal, or at least avuncular fashion. "You see things too black and white, even for your great black and white country. You took it for granted that your mother cared only for titles, but you see that you were wrong. And now you take it for granted that I care only about dowries. If that is true, of course, what difference should it make by which daughter I pick your father's pocket?" He shrugged and laughed again, but this time his laugh was gentle. "But I am a Frenchman, my dear. I have my discriminations. It is true that I cannot afford to marry without a *dot*. If that were not so, I would not be seeking a bride so far from home. But things are not desperate for me, my dear. I do not really have to marry at all. My younger brother is married to an Argentinian lady of many ranches, and he has a son who will be rich enough one day to keep up our poor old Conti properties. In fact, I had decided to return to Paris a bachelor when I met your sister."

He paused, and I watched him intently. "And she made the difference?"

"My dear, she might have been painted by Nattier!" he exclaimed, looking brightly down the lawn to the sea. "She's the most exquisite thing I've seen in your whole great country!"

"I thought you only cared about our factories," I protested with a pang of jealousy. It was as if I, with all my chatter, and America, with all its smoking industry, had been defeated by the silence, the very passivity of Cora. However one might wish a victory for Cora, the light which it cast upon the rest of us was hard to bear without blinking.

"Ah, your factories!" Antoine murmured.

"And Cora doesn't really *know* anything!"

"She doesn't have to!" He got up at this, agitated again, and we started slowly back towards the house. "She is one of those women who move through the pages of history dispelling an aura of loveliness. It is not necessary that she say anything. Like my ancestress, the Princesse de Conti, in Saint-Simon's memoirs. I am sorry to say this, Miss Gussie, but today we are being candid. Your sister knows that silence is the only protection from vulgarity in the atmosphere in which she lives."

I stopped, stricken. "You must think me very vulgar!"

"I think you very young."

"Oh, Antoine, must you really go to New York? We need you here!"

"No, I must go. Surely you see that?"

"I'm so sorry! For you and me and all of us!"

"Don't be sorry for me," he said. He picked up my hand suddenly and brought it to his lips. "Don't be sorry for me, Miss Gussie."

I was rather puzzled by this, but I had not long to wait for my elucidation. When Cora returned from her ride, he was gone, but when she joined Papa and Mamma and me on the big veranda before lunch she was holding a letter. I remember that it was a very beautiful, windless day and that I had been watching the sailboats almost becalmed on a heavy green sea. Cora seemed as calm as the day, but she had an odd new air of determination; she fixed expressionless, waiting eyes on Mamma who, in contrast, seemed hot and preoccupied, fidgeting restlessly with a little fan. Willie and Bertie had gone sailing, and Papa's absence from the golf club had been owing only to Mamma's insistence that he remain home for the interview with Antoine. That he hated it was evident from the way he was peering at a read and reread Sunday paper held down between his knees.

"Antoine is a very great gentleman," Cora said at last, holding up her letter. "He releases me from my pledge." She was addressing Mamma, but the latter did not even look at her.

"I wasn't aware that there had been pledges."

"Would it have mattered to you if you had been aware?" Cora demanded in a cold, clear tone.

"What do you mean by that?"

"Would you have behaved differently to Antoine?"

Mamma turned now to face Cora's stare. "What does it matter now that it's over?" she said peevishly. "I'm sure he's behaved handsomely, but shouldn't we expect it? He doesn't want a bride who cares for someone else, does he? What man would?"

"But suppose this bride refuses to be released?" Cora continued, striking a sharper note. "Suppose this bride chooses to consider herself bound by her word. Suppose she sends a telegram to his hotel in New York to say that she will marry him whenever and wherever he asks!"

"Cora, you wouldn't!"

"I already have."

Mamma was panting now, and her cheeks were mottled with anger. "You seem to be forgetting that in a marriage with Antoine the bride's consent is only one of many that are necessary. You seem to forget about Papa and the lawyers. I'm sure you'll find that Antoine hasn't!"

"I have forgotten nothing!" Cora cried, and her look of cold indignation had now hardened into one of positive contempt. "That's why I have decided to appeal to *you*, Papa." She turned and addressed her attention to him for the rest of the remarkable interview. "I want you to promise me here and now, Papa, that you will carry out your commitments to Antoine. I want you to redeem our family honor. Or whatever shred is left of it."

I waited, breathless, knowing that for Cora alone Papa might throw aside his native languor and oppose Mamma. For his usual acquiescence in her plans arose more from indifference than from any innate weakness of character. As long as he had his clubs and his beloved yacht, *The Wanderer*, he could allow the leadership at home to pass by default to his determined spouse. He put down his paper now and looked carefully at his pale, beautiful daughter.

"Can you promise me it is for your happiness?" he asked gravely.

"I promise."

"Yet you have given your mother and myself the impression that you preferred another."

"The impression!" Mamma cried. "Well, if she hasn't been running after Lancey Bell like a rabbit all over—!"

"Please, Eliza," Papa interrupted firmly, but without taking his eyes from Cora's. "Let her answer me."

"It's a matter of honor, Papa," Cora repeated simply. "Antoine has taught me about honor. It would be unthinkable for us to behave in any other way."

"But, my dear girl, your honor is not involved," Papa pointed out. "Antoine has released you from your pledge. It's one that could have been broken without dishonor, in any event. That's what engagements are for. So they *may* be broken."

"But, Papa, the way we did it!" Cora closed her eyes in pain. "The way Mamma and Gussie cheered for Lancey and the way he took advantage of it! And the way his mother talked it up everywhere! What could poor Antoine do in the midst of all that clatter and stamping but quietly withdraw? And release me? And he did it so beautifully!" Cora's eyes were full of tears now. "When I read his letter this morning, I felt so ashamed. So abysmally, unutterably ashamed! As if a lifetime would be hardly enough to make up for it!" Cora rose swiftly and walked to Papa's chair. She stood before him in earnest silence for several moments, her hands raised in clenched supplication. "I promise you, Papa," she said solemnly, "that whatever feeling I have for Lancey is fully under my control. And if Antoine will still have me, I'll make him a good wife. It's the last chance of happiness I'll ever have. To make up. Oh, Papa, if you *knew* how I yearned for it. It's the only thing in the world I do know how to do. To be Antoine's wife. He expects so little of me! I'll even become a Catholic. And we'll be married in Paris with nobody there but you, Papa, and Antoine's mother." She turned to me with a reproachful smile. Yet at least, I remembered afterwards, it was a smile. Cora did not begrudge me that. "Not even, Gussie, the Empress of Austria."

Papa looked at her for a long moment and then smiled himself. "You shall have anything you want, my darling," he said at last. "Every penny of it."

"Cyrus!" Mamma cried.

"Every penny of it," Papa repeated, without even turning his head, and we were all silent at the click of the screen door where Osborn had appeared to announce lunch.

6

CORA RECEIVED A telegram that very afternoon, and its contents must have been satisfactory, for she and Papa went to New York the following day. Mamma soon followed, and we heard nothing from the city until her return at the end of the week. She was very peevish and silent, but we managed to learn that Papa and Cora had sailed for France and that Cora and Antoine were to be married in Paris in a month's time. Cora had been inexorable in her insistence that only Papa should be present at the ceremony. Willie and Bertie and I were too awe-stricken at such a killing blow to Mamma's pride to worry at our own exclusion. Her mortification before Mrs. Bell and all of Newport was terrible to contemplate; there was no virtue to Mamma's friends in the acquisition of a titled son-in-law unless the package was delivered, so to speak, in one's lap. But Mamma was not one to repine under the blows of fate. She made a quick, cool assessment of the debris of her position; she measured the anger of Mrs. Bell and the triumph of Aunt Daisy and announced that she was closing the house for the rest of the season. Willie could go to Bar Harbor, I to Granny Millinder's and she and Bertie would cruise on *The Wanderer* until it was time to go back to New York.

In the general hum of cleaning and dusting that succeeded her announcement, amid the banging and hammering of the putting up of winter screens,
work that Mamma wished to see actually in progress before her departure,
I sat on my own little porch and wondered broodingly what screaming new
phoenix might arise for me from the ashes of her plans for Cora.

I was glad enough, however, to stay with Granny. It was my only consolation for the autumn. Granny, who was now a small, trim, neat, bustling
old lady, lived in an old yellow brick house in Fairfield, Connecticut, the
town where her father had once run the general store. In New York she
still had her third of the brownstone family palazzo, but in Fairfield everything was on a much smaller scale and she and her youngest child, Uncle
Jacob, a mild, smiling, soft-voiced, round-faced little man of retarded intellect, led a life of meticulous regularity on a schedule that had not been varied
since Grandpa's day. Granny was very sweet and very kind and remarkably
literal; she took everything that was said at its face value. In the same way
she was almost unaware of the absent; I believe that the reason she never
felt neglected by her sons was that she did not think of them when they
were not actually with her. If I suspected that she might have opened her
eyes just wide enough to encompass and disapprove the social careers of
Mamma and Aunt Daisy, it was not from anything she said or even implied,
but purely from the fact that she never visited her daughters-in-law. The
only exception in her general unawareness of things outside her own home
was in newspaper headlines. She worried about the small and immediate and
about the distant and vast, raising her delicate veined hands and pursing
her dry thin lips in equal horror over the death of a canary and the attempted
assassination of the Russian czar.

I adored Granny in my sloppy, gushing way. It was quite the reverse of
her own restrained, quiet manner of showing affection for myself. I loved
to fling my arms about her—for if she did not like it, she did not, at least,
like Mamma, positively prohibit it—and demand loudly if she was happy. It
seemed to me that she must be very sad and lonely, because she was so old,
and I could not bear the idea of her suffering as I feared she might. Of
course I realize now that the reassurance I craved was all for myself—if
Granny, so near the grave, could be happy, would it not be proof that the
rest of us could and should be? And when she murmured that she was "quite
as happy as was good for her," adjusting her Indian shawl from the ravages
of my caress, I took it as the expression of the highest philosophy, never
dreaming that Granny herself might have had to build, in the very order
and routine of her existence, fortifications against doubts and fears as hideous as my own.

My own doubts and fears, however, despite all Granny's reassurance, grew
alarmingly as the season of my coming out approached. It seemed to me in
Fairfield that Mamma had been appointed by the furies to punish my interference in Cora's life with a long black winter of balls and dinner parties, at
which I would sit, twisting my handkerchief in cruel isolation, while my
indefatigable parent pursued reluctant young men to offer them my hand
and purse. Granny and Uncle Jacob were going to the Hôtel de Paris in

Monte Carlo, as they did every winter, and to accompany them had become my dream of unimaginable bliss. All my standards of pleasure, in fact, were at that time just the opposite of what a young girl's were supposed to be. A cavernous hotel dining room, silent except for a three-piece orchestra playing Strauss waltzes and filled with tables where ancient ladies, in glittering sequins and black chokers, dined with paid companions, was now my idea of utter peace and content. Just before I was to return to New York, I wrote in desperation to Papa to beg him to let me go abroad with Granny and skip my coming out year. The answer came promptly in a letter from Mamma which I fully expected to contain a sharp rebuke for having ignored the family chain of command. Imagine my astonishment, imagine my resentment, when I discovered that my project was readily assented to! She and Papa had been contemplating a cruise that winter to the Greek islands, and only the prospect of my coming out had intervened. She thought it best, on the whole, in view of all the strangeness surrounding Cora's marriage, if everything were postponed for a year.

Of course, when I got to the Hôtel de Paris I found the life there too slow even for my purposes. Boredom imagined can be serene and restful; boredom experienced is only boredom. We did nothing but walk, eat and sleep, and we did these things at the same time every day. Yet I suppose now that the enforced routine of that winter may have saved me from a nervous breakdown. Whatever was wrong with me at that time, those long, still days in the Hôtel de Paris acted to pad it in, as with cotton, and upon my return to New York in the spring I was able, more or less, to function as a daughter of Mamma. The thing that helped me most was going home through Paris, and being able to see for myself that Cora was happy. She and Antoine were settled in a great grey modern house that Papa had bought for them near the Parc Monceaux and were engaged in filling its vast, noble rooms with eighteenth century adornments. I could see then the beginning of Cora's reputation for perfect taste, though it has often struck me that if one settles, with unlimited funds, exclusively for late Louis XV, one cannot go too far wrong. Yet it was undeniable that Cora's serenity of demeanor and regal bearing was well set off by the furnishings of that period, and Antoine, arranging his pictures and objets d'art, so to speak, around her, seemed intelligently intent on providing the perfect frame for her beauty. I remembered that he had said she might have been painted by Nattier. He seemed to be bringing it about that she *had* been, for I began to think of her now as in eighteenth century court dress, a faraway expression in her eyes, with a hint of fountains and classic façades in the background, holding in a negligent hand the grapes and ear of corn that would be the clue to her identity as Ceres.

Did he adore her, as everybody said? Or did he regard her as a prize possession, the delicately wrought bas-relief on the golden casket that had brought her dowry? Did it matter? He was always gentle with her, always courtly, always charming to her relatives, and if he was unfaithful, no one, not even Mamma who stoutly professed that all European husbands were, had any evidence of it. Cora was popular in Paris. With the title of

princess, so admirably suited to her beauty, with the great, perfect house
behind her and with Antoine always at hand to supervise the machinery of
their entertainments, her silence was accepted for wisdom, her indifference
for simplicity and her occasional rudeness for a high honesty. Cora was more
right about what she wanted than any of us could have been for her. She
would have exasperated Lancey quite as much as she enchanted Antoine.
Perhaps she had been able to visualize the comfortable routine of her life
with the latter as I had visualized mine with Granny at Monte Carlo; if so,
I hope she found no similar disappointment. It would not be like her, in
any event, to betray it. Antoine died a hero's death in the first war, and for
the past three decades Cora has been living a retired life in the Conti château
in Normandy. She has a great farm, and she runs it with an efficiency that
has proved her, after all, a true granddaughter of Julius Millinder. Need I
add that she is adored by every tenant on the whole great place? We tried
to make her come home during the last war, but she refused to leave the
château, even when German officers were quartered there. When she talks
about that period, there is an excitement in her voice that was never there
before. I think that she blessed the opportunity that it gave her to live up
at last to what Antoine expected of her. It was after all, as the grave inscrutable chatelaine, bowing silently to the orders of the German commander
while waiting her chance to send provisions to American fliers in the barn,
that she made the most beautiful picture in a life that had been a veritable
gallery. I think Antoine would have preferred it even to his imagined Nattier.

No Millinder strain that I have been able to detect seems to have passed
through Cora to either of her two daughters. Mathilde de Rochechouart
and Eliane de Bourbon-Busset are utterly Gallic, very dark and smart and
thin and chic. They have beautiful manners and large families of beautiful
children, and they are absolutely charming to their old maid aunt whenever
she comes to Paris. But they make her feel, all unwittingly, a bit coarse and
red and countrified. Of course, they have an eye to possible legacies in my
will, and that is perfectly natural. However rich Cora may be, ten grandchildren is a goodly number to provide for, and Mathilde and Eliane would
be deficient in their duty as good French mothers if they did not see that
"Tante Gussie" was diverted on her rare excursions to France. Nor is it
difficult. The old girl is perfectly happy with a round of night clubs. And
she will do her duty, too. I have remembered every one of Cora's family in
my will. They may belong to a class that has been for generations an anachronism, but it is an accepted and a rather charming anachronism, one that
is a perfectly valid part of an old Latin and Catholic civilization. They are
utterly free of the guilt and self-consciousness with which their richer American cousins are hag-ridden. They are distinctly old Julius' happiest and most
successful descendants. They need a good deal of money, but they will know
exactly what to do with it when they get it. I hope they will always keep it.
But at least they will enjoy it while they do.

THE YEARS FOLLOWING Cora's marriage were very flat ones for me. I did not seem to have any function either with my family or in social life. I read a great deal, and I sewed things for charity bazaars, and I drove out on calls with Mamma. I wanted to go to college, but this was opposed so violently that I did not persist. It may seem odd today that I should have been so weak of will, but my reader must remember Mamma's talent for making us feel that the unconventional was not only unpopular, but actually degrading. It was curious that she should have used her children's natural timidity to make them conform, seeing that her own conformity was so deliberate and voluntary. When, later in her life, she no longer found conformity useful for her purposes, she discarded it as easily as an old dress and added insult to injury by criticizing me for being "stuffy." Basically, Mamma could never understand that other people lacked her own force and will power.

There was, however, a more potent reason even than Mamma for my aimlessness at this period. With Cora living abroad I could no longer identify my emotions with hers. My own heart was now the vessel that had to contain them solely. Lancey Bell had been spending these years in Rome and Florence, studying the palazzos and churches that it was still the rage to reproduce as country houses or railway stations, and I could never wholly keep down the irrepressible little hope that when he came back to find all his old friends married and settled down, he might even be glad to find that the young girl who had once been his eager and devoted messenger had grown up into an intelligent, responsive woman. Was it not possible? He would be nearing thirty and ready to start his professional life. He would be through with his travels and knocking around. If I was tall, he was taller, and I was far more qualified to be his intellectual companion than any of the girls in his old set. And with the dazzling sun of Cora's beauty removed to shine on Paris, my own plain features might seem less dull. The complexion of my skin had improved, and I had good color. When I looked in the glass, as I did increasingly these days, it seemed to me that large brown eyes, a firm, straight nose, a high forehead, a hazel pompadour and cheeks flushed with health made up a picture that did less than repel. The threat of future weight might already have been there, but it had not yet materialized. If my features lacked a certain feminine delicacy, if my movements were still brusque and awkward, was there not appeal in the very struggle of honesty and enthusiasm for some niche in a coarse world? As I look back on my photographs of that time, standing behind groups on porches in the endless houseparties of Mamma's old albums, I can see that it was my critical year.

I have not mentioned among my attractions my potential inheritance. Parents in those days never discussed with their children their wills or how much they might leave them. It was one of the rare delicacies of a rather vulgar era and a constant bafflement to Europeans who could see in it only the grossest hypocrisy. I knew, of course, that Cora was an "heiress," for so the news columns always described her, and I thought of heiresses as being beautiful and marrying titles. And then, too, Grandpa had left his fortune unevenly, and Papa might very well do the same. In point of fact he did.

I should say also, in fairness to a much abused era, that there were not crowds of young men, eager for a dowry, hanging about our house. Mamma seemed to have exhausted her matchmaking appetite with Cora, while I had my heart too full of the secret image of Lancey to be looking for other idols. Occasionally, a young man would call, to be received politely but without other encouragement. He seldom came a second time. I was bookish and shy and, when aroused, inclined to be bossy. It may not surprise the reader that I have received in my whole life exactly one proposal. In Europe I would have had dozens.

The last summer that we spent as a family in Newport passed very much as other summers except for my being "taken up" by Mrs. Bell. She had always shown a preference for younger people, and now she selected me as the companion of her afternoon drives with as little apology for using my time as a queen might have vouchsafed to a lady-in-waiting. But whatever the arrogance of her manner, the pleasure of her company fully made up for it. Her conversation was pungent and refreshing, and if she sometimes embarrassed me by the sharpness of her references to my family, I was flattered into silence by her professing to find in my head a store of common sense rare among the "idle young noggins" of Newport. Mamma observed bleakly that Minnie Bell was after something and that I had better watch out, but I knew that Mamma was prejudiced. The only thing that concerned me about Mrs. Bell was that she was obviously ill. She stayed in bed all morning now to rest up from the previous night's party, and during our drives she would sometimes put her hand suddenly to her side and hold her breath as if in pain. But it annoyed her intensely to have anyone show the least solicitude, and I learned to hold my peace until the spasm had passed and she had resumed her conversation, more acid than ever.

Her distaste for the circle in which she so desperately tried to keep her place was evidently more than a parade of superior scorn designed to impress my young ears. Mrs. Bell in her moods of depression was genuinely misanthropic. What surprised me, as our friendship deepened, was that she should so unhesitatingly adopt the standards of people whom she despised. Her defiances, I began to discover, were all in minor things. She was forever being quoted around Newport for her "outrageous" statements, but what did these statements amount to but a kind of lofty badinage? When it came down to any issue of the group against the individual, Mrs. Bell could bay the loudest of the pack. This was most shockingly apparent on the afternoon when poor Mrs. Loring Taylor bowed to us as she passed in her landau. This small timid gesture of greeting slapped and broke, like a last, tired wave at low tide, against the flat rock of Mrs. Bell's stubbornly averted countenance. Mrs. Taylor had recently attempted to divorce her husband for what all Newport knew to have been his glaring infidelity. Unhappily for her, he had counter-claimed, charging her with like misconduct and naming the children's tutor. It was generally believed that he had suborned the witnesses, all servants in his pay, but the fact remained that he had proved his charges to the satisfaction of a jury of men.

"That woman has her nerve!" Mrs. Bell reached over and fiercely seized the hand with which I was about to wave to Mrs. Taylor. "How do you like that? Actually nodding to *me*!"

"Oh, Mrs. Bell!" I turned in distress to wave frantically after the retreating carriage, but it was too late. The back of Mrs. Taylor's large white hat, and one plume, quivering as if in pain, was all that I could see. "See what you made me do!" I turned back to my companion angrily, too agitated to be respectful. "You're worse than Aunt Daisy!"

"Do you want to be put out of this carriage? Do you want to walk home?"

"Yes!"

"My, my, what a vixen!" Mrs. Bell chuckled with instant pleasure at having so aroused me. "Come, child, don't let us waste our tempers on the likes of Mrs. Taylor."

"Then you believe all that about the tutor?"

"All? I don't know about *all*. I believe enough."

"You mean you really think that he—that he—?"

"Was her lover? I neither know nor care." Mrs. Bell tossed her head at such irrelevancies. "I believe that she's soft and sentimental. I believe there was enough between them to make the servants think there was more. And that's enough for me. A lady doesn't allow herself to be misunderstood!"

"But suppose she was only like Mr. Browning's last duchess?" I protested, resting my case immediately on what was then my favorite poem. "Suppose it was simply a case of her smiling kindly and innocently at too many people?"

"I'd have cut your last duchess, too. The simpering minx!"

I was shocked at such intransigency. "Even if she wasn't—even if she wasn't actually—immoral?"

"Don't talk to me about morals, child. It shows a middle class background. Talk to me about taste. The woman has no taste!"

I was silent for several minutes and looked out thoughtfully over the water. I knew that morality was by no means limited to what Mrs. Bell considered the middle class. Everyone talked morality in those days, including Mrs. Bell's own circle. But she had lived a great deal in England as a young woman and liked to affect the brusque independence and bad manners of an old duchess unreconstructed by Victorian ideas.

"Well, it seems very peculiar to me," I remarked at last.

"Aunt Daisy cuts poor Mrs. Taylor because she says she's immoral. And Mamma—"

"Your Aunt Daisy would *like* to cut her, you mean," Mrs. Bell interrupted testily. "How can she cut someone she doesn't know? Even to be in the swing?"

I had to smile at such pettiness. It made me feel for the first time almost the equal of the terrifying Mrs. Bell. "I'm afraid I have to correct you there," I insisted. "Aunt Daisy *does* know Mrs. Taylor. Or did, anyway. So does Mamma. But Mamma doesn't care about what Mrs. Taylor did or didn't do. She cares only about what people say about her. Mamma thinks it's immoral to be suspected. Poor Mrs. Taylor! She hasn't a chance."

"Poor Mrs. Taylor, indeed!" my companion retorted. "I know *her* kind. And I can just see her with that tutor, too! Letting her long tresses touch the top of his head as she leans over to look at the children's copybook. Sitting and sighing by the piano while he plays Chopin! Ugh! It sickens me!"

I began to notice then that Mrs. Bell sickened easily of anything that smacked in the least of the romantic or, to put it more simply, of love. She always made fun of love, sometimes with a bitterness that made one speculate on things that might have happened in her own youth. She and Mr. Bell had a great respect for each other, but they lived apart half the year. Her enthusiasms for parties appeared at times a need to turn life into a lurid and blaring carnival that would have no quiet corners or moonlit terraces, and in her angrier moods these frenzied gatherings seemed to take on the tones of a vicious parody of life itself. Mrs. Bell was always seeking greater and greater diversion; she was always devising a dinner on a boat, on an island, on a raft, seeking in some fashion to bring variety to the eternal evening meal, until at last even her brilliant imagination scudded on the shoals of farce and her little group tried to laugh at such things as trained seals in black ties lurching about the dinner table to impersonate waiters. The new and more serious Newport at length began to feel the wear and tear of her humor, and there were signs of something like a rebellion. Society had been too hard for most people to get into to be treated altogether as a joke. It was all very well for Mrs. Bell, who had been born to her position, to see it in this light, but others had invested years of effort and millions of dollars in the enterprise. Some values had to be preserved. But criticism only made her more violent. As that last summer wore on, I began to understand that she was slipping into the darkest kind of melancholy.

One Saturday when I went to her house for a ladies' lunch the old butler asked me gravely if I would go up to her bedroom. Half the ladies were already gathered in the drawing room, he whispered, but his mistress still refused to come down. I found her fully dressed, but sitting on her bed staring moodily out the window. She hardly looked up when I came over to her.

"I know," she muttered, "you've come to get me. But why should I come down? There's not a soul in that drawing room who gives a hoot whether I'm there or not!"

"Of course they care," I protested. "A lunch party without a hostess is chaos."

"Chaos? What are their very lives but chaos?"

But I was not impressed with her Shakespearian tragic mood. I pointed out that she had invited them.

"Of course I invited them!" she retorted. "I didn't want to be alone, when

I invited them. But now I've moved on a step. Now I want to be alone. Oh, Gussie," she murmured in a suddenly weakened voice, "if you *knew* the visions in my mind! The horrible, horrible visions. I try to drive them away with people, but it doesn't work any more. Now people only make them worse!"

"I'll tell them you're ill!" I cried, alarmed. "Why don't you go to bed? I'll come back and sit with you."

"No, no," she said patiently. She rose and stood for a moment with her hand clasped to her side. Then she shook her head briskly and started towards the door. "I'll go down. I'll go down. Come on. Let's face them together." She paused at the threshold and turned back to me. "You're a good girl, Gussie. Be sure you never end up an old fool like me." Then she grunted, and some of the old hostility came back into her eyes. "I've had my good times, though. I've had my share of fun. People will write about me some day and the merry dance I led old Newport! Except, no." She laughed with sudden harshness. "Because gossip columns make history, and they'll be all about your Aunt Daisy! Poor soul, they'll call her the Queen of Newport! That's it! To be immortal one must have been a real donkey!"

I bowed my head and said nothing. I was afraid that anything I said would only make her worse. She stared at me for a disdainful moment and then snorted and went downstairs. I have never seen her more amusing than she was that day at lunch.

I had no confidante at home without Cora, and I told more things to Mamma. She was not the most sympathetic of listeners, but she was interested in any news of the summer colony that might have escaped her, particularly in anything about Mrs. Bell. It pleased me to be intimate with a woman whose friend she had wanted to be; it was the first time in my life that I found myself in possession of anything that she valued. When I came home that afternoon from Mrs. Bell's lunch, I was glad to find Mamma alone on the terrace with a book that she wasn't reading and a glass of iced tea. Mamma, alone, inclined to let herself go a bit. She looked crosser and squarer and hotter than when in company, and she sat with her knees apart. She looked at me obliquely while I told her of Mrs. Bell's near refusal to attend her own lunch party.

"I daresay she's got plenty on her mind," she observed. "Your father says Mr. Bell was mixed up in that phosphate collapse in Georgia. Probably lost every penny he put in. And they're not rich, either, you know, for all her grand airs. I'll bet she spends double her income."

"Mrs. Bell doesn't worry about things like money," I replied, a bit loftily.

"Rather hard on her family, isn't it?" Mamma retorted. "Seeing what she does to their inheritance? But I suppose she figures the girls are settled and Lancey can always look after himself."

"Of course Lancey can look after himself! He's going to be a great architect!"

"He won't make any money in that. Real money. But I guess he can always marry it. He'll be coming home one of these days to take care of that. After all, he'd have had Cora if he hadn't dallied so about it."

I tried to make my voice calm and sarcastic, but it still trembled with indignation. "If you think Lancey intends to make his fortune at the altar, you have totally misconceived his character."

"What makes you so high and mighty?" Mamma demanded, instantly aroused. She put down her glass smartly on the table and glared at me. "Don't think you can put on Minnie Bell's airs with me, my girl. Not in my own house!"

"I am simply disagreeing with you, Mamma," I explained with as much dignity as I could muster. "You haven't heard Lancey tell of all the things he's done. You haven't heard of the three days and nights he was lost on Mount Shasta. You haven't heard how he saved the guide from that grizzly bear!"

"Everyone in Newport's heard that!" she said cuttingly. "Your Lancey could never be accused of hiding his light under a bushel. But what you're too young, or perhaps too stubborn, to understand is that a man like that might be able to live for six months in an igloo on the North Pole, but he could never shine his own boots. Don't I know the type! They can cook an antelope on a safari, but back in New York there has to be a butler behind every chair. And Lancey will have his butlers. Wait and see if he doesn't!"

I refused to go on with the subject, but I was struck a bit unpleasantly by what she said. Lancey had certainly shown me that he had a tooth for luxury. I well remembered how excoriating he had been on the subject of inferior wines in Newport. But such things were surely not basic. Mamma always thought everyone was like herself. It was one of her fixed principles that every human being was fundamentally motivated by a financial goal, and that those who would not recognize this were either fools or hypocrites. My reader today may shrug his shoulders and ask if she was not simply typical of a crass and money-minded era. But she wasn't, for that era was also characterized by a sticky coating of sentimentality. Women reveled in the dramas of Stephen Phillips and the novels of Marion Crawford. Money was something in which they theoretically had no part, that adoring men naturally lavished upon them. Mamma, resentful of fantasy, carried her reaction too far. If we were to worship graven images, she saw no virtue in concealment. Let the old gods have their altars! She challenged her world with a touch of magnificence, standing like Athalie, defiant at the gates of her old pagan temple.

As the summer wore on, Mrs. Bell seemed more and more dispirited. She looked very badly, and people began to talk about her health, though never to her. They would not have dared. When she had her spasms of pain, they learned, as I had, to look the other way, for a tart retort was the only reward for the least demonstration of solicitude. I suffered for my friend and for my helplessness and prayed that she might collapse and take to bed before it was too late to cure her ailment. Collapse, at any rate, she did, and ironically enough, at a fancy dress ball given by Aunt Daisy. All of the guests were decked out in historical costumes sent up from New York except Mrs. Bell who appeared in an evening dress of black sequins which she had bribed a servant to filch from Aunt Daisy's own wardrobe. When asked what she was intended to represent, she let it be known among her snickering circle that she had come as a "social climber." But the last laugh was on her, for when Uncle Fred, a resplendent Ivan the Terrible, approached her across the ballroom to ask her for the first waltz, Mrs. Bell arose with a strained smile and then fell back suddenly in her chair. I was in the next room when I heard the screams of the ladies. Before I could do anything to help, my poor friend had been taken home.

I called the next day and found that she was better, but still in a critical condition. Telegrams had been sent to the children and a cable to Lancey. Mr. Bell was on his way down from the Canadian woods. I was allowed to see her only for a few minutes while she lay stiffly still and hissed at me what the nurse told me had already become her obsession. She *had* to get back to New York. She could not bear to have her family see her in this state in Newport. That evening she seemed better, but was even more violently insistent, and the doctor told me that he thought it would not be advisable to oppose her if comfortable transportation could be arranged. I went straight home and begged my parents to let me have their private railway car, which was in Providence. Mamma, of course, objected. She pointed out that we should not make ourselves responsible for the health of a dying woman and one, too, who had insulted the family by her costume at Aunt Daisy's ball. But Papa was as suddenly firm as he had been with Cora's marriage. He could rise to great occasions.

"She is Gussie's friend," he said. "And if Gussie wants the car, Gussie shall have it."

The next day, Mrs. Bell was moved by ambulance and ferry to Providence, and we started the long railway trip to New York. She seemed more comfortable when we were actually in the car; she sat up that night in Mamma's gilded mahogany berth and looked out at the faintly moonlit countryside. Towards midnight she showed a desire to talk. Her voice was a bit stronger, but she was still very pale, and her hands, which I from time to time leaned over to grasp, were cold.

"It's typical of my life," she observed bleakly, "that my last ride should be in an overdecorated caboose."

"Last ride?" I reproached her. "Don't even think it. I hope you and I will be taking many trips in this car."

"Don't be fatuous, child," she retorted peevishly. "You and I both know I'm going to die, so why pretend? It's not dying I mind. Anyone can die. You'll die yourself, Gussie. Wait and see if you don't!"

I was about to protest my faith in her speedy recovery, but those hard green eyes stopped me. They seemed to warn me that the remaining hours were not to be wasted in sentiment.

"The only thing on my mind is my family," she continued, her eyes fixed again out the window. "People say I've neglected them, and it's perfectly true that I have. But what people don't realize is what I've had to contend with. Myself, Gussie. Myself! If I couldn't have got away every summer to play the fool in Newport, I'd have driven everyone at home crazy. Believe me, Gussie, I would have! When I first knew this thing in my side was eating me up, I thought I'd go home to be with Rutherfurd and the girls. Besides, it would have given the show away. They'd have known I must be dying if I'd spend a summer on the Hudson. No, Gussie, repentance is a mealy-mouthed kind of thing. It's better to play out the part you've chosen. There's nothing I can do for my family but make the end as easy as possible for them."

She closed her eyes here and was silent for a long time. I was afraid that she had become unconscious and was about to get the doctor when she opened them again suddenly and cried: "Except for Lancey! There must be something I can still do for Lancey!"

"He'll be home soon now."

"Yes." She grunted and closed her eyes again. "I was angry when they told me they'd cabled him. But maybe it's all right. Maybe it's just as well. I shall have to live till he comes. Gussie!" She seized my hand suddenly with both of hers. "I want you to promise me something! Will you?"

"Anything, anything, dear Mrs. Bell."

"I want you to promise me—" Her words were very slow and clear, but the pause seemed endless. "I want you to promise me that if Lancey should ever ask you to marry him, you will accept!"

Only the unreality of my hurtling through the dark night with a dying woman, of my playing the role, so unexpectedly, of a female Charon, so that it almost seemed as if Mrs. Bell and I were already holding hands in the black void of eternity, kept me from feeling to the full the shock of her suggestion.

"Lancey!" I exclaimed. "Whatever makes you dream that he would ask me?"

"*I'm* asking the questions, not answering them," she retorted with her old sharpness, and I felt her nails press into the hot palm of my hand. "I ask it again. *If* he does, will you promise?"

"But, Mrs. Bell, it would depend on so many things!"

"On what, for instance?"

"On whether we loved each other, or whether we thought we could be happy together or—"

"Stuff and nonsense! With a man like Lancey? Of course you'd be happy. You'd be happy as a lark!"

"But it isn't only a question of what Lancey can do for me," I protested, flushing. "I have no doubt of that. It's a question of what I can do for him."

"Leave that to me," Mrs. Bell said gruffly. "I've thought it all through. You'll be fine for him. Just fine. You have only one danger, my dear, I'll tell you frankly, and that's turning into an old maid. But, don't you see, that's just what Lancey would cure?"

"It might not be so bad to be an old maid."

"That's what *you* think. Wait till you've tried it. America's full of old maids who were terrified of being married for their money. Idiots, the lot of them. At any rate," she added, feeling perhaps she might have gone too far, "that's one thing you'll never have to worry about with Lancey. He hasn't a mercenary bone in his body, God bless him! He'll make money easily, that boy, and he'll spend it more easily yet. He'll spend yours, too, and it's just as well, because you'd never spend it yourself. And if you did, you'd buy ghastly things. But my Lancey has the taste of an angel!"

There was a jealous note in her voice now, as if her son were already mine, and like an Indian giver, she repented of her own generosity. When she turned her head from the window to stare at me, her eyes were almost hostile.

"You seem to forget, Mrs. Bell," I said timidly, "that this is all the merest speculation. He hasn't asked me yet."

"But he will!"

"Then time will tell."

"But I have no time!" she cried suddenly. "I want you to promise me now that you will have him!"

"Mrs. Bell, I can't!"

"Can you deny me, Augusta Millinder? A dying woman!"

There was a sudden note of panic in her voice which frightened me. Quickly I leaned down and kissed her hand. "Dear Mrs. Bell," I murmured, "I promise."

She closed her eyes at this and seemed at last to sleep. At any rate she did not speak again that night. I sat awake until the early morning, staring out the window. I think I hardly moved except to put a blanket around my shoulders when it grew colder. It was as if I had been paralyzed by an excess of strong emotion. I know now that it was the happiest night in my life. It was not that I did not love Mrs. Bell or that my heart did not ache at the prospect of losing her—she was indeed, despite the great difference in our ages, the closest friend I have ever had—but I was not then afraid of death myself, and it seemed distant and rather beautiful in others. More importantly, Mrs. Bell's death and the prospect of my life with Lancey were now indissolubly united, so that the sadness of one and the joyfulness of the other were interwoven, and I hovered in a wonderland of grief and ecstasy. It seemed, too, that they could only be true together, that only the terrible sureness of Mrs. Bell's imminent demise could justify the presumption of my raising my eyes to Lancey. All my heart tugged at me to live and to love, and when I finally wept at the implied disloyalty to my dear old dying friend, I fell asleep out of sheer exhaustion.

Mr. Bell met us at Grand Central, a tall, grave, bearded man, already in black, accompanied by his two tall, handsome married daughters. They were all perfectly polite to me and very solicitous, but when they had taken my friend away, and I had gone home alone to the Fifth Avenue house, I was chilled and depressed. I was paying for my binge of the night before in the flat nothingness of daylight.

I did not see Mrs. Bell again. She failed rapidly in the next few weeks and could see no one but her immediate family. I did not even see Lancey until the rainy morning when he called to tell me that it was all over. We met in the dark library where the remnants of Grandpa's picture gallery were hung, and I remember how pale and thin he looked and how he had grown a little black Valois beard that I thought enormously becoming. I remember, too, his smiling at a painting of two very earnest Italian lovers seated, hand in hand, on a prostrate column in the ruins of the Forum. When he

told me how all of his family and particularly he himself appreciated my
kindness to his mother, I was overcome with guilt at the memory of my
happy night in the train, and, much to my own shame and his dismay, I
burst into racking sobs. For almost half an hour I sat on the sofa and wept,
without restraint. Poor Lancey. Only a few hours after taking his last leave
of the mother he adored, he had to comfort me.

My parents were back in town now, and, somewhat to my surprise, they
were very kind and sympathetic about Mrs. Bell's death. They went to the
funeral at St. Bartholomew's and sat on either side of me. Mamma told me
afterwards that any time I wanted to ask Lancey to the house for lunch or
dinner, to let her know and she would arrange, in deference to his mourning, to have only the family present. I began to feel that I was at last a
personage in my own right. But at twenty-three, perhaps it was high time.

Lancey did call on me. He had decided to remain in New York and help
with the settlement of his mother's estate, of which he was an executor. He
was a far more serious Lancey than Cora's old beau; he had worked very
hard in Italy and was anxious now to be started with his architectural career. When he took me for walks, he would descant in fascinating detail on
just what castle or château had been the inspiration of each house on Fifth
Avenue and how and why the particular American architect had failed to
transmit the spirit of the original. He was still opinionated and cocksure,
but one felt there was more substance behind his thinking. He was less distracted by girls and parties and the vision of travel to exotic hunting areas.
He was just as proud, but more practical, just as bright, but more sympathetic. He was, in a word, more available. The Lancey of Cora's day had
been kind to women without beauty, but he had never looked at them as
he now looked at me.

He was wonderfully nice to me. He professed to find advantages in mourning, in that one saw only "old friends." He talked, of course, more than he
listened, but he did listen. He wanted to hear what I had been reading, what
plays I had seen. He urged me to take courses at Columbia and offered to
plead my case with Mamma. He wanted to hear every detail of his mother's
last summer, and he told me with strong emotion how tortured a soul she
had been. It was his belief that she had found no outlet for her creative
powers except in a fantastic social life that was bound to give a pound of
pain for every ounce of distraction. He was firmly convinced that had she
been properly oriented early in life, she would have been a great woman,
the Isabella d'Este, as he put it, of her generation. It was evident that he
regarded himself as heir to the same talent, but not to its same misuse. Lancey
was devoted to his father and sisters, but he and his mother had belonged
to a different race. His belief in his own great future was infectious, and
I shared it delightedly. Lancey's companionship was a series of brilliant
entertainments. If I felt at times a bit as though I were sitting out front in
the dark of the orchestra pit, it did not make the show any less diverting.
Lancey was an egoist, but he was a bright, amiable egoist, and I was far
happier listening than talking, observing than being observed. Had I been
invited up to the glaring light of his stage, I could only have hid my eyes
and mumbled for words. It was better to adore him from the pit.

It was for this reason that there was almost as much pain as pleasure in the moment when he finally stepped to the footlights and called my name. The actual setting, to drop my theater images, was Central Park. We had paused before the statue of Shakespeare in the Mall while Lancey disposed, in a few devastating sentences, of nineteenth century American sculpture. Then he asked me suddenly to sit down on a bench.

"Of course, I know what you promised Mother," he began as soon as we were seated.

"Oh, Lancey, no!"

It was the one thing I had counted on, that she would not have told him. He was smiling, but it was the friendliest smile, not in the least foxy or superior.

"I made her a promise, too," he continued. "And, what's more, I always keep my promises. But before I fulfill this one, I want you to know that I release you from yours."

"Release me?" I stared, half in surprise, half in sudden, absurd disappointment, not following his gaze. But those smiling eyes reassured me, and I felt suddenly bold. "By what authority do you release me?"

"I'm Mother's executor. Executors have that right."

"Then so do legatees!" I cried excitedly, clutching at the gaiety of his mood. "Your promise was made for my benefit. And I release *you*!"

"For your benefit, my dear Gussie! What do you know of the nature of my promise to Mother?"

"I can guess!"

"Then you're very modest, indeed," he retorted firmly. "The promise was made entirely for *my* benefit. It was a promise to do something that I should have done long ago. And something I *would* have done long ago had I not lost my head over a pretty girl whom I fancied was being married against her will to a French princeling." He picked up my hand with an easy confidence and held it in both of his while he looked at me earnestly. "Gussie, my dear, will you do me the honor—the unimaginable honor—of becoming my wife?"

I couldn't look at him; I even tried to pull my hand away, but he held it firm.

"But how can you, of all people," I exclaimed in sudden panic, "you, who care so about beauty and having things beautifully done, how can you care about *me*? You who loved Cora?"

"I am not going to pretend that you are better looking than Cora," he said calmly. "Nor will I credit you with accomplishments that you lack. But because I was once a young cub doesn't mean I have to be a young cub forever. Because I once had low standards doesn't mean that I always must have them. I have seen a lot of the world in the past three years, Gussie. I have been in Rome and Florence and Paris. And everything I have seen has made me appreciate more the qualities of honesty and directness and kindness that I think of when I think of you."

I have set down his words just as he uttered them. I know that I have remembered them correctly because one does remember correctly the most important moment in one's life. I suppose they sound dated today. I'm sure my nephews and nieces would shout with laughter at them. For that matter, I'm sure Lancey himself would if I were to recite them to him today. But they meant everything to me then, and they mean everything to me still.

"Cora had all those qualities," I said clumsily.

"And I adored Cora!" he exclaimed. "Have I ever tried to hide it from you?"

"No, I guess not—but—oh, Lancey, you've *planned* this!"

"Of course I've planned it. Men always plan their proposals."

"I mean you planned it because your mother wanted it."

"Gussie!" he said severely. He reached a hand to my chin and turned my head towards his. "Gussie, kiss me."

And we kissed, right there on a bench in Central Park, with people walking by, as I had been led to believe only streetwalkers behaved. But I had a suspicion that ours was a rather chaste kiss. I had never been kissed before, but I nonetheless suspected this. Was Lancey only engaged in the fulfillment of a deathbed vow? Or was this the way gentlemen kissed? I didn't know. I don't know to this day, but I have often wondered if I did not receive a better kiss than I realized.

"Lancey!" I cried, pushing back from him. "You don't have to, you know! You really don't!"

"Don't be a goose," he said gently. "These things are always a bit constrained at first. Take it from me. I *know*."

I told him that I could not give him my answer then and begged him to take me home. On the walk back I was too upset to say anything. I was trembling all over and terrified that I was going to burst into tears. When we got to the house I ran up the steps to the front door without even turning to say goodbye. For once in my life I felt a feverish need of Mamma. By a lucky chance I found her in the hall, about to go out, but when she saw the expression on my face, she led me quickly into the library and closed the door.

"What's the matter, child? Did Lancey do anything to upset you?"

"He wants to marry me!" I cried, and sitting down suddenly on an old Italian chest, I burst into tears as if it were the saddest thing in the world.

Mamma stood before me, smiling now as she tucked her veil up under the brim of her broad-brimmed hat. "I would have thought that was good news myself!"

"But *me*!" I wailed. "Why should he want to marry *me*?"

"Because you're a very nice girl," Mamma answered in her most positive tone. "And because he knows you'll make him a very good wife. You're a good deal more attractive than you think, my dear. You've always let Cora put you too much in the shade."

She was obviously pleased; there was no doubt of that, even though it was too late for a friendship with Mrs. Bell. But I was alarmed at how much her tone took for granted. "I haven't accepted him yet," I murmured.

"Quite right," she agreed. "Keep him waiting a bit. Not too long, though. The timing of these things can be a bit tricky. Your Aunt Daisy almost lost

Uncle Fred that way. She had to do a bit of scrambling at the end. You may think Aunt Daisy incapable of scrambling, but she can jump when it comes to it!" Mamma turned to the door. "I think we'll go now and tell your father."

"Mamma!" I cried desperately. "You don't understand! I'm not sure! I don't know if I'll have him!"

She paused with her first note of uncertainty. "Are you out of your mind? When it's as plain as daylight that you're head over heels in love with him?"

"Is it that obvious?" I half whispered.

"Of course it's that obvious! You've been mooning all over the house like a sixteen-year-old ever since he came back from Europe. And didn't I tell you he *would* come back?"

It took me a few moments to comprehend her reference. "But he came back because his mother was dying!" I cried indignantly. "*You* said he would come back to marry money!"

Mamma's stare of astonishment was eloquent. Twice she opened her lips, and twice she closed them. It was always difficult for her not to blurt out whatever was on her mind, but this time she didn't. I will always give her credit for that. She didn't. If the exclamation: "Well, what in the name of glory do you think he's doing *now*?" rang in my head as loudly as if it had been shouted at me from her distance of six feet, it had nonetheless not been uttered. But I wanted it to be uttered. I tried now almost savagely to goad her into it with the wounded cry:

"You think he only cares about money, don't you?"

"Well, I don't suppose he imagines that he's marrying a pauper," Mamma retorted, taken aback by my violence. "But if money was all he cared about, I daresay he could do better than you, with all these new oil fortunes around. Not that your father won't do what he can, but I'm afraid it won't be quite what he did for Cora. Times are harder now, and, frankly, Antoine's mother rather held us up. But with the Bells I'm sure there'll be no trouble. They're reasonable people and not grasping foreigners."

"If Lancey marries me," I exclaimed proudly, "he can marry me *without* a fortune!"

I can see in retrospect how intensely irritating my attitude must have been to Mamma, who always regarded the mildest disdain of money as insufferable hypocrisy. But whatever the price of her frustration she was determined not to let me lose the match. She was very fond of Lancey, and she cared, in her own way, about my happiness. She cared, too, that no daughter of hers should make such a fool of herself.

"I think we can leave all that to Lancey and your father," she said placatingly. "I see no reason why you should be bothered with such matters. You've got a marvelous young man who's in love with you and who wants to marry you. I should think that's enough for any girl to worry about at one time!"

I got up at this and ran to Mamma, and she allowed me to throw my arms around her neck and kiss her. I then drove out with her while she left calling cards, sitting in the carriage in silent ecstasy while I composed in my mind the letter of acceptance that I would write to Lancey. I did not find out until afterwards that, while I was writing it in my room that evening, Lancey called upon Papa, at Mamma's instigation, and was once more accepted into the family as a prospective son-in-law.

8

MAMMA'S GOOD MOOD continued in the weeks that followed the announcement of our engagement. It was a new and agreeable feeling to have her so wholeheartedly on one's side, but it had also the effect of snatching my engagement away from me and tossing it to the outstretched hands of what struck me as a vociferously clamoring world. Indeed, with the announcement to the press and the subsequent, hardly complimentary explosion of congratulation, I began to wonder if everyone did not have a larger share in it than myself. Mamma, however, was equal to every occasion. When I stuttered, she answered smoothly, when I blushed, she dazzlingly smiled, when I faltered, there was ever a firm hand at my elbow. She seemed genuinely anxious that I should enjoy my engagement as much as she did. Perhaps she was determined not to fail with me as she had failed with Cora. I realize that Mamma has usually appeared in these pages as a cold woman, but she was far from inhuman. The only trouble was that as an affectionate mother she was even more overwhelming than as an ambitious one. I felt a bit like the white captive in Grandpa's gallery, paraded triumphantly before Mamma's big world and my small one.

Society, indeed, smiled on my engagement. Everyone was glad, no doubt, to see a plain girl provided with a husband and a brilliant man provided with a fortune. A date was fixed for the wedding, and presents began to fill the library, where long boards had been placed on sawhorses and covered with white linen to receive them. After the first pieces of jewelry arrived, there had to be a detective always on guard. Uncle Fred and Aunt Daisy, who had congratulated me rather pompously on entering so "distinguished" a family as the Bells, sent me an enormous diamond tiara which was the subject of many unkind jokes between Lancey and Mamma. Papa gave me a diamond necklace, and Granny Millinder a ruby and diamond choker. The newspapers made wild estimates of the value of my presents. I avoided the library as much as I could, with its mounting piles of gold and silver. It alarmed me that my dreams should be redeemed in such heavy coin. Would there be even a chink left through which, like Freya in the *Rheingold*, I could still be glimpsed?

The alarm was part of a growing obsession that everyone had conspired to turn me into something that I wasn't. As in "The Emperor's Clothes" I felt that I was being borne through streets crowded with people professing to admire my wedding garments when actually I had not a stitch on. Other girls treated me as if I had always been like them, pretty and courted and party loving, and asked me to dinners and dances as if I had been a "real" bride. It terrified me. If Lancey had always kept my hand in his, if he had whispered to me occasionally that he, too, saw the joke, I might have been able to stand it. But Lancey, of course, had no conception of what I was going through. Parties and people were an integral part of his life, and it never occurred to him that they could really scare anybody. Like all the naturally gregarious, he believed that shyness was little more than an affectation. He adored the presents and adored taking visitors into the library to show them off. He even seemed to adore meeting my relatives. Wherever we went, he enjoyed himself. I saw his green eyes, easily distracted, constantly darting from face to face, from group to group, his lips half open to emit the retort that always hovered on his tongue's edge. He was affectionate to me and kind, it was true, but when I tried to keep him beside me at a party, those eyes would flash at me with the sudden resentment of a child held back, and then he would rush off, anyway, and in a few seconds, from another corner of the room, I would hear that high, shattering laugh.

Where was the intimacy I had dreamed of? Where were the long, delicious evenings of exchanging reminiscences and vows? Where, even, was the opportunity, in the midst of so much euphoric chatter, of developing myself into the kind of woman worthy of such a man? Spending my mornings writing thank-you letters for presents that I had not wanted and sometimes had not even seen, could I become an Isabella d'Este?

I think I can see now that Lancey was simply not a man of intimacies. He was too awake to everything that at the particular moment impinged on his senses. He had no need to be alone, because he had no fear of saying private things in public. It was part, again, of the renaissance prince in him. Accustomed to courts, he was hardly aware of crowds. We went to shops and galleries with Mamma to purchase pictures and furniture for our new house, and he and she would chatter and laugh and joke about the things we saw as if no salesmen or other customers had been about. They rarely consulted me, for I was moody and preoccupied. Besides, Mamma, who was beginning to be fascinated by objects of art, was eager to pick up everything that Lancey had to teach her. "She has a lot to learn," he would tell me with his usual outrageous condescension, "but I'll say this for her: she's quick." If I had only seen that Lancey was the way he was by nature and not because of *my* deficiencies, everything might still have been all right.

I had to keep telling him of my doubts, even though he ridiculed them and explained that all brides suffered as I did. Only once was he serious, and that was at an opera party given for me by Aunt Daisy when I thought he had paid too much attention to my cousin, Gwen Myol. In the middle of the first act I retreated by myself to the little anteroom of the box and burst into tears. Lancey had seen me go and followed. Closing the curtain tightly behind him, he stood and looked down at me reproachfully. It struck me suddenly that he also looked tired.

"You're going to make yourself sick," he warned me in a low, firm tone. "Miserably sick. You're going to get yourself stuck in some little emotional hole where nobody will be able to reach you. Now, don't do it. Pull your-self together. This is life, Gussie! And life is meant to be enjoyed!" Oh, how I wanted to believe him! I looked up imploringly and tried to believe him. But just then he laughed. "Don't look so solemn!" he exclaimed. "An engaged girl is permitted occasional little spring showers of tears. But never solemnity. She has plenty of time to be solemn later!"

How could he always laugh? To keep his own nerve up? He was trying to be nice, even I could see that. Oh, yes, if it tore my soul to tatters, I could see it. He had been caught by circumstance, and he was too much of a gentleman to back out. There was the deathbed promise and the loss of his adored mother; there was the lonely aftermath and the romantic aura of my older sister that may have still lingered about our name and house-hold. And if he was in the smallest degree mercenary . . . but, no, I would not think of that. Poor Lancey had enough good motives for marrying me without my stooping to give him a bad one.

I finally gathered enough courage to hint to Mamma that I might have to break the engagement. But, like Lancey, she refused to take me seriously.

"Don't use the best notepaper," was all she said, referring to the number of times that any such letter was bound to be written and destroyed.

Then there was the trouble over my bridesmaids. I didn't want brides-maids, but if I had to have any, I insisted on my friend Penelope Bridley, from Miss Dixon's Classes, a stout, hearty girl, as full of good nature as she was deficient in humor, who had a perceptible mustache on her upper lip and a father who had killed himself to avoid an investigation of his bank-ruptcy. Mamma insisted, with some degree of accuracy, that I had selected Penelope more out of loyalty than affection, but at this point I felt that I had been dominated enough, and I refused to yield. The ultimate victory, however, as always, went to Mamma, for in return for granting me Penelope she was able to stipulate that I should ask one of her Marston nieces and Agnes Courtland, also of Miss Dixon's Classes, but very beautiful and the daughter of one of Mamma's oldest friends. I detested Agnes and was sur-prised that she even accepted. Cora, of course, was to be matron of honor and would cross the ocean for my wedding. It all seemed very elaborate and large to me, and I protested to Lancey, only to be told that he had already asked fourteen ushers!

If Cora had only been there, if Mamma had only been more communi-cable, if Lancey's sisters had only been younger or more sympathetic, if I had only had one true friend with the smallest degree of sophistication! Any of these ifs might have kept me from seeking the advice of Granny Millinder. Granny was very old now; she was not to survive that year. She spent all her time at needlework, sitting in an armchair that overlooked the court-yard, and was remote from family problems. But in my perverse habit of sentimentalizing every relationship except my own with Lancey, I had long since constructed in my mind one of happy trust and confidence between a worldly-wise old woman and her adoring granddaughter. It was to take advantage of this fictional intimacy that I called one afternoon at the big house.

"Were you ever nervous when you were engaged to Grandpa?"

"Nervous? How do you mean, nervous? It wasn't a word we used."

"Well, did you ever feel that you might be making a terrible mistake in marrying him?"

"Never!" Granny looked up at me suddenly with her eyes of light sapphire. They were beautiful eyes, her only beautiful feature, but now they seemed to have hardened in an odd defiance, as though she were defending something old and precious from a rough intruder. "Never!" she repeated sharply. "I had complete confidence in your grandfather from the very beginning. And in the strength of my attachment."

"But I don't mean so much what you felt. Did you never doubt what *he* felt?"

"But he offered me his hand and heart!" Granny exclaimed, with the same distrustful stare. "He asked my father. How was I to doubt him after that?"

I reflected that Granny, of course, had had no fortune. And surely Grandpa's old mother in Hamburg had bound her son to no deathbed promise. It suddenly seemed to me that life had been much simpler in those days. "But supposing you *had* doubted him?" I persisted. "No, I don't mean him, but his affection. Supposing you had thought he was asking you to marry him to oblige someone else?"

"Good heavens, child! Whom?"

"Well, say his mother."

"I never knew his mother."

"But supposing, Granny!"

"I should think a young girl would have something better to do than sit around supposing such things when she's engaged to be married!"

"Oh, Granny, don't scold me!" I cried, with sudden tears in my eyes. "I can't help it if I doubt Lancey. I doubt him, that's all. I do!"

Granny looked very severe at this. "Then you have no business marrying him. You must go to your mother at once and tell her. She'll tell your father, and he will tell Lancey."

"No, she won't! She'll just tell me I'm an idiot!"

"Better be called an idiot than marry a man you don't trust."

"But mightn't I *learn* to trust him?"

"My child, marriage is no time for experiments!"

When I recrossed the courtyard to our house, my heart was low indeed. I walked through the hall as one in a trance, hardly noticing that there were people there. There were always people in the house those days, people with presents, caterers, dressmakers, bridesmaids, ushers. At the door to the library I paused and looked in. There were two people there, Lancey and Agnes Courtland. They were standing by the big table, looking at the wedding presents, the only things in the house that Agnes ever did look at. I could see that she was sneering at the big gold punch bowl that Aunt Euphemia Hoyt had given me, but I did not mind that. I knew that she was simply jealous. What I did mind was that Lancey was laughing with her. And as I started, I saw him pluck a rose from a vase on the table and hand it to her. I could see, even in the sudden, violent explosion of my anger, that it was one of his mock-gallant gestures, for I could hear the tone of the laugh that accompanied it. He was probably just giving her a playful prize for one of her epigrams. But something tore within me, and all the feelings erupted that I had stored for weeks. Hurrying across the room, I grabbed the rose from Agnes' hand and flung it to the floor. She stared down at it for a moment, astounded, then up at me, and then laughed.

"I'll thank you for my rose, Augusta."

For answer I simply stamped on it.

"Charming manners," she murmured, turning to Lancey. "Don't you agree?"

"Please go!" I almost shouted at her. "Please leave this house!"

"Go!" Agnes really drew herself up at this. "Do you think for a minute I'd ever have *come* if Mummy hadn't begged me? Daddy, of course, was right. *He* said from the start that no good could come of cultivating your family!"

When she had gone, Lancey strode quickly to the library door and closed it after her. Then he turned to me, very pale and exasperated.

"Gussie, what in God's name has come over you?"

"I want to break our engagement!" I cried.

He was close to me now, but he did not touch me. "Will you pull yourself together? Will you try, please?"

"You don't know me! You don't know the kind of person I am!"

"I think you'd better let me be the judge of that."

But there was no stopping me now. "You think you understand me!" I exclaimed. "You think I'm healthy and good. You've seen a lot of beautiful women, and some of them have treated you badly, and you're disillusioned. So you say to yourself: 'But there's always Gussie, Faithful Gussie, who's waited for me all these years.' And then you promised your mother . . ."

"Now don't bring that up again!"

"But you did! I've got to think of everything. Who else will?"

"I think you might trust me for something," he said with a sigh. It was a deep sigh. I was not in too much of a state to miss its depth. It was a sigh of more than passing perplexity. I knew with a sudden horrible clarity that *now* was the time to strike. If I hit him hard enough now, right after the shocking scene that I had made with Agnes, I had a chance of antagonizing him forever.

"You can't imagine what I'm really like!" I almost shouted. "You can't imagine how jealous I am! How possessive! I'd be morose and sullen every time I saw you talking to a pretty woman! Oh, I would!" And as I said it, I felt it was true. I knew that I was beginning to flush unbecomingly, that I was assuming the very role I described. I could tell by the sudden line of apprehension on his brow that he was seeing a new side of me. Oh, I was repulsive! "And eventually I'd just sulk at dinner parties and glare down the table at you. Or like Cousin Sally Marston, drink too much wine and maybe even insult you! Yes!" I hit the table a sharp blow with my fist that made the smaller presents jump. "And there'd be scenes and tantrums, and I'd open your mail and go to your office to see what your secretary was like! I'd let my looks go and get fat and messy . . ."

"Gussie, for God's sake!" he cried in horror. "Will you stop!"

"I want you to see me as I am! It's for your own good!" And I sat down suddenly in a chair and burst into sobs.

"My poor girl," he said, very gently. "You've got the worst case of bridal jitters that's ever been. It's all these silly preparations and parties. What you need is a complete rest."

"No!"

"Listen to me, Gussie." He put his hand under my chin and turned my face up to his. "I want you to drop everything and cancel every party. I want you to go away by yourself for a week. Perhaps to Newport. There's no one up there now. I want you to be absolutely quiet and think things over. If when you come back, you still feel the same way—if, after really thinking things over, you still do—then, I promise to release you from your engagement."

I looked into his green eyes, so grave now and so rigidly composed. What was his face but the face of a man doing his duty? I had been right, more right than I could bear to contemplate. If he had loved me, would he not have taken me in his arms and kissed my doubts away? I covered my face suddenly with my hands.

"Is that understood?" he asked.

I nodded quickly.

"And if you're really rested and calm when you come back, if you can convince me that this is your own decision and not just a case of nerves, then, as I say, I will release you."

"Yes," I murmured.

"Is that fair?"

"Oh, very fair."

"Are you satisfied?"

I nodded again, and he paused, irresolute, probably debating whether or not he should kiss me before he left. But he must have decided that it would not be consistent with his promised attitude of neutrality, for he turned on his heel, with the tiniest shrug of his shoulders to indicate that he, at least, had no part in such female nerves and doubts, and left the room.

There was only one more thing that I had to do, and that was to tell Mamma. I had just strength to do it. I was like a person who had been walking in the wilderness for days and had at last found shelter. With my final mite of energy I could just identify myself to those who took me in before falling to the ground.

I found Mamma upstairs alone in the long drawing room with her back to a window in the hard autumn light. It made her skin seem paler and the circles under her eyes darker. She remained absolutely immobile while she listened to me. As I look back upon that room, I can see that it must have contained the first signs of the taste that was later to make her so remarkable a collector. It was truly dazzling, all Louis XVI, with great yellow brocaded chairs, high, dim mirrors, panels after Fragonard, an exquisite marble mantel and a vast crystal chandelier. But she had cluttered up the tables and cabinets with shepherdesses and gallants blowing kisses and smiling, well-fed cardinals. It was the only way she liked her romance, in contemporary porcelain.

When she finally answered me, her tone had recovered its old hardness. For she knew as well as I that this was more than a bride's tantrum. "Well, if you're determined to wreck your life, there's very little I can do about it. It's everyone's prerogative." She sighed in discouragement. "But you can write all the letters yourself. You can cancel all the plans and send back the presents. For *I* shall be in Europe!"

"Would you have me marry a man who doesn't love me, Mamma?"

"And why," she asked, now in a bored tone, "are we so sure that Lancey doesn't love you?"

Slowly and stammeringly I told her the story of the deathbed promise. She listened without expression, but without taking her eyes off mine.

"It doesn't mean a thing," she said flatly. "Where he's concerned, anyway."

"It means everything to me," I affirmed solemnly.

"That's because you're a fool," Mamma said coldly, getting up. There was a finality in her tone and in her measured pace to the window. For a silent minute she stood looking out. "What a clever woman Minnie Bell was," she said pensively.

"Why was she so clever?"

"Because she thought things through. She wanted to look after her boy and see him properly settled. Maybe she saw that he might have too much delicacy to propose twice in one family. Maybe she was afraid he might bring home an Italian flower girl for a wife. He would be quite capable of it!" Mamma, warming to her theme, gave a little laugh. But her eyes were still fixed out the window. "What a brilliant stroke to square his conscience with that promise! To guarantee him for the future against the vagaries of his own nature! She was a great woman, Minnie Bell. It was almost worth dying to carry a point like that!"

The wide outer space of uncharted emotion through which I had been recklessly careening ever since my night on the train with Mrs. Bell suddenly straightened itself out into a dark wall which flung me back to earth and at Mamma's feet. I wanted to shut my eyes, but I could not take them from that stiff back which seemed to control the pattern of my world. I told myself that Lancey's first kiss had been as cold as I had imagined.

"If it was such a clever plan," I said in a barely audible tone, "it seems more a pity that it should miscarry."

"Yes. But she didn't calculate on the girl's being a fool."

"I don't care what she calculated upon," I said, shaking my head stubbornly. "There's only one thing I care about. Perhaps everybody's after the money. I can't help that. But I can help being married for it!" And then because I was sore and weary and had twice been called a fool, I added: "Unlike Papa!"

Mamma turned from the window as if she was going to strike me. I had never seen her in such a temper, and she said terrible things. I bowed my head, for I could not look at her. "Who do you think you are?" she fairly shouted. "What have you so wonderful to offer a brilliant man that you should scruple about a dowry? Are you so beautiful or so witty or so fascinating that you expect the pick of the land? What's the good of your father's money but to give you a great position? Do you realize that it's a challenge to live up to? My God, when I think of a woman like Minnie Bell scheming, actually dying to arrange this match, and you stand there simpering and mouthing stale clichés, I wonder if you are worthy of it? It's your choice, my girl! You can be a great woman or you can be a stupid, sentimental old maid. Smiling fatuously at attentive nephews and nieces who are only waiting for you to die!"

"Oh, Mamma! Please!" I covered my face with my hands.

But I couldn't stop her. Nothing could stop her. The memory appalls me to this day of how she tried to strip my soul of every last bit of its tinselly protection. There was something fiendishly compulsive in the way she did it, as if all my little protective masks and disguises were so many personal insults to her. And so we stood, the two of us, at the end of that terrible interview, the floor covered with the sequins and spangles of love and honor and faith, cut off, exposed for frauds, abandoned. But I had learned while carrying those silly notes between Cora and Lancey what the image of love could be. If there was an image there had to be somewhere a reality. And if there was a reality, there could be no compromise. Such was my desolate logic. I went to my room when Mamma had finally given me up and wrote a letter to Lancey to tell him that two lives could not be constructed on a deathbed promise. I was very firm and very clear. I told him that there was no need for me to go to Newport, that I should never know my mind better than I knew it then. I begged him not to try to see me, and, to my infinite relief and agonizing disappointment, he didn't. He returned instead to Europe where he finished his studies. Contrary to Mamma's expectations, he did not marry a fortune. He did, however, marry an Italian girl, the other possibility that she had suggested, but, far from being a flower girl, she belonged to a noble Roman family. Emilia was and still is very beautiful. She has never been anything but calm and tranquil in the face of Lancey's high spirits and high temper, and she has borne him six children who have all the arrogance and brilliance of the Bells. Lancey, as everybody had predicted, became a most successful architect. He has been particularly good with country houses, clubs and railway stations; his Florentine manner is known now over the whole country. In the past twenty years, with the immense growth of the modern style, he has fallen a bit into disrepute, but even as an old man he has enough business to keep him going. He has maintained his interest in all the arts and in the best food and wine. Like his mother, I doubt if he has ever lived within his income. I have dined there at times when Emilia has done the cooking, but we have still drunk champagne. She has been a superb manager and has made him a perfect wife.

One time, not very long ago, when I found myself next to Lancey at a dinner party, I asked him suddenly, surprising myself as much as I surprised him: "Did you really mean it when you proposed to me? Or were you only doing it because you promised your mother? You can tell me now. It's quite all right. I'm simply curious."

He looked at me soberly for a moment with a little frown. Perhaps he was trying to recapture the features of youth in the large old brown woman with the big diamonds at his side. Then he smiled and seemed about to answer, and then he frowned again, and I knew that we were going to be very serious indeed.

"No!" I exclaimed in sudden panic. "Oh, no, please! Don't tell me! It's better not to know! Much better!"

He nodded, smiling again, and said nothing. Obviously he thought I was afraid that he was going to tell me that he had been acting only at the behest of a dying parent. He must have thought that I wished to cherish, in sterile romantic folly, the illusion that I had once been loved. If so, he was wrong. What I could not bear to contemplate was the idea that Mamma had been right and that I had wrecked my own life.

9

I WAS TWENTY-FIVE before I first really asserted my independence of the family. Lancey had taught me that it was possible to act on the universe as well as be acted upon, and the fact that my parents were living more apart now and more away from New York had warned me that, unless I took measures, my status in Mamma's household might soon change from that of resident daughter to that of traveling companion. Cora was living in France; Willie, who had married Julia Lydig, was on a year's honeymoon around the world and Bertie had a bachelor suite at Delmonico's. When Papa announced that he was taking a group of scientists to the Pacific on *The Wanderer* to collect marine specimens, and Mamma that she was spending the winter in Paris, I saw my chance and seized it. I announced boldly that I planned to stay in New York and take courses in history and art at Columbia.

Well, then there *was* a storm. Where, if I pleased, was I going to live after the house had been closed up? I pointed out that I could subsist comfortably enough on the second floor with the caretaker and my maid. Well, then, had I no feeling for my own mother, living alone in Paris? I pointed out that she would have Cora. Did I want, finally, to turn into an old maid, a sour old bluestocking? Why *not*? My father laughed at my last answer, and I was at least assured of his lazy, halfhearted support. But Papa rarely cared enough about anything to put up much of a fight; he loaned you his charm, but you always knew that he would be wanting it back. If Mamma, in the course of marital retaliation, had become a bit of a joke to him, could her children be taken altogether seriously? I can see now the fear of failure that must have underlain Papa's reluctance to engage with the world, but at that time he seemed immeasurably strong, and I could only attribute his failure to take my side more wholeheartedly to an indifference that I had learned to look upon as my just desert. Oddly enough the person who came to my assistance at the last moment and made my project feasible was my Aunt Euphemia Hoyt.

Aunt Euphemia was one of Papa's two sisters and very much like Granny Millinder. She was a small, neat, quiet, homelike, thin-lipped lady, conservative, sweet and dull. She was, of course, an heiress, but her generation had not yet learned the power of the purse, and she was utterly dominated by her husband. This did not deter Sargent from painting her in the usual regal pose, and I was always amused by the contrast between the lady in the great canvas in flowing scarlet with high, pale, aristocratic cheekbones and the ebony eyes of the Millinders, and the small, submissive, actual figure of my aunt who used to sit beneath her magnificent likeness, patiently doing needlework. Yet whether it was a prescience in the artist, or the effect, over a period of years, of the painting on the subject, it is certainly true that Aunt Euphemia, who survived her awe-inspiring husband by forty years became in the end a rather formidable hostess herself and what is now loosely described as a "grande dame." But there was no hint of that in those days. Aunt Euphemia's interest in me must have originated in the emotional void created by the absoluteness of her husband's rule. There was perhaps an unconscious sympathy with my desire not to marry except on my own terms. At any rate she took Mamma quite by surprise in suggesting that she could keep an adequate eye on me in the city from her house next door and that I could spend all my weekends with her in Bedford. Mamma, who was not used to suggestions from Papa's sisters, had no answer ready, and when Aunt Daisy came unexpectedly to my aid by stating her unqualified opposition to my "plan of emancipation," I knew that my scheme was safe.

I shall never forget the heady freedom of that winter. With the obligations of social life removed, I entered into a paradise of courses in Italian art and literature. It was incredible luxury to be able to sit whole evenings alone by a fire with my books. It hardly occurred to me that it might have been more fun to be doing it in Florence or Rome. One step was enough at a time. I even made a few friends at Columbia, despite my promise to Mamma, faithfully carried out, not to go to and fro alone. Each morning I set out with my maid in a small tan brougham with a coachman arrayed in tan whipcord and a high hat. It was a special concession that he did not have to wear the Millinder livery. My maid even had to attend me to class where she sat in the back of the room. Obviously I became an object of general curiosity, but it was not an unfriendly curiosity, and it may have helped me to meet more people than would otherwise have been the case. I went so far as to give a couple of dinner parties for my new friends and induced the reluctant caretaker's wife to take the white covers off the chairs in the dining room. These parties, it is true, did not go off very well, for my new friends were a bit awed and silenced by the musty, sepulchral quality of the vast closed house, but I could still appreciate that they would rather have come there once than not have come at all. I have always had to recog-

nize that the life of the rich has a fascination to the general public, and at
the end of the last century this fascination was at its most intense.

Another pleasure of that winter was getting to know my brother Bertie.
He had never before shown the slightest interest in me, or, for that matter,
in any of the family. He was not handsome or athletic like Papa and Willie,
and I imagine he was ashamed of this. He had a friendly but slightly comic
frog-shaped face and was very short. He seemed, indeed, a sort of male
parody of Mamma, and it may have been because of this that she favored
him the least of her children But like her, he was very intelligent, and had
an even more wounding wit. Because Grandpa had left a million dollars to
each of his grandsons, Bertie was independent of the family and showed it
in his peremptory refusal even to consider a serious occupation. He moved
with a very sophisticated set, and his year was divided elaborately into a series
of "seasons" up and down the Atlantic seaboard. He owned a three-masted
schooner and a small racing stable, and Mamma used to say that she was
postponing further advice until he had got through his million. In the
meantime Bertie seemed without apprehensions. He could make devastating fun of his friends and his life, but he would never admit that,
however low their standards, anybody else had better ones. In this, like
Mamma, he was a true cynic. He gave several parties at the house to which
I was not invited and of which, judging from the sounds, I hardly think
Mamma would have approved. On these occasions all covers came off the
furniture in the big parlor as well as in the dining room, and waiters were
brought in from Delmonico's. I suppose the caretaker and his wife were
well tipped for their silence, while I was "squared" by Bertie's increased
affability He could be very agreeable indeed when he wanted. He sometimes dropped in of an evening on his way to a party and smoked by the
fire in my sitting room, a whisky and soda in his hand, while I worked on
my art notebooks. But he simply laughed when I tried to persuade him to
take the course.

"Cultivation in social life is quite superfluous," he assured me. "In fact,
it's inclined to make people suspicious of you. A smattering of French doesn't
hurt, but basically, a few words of English are all that's required."

"And a lot of money."

"Of course," he agreed, entirely serious. "It's possible to be in society
without it, but you're only a hanger-on, and that's hell. If you have money
and aren't positively repellent and if you can care enough to get the hang
of who's who in a few little groups, it's all you need to be a resounding hit.
Oh, there are trimmings that help, sure, like charm, ability to entertain, a
good polo game, but they're not fundamental."

"Bertie, how can you waste yourself so?" I exclaimed indignantly. "You
have the best brain in the family. You should use it."

He was irritated by my vehemence, for he got up and walked to the fire
to kick the logs. "What do you do up in Columbia but study history?" he
demanded sharply. "And what is history but a study of the acquisition and
misuse of power? Well, I prefer to live history. You can laugh at Bertie
Millinder today, but tomorrow he will be a perfectly respectable subject for

some dreary little pedant's thesis. Look at all the books they've written on Marie Antoinette!"

"You can't really think anyone is ever going, to be concerned with the goings-on of your little set?"

"My dear Gussie, your art, if you will only reflect upon it, is exclusively concerned with the upper classes. Portraits, busts, novels, verse dramas, paintings of courts and battles. It's only quite recently that the lower elements have begun to creep in."

"Upper class! Do you honestly believe that a few dollars of Grandpa's money puts you in an upper class?"

"Of course it does!" he retorted. "Not that I'm proud of it. Any more than I'm proud of *him*. Far from it. But I observe more than you think, Gussie. I observe that the qualities that get a man into society today are the very ones that used to keep him out: greed and trickiness. Instead of an aristocracy based on the sword, we have one based on usury. And don't think that hasn't put its stamp on the whole face of America! I don't have to go up to Columbia to learn my history, thank you." He looked now at his watch. "I must be off. I'm dining with our sainted Aunt Daisy on the stroke of eight."

"I thought you never went there."

"Once a winter. It's a whole history chapter in itself!"

When I got up to kiss him his mood had already passed, and he was laughing at me. But I had had my glimpse of his bitterness. Unhappiness behind a façade of trivia is always appealing, for we resent the idea that foolish things can bring content to others. "If you're doing the family again," I urged him, "why not come up with me some weekend to Aunt Euphemia's? She'd love it so!"

He burst out laughing. "Of course, when you're in prison, you want everyone else to join you there. It's quite understandable. But remember, my dear, that *I* didn't have to promise Mamma anything when she went away. And the next time I set foot in Aunt Euphemia's house will be the day she becomes a widow!"

This was typical of my family's attitude towards Uncle Josiah Hoyt. But Uncle Josiah had started it. He had despised all the Millinders from the very day on which he had "honored" Aunt Euphemia with his hand and had taken it arrogantly for granted that this same hand would be allowed to wallow freely in the till of her money. When Grandpa had died and left half of her fortune in trust, he had not scrupled to try to break the will, albeit unsuccessfully. Why he felt himself so far above us, I have never known. He came I suppose, of old colonial stock, but then, it is far easier for people of obscure ancestry to claim distinguished pedigrees than those of a notorious one. For example, there are plenty of people in New York today who still bracket the words "parvenu" and "Millinder," whose own grandfathers, perhaps unbeknownst to themselves, were of humbler origin than mine. Uncle Josiah, however, not only had the pride of descent; he had the pride of a potential ancestor. He had some nebulous goal, I imagine, of founding a Hoyt dynasty with Millinder money. The house in Bedford was a great square of red brick, magnificently situated on the top of a hill, with porticoes of white columns in the center of each of the four fronts. It was a better building than the renaissance replicas of his wife's family, but it was too bare and stern, like my uncle himself. When Aunt Euphemia died, only a few years back, the wreckers who bought it found it so well constructed that the cost of demolition wiped out their profit.

Uncle Josiah was very tall and gaunt, and he had long grey whiskers and a high bald formidable dome. He was a rigid Presbyterian, so that his passion for pomp and display had to be satisfied with a mournful pomp and a funereal display. The great halls of the house were filled with dark tapestries and carved black Italian furniture. Only in his own study, with its bronze figurines of naked girls at the slave market, its gaudy paintings of near-naked Christians in the arena and its shelves of memoirs of the mistresses of French kings, all bound in gold leather, did one become aware of the pruriency of the Victorian gentleman. Having read a bit in modern psychology, I can now imagine with what relish Uncle Josiah must have retired to his study to dwell on the problems of those Christian pioneers who had such trouble keeping their clothes on. But, needless to say, there was no hint of this in the long, grim meals at the family board where he lectured his family on the godlessness and degeneracy of the age. I suppose they were all so used to it that they barely heard. Aunt Euphemia would smile benignly down the table at him and gossip when she could of neighbors' doings while the two girls, Leila and Isabel, giggled at each other and communicated about men in secret signs and winks. I did not have to spend more than two weekends at "Great Lawns" to discover what everyone but Uncle Josiah knew: that Leila was madly in love with the young landscape architect who was helping her father to break the back of the stubborn countryside so that, like the parks at Versailles, it could be converted into a series of grand alleys leading to the house. I could have taken a romantic enthusiasm in a plot so sure of parental opposition if Leila had shown the smallest interest in me. But she and her sister, silly, giddy, pretty girls, made no secret of their disdain for a bookish cousin whom they regarded as already a hopeless old maid. Aunt Euphemia was always sweet and kind, but her outlook was tightly limited, and she could not comprehend that I was different from herself at the same age. It was in Lucius, the son of the house, that I found my sole friend and companion on those long winter weekends.

Lucius was the oldest child, being only two years younger than I, and the sole male heir for Uncle Josiah's dreams. But he had, in what I now understand to have been simple self-protection, barricaded himself from early childhood behind a solid wall of asthma. From the battlements of his sickroom, where he accepted in regal silence the crooning administrations of women, he peered down with an air of reserved suspicion at the pacing, impatient figure of his enormous father. Lucius' illness represented sanctuary, for himself and others; even Aunt Euphemia, sitting by her restlessly sleeping child in the warm, scented air of his chamber, dared to raise a stern finger to her lips when her husband appeared at the threshold. As the boy grew precariously older, this sanctuary was extended until there were evidences of it in every part of the house except for his father's study itself. Lucius could have his own cushioned chair at the dining room table; for Lucius the west porch was glassed in and for him the tiny grilled box of an elevator was installed to ruin the looks of the Adam stairway. Paintings and photographs crept over the walls and tables to show Lucius, tall and languid with rippling blond hair, with lace collars and velvet knickers and pointed black pumps, or leaning against a column in a silk shirt open at the neck, holding a Siamese cat. The one I remember best is a Boldini showing him sprawled on a Chinese rug, his head twisted up at a painful angle so that he could stare with opaque, adoring eyes at an emaciated, elongated, cryptically smiling Aunt Euphemia. There was a terrible crisis when Lucius was fourteen and had the indiscretion to gain in strength. His father had promptly invaded the sickroom to crop his hair, to put him in shorts, to take him outdoors and throw balls at him, to talk cheerfully of dark, distant, drafty New England schools. Small wonder that Lucius had promptly resumed his cough and fled permanently back to sanctuary. At twenty-three he was well enough to do anything he wanted and ill enough to be excused from everything else. Uncle Josiah had been checkmated and could only watch from his corner with a gruff solicitude. It was still possible, after all, that Lucius might marry and have a son.

Lucius was imperious and spoiled and utterly selfish, but he had great intelligence and a dry humor and could be kind when it suited him. He would summon me to his sitting room on the second floor, heaped with books and Chinese porcelains and odd, modern French paintings, a chamber which nobody entered except on his express invitation, and, safe from Uncle Josiah's fulminations, I passed my Saturday evenings. Lucius would lie on his chaise lounge, puffing at Turkish cigarettes, and eye me as closely as a cat.

"You're very lucky, you know," he said one night. "About Lancey Bell. Mummy told me all about his promise to his mother."

"How did *she* know?"

"Families always know those things," he answered calmly. "Don't get ruffled. But isn't it lucky you knew about it? Otherwise you might have married him."

I was nettled at all he took for granted, this insolent young man. "Maybe I should have!" I cried in pain. "Maybe I'd have been happy!"

"Maybe. But it would have been a bovine happiness and a bovine life. You're made for better things, Gussie. You've got the only commodity in the world that matters. Freedom. Don't let any man ever take it away from you. Believe me, they're all the same. I *know*."

"But they can't all be like Uncle Josiah!"

"Can't they?" Lucius' eyes assumed immediately a look of stubborn hostility. "*I* think they can. Daddy should be a very valuable person for you to study. *He'll* teach you to keep your money for yourself!"

"Do you think it absolutely impossible," I demanded indignantly, "that I should ever meet a man who wasn't interested in my money?"

"Absolutely," he retorted coolly. "Because it's your misfortune to be completely identified with it. No man could escape your money. Even a nihilist might marry you only to throw it away!"

I should have known better than to discuss such a subject with Lucius. A cold appraisal was the last thing I wanted. But I felt now that I had to elicit some spark of sentiment from him, for his own sake as well as my own.

"You say that freedom is such a wonderful thing," I protested. "Mightn't it be lonely?"

He shrugged. "You can't expect something for nothing. In this life we pay."

"What about yourself? Don't you ever want to marry?"

"Marry!" His eyes widened, and the Siamese cat leaped suddenly from his lap to the floor. "And have my life messed up by some chattering girl like Leila or Isabel?"

"They're not all like them!"

"*Aren't* they?"

The suggestion that I was not died on my lips before his quizzical stare. Evidently I had been promoted, along with himself, to some bleak neuter altitude of superior sexlessness. It was a compliment that did little to lift my spirits. "You talk about freedom," I grumbled. "But how much freedom is there in the life of a fussy old bachelor? Or a sour old maid?"

"As much as they put into it!" he cried. "As much as they take out! Don't be afraid of labels, Gussie. Be a great old maid! Be a magnificent old maid!"

How often since have I thought of those words! They were to be echoed by Ione, years later, when I was on the verge of nervous collapse. But at the time I was saddened and hurt. I was not in the least in love with Lucius, but I wanted to play with the idea. It was a blow to my female pride that he should refuse so bluntly even to fancy me in any role other than that of cousin. For I needed some game to salve the wound of Lancey Bell. The game would not have required that Lucius should have any knowledge of it or take any active part in it, but it would have required at least once in a while that he should utter a phrase that would not utterly repudiate the poesy of his looks. For Lucius, white and thin and delicate as he was, had a certain fragile beauty, a certain wasting, romantic pallor. His hands were small and perfect, his brow high, his nose small and aquiline, his lips a pursed, scarlet red. But there was nothing in the least romantic in his prosaic grey stare, which, like the dryness of his philosophy, announced a different person than his skin and hair, announced the gradual emergence of his father's son, announced the coming corpulence and the pompous manner. The passing fit of beauty that I then witnessed was to be regretted less by Lucius than anyone. When barely a year later his hair fell out, all in a few months' time, and his jowls thickened into something like health, he seemed hardly aware of it. I, who had wanted to place the soothing hand of Florence Nightingale on the fevered brow of John Keats, was the sole mourner for his beauty.

We discussed many things, but rarely poetry. Lucius, I think, enjoyed our talks as much as I; he was very petulant when anything interfered. He loved to gossip, particularly about the family, and he adored talking about money.

As a Millinder grandson, though on the distaff side, he, too, had inherited his million, but unlike my brother Bertie he had lovingly invested and reinvested every penny of it, including the income. This was my first introduction to Lucius' financial side which he kept strictly concealed from his parents. The drab statistical reports of railroads and oil wells and mines that he loved to pore over were smuggled into the sitting room where I'm sure Uncle Josiah pictured him sighing over a slender volume of sonnets. In those days it was not the custom to settle money on unmarried daughters, but I had my share of Granny Millinder's estate, and Lucius undertook to manage this with his own. I, too, began to take an interest in finance, and together we even planned a biography of Grandpa Millinder, whose memory Lucius revered. This plan Lucius eventually was to carry out, though by himself. It is not much read today, for it is very dry and statistical, but economists have always regarded it as a small classic. Such was my Keats's *Endymion*.

I wondered why Lucius would never show off his learning before his father, who would have been so proud of it. Uncle Josiah had been a lawyer until his marriage to Aunt Euphemia, and by reputation a rather tricky one. "He'd bluster and rant until the going got rough," my father used to say, "and then steal out through a back door of small print." With Aunt Euphemia's money he had abandoned the law for the wider fields of business. The fact that he despised businessmen in no way deterred him; on the contrary, it had made him assume that theirs must be an easy trick to learn. If one had to live in a world of parvenus, he might have said, one had to beat them at their own game. He had been working for several years now to unite a series of small New England railways into the kind of empire that he imagined Grandpa to have formed. But, as Lucius sarcastically pointed out to me, the difference in profits from Grandpa's operations showed that his father was no mere Chinese copyist.

The peculiar aspect of my uncle's management of his lines came out one Saturday night at dinner when he revealed to us his plan of suspending the operation of his trains on Sundays. He had long, he soberly explained, been deeply concerned with the increase of public travel on the Sabbath and his own involvement in its promotion. The argument that the poorer classes in the city would lose their opportunity to visit the country on holidays, which was gently advanced by Aunt Euphemia, was roundly denounced as "specious." Was God any closer because of flowers? Was it not His sky over the slums as well as the forests? These remarks come to mind today when I hear young people, in reaction against reaction, wax nostalgic about those days. Of course, they never knew anyone like Uncle Josiah. They can't really believe he existed.

"Your competitors will welcome the step," Lucius intervened in his mild, half-bantering tone. "They may even contribute to your church funds."

Uncle Josiah looked gravely at this son whom he could never hope to understand. "What do my competitors have to do with my duty to God?"

"Nothing whatever, I quite agree. And what you have just said clarifies my understanding of the management of your lines. You are serving

God. Very good. It makes sense now. I had thought you were serving Mammon."

There was a sudden hush at the table, followed by stifled giggles from
Leila and Isabel. Aunt Euphemia shook her head quickly at them. Lucius,
of course, enjoyed a certain immunity from his father's terrible temper, but
it was an immunity rather precariously fenced in by his own sometimes too
mocking good manners. Uncle Josiah glared at him ominously for several
moments and then coughed.

"I don't think I care for your tone, sir," he said, frowning. "I don't think
it shows a proper respect."

"But there is no lack of respect, Daddy!" Lucius' tone, for all his winning smile, betrayed a little throb of apprehension. "It's merely a question
of what your motive is. Is your motive to draw down the largest possible
revenue or is it to ensure a strict observance of the Sabbath? I take it, it's
not your intention to accomplish both?"

"Why should it not be?"

"But, my dear father, who will make up to you the lost revenues of every
seventh day?"

"He who provided wine at the Marriage at Cana and loaves and fishes
for the multitude on the Mount."

"Ah, then, I have no more to say!" Lucius gave a little snort of laughter.
"I didn't realize you had *Him* on your board of directors!"

"That will do, son!" Uncle Josiah's fist fell on the table, and Lucius, with
suddenly flushed cheeks, stared down into his plate. "I will tolerate no trifling with holy things! Watch your cynicism, my son. Watch it carefully! It
is the devil's surest weapon. It is especially important for you to be on guard,
for you inherit the tendency from your mother's father. Cynicism was his
besetting sin!"

In my sudden anger I lost all fear. I turned to Aunt Euphemia to see if
she would defend Grandpa, but her eyes, like Lucius', were fixed on her
plate. I then faced Lucius and raised my voice loudly:

"Grandpa Millinder was a great man! Don't you agree, Lucius?"

Lucius glanced up at me for a second. It was a quick, baleful glance. "I
don't classify relatives, Gussie," he retorted. "Relatives are relatives."

We all turned as Uncle Josiah rose. I think he was choking with frustration at being unable to berate me, as he would have berated one of his own
daughters.

"Euphemia, will you please have the rest of my dinner served in my study?"
he gasped in a hollow sibilant tone. "I seem not to be regarded at my own
table."

"Oh, Gussie," Aunt Euphcmia wailed when he had gone, "you *do* have a
bit of your mother in you, don't you?"

"She would never allow Papa to say such a thing about *her* father!" I
exclaimed, too excited now for apology.

"No, dear, I suppose not." Aunt Euphemia shook her head sadly. "But
then Cyrus *does* spend a lot of time away from home on that boat, doesn't
he?"

I almost bit my tongue off in my effort not to wish Uncle Josiah in one, and a sinking one at that. I turned once more to Lucius. "You didn't stand up for Grandpa!" I reproached him. "And you talk about freedom!"

"Grandpa Millinder has no need of *my* voice," he retorted sharply. He acted as if he had found my outburst in the worst possible taste. I flushed as I suddenly saw myself through his eyes. Instead of a spirited and gallant girl, standing up alone for her grandsire, I saw a noisy, perspiring virago. How red and crude I must have seemed before the small, grey coolness of Lucius! But even in my mortification I could feel an angry little pride that I was not as he.

My small outburst, however, was soon forgotten in the greater crisis that enveloped the family. The landscape architect finally worked up the courage to ask his employer for his daughter's hand and was promptly ordered off the place in a thunderous scene during which my uncle was heard to shout that not only would he be blacklisted, but that he would go unpaid for the work already done. The distracted Leila was to be sent abroad to stay for six months with Uncle Josiah's sister who had married a Scottish baron and lived in a dark, damp castle near Glasgow. Leila has told the story herself recently in a vulgar book called *The Omnibus of Me*, so I need not go into it. But I might add in the interests of truth that she says she was prevented from eloping by being locked in her room at "Great Lawns." This was not the case. She was prevented from eloping by the understandable reluctance of the young landscape architect to tie himself to a wife whose inefficiency in matters domestic was not to be balanced by any private means. When I think how many times Leila has subsequently married, it seems quite unimportant that the architect should not have headed the list, but, of course, I could not know this at the time, and Leila's suffering was distressing even to those who did not like her. Our weekend meals were held in an awful silence interrupted only by an occasional sob and Uncle Josiah's mournful reflections on the perversity of the female sex. Deception of parents was, it appealed, a crime even graver than cynicism, and Leila, in his evident opinion, was suffering only a temporary check in her headlong rush to the fiery regions.

"Stop, Josiah!" Aunt Euphemia cried one night when Leila had left her seat to bury her face in her mother's lap. "You've said enough! The poor child has suffered too much!"

"He's cruel! He's wicked!" shrieked Isabel, rushing to her mother's other side, and the three of them stared down the table at the head of the family in unprecedented defiance. Uncle Josiah once again had to fling down his napkin and quit the room, and Lucius, sitting across the table from me, simply sipped his wine and smiled. But I could not smile back. I was too disgusted by his neutrality. He made no secret of his opinion that if there were things worth fighting for, they did not include his sister's happiness. I deduced wrongfully that if he would not fight for Leila he would not fight for anything.

It was decided that Aunt Euphemia and Isabel were to accompany Leila on the ocean voyage to deliver her to her castle, and on the weekend after their departure, my last in Bedford during my uncle's lifetime, there were only he and Lucius and I in the house. I had been for a walk alone on the grounds in the chill early spring, and when I came in to the great hall with the surrounding balcony and double-storied white Corinthian columns, Uncle Josiah's butler, who had a demeanor as grave as his master's, told me that my uncle wished me to join him in the study. When I entered, I found Lucius, looking very still and collected, seated by the fire. His father was standing by the closed red curtains of a french window, staring at the Persian rug. He looked up gravely as I came in, nodded and then fixed his stare again on the rug. I sat down opposite Lucius, who glanced at me with a sudden quizzical smile. I could not make out his message, and I turned to the fire to warm my hands.

"I will be candid with you, Augusta," my uncle's voice came to me across the room, and it startled me to realize that he had never before addressed me by my Christian name. "It was not my original idea to have you at this conference."

I rose immediately. "Surely you can't imagine that I wish to intrude?"

"I will deem it a favor if you remain."

The grey eyes gazed at me with silent reproach, and, defeated, I resumed my seat.

"You are here at the insistence of my son," my uncle continued. "This is a business matter, and he has told me—somewhat to my surprise, I confess—that you and he have become financial partners."

"Well—I—I don't quite know—" I stared in confusion at Lucius.

"What I meant, Gussie," Lucius intervened, "is that you and I have been going into things together. I have told Daddy that I now propose to carry it one step further. I shall not go into anything without you."

"I'm very flattered, but what are we going into?"

"That is what we are meeting to discuss."

He bowed now to my uncle, as though to give him the floor, and the latter cleared his throat and started to outline his proposition. It was evidently a distasteful procedure, for in the pauses between his clipped syllables I could sense the suppressed sighs. "I have invited Lucius to associate himself with Hoyt Railways," he concluded with a loud cough. "I make the same offer now to you both. I am willing to turn over half of my own holding of the company's common stock, amounting to fifteen thousand shares, at its book value of fifty dollars a share."

"Three quarters of a million," Lucius calculated with a rapidity that startled his father.

"That is correct," the latter continued, nodding. "Of course, the stock is worth vastly more than book. But it is closely held, and there is no ready market. And, naturally, I wish to keep control of the company in my family."

"Why, then, do you sell it at all?"

My uncle's eyebrows went up slightly. "It so happens I could use additional capital in the business."

"For what purpose?"

"What purpose?" My uncle's tone became stiffer. "Isn't that a question for management?"

"I should think so!" Lucius' feet had reached the firm soil of his specialty, and there was a provoking sureness in the rising note of his voice. "Indeed, it is a question for management! But isn't management exactly a question for Gussie and me? Surely, my dear father, you don't expect us to plunk down three-quarters of a million dollars without a thorough review of what management's policy has been?"

"I had hoped that you might regard this in the nature of a happy opportunity," his father replied with injured dignity. "An opportunity, as I believe they put it now, 'to get in on the ground floor.'"

"But I first want to be sure there's a roof over my head!"

"Lucius!" Uncle Josiah took a threatening step towards him and stopped. "You seem to forget that I am president of the company. When you question the management, you're questioning me!"

I saw Lucius flush, and his long white hands grasped the arms of the Italian chair. I suddenly realized why he had raised no finger to help Leila. He had not deemed her worthy. Lucius must have conceived of himself as an outmatched David who had to conserve all his energy and skill for the one perfect cast of the pebble that was to deliver him from the Goliath of annihilation. As he slowly rose now and stood with his back to the fire, I knew that he had his slingshot in hand. And I knew, too, with a sudden intuition, that his aim would be deadly, that the contest before me was to be entirely one-sided.

"I do not mean to question you, sir," Lucius was saying in a high, bleak tone. "But I am obliged to question the president of Hoyt Lines. I am obliged to discover the reason for this sudden, pressing need of capital. I am ever obliged to wonder if it is not to cover the mistakes of management."

"You forget yourself, sir!"

I gasped as Lucius actually shrugged. I doubt if Uncle Josiah had ever seen anyone shrug in his house before, let alone in his study. "You see, Daddy?" he said condescendingly. "It won't do. You and I could never do business together. Let us not spoil our relationship. Let us forget you ever made this proposition." He turned to me with a sudden, bright smile. "How about it, Gussie? Shall we forget it?"

"Most willingly."

"Please sit down, Lucius, Augusta," my uncle asked us, and his voice was suddenly ragged with weariness. I looked up in surprise and saw that his eyes were troubled and shifted back and forth from me to Lucius. "Please," he repeated, and we sat. "I have been too hasty perhaps. You are undoubtedly right that an investor is entitled to know about the company in which he invests. Even when it happens to be managed by his own father." He sighed deeply. "What is it, then, that you wish to know?"

"Everything."

"Everything? You mean you would like the dividend record and a statement of assets and liabilities?"

"Well, those things, of course, as a starter. But I will wish to know every detail about every line you operate, what is your labor policy, who are your creditors and competitors, how strong is your officer personnel and what are your plans of expansion. I know you keep your files in here, sir. Would you like to make a start this very afternoon?"

I shall never forget that afternoon. It was the sheerest agony. Had anyone told me beforehand that I would suffer misery at the sight of Uncle Josiah's discomfiture, I would have called him a rank sentimentalist. Yet such was the case. My uncle and Lucius sat opposite each other at a tall Renaissance table with gilt legs and a marble surface and passed documents back and forth. Lucius, like a pale young Napoleon, snatched up paper after paper and digested their contents in a brief, fixed glare. He kept jotting down figures on a pad. Uncle Josiah watched him with a look of stony but helpless awe, mumbling rather incoherent answers to short, staccato questions. He must have wondered what fiend had changed his dreamy, poetical son into this driving, imperious accountant. The relationship between father and son had altered in a single hour to reflect the financial acumen of one and the business incompetence of the other. It all happened so fast that I was not even surprised when Lucius suddenly threw down his pencil and snapped:

"Of course, I couldn't make a final decision before I had inspected your lines and the company's books had been thoroughly audited. But I can tell you two things right now. Only I think I should warn you first that you won't like them."

"They won't be the first things this afternoon I haven't liked."

"You'd rather not hear them?"

"It appears I must."

"Very well, then. In the first place I can see at once from your annual statement that the actual value of your stock is nearer fifteen dollars a share than fifty. In the second, purchase of the stock at any price could only be premised on a total change of management."

Uncle Josiah stared at his strange new son for several seconds and then rose to his feet.

"Am I to understand that you would oust your own parent from the management of his lines?"

"The alternative would be even less agreeable."

"And what do you deem the alternative to be?"

"The contemplation of his imminent bankruptcy."

Uncle Josiah turned very slowly to the table and started to gather up the papers. "It must be my punishment for a crime of which I am not conscious," he said in a puzzled, hollow voice, speaking as if to himself, "to have been given such a son. But if the Almighty plans my suffering in this world, it may be to lessen it in the next."

Lucius' face at this became suddenly contorted with a violent anger, and he stamped on the floor. "It may be for the same reason that He gave me such a father!" he screamed.

"Lucius!" I cried. "You can't say such things!"

"Didn't *he*?"

"But he's your father!"

"My father! What does he know about being a father? I disown him as a father! And when he goes bust, may God be my witness, I'll never pay a debt of his!"

"Get out of this room, you blaspheming heathen!" Uncle Josiah shouted at him hoarsely. "And you, too, you scheming hussy! It is *you* who have corrupted him! He never dreamed such things before you came to my house!"

I fled away in horror, my hands clapped to my ears for fear of hearing even more terrible things, and Lucius followed me. His cheeks were flushed scarlet, but his eyes were shining.

"I did it, Gussie!" he cried after me as I hurried up the stairway. "You see, I did it! You saw me give it to him, piece by piece. Oh, Gussie, if you only *knew* how long I had planned that!"

It was obvious that I could not remain under my uncle's roof for another night after what he had said to me. I begged Lucius to go with me to the city, warning him that he would probably suffer a terrible reaction and beg his father's forgiveness before nightfall, but he assured me that there was no danger of this and promised that he could handle his father alone. Apparently he was right, for he and Uncle Josiah were again on speaking terms when Aunt Euphemia returned from Europe. And why not? So complete a victor could afford a degree of magnanimity.

Uncle Josiah's little railroad empire fell apart a few months later. His creditors took every penny that he had and all of Aunt Euphemia's money that had been invested in the business. There were many charges of mismanagement so shocking as to amount almost to a crime, and ugly stories about the Millinders which had not been heard since Grandpa's day were re-aired. But it all passed quickly enough. Uncle Josiah was too small a financier to make much noise in that age of titans. Aunt Euphemia still had her five millions in trust that he could not touch, and although they had to sell their house in New York to Papa, they continued to maintain "Great Lawns" on almost the same scale. Lucius continued to live with them, and it was his voice that was now raised with ultimate authority in family discussions. Uncle Josiah never recovered from his business failure. Gaunt and brooding, he would sit at the end of the great dining room table without saying a word, and little by little his wife and daughters, like warblers who have decided, after cautious inspection, that the immobile owl is blind, broke into chatter around him as if he had not been there. Indeed, he barely was. Less than two years after the disaster he slumped to his death in that very dining room, and several moments had passed before Aunt Euphemia's cry brought it to the attention of the others.

I have dwelt at some length on Lucius' defiance of his father because it was the one dramatic event of his life. All his life before it was a preparation, and all his life subsequent was a result. He must have husbanded every scrap of his wit and energy for twenty-five years for the terrible struggle, and once the image in the temple had been struck down, he knew the other that he wanted to put in its place. Happily for her, it was the image of Aunt

Euphemia. The girls married and left home, but Lucius and his mother remained together in total, almost excluding congeniality until her death when over ninety. I don't think that Lucius ever really loved a human being other than his limited, kind, silly, ultimately rather pompous little mother. All her remarks delighted him, and to her, of course, he was the very fountain of charm and wit. Had he not rescued her, a chained Andromeda, from the devouring serpent? Had he not become a trustee of her trust and tripled its value? Had he not made a fortune of his own? Oh, they were rich, Aunt Euphemia and Lucius, now, richer than Uncle Josiah had ever dreamed of making them, richer, in the end, than many of the Millinders who had inherited larger shares of Grandpa's fortunes. Aunt Euphemia became almost as grand as Aunt Daisy herself and held bridge tournaments at "Great Lawns" for as many as three hundred ladies. She adored people, and she adored cards, and she developed to the fullest in her old age the Millinder love of display and grandeur. I have never seen a woman so easily contented who had so much to content her. Lucius could have secured his mother's happiness for a tiny fraction of the price he paid. But it was the single tenet of his faith that he could not pay too much.

He flung off his asthma with his youth; after all, he no longer needed it. He became stout and bald and rather owl-like; he dressed elaborately, moved sedately and cultivated a superior demeanor and a high, sneering tone of voice. He had to have his own way in everything; with the exception of his kindness to Aunt Euphemia, he was totally selfish. He despised his sisters and all his cousins, except me. He had a large acquaintance, but few intimates. There was at one time, I have been told, a certain discreet procession through the house of doe-eyed young men, but Lucius never allowed any of them to gain too strong a hold on him, and when he was through with one of them, he was through for good. I have always found his advice excellent, perhaps largely because he cares so little about people. He is good company when one has resigned oneself to the absence of a heart. Since Aunt Euphemia's death I suppose he has been lonely. If he called me, I would go to him. But he has not. He sits in his perfect penthouse, surrounded by his perfect collection of French impressionists. They, too, have been good investments. He could sell them today for several times their cost.

10

IT WAS AFTER the turn of the century that Mamma's interest in objects of art began to be her main preoccupation. It has always seemed to me that I could pinpoint the moment when she crossed the borderline between shopping and collecting. It was when she purchased the large baroque Bavarian reliquary of silver gilt that gleamed with more whorls and curlicues than one would have thought possible for a metalsmith to fashion. Mamma set it up on a table in her dressing room and sat before it for minutes on end, staring at it with her peculiar, blank look. She would not even look up when I came in, and I used to wonder what strange repose she drew from its garish symmetry. But its chronological importance in the history of her hobby was that it lacked even a nominal function in the decoration of her home. The true collector is no utilitarian.

Ever since I could remember, Mamma had been a lavish shopper. It was always difficult for her to pass a window on Fifth Avenue or on the Rue de la Paix. She dug at stores with a kind of fury, as if to drag up from their very bowels the hidden beauty whose sample glittered so alluringly in the show case, and she never ceased to be mystified by the loss of gleam, the advent of shabbiness, that occurred almost simultaneously with the transfer of title and the taking of the object home.

"But it looked so much better in the shop," she would always protest, shaking her head. "I wonder why it looked so much better in the shop."

"Because it wasn't *yours*," I would point out, but she could never wholly accept this, and her refusal to accept it was the cornerstone on which she ultimately built her collection. For to turn herself from what she had been into what she became required some form of idealism, and I do not know what Mamma's could have consisted of except her passion to enshrine in permanent form the beauty that she saw in a shop window.

She had been buying art long before the acquisition of the Bavarian reliquary, but it had been ostensibly to fill the great rooms of her houses. There had been periods and periods, and as children we were quite used to the experience of discovering in the fall that the living room of the Fifth Avenue house had been changed from an austere and oppressive Louis XIV, with great canvases by Rigaud and Largillière of big-nosed, long-wigged Bourbons in armor with batons and tricky, watery Medician eyes, to an intimate, even a rather romping Louis XV, with cherubs and ladies in swings and grey panels and quantities of biscuit de Sèvres. She tired of her things rapidly, and when she tired of them, she immediately got rid of them. Storage would not do; they had to be disposed of, no matter what the loss. Yet it was more than simple restlessness; her taste changed as it developed. She had started, after all, in absolute ignorance. The Marstons, for all their vaunted old blood, had less taste even than the Millinders. But her ignorance had been happily devoid of prejudice, and it was her open-mindedness that accelerated her discovery that the Sun King was pompous and his successor cloyingly artificial. She turned to porcelains and to tapestries and, occasionally, to paintings. In the latter category, she had some arguments with Papa. It was not that he was stingy—her bills were usually paid without comment—but he was too much Grandpa's son to be able to understand how anyone could pay fifty thousand dollars to cover a few square feet of wall space, particularly when there were so many amusing pictures to be had for a song. What, indeed, about Grandpa's own collection, which Mamma now relegated to upstairs corridors and guest rooms? What was wrong with *those* pictures?

I did everything to encourage Mamma to collect, and it was I who persuaded Papa that it would be untactful to laugh at the reliquary. She desperately needed a new outlet. Although I still lived at home, I had established my independence and now taught a course in the history of art, three mornings a week at Miss Dixon's Classes. I was approaching thirty, and Mamma had given up all hope of my marrying. Willie, Cora and Bertie had all left home. Our social position had been solidified, by time and by marriages to such families as the Lydigs here and the Contis and Myols abroad. Nobody laughed at Aunt Daisy in Newport any more, or if they did, they took the trouble to hide it. There were still, I am sure, plenty of grey heads that wagged behind brownstone fronts at our ostentation and display, but it was an age of ostentation and display, and the Millinders were not much worse than many of the older families. We had, in short, "arrived," and Mamma had no further difficulty in making her dinners as select as she chose. It was, of course, for this very reason that she lost interest in them. She lacked Aunt Daisy's complacent delight in the regal existence which was to give her the same satisfaction at eighty that it had given her at thirty-five. Mamma saw life instead as a series of challenges that became boring as soon as they were met. She was fundamentally not interested in human beings, either rich or poor; she cared no more for the patients in the Eliza Millinder Nursing Home than she cared for the dinner guests whose acquaintance only a few years back she had so assiduously cultivated. She looked about grumpily at her tinseled life as though to say: "Is *this* all I get for having married a Millinder?"

It was a pity that Papa was no more comfort to her than she to him, but that was the way of their marriage. According to the oddly reversed double standard of Mamma's philosophy, a gentleman owed a lady, or at least Papa owed her, a lifetime of devotion in return for her hand. A hand was all he got, too, and what sometimes seemed more like the back of it. Mamma would have regarded the idea that she had a duty to remain soft and feminine to please her husband as not only immoral but actually disgusting. It was small wonder that from almost the beginning he had sought consolation with others. Papa, too, was bored with society, but he had been bored from the beginning. He had made one brief excursion in politics and been defeated in his effort to obtain the Republican nomination for lieutenant governor of New York. Since then he had been inclined to find a salve for his bitterness in rather bizarre theories of history, usually with anti-Semitic or anti-Catholic undertones. Yet he was fundamentally a kind man with no prejudices against individuals. He spent a great deal of time on expeditions for marine specimens, but at the period I am now describing these had given way to a new and absorbing interest in an actress called Cecilia Dart. At least she had started as an actress. In those days one could, on looks alone. Cecilia Amory was one of those cold marble beauties of a type then popular who without a shred of histrionic talent had made a great if brief success in sentimental comedies where she played such roles as that of the tweeny who captures the heart of Lord Alistair and turns out to be an heiress in the third act. Nobody ever knew quite where she came from, but she had a dear

old chattering Kentucky aunt who needlessly supplemented the chaperon-
ing function of her niece's frosty nature. Poor old Mr. Winny Dart, the
clubman and bachelor, who had been a feature of stage doors for forty years,
found himself caught, chastened, taken off liquor and tobacco, brushed,
dusted, and led to the altar with a flower in his buttonhole while the press
carried moving stories of how Miss Amory was giving up the stage for love.
It was too much for Winny, and in six months' time the same firm, fair
hand that had published the banns offered for probate a last will and testament that bequeathed to the testator's widow the remnants of a life of spending. But it was enough to enable Cecilia to set herself up in a charming
little house on Washington Square, isolating the aunt in an upper story, and
to receive a judicious mixture of the more respectable members of the theater world and the less respectable members of the Racquet and Tennis Club.
If one group hoped to enter society and the other to find Bohemia, both
were satisfied by Cecilia's ingenuity, and in time her salon developed the
enviable reputation of being at once "daring" and safe. It was this that
attracted my brother Willie's wife, Julia, who made a great deal of her boredom with "stuffy people," and she and Cecilia became inseparable friends,
which was, of course, how Papa met Mrs. Dart. In a scant month the amiable philanderer of sixty was as moody as a lovesick schoolboy. I will add,
in justice to Julia, that it could not have been predicted. Papa was already
well past what was then considered the "dangerous" age.

When Julia asked me to spend a weekend with her and Willie during that
spring, it never occurred to me that Mrs. Dart would be there. I did not
know how fast things had gone. Julia herself, as I found out later, had lost
the battle before she had even begun to fight. When she and Willie had
finally awakened to their friend's designs, it had been too late to oppose
them without alienating Papa.

"Come for the weekend," Julia had said casually. "Your father says he
never sees you, even living under the same roof. I know you don't hunt,
but Willie will fix you up with a quiet mare, and you and Mr. Millinder can
go off for a trot."

The improved social position of the family was exemplified by Willie's and
Julia's house. They laughed at Newport as an English hunting squire might
laugh at Brighton and had purchased five thousand acres in Bernardsville,
New Jersey, where they had built a great sprawling structure of red brick
and shingle, with high gables and here and there a turret as a concession to
decoration, with two dozen bedrooms for winter and fall weekend parties
and a main floor of dark, comfortable leathery rooms in which one made
out the spread of antlers and the gleam of ivory tusks in the flickering light
of large fires. It was a masculine house and a masculine place; from its great
stable to its nine-hole golf course it was dedicated to the propulsion of balls
and the slaughter of animals. Julia, so tall and thin and angular, with her
twitching shoulders and her constant smoking, her high cheekbones and
red hair, her general air of high intelligence and impatience, might have
seemed at first blush rather out of place in an establishment seemingly
designed for her lazy, handsome husband with his dogs and his guns. But

this was only at first blush. It was actually Julia who was the better eques-
trian, as it was Julia who returned in the early morning with the larger bag
of ducks. For if Julia had a brain that could encompass literature and the
other arts, the act of encompassment seemed more with her an exercise than
a pleasure. She was always taking your measure and matching you, whatever your field; she seemed to be saying: "Dante? You read him in *English*?"
or "Newport? You still go *there*?"—as if literature and society were mere
semi-precious stones of equal value which she had discarded in favor of the
true article of sport. But, however discarded, they were still hers. She was
like a hawk of brilliant plumage, but like a hawk she had a hard beak
and claws—but no, I am going too far. I am seeing her as I see her today
when we are no longer friends. You must think of her as in the painting
by John Sloane in the Museum of Modern Art where you can almost hear
the zestful harshness of her laugh and the jangle of her bracelets. Willie was
not to remain faithful to her, nor she to him, but it was not he who started
that chapter. Julia, for all her near ugliness, was always exciting to men,
and even Mamma, who used to maintain that Willie had married a piece
of Tiffany glass, had to admit that one could not expect to keep her on a
shelf.

Everybody was nice to me when I arrived in Bernardsville that Friday
afternoon, suspiciously nice. But nobody is more easily disarmed than one
who has expected to be snubbed, and after Willie had taken me to his ken-
nels, and Papa had asked me to ride with him the next day, I felt warm and
happy all over. Papa was even giving up the hunt for me! Later, when Julia
and I were having tea alone by the fire and discussing the guests who were
coming, I felt almost at home.

"Is everyone coming tonight?" I asked.

"Everyone but Cecilia. She's coming down in the morning."

"Cecilia?"

Julia looked at me calmly. "Cecilia Dart."

My new sense of belonging went out as fast as it had stolen in, and in my
embarrassment I did the only thing that could have made matters worse. I
snickered.

"Why do you laugh?" Julia demanded.

"Because I'm surprised to hear what you just said."

"Why should you be surprised?"

"Well, don't we all know what—well, what she was?"

"Was?" Julia's cool monosyllable seemed to imply that who, after all, were
the Millinders that one of them should use the past tense to a Lydig. "I
don't think who one *was* is of much importance these days."

I had too many points of obvious inferiority to Julia to be able to give in,
even on a small matter. "I didn't say 'who,'" I insisted. "I said 'what.'"

"You object to her having been an actress?"

"Not an actress, no."

"Well, I don't pretend to know what you're driving at," Julia said airily.
"All I know is that Cecilia Dart is one of my very good friends. Surely, Gussie,
I can depend on you to be civil to her. For one weekend?"

"I shall certainly be civil. But, to be quite frank with you, I wonder if it would be loyal to Mamma to be anything more."

"Ah, well, so long as you bring it up." Julia plucked the cigarette out of her long red holder and flung it in the blazing fire. "Should we talk about that for a bit, do you think?"

"That?" I asked, startled.

"Well, your mother and father. Or, to be more exact, the question of your loyalty to them. Or, to be absolutely precise, the question of whether or not there's even a question of loyalty. Of course, if you put it all on religious grounds, if you believe that marriage is a holy sacrament, then I suppose that's that. It doesn't matter how incompatible the couple, they must stick together, and there's the end of it. But you're a highly educated and intelligent woman, Gussie, and I didn't think you'd be so arbitrary."

"I don't disapprove of divorce under all circumstances, if that's what you mean," I said guardedly. "*I* wouldn't chain two people together who have no reason for staying together. But if you're talking about Mamma and Papa, I had no idea there was any question of divorce!"

"My dear Gussie, it's precisely the question that concerns us!"

"Mamma doesn't know it, then!" I exclaimed, getting up. "And certainly I don't!"

"Of course you don't," Julia said calmly. "Since you're the one who will tell her. *If* she's ever to be told."

"I!"

"Please sit down, Gussie, and hear me out. If your father ever needed his children, it's right now. I know I'm only an in-law, but maybe that's the very reason he's confided in me. Maybe he's too embarrassed to tell his own children. Will you hear me?"

Slowly and reluctantly I sat down. My mind was already a jumping flame of suspicion. Why was Julia so proprietary about Papa? She had always made as great a fuss over him as she had made a small one over Mamma. Did she hope that he would leave his money unequally, as Grandpa had, and favor Willie? "I will hear you, Julia," I said sullenly.

"Your mother and father have been married for thirty-four years," she began in her sharp, emphatic tone, "and their four children are fully grown and fully able to take care of themselves. Would you admit that they have no obligation to preserve their marriage for your sake? Or for Willie's or Cora's or Bertie's?"

"For ours, perhaps not. But for each other's?"

"Well, certainly not for your father's. I know what *he* wants. That leaves your mother. Can you honestly say that it makes so much difference to her whether he's home or away?"

"But there's more to a marriage than that!" I protested. "There's more than just missing a person or not missing a person. There's a whole shared life and children and grandchildren and—well, all sorts of things!" I was beginning to feel a tiny bit hysterical. I wanted to shout at Julia that of course my parents had a duty to remain married for my sake! And then, as I realized that Julia would only laugh at me, that I was too old to expect that anyone owed any duty to preserve *my* illusions or protect *my* faiths, I felt suddenly lonely and abandoned. But who was Julia to take those things from me? "Marriage isn't something one breaks for—a whim!" I cried.

"Not for a whim, I concede," Julia said quickly. She must have sensed that she had gone too far, for she quickly altered her strategy. "And I concede, also, that marriage is something more than missing or not missing a person. What I want to find out is whether that something more in your mother's case is enough to warrant your father's giving up the one hope of happiness that remains in his life."

I stared. "You mean Mrs. Dart is *that?*"

Julia was almost solemn now. "I mean Mrs. Dart is just *that.*"

I do not know what I might have said had Willie not come into the room. He looked embarrassed and shy, and I wondered afterwards if it had been arranged between them that he should hover outside and enter at a given cue. But if Julia had a hidden motive for plotting, I am sure he had none, other than a good-natured desire for his father's happiness. Willie might have been lazy and selfish, but he was not a schemer, and he was devoid of malice. He stood before me now, a younger image of Papa except for his thick curly brown hair, trying with a radiant smile to conceal his uneasiness at what his bright, determined wife was up to. As the oldest he had always had the least to do with me, but now my heart rushed out to him.

"Willie, you don't think Papa should marry this woman, do you? You don't think he should divorce Mamma?"

"Not if you don't think so, Gussie. Not if you think it's going to hurt her."

"But of course it's going to hurt her!"

"Then that's that." He turned to Julia who bowed, as if in reluctant agreement. "The old boy will have to contain himself. We said we'd be ruled by Gussie, and we will be."

I was overwhelmed by such deference, as I see now I was meant to be. "But can't he and Mrs. Dart—?" I hesitated. "Can't they—go on being good friends? I don't think Mamma minds *that* so much."

"Despite what you and your mother take for granted," Julia said with dignity, "Cecilia is not the kind of woman who consents to be 'good friends.'"

I wanted to ask when she had graduated from *that* stage, but I had not quite the boldness. Besides, I was troubled. It was charming to have my oldest brother, always so removed by a superior and dazzling masculinity, turn now to me, almost humbly, to ask for my decision. Nor was I unaware that a refusal on my part to treat with Julia would slam closed the door so temptingly ajar.

"Of course, I suppose I could sound Mamma out," I said doubtfully. "I could feel my way as to how much she does care."

"But that's all we even suggest!" Julia exclaimed.

"Exactly," Willie agreed eagerly. "If you could just broach the subject gently to her. If you could make it seem funny, even pathetic, so she wouldn't get her dander up. And then if you could sort of ease her into speculating on what her settlement would be—just on the hypothesis, you see, of a divorce. Well, once she'd gotten used to the idea, I wonder how much she'd really mind."

"Terribly!" The one thing I would not permit from either of them was the least minimization of what Mamma and myself would have to go through. If the drama were pitched to the highest note, it somehow made my disloyalty seem less shabby. "She'll mind terribly! She might in the end give way, but don't think for a moment it's going to be easy. You should know Mamma better than that, Willie!"

"I think I know Mamma and love her as well as anyone," Willie replied, flushing slightly. "I don't want to see Mamma cast off like an old shoe any more than you do. But if she and Papa separated quietly and with dignity, if she was free to travel all over the world and buy all the art she wants—"

"Willie!" his wife warned him. She at least had the sensitivity to feel how offensive to me would be any idea that Mamma could be "bought off." "It is purely a question of your mother's realism and magnanimity. And then, too, you must remember that in her generation divorce is almost unknown. That is why Gussie is the only possible person to approach her. Gussie understands her mother and the whole point of view of that generation as nobody else does. And she's at the same time a modern woman with a college education and a responsible job. If Gussie can't put the matter up to your mother without exciting her beyond the hope of compromise, depend upon it, nobody can."

Well, of course, it *was* a bit thick. I knew that Julia was flattering me, but flattery was very sweet. As I stood up to go to my room and consider the whole thing, I contemplated the appealing eyes of my magnificent brother and sister-in-law and felt, half with shame, my bosom begin to fill with something like pride. When I turned to the door I wondered if this was the way Mamma herself always felt, if *this* was what it was to hold the attention of others!

Of course they saw their advantage and worked on me that night, as did Papa himself. Everyone at dinner asked me questions about Miss Dixon's Classes, and I talked a great deal and drank three glasses of champagne. There was a good deal of hilarity at my stories, and I went to bed feeling that I had made a great hit. And when, the next morning, Papa and I took off on a ride through the early spring misty woods, I felt in my exhilaration that there was nothing I would not do for him.

He was still the handsomest man I knew, handsomer even than Willie. The steely grey curly hair, the long firm nose and high clear brow, the arched bushy eyebrows, the broad shoulders and trim figure, all blended into a perfect mixture of the easy sportsman and the intelligent, responsive companion. When he reached over to adjust my reins, when he gently admonished me to sit forward, when he smiled at my protests of incapacity, he might have been the most charming instructor in the world and I a young thing whose giddy love for him he was too kind not to ignore. I began to wonder if Mrs. Dart had to be either cold or calculating. Maybe she was simply in love. Maybe Papa's charm could bridge the thirty-year gap in their ages. Did it not with me?

"I know I've never paid you the attention I should have, Gussie," he said after a half hour of riding, shifting into intimacy as easily as if he and I had been accustomed to such talks. "For that matter I've never paid the proper attention to any of my children, except possibly Willie, because he and I like the same sports. But it doesn't mean that I don't care or that I haven't watched you. I think it's splendid the way you've taken up teaching in the face of your mother's opposition. I admire you for it more than I can say. If I'd stood up to your mother a little more myself, we might all have had a better home life. But there you are, it's water under the bridge."

"Oh, Papa!" I exclaimed. "*I* think you've been a good father!"

"You're a darling to say it, but you must allow me to disagree. I have *not* been a good father, any more than I've been a successful man. But at least I have the honesty not to blame the first on your mother or the second on my money. On the contrary, they have each supplied me with what little discipline I possess."

"You mustn't say you're not successful!" I protested eagerly. "Think of all those fish specimens you've brought back from the Pacific! Think of the expeditions you've paid for!"

"Well, maybe I have my tiny niche in the marine hall of fame," he assented, more, I was sure, to relieve me than from any conviction. "But be that as it may, I want you to have yours."

"Mine?"

"Well, wouldn't you like to run your own school? I should be delighted to start one for you. Would you let me?"

"Oh, Papa!" Joy and disappointment pounded on me together, like two ravening buzzards. "Is that a bribe?"

He smiled. "A bribe? A bribe for what?"

"To be your ambassador to Mamma!"

It was wonderful how easily he took it. He simply threw back his head and laughed. "Of course it is! But it's a funny kind of bribe. You get the school even if you refuse!"

The tears jumped to my eyes. "Mrs. Dart means that much to you?"

"You've heard the old adage, Gussie. There's no fool like an old fool!"

When I turned, I saw that his face was suddenly serious, and I felt a prick of jealousy. "But, Papa, how do you know she's not after—that she's not just after—?"

"The money?" he finished for me. "My dear Gussie, when you reach my age you're very careful not to inquire what they're after. When I was young and beautiful," he continued, once more in his old bantering tone but now with a tinge of bitterness, "I had the world at my feet. But do you think—for one single, solitary second—that your mother would have married me had I carried my fortune in my *beaux yeux?*"

I turned away and reluctantly shook my head. The picture in my mind of Papa actually needing a woman was far more painful than any suspicion of the woman's motives. Indeed, it seemed to me that my whole pleasure in the morning was suddenly gone. But I was committed too far to go back now.

"I will do my best for you, Papa," I said abruptly, and prodding my horse sharply, I cantered on ahead.

I wondered as I came downstairs that noon, where the hunt breakfast was assembling, how Mrs. Dart would conduct herself in a world of sport where I imagined that she would be at a disadvantage. But it was quite easy. She simply refused to recognize the existence of any such world, never referred to it, and on weekends always managed to arrive after the main sporting event. She was in the living room ahead of me, in radiant blue, and I was mortified to see that she had caught me looking for her, for she was already smiling at me when my gaze fell upon hers. It could only have been she. She had the good looks of an actress, very blond, very pale, a heart-shaped face and large, rather staring eyes. I later made out that they were grey. But what did not seem like an actress was the total want of animation, not only in her features and skin, but in the listless mechanism of her movements. When she smiled, it was without warmth, certainly without humor, and when she reached out her hand, on Julia's introduction, she allowed it to remain inertly in mine until I let go. Yet it was evident even on a first meeting that this seeming limpness did not spring from any ailment or from any natural deficiency. On the contrary, one could see by the breadth of her peerless shoulders, by the contour of her breasts and figure that she was a specimen of remarkable health. What was shocking to another woman was to find her so cold. Men think they perceive this, but they don't, at least American men. What I knew that night about Cecilia Dart was that she had been given every grace but that of enjoying her graces. She might have been a disembodied intelligence, for all the identification that she seemed to have with her beauty. She would use it—ah, yes! She would use it as she had always used it, as a clever beggar might don a ragged dress before ringing at the great door of wealth. But she knew that it was *all* she needed to use; charm and warmth and love were so many spangles to be scattered, if one had time, on one's attire. Her fine intelligence, even, she could keep, as she has always kept it, for herself. I can never think of her without thinking of the idiocy of men!

She stood by me now with her back to the fire. She would not look at me again, for she could not have it thought that she distinguished me in any way. She inclined her head closer to mine, but her eyes were directed across the room.

"I hear it's all arranged," she said. Her matter-of-fact tone, tinged with the faintest note of amusement, might have been dealing with the organization of sports for the afternoon.

"What is arranged?"

Her eyebrows rose the least bit. "Why, I hear you're going to 'square' Mamma."

For several moments I was incapable of answering. My throat was constricted with sudden fury. I do not know which was the more irritating, her casual, familiar reference to my mother as "Mamma," or the vulgarity of her conception of my "squaring" her, or her basic attitude, carelessly unconcealed, that my own role in the scheme of things was a minor, albeit useful assistance that could be easily dispensed with if I chose to see it in any other light. Mrs. Dart had too much faith in the lethal power of her own beauty to admit that custom, law or even the opposition of an outraged spouse were more than matchsticks to oppose its onward and ultimately triumphant progress. She was afraid of nothing in the world but of having to offer the least demonstration of gratitude.

"I don't think it fitting for you and me to discuss my mother," I was finally able to whisper.

"But I couldn't agree with you more!" she exclaimed with a brilliant smile. "Your mother is the last person in the world I would care to discuss. We leave her, my dear, entirely to you!"

Her "we" swept away the last dike of my discretion. "I'm glad I've met you!" I exclaimed in the same passionate whisper. "I had no idea what my function was really to be. But now I think you've taught me!"

"*I* have?" She faced me with a bland, quizzical stare. "And what, in the name of mercy, have *I* taught you?"

"That my real job, my only job, is to save Papa! From the likes of you!"

There was not even a flicker of shock across that pale face. She continued to stare at me as if I were an unpredictable, emotional child whose parents, from mistaken motives of family pride, had allowed to put in a painful but presumably brief appearance in the drawing room.

"My dear Julia," she said as the latter came up, "your sister-in-law is too extraordinary!"

I promptly left the room and went upstairs. Julia was close behind me, but I would not turn and give her ear until I had reached the threshold. Then I anticipated what she was going to say.

"I'm going back to town!" I cried, breathless after my rapid climb. "Would you be good enough to have someone send for my maid and look up the trains? I'm sorry to do this to your houseparty, Julia, but I can't spend another hour under the same roof with that woman!"

Julia, in her desperation, tried a high, amused smile.

"Surely, Gussie, you're not a woman to make mountains out of mole-hills!"

"Aren't I?"

"But, my dear girl, think of your father. Think of the pain you'll cause him!"

"Think of what he's doing to Mamma!"

Julia's smile disappeared immediately, and her stare became grave. "Think of the scandal," she said harshly. "Everyone at this party will know just why you've gone!"

"Let them!" I retorted defiantly. "*You're* the one who will have caused the scandal by having a woman like that in your house! And by encouraging her to make a fool of Papa! What sort of behavior is that for a daughter-in-law? You and Willie should be ashamed of yourselves!"

Julia looked at me for a long moment with an expression that I can only describe as hate. Then she turned away. "I'll tell them to send your maid" was all she said as her tall figure retreated down the stairway.

When I got back home late that afternoon I found that Mamma had gone up to Troy to see a tapestry in the collection of an ironmonger who had recently died. I had to wait in wretched impatience until she arrived late that night. When I went to her room I knew by the gleam of possession in her eye that the tapestry was hers.

"What on earth brings you back from the country?" she asked good-humoredly and started to brush her hair.

"Gervaise," I said to her maid, "could you leave us for a moment?"

Mamma stared as the girl left. "My dear Gussie, you look positively green. Are you engaged to be married?"

"Papa was at Willie's," I said in a half whisper. "With Mrs. Dart."

Mamma flung down her brush at once and turned to me angrily. "You mean Julia asked them? *Together?*"

Her breath came in little gasps as I related the story of my interviews with Julia and Papa and of my abrupt departure. But when I had finished and was waiting for her wrathful denunciations to fill the room, she said nothing for several moments. When she did speak, her tone was cold and controlled.

"Why are you telling me this?"

"But shouldn't I?" I cried. "Don't you want to know?" It seemed in my sudden agony as if all the world had deserted me. "Aren't you my mother?"

"There's no law that says you have to take your mother's side."

"Oh, Mamma!" I sank down on the end of the chaise longue and started to sob helplessly. "Oh, Mamma!" I repeated aimlessly and covered my burning face with my hands.

"Thank you, child," she said at last in an odd rough tone. Then I heard her get up and felt her hand on my head. I seized it and kissed it passionately. "You will find that I'll never forget what you've done." Her voice was solemn. "Never in my life!"

I was excited that night, much too excited to sleep. If it was distressing, it was still exhilarating that the parent who had never needed anything from her youngest child should now find herself deserted by everyone else. For Cora was away in France, and Bertie never cared about anything, and Willie and Julia were the rankest traitors. Would not Mamma turn, the formerly self-sufficient, to clasp hands gratefully with the loyal child whose despised qualities of sentiment she would now learn to value? And oh, how willingly would that child forgive! How happily would she raise her standard with that of her wronged parent and carry war into the very heart of the enemy's country until that complacent smile had been rubbed off the pale face of Cecilia Dart, until Papa, poor, unhappy, foolish Papa, had been saved and Julia reprimanded! Until life had been restored once more to its ancient dignity, with the jackals of lasciviousness left to howl outside bolted doors!

When I awoke, however, the next morning, I found that the guns of Mamma's opening broadside had started booming without me. It was the old, old difference between reality and my dreams. She might have needed a spy, but I had been vain indeed to think she needed an ally! She would always do her work alone, and she was right, too, for allies would always object to her methods. I was appalled, for example, to find that all Papa's clothes had been packed in trunks and were already stacked in a row on the sidewalk outside our front door! Happily I was able to get hold of Bertie and have them removed to Papa's club before any roving journalists had been called to the scene.

I was unable to see Mamma until lunch time for she was closeted with Mr. Ezra Font. Mr. Font was a notoriously successful lawyer in matrimonial matters, but he was hardly the kind of advocate that members of our family were supposed to consult. All the Millinders went to Julia's father, Judge Lydig. But undoubtedly both his clients and his daughter had disqualified him in Mamma's eyes. When she finally sent for me in the early afternoon it was to announce that she proposed to sue Papa for a separation, naming Mrs. Dart as co-respondent. The publicity of such an action was calculated to chasten him without at the same time freeing him to marry his "mistress." In the meantime Mamma and I were to call on Aunt Daisy and demand that Papa's family form a united front behind their injured sister-in-law.

"Of course, she'll be glad enough to see your father and me separated," Mamma said with a sniff as we drove up the avenue to the great pink stucco copy of Chambord that Aunt Daisy and Uncle Fred had built after selling their wing of Grandpa's brownstone. "It'll give her the excuse she's always wanted to call herself plain 'Mrs. Millinder.' Do you know she had the gall to tell me once she was really entitled to because Uncle Fred got the bigger share of the estate?"

But if Aunt Daisy welcomed dissention in the Cyrus Millinders' household, she was too wise to show it. She had always been too wise to betray the least sign of gratification; she knew that life brought its richest reward to those women who simply waited and accepted. Effort or gratitude would equally imply doubt as to one's proper due. She sat now in the red and gold parlor that seemed as pointlessly large as an opera set and shook her head slowly as Mamma outlined her wrongs and their proposed satisfaction. Aunt Daisy's gesture seemed to imply an equal reproach to both spouses.

"Should you tell me such things in front of Augusta?" was all she asked when Mamma had finished.

"Augusta was exposed to it by her own father and brother!" Mamma exclaimed.

"Even so, even so." Aunt Daisy's disgust seemed now to reach out to embrace me as well. "That a young girl should hear such things!"

"Augusta is twenty-eight, thank you!"

"But unmarried, Eliza. She's still unmarried!"

"Really, Daisy, you have a genius for the irrelevant. I won't be sidetracked. Are you and Fred going to stand behind me or are you not?"

"We never take sides."

"Sides? It isn't as if there were any sides. Who could be on the side of adultery?"

"Eliza, I must ask you, in my own house, to remember that an unmarried girl is present!"

"What will you do, then, to save her from a stepmother like Cecilia Dart?"

"I've told you, Eliza. My husband and I never take sides."

Mamma contemplated her for an exasperated moment and then saw it was hopeless. She rose. "You repeat that as if it were a moral principle of which you should be proud," she said scornfully. "When it's only a blind for your own laziness. Everything in the world you do or don't do has to be a moral triumph. When will you learn that people care nothing for your morals, Daisy? When will you learn that all they care about is your money?"

She marched out of the room, and I stumbled after her, too embarrassed to take leave of Aunt Daisy who was simply shaking her head again. I do not believe that she and Mamma ever spoke to each other again, although Aunt Daisy, in her extreme old age, with the forgiving spirit of a survivor, used to speak nostalgically of those early long ago days when two young sisters-in-law had, hand in hand, approached the joint adventure of Newport.

Papa, fortunately for the reputation of the family, showed none of Aunt Daisy's stiffness. If he had legal remedies against eviction from his own house, he did not use them. He simply moved to his club and ceased all communication with Mamma and myself. Judge Lydig wrote Mamma and asked her to come to his office to discuss the situation, but Mamma referred him contemptuously to Mr. Font whom he, with equal contempt, refused to see. And so matters might have remained until Mr. Font had filed his fatal petition in court had not Willie and Bertie both called on me and solemnly represented that it was my duty to persuade Mamma at least to listen to Judge Lydig. When I had gone to her room and made my plea, she looked at me fixedly.

"Very well, Gussie," she said, "I'll do it for you. But I shall consider that I have paid off a portion of my debt. Will he come to me?"

"I shall write him."

But no, he would not even do that. Judge Lydig had never gone to a client in his life, not even to Grandpa. Mamma was made to feel that her request had been an impertinence, and the first round went to him in the exchange of letters and in our subsequent appearance in the big dark varnished office on top of the Flatiron Building, decorated with the likenesses of America's great businessmen, bearded and dry, in rumpled suits, with legs crossed and dusty boots, giving out the dry, hard sense of a western plain. On the wide bare surface of the judge's desk I made out a photograph of him as a young man standing on the platform of a railway car with Grandpa and several other men in derbies. That the room should be so devoid of accessories, without any of the hurrying clerks or clacketing typewriters of the usual lawyer's office, served to emphasize that Judge Lydig dealt in one commodity and one alone: his own formidable intelligence. One felt sure that all the law in the world had been stored away in rich reserves behind that high, clear brow and the still grey eyes that took one in so blankly yet so comprehensively. One even felt that law somehow circulated through the whole small wiry black-suited body down to the thin ankle, resting on the knee, that was constantly slapped by a ruler. Anthon Lydig practiced law as he had done everything else in life, exactly as he had wanted to. He had collected "tycoons," as deliberately as Mamma collected snuff-boxes; they were the men who intrigued him; and it was in their problems that he was surpassingly expert. Their companies he left to the corporation law firms; he was content to be "personal counsel" to a handful of big men and to direct the consolidation and expenditure of their fortunes and ultimately, as executor and trustee, to administer their estates. It was a surprise to nobody, when he died, that he left a fortune himself. The Millinder family had been his greatest single "catch," and I have often wondered if he had not molded and patted us, shaped us to his fancy, to bring us up as an ideal "tycoon's family," to water our family tree until his long white fingers could ultimately pluck, from the highest branch, our Willie as the perfect mate for his Julia.

"I think I should tell you straight off, Anthon," Mamma began, "that my lawyer thinks it most unethical of you to see me without seeing him."

Lydig twitched around in his chair to give her a sharp glance and then banged his ankle again with the ruler. "I wouldn't have that shyster in my office!"

"I very much doubt if he'd come," Mamma retorted.

"But he let you come, didn't he?" Lydig thrust at her suddenly. "He didn't threaten to drop the case, did he?"

"He said that I might as well find out what you had to propose," Mamma said with dignity. "That is why I have brought Augusta. To be sure that there is no misunderstanding."

"Gussie's a better lawyer than Font any day in the week," the judge said gruffly, giving me a little wink. "I think Gussie and I will understand each other perfectly. But to save Mr. Font's feelings—and, of course, the more unprincipled the shyster, the more delicate the feelings—let me state at the outset that I have not asked you here as a lawyer, nor am I charging anybody a fee. I have been a friend of the Millinder family for forty years. My daughter is a member of that family. I have asked you to see me, Eliza, in my capacity as family adviser. There is no place in our meeting for such a man as Font."

"Very well." Mamma gave him a grim little nod. "You're probably right. Mr. Font's time will come later. In the courtroom."

"That's just where you're wrong, Eliza!" This time the judge emphasized his words by striking the table a sharp blow with his ruler. "Mr. Font's time will never come! I do not propose to allow you to destroy the reputation of the Millinders to satisfy your pique and his greed!"

"And how, I should like to know, do you propose to stop me?"

"Very easily. By giving you five times the biggest settlement that Font could ever dream of!"

I glanced quickly at Mamma and saw her pale stare. "Do you think you can bribe me, Anthon?" she asked coldly.

"Of course I can bribe you!" he retorted. "I regard you as one of the most intelligent women of my acquaintance. Only fools can't be bribed. How would you like to reserve your judgment until you've heard what I have to say?"

Mamma continued to fix him with that stare. "Go on."

"I'm sorry to say all this in front of Gussie, but I guess she's old enough." Judge Lydig threw his ruler suddenly on the desk and leaned back in his chair, resting his chin on his clasped hands. He seemed to shrivel up in this posture to a small round bug of attention. "Let's not try to pretend, Eliza, that you and Cyrus are necessary to each other. In the past five years you have certainly not spent more than a third of your nights under the same roof. Cyrus, I grant you, is an old fool to want to marry this woman. But I'm convinced that nothing will cure him. He's like a man possessed. He's going to get his divorce, even if he has to go and live in the Fiji Islands. Would you like to know what I told him?"

"Go on," Mamma repeated.

"I told him that he owed it to you to see that a divorce should not in any way affect your scale of living. I pointed out that it would cost him nothing to give you a third of his fortune. He could hardly spend the income of what's left, and as you both have the same heirs, the ultimate division would be the same. He said you might spend it all on art, and I said fine! With your eye, I told him, it's the best investment you could make!"

I could see that Mamma was plainly taken aback. She was trying to look grim and unaffected, but there was a twitch in one of her eyebrows. She was evidently thinking of her collection. She could never build a great one with Papa looking over her shoulder. The Millinders were lavish, but it was the lavishness of display. In their private corners they could be as saving as French peasants.

"A third," Mamma murmured in a bemused tone. "How much would be a third?"

When he told her, she must have had a vision of the future and those rooms of gleaming treasure, for she closed her eyes, and I heard her long sigh.

"And, of course, the houses would be yours," the judge continued, "both here and in Newport, and all their contents." He picked up a paper and read through a list of other commitments in a dry, droning, legal tone. It must have amused him to know in advance that Mamma would have to accede to so princely a bribe. She had always so gloated over the downfall of others who had shown "hubris" towards the power of gold. Now it was her turn. But the decision, if inevitable, was not an easy one. Mamma was like an Italian nobleman who has been forced to give up the family castle, which he could just afford to run, because of an American offer absurdly disproportionate to its true value. He would sign the deed, yes, and vacate the premises, but he would do so with anger in his heart at the extravagance of the fool who was evicting him.

"I will discuss it with Mr. Font," she said.

But the judge was inexorable. She was not even to be allowed this last shred to hide her defeat. "Don't be a fool, Eliza!" he warned her brusquely. "If you tell Font, he'll claim he made the deal and charge you the biggest fee in legal history. Tell him the matter is to be privately negotiated and to send his bill *now*."

"I will consider it," she said, rising.

The judge rose with her. "Don't consider it too long, Eliza! You're staring the greatest gift horse in the mouth that any woman ever stared!"

Mamma and I had no conversation in the carriage going uptown. She simply gazed out the window, and I respected her need for silence. Either consolation or congratulation would have been equally insulting. And what need was there for advice when I knew her Rubicon had already been crossed? Mamma and I, it appeared, were not to be allies, nor to have our clean and heady victory over vice. Mamma could return to the old self-sufficiency that she had indeed never abandoned, and Cecilia Dart could have Papa. And I? What kind of fool was I to have expected anything else? I had simply lived to see the family money triumph once again.

The process of being "bought off" was swift. There were no tax problems in those days to encumber the transfer of great blocks of stock. A fortune could be deeded over in the twinkling of an eye, and Paris was as good as Reno for divorces. It was agreed that Mamma would go there to bring her suit, and I, of course, would be her companion. Prior to our departure she made a round of visits to the family and friends in a last effort to close as many doors as possible to her successor. But the terms of her settlement were already known, and it was generally felt that she was trying to keep the cake which she had eaten. Papa was paying a monstrous price for his Cecilia, and even the morally minded among his contemporaries believed, deep down, that a man should get *something* for that kind of money.

11

WHEN I THINK back on the decade that followed my decision to give up teaching and help Mamma with her collecting, it seems that it should have been the happiest and most exciting period of my life. But although it had its great moments, as when we arrived in Cyprus ahead of Mr. Morgan's agent to capture the recently unearthed gold plates of the Emperor John Commenus or when we found the twin to Mamma's great Meissen swan in a pawnshop in Trieste, and although we traveled all through Europe and to the Orient, there was never a time when I was a real partner in the project. It was not simply that the collection was paid for by Mamma and ultimately disposed of by her will. It was more that the entire philosophy that went into its assembling was hers. It was always this way with Mamma. If she could not have her own way in anything, she would give it up. It was impossible for her to work except as a boss. She made full use of my knowledge and research, it is true, and had I left her, it would have taken two persons to replace me, an art expert and a secretary, but it was nonetheless always clear to me that two such persons *could* have been obtained. There were only two things that were indispensable to Mamma, her vision and her money, and as time went by she became even more remote from other humans. She lived only for this new and final passion.

Why then did I stay? Why did I give up for Mamma's hobby even so much of a teacher's career as I had? For a long time I tried to think it was because she had developed heart trouble and that none of the rest of the family seemed to care. I insisted to myself that I was no mere weak virgin daughter, transformed into a body servant by a stronger will. Had I not fought for my own education and my job at Miss Dixon's Classes? If I had chosen to throw in my lot with Mamma after all that, if the liberated child had turned back to sew up the severed umbilical cord, my defense had to be that the choice was a free one, made with full knowledge of the facts. But as time went on and Mamma's heart continued as strong as the continued indifference of her next-of-kin, I began to have misgivings as to whether such insistence on my unviolated will had not taken on the shrillness of a whistle in the dark. Had not my life become a vacuum which Mamma, like nature, had simply filled? The hardest thing for me to bear to this day is the suspicion that Mamma never even knew of my resentment. It is often said that to a mother her offspring are always children. But in our case it was Mamma who saw my age most clearly, and I who basically wanted to throw off the years when I was with her. I suppose it was my final effort to attract her attention. Of course it is by now obvious to my reader, as it was obvious to my friends, that I was utterly dominated by Mamma. The reason it has taken me so many years to recognize this is that I had always assumed that in such cases it was the parent who sought to dominate the child. We did not know in those days of the yearning to be dominated.

Mamma wasted no time in getting to work on her collection. She and I spent the winter in a hotel in Paris where she obtained her divorce, and in three months she must have visited every antiquaire in the city. Antoine de Conti politely offered to escort her on her first expeditions, but his idea of collecting was to spend a morning at Wildenstein's, sitting back on a sofa in a private room sipping sherry, while a single Watteau or Lancret was exhibited for his delectation. Mamma found him as overrefined as he found her indiscriminate, and they soon abandoned the idea of shopping in company. In any event, Antoine could have never kept up with her. She moved about the city at a furious pace and bought far too much. It was inevitable. Granted Mamma's enthusiasm, her basic ignorance and the sudden possession of unlimited funds, she was bound at first to overdo it. She overdid it, in fact, for the first two years.

"Yes, yes, I know," she would murmur impatiently when I remonstrated, "but I've got to get my eye in. When I get my eye in, I'll be all right. And don't forget, Gussie, these things aren't paintings that lose their value when the public taste changes. They'll always be worth something."

This idea, I confess, had a good deal of truth in it. Mamma ultimately disposed of most of her purchases of those early years at a profit, and had she waited longer her profit would have been greater. The market for the decorative arts has always been smaller but steadier than the market for paintings, and the things that Mamma bought did not go out of fashion. She concentrated mostly on perfection of workmanship and of condition; she was not in the least interested in acquiring anything because it was by a particular master or because it had once been beautiful before it had been unhappily chipped. The object had to speak for itself, without the least introduction or explanation; it had to strike a twentieth century eye, beholding it isolated on its pedestal, as inherently beautiful without regard to its function or place of origin. When we returned to New York it was to fill the rooms with Mamma's loot: reliquaries, goblets, models of galleons, shields and armor fantastically wrought for princes on state occasions, gold and silver centerpieces, medallions, rapiers with jeweled hilts, baroque clocks and music boxes, urns of malachite and a gilded Venetian sedan chair which was placed in the middle of the front hall. Mamma now asked to dinner only people whose opinion of her things she valued, and conversation dwelt largely on the history and purchase of each object. She may have started in near total ignorance, but as she never forgot anything that she had learned about one of her own purchases, her knowledge grew as rapidly as her collection. The first time that she was interviewed by a newspaper she showed little humility in airing her new opinions. Her biggest purchase to that date had been a magnificent third century Roman sarcophagus, unearthed near Florence, with an exquisite frieze of male nude mourning figures in stately procession from the decedent's villa. Some public interest had been aroused in this, and the *New York Times* critic had irritated Mamma by describing it as "a fine specimen of a decadent period when workmanship exceeded inspiration."

"It takes a decadent to smell a decadent!" Mamma retorted angrily in print. "In a finicky age like ours where men aren't men they try to suck virility from crude and barbaric forms of art. The truly vigorous artist is never afraid of perfect workmanship. He does not throw his chisel down when the job is half done to give it the appearance of 'force'!"

This comment of Mamma's was widely discussed and was received by Aunt Daisy as the ultimate proof of her essential coarseness. But Mamma was way past caring what her ex-sister-in-law thought. She was already engaged in her first extensive job of weeding. She planned another assault upon the markets of Europe, but she had first to put her acquisitions through the strainer of her afterthoughts. The effect was devastating. She reduced the collection to a third of its size and, far from relinquishing any of the pieces with regret, she seemed positively to hurl them out. She would sit by the hour in the Venetian chair, which had become for some reason the tribunal of her justice, and fix her white blank stare on the things that were placed in turn on a table before her. When she had once made up her mind, she would never reconsider. The poor object would be hurried away like a trembling offender from the presence of an implacable despot.

"It won't do," she would mutter. "It's let me down."

"But Mamma," I would sometimes protest. "It's beautiful!"

"It's not. It's vulgar."

Which was always the damning word. "Vulgar," as I gradually made out, was the quality of having looked better in the shop window. Mamma would never define it herself, but she maintained peremptorily, and sometimes with a dry laugh, that vulgarity was something she knew a great deal about.

On our second expedition to Europe, which lasted over a year, I exerted for the only time in my life a brief influence over her field of choice. I induced her to have a fling at painting. It was not a happy phase, and it lasted only one winter. Mamma was not fundamentally sympathetic with oil and canvas; she liked to peer into the corners of a picture with a magnifying glass to study the artist's handling of detail. It is significant that the only two paintings of note that she bought, which are both now in the Metropolitan, were the Holbein of an unknown English lady (*aetatis suae* 37) and the tiny Vermeer of a housemaid holding a blue and white cup. The Holbein, of course, is a perfectly executed and finished picture, and the subject even looks a bit like Mamma: white, square-jawed, intelligent and perfectly at home in a world where humor and death were like partners at a dance. Mamma would have understood the Tudors.

"It's not that I can't see what people like," she told me one day in a gallery whose owner was trying vainly to interest her in a Manet study of a bullfighter. "If I were buying to cash in later, I'd pick up every Renoir and Manet in Paris. Lucius Hoyt's putting his money in impressionists, and I'm sure Lucius is never wrong. But they bore me, and I'm not out to make a fortune. Your grandfather was good enough to do that for me. I'm sorry," she said to the dealer as she rose, "I don't like it. But keep your courage up. Mrs. Havemeyer's in Paris!"

It is probably significant that the Vermeer, the last painting of any importance that Mamma was to purchase, should have contained a blue and white bowl. In fact, it is more of a still life than a portrait, for the housemaid has her head turned away, and the bowl is the focal center of the canvas. Certainly it was what caught Mamma's eye. She had been taking a greater interest in porcelain at the time, and after her painting phase had ended she was to devote the next five years largely to that field. In the end, her collection was to be more than half porcelains and to include the world's finest examples of eighteenth century French cabinets with porcelain plaques.

It was during the second great weeding out that Mamma and I had a conversation which threw a chilling insight into the philosophy behind her acquisitions. We were standing in the great hall of the Fifth Avenue house where the pieces and pictures that were to be sold had been placed on long trestles for a final inspection. As I paced up and down before the great dock of the condemned, a thought suddenly struck me.

"You know what it is?" I demanded. "You don't like people!"

Mamma's eyes betrayed no sense of shock, but simply a mild amusement. "What do you mean by that extraordinary statement?"

"You don't like human beings!" I continued, excited as the truth of my discovery began to dawn on me. "You don't like the human figure. Wherever it's represented, whether on a plate or a cup or a canvas, you want to get rid of it!"

"I'm keeping the Holbein," she said gruffly.

"Ah, but that's you!"

"And the Houdons."

"But they're not really human!" I insisted, refusing to give up my theory. "They're softer and milkier and quieter."

"It's not hard to be better than human," Mamma retorted with a grunt. "Personally, I've always thought the human figure a vastly overrated thing."

"Ah, you admit it!" I cried.

"Of course I admit it. Have you ever looked at one of those magazines that nudist camps send out?"

"No! And I never shall!"

I did not go on with the subject, but I was never to forget it, nor was I ever to feel again the same enthusiasm about Mamma's collection. Of course, my theory would not exactly fit the facts—among the procelains alone there were dozens and dozens of cupids and shepherdesses and soldiers and kings, human figures, indeed, galore—but the tendency was still there: the human figure was either absent or present as part of the decorative scheme. The body to Mamma was not only unlovable; it was a symbol of decay. She resented furiously the deficiencies of her own; it could never, she always complained, keep up with her. When she thought of a tooth, she thought of a toothache; when she thought of skin, she thought of a rash. She would have liked to have had bones of sapphire and flesh of ivory. In the things that she bought she sometimes seemed to be reaching into eternity not through the spirit, but through its very opposite, through the hard materials out of which her objects were fashioned. I shuddered when it struck me that Mamma was engaged in converting the fortune of the Millinders, the true possession of which seemed always to have eluded her, into a tangible form that she could literally grasp and stroke. Sitting in her Venetian chair in the great hall she was simply another old miser counting his goldpieces.

It was this image that rose suddenly to repel me when she asked me if I wanted the collection.

"In my will, I mean," she explained impatiently as I simply stared. "I'm doing my will over. Shall I leave it to you? There's nobody who knows more about it."

I had answered before I could think. "No!" I cried. "No, please!" It suddenly seemed to me that nothing in the world mattered more than my escaping such a legacy, that if there was to be any fragment of happiness left over for me after Mamma should go, it would depend on this. "I don't want it!" I exclaimed. "Really, I don't!"

"Well, you certainly shan't have it then," Mamma said tartly, and I knew that for the first time in my life I had hurt her feelings.

The great collection continued apace, but after this brief altercation I had less and less to do with it. I turned more to social welfare work, and Mamma seemed hardly to notice my defection. The Fifth Avenue house where she and I continued to live (we went to Europe every summer and never to Newport) was more like a museum than a home. The guest rooms, one by one, were stripped of furniture and filled with glass cabinets. The great hall could no longer be used for dinner parties; it was bisected now by a huge choir screen that Mamma had acquired in Spain, and the porcelain tables were raised on little stands for better viewing. The walls were covered with brilliant Persian rugs, and everywhere in the house was the gleam of Meissen and Sèvres and Lowestoft. As one approached the main living room on the second floor down a corridor lined with armor and interspersed with baroque marble and bronze busts of popes and cardinals by Ottoni and Cafa one was prepared for the coming change to the Orient by seeing through the double doors ahead a great calm gilded Buddha. And passing through these doors one entered the holy of holies, the great room of Chinese porcelains and jade screens and goddesses. For Mamma had traveled steadily eastward from the Brooklyn of her birth.

In the last few years, mostly to replace me, Mamma retained a young art student, Jules Meisner, a quiet, charming young man with pale skin and the blackest hair I have ever seen, to help her in her acquisitions. They seemed to understand each other perfectly, for Mamma could soon hardly be without him. Willie and Bertie were constantly trying to agitate me, saying that he would supersede us all in Mamma's will, but I simply did not care. Anyway, they were quite wrong. In the end, Jules received a legacy of twenty-five thousand dollars and a pair of Rose Pompadour urns, decorated after Boucher. But had he wished, he could have had anything. At the least, he could have been director of the Eliza Millinder Museum for the Decorative Arts at an annual salary of the full amount of his legacy. The Millinders would never believe it, but it was Jules who talked Mamma out of this. He saw in the collection what I saw; he felt the chill of its assembled array. At least I assume he did, for it was his plan to divide it all among the major museums of the country. It was worthy of the genius of Jules, as exemplified in his later books, that he saw that the parts were greater than the whole.

The final stage was in China. Mamma and Jules traveled feverishly, as if they knew they were working against time. In Canton they snatched the great set of canary yellow and *sang de boeuf* vases of the K'ang Hsi period out from under the very nose of Mr. Altman's agent, and in Korea they made the first important purchase of that country's pottery. They were concentrating on jade screens when Mamma had her stroke and was taken to an English hospital in Hong Kong. I had just enough time to get out there before she died. She was unable to speak, but she knew me, and I sat by her bed in the two days that remained. She hardly moved her eyes from the table by her side on which Jules had arranged the particular treasures of their Eastern expedition. In the center was a small yellow glaze jar, of a simplicity and depth of color that made it a perfection among man-made things. I believe that her brooding stare was on it when she died.

Part Two

1

Mamma's death was the natural semicolon in my life. While she was still living I could cling to my old fantasies and excuses: that I was still a child, that I was kept down, that some day I would grow up and things would be different. Mamma was a wonderful person to blame things on because she never cared enough to answer back. Her indifference was like the indifference of the world; one might have even supposed it a good preparation for the latter. Yet for me it was just the reverse. For I had somehow clung to my childhood illusion that the world *did* care, perhaps for the very reason that Mamma so obviously didn't. When she was gone, I was stunned by my sudden sense of the surrounding unconcern. It even made me think of Mamma as the one person who had shown an occasional interest, and, quite irrationally, I began to miss her and to sentimentalize her memory. If I had grown up at last, it seemed to me that I had overdone it, both in years and in flesh. I was halfway through my forties and on the wrong side of a hundred and sixty pounds.

The blow of self-recognition, however, was delayed for two years by world events. Mamma died in 1916, supremely indifferent to a European war that had affected so little her Oriental area of operations. I was not to remain so detached. When I returned from Hong Kong, I was immediately swept up in Red Cross work, and I continued to be so occupied until the Armistice. With my inspiring friend Miss Grace McElway, I toured the country on a fund-raising drive and crossed to Europe on a troop transport as member of a delegation appointed by President Wilson to inspect the movement of hospital supplies to the front. I had never worked so hard or so regularly, and I found it exhilarating. When I look at my photographs of the period and see the straight hair pulled back from the high forehead, forming a bun behind, the big, staring eyes under the pince-nez, the small, tightly closed lips, the plain suit over the expanding girth, the buckled shoes, the general air of repressed, heavy emotionalism, I see the dedicated female of good works who battens on war and disaster, a fifth rider to come puffing up after the four grim ones of the Apocalypse. I do not intend to describe my wartime activities, because I know from the memoirs of others, including those of the late Miss McElway (who was indeed a saint), that there is no duller reading than the good works of others. Besides, this book is about my family, who, except for Antoine de Conti who lost his life at Verdun, were either too old or too young to have been much affected by the war.

Suffice it to say that the Armistice came as an anticlimax for me. Bertie and I decided to spend the winter of 1919 in the Fifth Avenue house which we now jointly owned. Stripped of Mamma's collection which had been sent to the various museums named in her will, it seemed very bare, but we were both attached to it, and there was certainly enough room so that we did not get in each other's way. Mamma had divided her fortune, or what was left of it after her enormous purchases, equally, like the house, between Bertie and myself. Cora, she considered, had already enough with her marriage settlement, and Willie would have more than any of us from Papa. And so, at last, I really was grown up, not only grown up but rich. I was not fabulously or even dazzlingly rich, but I was certainly rich. I could afford to live in a house that was twelve times too big for me and be waited on by twelve servants under the leadership of the aging and mournful Osborn, Mamma's old butler, who had disapproved of my war work as much as he had disapproved of her collecting, but who felt that it was his laborious duty to see me through. I could afford a summer place in Bar Harbor, any number of automobiles and an opera box. My friends have always thought me richer than I was because, like a true New Yorker, I have never hesitated at a pinch to invade my capital. But in that first postwar winter I had no pleasure in such things. The only thing that I felt I could afford was a nervous breakdown.

I had all the black hours of loneliness and despair that might have been expected of an old maid who realizes for the first time what she has missed in life. It seemed to me that my money and my independence had come too late, that my life was over and that I would never be loved. I sat morning after morning looking down at the traffic on Fifth Avenue and weeping large, slow tears. My wartime friends had scattered to their homes, and it seemed too flat to go back to the old faces of Miss Dixon's Classes. There was nothing ahead for me but death, and I was afraid of death. It was a hard, chilly world, as hard as the pavements on Fifth Avenue, and the hurrying crowds below my windows evoked pictures of crowds elsewhere, swelling crowds in Russia, Africa, China, indifferent crowds, spreading into one fetid oleaginous mass of human matter to cover every inch of the globe and smother the last aspect of individuality and romance—and of *me*! My mind was full of grisly pictures, some that I had seen and some that I had not: amputations at the hospital in Nancy, people burned alive in the fire that had occurred in the next block, the beautiful Czarina and her daughters in that cellar in Ekaterinburg. I had known two wonderful women, twins, unmarried like myself, who had gone to France as nurses and who had leaped to their death, hand in hand, from the deck of the returning steamer, their minds affected by what they had witnessed. I thought of them sometimes with envy and sometimes with horror. Had they seen that there was no place in the new world for such as we?

Bertie was precious little help. His own life had frozen into the routine of the exquisite, middle-aged bachelor; he pursued his pleasures with the same grim methodicalness that Grandpa Millinder had applied to business. Mamma's money had been a godsend, for Papa had been a reluctant provider to so uncongenial a son, and poor Bertie had been running short. Now his small, dapper figure, clad in English tweeds, and his cheerful, froglike face could be seen again at all the right places at all the right seasons: July in Newport, September in Scotland, December in New York, April in Warrenton. He still had a sense of humor, but the years had eroded it.

There was nothing in the least funny to Bertie about my inability to count trumps or about poor Osborn's failing memory when it resulted in red-wine glasses being used for white.

But the really disappointing thing about Bertie was that he had none of even that dilettante interest in arts and letters that so often accompanies the pursuit of elegance. He had instead all the Philistinism of the businessman with none of his creativeness; he liked barroom stories and the conversational lynching of radicals and "pansies." His taste in women dropped directly from the society hostess to the streetwalker; he recognized no intermediate ranks. He hadn't married, at least in my opinion, because he was too selfish. Certainly he had no patience with female temperament, or what he called "fussing." When it began to be apparent even to him that my nervous troubles were more than a prolonged bad mood, he was briefly sympathetic. He gave up a whole weekend in Long Island to stay in town and draw up a list of occupations that would keep me from "brooding." I was to take bridge lessons; I was to resume my teaching on a part-time basis; I was to go out more and see more people. I was even to get a dog. It all made perfect sense, but what was the use of placing meals before a patient to cure a loss of appetite? When I failed to take any of the steps that he recommended, he washed his hands of the case as briskly as a doctor who is too busy to waste time on persons who will not carry out his prescriptions. He felt that he had offered me an alternative to self-pity and that I had voluntarily rejected it. The only thing that saved his time from having been completely wasted was that he had absolved himself from the duty of further sympathy. From now on I was on my own, with the inarticulate commiseration of old Osborn.

It was all very well for Bertie to ignore me at home, but it was harder for him to be so detached when we dined out together. Of course, as we moved in different circles, this occurred infrequently, but he did have the mortification of witnessing the terrible scene that I made at Aunt Daisy's dinner party for my cousin Gwen and her husband, the Earl of Myol, on the occasion of their first visit to New York after the war. Fortunately for Bertie, the party had been limited to a dozen guests as Aunt Daisy was still in mourning for Uncle Fred who had died in the same year as Mamma.

I had been feeling particularly low that day, and I sat in gloomy silence, listening to Lord Myol hold forth across the table. There was a striking resemblance between his wide, red, fatuous features and those of the Prince Regent in the big portrait by Lawrence that hung directly behind him. As he ranted on, with the incredible arrogance of his generation of British peers, about how England had won the war, how little our late entry had contributed to the victory, how dirty New York was and how poor the service in our clubs, I began to have a curious illusion that the portrait itself was speaking, that Prinny had appeared in the flesh to scorn these burghers who had dared to buy his likeness. And as I continued to stare, gradually hypnotized, the voice that I heard ceased to be that of English superiority; it became simply the voice of hardness, of indifference; it became the metallic tapping of a hammer that seemed to be repeating and repeating, to the point

of driving me mad, that the world did not care, that the world, like the
wall on which the portrait hung, had no function but to reject me forever.

"Speaking of your great experiment in democracy," the voice went on,
"I had a curious illustration of it only this morning. I was up at Ninetieth
Street to see George Millinder's new house, right in the center of Harlem,
I should say. Well, nobody was kind enough to offer to send me back to
civilization in a car, and you can't find a cab up there for love or money,
so I was constrained to hail a Fifth Avenue omnibus. I finally got a seat to
myself and was prepared to have a look at that monstrous row of white
elephants you all love so, when an evil smelling old black hag—I'm sorry,
Mother Daisy, but she positively reeked and must have weighed twenty
stone—squeezed her way into the seat beside me and kept asking if each
stop was Fourteenth Street. She wouldn't believe me when I told her, but
kept leaning over to see the signs, half asphyxiating me with her fumes. Well,
I can tell you that by Seventy-ninth Street I'd had my fill, and I turned to
her and shouted: 'Here you are, Madame, here's your stop, quick now before
you miss it!' Dear me, you should have seen her jump and waddle down
that aisle. She landed on the pavement with her bundles in a positive heap!
I wager that'll teach her to treat strangers with more consideration!"

Before I even knew that I was going to speak I heard my voice, far away
and shrill, like a child locked in an attic: "Do you realize she might have
been taking those bundles to a sick family? And had only one fare? Do you
realize she may have had to trudge all the way from Seventy-ninth Street to
Fourteenth? She may have arrived too late! Maybe she was a midwife. Those
people have midwives. Maybe the mother and baby are dead! And you're
the murderer, Lord Myol! Have you stopped to think of that? You're the
murderer!"

There was consternation around the table. Myol's face flushed an even
deeper red as he stuttered: "Oh, I say, that's a bit thick. Come now, isn't
that a bit thick?"

"Really, Gussie, take hold of yourself!" Bertie hissed at me.

"Alistair was only making it up, I'm sure," Gwen Myol murmured
placatingly.

"Most extraordinary," commented Aunt Daisy.

"But you don't understand!" I wailed. "The poor woman may have had
only one fare! None of you know what that means! You haven't worked
with poverty and disease. I'm going to ring up the British Consul tomorrow and ask him if Lord Myol is behaving as a guest of this nation should
behave. I may even call the Ambassador in Washington! I think his visa
should be revoked!"

"Oh, come off it, Gussie!" Bertie cried, angry now. "Enough's enough!"

"I doubt very much if Alistair will tell that story again," Gwen remarked
with a shadow of a smile.

"I think Augusta is forgetting that she's my guest," Aunt Daisy said solemnly.

"But it's just what she's remembering, Cousin Daisy!" a soft, firm voice
suddenly remonstrated. "We are all your guests. I don't think Lord Myol's

story showed a proper recognition of that. It was a cruel story, and it is embarrassing for guests to have to listen to a cruel story. If we protest, we seem rude. Perhaps we're too afraid of seeming rude. After all, there are principles. And I, for one, will take Miss Millinder's!"

At the time my only impression of my champion was one of general loveliness, but I shall describe her as she appeared to me later. Mrs. Locke was several years younger than I, being then in her late thirties, and was dressed in the heavy black of her tragic bereavement. Titus Locke had been killed in the last week of hostilities. She had the whitest skin and the bluest eyes I have ever seen, and a high crown of golden hair. With her small aquiline nose and scarlet lips, as perfectly shaped as those in the illustrations of prewar novels, she might have been the heroine of a tale by Howells or Harold Bell Wright, quiet, reserved, gentle, but full of patrician pride and strength to meet the crisis which the plot was sure to entail. Yet the simple fact that she looked so much a heroine of fiction should have been enough in itself to suggest that she must have been something greater or lesser than that. She must, for example, have wanted to look the part and wanted to look it for a purpose. There was in her quick, charming, self-conscious smile, in her high, agreeably strident tone, in the brusque movements of her head and arms, something which offered a vivid contrast to the almost languid stillness of her high brow and gold hair, something which hinted that this woman was a good deal more contemporary than one might at first suspect. But, of course, I saw none of this at the time. At the time I simply burst into tears.

"Oh, dear me, this is too bad, it *is* too bad," I heard Aunt Daisy mutter. "Bertie, you'd better take your sister home. I don't think she's feeling much like a party."

"May I go with you, Miss Millinder?" asked Mrs. Locke, rising. "Excuse me, Cousin Daisy, but I think Bertie needs a little supplementing here. Not, of course, that he isn't the greatest help." She walked to my seat and leaned over to murmur in my ear: "Would you let me go home and sit with you for a bit? Please say yes. I should like it so much!"

Even in my state of emotional tension, as she led me sniffing from the room, I was able to note that she had called my aunt "Cousin Daisy" and that she must have known Bertie before. It came back to me vaguely that Aunt Daisy had spoken of an unfortunate cousin who had been left unexpectedly poor and whom she had asked to spend the winter in the Fifth Avenue house. It also came back to me that Bertie had mentioned a beautiful and fashionable widow who was going to die of boredom at Aunt Daisy's. But all I cared about was that an angel had suddenly appeared to take my side, and in the car driving home I resented the presence of Bertie's back on the jump seat, stiff with mortification at my behavior.

"There's no need for you to come home, Bertie," I told him. "I'll be quite all right with Mrs. Locke. Why don't you go back to the party?"

"And interrupt the happy little post-mortem they're enjoying right now?" he replied testily. "I wouldn't think of it. We've done enough to Aunt Daisy for one night."

"If you ask me, Bertie, I think your sister rather improved the party," Mrs. Locke reproved him. "If you had to spend as much time in that house as I do, you'd learn to appreciate a little excitement."

"It can't be too dull if you're there," Bertie said, turning around and giving her a rather toothy smile. We were being treated to Bertie's "gallant manner," and I stared back at him balefully. "Except even you couldn't do anything about the cooking. It's worse than ever, isn't it? I think Aunt Daisy must feel there's something moral about burnt soup."

"You never change, Bertie, do you?" Mrs. Locke asked in a drier tone. "A world war breaks out, and empires fall, but Bertie Millinder still thinks of burnt soup."

"Does general catastrophe make it taste any better?"

"It makes other things taste worse."

Bertie tapped on the glass. "Let me off here," he said to the chauffeur. "I think I'll finish my dinner at the club. You ladies are obviously in a more philosophic mood than I." He got out, and holding the door open, bowed to Mrs. Locke. "I'll come and call some afternoon," he continued with the same toothy grin, "if you will allow me. Despite what's happened to your taste for soup. And, by the way, if you're going home, give my sister some tips about the house." He turned to me. "She's a bit of a genius, this girl, Gus. Best damn decorator in New York!"

But I didn't want to hear about Mrs. Locke's accomplishments or even that she had any life outside the shadow of Aunt Daisy's precarious favor. All I wanted was that this beautiful creature should come to sit for an hour with me and let me pour out my heart. I was delighted to be rid of Bertie. At home I took her to the Louis XVI drawing room, or what was left of it after Mamma's bequests, and ordered scrambled eggs and a bottle of wine from the silently outraged Osborn. I even ordered a fire, and stared into it as I related to my new friend my melancholy and morbid reflections of the preceding months. I never asked her permission; I simply plunged right off into the dreary tale of my war work and its aftermath and the bleakness of everything at present. Somehow I had to explain my outbreak at dinner to this golden-haired creature in black who sat so quietly listening, with no movement but the almost surreptitious lighting of a cigarette.

"I feel such a fool," I ended mournfully. "Such a perfect idiot."

"My dear Miss Millinder, you mustn't." Mrs. Locke took firm possession of the first real opening that I had allowed her. "We all live surrounded by densities of incomprehension. We smile and nod like so many monkeys out of fear of being considered boorish or unpleasant. Is it so vital to keep the peace at your Aunt Daisy's dinners? Must everything be sacrificed to that?"

"No, but, after all, it was a family party."

"Do you want me to tell you something?" Mrs. Locke asked abruptly. "There wasn't one person at that table, except for old Myol himself, who wasn't a hundred per cent on your side!"

"Surely not Gwen!"

"Oh, Gwen most of all!"

"But why? Her own husband?"

"My dear Miss Millinder, where have you been? Myol has been shockingly unfaithful to her from the very beginning. He's never made any secret of the fact that he regards her as a cashbox, pure and simple. And now it's reached a point where it's positively repulsive. Every maid, every tweeny, the school friends of the girls, even the curate's wife, it's pinch, pinch, pinch, all the time. They call him the Lobster of Kent! And if you ask me, that's the real reason the old colored gal got off the bus. She preferred to walk!" She threw back her head at this and burst into a sudden startling laugh. It was a high, gay, rather gasping laugh, and it had a roughness of edge that was oddly infectious. She gave herself up to it as if it were a coughing fit; she held her body straight and her head tilted back in a gargling position. It is impossible to describe why this laugh should have been so charming, but it was. It was in such odd contrast to the immediately preceding mood of high melancholy and to her widow's weeds; it seemed to say that if love and death and moral principles had their place in the universe, so did laughter, raucous laughter, possibly even indelicate laughter, possibly even gross.

"Does Aunt Daisy know all that?"

"Bless you, of course she knows! She gave her only two pretty maids strict orders to remain below stairs during Myol's visit. I wonder how Gwen stands it."

"Well, if he's always been that way," I pointed out, "maybe she's used to it. Maybe she thinks all husbands are like that."

"Poor precious, I hope so." Mrs. Locke became serious again with the mention of husbands and lit another cigarette. "I pray for her sake that she may never know what she's missed. If you've had what I've had, that's about all any woman can ask. Did you ever know my Titus, Miss Millinder?" I shook my head regretfully, and she got up to roam about the room. "He was divine, that's all. Simply divine." She paused to examine a tiny Chelsea cat, one of the few items in her collection that Mamma had given to me. "What a gorgeous thing," she said without changing her tone, and I reflected on the eye that had so quickly isolated it from the rest of the bric-a-brac. "You should have more, many more. Life with Titus was so full," she continued, reverting to her husband, "that I sometimes think children would have detracted from it. Yes, I'm almost glad we had no children. Even now." She squinted at the fire screen and nodded in approval. "Charming. Perfectly charming. But I have such a feeling that there used to be *other* things," she added, gazing vaguely around. "There are so many blank places."

I explained briefly about the removal of Mamma's collection.

"Oh, I see," she said nodding. "I see. Well, you must fill up the blank spots, that's all."

"I don't collect."

"Oh, I don't mean with treasures," she said hastily. "Just with things. Things that are you. Yes, I begin to see it." She glanced at me critically for a moment and then back around the room. "It can be done. It won't take too much, either. Basically, the house is right for you."

"This mausoleum?"

"Aha! How you say that! I can see you love it. If I called it a mausoleum, you'd be very angry. But we can cheer it up a bit. I always believe in making do with what one has. I distrust the clean sweep." She lifted up a fold of curtain and examined it. "Filthy," she said. "Get after those maids."

"I'd be so pleased if you'd help me do the room over," I ventured timidly and waited in suspense.

"I should be delighted." She turned and made me a little bow. "But, as I say, it won't take too much. It suits you. The way your Aunt Daisy's house suits her. Gwen wants to get her out of it into an apartment, but who would Mrs. Frederick P. Millinder be in an apartment? Nobody, don't you see?" I didn't quite see, but I nodded eagerly. "One thing I've always liked about your family is that they spend more where it *shows*. After all, isn't that what it's for?"

"You don't find that . . . a bit vulgar?"

"But I adore vulgarity!" And again she laughed that laugh. "Titus and I could never stand the kind of people who hide their goldpieces under their good breeding. Vulgarity is at least alive! I even like the name," she went on. "Millinder. Millinder," she repeated and smiled in approval. "Augusta Millinder. Oh, yes, I like it."

"Then I'm sorry you can't use it," I said, my heart beating a bit faster, "because I insist that you call me Gussie."

"Gussie?" Her nose seemed about to wrinkle as she considered it. But then her laugh rang out a third time, and again it warmed and thrilled me. "Oh, I like Gussie, too. It goes with you. 'Gussie,'" she repeated more pensively. "Yes, it's as loyal and good as a dear old sheep dog. And mine is Ione. Will you call me Ione?"

"I'd love to," I answered eagerly. "What a pretty name—Ione."

When I went to bed that night I slept well for the first time in weeks. There was a therapeutic quality in Ione's conversation and charm that I felt already I could not do without. How could I attach her to myself? That was my sole concern. Would she come and visit? Could I employ her to do over the house? Could I take her on a cruise? I hated having to go to Bertie for information in such a matter, but as I did not know where else to turn, I came down the next morning to interrupt his breakfast in the dining room. The look that he gave me over his newspaper made me feel that it was just as well he was going south the following week.

"I want to ask you about Mrs. Locke," I began as casually as I could. "Is she a professional decorator? I mean, could I retain her to do over the big room?"

"She doesn't have an office, if that's what you mean. But I believe she does jobs for friends. Titus left almost nothing, they say."

"Did you know him?"

"Of course I knew him. Everyone knew Titus. He and Ione were the most popular young couple in town."

"In *your* town," I couldn't help adding.

"Well, of course, in *my* town," he retorted, nettled. "That's what you came to ask about, wasn't it? I don't imagine you find many Iones in yours."

I let this pass. "I suppose she entertained very well."

"Superbly," Bertie said emphatically, and praise from him was never lightly bestowed. "The best I've ever seen. She could do with a hundred dollars what Aunt Daisy couldn't do with a hundred thousand. That's why Aunt Daisy wants her. As long as Titus was alive, she couldn't have her. But now that Ione is a poor widow and out of the swing, it's the old girl's chance to put her in a cage and see if she won't warble. That's the eternal faith of people like Aunt Daisy," he wound up with a snort. "They believe in osmosis through ownership. Aunt Daisy thinks that if she pays for Ione's board and lodging, Ione's taste will be somehow transmitted to her!"

"Poor Mrs. Locke," I murmured. "Does she have to stay with Aunt Daisy?"

"Oh, I don't suppose she *has* to. It's probably a convenient berth for the winter."

"Do you think she'd come here? I mean, wouldn't it be more convenient if she was working here?"

Bertie looked up quizzically for a moment. Then he shrugged and returned his attention to his egg. "You'll have to square yourself with Aunt Daisy. But I daresay Ione would jump at the chance. Only I think it's rather mean of you to start filling the house with beautiful women just as I'm on my way to Florida."

I invited Ione to the opera that night, forgetting what a dose of the Metropolitan she must have been getting with Aunt Daisy, but she came and adored it. After all, it was Caruso and Farrar. Two days later we lunched at the Colony Club, and Ione told me the story of her life with Titus. Had I heard of this before knowing her, I might have drawn a comparison with the Rawdon Crawleys in *Vanity Fair*, but now I could see nothing but gallantry and high spirits and vivid imagination in their determination not to allow any lack of fortune to deprive them of any fun that was going around. I did not in the least ameliorate any of my harsh judgments of Bertie's set; I simply concluded that the Titus Lockes must have been the exception that proved my rule. After all, as Mrs. Bell used to say, there's no friend like a new friend.

"I know we're very different kinds of people," I finally dug up the courage to tell her. "I've never gone in for a social life except when I was made to, and you, of course, have been pursued by the world. But if you decide to do over the big room, and while you're still in mourning, it might be convenient for you to stay with me. I'm sure you're very well off at Aunt Daisy's," I hastened to add, trying to construct the setting of a joke about my bribe, "but I can offer you breakfast in bed, your own maid and a car. And no interference whatever!"

"Why, Gussie, you old princess!" Ione gave herself up again to that gasping laugh. "You know perfectly well I get nothing like that at your aunt's. If I'm not downstairs by half past eight, I don't even get a cup of coffee! It's discomfort on the grand scale. But, to be serious, my dear, I think we're very much the same kind of people. We both believe in speaking our minds, and we've' both got the nerve to do it. And then I think we're both a bit lonely." She paused and looked down at the table, and when she spoke again, her voice was very low. "However little we care to admit it."

"Would you come, then?" My voice had dropped, too, in fear of a negative answer. It suddenly seemed to me that I should die of loneliness if Ione would not come.

"Why, you goose, I'd like nothing better!" Ione exclaimed. "But you know my situation with your aunt. I told her I'd stay the winter."

"Oh, I'll fix Aunt Daisy!" I assured her.

I realized later that afternoon, as I drove up the avenue to Aunt Daisy's to see Gwen Myol, how far my precipitation had carried me. How little in the past would I have talked of squaring Aunt Daisy! My only hope was that she had become rather less formidable since Uncle Fred's death. She had not even now, three years afterwards, developed that widow's wind that was to see her through the final magnificent decade of her life. Without Uncle Fred to sustain the fantasy that the dreary, gilded pomp of their lives was somehow demanded of them, as a kind of American Victoria and Albert, she was temporarily lost, and almost agreeable. She would ask me to lunch now, just by myself, and make timid advances, rapidly withdrawn if successful, towards something like friendship. Poor Aunt Daisy! She had less flair for human relationships than anyone I have ever known. I'm sure Ione was right in guiding her back to the old life of stately pageant where only the brief, formal and multiple relationships of the hostess had to be coped with.

Gwen Myol, who met me in a stiff little Venetian library off the front hall that I had never seen used before, made my mission easier than I would have thought possible. Gwen had become so English that it was hard to believe she had been born American; her big, lanky body, her bluish-white skin, her baggy tweed suit, her slurred syllables and projected chin seemed to belong to a foggy weekend in Norfolk. Like her husband, she was always referring to "you Americans." Yet from all accounts Gwen had not been a success in England. Her children, now grown, were as rude and insensitive as their father, and as Gwen always backed him up, and he never her, they simply assumed that the "mater," probably because of her Yankee birth, was a bit of a troublemaker. Gwen could have found plenty of friends had she not been so blindly loyal to the Myols, had she not spent her life battering her head in vain against the wall of xenophobia that existed only in their tiny, stupid set. She was unhappy, too, in the choice of her sole retaliation, which was boasting about her country and her grandfather and the energy that teemed beyond the seas. Gwen was like the unhappy Empress Frederick, a jingoist abroad and an internationalist at home. There was something pathetic about the way she turned more and more back, as she grew older, to the land of her birth and her small, impersonal, tightlipped American mother. It was as if Gwen, in coming across the Atlantic to see that Aunt Daisy was amused and diverted, to check up on her afternoon drives and her nights at the opera, had found at last a person who would accept her unwanted ministrations. Aunt Daisy, of course, had always accepted everything.

"To be absolutely frank, I don't think Mother would mind at all if Ione went to you," she answered readily when I had stammered out my proposition. I even had a rather uneasy sense that she had anticipated it. "Ione's a dear, of course, and she's been an angel to Mother, but she's not very practical, and if one's not practical in this topsy-turvy new world, where is one?"

"How is she not practical?"

"My dear, it's so simple. She looks at life through the eye of a decorator. And not a very good one at that, I'm afraid. I couldn't get home when Father died, because of the war, so I'm a bit late in helping Mother to readjust. But there you are, better late . . ."

I looked at my big, rawboned cousin blankly. "Readjust to what?"

"Why, my dear Gussie, to a whole new world! You don't think *this* sort of thing is going to continue, do you?" She waved her arm as though to take in the whole house. "Not for a minute. The handwriting's on the wall. My job is to sell this place and the one in Newport and get Mother on what you Americans call a 'paying basis.'"

"You don't think, then, she'll miss Ione?" I asked, returning to the main point. I cared very little what Aunt Daisy did with her real estate.

"Bless you, no. Just between ourselves, Ione's been a bit inconsiderate. Of course, it won't matter with you, because you can control it. But Mother's getting on, you know."

"What did Ione do?" I demanded, with a touch of heat.

"Oh, nothing really." Gwen shrugged it off. "But the other day, when Mother loaned her the car, she sent it back fifteen minutes late for Mother's drive. And she never even gave the chauffeur a dollar for lunch. Small things, of course, but they tell."

It angers me even today to write these lines. Gwen and Aunt Daisy, different as they were in other respects, were at one in their reverence for money. All of Ione's charm and sympathy could never make up in their eyes for her poverty. If one received the smallest financial favor, even in the form of a room and board for the winter, one became at once a kind of servant, and when servants left, didn't one count the silver? The fact that Aunt Daisy could possibly owe anything to Ione would never have occurred either to her or to her daughter.

And yet she did. She owed, in brief, the rest of her life, and to that very "decorator's eye" that Gwen so scorned. Without it Aunt Daisy might have succumbed to Gwen's efforts to modernize her and have become another rich widow, traveling, playing cards and taking a fierce little pride in her curiosity about "what's going on" and "the young people." It was Ione who saw that her only interest to the latter would lie in her very anachronisms. It was Ione who fortified her in her resolution to keep to her dying day (and ultimately at the price of a good deal of capital) the immense old gilded palaces in New York and Newport. "Survival is everything," Ione used to say, "and your aunt will survive." She was right. Aunt Daisy survived everyone who had laughed at her, everyone, even, who had been bored by her, and her last years were by far her best. What Mrs. Bell's friends in my childhood had found merely pompous and dull, their grandchildren in the nineteen-thirties were to find stately and impressive. Aunt Daisy's "nevers" which had once seemed so pretentious—she would never go into a department store or talk on the telephone or attend a movie—came to be regarded with a kind of awe by a generation that could not imagine life without such things. The newspapers took her up and ended by making the public share in what I had always suspected was Aunt Daisy's private fantasy, namely that she was a queen. Her disapprovals were quoted everywhere, for Aunt Daisy disapproved of everything: of smoking, of drinking, of short skirts and tall buildings, of traffic, of taxes and ultimately of the depression itself. She was an incredibly simple woman who seemed to have almost succeeded in simplifying the world. Reporters began to dog her steps, at the opera, at family weddings, on Easter Sunday. In the strange pattern of this hunt, pursued and pursuer performed their roles with equal meticulousness and equal delight. I went with Aunt Daisy to her last opening night at the opera and suggested, because she was then so feeble, that we avail ourselves of the director's kind offer to let us slip in by a private side door. I might as well have suggested to Queen Victoria that she slip unnoticed into St. Paul's on her jubilee. "Thank God, I can still do my duty!" was her indignant rejoinder as she and I descended from the tall old green Rolls-Royce, like two big dolled up, gaudy bugs, and made our slow way through the crowd of cameramen, our evening bags held resolutely up to cover our faces. The men shouted familiar but friendly greetings to Aunt Daisy like "Go it, old girl!" and I was sure that behind her pursed lips and forward-looking stare her heart was beating with a fierce pride at so fitting a Nunc Dimittis.

2

Ione, in the first weeks that she stayed with me, struck me as the perfect house guest. As I look back on it now, I can see that she continued to be that, not only for those first weeks but for the whole six months of her visit, both in New York and in Bar Harbor, and that what I came to regard as a love of social life excessive in a guest was in fact a possessiveness on my own part unpleasant in a hostess. But in those early weeks we were never out of tune. Ione seemed utterly contented with our quiet evenings at home or at the theater, and in the daytime she rummaged about the house or shopped for new furniture and materials. Her gaiety infected my whole household, not one of whom resented the extra work which her presence entailed. She planned amusing little expeditions on weekends, and as spring approached we motored as far north as Concord and as far south as Williamsburg. I trembled only that Ione would become bored, and I did what I could, as surreptitiously as possible, to make her life easy and luxurious. She had my car and chauffeur whenever she wanted; she had her own maid and Mamma's old bedroom; she had as many presents from me in the way of bits of jewelry and bric-a-brac as I could induce her to accept. I am sure that my family, particularly Julia and Gwen Myol, thought I was being richly fleeced by a person who in their eyes was little better than an adventuress, but I knew then, as I know today, that Ione always gave more than she received. I simply gave her a few dollars, and she simply showed me the way to a whole new life. Yet such are the values of a merchant's world that in the eyes of the Millinders those few dollars colored our whole relationship, to make me a dupe and Ione a "sponge."

Ione operated under the same principle, both as decorator and friend, which was to preserve as much as possible of the materials with which she had to work. Although she could have made more money by exploiting my willingness, at her behest, to strip the whole house and start afresh, she insisted on keeping three-quarters of what was already there. "We mustn't lose sight of the basic swagger," she would say. "If we lose that, we've lost everything." Curtains could be replaced in lighter shades, rooms repainted in lighter tones, certain old dark mahogany pieces sold and stained glass windows removed, but at the end the house still had to suggest, albeit pleasantly instead of vulgarly, some of the pushing spirit of the decade of its construction. I can tell how successful Ione was by the number of people today who think that I have never changed it.

"You're a bit like your own house," she told me once. "You don't appreciate your good points. You'll never be happy till you accept the fact that you're a rich, respectable, intelligent old maid. Why isn't that a perfectly good thing to be?"

"How would you like to be it?" I asked sulkily.

"Perfectly well!" she exclaimed, raising one hand in a gesture of oath-taking. "Perfectly well!"

"People have always cared about you for yourself. You can't imagine what it's like to suspect they're only interested in your money!"

"That's another obsession of yours!" she retorted. "What is yourself? We're all bits and pieces of our background, our tastes, our inheritances, even our clothes. It's only natural for people to be curious because you're a Millinder and live in a big house. It's up to you to turn that curiosity into something better!"

It was the simplest idea in the world, yet it changed my life. I had become ashamed of my stoutness and my spinsterhood. In anticipation of people's prying curiosity, I had become disagreeable. Now I began to see myself in a different light. Of course Ione dramatized me, as she dramatized everything. It was as if she could not bear the drab, everyday aspect of things in which most people were content to loll, like manatees in a dirty tank. She convinced me that the role of an old maid could be a far bigger one than I had ever imagined, that an old maid could reach the young because she was neutral in the conflict between generations and the old because she was the priestess at the shrine of tradition. An old maid, at least a rich one, could wear big jewelry and drive around in an antique town car and wear fussy clothes out of fashion and weep at the opera and threaten naughty street urchins with her stick; she could join the boards of clubs and charities and be as officious and bossy as she liked; she could insist on giving the family party on Christmas Eve; she could even, in her new, shrewd, noisy way, become the head of the remnants of the Millinders. She could become, in short, to two generations of relatives and friends, the redoubtable, the indomitable "Aunt Gussie" and earn for herself, as much as Aunt Daisy, the ultimate compliment of an easily hoodwinked world: she could be "wonderful."

This side of myself, of course, was not to be realized yet. At the time I was still the victim of the misty moodiness that had made me so unlovable a child. I could never leave well enough alone. I had to reach in with my busy fingers and mess things up. Ione had not been in the house for six weeks before I began to be perturbed by the idea that she was hankering for a gayer society.

"Have your friends in," I urged her. "Just tell Osborn how many you want for lunch or dinner. Don't be afraid of his gloomy air. Be firm."

Ione acted on my suggestion, and her friends, one by one, and soon in twos and threes began to appear at lunch time. They were always ladies of the most elegant and sophisticated sort, they always knew Bertie and they invariably treated me with a politeness in which I read every nuance of condescension. I would sit brooding in a steamy silence at the end of the table while the chatter went on around me, wondering how Ione, with her crushing sorrow and her fine sympathies, could abide such a trivial, gossiping lot. Yet even I could see that it was more than a question of abiding it. Ione adored it. From lunches she progressed to dinner parties, and with the presence of men her spirits seemed to soar. Down the table would peal her laugh, that high, rough, hearty, infectious laugh, breaking over the general conversation like a wave, whirling and eddying about until even the most tightly wedged pebbles of complacency or disapproval had been dislodged. She would appeal to me, quote me, draw me out—"But you should have heard what Gussie said today" or "You should have seen Gussie give that salesman what for," until like a truculent child with a boasting mother, I could no longer bear it and wanted to behave badly, to make a scene, to flee from the room and sulk upstairs to the consternation of the glittering assembly below. I never quite dared do this, but one night I retired early and lay awake for two hours until I saw my door open a crack and heard Ione's sibilant:

"Gussie, are you asleep?"

She had come to bid me good night, and in my sudden, eager gratitude I sat up in bed and turned on the light and poured out my heart to her. She would have to learn to be magnanimous with me, I told her. Of course she was bored, cooped up with me all day. Of course she wanted to see people. What could be more natural? Only, in the future, she would have to realize that her friends were not the kind of people who interested me, that undoubtedly this was my fault, but that still it was so, and would she mind terribly if I had my dinner upstairs when she entertained?

Ione looked very sad as she sat by my bed. Her blue eyes seemed darker with their sudden air of despondency.

"You must think me a terrible butterfly," she said in a low, regretful tone. "You must think I've forgotten all about Titus. And he was killed only in October! Oh, but I haven't, Gussie, I haven't!" She leaned over, and in another moment her body was shaking with sobs. "This is all distraction. Silly, absurd distraction. Take me away, Gussie, please! Is it too early, do you think, to go to Maine?"

I had a momentary misgiving. Who, after all, was I to play the role of grim reminder to this recovering child? For it was as a child that she suddenly struck me, her head bent over so that I could see only her crown of golden hair and quivering shoulders. Who was I to enter the scene like some dour old relative of Titus', swathed in reproachful black, and frown on her simple diversions? But this reflection was soon dissipated by the memory of that chattering, laughing group about my board, whose only proffered assistance to Ione, even if kindly meant, was to blot out the pain of Titus' death with the great sponge of gossip. Surely, if Ione wanted time and quiet in which to develop a fortitude consistent with the deeper part of her nature, it was not up to me to play the fool, to put on a silly hat and jangle bells and leap about, to make her think of absurdities that would vanish the moment her head touched the pillow and the struggle for sleep began.

"I'll open the house tomorrow!" I exclaimed stoutly. "June is the best month up in Maine!"

The last house that Mamma had built had been in Bar Harbor. It was on the end of a point, out beyond most of the other summer cottages, and had an open view on three sides of the rocks and sea while in back the pine trees almost touched the roof. It was a big, plain structure of stone and weather-beaten shingle, with no pretence of looks, built to withstand the winter storms to which it was so nakedly exposed. Inside it was full of leather sofas and animal skins and large fireplaces with soaring hoods and here and there some of my old favorites of Grandpa's gallery, including the assassination of the Medici by Gérôme which hung over the black walnut sideboard in the dining room.

Mamma had built this house as a means of getting away, from time to time, from her own collection. "Too much beauty," she used to say, "puts the eye out," and she would travel up to Mount Desert Island to sit by the sea and play cards with a few old cronies. She never took any interest in the social life of the island; she had not given up Newport, she would dryly comment, to play the same game in lesser resorts. There was consequently no circle out of which I had to break, and my comings and goings were scarcely noticed by the summer colony. I loved the mountains and the pine woods and the screaming sea gulls; I even loved the wet fogs that floated in from the Atlantic and enshrouded the house for days at a time. It made one appreciate more fully the beautiful days when they did come, when everything sparkled like a world of make-believe, from the glittering waves and foam to the spoked wheels of polished town cars delivering old ladies in white to the brightly painted stores of the village. I was sure that Ione would love it.

For three weeks, indeed, it was perfect. I chartered a motor launch and we went on expeditions around the island; we drove to picturesque sites for tea and in the evenings we read poetry aloud. Ione loved to swim, and as the ocean was still too cold I took her to the club where I would sit alone at an umbrella table and watch her breast-stroke slowly around the huge square pool that jutted out into the sea. I was always afraid that she would run into friends, but it was early in the season and I was still safe. I had the delicious feeling that we had the island to ourselves.

It was Bertie who broke up our happy existence. I was particularly irritated by his arrival, as he had never come to Bar Harbor before and was obviously doing so only to see Ione. Of course, legally, the house did belong half to him, but it had been understood between us that it was to be included in my share of Mamma's estate, and I resented the bland air of proprietorship with which he and his valet moved in. I resented even more his attitude that it was our duty to "cheer things up" for Ione.

"Fresh air and pine woods are fine as far as they go," he told me briskly, "but Ione needs people. As Titus used to say, she's not the kind of dog one can keep in the country. She likes all the smells of pavement life."

I did not dignify this with an answer, and Bertie must have taken my silence for assent, for he proceeded at once to telephone to every friend whom he had on the island and to stir up a hornet's nest of social activity. I could hardly refuse my brother a dinner party, even two; I certainly could not prevent his organizing his own picnics, and as for going out, when he called across the breakfast table to Ione: "How about driving over to Northeast today and lunching at Anya's?" and she shrugged and nodded, what could I say? If I stayed home Bertie was only too delighted. If I accompanied them, he would keep up a monologue of gossip about friends of his and Ione's whom I didn't know, leaving me to stare grumpily out the car window. A week after his arrival I was thoroughly wretched, and Ione made matters worse by taking it for granted that I found his addition to the household as enlivening as she did.

"Your brother is a bit of a fool," she admitted once when I had criticized him too bitterly, "but let's face it, Gussie. When two women are alone in a house, the presence of a male, any male, is a bit of a godsend. Even if he's a brother and even if he's Bertie."

A male, any male! I couldn't have been more shocked. Why should a woman who had enjoyed the love of such a man as she was always describing her Titus to have been find Bertie a godsend less than a year after his death? I reflected how many years had passed since my engagement to Lancey Bell and how completely the memory of that frustrated romance still filled my need for the other sex. How could a trivial idler like Bertie have such an effect on a woman? I began to regard him with a grudging curiosity. I had to admit that despite his short size and unprepossessing looks he managed to dominate the little group that he assembled about him. Not, Lord knows, that they were such strong characters. But the act of domination is more significant than the type of personality dominated. Bertie, high-spirited, intelligent, an excellent organizer and a bit of a clown, was certainly good company at his own parties, and his dogmatism and bad temper ensured him a respect not always accorded to men of his superficial tastes. As for Ione, he was constantly humming and buzzing about her, paying her the most extravagant compliments, running upstairs to fetch her sweaters and scarfs, while she responded with a tolerant but charming smile, a perfunctory shrug, an occasional sarcasm. Their relationship might have been a parody of the Edwardian hero and heroine of twenty years before, he all ardor and she a wall of cool aloofness—until the final chapter. But it was just the prospect of that final chapter that haunted me.

On the morning of the Fourth of July the three of us were seated at an umbrella table at the club before lunch. Ione had finished her swim and was dressed and ready to go home, but Bcrfie had insisted that we wait until he should have finished his noontime tonic water. Certainly the big pool and the children in brightly colored bathing suits and the little orchestra in red coats on the balcony playing Victor Herbert made a pretty sight, and in one direction we could see over the roof of the pavilion to the green top of Green Mountain glittering in the sunshine and on the other to the blue sea and the long pine profile of Bar Island. But I knew that people would soon be coming over to speak to Ione, and I felt self-conscious in the old red tweed skirt and buckled shoes that I had worn for my morning hike. Bertie, of course, was patriotically immaculate in a blue coat, red tie and white flannels, and Ione perfection in her mourning white. She must have seemed an odd captive of the big, plain sister and the small, plain, dapper brother who were so unlike except for a certain family similarity about the eyes and chin. Bertie was complaining that there were too few men in Bar Harbor to allow of proper dinner parties.

"Gussie thinks me an idle peacock," he said to Ione, when I had pointed out that some men had to work. "She has no understanding of my function in the modern world."

"I wasn't aware you had one," I retorted.

"Oh my, yes," he said emphatically. "And a valuable one, at that. You see, Ione, every Tom, Dick and Harry hopes to make a fortune today. The little orchestra leader up there is probably thinking at this very moment about buying five shares of U.S. Steel. Why not? It's the American dream, isn't it? My function is simply to show them what their grandsons will be like, once the fortune has been made and handed down. Now, whether or not they like this example is no affair of mine. That is entirely up to them. I make no claim to be anything but a representative American gentleman of leisure. The choice is theirs. To stay in their present humble bracket or to sweat out a lifetime and produce one Bertie Millinder!"

"You're absurdly cynical," I said.

Ione had been listening with evident impatience. "But he means it, Gussie!" she exclaimed. "He actually means it. Bertie's as serious about spending the money as your grandfather ever was about making it!"

"Serious?" Bertie demanded, nettled by her tone. "Of course I'm serious. Spending money is a serious matter."

"Must it be a grim one? Is that, too, part of the American dream? To miss the joy? The gaiety?"

"You'll find even gaiety has to be paid for, Ione," Bertie retorted with sudden testiness. "Even yours!"

Ione flushed instantly and was silent. I had never seen him so sharp with her before, and I wondered uneasily if it might not increase her respect for him. Nothing further was said on the subject, but that night at a picnic with fireworks which Bertie gave on a sandy beach on the other side of the island, he was so noticeably attentive to Ione that he must have been repenting of his rudeness. He shouted with laughter at her jokes; he toasted her health in the champagne that he had insisted on bringing, and he even made what I thought a rather drunken little speech on how she had converted him from Newport to Bar Harbor. Furious, I decided that he was compromising her and that I must make my position clear.

I had my chance that same night as Bertie and I were walking down the beach to the cars. It was dark, but we could hear the others ahead talking gaily and every now and then the high shrill note of Ione's laugh. Bertie had no desire to make up the rear of a procession with me and was accelerating his pace when I caught him by the elbow.

"I want to talk to you a minute," I said gruffly, coming to a halt.

"What is it, Gussie?" he demanded impatiently. "Have you lost something? We can send back tomorrow for it."

"Wait." I cocked my head and listened. Ione's laugh sounded thinly through the night air. They were already too far away to hear us. "How could you carry on that way?" I began fiercely.

"What way?" His face in the dark was a small round moon of surprise.

"Making up to Ione like a sophomore at a barn dance! I should think you'd have more respect for the dead!"

"The *dead?*"

"Titus Locke hasn't been dead a year!"

Bertie with this seemed immediately to recover his self-possession. He even had the gall to chuckle. "Don't you think it might be a bit presumptuous for me to go into deeper mourning than his widow?"

"Ione mourns him sincerely!" I cried, stung. "Her real life ended when Titus was killed!"

"Then why are you so wrought up about a little summer flirting? Obviously, it can have no consequences."

"I'm not in the least concerned about the consequences," I retorted, in a hasty effort to restore the dignity of my grievance. "I have far too much faith in Ione. What concerns me is that a brother of mine should show so little delicacy towards the widow of one of our war heroes."

"Is that a crack about my not being in the army?"

"No. But I think those who were lucky enough to have spent the war in safety might show a little respect for the widows of those who gave up their lives."

"Hoity-toity!" he cried. "Don't we take a high line? Who put *you* in charge of Ione's life?"

So direct an onslaught left me trembling all over. "I don't know if I care to have as my house guest a person with so little feeling for tragedy!"

"House guest!" he exploded.

We faced each other now, on the old, familiar well-trodden ground of childhood rivalries. "I never interfere with the house in Newport," I pointed out, "and if you were half a gentleman, you wouldn't interfere with the house up here."

"I shall leave tomorrow!" he said irately. "If you think it's *gay* staying with you!"

"It's not intended to be," I said cuttingly, and we proceeded on through the dark for several long moments of silence. Unfortunately, we were both too angry to give up the argument. I felt it a minor victory that Bertie should have been the first to speak.

"I suppose I should take it as a compliment that you're afraid of my influence with Ione."

"I told you, I'm not in the least afraid of it. I want to give her a peaceful summer, that's all. Free of molestation."

"Oh, come, Gussie. You've got a bird of paradise trapped up here, and you're scared she'll fly the coop. I hadn't realized I was doing so well. *Merci!*"

I almost turned my ankle at this. My foot slipped on a rock, and I paused, breathing heavily. Bertie came right up and stood beside me; in the moonlight I could just make out his offensive grin. "What are your plans for Ione?" I demanded abruptly. "Do you expect her to be another of your chorus girls?"

"I think it unseemly for maiden ladies to discuss things they cannot understand. However *curious* they may be. But in view of the scene you're making, I suppose I may as well tell you that I'm planning to ask Ione to be my wife."

My anger at once dropped to pieces. There was no further time for such a luxury. Bertie as a flirt, or even as a would-be seducer, might be simply a bore, but Bertie as a suitor was dangerous indeed. "And do you flatter yourself that she'll have you?"

"I think it entirely possible."

"After being married to a man like Titus?"

"You forget that I knew Titus," he said with a sniff. "He wasn't all you crack him up to be. He's been covered with posthumous glory, but so would I, if I'd been clumsy enough to step on that mine. Titus was a charming fellow and had a way with the ladies, but he was no heavyweight, believe me."

"Then he'll have a worthy successor in you!"

"Really, Gussie, what an ugly mood you're in. You should be glad for Ione. I simply propose to put her back in the setting where she belongs. She was the best hostess in New York on a pittance. What will she be with what I can give her?"

"Is that all you want her for? To be a hostess?"

"Never mind what I want her for," Bertie said with a maddening chuckle. "That's another of the things one doesn't discuss with maiden sisters."

I shuddered at the prospect of his small greedy hands on Ione's white skin. I thought of Alberich, the dwarf, and then of the nude captive in

Grandpa's gallery; I remembered her proud, reproachful stare. I became reckless. "If she married you so soon after Titus' death, what do you think she'd do after yours?"

"Marry somebody else," he said promptly. "As I should wish her to. Ione has the warmth and friendliness of a beautiful poodle. She is perfectly devoted and loyal to one master." He paused. "To one master at a time."

"A poodle!" I cried in outrage.

"I suggest you see a psychiatrist, Gussie. They're quite the coming thing. He might be able to tell you some illuminating things about your resentment of me and Ione."

"You'll leave my house tomorrow!" I shouted hoarsely.

"*Our* house," he corrected me coolly, and I stamped on ahead of him down the beach.

I knew that I would never sleep that night if I did not talk to Ione, and I insisted that she drive back with me alone in the Pierce-Arrow, although this assignment crowded the others into the remaining vehicles. As soon as I had reached forward to tap the glass partition to make sure that it was closed, I sank back in the seat and burst into tears.

"Gussie, my poor Gussie, what is it?" Ione cried in dismay.

Sobbingly, I related my conversation with Bertie. Even in my shaken mood I noticed that there was a certain intensity in the stillness with which she listened. I was too upset to edit any part of what had been said; I told her the whole thing down to his final remark about the poodle. It was the second time, I blurted out, that he had likened her to a bitch! But Ione gave a sudden, startling hoot of laughter.

"You've always said he had a low opinion of women!" she cried. "What could prove it more than his being reduced to propose to a poodle? But don't worry, my dear," she continued, shifting suddenly into the high sad tone that she always used in discussing Titus. "You're quite right that I'm in no mood to consider any proposal of marriage." She raised her hands to emphasize the sheer absurdity of such an idea. "But that doesn't mean, of course, I resent them. No woman ever really resents them. For all his reservations, I am highly sensible of the compliment from so confirmed a bachelor as your brother."

"Then you'd rather he stayed?" I asked gloomily.

"Certainly not," she said firmly. "I think, all things considered, Bertie had much better go."

And Bertie went. Ione got up earlier than usual to breakfast with him before he motored to Islesboro to stay with Willie and Julia, and from my bedroom window I had the mortification of hearing the sound of their laughter. Evidently it was a cheerful leave-taking. In the days that followed, Ione and I resumed our old routine; we motored once more to distant parts of the island to dip in odd warm nooks of the chilly sea and to picnic afterwards on sun-heated rocks, finding seals and eagles and even once a black bear, but there was a new, false note in our Arcadian simplicity. It was the difference between the house from which electricity and telephones have been arbitrarily banished and the house into which they have never penetrated. Bertie had opened up to us the social world of Bar Harbor, and to keep it now at bay seemed, at the least, artificial. Ione uttered no complaints; she was as cheerful and charming as ever, but her silences were longer, and my pleasure in our summer was tarnished by the renewed fear that she was bored. I even began to wonder if it might not be wise to organize a dinner party, but when I finally drew up a guest list I realized in disgust that I had simply duplicated one of Bertie's, and tore it up. If I was to compete with my brother, I could never do it in his own territory. Yet when I looked about with saddened eyes at the stubble which he had made of my own fields, I wondered where else I could carry on the fight.

3

IT TURNED OUT, however, that there were to be other contestants in the battle for Ione. She and I were having tea one hot July afternoon on the terrace when our eyes were dazzled by the apparition around the point and close in to shore of a great schooner, a vision of billowing sail and diaphanous grace which, as it passed abeam, broke out its flags in an explosion of color. Ione, watching intently as it went swiftly by, gave a little cry of recognition.

"It's the *Endymion*!"

Even I knew that the *Endymion* belonged to Harold Fay. He was the friend whom Bertie talked most about, which meant, of course, that he was rich, not rich like a Millinder, but really rich, the only son of an original Standard Oil partner. I was even capable of a sudden twinge of jealousy at the thought of how antiquated Mr. Fay's fortune must make ours seem to Ione's eyes. His oil was like his sails, smooth and new; it might make us appear as dowdy and out of date as love seats or Turkish corners.

"My cousin, Sandy Herron, must be on board," I said, immediately trying to connect myself with the object of her attention. "Aunt Polly wrote me from Newport that he was cruising with Mr. Fay."

"Will they come and call?"

"They?" I glanced sideways at her. "Sandy might. But I don't know Mr. Fay. I suppose you must. You and Bertie seem to know everybody."

"Yes, I know him."

Something in her tone made me want to abuse Mr. Fay. "Is he as disagreeable as they say?"

"Oh, he can be. But if you agree with him and flatter him, he can be nice enough. He's like an absolute despot on some small cowering tropical island."

I sniffed. "Does he have any brains?"

"Some." Ione shrugged. "Not as many as he's supposed to have. But then, people have to credit him with all sorts of virtues to persuade themselves they're not cultivating him for his money. Isn't that your theory, Gussie?"

I decided to drop that part of the topic. There were moments when Ione struck me as almost too sophisticated. "Is he married?"

"Oh, no, he's a confirmed bachelor. Titus used to say that Harold would never marry until he found a woman richer than himself. And that he'd hate her worst of all!"

The good manners of the Herrons were proverbial in our family, and that very night Sandy telephoned to ask if he might pay a call the next day and bring his skipper, Mr. Fay. I asked them for lunch, and rather to my surprise, they both accepted. That Sandy should take off a little time to call on an old maid cousin I expected from a son of Aunt Polly's, but that he should grace her board for a meal and bring a friend to boot was surely beyond the call of duty. I decided that they must have heard about my house guest and that Mr. Fay was less of a misogynist than commonly supposed. This impression was confirmed the following day when neither of them showed the least surprise on seeing Ione.

Sandy Herron was the baby of my generation, the youngest of all Grandpa Millinder's grandchildren, having even missed out, because of his posthumous birth, on the million-dollar legacy left to each of his male cousins. He was a tall, broad, muscular young man with a rugged, craggy countenance and thinning blond hair which kept popping up from his head in cowlicks. He had mild blue eyes and a gentle, lazy disposition and was adored by his mother, his sisters and plenty of other women. Yet although he had passed thirty he was still unmarried. There was a family theory that Sandy thought of only one thing at a time and that marriage had not yet occurred to him. He was a customer's man in a stockbrokerage house and devoted the greater part of his time to violent athletics. His peculiar characteristic was the ease with which he adapted himself to the exigencies of a society more artificial than one would have thought his simple nature could tolerate. It was difficult, for example, to imagine Sandy spending the time and care that he must have spent on his elaborate wardrobe. It was easier to imagine him as somehow growing his clothes, like feathers.

I was always glad to see Sandy, who brought me friendly messages from Aunt Polly in Newport and from Willie and Julia in Islesboro. I was less glad to see the captain of the *Endymion*, but I had grudgingly to admit that for a man who must have been nearing fifty, Mr. Fay was still almost romantic looking. He was very tall and bony and thin, and he had long thick black greying hair and large, dark, hostile, evasive eyes. He was ungracious and moody; his abrupt movements and swinging jerky walk seemed to anticipate pursuing hosts of trivial admirers, but I could perfectly see how some foolish, misguided woman might think that if she ever seized his affections they would prove, like those of Byron's Corsair, to be worth a world renounced. He was not exactly rude to me at lunch, but I kept expecting that he would be at any moment. He answered my questions about his boat in the manner of one who felt his time being wasted and after the meal paced up and down the porch alone, paying no attention to any of us. Ione sat up straight and smiled sweetly at Sandy who was talking about the cruise, but I had a distinct impression that she was very much aware of that pacing figure. I had just picked up my needlepoint when Fay suddenly turned back to Ione and blurted out, with no more apology to Sandy for his interruption than if the latter had been a hired deck hand:

"Would you like to come out on the boat this afternoon? I'll sail you round the island."

Ione's eyes had a smiling, bemused look. "Are you asking just *me*?"

"Certainly I'm asking just you. Who else should I ask?"

"Well, don't we both happen to be guests at the moment?"

Fay stared at her, puzzled, and then turned abruptly to me. "I should be very happy, Miss Millinder," he said gruffly, "to have you as my guest on a trip around the island."

"It's very kind of you," I said hastily, "but I have things to do here. Take Ione. It's such a lovely day."

"Do you really mean that, Gussie?" Ione inquired with a slight lift of her eyebrows. "Are you absolutely sure the idea doesn't appeal to you?"

"You heard her, didn't you?" Fay demanded. "She says you're to go. You have her permission, if that's what you want."

"What I want is not Gussie's permission," Ione replied with the smallest edge in her tone. "What I want is the assurance that in declining your invitation I shall not be depriving her of an expedition that she might enjoy."

"You mean you're not coming?"

"How quickly you understand."

Ione and Fay stared at each other as his frown deepened. "You make me feel that I've committed a gaffe in asking you. Would you mind telling me why?"

"No, Harold, I would not in the least mind," Ione answered in a cool, metallic tone, but with her same smile. "I will not come out on your boat this afternoon for the simple reason that you assume I will. You assume that I am a poor female who has nothing to do but wait breathlessly to be asked. You are arrogant, Harold. You are repellently arrogant."

"Oh, stuff!" Fay retorted, turning away as if he had expected better things than a repetition of so stale an indictment. "Frankness isn't arrogance. Or if it is, we need a lot more arrogance in this world."

Any embarrassment that I might have felt vanished at the sight of Sandy's pink cheeks. Sandy, like his mother, had no place in his scheme of things for bad manners. It was not that they shocked him, or even frightened him. It was simply that there was no accepted way of handling them.

"Oh, come off it, Harold," he muttered, plunging his hands in his pockets. "That's a bit thick."

"Was it frankness," Ione continued to Fay, raising her voice, "that kept you from writing me when Titus died? That even kept you from calling? Was it frankness that made you the only member of his form at Chelton who failed to contribute to the memorial gates? The only one as well as the richest?"

"Oh, come now," he muttered, turning very red. "I never got the appeal."

"I wrote you myself, Harold!"

"Well, I guess my secretary never forwarded it. She knows I only give to my foundation." He shrugged as if it were simpler to settle the matter than to discuss it. "I'll build Titus another pair of memorial gates. Or a drinking fountain. Or a marble bench. Anything you think proper. How about it?"

"I'm afraid it's too late for that now!" Ione exclaimed tensely, shaking her head. "My object in telling you was not to extort another memorial for poor Titus. His gates at the school are under construction now, and very beautiful they will be, no thanks to you. My object was to teach you a very simple lesson: that there are some things in this world your money can't buy." She turned to me now with a brilliant smile. "There, Gussie! You see I have learned from your example. There are times when it's better to speak out!"

Harold Fay turned on his heel and marched around to the front of the house where his hired car was waiting. Sandy lingered, stuttering, not quite sure whether to offer or accept apologies, and finally scurried off after his friend. Ione talked with great spirit about the episode all during our drive that afternoon; she was terribly excited and more than a little scared by her own daring. Then she fell to brooding, turning from the sea view to ask:

"You think I did right, don't you? You don't really think I went too far? After all, he was rather a friend of Titus'."

She hardly listened to my reassurances. When we returned from our drive, we found, as I had feared, a letter that had just been delivered by a sailor from the *Endymion*. Ione read it quickly and handed it to me. It was, of course, from Harold Fay. He apologized very handsomely for his remissness in failing to contribute to Titus' gates and announced that he had sent his pledge that very afternoon to President Hadley of Yale for twenty-five thousand dollars towards a memorial for Titus to take such form as his widow should designate.

"It's just as you say," I remarked uncomfortably as I handed back the letter. "Mr. Fay thinks he can buy his way out of anything."

But Ione had obviously been softened by his gesture. "Perhaps he can," she mused. "Perhaps that's just the beauty of money. I can't help it, Gussie. It touches me to think I can start a scholarship fund in Titus' memory. He always felt so sorry about boys who couldn't afford to go to college. It came so near being his own case."

The next day another invitation came to board the *Endymion*. Ione said she wouldn't go without me, and as she obviously wanted very much to go, I reluctantly agreed. It was a dreary day for me. The boat was very beautiful, and we sailed out to Egg Rock and circled the lighthouse, and Harold Fay in his skipper's cap was like a little boy with his unfamiliar good manners and his pride in showing Ione everything, but I was miserably sick, and Sandy had to take me below to a cabin and sit with me during the balance of the trip. The invitation was repeated the following day, but I declined firmly and finally prevailed on Ione to go without me.

"You love it, and you ought to go," I kept insisting morosely. "Besides, you've been entirely too much cooped up with me. It'll do you good to get off for a bit."

When she came in late that night, flushed and excited, I tried in vain to elicit the information from her that I dreaded to hear. I kept turning the conversation to Fay himself and the kind of man he was and what he wanted out of life, but Ione would not talk about him, telling me instead about the sea and the wind and the islands and the charming picnic they had had at the end of a long wooded point. Her spirits were high, but her remarks were general. I had no idea if she was in love with Fay, or with Bertie, or with anyone at all. It even occurred to me that she might be simply in love with attention. I had never felt more distant from her.

Every day now she went out on the *Endymion*. It became an understood thing. Twice Harold Fay dined with us, hardly addressing a word to me, never taking his eyes off Ione, and once he took her after dinner to the movies, asking me to accompany them in an offhand manner that ensured my refusal. Then Sandy called one morning when the *Endymion* was out. He was in a business suit and on his way to Ellsworth to take the train.

"Harold was due to leave Bar Harbor three days ago," he complained, his blue eyes vivid with a vague bewilderment, "but he simply refuses to go. I have to be in Newport tomorrow, and I've got to take the train. So do a couple of the other fellows. They're furious, and I can't say I blame them. It's a hell of a thing to ask a fellow off on a cruise and then maroon him up here!"

I was beside myself when Ione returned that night, and we had our first real fight. I told her that she was encouraging Harold Fay in his rudeness to his guests, and she retorted with an airiness of which I would not have thought her capable that Harold's orders for his own vessel were not matters in which she had any concern. He had given a memorial to Titus, and if he chose to ask her to go sailing, which she adored, it was the least she could do in return.

"You said it was not good for us to be so much cooped up together," she finished on a lofty note as she rose to go to her room. "Well, I'm simply taking your advice. To expect me to worry about a few idle men who have to take a train instead of a yacht to fulfill their silly social obligations seems to me the height of absurdity. If you think it over dispassionately, I think you'll find I'm right. Good night, Gussie!"

I sat up late that night brooding, and then I did a strange thing. I telegraphed to Bertie who was still with Willie and Julia at Islesboro. My telegram read: "If you still want what you wanted, come back immediately. Fay and *Endymion* objects of an alarming interest." I had faced in those long quiet nocturnal hours the fact that Ione was lost to me. I had even faced the fact that she had never belonged to me. Ione, even more than most women, was peculiarly a creature for men. Such was her nature, and resentment was idle. But there was still one thing I could do, for her and for the Millinders. I could keep her for our team. I could keep her from the all-clutching grasp of Harold Fay.

The next morning I went into Ione's bedroom, while she was having breakfast, with Bertie's telegram announcing his arrival that same day. Ione read it at a glance and then broke into a loud, long laugh. It was a cheerful, disarming laugh, and I had no idea what it meant.

"Oh, Gussie, you old darling, you *asked* him to come, didn't you? You actually did!"

I stared in bewilderment. "You mean you *wanted* me to?"

"Of course I wanted you to! Gussie, my own dear sister, Bertie and I are engaged! We have to wait to the end of my year of mourning, but then we'll be married. Very quietly with just you and maybe Willie and Julia and Titus' darling old mother." She jumped out of bed to embrace me, kissing both my burning cheeks. "Titus would have wanted it this way, I know. He never could stand widows. He used to say that remarriage was the only civilized substitute for suttee!"

Everything in my mind seemed to slip and crash, like tableware in a storm at sea. "But when he left, you told me he hadn't a chance. Were you fibbing, Ione?"

"Not a bit of it! He didn't have a chance. *Then*. But he's written me every day since. With a typewritten address so you wouldn't know. We became engaged by mail. Think of it, Gussie! I'm a mail-order bride!"

Well, I didn't know what to think of it. It was all too much for me. "And Harold Fay?" I demanded. "How will he take it?"

"Oh, Harold should be glad," she said, smiling a bit mischievously. "Now Harold can go back to Newport. Now Harold can marry the richest woman in the world! He's had a tiny lesson in humility that he very badly needed. He's in my debt, actually, if he'll only see it. And if he doesn't, well—we've both had three charming weeks!"

"*He* has. But what about you? How could you enjoy yourself, thinking of Bertie all the time?"

Ione laughed even more loudly. "Oh, my dear Gussie, how *much* you have to learn!"

Well, perhaps I did. I had learned a lot already. I can almost hear the guffaw from my reader's lips that I should have believed for a moment in the sincerity of Ione's mourning. But I did believe in it, and I still do. Bertie's Ione and Harold Fay's Ione both existed, but so did mine. Life is complex, and if the beautiful creature who came to redecorate my house and life should have helped herself at the same time to a slice of personal happiness, was it not for the ultimate good of all? Ione always gave more than she got, and nobody ever got very much from the Millinders.

4

Bᴇʀᴛɪᴇ ᴡᴀs ᴄᴏʀʀᴇᴄᴛ in his prophecy that Ione would make a great hostess. Half of that job is enjoying it, and Ione took a childish delight in every bauble that Bertie's money could buy. Having always been relatively poor, yet at the same time linked by ties of blood and marriage to several fortunes (to ours, for example, through Aunt Daisy), she had spent much of her life in the antechamber of wealth and was well qualified to judge how much better money might be spent than it usually was. At first she was a trifle too ebullient. She showed off the pearls and diamonds that Bertie had bought for her with a candid enthusiasm that was meant to be disarming but that might have been considered vulgar in anyone less irreproachably born. This stage once behind her, however, she settled down with relish to the serious business of being a Millinder. Like the rest of us, she was extravagant, but she was extravagant with a flair. She sold Bertie's share of the family brownstone to me and erected a Palladian villa on Seventieth Street with an interior as exotic as its exterior was chaste: panels of jungle birds and mythological beasts painted by Robert Chanler, Japanese screens and huge jade lamps, Persian rugs and Tiffany glass chandeliers in the shape of clusters of flowers. In Bar Harbor she built a white stucco Spanish convent with a red roof and a great patio that commanded a breath-taking view of Frenchman's Bay. If I had once thought of her as Edwardian, I now saw her as more appropriately postwar, with a touch of the vamp and the enigmatic moodiness of a Fitzgerald heroine. I think of the Ione of this period in a kimono, holding up a long cigarette holder and looking soulfully at her dinner partner while she mused on the radiancy of her own golden hair. But then would come that laugh, the famous laugh, raucous and flinty and down-to-earth, and out of a D. W. Griffiths frame would step the eternal, practical New York hostess. It was as if she had been playing tableaux, and someone had cried "Cut!" And, of course, it charmed everyone, for those who had liked the tableau had been able to take their fill of it, and those who had not could think it had been made fun of. There were very few people who were impervious to Ione's charm.

Was she really the great hostess that people believed? It is hard to say. Society is kind to its favorites, contrary to popular belief. To hear her friends talk about her, one would have endowed Ione with the energy and the imagination of a Michelangelo, simply because she liked to fill her rooms with crowds of people. To some of my family, on the other hand, particularly to Julia, she was always a bit of a joke. Julia and Willie who, thanks to Papa's partiality, were far richer than Bertie or I, moved in that solid, conservative homogeneous world of sportsmen and bankers who occupied the great Tudor and Georgian country places indigenous to northern New Jersey and the north shore of Long Island; they looked with pity and amusement at people who found any social merit in the meretricious gaudiness of such silly watering places as Newport or Bar Harbor. I have known Julia actually to apologize for Ione in such terms as: "I hope you don't mind, we've asked Willie's brother and sister-in-law for the weekend. She's rather a dear, actually, despite the silly things the papers say about her. But who in the world can I get to play bridge with them while we're hunting?" And the visitor, who might have previously thought Mrs. Bertie Millinder was a queen of the fashionable world, now changed his mind, as he was intended to, and concluded that she must be nearer the fringe.

Julia even went so far as to maintain that Ione had been a better hostess before her marriage to Bertie, that she had the kind of talent that flourished on challenge and that, with too large a purse at her disposal, she tended towards the showy and obvious. There was some truth in this, but there was also a good deal of Julia. Julia never took into consideration, for example, Ione's remarkable facility for controlling all the machinery of entertainment at her own parties while seeming as unconcerned and as much at ease as one of her guests. But then Julia never entertained well herself; she regarded the machinery as too much beneath her. She could not understand the amount of organization required for a successful party or that Ione's concealment of it was the purest art. I never even saw Ione glance over the shoulder of the person to whom she was talking, yet she always turned at the right moment and with the same charming air of "*You*, at last!" to each newcomer.

I should say immediately that, as a sister-in-law, Ione was perfectly lovely to me. Sometimes I thought it was because she had so little family of her own, sometimes simply because she liked me. There was never any idea of crossing off Bertie's old maid sister with a standing invitation to Sunday lunch. Ione would call me every day to tell me about the parties she was planning and to offer me my pick of them. I knew she was sincere, for my prickly nature would have rung with alarm bells at the first false note. I went to some of the parties, but it irked me to see the attention that Ione poured out on people whom I deemed hardly worthy of it. Ione, for all her taste in things, was strangely undiscriminating about people. It may have been part of her charm, that instinct for sympathy with the most boring individuals. But what I objected to, more than her lack of discrimination, was her lack of consistency, or as it gradually struck me, her lack of principle. Ione, chameleon-like, took on the colors of her interlocutor. If it happened to be a banker, red-faced and red-baiting, she would deplore the dangers of Bolshevism; if it happened to be an artist who sensed the desert of Philistia closing in around him, she would sigh over the materialism of the American scene. She vibrated with the passions of her friends, but with no sense of the conflicts between them. When I taxed her once with this, she laughed in sheer pleasure. It was not cynicism; Ione had not a cynical bone in her body. It was the same habit of falling in with the views of others.

"Oh, Gussie," she exclaimed, when she had stopped laughing, "you really make me sound too awful! You must think I don't have an ounce of character. Now promise that the next time you catch me at it, you'll stand up before the whole room and denounce me!"

But, of course, I did no such thing. Only a week later I heard her tell one guest that the tragedy of our age was America's failure to join the League of Nations and agree with another that Henry Cabot Lodge was the greatest man of the century. I was learning that it was simply the way Ione was. She believed in the value of feeling rather than in the value of what one felt. And perhaps she was right. Perhaps nothing in the world justified one in being rude at a dinner party. Yet had it not been just such rudeness that had brought us together in the first place?

One of the beneficent results of Ione's philosophy of compromise was my reconciliation with Papa. Being incapable of bearing grudges herself, Ione was incapable of understanding them in others. She knew Cecilia and found her amusing. Why should we not all be friends? It was not difficult for her to effect a reconciliation between Bertie and Papa, as they had been too little congenial from the beginning to have noticed much the further breach, and Bertie and Cecilia immediately hit it off as persons of cold nature often do. With me, of course, it was harder. I would not be the first to call on Cecilia, and, as my stepmother (though I had never regarded her as such), she could hardly be the first to come to me. Eventually we met at Ione's and exchanged the necessary formalities. Our mutual dislike has never altered and persists to this day. But we have been perfectly civilized; we exchange gifts at Christmas and postcards on our birthdays. When I first called on Papa, however, I was so overcome at how he had aged that I threw my arms around him and burst into tears. Thereafter I went to see him every day for the remaining two winters of his life. Cecilia always left us alone; she was glad enough, I am sure, to have somebody else take over her duties at the side of an aged and ailing spouse.

Papa may have showed his age, but as in everything else, he did it charmingly. How many times do we hear that the sportsman is lost when he can no longer shoot or ride to hounds or even putt on his own front lawn! Yet Papa, who had no resources in books or pictures or music, accepted boredom and inactivity with a grace that astonished us all. I blessed the radio to which he listened incessantly and the solitaire which he incessantly played. He was always cheerful, always concerned that Cecilia should not waste her time by staying home with him. He need not have been. Cecilia was making a great name for herself in social welfare work; her voice on the radio and at public dinners, eloquent and moving, was known to hundreds of thousands. She had at last found her greatest role. With Papa she was very correct: cheerful when present and strict in the running of his household. She was his Catherine Parr, his Madame de Maintenon. I suppose many great lovers have ended in the care of such women. What Papa thought of her, whether he was satisfied with the wife for whom he had sacrificed so much, I could only surmise. He had always detested the personal note in conversation, and old age had not changed this. He and I used to talk about everything under the sun except what was closest to our hearts. It was restful, it was pleasant, but it did not help to fill in the gap which the years of our estrangement had created. The closest that we came to doing this was on an afternoon a few months before his death, when after a good deal of coughing and throat-clearing, he brought himself to speak of his will.

"I haven't left you anything, Gus," he said at last. "Because you and Bertie got your mother's money. But I can change it if you'll say the word. How about it? How are you fixed?"

Unlike Cordelia I didn't even have to say I loved him. I simply had to ask, that was all. To hold out my hand to have it crammed with gold. But as I sat in silence, considering the magnanimity of this offer and what I should answer to it, I was shocked by my sudden confrontation with the indubitable fact, that, again unlike Cordelia, I *wanted* Papa's gold! Bitterly now I remembered what Ione had said about my growing obsession that people cared only for my money. Would I not want more and more, as the years went by, to guard against future disaster, to assure my timorous self that I could always at least purchase the loyalty of my own household? Or, at the very least, Osborn's? I saw in a flash that there would be no end to this kind of thinking unless I refused Papa's offer immediately, unless I took a stand once and for all against the creeping paralysis of my panic.

"No, no, Papa!" I exclaimed. "I want nothing. Nothing at all." I looked about the room desperately until my eye fell on a portrait of Granny Millinder, a miniature, depicting her working on her needlepoint, the pose in which I remembered her on the fatal day when I consulted her about Lancey. "Except that!" I cried. "That will always keep me from making too great a fool of myself!"

Papa grunted, and the miniature was all I got. Cecilia and Cora had had lifetime settlements; the whole estate went to Willie and his sons. But that, I comforted myself, was what Papa really wanted. Willie was the child whom he had always adored, and Willie's boys, Lydig and Oswald, were the consolation of his last years. And then, too, according to Bertie, there may have been a subdued little jealousy in Papa at the concentration of his father's fortune first in Uncle Fred's hands and then in his son George's. If our branch of the family was ever to keep up, it would not do to dissipate our share. With such hopes, it was a merciful providence that kept him from seeing the later careers of Lydig and Oswald.

But to return to Ione. Her relationship with Bertie had always baffled me. I am sure that she was never a demanding wife, either emotionally or physically. She was the kind of woman, as Bertie himself had once put it, who was perfectly satisfied with one man—so long as he belonged to her. But there was the trouble: Bertie belonged to himself. It was as much as he could do to suffer himself to be loved. In the years that followed his marriage he became, if possible, even more of a bachelor than he had been before. When Ione, who had tried desperately to be a worthy partner at the bridge table, finally gave up the game, he simply continued to go to his card parties without her. Bertie would no more have given up an evening of bridge for a wife who didn't enjoy it than a surgeon would have refused to operate because his wife was afraid of the sight of blood. His pleasures were his business, and they continued as rigidly as if Ione had never existed: cards, golf, billiards, beagling and men's dinners at all his different clubs. I have never known a husband who made fewer concessions to his wife in the arrangement of his own schedule. He allowed Ione to entertain whom she pleased and go where she pleased, and I think he was rather proud of her parties, but he detested her artistic and musical friends and refused to budge an inch from the protective covering of his small, familiar, epicurean, Philistine world.

Everyone assumed that it was only a matter of time before Ione would console herself with someone who knew better how to appreciate her attractions. She was beautiful and but recently forty; she had no children, and her husband gave her free rein. I believed that she had too much taste, and I stoutly maintained my faith in her long after the regular appearances at her side of my cousin Sandy Herron had become a matter of public comment. Sandy never missed a party at Ione's and hardly any that she went to. As Bertie was frequently otherwise engaged, it became the practice in New York social life to invite Sandy in his place. Most people, anyway, preferred him to Bertie; he was polite, agreeable, easily amused and had a shaggy blond muscular look that was very winning to women. And then, too, his obvious devotion to his beautiful, gay, older cousin-in-law made a tableau that her friends liked to watch and whisper about. Sandy always seemed to have a corner of one eye ready to spot Ione's least discomfort or need. One imagined him pining for danger that he might have occasion to draw a sword in her defense. When the Bertie Millinders came to Bar Harbor, Sandy followed and stayed at the Malvern Hotel; he kept his sailing sloop there and a long, rattling, yellow Mercedes in which he could be seen racing down West Street to or from Ione's house. Ione appeared to take his being there entirely for granted and almost to ignore him. Yet even I noticed that whenever she turned to speak to him, she always turned to just the spot in the room where he was standing.

By the beginning of Sandy's second summer at the Malvern I suspected that I had been naïve. When Julia came over from Islesboro on her motor cruiser to watch young Lydig and his new bride, Elsie, race at Northeast and lunched with me afterwards, I found her of the same opinion. Julia and I had got on better since my reconciliation with Papa, but she was as condescending as ever.

"Why, it's as plain as the nose on your face!" she exclaimed, crossing her long legs under her white cruising dress. "You can't expect a woman like Ione to play dummy every night!"

"Do you suppose Bertie knows?"

"It's like having a fatal disease. You don't want to know."

"But if you do!"

Julia shrugged. "Why should he care? He wanted a hostess, and he's got a hostess. I daresay he's satisfied with his bargain. In the set he plays with that kind of thing makes precious little difference."

I soon found myself going to the swimming club each day at noon and peering about to see if Ione and Sandy were there. I found that I was reading the social columns of the *Bar Harbor Times* to see what dinner parties the Herbert Millinders had attended and if Mr. Alexander Herron had been present. But what surprised me most of all was to find myself ringing up Sandy one morning and asking him to a picnic that I had never planned to give. I was taken aback by the bluntness of his response.

"Will Ione be there?" he asked.

"Ione? Don't you think it's rather dull to have the family together?"

"I just thought she might be coming."

"Can't you go anywhere without Ione?" I demanded in a tone that suddenly rasped. "Are you so tied to her apron strings? I'm surprised at you, Sandy," I went on, adopting without the smallest authority, the tone of an older sister. "Where are the famous Herron manners? I can't imagine what Aunt Polly would say if she knew her son required a guest list before making up his mind about an invitation!"

"It's not that, Gussie," the friendly, embarrassed voice drawled. "But Ione and Bertie and I have been sort of doing the same things together."

"I see!" I exclaimed sarcastically. "Well, I shall remember you the *next* time I ask Ione and Bertie!" And I hung up, so excited that I was trembling all over. The same things! Had there ever been so brash an excuse?

When I called on Sandy's inseparable friend that same morning, I found her, by a rare chance, alone. It was a hot day, and Ione was sitting on the patio in a listless mood, gazing out at the mist over a dead sea. She gave me none of the openings that I had expected, and I had to keep introducing Sandy's name rather clumsily into our lagging conversation.

"You seem to have Sandy on the brain this morning," she observed finally.

"It seems that way, doesn't it?"

"Have you fallen in love with him, Gussie?" she asked in a sudden mocking tone, giving me a bold look before which I quailed. "I think you ought to know that I very much disapprove of older women who run after young men."

"But I agree with you!" I cried.

Ione glanced at me obliquely. "Of course it's different if the young man does the chasing."

"*Does* he?" I asked pointedly.

"Yes, he does, believe it or not," Ione retorted sharply.

"Now, is *that* what you came for? If I'd left it to you, we'd have been at it all afternoon."

"No," I said sulkily, ashamed of my awkward subterfuge. "I came to suggest it was high time that Sandy thought of marrying and settling down. And that you're hardly helping him!"

Ione's eyes were faintly amused. She seemed to be debating her different tacks. But the obvious one, that it was none of my business, she eschewed. "I don't know why you should be such a champion of marriage. You've managed to give it a pretty wide berth yourself!"

"Oh, me," I said, raising my hands in a deprecating gesture. How could anyone compare the predicament of a blond, muscular young man with that of a middle-aged old maid? I was still the victim of the American cult of youth and marriage. "Sandy is obviously the marrying kind," I continued. "He's gentle and dutiful and sweet. Don't you agree he'd make a marvelous father?"

"What about his making a marvelous husband?"

"To be a marvelous husband, mustn't one first be a husband?"

"What rot we're talking," Ione answered impatiently. "A man can marry at any age. And believe me, Gussie, Sandy will be a better husband for having known me!"

She rather drew herself up as she flung this at me, and I promptly assumed the worst about her and Sandy. For didn't vice always lend strength? Had not Cecilia prevailed over Mamma? That Ione should flaunt in my face her affair with poor Sandy, that she should brag of the advantages to him in whatever little tricks she might have taught him, tricks that in turn he might teach to the innocent girl who would one day be his bride, struck me as sordid in the extreme. I abominated the Latin philosophy of love. I believed firmly that spontaneity was everything, that the least premeditation, the smallest amount of planning, would be fatal to the bloom of a natural emotion. It made me tremble with resentment to think that Ione, who had passed her brief widowhood with me, who had made me throb with her sorrows and her "lifelong grief," should now be lecturing me, like a demimondaine, on what *she* could do for my own cousin!

"You sound like a chapter in a dirty French novel!" I exclaimed angrily.

"You're beginning to make me cross, and I don't like to be cross." Ione had got up and was pacing slowly down the patio. But when she turned and faced me, there was no trace of anger in her eyes. Instead, she wore a sudden, pleading expression. Even in my indignation, I was impressed that I should have driven her to use her famous charm. "Look, Gussie, you've always tried to be a realist. Can't you leave me and Sandy alone for a bit? It's not going to last forever. *Je n'ai pas vingt ans, ma cherè!*"

I left without deigning to answer her and went straight to the swimming club where I knew I would find Bertie, in one of his striped blazers and shimmering white flannels, sitting at an umbrella table and sipping his noontime tonic water. He greeted me in an uninviting, brotherly way, but I sat firmly down in the canvas-back chair beside him.

"If you're looking for Ione," he said, "I believe she's gone for a walk. Around Jordan's Pond."

So that was how much he checked up on her! "She never used to like walking," I retorted. "At least, so she always told me."

"So she always told me," he agreed with a shrug. "I suppose it depends on who she walks with."

"Ah." I paused significantly. "You mean she's out with Sandy?"

"Who else?"

I allowed a longer pause. "It seems to me you're very philosophic."

"What on earth is there to be philosophic about?"

"Honor!" I exclaimed boldly.

Bertie looked at me in astonishment for a moment and then cackled loudly. "You think I'm a cuckold, don't you, Gussie? Don't deny it. It's written all over your face, like righteousness. It must give you the most delightful sense of superiority!"

"Do you possibly imagine," I replied with such dignity as I was still able to muster, "that I could derive any pride from anything so disgraceful?"

"Pride? I didn't say anything about pride. I imagine you're very much ashamed. But pleasure and shame go hand in hand. They're even twins!"

"If you care nothing for what *I* think," I said in a tone of reproach that was now the only feasible substitute for anger, "you might at least consider what others do."

"And what *do* others think?"

"You should know better than I. You're always telling me how well you know your world.'"

"Well, if it's a scandal, I know who's made it one!" Bertie was suddenly very angry. He sat up straight and glared at me with eyes that jumped. "I've seen you spying on Ione and Sandy, day after day, right here at the pool." He tapped the table warningly with his forefinger. "You're right, Gussie, I *do* know my world. And I know exactly what you're up to. Now you listen to me, my girl. If there is a scandal about Ione, you can be sure I'll see that Sandy clears out of Bar Harbor the very same day. But I'll never forgive the person who started the scandal. Never! There are ways and means to handle everything in this world, and scandal isn't one of them! Do you understand me, Augusta? Scandal isn't one of them!"

Was there an appeal in his tone? Was he pleading with me to find that way? I thought so, anyway, and it took the sting from his words. What I had been meaning to suggest, I now decided to carry out myself. I went directly home and wrote a letter to Sandy's mother. In defense of my officiousness I can only add that I had reached a certain time of life and that my nerves were unusually on edge.

5

AUNT POLLY HERRON, in our family, was everyone's favorite aunt. The difference between her and Aunt Euphemia Hoyt may have simply boiled down to the fact that they had such different husbands. For Uncle Stuart, a stout, twinkling, genial, hand-rubbing personal trust officer at J. P. Morgan & Co., who adored club life and spa life and who sat on every charity board that anyone could think of, was as kind to Aunt Polly as Uncle Josiah had been disagreeable to Aunt Euphemia. He was proud of her looks, proud of her fortune and proud of her, and even Grandpa Millinder had succumbed to the genial charm of this friendly son-in-law to the extent of leaving him half a million dollars. With such a husband, how could Aunt Polly fail to enjoy herself? It was said of Louis XIV that every organ of his body was perfectly adapted to the demands of life at Versailles; it might have been said of Aunt Polly that she was similarly equipped for the Newport season. Her black, marcelled hair, now greying, was always in place as in a statue; her white Millinder skin, aquiline nose and blinking black eyes never changed color or betrayed fatigue, either at the latest dinner parties or under the brightest sun at Bailey's Beach. She carried herself erectly and stuck her arm out very straight to greet you and never altered her mannered little sing-song way of speaking. Yet if the picture so conveyed is of a cold, formal woman, it is totally false. Aunt Polly fairly trembled with the violence of her passions: her passion for her family, her passion for her friends, her passion for clothes and parties and scrapbooks. She seemed not to know what privacy was and yet at the same time to enjoy with her daughters an inarticulate intimacy, as if they were all children together in the nursery of good manners. There was something lovable in the violent optimism behind Aunt Polly's naïveté, an optimism that seemed almost to make the world what the advertisements said of it. The dinner party she had been to the night before had always been "so interesting," the Englishman on her right "so stimulating," her hostess "so charming," the house "so attractive." She went to Europe every other year, always with the excitement of a sixteen-year-old, and kept huge red leather albums to commemorate the exciting events of her wonderful trips. It was impossible not to love Aunt Polly, but it was equally impossible to be close to her. She talked about the same things with the same people. With me it was the Red Cross, girls' schools, Italian art and what a pity Mamma had not liked the impressionist painters. I had tried in vain as a girl to strike a more intimate note and had finally given up. When I listened to her chattering with Grace, Nancy and Pamela I might as well have been listening to four brightly plumed macaws in the bird house at Central Park.

I was not so stupid as to say anything in my letter about Ione and Sandy. I knew that Aunt Polly would allow none but herself to criticize her "baby," who was adored as only a long-awaited son can be adored. I simply said that it was a beautiful summer and that it was such fun to have Sandy on Mount Desert, and wouldn't she and Uncle Stuart like to take a week out of their Newport season and come up to stay with me? My response was immediate and couched in the same enthusiastic language. Uncle Stuart was fishing in Canada, but Aunt Polly "craved" a week in Bar Harbor, provided I promised not to "put myself out" for her. There were to be no parties or picnics planned; all she wanted was a chance to look at the mountains and sea and to "catch up" on Bertie and myself.

When I met her train at Ellsworth in the early morning she was as bright and neat and brisk as if she had spent the night in her own bed. She darted down the platform to seize my hands in hers.

"Gussie, my dear, you look so well! I think the Millinders who've chosen Maine must have chosen wisely. So Sandy's always telling me!"

It was only at the mention of his name that I realized how brave were the good manners that kept her eyes and smile for me when she must have been pining to look about for her son.

"I didn't tell him you were coming," I confessed. "I wanted it to be a complete surprise."

"Oh, good!" she exclaimed, clapping her hands. "Then it really will be one, for I haven't written him a word!"

I was surprised, for I always pictured her as in constant communication with her children. It became obvious to me later that her prompt acceptance of my invitation, together with her omission to warn Sandy of it, was part of a carefully conceived plan of action, but her explosion of enthusiasm over Mount Desert and her little popping inquiries about all my friends and habits concealed it from me at the time. When we went to the swimming club at noon to sit at the umbrella tables, Aunt Polly held a little court amid all the ladies who hurried over to speak to her. I have never known anyone who knew so many people. She was still greeting friends when Bertie, Ione and Sandy appeared on the steps of the clubhouse. The latter at first turned a bright red and then, with a little shamefaced smile, hurried over to throw his big arms around his mother.

"Why, Mumsy! How on *earth*?"

Then everybody babbled excitedly about the surprise arrival. Bertie seemed delighted to see Aunt Polly, though I had never before considered that he was particularly fond of her. He laughed and chuckled as she told him the Newport gossip, asked her to dine the next day and promised to give her a dinner party on Saturday. There was general talk of a sail on Sandy's sloop followed by a picnic. Ione was the only silent member of our little group. I thought she kept trying to catch my eye with a quizzical stare, but I was careful to avoid it.

My life in the next days took on an unprecedentedly social pattern. Aunt Polly had insisted that nothing be done for her, that "a whiff of sea air" was all she wanted, but to have taken her at her word would have been like inviting an alcoholic for the weekend and hiding all the bottles. Besides, we were invaded by the social world; the telephone rang insistently and chauffeurs with cards kept appearing at the front door. Aunt Polly protested, but I begged her to treat the house as her own, which she finally did. This, too, as it turned out, was a part of her plan, and she was to make it up to me with expensive Christmas presents for years to come. Sandy was at the house most of the time; his filial nature was evidently upset that his old mother, two summers abandoned, should have to travel north to seek him out. The least that he could do was to devote himself to her during her little visit as attentively as he had devoted himself to Ione. The latter was obviously frantic, but she found that Sandy could be as stubborn as he was simple and as filial as he was faithful. She telephoned him continually and left the most imprudent messages. Usually the focal center of any party, she became abstracted and dull. She said nothing to me, however, until after a ladies' lunch that I had given for Aunt Polly, when she and I were sitting alone on the terrace while the others were out on the point inspecting the view. Ione was tense and nervous; she smoked cigarette after cigarette and threw the butts carelessly on the lawn, a habit that she knew I detested.

"You're tickled pink with yourself, aren't you?" she demanded in a sulky drawl." For bringing the old trout up here?"

"Really, Ione! She's your aunt, too!"

"I don't care if she's my bloody grandmother," Ione said crudely. "She's come up to take care of her precious cub, and she means business. I can't shake her even for an hour. It's 'darling Ione' this and 'darling Ione' that." She mimicked Aunt Polly so loudly that I was afraid her voice would carry down the lawn. "The amazing thing is she may actually mean it. She's so crooked, she's almost straight!"

"I thought Bertie seemed particularly glad to see her," I said mischievously.

"Bertie likes old ladies. Or was that, too, part of your nasty little plot? What I can't see is why Sandy is *your* responsibility. What did I ever do to *you?*" she demanded in a suddenly aggrieved tone. "Why should you bedevil me so? I always wanted you to be happy!"

I quailed before that angry stare. "After all, Bertie *is* my brother," I murmured.

"Oh, fiddlesticks!" Ione retorted rudely. "You wouldn't give a hoot what Bertie's wife was up to if she didn't happen to be me. It's *me* you're jealous of. You can't bear to see me have anything you haven't got yourself. You're a jealous, bitter old maid, Gussie Millinder, and it's high time somebody told you so!" I stared, thunderstruck, into those blazing blue eyes while the tears started into my own. I remembered when she had urged me to be a very different kind of old maid. And now, as the terrible picture of what I had become instead sprang up vividly in my mind, I covered my face and sobbed.

"Oh, Gussie!" Ione protested with a little wail. "Don't! You know I can't bear it! Please, Gussie, your guests! They'll be back any minute!" I felt my hands pulled from my face and Ione's handkerchief daubing my eyes. "I'm sorry, you old silly-billy, I didn't mean to go that far. Do pull yourself together. Honestly, it's too unfair, my having to comfort you!"

"No, no, you're right," I insisted, swept along in the full tide of my remorse. "You're absolutely right. I'm a jealous, bitter old maid. I was jealous of your having a lover! It's why I wrote Aunt Polly!"

"A lover!" Ione exclaimed, shocked. "But Sandy wasn't my lover. *Then.*"

I gaped. "He wasn't. What was he?"

Ione threw back her head and laughed her old rasping laugh. It was the same laugh except for a faint new hint of hysteria. "Why, you may well *ask!* I was too scared to let him be anything. Too scared of Bertie and you and your whole family. Too scared of what Sandy himself might think of me afterwards. I was paralyzed, and he, poor lamb, was good as gold. Except for that little naughty question in his eyes. Like the eyes of a faithful dog that wants to be taken on a walk. Oh, Gussie, what I've been through!" She got up and took a few steps down the terrace. "We might have gone on forever that way if it hadn't been for you!"

"For *me!*"

"Who else? Who threatened me and put me into a panic? After your call the other day I saw Sandy being taken away from me. I saw myself being punished, and for *nothing!* Oh, I was wild!" She strode back to my chair and faced me with a sudden defiant air of triumph. "I went to him that day, Gussie. That day! We became lovers that day! I owe you that! I'll always owe you that!"

When I could speak, I could only utter one word. It surprised me as much as it surprised her. "Where?"

Her brows knitted. "Where?"

"I never know where people go to do that sort of thing."

She stared at me for a blank moment and then gave another wild whoop of laughter. "Gussie, you're marvelous! You really are! Well, it turned out that Sandy had rented a camp at Indian Point. He'd had it ready all summer, just in case." Her face clouded over as she saw Aunt Polly with her chattering group reappear around the side of the house. "But don't worry," she concluded bitterly, as the returning group bore down on us across the lawn. "Your little trick has worked to perfection. We haven't been to the camp since your aunt blew in. And trust her to see to it that we never go again!"

I truly believe that if there had been any way in which I could have enabled Ione and Sandy to have protracted their affair, I would now have seized upon it. But the whole matter was about to be taken effectively from my hands.

"I've decided to take one of the Malvern cottages for the rest of the season," Aunt Polly announced. "I don't want to impose any more on you, dear Gussie, and I'm having such a marvelous time that I simply can't go back to Newport. Besides, if I left now, poor Sandy might feel he had to see his old ma safely home. And I wonder if it wouldn't be *rather* hard on him," she continued with a sly little wink to us all, "to have to tear himself away from Clara Bartlett at *just* this juncture!"

It might have seemed that this was overdoing it, but facts themselves wilted before the brazen boldness of Aunt Polly's presumptions. Clara Bartlett was a small, pretty, silent Boston girl who had been seated next to Sandy at every dinner since Aunt Polly's arrival. Ione was being surely strangled by the thin gold wire in which the Newport invader had enmeshed us all.

I was particularly conscious of this at the dance that Aunt Polly gave at the swimming club for her friends and Sandy's, to pay back, as she told me, "some of the kindness that Mount Desert had heaped on her that summer." It was a great occasion for all ages, and Aunt Euphemia Hoyt came up from Bedford to stay with her sister and help out. It was appalling to see what delight these two small, smiling, handshaking old women got out of a party. They might have been, as they hurried about, greeting guests and laughing, two little girls at a birthday celebration, blissful in a glittering, sexless world of tall cakes and spun sugar. Uncle Stuart in Canada was as absent as Uncle Josiah, dead. My aunts that night were sufficient unto themselves. I sat with Ione, who was dressed almost insultingly in a Chinese robe and pajamas, in a corner of the long glassed-in porch opening onto the ballroom. It was the first time I had ever seen her when she had had too much to drink. She kept slapping her fan hard against her knee as she stared moodily over the dance floor.

"Did you ever see such an ordinary party?" she asked sourly. "The same old clubhouse, exactly as it is every Saturday night. But just look at your silly old aunts. How they adore it! When I *think* of what I've tried to do with parties up here! This little touch, that little touch." She closed her eyes in pain. "What's the use? All they want is a barn to meet in and chat, chat, chat." When she opened her eyes again, she caught sight of Sandy and started. "Oh, look, he's dancing with that little Bartlett girl. Isn't it *too* sweet? Isn't she *too* adorable? Aren't you crazy about Boston girls?" She was again mimicking Aunt Polly in that shrill tone that had struck me so unpleasantly at my lunch party. "And such a nice family, too. Don't you like Boston families? Don't you find them 'attractive'?"

"Please, Ione. Someone will hear you."

"Let them! Let the little mouse from Boston hear me! The gold-digging little mouse from Boston!"

Someone had cut in on Sandy and his girl, and he crossed the floor now to the porch, and, bowing, gravely asked Ione if she cared to dance.

"No thanks, dearie," she said bitterly. "I don't 'care' to dance."

Sandy turned to me. "I hope you won't disappoint me, Gussie?"

"No, dear boy, I'm tired tonight. I think I'll just sit here with Ione."

He bowed again and was turning to go when Ione called out: "Are you going back to your little brown bean? Will you take her to the camp afterwards? Mumsy wouldn't mind *that*, would she? Not half!"

Sandy's eyes searched mine for a long, quiet moment as he took it in that I knew all there was to know. But he did not flush or lose his head. He simply accepted the situation and trusted me. As he turned those sad, puzzled eyes back to Ione I understood, with a little tug at my heart, why she loved him so. "I think you should go home, Ione. I think you're tired."

"You mean I'm plastered. Why don't you say so?"

"I think you shouldn't have any more champagne."

"Are you afraid I'll embarrass you before Mumsy and the little brown bean? The little brown, greasy bean?"

He turned once more to me. "Gussie, she ought to go home. Please tell her."

"I'll go if you'll take me to the camp!" Ione exclaimed. "Will you take me to the camp in your long yellow Mercedes?"

Her request fell among the three of us, fell at our feet into as many pieces as cheap glass. Ione was not that drunk; Sandy and I knew it, just as we knew that it was her way of saying goodbye. The silence that followed her little explosion was a very sober one. Then Sandy turned for the last time to me and said: "Would you take her home, Gussie? I think it would be better. I think it really would."

"Of course."

Ione's excitement seemed to have suddenly subsided. She shook her head in a listless way. "He'll be married to the mouse before Christmas," she murmured, as if to herself. "Mark my words. Before Christmas!"

"Good night, Ione," he said gently, and turning, he walked firmly away. There was nothing evasive or shamefaced about that departing stride. He was simply leaving her to me as he had to leave her. In the Herron world everything was done by the code, and nothing was left to passion. The young man had his affair with the older woman; he even loved the older woman. But that was that. When the time came, it was not necessary for his father, as in *Traviata*, to appeal to the woman. It was only necessary for his mother to arrive with his bride.

"Oh, Gussie," Ione murmured in a voice that would surely have ended in a sob had Bertie not stepped onto the porch at just that moment. He was smiling as he always smiled when he was nervous. I realized suddenly that he was frightened, too. It was a new Ione to him, as well as to me.

"Do you care to dance, Ione?"

She did not even look at him. She turned away, with one hand over her eyes, as if he were nothing but an intruding ray of light in the dark room of her sorrow. I tried to cover the pause. "Ione is tired, she's not feeling well," I explained. "I thought I'd take her home."

"*I'll* take her home, Gussie."

"But I want to go, anyway, and—"

"I know, Gussie." His interruption was firm but kind. "I know all about it. Don't worry about Ione. I'll get her home to bed."

I watched anxiously as he took her hand in his and murmured, "Come, dear." Ione made no move for several moments and then got up suddenly with a sigh, still without looking at her husband, put her arm under his and left the porch. My aunts remained until the party broke up at three.

Ione was right in her prediction. Aunt Polly left Bar Harbor for Newport the next day, and Sandy went with her. The following November he and Clara Bartlett were married in a huge wedding in Boston attended by most of the Millinders including myself. They appear to have been happy, but it is hard to tell with anyone as easygoing as Sandy. The finest stroke of Aunt Polly's genius—how it was done I have never known—was to persuade Clara that it was her charm and not her future mother-in-law's maneuverings that had extricated Sandy from the clutches of Ione. Yet obviously she could not hoodwink Ione. The latter has never forgiven Aunt Polly for defeating her singlehanded.

I began to realize, as I pondered my own role in the affair, that Ione had asked very little of my family. We, on the other hand, had resented her for having the charm and gaiety that we lacked ourselves. It was one of the dangers of being rich in my generation, and surrounded by cousins and friends who were as rich or richer, that it was difficult not to believe, at least subconsciously, that the money could purchase the things we lacked. Seeing Ione, I had done what Aunt Daisy had done before me; I had tried to possess her by purchase, as if her charming qualities would become mine with the chink of coins on the counter. I was like a German in occupied Paris, ordering lobster and champagne, and wondering in my naïveté why the city of light had become so dull. Bertie had been more understanding, but he, too, had been possessive. He, too, had wanted to warm his fingertips at the little crackle of Ione's cheerful blaze. As had Sandy. Was it any wonder that with all of us stamping and blowing, the little blaze should have subsided to a few hard, glowing coals?

For subside it did. Ione was never quite the same after that summer. Bertie died a few years later, in the summer of 1929, of a heart attack, while still in his middle fifties. He was the first of my generation to go, and his death hit me much harder than I would have anticipated. He and Ione had seemed to be getting on together well enough; at least there had been no repetition of Sandy. Yet his will was hardly generous to her. He left her half his estate, in trust until her remarriage. The other half he left to Cora's and Willie's children, whom he had never seemed to care about in his lifetime and who were far richer than Ione, anyway. It may have been part of his natural conservatism to keep Millinder money for Millinders. At any rate, as he and Ione had dipped heavily into capital for years, there was not too much of it left, and in the depression that followed his death, Ione was obliged to sell her houses in New York and Maine and drastically to reduce her scale of living. She went into a sort of panic which surprised me; after all, she was still far from poor, except by Millinder standards. But in her second widowhood and in the gloom of those depression years she seemed to lose her old sense of balance; she saw nothing ahead but loneliness and old age and eventually, destitution. When Harold Fay, who was still a bachelor, still surly and almost untouched by the crash, again proposed to her, she accepted with what struck us all as indecent haste. Once more the famous laugh rang out at her parties, bigger parties than ever before, so big that a cross and brooding Harold was barely noticed in them, silenced at last, a petulant old man, defeated by a woman with his own money. But to me, at least, the famous laugh had developed a faintly mechanical tone.

So Ione at last was richer than all the Millinders, richer even than George. She became an even more famous hostess than she had been, and her name today is synonymous in newspaper columns and on the lips of all the unthinking persons who make up society with "charm" and "graciousness." Perhaps it is only in my imagination that her history illustrates the rule that charm cannot survive too great wealth. Perhaps, as in the past, I am still jealous of Ione. But it seems to me that as she has grown old, all her attitudes have become frozen repetitions of a long-dead past. The dyed gold hair, the marble cheeks, the clipped, unfinished sentences of one used only to speak in crowds, the pointless, endless laugh—to me it is all the slightly macabre ghost of the Ione Locke who came to stay and do over the big room and who taught me to live when I no longer wished to. But what else could I expect? In all the years of our friendship she had asked me only one favor, and I had refused her that. I had treated her as the world had treated her, and who was I to complain of the result? We had made her in the end a true Millinder.

6

THE LATE NINETEEN twenties and early thirties were the happiest period of my life. I was in my sixth decade and long clear of the emotional complaints that had afflicted me at the end of the first war. I no longer resented it if a bank teller failed to recognize me or if I was made to wait when I had an appointment with my doctor. Such things no longer seemed the manifestations of a universal conspiracy to degrade me. I also discovered that with the return of my confidence, the number of these incidents diminished. As, little by little, I began to assume the role in which Ione had long tried to cast me, that of the magnificent and indomitable old maid, I found that people were only too happy to treat me with the respect that such a conception of myself required. Civilized life is a fancy-dress party, and everyone is encouraged to don a costume. It makes for color to have queens and cardinals about, and for enough color nobody minds doffing a hat. The illusion is created as much by him who performs the reverence as him to whom it is made. Both, after all, are members of the same cast. And so when I made my early appearances in the public eye, as the first woman trustee of the North American Ornithological Society, as president of the Institute to Save Historical Land Marks and Battle Sites, as vice-chairman of the National Women's League for Repeal of the Eighteenth Amendment, as my considerable figure and my big hats became familiar sights at the speakers' tables at public lunches, and my buckled shoes well known to Fifth Avenue parades, I learned what so many have learned before me, that publicity is easily come by, but hard to shake. I made all kinds of new friends; public causes are thronged with old maids and widows, many of them poor, and my invitations to dinner in New York and weekends in Maine were gratefully accepted. I surrounded myself, in short, with a cackling, appreciative female court which provided me with little whiffs of my first incense. There is no loyalty more steadfast and no admiration blinder than that of the faded, genteel, poverty-stricken single female for her patroness. In time I added men to the ranks of my courtiers, old bachelors who could afford to live only at their clubs and needed to pick up extra dollars at the bridge table, younger, giggling interior decorators who "adored" my old house and found me "superb," and bald, monocled European noblemen in search of a second or third American wife. The latter included a rather fierce Caucasian prince who I believe would have proposed to me had I not always laughed at him. I would take my whole group up to the boat races in New London or to the Harvard-Yale football game in a private railway car and lead them in college songs. Oh, I know it all sounds foolish enough, but it was great fun while it lasted, and my only regret today is how little I did for all of them and how much they did for me. Ione always said that she had learned in her poorer days how little one got out of the rich, and I fear my friends made the same discovery with me. As I look back on those years now, my heart aches to think how much I could have done for them and how easily I could have done it. But my largesse was confined to beds and meals and transportation, and what was all of this but a way of filling in the void of my own loneliness? I still wanted to be loved for myself—heaven help me!—and I was afraid that a checkbook too often opened would tend to instill mercenary motives in the simple souls who gathered about me. It served me right to discover, when poor little Annie Trig died, the gentle old virgin who left her tiny room at the Abigail Adams only to come to my Sunday night suppers, that she had no armchair and shared a bathroom with twelve others. She could have lived more comfortably in my attic, and I need never have known she was there!

I was encouraged in my egotism by my devoted Italian maid, Teresa. Her passionate espousal of my every wish was very spoiling. Osborn, Mamma's old butler, had died in his eighties, still working for me and still disapproving, and Teresa, though my personal maid and not a housekeeper, had taken his place as director of the other servants by sheer dominance of personality. No one thereafter remained in my service who ran afoul of Teresa. What she did, how she got rid of them, I was never quite sure, nor did I ever really want to find out, for I depended increasingly on Teresa's crooning over me when I was tired or depressed and on her brisk imperious attitude to the others that everything in the house be managed for the greater comfort and glory of "Signorina Gussie." Elderly households tend to freeze into formal routines that ultimately enmesh even their employers; Louis XVI always claimed that he was as much a prisoner in Versailles as his humblest lackey. Teresa, however, burnt her way through domestic red tape with temper and tongue and arranged everything for my total comfort. She seemed sincerely to believe that I was a sort of superior being, a kind of princess. The adage is false which claims that no man is a hero to his valet. It would be better for us all if it were true.

To return to my family, who, after all, constitute the subject matter of this memoir (I consider my own story revelant only insofar as I am a Millinder), this was the period of my life when my emotions were primarily occupied with the career and problems of my nephew, Lydig Millinder. I shall have to turn back in my chronology to introduce him properly. Lydig, and his younger brother, Oswald, were the sons of my older brother, Willie, and of my sister-in-law, Julia, who was the daughter of our old family lawyer, Judge Lydig. They were born at the very end of the last century and were generally considered to represent the hope and future of our branch of the family. There is a portrait by Sargent of Julia and her two boys that has always hung at the turn of the black oak stairway of the house in New Jersey. It is revealing in its assurance that the future will be conquered by beauty and privilege, though there are intimations in the pallor of the boys' skin and in their gentle, staring eyes, in the long white maternal fingers resting on their shoulders, in the background of gold curtains and French chairs, that the future to be conquered may not really be worth the effort of creatures so elegant. Of course, that was Sargent; he had a habit of painting children that way. Lydig, pale and tense, with raven curly hair, is dressed in a sailor suit; he is standing up very straight and stiff as if to announce to a snarling crowd that he will guard with his young life his threatened, regal mother. Oswald, very small and *gamin,* with a lace collar, velvet knickerbockers, long black socks and pumps, his red hair seeming to rise like a bush from the oval top of his head, has more the air of one who knows that, given the chance to talk, he could cajole that crowd out of anything. But leaving aside the mannerisms of the artist, it still seems to me that the essence of Lydig and of Oswald is contained in that painting. Whenever I study it long enough, I feel a small, worrying pain in my heart, akin to the pain I have felt in the Prado contemplating the grave, charming faces of the little Hapsburg infants and infantas and knowing that outside the walls of the palace where Velasquez painted them lay a world of carnage licked by the flames of a thousand autos-da-fé. The beauty of children is a reminder of how beautiful life *could* be. When we contemplate it, we are sad because we know what men will do to life and how soon these same children will be men.

The attitude of each boy, as shown in the painting, may have been his defense to his mother's ambition. For Julia was as Roman a mother as her name implied. We have heard a great deal in recent years about the possessive American mother. The ambitious one is less indigenous. I suppose the easy explanation is that her eldest son had to make up to Julia for the career she herself had never had. Yet why had she never had it? Nobody would have opposed her, least of all Willie. She could have painted or sculpted or run for Congress, and everyone would have applauded. Yet instead she wasted her energy inconceivably on sport and travel and cards. Whatever she did she had to do better than anyone else, but it spoiled her pleasure in victory to know how she had limited the field of competition. She was a very intelligent but at the same time a very cynical woman; her contempt for goals may have intensified her feeling that the contest was everything. But if this was so, did one need a goal at all? When I think of Julia I see her thin and bony, with hair still red, lying full length on a sofa, ignoring guests whom she always treated as if they had invited themselves, and talking in her deep voice on a telephone to her trainer while patting two enormous sheep dogs with a free hand on which a bracelet of gold golf clubs, each a trophy, jangles. Yet if Julia had found in her own life nothing to reward effort but effort itself, she was more optimistic about Lydig's. For him, evidently, the goals were to have more validity. She may have seen that men needed goals more than women; she had certainly seen that Willie had weathered their life together worse than she. Willie had Papa's looks and a good part of his charm, but he lacked the sunny benignity of Papa's disposition. As a young man it had briefly seemed that he might develop this, too, but with the years had come instead a bitterness of general attitude and a sarcasm of manner that reminded one more of Bertie. He also took to heavy drinking, the first of the Millinders to do so. He had a hunting accident in his late thirties which left him with a slight limp for life, and he had to give up the violent sports that he so loved. It may have been in those long mornings when Julia was following the hounds and he was sitting in the library with his old police dog that he started to drink for solace. He never appeared unpleasantly intoxicated, but at almost all times in the afternoon and always in the evening one was conscious of a thickening of speech and slowness of movement that ultimately seemed his natural characteristics. Julia went out more and more without him; she and Parmelee Everett hunted together and beagled together and even ran a racing stable together. Their names were constantly associated, and as Willie never seemed to mind, nobody else did. At least nobody but Lydig.

I have never seen a mother demand as much of a child as Julia did of Lydig. It was the more remarkable in that she demanded so little of Oswald. She seemed to have crossed off the latter, perhaps because he was small and not adapted to sports, to have marked him, like an English younger son, for the church or the colonies. If it was so, it was certainly not protested by Oswald who regarded his exemption with open relief and treated his older brother with a friendly hut contemptuous pity. And, indeed, to be subject to Julia's high standards was no enviable experience, for it did not appear to be accompanied by any correspondingly larger share of the maternal affection. If Julia loved Lydig—and, despite all that has happened, I have still no doubt that she loved him fiercely—she concealed it as a teacher of old-fashioned principles might conceal it from his pupil, evident only to those who caught the flash of pride in that stubbornly averted eye. Julia had a strong distaste for what she called the "sloshy." It was "sloshy" for a mother and child to kiss in public or to use any terms of endearment or even to pay any marked attention to each other; it was "sloshy," too, to be negligent in clothes or cleanliness or even to refer to one's health to excuse a bad performance. It was "sloshy," it sometimes seemed to me, to admit that any weakness tied one to the rest of the human race. I have seen Julia, after the tennis finals at Chelton School, turn away from Lydig, when others were congratulating him for his near victory over an older boy, because she thought he should have won. There was no field in which she did not want him to excel; he had to be a leader in the classroom as well as on the playing field. I used to protest that she was driving him too hard, but she always retorted that she judged him according to his capabilities. "With another boy it might be too much," she would admit. "With Oswald, for example. But Lydig has a fatal facility. Left to himself he would be content to be second best in everything and loaf. Why not work a little harder and be first? After all, Gussie, you can't claim he looks done in. Have you ever seen anything more blooming?"

Well, I had to admit I hadn't. Lydig was beautiful to behold. With his black curly hair and shining black eyes and white, perfect teeth, with the build of a gladiator and the tiniest crook in his aristocratic nose to suggest some remote, brilliant Jewish ancestor, he might have been an illustration in a boy's adventure book. I never could look at Lydig without feeling a pull at my heart. He had excellent manners, too, if a trifle on the hearty side; he gripped one's hand very hard as he shook it and looked one deep in the eye. He was a child during Theodore Roosevelt's administration, and Julia, a passionate admirer of the President, who as police commissioner had given Willie the only job he had ever held, took Lydig on two occasions to see the great man at Sagamore Hill and learn that it was possible for one human being to do all things: to ride and write, to read and hunt, to be a student of natural history and President of the United States. If Lydig had a fault, it was in being what young men today might deridingly call a "boy scout." Yet to me his particular charm was in a certain halting shamefacedness at the very brilliance of his own achievements. He seemed to be apologizing alike for his dark good looks and his smashing tennis serve, to be shrugging in embarrassed irritation as though to say: "Oh, all right, heck, I know it looks like a terrible show-off, but what do you do if you can't *help* it?" I used to tremble for Lydig because I knew how envious the world was. It would forgive Willie his fortune because he drank and Bertie his because he led a fool's existence, but how could it forgive Lydig?

I hope it's fair to say that Lydig was fond of me from the beginning. I was just the opposite of Julia, of course; I applauded him and fussed over him and bought him every kind of expensive present. In fact, I was "sloshy" to an appalling degree. Yet Julia did not seem to mind. She may have had the sense to realize that Lydig needed at least one large, cozy female relative, all-loving and uncritical, in whose warm embrace he could find occasional solace, and she no more resented me than that noble English mother, to whom I have already compared her, would have resented her children's nanny. She let me see the boys as much as I wanted (I say "the boys," for although I never really cared for little Oswald, I did my best to appear to love them equally) and let them visit me in Bar Harbor when she was in Islesboro. I was invited to weekends in New Jersey, and, indeed, through my nephews, the breach that Cecilia had opened between me and Julia was healed long before the breach between me and Papa. I was even encouraged to visit Lydig and Oswald when they went off to Chelton, and Julia did me the signal honor of consulting me on minor questions of their curricula. She was and is a remarkable woman. She has never allowed her almost unconcealed dislike of me to stand in the way of my being useful to her children.

It was Julia who suggested that I go up to see Lydig in the spring of his next-to-last year at boarding school.

"He may talk to you; he won't to me," she informed me in her brisk, shoulder-shrugging way. "I'm afraid he's developing some queer ideas. Of course, they were bound to come."

"What kind of ideas?"

"Well, he's getting very anti-school and arty and writes poetry all the time. I know it's a phase, but these things bear watching."

I loved visiting Chelton School, particularly in the spring. I loved the red brick and the broad green playing fields and the quiet memorial gates and fountains and bosky walks, blowing leafily on afternoons pregnant with rain. Strolling around the campus one could pass in a hundred yards from the shouting atmosphere of *Tom Brown's School Days* to a cool, emerald scene that might have been painted by Hubert Robert. Oswald, who was always on probation or working off demerits, had time to see me only for meals at the inn where he would bring his friends (always the most prominent boys in his form, for Oswald was as political as Lydig was not) and where we would have rather noisy, hilarious feasts. Oswald had Bertie's party spirit. Lydig sometimes brought a friend, never more than one at a time, and he rarely brought the same friend twice. When I would ask about the former one, he would always answer evasively, and I began to suspect that Lydig was not the one who had cooled. He may have suffered from my old habit of smothering friendship by expecting too much of it. Attractive and brilliant as he was, he should not have expected to monopolize other boys. I am sure that he was hurt by their attitude, for at college he was to cultivate groups rather than individuals, reserving his intimacy for girls. On this visit to Chelton, however, there was no question of guests. Lydig wanted to talk to me alone, and we walked on Sunday afternoon through the great row of elms that led down to the river.

"Do you think Mother would kick up an awful row if I didn't play football next year?" he asked abruptly.

"But don't you *want* to?" I followed the school paper and knew that his forward passes were Chelton's hope for the coming season. "I thought you loved the game."

"Oh, the game's all right. As games go. But, Auntie, all our time here goes into games."

"That's never been my picture of a New England school."

"Well, games of one sort or another. Changing our clothes or washing our bodies. Throwing balls or going to chapel."

"I daresay it keeps you out of worse trouble."

"Like *thinking*?"

There was a quality in his tone that I promptly labeled fatuous. "Yes, like thinking," I retorted. "You're much too young to think!"

"Then there ought to be more girls and less rules!"

But I had no idea of getting into a discussion of the school and sex. I disapproved of Lydig's excited manner and of the way he now roughly tore off his tie and unbuttoned the stiff white collar that was part of the Chelton Sunday uniform. He was too self-consciously emulating the young savage who yearns to cast off the silly clothes of a stultifying civilization and bound away naked into the woods. My own vote had been cast long ago for the stultifying things. "Tell me about your poetry," I said gruffly. "How long have you been writing it?"

It so happened that he had several sheets in his pocket, and I sat down on the first bench to read them. Lydig, after a perfunctory protest, walked over to the riverbank and waited, tossing pebbles into the water. The poems were not bad for a boy who had just turned seventeen. As might have been expected, they were full of a passionate scorn for conventions. Why could not the human race be *free*? One was a bitter castigation, in Browning style, of an Italian Renaissance girl who lacks the courage to defy her ducal father and flee with her sculptor to the New World. Another was a dramatic mono-

logue by Cortez whose pride in victory is poisoned by the suicide of an
Aztec concubine who has loved him truly. Clearly Lydig, like any other
healthy young man, was obsessed with sex. There was a combination of prudishness and pantheism in his verse, of a yearning for licentiousness and of a
clinging to purity. What discouraged me was that it did not seem to contain any seeds of growth. I was pretty sure that it was as good as Lydig was
ever going to do. When he came back to the bench, therefore, I congratulated him. Why not? Even Julia could have seen no danger in that kind
of verse.

"They're nice poems, but they're not good enough to justify your giving
up football," I warned him, and his face immediately fell.

"Then they can't be any good," he replied, kicking the earth.

"It depends on the weight you give football."

"Compared to poetry? Oh, come, Auntie!"

"Well, then, it depends on the weight you give loyalty to your team," I
retorted, irritated by what I considered his airy tone.

"Football and team loyalty are essentially the same thing."

"I disagree with you!" I cried, sincerely shocked. "One involves only your
own prowess, and the other involves the feelings of others. Only a very real
talent would justify you in ignoring the team. If you were a Keats, I'd tell
you to go ahead!"

He whirled around at me. "Would you, really, Auntie?"

"Do you doubt me?"

"Perhaps not. But I can't help thinking of you as being on Mother's side.
As a kind of good-will ambassador from the big world of positive things."

If he had taken his poems and rolled them up tightly and struck me across
the face with them, I couldn't have been more hurt. I, who had loved to
consider myself his ally and confidante!

"Well, I can tell you one positive thing from that big world!" I retorted,
aggrieved and bitter now. "If you spend next fall with a pad and pencil under
the elm trees, instead of down on that football field with your friends where
you belong, only one good poem will come out of it. And do you know
what that poem will be?"

He flushed slowly as he stared at me. "What?"

"A dramatic monologue by the boy who let down his team to write it!"

Lydig said nothing, and we finished our walk in a rather sulky silence,
but I had an uneasy feeling that I had made my impression. It may seem
odd to the reader that he should not have seen his problem before as it
would affect the school team, but that was a direct result of Julia's fetish of
a man's doing his best for his *own* sake. Lydig's career to Lydig was a matter that concerned him and his mother only. But for all his new airs and
theories he had a naturally generous nature, and there was no further talk
of his plan to give up football. As it turned out, his forward passes were as
vital to the team as I had been led to believe, and Chelton won all its outside games. I know, for I attended every one of them. When I told Julia of
the talk Lydig and I had, she surreptitiously got hold of his poems and had
them magnificently printed and bound for his next Christmas present. It

was the worst thing she could have done. Lydig's boyish stanzas seemed shrill and jumping on the thick parchment and in the great black flowing script. At a later date he destroyed all the copies he could find. I still have mine, however, and I frequently take it out to turn those heavy pages and contemplate the effects of adult interference. I do not mean to imply by this anything so foolish as that I, singlehanded, prevented Lydig from becoming a major poet or even a poet at all. But the first manifestations of any gift are apt to be show-off, and the temptation to squash them irresistible. It is so hard to distinguish pose from talent at that age! At the very least, it was none of my business. At the most, I should have told Julia to do her own dirty work. Had I that part of my life to lead over, I would encourage Lydig in his every dissent. But that, of course, is hindsight.

Lydig, at any rate, wrote no more poetry at Chelton, nor afterwards at Yale. It was a distracting time for a young man to be in college. The war was raging in Europe, and President Wilson, to the disgust of Lydig and his friends, was still managing to keep us neutral. Many young men were slipping off to Canada to join up, and only Julia's most violent representations that it was Lydig's duty to finish his education had kept him from doing the same. As it was, his restless and frustrated energy exploded all over the place. He would appear in goggles in a white Rolls-Royce at my house on a Saturday morning, having driven down from New Haven, take me for a spin up and down Fifth Avenue and to early lunch at Delmonico's, drive down to Westbury to play in a polo match and then back to New York to take out a girl. He was always taking out girls. Some of them he introduced to me; some he did not. He professed to care very much for my opinion on this and on other subjects. I did everything I could to prepare for the role thus thrust upon me; I read the books that he talked about and learned the rules of the games that he played. I, who had hitherto avoided the subject of youth, now bored my friends with my constant questions about their children. I was resolved to make no gaffes in discussing with Lydig the mores of his generation. I kept my weekends free from other engagements on the chance that he might have a free afternoon to take me to a play or a picture gallery, which he frequently did. I suppose I must have offered him that total love and sympathy that with all his charm and passion he had never found in others. Who but a virgin aunt could give all? There may have been some egotism in his need and use of me, but this kind of egotism a woman can always forgive. I only dreaded the day when he would fix his attention on one of his many girls. There would then be no further need of the searching discussions between aunt and nephew of which the following is a fair example.

"What about that little Mary Bowden? She struck me as a sweet sort of girl."

"Oh, she's *sweet* enough." Lydig's shrug was monumental. "But you know her kind. One kiss, even just a peck, and a fellow finds himself being congratulated by her whole family."

"Well, then what about Eileen Denison? I imagine she's a bit—shall I say, more generous?"

"Generous to a fault!" he exclaimed with a snort. "Nobody ever accused Eileen of holding back. It was lucky for me I compared notes with my roommate!"

"I don't think I quite like that," I observed judiciously. "Is that the standard of gallantry of your generation?"

"It's self-preservation. *Women*, Auntie!"

"Women? Don't be impertinent. What do you think I am?"

"But you're different! You've risen above the limitations of your sex! Like Queen Elizabeth and Joan of Arc! Or the Dowager Empress of China!"

I shuddered. "Tell me about some of your other girls," I said gruffly. "Tell me about the ones you *don't* bring to see me."

"I can only tell you there's a very good reason for that!"

He said this with the flicker of a wink, and I had a sudden uneasy feeling that he was a good deal more sophisticated than his nineteen years warranted. I wondered if these girls whom I never met did not see a very different Lydig from the solicitous visitor who even now was closing the window behind me to shut off a draft. I did not then realize that college sophomores could be expected to have actual affairs or that Lydig was developing a bad name among the mothers of New York debutantes. However fickle as a swain, he was undeviatingly loyal as a nephew. The candies that he gave me on my birthday were ordered from Paris, and the flowers that he sent me when he came to visit were the most exotic imaginable. I think he must have rather enjoyed the little game of making a cult of his old maid aunt. But there was nothing fake about his kindness, nor was it confined to presents. When my maid, Teresa, brought me my breakfast one somber morning in the early winter of 1916 and told me that Lydig was outside in the corridor, I was afraid that he was in trouble. It turned out, however, that his bad news was for me.

"I'm sorry, Auntie. Gran's had a stroke in Korea. They want you to go out."

"Oh, Lydig!" I gasped in dismay.

"Daddy had a cable last night."

"Why didn't he tell me?" I demanded, half out of bed, already seeking a distraction from grief in anger.

"He did. I mean, he sent me. But when I got here you'd already gone to bed, and I didn't see the point of waking you. I thought you'd be better with a good night's sleep to face it all."

Teresa whispered to me that he had sat up all night outside my door to be sure that no other messenger would disturb me. I burst into tears, my face in my hands, but my tears were not all for poor Mamma.

Lydig's college years were difficult ones for Julia, but she was wise enough to let out enough line, so that after the first hectic years of girls and polo, when he came panting to the surface, she still had her hook in his jaw. She wanted him, of course, to be an eminent man on the campus. Although of a Harvard family herself, she made it her business to study the Yale standards of success, and she bored Willie by making him endlessly analyze the different advantages of the different senior societies. But although Lydig, who settled down to work in time to obtain a Phi Beta Kappa key and to become an editor of the *News*, would have been a natural choice for Scroll & Key, something intervened that was beyond the control of even Julia: our entry into the war. Lydig anticipated the actual declaration, despite all his mother could do, by resigning from Yale and enlisting in the Army Air Corps. It was one of the curious things about Julia that she never quite forgave this and never afterwards took quite the same rapt interest in his career. For all her sophistication, she had something of a child's attitude towards life. If she could not do a job entirely herself, she would rather not do it at all. She could look up at the heavens with a bold, defiant eye and say "All right. You interfered. Now you finish it!"

Lydig went through his training in Louisville as competently as he did everything else, but when the time came for his squadron to go overseas, he alone was held back to be a flight instructor. Immediately his angry letters began to pepper his family and friends, begging them to use any pressure that was needed to send him abroad. Telegrams followed letters, and, as time wore on, he began to sound almost hysterical. He was even desperate enough to appeal to Aunt Daisy who wrote him a long, severe letter about doing one's duty in whatever sphere one happened to be called. I wanted to go down to Louisville, but Julia dissuaded me.

"It's only a matter of weeks before he goes to France," she assured me. "I've checked myself with General Gage. It appears that Lydig is absolutely indispensable just now as an instructor. I can see that, can't you?"

At this point, anyway, I lost touch with the problem, for I went to France myself, and when I returned the first thing Julia told me was that Lydig at last had his orders to go overseas and that everything was all right. I found in my mail some poems that he had sent me while I had been away. The frustration about his orders, it seemed, had made him return to his muse. The poems were not remarkable, but they were good, better than I would have thought he could ever do. Even Lancey Bell, who was a devastating critic of amateurs, agreed to this when I showed them to him. They were short, pungent and bitter, and behind their brief stanzas was the feeling of a vast army of restless young men on the move. Lydig seemed happier with his new friends of simpler background; he had never, for all his success at Chelton and Yale, been truly popular with his peers. He was too serious, too intense, too inclined to worry and maul a topic when others were through with it, too competitive, too lacking in humor. Because of his looks and his competence, his fairness and his easy habit of command, he was looked up to by the less sophisticated youths who crowded into the camp at Louisville and placed their lives in the hands of their young instructor. Lydig's letters were full of his new friends and their problems and what sort of world it would be for them after the Armistice. His poems seemed to catch some of their sense of spiritual dislocation and some of their hope for the future that was already peeping over the red blanket of war. But there was also a strain of fascination with that very blanket, an odd yearning to bury his head in it, a melancholy feeling that if there was a beautiful future after Armageddon for others, it might not be for him. I found out more about this when he came to see me on his last leave. The blow had fallen. The Armistice had just been declared, and now he would never fly in European combat. I have never seen a face so dark in the midst of such tumultuous celebration. He stood in my living room, staring down at a Fifth Avenue where strangers were hailing each other with the joyful news of peace and hinted darkly that his mother might have been responsible for the delay in his orders.

"You mean, she pulled wires?" I protested, shocked. "Oh, Lydig, no, that's not like her! Besides, *could* she have?"

"Think of all her military friends," he retorted. "From Colonel Roosevelt down. Don't worry. When Mother puts her mind on something, she usually gets it. And besides, wasn't General Gage one of her . . . ?" He paused and swung around to fix his suddenly sneering eyes on me. "What was the polite term you used to use, Auntie? *Cavalieri serventi?*"

I had never seen that particular look of resentment on his face before, and I remembered Oswald's quip that his brother used to glower at Julia's gentlemen friends like "a Yale edition of Hamlet." I had been prepared for an ultimate reaction to his mother's domination, but I had not suspected that it would verge on the irrational. Julia had had her admirers, as I well knew. Talk had even come to my spinster's ears of her intimacy with a certain master of foxhounds in New Jersey. But to imply that she extended her benevolence to the military, and for such reasons, was the rankest absurdity.

"Your mother would never go to a soldier to keep her son from the front," I pointed out brusquely. "Pride alone, if nothing else, would stop her."

"Don't ask me *how* she did it," he retorted bitterly. "We'll never know. She's far too shrewd for that."

It suddenly struck me as outrageous that on this day of universal thanksgiving there should be nothing better for us to discuss than Lydig's personal disappointment. "What a pity they can't revive the war!" I exclaimed with indignant sarcasm. "Just for a few more weeks! A few more weeks of mild carnage. So that Lydig Millinder can earn his battle stars!"

"I know it's selfish of me," he conceded, "but I can't help it. I'm sick at heart that I've missed the great experience of my generation."

"Great experience fiddlesticks! It was a dirty, bloody, muddy mess!"

"You can say that, Auntie, because you saw it."

"I saw nothing! I was thirty miles behind the lines. While you were up in the air every day with crazy cadets who could have crashed your plane in the twinkling of an eye!"

"It's not the danger I'm thinking of," he insisted stubbornly. "I didn't care about the danger. It was the war I cared about. I wanted to see and feel the war. I wanted to take it into me. Maybe it wasn't the great experience for my generation. Maybe they'll all forget about it or talk it up into something it never was. But I have a feeling it was meant to have been *my* great experience."

"It might have been a final one," I pointed out.

"Exactly!" he exclaimed, suddenly very much excited. "That's exactly what

I feel! That's the image that sticks in my mind, of a plane descending in a silver arc to Flanders Field. Oh, I know that sounds morbid and sloshy. But there you are, Auntie. I can't get it out of my mind. That *that* was my destiny!"

I got up and went over to put my arms around him. "My dear child," I exclaimed with tears in my eyes, "let us thank God, then, it's been averted!"

Lydig kissed me and then laughed in sudden embarrassment at the scene he had caused. "Oh, come now, Auntie, don't take it too hard!" he said in a heartier tone. "Here I am, safe and sound, and before you know it, I'll be going back to Yale. Because I've decided to study law. What do you think of that, Auntie? They say law leads to everything!"

"Oh, I'm a sentimental old fool, my dear," I said, wiping my eyes. "I want you to be a poet."

"Well, maybe the law will lead to poetry!"

We continued in this more cheerful strain for the balance of his visit, but when he had gone, the memory of his previous utterances weighed heavily in my mind. It was aggravated by the feeling that the armistice had been for me, too, an anticlimax. Yet I, at least, had long faced the fact that I was a misfit. It had certainly never occurred to me that Lydig could feel the same way, unless, by the very fact of fitting too perfectly, of being almost too round a peg for his round hole, he might have deemed himself a special kind of maverick. Now, after the passage of yet another war that has covered my tables with other photographs of sons and grandsons of friends in uniform, I can look at my painting of Julia's boy aviator and reread my letters from Louisville with less pain and bitterness, fitting Lydig's story with greater resignation into the seemingly endless tale of world conflicts. But I can still feel a tug of misery at my heart in remembering that Lydig might have been right, that it might have been a better thing had he died a hero's death in Flanders and left a beautiful memory of early promise cut short. I know that this is evasive and sentimental; I am enough of an Aristotelian to realize that all that came out later in Lydig must have been latent in him then, that so early a death would have been no more than the accidental dropping of a curtain in the middle of a performance. But I don't care. The memory of Lydig as an American Rupert Brooke would have given my old maid's heart something to live for, down to this very day.

7

Lydig plunged into hard work at Yale Law School and obtained his customary high marks. When he came to see me, he would talk about his cases and his statutes in greater detail than I could follow, but I was happy to see him enthusiastic, and relieved that there was no recurrence of the melancholy mood of Armistice Day. Whether or not there had been recriminations between him and Julia on account of his fancied grievance I did not know, but I knew that he was seeing very little of his mother. He had a new girl, Elsie Courtland, who was taking up the major share of his free time. I had long had a mental picture of the bride I wanted for Lydig. My favorite theme in Victorian fiction had always been that of the libertine who meets his ultimate match in the lovely, industrious only daughter of a widowered curate, who, with all her housework, has still a finely developed ear for music and poetry, who is shy but not timid, sensitive but not frail, and who is transfigured by her love for the libertine which will, of course, be the only love of her life. Was Lydig going to prove that she existed in fact?

Alas, not. It seemed that the only function of my Victorian heroine was to enable me to recognize that Elsie was her exact opposite. Elsie was very fashionable and one of a large family with a scheming mother; she had no interest whatever in the arts, and she struck me as bold without being courageous. Furthermore, she gave no appearance of being the least bit in love with Lydig. She was far too sure of herself to find it necessary to conceal her frank interest in the sizeable portion of Papa's estate which Lydig had recently inherited. It was difficult for me to grasp what it was that Lydig saw in her, unless the very impossibility of impressing such a girl made her seem the symbol of the ambitious life that he had espoused. Perhaps the simple fact that she and Julia had despised each other on sight was my warning that she was Julia's destined successor.

Yet she fascinated me. She took it so completely for granted that the universe had no better function than to fill her lap with gifts. It even struck me that she assumed a greater generosity in the universe than she had cause to. It was true that she had lovely skin, rich auburn hair and fine, regular features, but she had a way of bunching the latter together in a rather cat-like little smile that she used for all occasions and which had nothing to do with amusement. She was tall and, to my mind, figureless (though, happily for her, the flat chest was then in vogue) and she walked with a quick, loping stride that was more like a boy's than a woman's. Yet she was generally considered to have great sex appeal, and her tranquil manner of looking the world, unimpressed and faintly shrugging, in the eye, was a casual acceptance of the verdict. Such, indeed, had always been the attitude of the Courtlands. It was her aunt, Agnes Courtland, who was to have been my bridesmaid and to whom Lancey had given that flower. They were handsome people with a family tradition of advantageous marriages. Elsie was very sweet to me; she was sweet to everybody, except Julia, but I never felt that I truly existed for her. Her only reality lay in the small group of her exact contemporaries who were equally rich, equally handsome and equally leisured, and their animals. Elsie was never impressed, favorably or unfavorably, by anything outside of her own small world; she would simply wrinkle her nose and shrug if you mentioned starvation in China or starvation in the next block. Yet she was undeniably intelligent; even Bertie was impressed with her bridge game. To watch her contemplate her cards, her eyes grey and grave, and then to see the quick movement of the brown shoulders and the reach of the long arm towards dummy where a scarlet finger just tapped, for a moment of fond reflection, the card to be played, was to see something beautiful. I had a suspicion, as early as my first meeting with her, that this purring kitten, as Lydig chose to describe her, had turned already into a lissome, bounding cat. If she had shown the slightest jealousy of Lydig's affection for me, we might still have been friends. But her cool assumption that I could be no more to Lydig than I was to her, a "dear, old thing" to be made up to on Christmas parties and laughed at behind my back, I could never forgive.

Lydig brought her to dinner alone with me right after they were engaged. Conversation progressed smoothly enough, for Elsie had been well brought up, but there were none of those loving questions about what Lydig had been like as a little boy that I had used fondly to imagine his fiancée putting to me. Instead, our talk dealt with wedding presents and the plans for the little yellow French château they were building on the Courtlands' place on Long Island. I didn't know if the subject of presents was intended for a hint, but after dinner I took Elsie up alone to my bedroom to show her Mamma's jewelry and ask her to select a piece. For the first time in our acquaintance I felt I had her undivided attention.

"Oh, Aunt Gussie, how divine! *Any* one?"

"Any one, my dear. I hardly ever wear them."

It was true. Unlike many old maids of my generation, I wore little jewelry except when I sallied forth to a big party, like an English princess, with most of the collection clipped to me. Mamma's jewelry was old-fashioned, elaborate and showy, but some of the big stones were very fine. Elsie turned them over, one by one, with a practiced eye, and finally selected the great choker of rubies and diamonds that Granny Millinder had first given me as a wedding present and later left me in her will. It was unquestionably the ugliest and the most valuable piece of the collection.

"You don't mind if I have this reset, do you, Aunt Gussie? I think I could get two charming clips and a bracelet out of it."

"Of course not, my dear. The resetting will be part of the present."

Elsie came over and kissed me on the cheek.

"You're a dear, Aunt Gussie. You really are. And will you forgive me now? I promised Aunt Agnes I'd bring Lydig in for a little family party after dinner."

When Lydig returned that night, for he was staying with me, he came up to my room where I was reading in bed.

"Isn't she marvelous, Auntie?" he exclaimed with shining eyes. "Aren't I the luckiest guy in the world?"

I gripped my book tightly and stuck my feet out straight under the covers. "It's awfully hard for those of us who *aren't* in love to feel quite the same enthusiasm," I began cautiously. "However 'marvelous' Elsie may be, you must remember she's walking off with my favorite nephew. That's bound to prejudice me a bit."

His smile dwindled slowly into something small and fixed. "Prejudice, Auntie? What's your prejudice against Elsie?"

"Well, she strikes me as just a bit—and, mind you, I couldn't find her more beautiful or attractive—but—"

"But *what?*"

"Well, mightn't she be *just* a touch worldly?"

"You think she shouldn't have taken that big choker." He was quick and definite, like a lawyer cross-examining. "You think she shouldn't have taken it and then gone off to her aunt's. You're right. I told her so. But jewelry means so little to Elsie. You must try to understand that."

"Oh, no, I wanted her to have the silly choker!" I protested, embarrassed. "I just thought maybe—, that maybe she cared rather a lot for things like that."

"Why don't you come out with it?" he demanded in a sharper tone. "Why don't you say she's marrying me for my money?"

"Well, are you so sure she'd marry you without it?"

I was surprised at my own boldness, but Lydig looked at me with immediate pity. "You're just like Mother," he said, shaking his head. "And the rest of your generation. You're obsessed with the idea that everyone's after the money. You think it's the only reason any girl would marry me!"

"But my darling boy, you're the catch of catches!" I cried, shocked at such an interpretation. "You could marry any girl in New York without a penny to your name! Any girl but this one!"

"How many times have you told me, Auntie, that it was the fear of being married for your money that ruined your greatest chance for happiness?"

"But I wasn't a handsome and brilliant young man!" I protested. "And Lancey Bell was no Elsie!"

"What do you know about Elsie?" he demanded, and I was silenced by his challenging look. "I'm sorry, Auntie, but you're out of your depth here. Elsie belongs to the new generation. The postwar generation. She'll be one of the leaders of it, the way she's now the leader of her own set. You just wait and see! Some people think that because Elsie likes to ride to hounds and is a crack shot she's not interested in other things. Well, they're wrong. She's got a brain, that girl! It's going to be a new world, and Elsie's going to have her part in it!"

"I'm not talking about Elsie's brain," I insisted stubbornly. "Or about her part in the new world. I'm talking about Elsie. I may not know about the new generation, but I know it would take more than a world war to change a Courtland. You forget that I went to school with her Aunt Agnes!"

"But I'm not marrying her Aunt Agnes! Please don't theorize, Auntie. This is me."

"Theorize!" I cried in agony. "Do you think I'm theorizing? Do you think I don't care about your happiness more than anything in the whole world? Who do I love if I don't love you?"

Lydig lowered his eyes in embarrassment before my appeal. "Of course you and I love each other, Auntie. We always have, and we always will. Nothing you have said tonight is going to affect that. If I had any doubts about Elsie, I might resent your attitude. But I have none. I know that when you've seen more of her, you'll be big enough to admit you're wrong."

"Oh, my darling boy, big enough!" I exclaimed, moved to tears by his fairness and moderation. "I'll be jubilant! I'll be happy as a queen to tell the whole world what an ass I've been!" I threw my arms around his neck as he came over to kiss me good night. "You're an angel to listen to a prejudiced, jealous old aunt. And I shall say my prayers that your Elsie will turn out to be everything you dream of!"

I was resolved that, having made my attempt and failed, I would accept Lydig's bride with open arms and appear to everyone in wedding smiles right through the date of the ceremony. And indeed I may say for myself that I succeeded in my resolution, and that nobody at the crowded reception on the lawn and under the big marquee at the Courtlands' place in old Westbury suspected that the large lady in blue lace with the big pearls and sapphires (for I had donned the best that remained of Mamma's collection), who toasted the wedding couple in a loud, hoarse voice that trembled on the verge of a sob, was affected with any emotions other than those appropriate to middle-aged female relatives at weddings. Nobody, that is, but my erstwhile bridesmaid, Agnes Courtland, now Agnes Goelet, who approached me across the lawn, still beautiful, still superior and with that same half-mocking smile that took me back thirty years to the unkindness of schooldays. I felt my whole body tingle with resentment.

"Hello, Gussie Millinder!" she exclaimed. "You see, we were fated to be in a wedding together after all. I adore that beautiful nephew of yours. They tell me he's had a thousand girls. I hope he'll be kind to our little Elsie."

"He took his vow, didn't he?" I answered stoutly. "You heard him. Lydig will not break his word!"

Agnes really stared. "My dear Gussie, it's easy to see you've never married. If we women had to rely on vows!"

"Lydig is the best thing that ever happened to our family. I shouldn't be surprised if he's the best thing that ever happened to yours!"

Of course this was very rude, but it was a hot June day, and I had drunk three glasses of champagne, and my nerves were on edge. Agnes was an attractive, controlled woman, tall and lissome like her niece, but I had succeeded at one stroke in uncovering the former bully of Miss Dixon's Classes.

"I see, anyway, that the years have not changed your manners," she said with a thin smile as she turned away. "I understand now why Lancey Bell preferred a gentle Latin for his bride."

Not for Lydig was the measured pace to success that his grandfather, Judge Lydig, had trod. He had, if not to ravish the bitch goddess, at least to capture her affections by storm, to keep her dressing room filled with flowers and her telephone always busy. To the alarm of his own and Elsie's families he invested the bulk of his inheritance from Papa at one fell swoop in a corporation called Millinder Enterprises, whose avowed function was to take over and revitalize certain worthy institutions that had become moribund. He rented a suite of offices on Fifth Avenue just south of my house and assembled about him a corps of enthusiastic young men. In the first two years of its existence Millinder Enterprises acquired a daily newspaper, three magazines, a radio station, a whaling museum and a repertory theater. Such philanthropy was less common then than it has since become, and Lydig was the subject of much favorable publicity. The aura of the rich young man who "wasn't content to sit on his moneybags" shone about him, and he was cited by countless mothers as a brilliant example to a wastrel generation.

It was all very satisfactory, and I was pleased for Lydig's sake, but the constant enthusiasm required for the launching of his different enterprises was a bit wearing to the friends and relations. I came to associate my nephew's broad smile, which would have once sufficed to cheer me in the darkest hour, with the revival of folk dancing or the endowment of bird sanctuaries. And also, I am afraid, with a request for favors. I knew now that an invitation to accompany him to the opening of "Rosmersholm" was apt to be followed by: "Oh, and by the way, Auntie, would it bore you horribly to loan me your house for a supper party afterwards? I've asked a good many theater people, and I want them to meet the cast."

Well, of course it didn't bore me. My household and I were glad enough to shine up the old Louis XVI drawing room to impress his friends, and actors were particularly satisfactory because they let it be seen when they were impressed. What I minded was feeling that I was part of a plan. But I discovered at that "Rosmersholm" supper party that one person was bored and that was Elsie. As thin and elegant as ever, despite the birth of two children in two years, she sat with me on the big sofa and glanced coolly about the room. Fortunately for Lydig's friends, one had to know the Courtlands to know all the superciliousness behind that stare.

"Funny-looking people, aren't they?" she said. "They can't forget themselves for a moment. Don't they give you the feeling that a curtain's about to go up?"

"Of course they don't hunt and shoot," I retorted. "I daresay they could pass a squirrel or a pigeon in Central Park without even the twitch of a desire to kill it."

"Oh, come now, Auntie, you think they're just as funny as I do! That's why you've got yourself all dolled up in red. To knock their eyes out!" There was something oddly attractive even to me about Elsie's detachment. It was the candid and honest detachment of a cool nature, and it reminded me of Mamma. "Daddy says that Lydig is going to be just like his grandmother," she continued, as if reading my mind. "He says he'll sink his fortune in art."

"But the things Mamma bought are worth many times today what she paid for them!"

"Yes, but they're all in museums."

"Well, maybe Lydig will give his to you. Maybe that will be the difference."

Elsie sniffed as she glanced again about the room. "I wonder if I want them."

I saw no reason that I should bow to her denigrating attitude. "Your husband is engaged in provocative and useful work," I reproved her, perhaps a bit pompously. "I think it's a pity you should sneer at it. You could be a great help to him."

But I aroused only a gleam of amusement in Elsie's stare. "You're determined to lecture me tonight, aren't you, Auntie? You have this *idée fixe* that I'm a bad woman. Perhaps I am. But I keep my eyes open, and I see a good many others around. Suppose I were to tempt you, Auntie? How proof do you think you'd be?"

"Tempt me?" I asked in astonishment. "With what?"

"Why, with Lydig, of course!" she exclaimed, with a bright smile. "*You*'re the one who could be the great help to Lydig. And you're the one who wants to do it. Well, go ahead! You have my blessing!"

"I'm sorry, Elsie," I said peevishly. "I haven't followed a word you've said."

"Well, then I shall be very clear," she continued briskly, putting down her cigarette and turning her full face to me. "I'm bored with philanthropy. I'm bored with arts and crafts. And I'm bored to death with parties like this one. I like life in the country with my own friends and my own dogs and my own children. What I suggest should please everybody. I simply suggest that when Lydig has to spend nights in town for this kind of thing, he stay here with you. *Alone!*"

I scrutinized those mocking eyes with caution. "There'll always be a room in my house for Lydig, if that's what you mean," I said stiffly. "Whether or not you care to accompany him. Is that my temptation?"

"Another woman's husband is always a temptation."

"Even when he's a *nephew?*"

"Oh, particularly when he's a nephew!"

I said nothing more, for I thought her tone flippant and verging on the disrespectful, but I was surprised to discover a week later that she had acted as if a true bargain had been struck between us. Lydig called to thank me formally and thereafter proceeded to spend two nights in the middle of each week under my roof. I gave him a permanent room into which he moved his own books and pictures, and he would come to my dressing room in the morning to breakfast with me on a tray. Of course the arrangement delighted me—how could it not have? Loneliness was always my besetting enemy, and Lydig was a most sympathetic companion. If he talked a good deal about himself, he was still willing to listen—and listen attentively—to my problems. At first I was afraid to ask people in on the nights when he was there, for fear of boring him, but in time I slipped back into my old routine. If I happened to be entertaining, and Lydig came in, Osborn had standing instructions to lay an extra place. After dinner I would whisper to him that he was not obligated to sit with us, but he always chose to, and, furthermore, he would stay until the party was over. His manners were perfect; if he was weary in the company of my old widows and broken-down noblemen, he never betrayed it by so much as a yawn or a glazed eye. He taught Osborn how to mix the drinks properly, acted as a host to the gentlemen in the library and joined enthusiastically and competently in our word games and charades. He learned all the iodiosyncrasies of the little group and even brought himself up to date on their gossip. I marveled at his interest and decided that it must be a reaction against too heavy a dose of Elsie's sophisticated hunting set. I resigned myself to the inevitable rebound, which, however, did not seem to come. One night, when my guests had gone, and Lydig was having a last drink before bedtime, he said to me:

"I like Prince Sherebenieff. He said you were his ideal of a grand duchess. Do you suppose he's in love with you?"

"I suppose he's in love with a free meal," I retorted with a little sniff. "When we go out, it's always to the Ritz. You can imagine who picks up the check. Last time he asked me to lunch, I said: 'I'm sorry, Andrei, I can't afford it more than twice a month.'"

"How mean of you, Auntie! After all, he'd pay if he could. Before the revolution, he'd have bought you the Ritz!"

"Before the revolution he wouldn't have asked me to lunch."

"You underrate yourself. If I were you, I'd think twice before turning him down."

"What!" I cried. "Have you taken leave of your senses? At *my* age? Besides," I added, pleased in spite of myself with the topic, "he hasn't asked me."

"That's because he's scared stiff. Shall I encourage him? Wouldn't you like to be a princess? Like Aunt Cora?"

"Is that a reason for marrying somebody?"

"As good as any," he said, and his voice took on a sudden bitter note that startled me. "What did *I* get? Not even a title." He laughed, but it was a rough, sardonic laugh. "No title that I care to use, anyway."

"Oh, Lydig!" I exclaimed in dismay. "Aren't you and Elsie getting on?"

I was too blunt, as usual, and he jumped up immediately and strode to the door. "Don't pay any attention to me, Auntie, I'm getting maudlin. Of course we're getting on. And it's high time I took myself to bed!"

I was worried enough to call Julia the next morning and make an engagement to lunch with her at the Colony Club. It was a long time since she and I had discussed Lydig in other than perfunctory terms, but when I hinted that he might be unhappy she looked up.

"What did he tell you?"

"Nothing, really. What is there to tell?"

"I wouldn't know anything myself if it weren't for Ione," Julia replied with a rather bitter shrug. "Nobody seems to think it important to keep me posted. But Ione tells me that Elsie's having an affair with Townie Fales."

"Townie Fales!" I gasped. "But he's one of Lydig's oldest friends!"

"Oh, yes. They're all thick as thieves."

"But why would any woman be unfaithful to Lydig?" I protested in bewilderment. "Unless she's one of those—one of those—nymphomaniacs?"

"Don't try to be modern," Julia reproved me. "It doesn't become you. Has it never occurred to you that Lydig might *bore* Elsie?"

As I stared at her, I remembered uncomfortably that it had occurred to me. It also occurred to me for the first time that he might have bored Julia. And were these the two women whom he had spent his life trying to please?

"What must it be like to bore someone you love?" I whispered, half to myself. "It must be a terrible thing." I shuddered to think of the narrow escape that I might have had with Lancey Bell.

When I came home that afternoon, I hurried immediately to Lydig's room. I knew that he had hung a large watercolor over the fireplace, representing himself and Elsie and all their little group at a cockfight, and I wanted to see if I could identify Townie Fales. I felt a bit guilty to be prying in his absence, and I was very short with Teresa when she came in after me and even shorter with the chambermaid who followed her. When I was at last alone, I went over to the fireplace and carefully studied the picture.

On a grass plot against the background of a red barn and blue sky two large cocks were engaged in a death struggle. One, with its beak drawn back and its black wings half spread, seemed ready to deliver the fatal stroke to the other, whose head was lowered at an ominously crooked angle. In white chairs around the fighting birds were seated a group of debonair, well-dressed young people, with drinks in their hands. I immediately recognized the tall, gaunt horse-faced man who seemed to be standing over the cocks as a sort of referee as Townie Fales. I could also make out that the smiling girl in the center of the watching group was Elsie and that the rather wooden figure in the blazer, standing behind her, was my nephew. The artist was an amateur, which gave to the figures a fatuous, smiling, comic-strip air, which formed a grim contrast to the contest in the center of the picture.

"Doesn't all appear to be for the best in the best of all possible worlds?" I turned, flushing with embarrassment at the mocking sound of his voice, to see Lydig standing in the doorway, a briefcase in his hand. "And yet all is not perfect," he continued in the same tone, coming over to my side, "even in paradise. This little girl in blue has been married to two of the gentlemen depicted, here and here." He placed a finger on the watercolor to identify the persons. "This other little girl has been the intimate friend of at least four of the gentlemen in the picture and has also been married twice, but, as it happens, outside the little group presented to us. This—"

"Lydig," I protested, taking his arm, "darling, *please*. I just wanted to see if you needed new curtains. I wasn't prying."

"This," he continued inexorably, pointing to the figure I had already identified, "is Mr. Townsend Fales. He is the intimate friend of . . ." He paused and then burst out laughing at my stricken expression. "Oh, Auntie, what a face! You're as subtle as a meat axe!"

It was too late, obviously, for anything but a vigorous offensive. "Why do you let her lead that kind of life?" I demanded. "Why do you expose her to temptation? You should take her away from those people! It's your duty!"

He laughed derisively. "Can you imagine Elsie away from Long Island? Oh, she might move to New Jersey. Yes, I think I could get her to Far Hills at a pinch. Or even Tuxedo Park. But that would be the ultimate limit."

"If she's your wife, she should go where you want!"

"Wait, Auntie." He went over and sat on the edge of his bed, leaning forward suddenly to rest his head in his hands. For several moments he sat in silence, apparently considering how much he ought to tell me. Then he looked up. "I have learned only one thing about Elsie," he said in a resigned tone. "She can never be changed. She's like an African bush girl. You can put her in a skirt and sit her on a chair for as long as you like, but the minute you take an eye off her, she's back squatting on the floor of a mud hut in her birthday suit. Oh, *I* was the fool. I quite see that now. She never tried to kid me for a single minute. She never even bothered to disguise the fact that she was after a 'good marriage.' But I couldn't believe, when I talked to her about poetry and painting and music, that I was getting no response. I couldn't believe that *all* my seeds were being scattered on a stone pavement. Yet they were. Nothing has ever existed for Elsie but the immediate environment of her childhood. And Townie Fales!" He glared at me suddenly, and his voice soared to shrillness. "Yet I, with three times his brains and twenty times his money, I who can beat him at his favorite game of squash and am probably even a more expert lover, have to sit here tearing my silly hair out because I can't turn myself into an African bush boy!"

"Why should you *try*?" I cried indignantly. "Why do you let them do it to you? Why should that girl ruin your life? Leave her!"

"And let her marry Fales?" he demanded passionately. "You don't know me, Auntie. I promise you, you don't know me!"

His tone was not one to induce me to continue the subject or ever to bring it up again. I left the room, and when we met at dinner that night we argued tepidly about abstract art. But for the rest of that winter he continued regularly to spend his two nights in the middle of each week with me. As he seemed to welcome a bit of festivity on these occasions, possibly to keep me off the subject of Elsie, I planned my little parties for the nights when he was there. I decided, or he had decided for me, that his marriage was not my worry. What I did worry about, as the months drew on, was that he seemed to be slipping into the status of a "regular" in my little group. I objected to this. It had been all right when he appeared in my drawing room like a young prince on his way to greater realms, who would condescend charmingly for a few moments to his aunt's old friends. That was the way I wanted it. But to have him spend a whole evening in heated argument with Annie Trig about the biblical prophecies or with Sherebenieff about the restoration of the Czar, was to reduce him to their level, to make him a part of the crazy world of make-believe in which they all fantastically lived. I had thought once that Annie Trig and my nephew could hardly belong to the same species, but to see them laughing together, or even fighting together, was to be made unpleasantly aware that not so very much separated human beings, after all, and that a withered little old maid and a stalwart young man could seem curiously alike in their joint amusement at one bad joke.

Lydig himself, obviously, shared none of my feelings. One of his points of congeniality with my friends was that he had, like each of them, an obsession. His was a rather embarrassing one about the frailty of women. He would hold forth, like a deluded Shakespearean hero, on the innate inability of my sex to adhere with any permanence to his own. Happy marriages were matters of habit, and fidelity simply the result of lack of opportunity. As almost all my friends were unmarried, the subject was not offensive, and Grace McElway, a devoted Victorian, regarded it as her titillating duty to persuade this handsome young cynic that his own experiences (never mentioned, but as pleasantly thrilling to my group as a ghost tale to a cozy circle about a fire) must have led him into error. They would sit in a corner and argue passionately for a whole evening, one with the sardonic bitterness of a Dumas fils, the other with the fiery purity of a Charlotte Brontë. When I came over once to interrupt them, Grace darted her bright eyes up at me and cried:

"I'm telling your nephew some of the wonderful examples the last century gives us of loyal wives." She turned back to Lydig. "What about Mrs. Browning?"

"She was an invalid. She doesn't count."

"And Mary Ann Disraeli? When she caught her fingers in the door of that carriage the night he had to speak—"

"She probably screamed her head off!" Lydig finished for her with a shout of laughter. "Anyway, she was years older than Dizzy and couldn't have caught another man."

"*Really!* Then let me cite the example of the Queen herself. Surely, there's someone you can't deny!"

"What about that gillie? Didn't the duchesses in London call her 'Mrs. Brown'?"

"Lydig Millinder! How can you *say* such things?"

I knew that they were both having a lovely time, and that Lydig's innate sweetness of temper was brought out in a simple, approving atmosphere where his high ideals and literalness of mind were not laughed at and his rather heavy humor could find mates. When he relaxed, he laughed too loudly, and I couldn't help reflecting that a mood of melancholy more became his dark, romantic looks. I wanted him to be happy, but not at the cost of unseemliness.

"You shouldn't go on that way," I warned him afterwards. "People see you here without Elsie, and they'll put two and two together."

"And get four! Why shouldn't they?"

"But it's not *done* to talk that way. It's not—well, it's not quite gentlemanly."

"Maybe I'm not a gentleman!"

I began to be irritated. "Then I hope you'll try to act like one. In my house, anyway."

"But, Auntie, if your friends don't mind, and I don't mind, what's the harm in it?"

"Because *I* mind."

He behaved better after this, at least under my roof. But there was a new development in his social life over which I had no control. My friends started asking him to their own parties. I had the mortification of meeting my nephew, whom I had held up to everyone as the most sought after young man in New York society, at Annie Trig's tiny tea parties in the lobby of the Abigail Adams, at Grace McElways's Sunday suppers at the Cosmopolitan Club and for vodka cocktails in old Sherebenieff's walk-up apartment. It could not have been snobbishness that caused me to resent this, for, after all, I went to these places myself. But Lydig to me was youth and beauty incarnate; I could not bear to have him associated with my little collection of old crocks. It seemed to me that they surrounded him, cackling, like a group of lepers who wanted to be cured by the proximity of his strength and vigor, but who at the same time, with unconscious spite, wanted to make him one of themselves. I ceased to give parties on nights when I expected Lydig at the house, and we dined together alone, with a new constraint between us. All I got for my pains was a drop in the number of his visits and a comment that was to haunt me in later years. Finding that he had missed a party that I had given on a Monday night, he expressed regret that I had not asked him.

"But, Lydig, my dear, you'd have been bored stiff!"

"Oh, no, Auntie. I sometimes think your friends are the only people left I can be myself with."

I suppose, in any event, that his visits would have dropped off with the decline of his interest in Millinder Enterprises. He was returning more and more to his old pastime of sport. When he traveled now, it was no longer to investigate hand weaving in New Hampshire or the restoration of old houses on the James River, but rather to fish in Florida or to shoot bear in Canada. He took up polo again, and I was shocked to hear that he played regularly on a team with Townie Fales. I was even more shocked to hear that he and Eales had won the doubles squash tournament at the Racquet Club. He sold his newspaper for four times what it had cost him, and his repertory theater, after a winter of sparse attendance at *Timon of Athens* and *The Jew of Malta* staged a popular revival of *Charley's Aunt*. The curious thing about all of Lydig's projects was that, when liquidated or turned to baser purposes, they showed an immediate profit. His gallery of nonrepresentational art was ultimately converted for a whacking price into a Buick salesroom.

"The thing about Lydig," his sarcastic brother Oswald told me, "is that he's basically a simple guy with an uncanny nose for a buck. If he'd only been born poor, he could have made a fortune."

"And would *that* have made him happy?"

"Happier than all this art business that he has no real feeling for. The trouble with Lydig is that Mummy had too much ambition, and his wife too little. He spends his life jumping through hoops, and Elsie's simply not amused."

"She seems to be amused enough with Townie Fales," I said bitterly.

"Exactly! So Lydig has to turn himself into a bigger and better Townie. Have you heard the latest? He's organizing an expedition to climb Dwandikar."

"What is Dwandikar?"

"A pile of rock in Nepal. They call it the poor man's Everest."

"A mountain?" I queried. "It seems such an obvious symbol, a mountain."

"But there you are! Lydig *is* obvious!"

The last time I saw Lydig was the hot June night that he dined with me before taking his boat to India en route to Nepal. He was moody and silent, and in the library after dinner he stood before an open window, looking down at the avenue from which I could hear the roar of starting buses. Watching that stiff back I was reminded of Armistice Day when he had stared gloomily out of the same window at the celebrating crowds.

"Must you really go, my dear?" I asked in a voice that suddenly trembled. "It seems so long and so far. Couldn't you wait and pick a smaller mountain?"

He did not turn. "No, Auntie. The plans are all made."

"But plans can be unmade," I protested. "That's the advantage of money. You can call everything off at the last moment."

"But I don't want to. I want to climb that mountain!"

"But why, in God's name?"

"Because that's where you all see me. On top of it!"

My hands flew to my brow. "Not *me*, surely!"

"Yes, Auntie, even you!" And he turned to give me a look of surprising hostility. "Even you!"

"But I only want you to stop, dearest, I only want you to rest," I implored him, agonized at the hardness of his tone. "All your life you've been giving things up as soon as you accomplished them. As if they were nothing but tests. Way back, it was football and high marks. Then it was poetry and polo, and then law. And then there was journalism and theater and your art museum. And now there's hunting and mountain climbing. You rip through one thing after another, faster and faster, and all to dazzle—that bitch."

I burst into tears as I uttered the unretractable word and sat heavily down on the nearest chair to cover my face with my hands. I felt suddenly that he was pathetic, and it made me angry. Lydig had no business to be anything but tragic. I knew that nothing would stop him and that no one could save him. He lacked even the imagination to extricate himself from the toils of his own stubborn obsession. But I loved him, both the idealized Lydig and the one I now knew better, and when I felt his silent kiss on my cheek, I threw my arms about him and clung to him until he had to call Teresa to come and help me to bed.

He was killed, two months later, with his party of six in an avalanche on Dwandikar. The bare statement of that terrible fact should suffice, and there is no need to pain the reader by dwelling on the black days that followed. They were the blackest of my life, but I cannot suppose that a picture of private grief would add to the story of my family. Besides, Lydig's death was an accident, a futile, ghastly accident, and the aftermath of such makes poor reading. It is enough to say that Julia showed her feelings only in her fixed, white mask and that Elsie surprised everybody by waiting a full year before marrying Townie Fales. I came in time to miss Lydig less acutely, but what I never got over was the realization that I, as much as his mother and wife, had failed him. All he had wanted from me was the gentle, friendly atmosphere of my dowdy little chattering group. It had been a small thing, but I had refused it, as I had refused Ione her lover. For me Lydig had to be a prince, and it was my punishment that he should die a prince's death in the snows of Dwandikar.

8

Iᴛ ᴡᴀꜱ ᴏɴʟʏ a year after Lydig's death that the stock market fell to pieces and the great depression began. It seemed to affect my family in inverse proportion to the amount of their individual fortunes. My cousin George Millinder, who had inherited the bulk of Uncle Fred's estate and hence the largest remaining share of Grandpa's, sold most of his securities before the crash and bought real estate in New York City by the block in the ensuing years of panic and mortgage foreclosure. He must have multiplied his fortune many times. Lucius Hoyt, who did the same thing, though on a smaller scale, used to boast, with a dry little cackle, that he and George had started the depression. Other Millinders did less well. Aunt Daisy, who had clung to certain old stocks which Uncle Fred had esteemed, with a stubbornness intended to be a moral example to a heedless generation of hasty buyers and sellers, was virtually wiped out, as was her daughter, Gwen Myol. Few people, however, were to learn this, because George Millinder, whose wise counsels they had ignored, made up at least the income that his improvident mother and sister had lost. In similar fashion my brother Willie's heavy losses were not generally known, because Julia managed to preserve her Lydig fortune and was able to take over the domestic expenses that he could no longer afford. Ione, as we have seen, was rescued from what at least she considered indigence by Harold Fay. As for myself, the fact that I lost only half of my fortune was attributable to the fact I took only half of Lucius Hoyt's advice. An ill-advised spurt of spinsterish independence, plus the fact that my "little court" contained an economic crackpot, was the cause of this folly. But what did it really matter? I gave up hiring a private railway car on my trips to Maine, closed off the top floor of the house in New York, dipped into capital and decided I was down to bare essentials.

Such events were everyday history in the depression. The really strange thing in our family was my experience with Collier Haven, the stockbroker who had married Aunt Polly Herron's youngest daughter, Pamela. "Colly" Haven was a son-in-law after Aunt Polly's own heart. Her two older daughters had married diplomats, but, being a true New Yorker, she preferred her success within the limits of Manhattan. Colly was not only handsome and what I still call "elegant"; he was senior partner of the old and respected Wall Street firm of Haven, Bryce & Co., and his surname had a flavor that was peculiarly aristocratic. The Havens were old New Yorkers, but not the kind who had allowed themselves to tumble into a pedigree-worshiping, servant-distrusting brownstone meanness. Like all true epicures, they had kept up with the times. If a Haven had been at Valley Forge and a Haven at Gettysburg, a Haven had also been president of the Erie Railway and a Haven had married a Vanderbilt. It was a family on a minor scale like the Adams family, associated with every chapter of American history, yet always standing, quite voluntarily a bit to the side, a bit aloof. I have never known how to grade the various tiers of New York society—I leave that to the gossip writers—but I venture to say that a shrewd social climber would have given more to be invited to the Collier Havens' than to any other house in the city. They were not as rich or as important as many other couples, but the climber who managed to dine there might hope to dine wherever else he chose. I went there myself but once a year, to their Christmas tree. Pamela was always very sweet, but she had the same air of formal coziness as her mother, part of a snobbishness so deeply imbedded in their characters that they were sincerely unaware of it. I liked her well enough, but I was determined that she was not going to condescend to me.

Pamela and I, however, were destined to meet at a party given neither at her house nor at mine, but at Victor Selmuth's, in the winter of 1934. Victor Selmuth was a dark, soft, pleasant, but rather damp young man, a curator of Chinese art at the Metropolitan Museum, who had a way of standing with his hands on his hips, his lips formed in an "o," as he listened to one and then breaking gently into what must have been intended to be an easy and charming laugh. It took me a while to discover that he concentrated too much on that laugh to hear the story that ostensibly provoked it. I had met him when he was doing research for an article on Mamma's jade collection and had added him to my dinner list. He flattered me outrageously, but this was my silly period, and I liked it. When he moved into a small apartment above a gallery on Fifty-seventh Street I loaned him his furniture, and he invited me in return to his little cocktail parties, made up half of young men—artists, decorators and actors—and half of elderly, fashionable women. I noticed with time that the latter were becoming more and more fashionable. When I arrived at the party that I have mentioned, after making my painful way up two flights of stairs, Victor greeted me at the landing, a drink in his hand, with his usual salutation:

"Glorious Miss Gussie! You've made it again!"

"Hannibal has come over the Alps," I muttered, pausing, one hand on the banister, to catch my breath. "Is that Hannibal's whisky?"

"Expressly made," he replied and placed in my hand my special concoction of rye, fruit and sugar. "I'm particularly glad you came today." He leaned closer as he led me into the living room. "I'm expecting your cousin, Mrs. Haven."

"What's a great lady like Pamela doing with the likes of you?"

"I sat next to her at dinner at Mr. Hoyt's, and I happened to mention that you were coming today. I hope you don't mind."

"So I'm only a rung in your ladder to Pamela Haven, is that it?" I demanded with an irritation that was only half assumed. It seemed to me that Pamela's New York should have been big enough for her without the addition of mine.

"A rung, my dear Miss Gussie!" Victor exclaimed in his most fatuous tone.

"But you're a true Millinder, a *princesse du sang*, and she's only the daughter of one!"

This was a bit fresh, but it was Victor's style, and, after all, I had encouraged it. I moved across the room to greet my old friend, Prince Sherebenieff, who clicked his heels and kissed my hand, and we were having a rather catty conversation about the young men present when I saw Victor hurry across the room to greet a tall lady with a black beret and a silver fox neckpiece who was standing in the doorway, pulling off a glove and casting a practiced eye about the little party. I was sorry to recognize Pamela, for I had already laid a wager with the Prince that she would disappoint our host.

"Dear Mrs. Haven!" Victor cried in a tone of exultation which I felt would be the end of our friendship. "How wonderful of you to come! You've made the stairs, and you've made my little party!"

Pamela Haven, then in her late forties, was the best-looking of the Herron daughters. She had Aunt Polly's high brow, white skin and small aquiline nose, but where Aunt Polly was compact and rather darting, Pamela was tall and a bit ungainly, with a tendency to overdress, particularly where feathers and furs were concerned. She had a habit of nodding her head too much and of making jerky gesticulations with her arms which reflected, or seemed meant to reflect, the naïveté of her trusting little girl's picture of the world. Collier Haven was reputed to be constantly unfaithful to her. Yet Pamela was not altogether stupid; she had her mother's remarkable instinct for the social right thing. I imagined that she had come to Victor's for a half hour of observation and maybe, like myself, to add one or two names to her list of available extra men. In the New York of those days it was the husband who made himself socially rare. Colly Haven would not have been seen dead at a party at Victor Selmuth's.

"Has my cousin Augusta Millinder arrived yet?" I was surprised to hear her ask. "Oh, yes, thank you, Mr. Selmuth, I see her now. Do you think I might go and talk to her a minute? You know how it is. One never has a chance to see one's family except at parties."

In a moment Prince Sherebenieff was on his feet, clicking his heels and bowing to her, but Pamela, while allowing her hand to be kissed, was quite definite about his removal.

"Would you mind terribly, Prince, if I took your place on this nice window seat? Just for a minute? I do so want to have a *tiny*, private talk with my cousin."

When we were seated alone in our corner, Pamela looked at me silently in an odd way, her head cocked to one side, her lips half open, as if about to speak. It suddenly struck me that the flicker in her eyes was nothing but simple embarrassment.

"What is this 'tiny, private talk' to be about?" I asked gruffly.

"I'm in trouble," she said abruptly and then laughed. It was a silly, nervous laugh. "Rather bad trouble, I'm afraid. It's about Colly."

"I'm sorry. What kind of trouble?"

"Well . . . financial trouble."

My back stiffened. Surely, the Collier Havens, who asked me only to their

Christmas tree, were not coming to *me* for money? "I guess we're all in that boat these days," I said coolly.

"But this is different." Pamela fixed her eyes on some spot of the wall opposite and appeared to be making herself recite a little tale which she had painfully memorized. "It isn't just ordinary money trouble. Poor Colly seems to have made an unfortunate mistake at the office. I'm not clear just what, but I gather it could be made to look a bit ugly. You see, he and his partners are always investing other people's money, and sometimes, particularly when they're investing their own at the same time, it's easy to get things mixed up. I mean, if you're buying a thousand shares for one account, and you put it in your own, because you happen to need *that* stock *that* day—well, of course, everything comes out right in the end, but it's like musical chairs, it depends when the music stops."

"You mean someone's always minus a chair?" I was too flabbergasted to do anything but continue Pamela's absurd analogy. One must have lived in those days and have known the position of Haven, Bryce & Co. to comprehend my shock.

"Not really, because the music's not *meant* to stop. Don't you see? It's meant to go on and on!"

"I'm not sure if I know what you're driving at, Pamela," I said in a graver tone. "If it's what I think it is, a cocktail party is hardly the place to discuss it."

But Pamela was not quite so childish as she appeared. Much of her attitude was probably a simple defense against terror, for now she looked at me with suddenly distracted eyes. "But where can I discuss it? I've never had to discuss such a thing before. I only came here today because I was told I might find you. I didn't know where else to turn."

"To turn for what?"

"Why, for the money Colly needs!"

"The money!" I gasped. "Surely his firm will cover him!"

"But that's just it, they can't! Or say they can't. You see, Colly made the mistake of telling one of his partners what he needed the money for, instead of just asking for it. Well, the partner, it seems, got panicky and went to the firm's lawyer, who said they couldn't do anything for Colly because they'd be compounding a crime or whatever the legal phrase is. Of course, as Colly says, the silly partner should never have gone to the lawyer. But now, don't you see, he's stuck? If he goes to anyone else for the money, they'll want to know why his firm won't put it up. And then the cat's out of the bag!"

"How much does he need?"

She lowered her voice and looked away as she told me. It was not a monstrous sum. Had Lydig been alive and needed it, I would have raised it soon enough. But I was still very far from willing to become the guardian angel of Collier Haven. I gazed pensively about the gay little room with its chatting couples and thought wryly how dazzled our host would have been to have his apartment used for such revelations of the downtown world.

"But why me?" I demanded in ultimate resentment. "Can't you put up the money yourself? Can't your mother?"

"You know how Daddy was about trusts. He made us tie everything up."

"But trusts can be invaded."

"Not without telling the trustee why."

"Well, what about George Millinder? He's richer than God!"

"Can you imagine explaining to George?" Pamela was now clasping and unclasping her hands. "No, Gussie, believe me, you're the only one. I've gone over the whole family in my mind a thousand times, and Colly's too, and you're the only one I could trust with this secret. You're the only one with the generosity to put up the money and not tell!" She shook her head sadly. "Of course, I can't blame you if you don't. But at least I can promise you that your money would be safe. Even if the worst came to the worst, I could pay you back out of my income. It might take years, but I could!"

Well, of course, I knew that she could and would. It was not Pamela who had forfeited my confidence. I began at last to feel sorry for her, poor driven creature, lost in dark, unfamiliar territory, turning her scared eyes this way and that in search of enemies until then not imagined. I tried to think of her visiting her husband in Sing Sing, but fancy failed. I thought of the whole smashed shelf of her lares and penates and recoiled at the picture of Aunt Polly, her proud lips quivering, her eager mind unable at last to find a saving cliché. Yes, Pamela was no fool. Her instinct had guided her to the one person in the world who could snatch her husband's chestnuts from the fire.

"I think you'd better send Collier to see me," I said abruptly. "I think I'd better hear the whole story from him."

"Oh, Gussie, you're a darling!" she cried, clasping her hands. "Could I send him tonight?"

"If you wish. At nine o'clock."

It was all very well for me to sneer at my poor young host, imagining the excitement that he would have felt had he known of our discussion, but I was very much excited myself. Had I been really honest with myself, I might have admitted that the pleasure of owning such a secret was almost worth the risk of the loan. For Collier Haven's position in the downtown world was a peculiarly trusted one. It was not so much his personal wealth or his wife's or his financial acumen or his directorships or even his partnership in Haven, Bryce & Co. It was more the unique charm that he had for other men, important men, men like my cousin George Millinder, and Harold Fay, who found his advice and companionship almost indispensable. It was his particular genius to be able to impress men of greater intelligence than himself. His exposure would have shaken every man's confidence in his brother.

He came that night a few minutes after nine. I am sure that those minutes were carefully timed to avoid the appearance of too desperate an anxiety. I had directed beforehand that he be shown into the library, and I kept him waiting a good fifteen minutes in my turn. When I finally went in, I found him idly turning the atlas with his long fingers and gazing at the blue expanse of the Pacific.

"Are you looking for a South Sea island?"

It was a rude opening, but it seemed to fit with his idea of my character, for he smiled as he came over to take my hand.

"I thought I had found it in your house, Augusta."

"That remains to be seen."

He was certainly a handsome man, though very thin and grey. Everything about him was grey, his long hair, his eyes, his silk tie, his pearl stickpin, his perfectly tailored suit. For color there was simply a spot of green in the irises of his eyes, a flash of gold from his slender watch chain, a gleam of claret from his polished shoes. Collier at first blush might have seemed too well turned out, almost too fragile to have been such a man's man, but I had heard from Ione that he made up for it by the excellence of his golf and the salaciousness of his humor. His charm was the charm of the unexpected. It was delightful to find a good fellow where one had expected a snob. It was the people who did not know Collier who regarded him as the worst kind of Porcellian Club aristocrat and who would have rejoiced at his downfall. I confess that I felt a bit of their hostility myself that night as he leaned forward, his feet apart, his hands in his coat pockets, and asked with a little cough:

"Where would you like to begin?"

"I think at the beginning, if you don't mind," I said sourly as I took my seat. "Omitting as little as possible and changing as little as possible."

He remained standing as he told me the story. He told it with more accuracy and in greater detail than Pamela had told it, but it was essentially the same story. He had embezzled from his firm's accounts. The sums taken had not been enormous; they could, in fact, have been obtained as easily by borrowing. As the Haven of Haven, Bryce & Co., he had simply become accustomed to using the nearest funds at hand. But now replacement could not be made, and disaster threatened. He related the facts concisely and clearly and without the least hint of shame. No doubt it was painful to his pride to have to come begging to his wife's cousin, but he was not one to complain about the bitterness of the remedy. It was even conceivable that he felt it a privilege for such a one as I to be of assistance to such a one as he. I began to see that his crime consisted more in arrogance than greed. He despised the world too much to obey its little rules.

"I suppose you realize that I have no choice," I said at last. "I can't let you go to jail. It would kill Pamela. And it would kill my poor Aunt Polly."

"Oh, I shouldn't go to jail, I don't think."

"How would you avoid it?"

"Well, it's not absolutely compulsory to live, is it?"

His words might have suggested a note of bravado, but his tone had none. Coriolanus would never stoop to impress a mob. I might have been impressed had I felt less a mob.

"You can have your money," I said grudgingly. "Pamela, of course, will go on the note with you. I'll have my lawyer, Barry Neilson, draw it up. You needn't worry. I shan't tell him what it's for."

"May I say that you're a very good cousin?" His smile and tone were more consistent with good manners than with jubilation. A person hearing him might have thought I was being thanked for the loan of my opera box. "Pamela will never forget this."

"I imagine she won't," I said, with a touch of grimness. But I liked his recognition of the fact that I was not doing it for him and that gratitude on his part might have been indelicate. "I have a condition to add," I warned him. "When you hear it, you may wish to find your money elsewhere."

"But there *is* no elsewhere. What is your condition, Augusta?"

"That you retire permanently from business."

I was astonished at his reaction. Instead of anger, it was one of curiosity, almost of amusement. It was the first time that I sensed his charm. I had never really believed in it before. But it existed. It seemed to consist of his basic belief that all men were created equal, but that some were luckier and some cleverer than others—it hardly mattered which. Gussie Millinder might be a tiresome old maid and not to be bothered with, but if chance happened to deal Gussie Millinder the trumps, well, good for old Gussie! Henceforth, she could play with the experts. Colly's arrogance was less arrogance than it was his capacity immediately to recognize and accept, with however brutal a frankness, the changes in position of those around him.

"Perhaps you wouldn't mind telling why you exact such a condition?" he asked.

"Not at all. In bailing you out, I am obstructing justice. Justice would keep you from harming other people. Mustn't I do the same?"

"Whom have I harmed?"

"Well, nobody, I suppose, now. That's because of me."

"And God bless you!"

"Next time there might not be a me."

"But I should never dream of appealing a second time to your generosity!"

"That's not what I mean at all," I retorted, afraid of being confused by his smoothness. "I mean, how else can I protect you from your own propensities? You're obviously not in the least ashamed of what you've done."

He did not deny it. Should a cuckoo be ashamed of laying its egg in another bird's nest? Or a magpie of taking bright objects?

"But how can you be sure I'll stay retired?" he asked.

"I'll have your word of honor."

"My word of honor," he repeated softly. "I call that charming of you, Augusta!"

"Your word of honor as a gentleman!"

"I see," he mused. "But surely you'll give me time to wind up my affairs? Time, for example, to pay you back?"

"How much time will you require?"

"Shall we say, a year?"

"Very well, then. I give you a year." Even faced with the loss of his occupation in life, he would not beg. He simply nodded and took his leave.

I had a terrible time with Barry Neilson the next day. He was a gruff, deaf, sour, cynical, leathery old lawyer of the ancient school, profoundly sensible and impossible to impress, who carried on the tradition and law firm of his late adored senior partner, Judge Lydig. He was bitterly suspicious of Collier and very reluctant to draw the note. When I finally convinced him that the risk was not his responsibility and that I simply wanted him to put the loan papers in proper form, he shrugged and muttered something about a fool and his money.

For all his gloomy prognostications, however, my note was paid promptly on its four quarter-annual installments. On the final payment, just a year later, I telephoned Collier to congratulate him. I had not seen him or Pamela in the interval. I had been too tactful to call, and they to invite me. But my heart had been softened by those punctual payments.

"If it were not for the oath I took to myself," I told him over the wire, "I should be tempted to let you off my condition."

The smooth voice never faltered. "Your condition?"

"Why, the condition that you retire from business!" I exclaimed in sudden suspicion. "Surely you're arranging that now!"

"Retire? My dear Augusta, at fifty-six? I hope to have many years in harness yet!"

"But you promised me!" I cried in sudden erupting anger. "You gave me your word of honor!"

"I remember that I promised to retire if I couldn't repay your loan in a year," he said coolly. "As indeed, I ought to have, if I couldn't. But, surely, you don't expect to lay down conditions now you have your money back? As the lawyers would say, what would be the consideration?"

"It serves me right," I shouted into the instrument, "for taking the word of a thief!"

He hung up at this, and I rang my bell cord so hard that it broke.

"Get the car!" I cried when I saw poor Teresa's startled face at the door. "I'm going downtown to see Mr. Neilson!"

But Mr. Neilson had very little consolation to offer. He sat with his hands clasped on the desk and grunted as I told him the sorry tale.

"So like a woman," he mumbled when I had finished, "to think that every handsome crook must have a word of honor. Serves you jolly well right, if you ask me."

I began to wonder if it wasn't just as well that the old-fashioned type of lawyer was dying out. Who would not prefer a little sycophancy to paying large fees for the privilege of being insulted? I decided that I, too, could be rude.

"I expect you to put on your hat and go right over to Mr. Haven's office!" I exclaimed. "And tell him we'll send him to jail if he hasn't retired by tomorrow morning!"

"You expect me to undertake blackmail? At my time of life and with my reputation at the bar?"

"But he promised me!"

"And what is that promise worth?" he retorted, with a snort. "Do you think a court would support it? A promise given in return for breaking the law? For that's what you did, Miss Millinder. You broke the law! You're an accessory after the fact, and if you make too much noise about it, you may find the district attorney rapping at your door!"

This finally subdued me. "What *can* I do, then?" I asked sulkily.

"You can forget the whole thing. And keep your fingers crossed that Mr. Collier Haven will keep *his* fingers out of other people's accounts. For if it ever comes to light that you kept him out of jail, you might be liable to his subsequent victims!"

I mastered my ill-humor as best I could, and I saw and heard no more of the Havens until a performance of *Traviata*, some weeks later. In those days I shared an opera box with Aunt Polly Herron. Ordinarily, we took alternate nights, but I would sometimes send her the tickets I could not use. It was on such an evening that Pamela slipped into the back of the box just before the first intermission and then moved up, while my other guests were strolling, to sit by the corner chair which I never vacated until the final curtain.

"I take it Collier doesn't like Italian opera?" I asked dryly. I assumed from her being there that she knew nothing of our bargain or its breach.

"Oh, no, he's here," she replied, quite innocently. "He prefers to sit with the opera club. There he is, over there. Talking to that lady in red."

Following her gesture I saw Collier Haven standing in the back of one of the boxes opposite, which he must have just entered, leaning forward to take the hand of a lady in a rather flaming red dress who had turned to smile up at him. Even I knew that the lady was Angela Cryder. Ione had pointed her out to me at a wedding reception only a few weeks before. She had been very explicit as to her relationship with Collier.

"Who is she?"

"I believe she's a Mrs. Cryder," Pamela answered without a flicker of the eye. "They say she's most attractive."

Was it possible that she didn't know? Was it possible that she *did*? I was more and more baffled with Pamela. "Well, if he were my husband, I'd go over and collar him!" I said with a grunt. "That dress is entirely too red!"

"That must be one of the advantages of being single: that you don't have to worry about red dresses." As Pamela said this, with her mannered smile, and gazed about at the other boxes, nodding here and there to an acquaintance, it was almost impossible to believe her concerned. But her next words showed that she could, after all, wear a mask. "I really came tonight because I want to thank you for all you've done." Still she did not look at me. "You can't imagine. My nightmares are all gone."

Had I been generous, I would have left the poor creature in ignorance, but I was still too sore and bitter. Should anyone be allowed to dwell in such complacency as Pamela's? Did we all have to be stagehands to keep her life a perpetual performance of *The Bluebird*?

"I know," I said grimly. "*I* have the nightmares now."

"You?" Pamela turned to me at last in surprise. "But didn't Colly pay you back?"

"Oh, yes. My nightmare isn't about the money. Any more than it's about going to jail. My nightmare is knowing that a certain suave 'gentleman,' whose likeness I see across the way, is moving confidently about in the most important financial circles of this city, trusted by everybody, and that *I* put him there!"

"But. surely, Gussie, it won't happen again! Surely, Colly has learned his lesson!"

It was too much, on top of everything else, that I should be expected to swallow the picture of Colly Haven learning his lesson, a fair-haired boy in an Eton jacket, extending his palm for a slap of the ferrule without a quiver of his manly little lip.

"Will you guarantee him?" I demanded angrily. "Will you exert your wifely influence to keep him straight? The same wifely influence that's keeping him away from that trollop in the box over there?"

Pamela's eyelids just flickered now, and she looked at me pensively a moment. "*Could* you be referring to Mrs. Cryder?"

"I know the Herron attitude that facts needn't exist!" I exclaimed. "But they can be stubborn things, you'll find! Once you get used to looking at them, you may discover there's something you can *do* about them. It's for your own good, Pamela!"

Her gaze became almost quizzical. Certainly poor Pamela must have associated me by now with the most disagreeable revelations. Yet her attitude conveyed neither shock nor indignation. There might have been a mild surprise at my poor taste; that was all. But then, suddenly, she turned away from me and, raising her opera glasses to her eyes, stared deliberately across the house at Mrs. Cryder. It was a long stare. Collier Haven observed her; he moved his arm in a greeting of evident surprise and embarrassment. His wife made no acknowledgment of his gesture; I had never seen her so motionless. Even in the agitation of that moment I noticed that stillness made her more attractive. Aunt Polly's daughters were all good-looking enough, but they were not very feminine; they were timid, startled, rather staring creatures, like tense antelopes, who might nibble out of your hand and then bound away. But the Pamela who now calmly put down her opera glasses and turned back to me was entirely a woman, and a woman who had sized up her rival.

"Do you notice that Mrs. Cryder has her sables over the back of her chair?" she asked me. "I think that's so common, don't you? Mother always taught us that ladies left their coats in the little vestibule."

"I suppose she wants you to see them. After all, you probably paid for them!"

But I was learning rapidly how much I had underestimated Pamela. "Really?" she queried. "I thought you had."

"Oh, but I've been paid off!" When Pamela said nothing to this, I decided she was ready for a direct appeal. "Why do you put up with it?"

She shrugged and raised her glasses again, but this time only to inspect the great yellow curtain. "What can I do?"

"You can take him away from New York! You can make him retire from business! He promised me he would!"

She said nothing for a moment, but I could see that she was disturbed. "He *promised* you?" she asked finally. Then she turned. "He did, really? He promised?" There was a note of incredulity in her voice.

I had a sudden inspiration. If dishonesty in the business world, which to Pamela was simply a distasteful and potentially embarrassing aspect of the male way of doing things, could be translated into terms that she had learned as a child at her father's knee, there was no telling what genie I might evoke in her behalf.

"He gave me his word of honor!" I exclaimed.

"His word of honor!" she repeated, suddenly awe-struck. "But if he gave you his word of honor, he must keep it!"

"He hasn't seen fit to!"

"Oh, but he will. You may depend on that, Gussie. If Colly gave you his word of honor, he will keep it!"

The others returned to the box at this point, and we could say no more. I noticed, however, that Pamela was very silent, and in the middle of the next act she whispered something in my ear and left. I was upset, for even in my moments of sorest irritation I had not really meant to do anything that would jeopardize the conjugal relation of so lordly a husband and so submissive a wife. But I had to admit to myself that there was nothing submissive about the straight line of Pamela's disappearing back. Had I misconceived that relationship, as I had misconceived so many others?

On Saturday matinees Aunt Polly and I always shared the box, and on the next such occasion, as she chatted happily to me through the first act of *Lakmé*, I had my first news of Collier Haven's retirement. It was a bit difficult to pick out the facts from a picture so "Herronized."

"It's really the best news," Aunt Polly whispered. "Poor Colly has seemed so tired recently, and now they can buy a farm, which will be so much better for Pamela and the children. And then, too, my dear," she continued in a lower whisper, one that could hardly be heard in the adjoining boxes, "between the two of us, it won't be exactly a tragedy if Colly is removed from the distractions of the New York social scene. I guess it's not altogether a secret that he has a bit of a wandering eye!"

I should like to have witnessed the scene between Pamela and Colly. It must have been a bitter experience for a man of his mental resources, one who could slide so easily over words and facts and who had handled so much money and so many men, to find himself brought to a halt before the raised oval chin and stubborn eyes of a hitherto compliant wife who now flung the word "honor" down between them and demanded that he keep his word. With what she knew about him, her success was inevitable; Colly not only retired from business, but moved, as Aunt Polly had predicted, to the farm in Connecticut which Pamela now purchased. Her trust could be invaded for that! But it seemed to me that she was carrying things a bit far. I had made no stipulation about living in the country. For Pamela to change her existence so completely gave the appearance of donning sackcloth and ashes in an almost carnival spirit. There was certainly no reason, either moral or financial, why she should give up her social life.

Before too many months had passed, however, I discovered that she hadn't. Considering my delicate relations with the Havens, I had never expected to be invited to the farm, but in this I had underestimated both

Pamela's gratitude and her faith in the healing powers of hospitality. She wrote to ask me to spend a weekend with them in the fall as naturally as though nothing had happened between me and Colly. She even put it out of my power to decline by asking me to drive up with Aunt Polly and keep her amused on the trip. I need not have worried about the embarrassment of finding myself alone with Colly. There were ten other house guests, and we never sat down less than twenty for lunch or dinner.

The farm, if magnificent, was still a farm. Everything was freshly painted white or red: the two vast barns, the silos, the stables, the chicken houses. Two hundred head of Swiss cattle and three hundred sheep grazed picturesquely on the rolling green of the soft Connecticut countryside. But Pamela, the rustic, had managed to bring Newport with her. To the old white farmhouse she had added a wing with a dining room of a size in which to hang her Romneys and Lawrences; she had erected a charming *folie* of an eighteenth century guest pavilion, and she had put in a swimming pool. The cocktail hour on the terrace was enhanced by the bells of the passing herd, but louder than the clanging of bells were the cries of the guests, led by Pamela's mother and sisters, who exclaimed at the beauty of everything, raising their hands and their glasses in a chorus of loyal female approval. There was something unquenchable about the spirit and enthusiasm of the Herrons. In the middle of the Sahara they could have turned a mud hut into a tea house and cut out a window to snatch a bit of view at the desert.

I had a distressing sense, as the weekend wore on, of the defeat and captivity of Colly. Stripped of his business, his city life and his city women, he seemed as docile and quiet as another animal on the farm, and I would not have been surprised to see a bell hung around his neck when the guests went out to the terrace at sundown for their evening libation. He seemed to take no interest in the farm and to have no say about it. He was thinner than ever, almost scrawny, and it was alarming to see his Adam's apple go up and down when he swallowed. On Sunday afternoon, when the houseparty was led off to see a newborn calf that was to be named for Aunt Polly, I lingered on purpose to be with him. Together we stood on the edge of the flagstone terrace and looked down the hill towards the nearest barn. His first, quiet words recognized that it was I and not he who had sought this interview.

"Are you satisfied with your handiwork, Augusta?"

"*My* handiwork! Pamela took everything into her own hands!"

"But those were the hands into which you delivered me. You taught her the joys of management. Do you deny it?"

"I gave her a weapon to defend herself against a husband who was mistreating her!"

"Mistreating her?" he demanded coolly. "What utter rubbish. Nobody could mistreat Pamela. She was perfectly happy being married to a man whom she had been taught to regard as successful. She had it all over her sisters, and that's what she really wanted."

"She didn't have Mrs. Cryder over them!"

"I'm not sure she didn't. Mrs. Cryder probably made me more 'interesting.' Isn't that the way your Aunt Polly would have taught her to face it?"

I had to admit to myself that it was, and I paused to gather my wits. "Does a husband, then, have no obligations?"

"But the Herron women don't have husbands," he exclaimed with exasperating patience. "They have governesses. I don't claim I was a very good governess. I suppose I took too many days off. But I always kept my temper—which is so important with children—and I was kind."

The image of Colly in a white uniform with a nurse's cap rose ludicrously to mind, but I knew that I was lost if I laughed. "Do you think it was kind to send her begging for the money you needed?"

"That was rather bad of me," he conceded pleasantly, "but even well-bred children must occasionally face the world. Besides, she was very clever about it. You were her idea."

"But it almost killed her that you broke your word!"

"Ah, that's where you're wrong!" Colly raised his eyebrows, and his voice was suddenly emphatic. "That's where she spied my weakness! And see how quickly she struck! Little girls can be fiendish when they have the chance. Governesses must beware. Behold me now, as helpless as one of those cows in the model barn, milked by the gentlest machinery! Surrounded by shiny bars and tinkling bells and Victor Herbert through a loudspeaker. Do you remember I told you once I'd never go to jail, Augusta? Well, here I am!"

It was certainly true that he struck me, while he said this, as some long grey canine creature, a wolf or wolfhound, self-starved and pacing restlessly his narrow cell. If one let him out, he would turn on his liberator as soon as on his jailer. But one could know this and still regret that pacing captivity.

"I don't understand people like you," I murmured. "You don't believe in anything!"

"Do you believe in *that*?"

I followed his pointing finger and saw that the rest of the houseparty had just emerged from the barn and were starting slowly up the gentle hillside towards us. Aunt Polly, then in her eighties, led the way, supported by a daughter on each arm. As long as there was further delight to be dug out of the countryside, as long as there were cows and pigs and emeralds and trips to town for matinees, as long as life could present itself as a perpetual notions counter, full of bright ribbons and buttons, the cacophony of my aunt and cousins would never cease. The captive wolfhound would slowly perish amid the cocktails, between the courses, as the conversation turned at dinner. Unless someone slipped the bolt.

"I give you back your word!" I whispered hoarsely to him, without turning my eyes from the approaching group. "I release you from our bargain! You may tell Pamela I release you!"

When he did not answer, and I glanced at him, I saw the smallest flash in the green irises of his grey eyes. He had counted on separating me from the others. He could always deal with a woman alone, except for a Pamela armed by me. But Collier was too consummate a gambler to rake in his chips with any greedy gesture. He liked to hazard his very victory by savoring it.

"You're not worried about widows and orphans?" he asked.

"Oh, I guess Mr. Roosevelt can look after them," I replied with a shrug. "What's the use of his New Deal otherwise?" I turned away, for the others had almost reached the terrace.

Collier Haven's return to Wall Street, only two months later, came as little surprise to the business world. It was generally agreed that he had retired too early and that, quite naturally, he had been bored. What came as more of a shock, however, was his failure to return to Haven, Bryce & Co. I knew, of course, that his former partners were aware of his defalcations. They would not expel him, so long as he was a member, nor would they betray him, but they would not have him back. Unhappily for Collier, their decision made him a marked man. The faintest aroma of something not quite right seemed to hover about that handsome grey head. When scandal breaks in the great houses of finance everyone always cries: "I can't believe it!" Actually, they can. They can believe anything. That is why they are so wary. Collier became associated in several speculative enterprises with men whom he would hardly have known in the past. Two of them failed. Then he worked briefly in the trust department of a bank and thereafter as a customer's man for a brokerage house. He became a familiar figure at the bars of fashionable clubs, always with a deal to propose to the first comer. People found it hard to understand. After all, there was still his wife's income. What did Colly Haven really want? Speculation increased to a fever pitch when he suddenly disappeared—vanished without trace—and then it exploded into headlines all over the nation when the district attorney revealed that he had embezzled a piece of one of Pamela's trusts. He had been a co-trustee, apparently, with a small, sleepy trust company that had not been cognizant of his slipping reputation. He has never turned up, although there is a rumor that one of his sisters knows of his whereabouts and sends him small remittances to this day. I hope that he has found that Pacific island, but I feel sorry for the natives who trade with him.

When I learned that the unfortunate trust company was being required by the Herron family to make restitution in full to Pamela's trust for what her husband had stolen, I was outraged. I went down to see Barry Neilson, who was also Aunt Polly's and Pamela's lawyer, and told him that it was a disgrace to the family. Of course he was entirely noncommittal.

"I have advised Mrs. Haven that the trust company is absolutely liable to make restitution," he said, leaning back in his swivel chair and touching the tips of his fingers together as Judge Lydig used to do. "The fact that the thief happened to be her husband is legally irrelevant."

"But it's morally very relevant!" I protested.

"I am not retained to make moral judgments, Miss Millinder. Your cousin and your aunt incline to a practical view of the matter. In my opinion, nine out of ten people would do the same. But if it's any comfort to you, their view has no effect on the matter. The Haven children are still under age, and a court would compel restitution for their benefit in any event."

"Then *I* must make it up to the trust company!" I exclaimed.

The swivel chair snapped back into place. "You'll do no such thing!" Mr. Neilson retorted. "You'll kindly go straight home and keep your mouth tight shut about the whole affair!"

"But you told me yourself I might be liable! If I'm liable, I want to pay. It was my fault that Collier Haven didn't go to jail. And my fault that he went back to business!"

It took me a long time to convince Mr. Neilson that I was serious, but I finally did. I think he was basically sympathetic. For all his wordly cynicism, he was a deeply moral man. He absolutely refused, however, to let me put up the full amount of the trust company's damages. He pointed out a series of factors in the problem, such as what the trust company had allowed Collier to do *before* my loan and what his chances had been of obtaining the loan elsewhere had I refused him, and so forth. He said he would have to think about it, and a week later he called on me at home with an elaborate computation of the amount of my "moral liability" to Pamela's trustee. I did not profess to understand it, and it bothered me that the final figure was only a third of what I had expected to pay, but I ultimately agreed. Mr. Neilson then arranged to pay it to the trust company as the anonymous contribution of a person who did not wish to see it penalized for "Collier Haven's malfeasance." One of the conditions of the contribution was that Mrs. Haven should not be instructed of it. I was afraid she might suspect. But it hardly matters, anyhow. Pamela has had nothing to do with me since Collier's flight. She is furious with me for releasing him from his vow and regards me as the origin of all her troubles.

9

THERE WAS A general expectation in the family, after Lydig's tragic accident on Dwandikar, that Willie and Julia would turn their attention to their hitherto neglected younger son. But Oswald, at least in their eyes, was impossible. He infuriated Willie by sneering at Scroll & Key, the Yale senior society which constituted the primary interest of his father's life, and he disgusted Julia by pointing out, on too many occasions, how integral a part she was of the social world that she professed to despise. Neither of his parents was sympathetic enough to understand that he was simply jealous of the preference which they had always shown for Lydig. But even under ordinary circumstances Oswald would not have been the type to suit them. He had grown up into a stringy young man with his mother's red hair, nervous limbs and eyes that were always laughing at one, in an irritating way. It was never possible in an argument to pin him down; he had a trick of shifting his basis that continually baffled me. After a good deal of world traveling and a disastrously expensive marriage to the toughest kind of Follies girl, he had settled down—if one can use the term—to a series of inferior hobbies and bad companions. He had invested money in a jazz band, then in a night club, then in a movie company in Long Island City. Fortunately, Papa had left him only a third of what he had left Lydig, and when that was gone, he found it difficult to get more than living expenses out of Willie and Julia. But even these were cut off, after his dip into radical journalism and the publication of a series of articles entitled "Tin Spoon, or the Memoirs of a Younger Son," and Oswald was obliged to start cultivating his maiden aunt. Of course I knew perfectly what he was up to, but he had a way about him, and there was still a void in my heart where his older brother's place had been. He amused me, even when he made me mad, on the subject of the family.

"Do you know the greatest opiate ever served up to the American masses?" he would ask me. "It's the old adage: 'Three generations from shirt sleeves to shirt sleeves.' The idea that all the great fortunes find their ultimate way back to the dirt from which they sprang. Nothing could be falser. Take the twelve living grandchildren of Julius Millinder. Every last blessed one of them is rich. Consider Aunt Cora's great farm in Normandy. Gwen's estates in Kent and Ireland. Cousin George's vast tracts in Canada and Mexico. Why, they're spread all over the globe! I figure that it takes no less than a thousand human souls to wait on the old pirate's progeny!"

"Now just a minute, Oswald!" I interrupted indignantly. I was never prepared to have Grandpa abused by anyone but myself. "You might show a little respect for the memory of the man whose money stands between you and the gutter!"

"Oh, but it doesn't, Auntie!" he exclaimed cheerfully. "I jumped in of my own accord!"

He was always quick and good-tempered, if inclined to be facetious, and always infectiously gay. Sometimes, when he was not talking, he would seem plunged in preoccupation, and I would catch what struck me as an odd, sullen gleam in his eye, but it would disappear the moment I asked the reason for it. There must have been many resentments under his clowning, resentment of his parents, whose love he had never enjoyed, resentment of his older brother, whose intellectual superior he had deemed himself, resentment of the whole Millinder family under the weight of whose name he suffered, but the strings of whose compensatory purse he found tightly closed.

I can see now that it was a natural thing that he should turn to the left and fill his perfect little federal house in Greenwich Village—he never, whatever his friends, lost his taste in things—with the flotsam and jetsam of Bolshevik thinking. Radicalism was outspoken in that discontented era, and Oswald made no secret of his intimacy with the editors of *The Daily Worker* itself. When he asked me for money I refused, apprehending the pockets into which it might be dropped, but I did take over some of his fixed expenses, such as the mortgage on his house and his bills at Brooks Brothers. The reader may wonder why I did as much as this, and I suppose it was simply that Oswald charmed me into it. All the grimness of the long-haired

artists and intellectuals who slumped on his Empire furniture, burned holes
in his Aubusson carpets and drank his vintage wines could not dampen the
vivacity of Oswald's spirits or make headway against the stubbornness of his
sense of humor.

My own sentimentality, however, was at least as tough a weed as Oswald's
humor, and I clung to my theory that the right wife might guide him to a
useful life. He always exploded with laughter when I brought up the subject, but I wondered if I might not be making some headway when he invited
me to the theater to give my opinion of a certain young actress who was a
friend of his. The play was a modern dress version of *A Doll's House* put on
by the experimental workshop of a repertory theatre. Oswald did not specify
whether he wished me to judge the girl who played Nora as an actress or as
a possible spouse, but after one act I decided that it could not be the former.
His eye was too good, and the girl was terrible. She was big and lanky and
awkward with dirty blond hair and wide, haggard eyes. The only quality of
Nora that she conveyed was helplessness; I knew that I was never going to
believe in that slammed door at the final curtain. The best that one could
say of Miss Camilla Larkin as an actress was that she appealed to the sympathies. She was the kind of girl who was always going to get hurt, but the
people who hurt her were going to feel badly about it.

"What did you think of her?" Oswald asked me in the intermission. "Too
much of a hick?"

"But, my dear boy, I *like* hicks! I'm a bit of a hick myself."

"You, Auntie? Why, I thought you were the last of the great ladies of old
New York!"

It was all very well for him to be sarcastic, but I noted that he still cared
who was a "hick," in spite of Trotsky. We went afterwards in my car to his
house in the Village where he was giving a party for Miss Larkin. It had
always been a pet illusion of mine that I would be happy in the company of
intellectuals, but if Oswald's guests were typical, it was certainly an illusion.
They plainly regarded me as a rare survival, a whooping crane or a great
auk, and asked me, with the bold candor of badly brought up children, how
many servants I kept and whether I was more "exclusive" than Helen Astor.
I would have left, had I not been anxious to meet Miss Larkin, and I finally
signaled to Oswald to bring her over. When she was seated beside me on
the sofa, staring at me with big frightened eyes, I congratulated her as con-
vincingly as I could on her performance.

"Oh, I was terrible, Miss Millinder, and I know it," she responded in a
breathless tone, but with a sincerity that silenced even a weak remonstrance.
"It's not my kind of part at all. The only thing I'd be any good at would be
the movies. I could be the girl who goes into darkest Africa with Ronald
Colman. You know, the type who simply screams at everything, in enormous close-ups? At spiders and snakes and rogue elephants?"

I couldn't help laughing at the fitness of such a part for her. "Then why
do you play Ibsen?"

"Because your nephew happened to know a man who was doing Ibsen!"
she exclaimed simply. She was never still for a moment. When she was not

pulling at her hair, she was thrusting her chin at the mirror behind the sofa and scratching at her make-up.

"Why are you so restless?" I asked in my blunt way. "I thought actresses were only nervous on the stage."

She spun around quickly and gave me a frank little smile. "Oh, because I'm scared of you!"

"Am I a rogue elephant?"

We both laughed, and in that moment we almost became friends. There was indeed something of the elephant about me, filling most of the little sofa with my near two hundred pounds and with my gouty leg, for which a cane was at times necessary, stuck out stiffly on a chair before me.

"You see, I've never met any of Oswald's family before," she explained. "I've always imagined them as terrifying. Particularly you. The wonderful 'Auntie' he talks so much about." She reached out a hand timidly as though to touch mine and then hastily withdrew it. "But now I see you're kind."

I grunted. I had not taken that proferred hand, not from any sense of unfriendliness, but because it had seemed to me premature. Things between her and Oswald had obviously gone further than I had suspected, and I wanted time to think it over. "Since you admit Ibsen is not your cup of tea, I don't have to say you're a Nazimova. But then you don't need to be, my dear, for Oswald's family. You'll find us much less exacting than the critics."

When I left the party, a few minutes later, she and Oswald both saw me to the door where my chauffeur was waiting. Some of the other guests pressed behind them, probably to enjoy the phenomenal sight of an elderly female capitalist getting into a limousine. I observed to Millie on the stoop that she must be tired after her performance, and I offered her a ride home. She shook her head quickly, unaccountably embarrassed, and Oswald looked away. Someone behind them laughed in a sneering manner. Indignantly, I hobbled down the steps and across the pavement to my car and did not even turn to wave as I was driven off. Perhaps I had been naïve in failing to realize that Millie lived under his roof, but I was determined to have nothing more to do with Oswald's mistress.

I was surprised, however, one morning several weeks later, while I was still sitting up in bed, my writing board covered with bills and appeals, dictating to my secretary, to receive a card on which the words "Miss Larkin" were scrawled in a large, childish handwriting. At first I did not recognize the name, but when Teresa told me that she claimed to be a friend of "Mr. Oswald's," I allowed her to come up. I sent the secretary and Teresa out of the room, telling the latter to remain within call, but I soon realized that little violence was to be expected from the pale, trembling creature who crept in and stood at the end of my bed.

"I'm sorry to receive you so informally, Miss Larkin," I began gruffly. "But I gather from the hour of your call that your business is urgent. I hope Oswald is well?"

"Oh, Oswald is fine, Miss Millinder, and you're very kind to see me." Saying which, she burst into tears. I thought it all rather stagy, and I simply sat and watched her until she had recovered sufficiently to proceed. "Perhaps you've suspected the terms that I'm on with your nephew?"

I wrinkled my nose in distaste. "I understand you are living in his house."

"I'm going to have his child."

I shrugged callously. "I suppose that follows from living in his house."

Millie gave a little cry of pain and turned to the door. "I'm sorry, Miss Millinder, I shouldn't have come. I should have realized how I would appear to you. Please forgive me!"

With a hand over her mouth she was walking rapidly to the door when compunction overcame me. "Sit down, Miss Larkin, please," I called to her, and she stopped and turned timidly back. "You'll have to get used to louder barks than mine, but I hope not to bigger bites. Sit down and tell me about it." Millie, dazed, sat slowly down in my secretary's chair. "I suppose you want the money for certain illegal medical attentions about which I have no wish to be told. I'm surprised that Oswald has not already offered it."

"Oh, but he has!" Millie exclaimed. "Only I won't take it!"

"Why not? Is it pride? You can't afford much pride, Miss Larkin, in your position."

"But I *can!*" Millie protested in a sudden, startling burst of boldness. "I can afford all the pride in the world! Not because of my shabby life with Oswald, but because I'm going to be a mother! For I mean to have this baby, Miss Millinder! I mean to love it and bring it up and make it into a fine man or woman. You'll see!"

"How will you give it a name?"

"I'll make up a name for it! And when I go home to Pasadena, I'll say I've been divorced. People may not believe me, but it won't matter. They'll accept me in time. And I'll get a job and work hard. All I need from you, Miss Millinder, is a loan to see me through till the baby's born. Oswald thinks my idea is crazy and won't pay for anything but an abortion."

As Millie clasped her hands in appeal, she looked almost beautiful, and my heart was suddenly heavy against my nephew. I reminded myself that she was an actress and that I might be witnessing another scene from her repertory. But then I remembered that she had proved herself a very inferior actress. If her present scene was convincing, might it not be because she was sincere?

"Maybe I can get you more than the money, my dear," I said at last with a sigh. My head ached already at the prospect of troubles ahead. "Maybe I can even get you a husband. We'll see, anyway. In the meantime, you can stay right here in this house. You can have the room at the end of the corridor that used to belong to Oswald's brother. I'll tell Teresa." I reached for my bell. "And I'm going to get my doctor to come around. I want you to have a thorough checkup, young lady. No mishaps!"

Millie proved utterly docile. She placed herself in my hands entirely. In fact, she collapsed. Teresa, whom I sent down to Oswald's to collect her things, proved less tractable and used some horrid Italian expressions about my new guest, but when my blood was up, I could even cope with Teresa. I gave her a note for Oswald, asking him to call that afternoon, and, a little to my surprise, he came. We sat in the dark library while I described my scene with Millie, ending with the expression of my fervent hope that he would marry her and give his child a name. His lips wore a small, patient smile during my recital, and he made no move to interrupt me. When I had finished, he shrugged.

"So she took you in? Really, Auntie, I would have thought better of you."

"I don't know about taking me in," I retorted, irked. "She convinced me that she wanted the child."

"What she really wants is *me*," he said with a snort.

"Why, you conceited dog! What should she want with you after the way you've behaved?"

"Don't ask me. All I know is that she does. She's one of those women who can never give up a man once she's—well, once she's been a friend of his. It doesn't matter how much he bites and scratches, she pulls him slowly and irresistibly to her breast with long, white tentacles. Don't shudder, Auntie, you're the one who's helping her. You're the one who's throwing me to the octopa!"

"I'm simply trying to make you see what's for your own good. Millie will give you a child and put you on a pedestal. She'll work her fingers to the bone for you. She might even be the saving of you!"

"Poor Millie," he said with a sigh. "And poor me. And how, pray, am I to afford this salvation? When I can barely support one, how am I to assume the responsibility of three?"

"Haven't you already assumed it?"

"I don't see why," Oswald answered coolly. "Millie finds herself in her present predicament because she failed to take certain precautions. In my opinion, her failure was deliberate. This baby is her idea, as this marriage is yours. For neither do I feel the smallest responsibility. Therefore, I repeat, how am I to afford it?"

I felt a bit sickened by such a picture of his relationship with Millie. It was always impossible to keep anything unsullied when Oswald talked. His little spray of mud touched everything. "Of course, I'm prepared to pay," I said grumpily. "I've long since learned there's no point my proposing anything unless I'm willing to pay for it."

"Who is that not true of? But how *much* are you willing to pay?"

"Well, I thought if I made up your debts and gave you your house free and clear, that might be an inducement," I began reluctantly.

Oswald, obviously, was not suffering the least embarrassment My own distaste for the subject, if anything, seemed to enhance his pleasure in it. "An inducement," he conceded, "but hardly a sufficient one. I would suggest, in addition, a small annual stipend, shall we say . . . ?"

We bargained thus for an hour, and he would have bargained further, but I was exhausted and gave in. I was sore and angry and humiliated. Oswald robbed me of any pleasure that I might otherwise have enjoyed in performing a good deed by making me feel at once sentimental and swindled. Any credit due to anyone in the whole sordid transaction was evidently due to him for putting himself out to oblige the whim of a capricious old aunt.

My only satisfaction was in stipulating that the duration of his allowance would be the duration of his marriage to Millie. At least I had maintained the whip hand. Or I thought I had.

It was agreed that Millie would stay with me during the time necessary to procure the license. She turned out to be more of a visitor than I had bargained for; she clung to me like a stray dog that had been picked up starving in the street. It was not that Millie in fact had ever been hungry, or that her background was one of indigence. Her father was a perfectly respectable druggist in Pasadena who had been able to send his daughter to a junior college. But since she had fallen in love with Oswald, nothing existed for her but him. I have never seen such blind adoration in a woman for a man. The crass commercial transaction that had preceded his proposal must have been known to her, but she was evidently able to sweep it out of sight under the copious carpet of her wishful thinking. She was happy to bring any money, even mine, to her lover. The moment her marriage was arranged, she could see herself in no other guise than that of a blushing bride and Oswald in none but that of an impatient suitor.

She even tried to prepare herself to be accepted by Oswald's family. She wanted to hear every detail about his upbringing, and she pored over my scrapbooks. She learned to recognize each member of the family, whether living or dead, and when she had exhausted mine, I took her to call on Aunt Polly Herron whose scrapbooks were truly magnificent and who adored showing them. Aunt Polly seemed much taken by Millie, and on the strength of her enthusiasm I invited Julia to lunch to meet her future daughter-in-law. It was a disaster. Millie was terrified and could hardly utter a word. In the middle of the meal she excused herself and hurried upstairs where I later learned she had been sick.

"Is that what you're trying to sell me?" Julia demanded, as soon as we were alone. "That mawkish creature?"

"You've scared her, Julia. She's not always that way."

"She must scare easily." Julia shrugged impatiently. "I know the type. Runs from every woman and sleeps with every man."

"You have no right to say that!" I began with indignation, but I dropped the subject immediately when I remembered that Julia might still not know what I knew.

Millie and Oswald were married in City Hall and came to drink a glass of champagne with me afterwards. Millie was in such a trance that she made no sense at all, and when she said goodbye, she threw her arms around my neck and sobbed like a child. I was touched but embarrassed, for it was perfectly evident that Oswald regarded such emotional display as excessive.

"You've opened a Pandora's box of respectabilities," he told me when Millie had gone upstairs to get her things. "I hope you'll take the responsibility for what happens."

"I've never been afraid to take responsibility in a good cause!"

"You've taken away a docile mistress," he continued with a thin smile. "And saddled me with what I shouldn't be surprised to find a nagging wife. Strike one, I suppose, for law and order?"

"I've given you a child!" I declared stoutly. "Maybe a son, whom one day you'll be proud of!"

"We'll christen him Julius Millinder!" Oswald exclaimed with a sudden whoop of laughter. "Wouldn't that please you, Auntie? Do you realize I'd be the first Millinder to name a son after the old pirate? Why do you suppose that is? Are they ashamed of him, deep down? Take care, Auntie! I may end up the most respectable of you all!"

Five months later, when his son was born, Oswald, to the astonishment of the family, carried out what I had thought at the time was only a mocking suggestion and named the boy for his great-grandfather. It was widely considered a hopeful sign of reform.

10

THE CHANGE IN Oswald during the next two years continued. The reorganization of his financial affairs (effected, of course, by myself) was only the preface to the reorganization of his social and political activities. With amazing speed, efficiency and, I imagine, ruthlessness, he swept his house clean of the old crowd of ragged and dirty intellectuals and started to give more decorous parties for more decorative people. They were still artists and actors and journalists, but there was the difference now that they were the successful rather than the unsuccessful of their respective professions. Oswald's name, his wit and the notoriety of a trashy but sensational novel that he published at this time, transparently taken from the life of Colly Haven, attracted people to the perfectly appointed little house on Hone Street. His parties were like the parties in Thomas Wolfe's novels of the period; in fact, some of them *were*, for Wolfe was taken there by a Mrs. Bernstein whom I met and liked on one of the rare occasions when I attended. After Oswald had been employed as public relations officer of George Millinder's medical foundation, his reputation as a respectable liberal was firmly established. There was even talk of his getting a diplomatic post. People, of course, assumed that he was rich, and, indeed, there was every possibility of his becoming so, if Julia continued to watch the career of her prodigal son out of the corner of an increasingly favorable eye.

I knew, of course, that Millie would be the final casualty of Oswald's housecleaning. It was inevitable. He had no further need of me once he had his hooks in George Millinder, and Millie's tenure depended utterly on that need. I will have to admit, for all my disapproval of Oswald's behavior, that she was only a liability to him. I had hoped that little Julius might have diluted some of the intensity of her concentration on Oswald, but such had not been the case. That concentration had remained as intense as ever, except that Millie had taken to wearing a defeated expression in which the dawn of a permanent sullenness was already visible. Her wide reproachful eyes seemed to be saying to her husband: "I can't help it if I'm stupid—is it *my* fault that all I can think of is you?" No wonder Oswald looked the other way. If Millie's theory was that a woman was a man's chattel, she was not a chattel neatly put away on a shelf, but one left on the floor where he would always stumble over it. It was even apparent in the way she wore the clothes that Oswald bought for her. For he would no more allow Millie to select her own clothes than he would allow her to change a single curtain in the little house where she lived more like a guest than a wife. The color of a dress might be perfect for her hair and complexion and the style ideally suited for her lanky figure, but she would sit in it at one of Oswald's parties as awkwardly as a little girl dressed up in Mummy's finery, rejecting it with all the force of a personality that was too stubbornly passive to be truly passive at all. Guests would take one look at her and quickly let her be. They hardly noticed when she was no longer there.

I was glad enough to help her find an apartment for herself and the baby and to give her the furniture, for I was afraid that if I put her up at home, I would never get rid of her. She appeared very listless and low in spirit. She would ask me the same questions over and over again, and if I reminded her that I had already answered them, she would put a hand to her forehead and shake her head impatiently as if deploring some dreaded mental affliction. She was frequently out when I called to see Julius, and I was surprised to hear, brokenhearted as she claimed to be, that she was already seeing other men. Once I found her at home with gentlemen callers at the cocktail hour, "gentlemen" who rose to their feet at my entrance and gave me what I considered rather ill-bred little bows. I supposed that it was all right for Millie to be emerging from the black pall of her desolation, but I was decidedly of the opinion that she was not doing it in the right way or with the right people. I hated to see my niece-in-law associating with men who bowed from the waist and spoke of "the honor" of meeting me.

One morning, while I was playing at her apartment with little Julius and the toys that I had brought him on my visit, Millie leaned near me to pick up a cigarette, and I distinctly detected the smell of liquor. Abruptly, I called for the nurse and sent Julius to his room.

"You've been drinking!"

"Oh, Auntie, what of it?" She stared out the window, bored. "You'd drink too, if you had my dreams."

"What dreams?"

"About Oswald. And the terrible men who have control of him. Oh, Auntie, if you *saw* them! The men who used to come to the house!"

"At the parties? What's wrong with them?"

"Oh, no, *after* the parties. Late at night. The dirty little men who make him give the parties! The men who made him give me up!"

I considered her wild idea for several moments and then decided that it was indeed a dream. I knew that Millie could never abide facts and that she would invent any romantic tale to explain how Oswald could love her and still reject her. These men who came at night were undoubtedly late-staying guests who provided Oswald with a needed excuse to let his wife go to her bedroom alone.

"Never you mind the men," I said brusquely. "It's your child we've got to think of. What kind of mother are you with gin on your breath in the middle of the morning?"

This scared her a bit. "It hasn't happened before," she said quickly. "And it won't happen again."

"You'd better make that a promise, young woman, or I'll go to your husband."

She jumped up, her eyes begging me. "Oh, please, Aunt Gus, I promise!"

All that my bluster accomplished was that I saw even less of her. When she came to my house now, she was always on her best behavior. She would ostentatiously refuse a cocktail before dinner. But I hated the things I heard about her. Ione, who, as always, knew everything about everybody, told me that Millie had been drunk at a charity ball at the Waldorf and that people were gossiping openly about her private life.

"You can't mean that she's having . . . an affair?" I demanded, shocked.

"Not one. A dozen!"

"Ione!"

"I'm sorry, Gussie, but I think you ought to know. People say she's become a regular tramp. Of course, *I* don't say that." Ione's eyes, in circles of dark skin over white, drawn cheeks, waxed nostalgic. "People don't understand about loneliness. It can make one do very odd things. I know a bit about that. But you ought to warn her. Julia's out for her blood."

"Julia? Why should Julia care?"

"Because she wants that child. Elsie Fales hardly gives her a peep at her other grandchildren, so little Julius is her last hope. She wants to try again, as she tried with Lydig!"

I shuddered and went that same afternoon to see Millie. But when I told her what Ione had said, as tactfully as I could, she simply burst into tears and protested that New York was full of the vilest slander. The very next day Ione sent me a gossip column, marked in red pencil, asserting that Mrs. Oswald Millinder had been seen in Harlem, escorted by a colored band leader. I told myself that I would have it all out with Millie when she next came to see me, but she did not come until it was too late. She burst into my library one morning at noon, haggard eyed, where I was doing accounts, and cried out:

"She's taken him, Aunt Gus! She's taken Julius! She wouldn't even let me in!"

Of course I knew immediately what had happened, but I had to sit for ten minutes on the sofa beside an almost hysterical Millie before I could get an articulate story out of her. It appeared that she had sent little Julius to his grandmother's for a week's visit a month before. Then, for one reason and another, she had not been able to take him back. She had had flu; a dear friend of hers had been sick; her mother had come east to visit her. But Julia had seemed entirely understanding and had even volunteered to look after the boy as long as Millie cared to leave him. Yet when Millie had finally called for him in New Jersey early that morning, Julia had met her in the front hall, with a fixed little smile, to announce that she had decided to keep Julius until Millie should have proved herself a fit parent. She had thereupon boldly offered her twenty-five thousand dollars a year to accept the arrangement and had warned her to consult a lawyer before refusing. Finally, she had turned her back and walked away, leaving Millie in the hall to scream for her child until the butler and a detective had forcibly ejected her.

"Can she do such a thing to me?" Millie cried. "Is there a law that allows it?"

"I don't know how much she knows about you," I said with a doubtful sigh. I saw that I was destined for a long and bitter struggle that would probably alienate me from my whole family. I visualized the consequences in a dreary pause, but in that same pause I grimly accepted them. For whatever Millie might have been, she was still my protégée, and her child still my responsibility. However bad a mother she might turn out, while he was with her I could to some degree control the situation. If he went to Julia, I was helpless. Heaven knew, I had seen what Julia could do to children! "I think you and I had better go down and call on Oswald."

"But he won't see me!"

"I fancy he'll see *me*!"

When I called Oswald, however, I found that he was spending the weekend with the George Millinders in Greenwich. I then called Willie in New Jersey, but he gruffly refused to discuss the subject with me at all. He said that it was entirely Julia's doing and that she had just left for Greenwich to confer with Oswald. I decided to leave Millie, who was in no state to face so many of the family, and drive up to Greenwich to have it out with all of them.

I had always been told that my cousin George, who was Uncle Fred's son and heir and the richest of the Millinders, was the "best type" of modern millionaire. In fact, I had become a little tired of hearing it. He had created the Millinder Foundation for research in degenerative diseases (the ones, as Ione used to say, of which George was personally frightened); he had employed a historian to clean up the family name and he had sent his sons, like so many princes on viceregal missions, to Dartmouth and Cornell and Brown rather than to Harvard or Yale or Princeton. Julia, before Oswald's employment by George, used to sneer at his policy of "pompous concealment." The boys, she claimed, drove Fords with Cadillac motors and had to hide their whisky in milk. But Julia, of course, was bitter about her own failure with Lydig. She had raised her sons on the standards of "The Prince" of Machiavelli, while George had raised his on those of the Prince Consort. Julia's may have been the more romantic conception, but it had been out of date and doomed to failure, and much of the jealousy that she feels to this day about George's sons is that they are having the careers that Lydig should have had. It is a jealousy which I share.

The great place north of Greenwich was the symbol of George's philosophy. It contained every comfort and every luxury, but all carefully camouflaged. The sybarite in George was clad in the simple garb of a Spartan. Two thousand acres were surrounded by a tall picket fence with high-tension wires on top, and the gates were opened and closed for each automobile by a man on duty. Once admitted, one glided over a macadam road through forests and past fields and lakes, never seeing more than one structure at a time: in one place, the outdoor courts, grass and clay, with their pavilion; in another, the indoor court, surrounded by pines and covered with ivy; half a mile further, the swimming pool for adults; then the swimming pool for infants; and then signs to other roads leading to the guest houses for visiting sons and friends. And, finally, suddenly, one came around a corner to the long dark many-porched ark that Frank Lloyd Wright had built for George himself and saw the colored butler (to whom the man at the gate had telephoned), in black pants with a white coat, standing on the steps and smiling in anticipation of his habitual greeting:

"Welcome to Keewaydin, Miss Gussie."

I suppose it was the impression of perfect upkeep that made it all seem so much richer than Aunt Daisy's more ostentatious splendor had ever seemed. One knew that a single crack in that macadam drive would be repaired the next day, that the water from the tap in the bathroom would plunge into the basin in a strong hissing stream, that the used towel would be removed as soon as one left. The servants, if invisible, were miraculously efficient. It had been just the opposite at George's parents' in the old days, where the function of liveried footmen had been, as in Renaissance palaces, to show off the greatness of their master rather than to minister to the wants of his guests. I can remember, visiting Aunt Daisy as a girl, going up to my room after a dinner where there had been a man behind every chair, to find my bed unmade from the night before. Such a thing would have been unimaginable at "Keewaydin."

And yet I wondered, as I was ushered into George's high-ceilinged library where he kept the cream of his pre-Columbian pottery and the best of his Rouaults, if some of Aunt Daisy's prudishness and moral snobbery did not lurk behind the placidity of her son's determined good cheer. George was older than I and nearly as stout, but his skin was still unwrinkled and his long, thick hair of a distinguished white. He always smiled and nodded as he talked and moved objects back and forth across his desk. George's attitude was that the truth must always be halfway between two divergent points of view.

"I want you to tell me everything that's on your mind, Gussie," he began in his most genial tone. "I want to talk this thing out frankly and openly. And when we've each heard what the other has to say, I suggest that we join my good wife and Julia and eat some of the excellent trout I caught in Canada!"

I felt flushed and cross as I stared across the desk at those twinkling grey eyes. "I'm not sure that I want to eat any trout with Oswald," I muttered. My nephew, the only other person in the room, who had remained standing by the window looking out, now turned around to smile at me impudently.

"Come now, Gussie," George reproved me. "Things can't be quite that bad, can they?"

"Can't they?" I demanded, irked at being soothed by George. "Do you know what Oswald and his mother are doing to Millie?"

"In a general way, yes. Oswald is now a member of my office family, and I make it a practice to be available to my staff for consultation on personal problems. If they desire it, of course. In this case, at Oswald's request, my lawyer has already conferred with Julia's."

"You know, then, that they've taken Millie's child?"

"I know that Julia is keeping the child," George corrected me. "I am told that she proposed a temporary custody arrangement that was perfectly reasonable. Are you planning to talk Millie out of it?"

"I'm planning to talk her out of selling her child!"

"Isn't that a rather emotional way of putting it?"

"It's a precise way!"

"You beg the question of Millie's fitness as a mother," George pursued patiently. "Has it ever occurred to you that Oswald might be a better judge of that than you?"

"Oswald deserted her!"

"Ah, but *why?*"

"Because he's selfish and unprincipled!"

"Oh, Auntie!" Oswald exclaimed with a burst of his high, mocking laugh. "And to think what friends you and I used to be!"

"Did you tell George that your child would have been a bastard if I hadn't intervened?" I demanded heatedly, turning on him. "Did you tell him you had washed your hands of the girl you seduced?"

"Oswald told me all about that," George intervened with a little cough that was the first hint of his irritation. His raised eyebrows deprecated my expressions. "It seems perfectly evident to me that marriages made with a shotgun are not made in heaven. However morally indignant you may be, Gussie, you ought in fairness to recognize that the problem before us is of your own making."

"You think, of course, that Millie should have got rid of the child and been discreetly paid off!" I retorted indignantly. "That, of course, would be the *moral* point of view. Well, I don't happen to believe in the moral point of view. If Julia doesn't return that child immediately, I shall instruct my lawyers to sue her on Millie's behalf!"

"You don't care, then," George demanded, thoroughly irritated now, "about how the family will be made to look? You don't mind a public washing of filthy linen?"

"It won't involve you, George," I reassured him coldly. "It will involve only our branch of the family."

"But the public thinks of us as one."

"The public be damned!"

"I think you'll find that attitude's a bit out of date, Gussie," George retorted. "But if the family means nothing to you, perhaps you'll consider the waste of your own time and money. My lawyer's impartial opinion is that Julia's case against her daughter-in-law is airtight."

"But he has only considered the case against Millie. *I* shall present the case against Oswald!"

"I don't think any judge is going to be very interested in a rehash of sown wild oats," George said dryly. He turned and conveyed a fatherly smile to the young prodigal cousin who simpered behind him. "Oswald may have been a bit of a rake in his day and a bit of a radical. But I can give my personal testimony that he has thoroughly reformed. Oswald has been invaluable to me for a year now. He's like one of my own sons. There's an old saying that any man with brains and spirit is going to be a communist at twenty-one, a liberal at thirty and a conservative at forty-five. Well, Oswald is not quite a conservative yet, but he's one of the most intelligent liberals I know!"

I was appalled at such obtuseness and felt that I would stifle if I heard another cliché. How was it possible for a man to accomplish all the good that George was supposed to have accomplished if he was so easily taken in? Oswald was smiling even more broadly, but as I rose angrily to my feet I noticed that his fists were clenched. He saw my glance and relaxed them again instantly, but his gesture only clarified my sudden realization that he was tense, desperately tense! I recalled now what Millie had said about the men who came to the house, and a devastating light flooded a hitherto murky picture in my mind.

"A liberal!" I cried with a snort, and Oswald turned away quickly to the window. "I'm glad I don't have that kind of liberal handling *my* affairs! And I'm glad I'm not fool enough to believe that the Communist Party is a social club that you can resign from at will! Mark my words, George, that young man, standing so smugly behind you, was probably assigned to your case by a council of unshaven Bolshevik ghouls, plotting up in some loft in Greenwich Village!"

For just a moment the full horror of my idea caused George's eyelids to flicker and his mouth to fall half open. Then, quickly, he coughed and moved a paperweight across his desk. "You make it all sound so dramatic, Gussie," he said, his eyes moving from side to side. "I wish life could be half as exciting as that, don't you, Oswald?"

But Oswald's answer was lost as the door opened and Julia, in white and black, a cigarette holder in her hand, appeared, smiling at us all. Julia had lost some of her distinction with advancing age. Her personality had become as artificial as the red dye in her hair. She was still arrogant, still thin and bony, still perceptive and shrewd, but the emptiness of her life had begun to show in the growing extremism of her habits: collecting too many dogs and parrots, playing bridge until dawn, having séances with fortunetellers.

"Haven't you all finished?" she demanded. "I'm starved for lunch."

"We'll go right in then," George said testily, getting up and walking to the door. Obviously, Julia's invasion of the master's library, without so much as a knock, was without precedent in that house. "I thought it had been understood that we could have until half past one." He turned briskly to me. "Will you lead the way, Gussie?"

"You can't really think I'm going to sit down at the same table with Oswald after what's been said?"

"You must do as you please," George snapped, and with a little jerky bow to express his impatience with the whole subject, he left me alone with Julia and her son.

"Oh, come now, Gussie," Julia said in her old bantering tone. "The world's not coming to an end because you've taken Millie's side."

I drew myself up. "You had better know, Julia, that I intend to take legal proceedings against you!"

"All right, all right!" Julia threw her hands in the air and shrugged to protest my making so much of it. "What's a bit of litigation among sisters-in-law? Frankly, I can't imagine why you should resent my efforts to save my own grandson from a woman of Millie's morals, but win, lose or draw, can't we have our old peppery friendship? It *has* been peppery, Gussie, but it has been a friendship, too."

"That will depend on how you feel after my testimony."

"After *your* testimony? What on earth will *you* testify about?"

"You have questioned Millie's fitness as a guardian for her son. I intend to question yours."

"On what grounds?"

I was relieved by the hard, sudden note of hostility in Julia's tone. Anything was easier to face than her assumed air of friendliness. "I'm learning things, Julia. You object to Millie's morals. Very well. I object to yours!"

Julia evidently did not know whether to laugh or to burst into one of her tempers. "What sort of a bad joke is this, Gussie?"

"It's no joke. I'm deadly serious. If your lawyer brings in testimony about Millie's love affairs, I shall testify about *yours!*"

"Love affairs!" Julia laughed shrilly. "Who will believe you?"

"That's not my concern. I shall have done my duty."

"But it's not even relevant!" Julia cried in a suddenly strident voice. "They won't allow it in evidence!"

"In that case you have nothing to worry about."

The silence that followed this was broken only by Oswald's impudent laugh. But a glance from Julia silenced him. She stared down at the floor while she considered her position. I had no idea of her legal rights or of mine, but I knew that I had upset her.

"My God, Augusta, you're talking about the Dark Ages!" she exploded at last. "You don't expect a judge to sit there while you drool out all the ancient gossip that your suspicious old maid's mind has been accumulating since the year one!"

"If he won't, then, as I say, you have nothing to worry about."

"Except the mortification of seeing my own sister-in-law make a public spectacle of herself!"

"You evidently don't mind the prospect of making a public spectacle of your own daughter-in-law."

"But that's different! That's for the child's sake!"

"So is what I'm doing for the child's sake."

"How do you have the nerve to say that?" Julia demanded irately. "What do you care for that child? You simply enjoy spiting me. Very well, let's assume I had some affair in the dim, dark past—which I don't for a minute admit. Can you honestly tell me there's no difference between a woman of the world who knows how to run her house and family and enjoy a discreet little fling on the side and a drunken slut who tumbles into bed with the first man who asks her?"

"None whatever," I maintained stoutly. "Except the slut is more honest."

"Honest! You can't be so idiotic!"

"If you go on with this suit, Julia, you will find just how honest I can be!"

"How dare you!" Julia shouted, and now she pounded on George's desk with both her fists. "How dare you! I'll never speak to you again as long as I live! You're a prejudiced, vitriolic, sour, frustrated bitch of an old maid!"

The magnificence of her final explosion was again dampened by Oswald's gleeful laugh. But Julia enjoyed losing her temper; there was something oddly unwounding about her harsh words and the way she spat them at me. I simply turned and marched out to the hall. As I reached for the front doorknob, however, a hand intervened to catch my arm. It was Oswald.

"May I see you to your car, Auntie?"

"I can see myself to it."

"Oh, come!" The laughing eyes pleaded with me. "You have that look of someone who's never going to speak to me again. But if that's so, isn't it all the more reason to say goodbye nicely?"

I pushed my way through the door into the damp, autumn air, but halfway down the flagstone walk to my car I turned to look back at him.

"Goodbye, Oswald!" I called. "I hope for everyone's sake you're a great deal better than I think you are!"

He hurried immediately down the walk after me and seized my hands with both of his. "Goodbye, Auntie! Will you be angry if I tell you you were magnificent? I wouldn't have missed that scene if it costs me my job with Cousin George!"

"Which, unfortunately, it won't."

"Don't be too sure! The rich are easily scared. Their very immunity terrifies them. And what a bogey you put in his mind! I'll have to warn Moscow about *you*!"

That red head seemed even less real against the background of red and yellow foliage. In a sudden damp gust of wind from across the lawn I shuddered. "Tell me, Oswald," I asked gravely. "Do you really have no morals at all? Is it all just play acting to you?"

He stared at me for a moment and then turned to gaze across the lawn. He shrugged, but at least he had stopped smiling. His expression was still amused, but it was a wistful amusement, and his tone, when he spoke, was nostalgic. "Dr. Pratt used to give a sermon at school that always struck me. He said there were too many long words to excuse bad behavior. Too much about complexes and compulsions. He wanted to revive the use of the simple word 'wicked.' That was it. We were wicked." He nodded in satisfaction as he repeated the word. "Wicked."

"Do you think you've been wicked?" I pursued grimly.

"I don't know." His tone was curious. "But I'd like to know. And if anyone could help me, you could. Because you're my nemesis, Auntie. I have never resented you. Your fulminations are—well, let's say they're—relevant. Yes, that's the word—relevant. While the fulminations of others seem somehow not to be. Maybe it's because you have a place in my life. As a kind of substitute mother. If you're real—well, then I'm wicked. Do you see? But are *you* real?"

His eyes, usually so furtive, met mine now in a sudden bold stare. There was a challenge in that blue gaze that startled and unnerved me; it was I this time who looked away. But at the same time I thought I could sense a glimmer of fear beneath that boldness and the suggestion of an appeal to me, a frightened little boy's appeal to an adult who should be adept in miracles. I suddenly held my breath with the feeling that a moment of crisis had arrived that might never come again.

"Oswald, dear child," I exclaimed, putting my hands on his thin shoulders and giving him a little shake, "give it all up, whatever it is, and come back to us! If you're involved in any way, I can buy you out—there's always a way out! If you'll only let me help! What else, in God's name, is the money for?"

It was his turn now to be startled, but I could see that my idea had momentarily caught him. "You mean you'd buy off those Bolshevik ghouls, Auntie?" He was smiling again, but there was a rueful note in his voice. "You'd really do that for me?"

"I'll give you the cash, and I'll ask no questions."

He backed suddenly away from me, and my arms fell to my sides. I knew that our moment was over.

"But supposing I used it on homemade bombs?" he exclaimed with a desperate peal of his old laugh. "Or to redecorate that loft where the ghouls meet? Or to buy them all a shave? Oh, no, Auntie, keep your money. And spend it while you can!"

I shrugged sadly and mounted slowly into the back seat of my waiting car. As I was driven off, I again heard Oswald's mocking laugh and glancing back, saw his fist raised in a parody of the Communist salute.

Julia never offered to compromise and never sent me a direct communication of any kind. Her lawyer simply instructed Millie the following Monday that the child would be delivered to his mother's apartment that same day. Julia asked no visitation rights for herself and no assurances of Millie's good conduct in the future. It was evident that if she could not save her grandson altogether from the toils of a delinquent parent, she preferred to cast him loose. There was to be no bargaining between Julia Millinder and the likes of Millie.

Millie seemed stunned by her victory. For three months afterwards she hardly left home without taking little Julius and his nurse with her. She told me that she was convinced that Julia was having her shadowed. But as time wore on, it began to be apparent, even to Millie, that Julia had washed her hands of the whole affair, and I am afraid that Millie rather missed the drama of their conflict. In a curious way this very drama may have served to keep alive for her some of the wild abandon of that love for Oswald in which she had so stubbornly and recklessly invested her emotional life. To enter a convent had once been a way of explaining to one's friends and family that one had lost one's interest in this world. Perhaps now promiscuity had become the substitute for chastity as a means of expressing the same loss. Many men or no men, what was the basic difference to the heart? The fact that the world should have misconstrued Millie's conduct, that the Millinders should have threatened to crucify her in court, what was that but the final touch to her sackcloth and ashes? Without Oswald how could Millie stand but alone? And as long as she was bound to be alone, was not hostility more exciting than indifference?

During the second world war, which followed shortly these events, she slipped back to her former habits. She worked in an officers' club until she was asked to leave. She had started drinking again. After that, it was a case of one man after another. She actually married one of them, but he left her in a year. She lived on an allowance from the money that Julius inherited when my brother Willie died, spending most of her time in Florida, while Julius lived with me. My elderly household was delighted to have this small stake in the future; they fussed over the boy until I began to feel almost neglected myself. Things were done for him voluntarily that I would never have dared request; two bedrooms and the upstairs living room were stripped of furniture and rugs to make room for the hundreds of feet of track of his electric train. With elaborate planning I managed to maintain a steady procession of other children through the house to keep him company. If anything, the poor child may have yearned for solitude in a life as crowded as that of a little prince. It was inevitable that Millie should ultimately resent my appropriation of her son. Drinking and parties had improved neither her looks nor her temper, and she was finding it increasingly difficult to obtain grants from the funds of a child whom she so rarely saw. When she came one day to ask that Julius should spend the summer with her on Long Island, purely, as I believed, on the advice of her lawyer, I brusquely made my counterproposal. I would give her twenty-five thousand a year so long as the child lived with me. My offer was followed by long silence. Then Millie suddenly smiled at me, very sadly, with more than a remnant of her old, pathetic charm.

"I don't suppose I could get anything on you, Aunt Gus," she said. "The way you did on Mrs. Millinder. You're quite impregnable, aren't you? And, after all, why should I want to? The boy is happier here. Mrs. Millinder was right. I'm good for nothing. But I'm still glad I fought her. I'm still glad I got him back if only to give him up to you. He will never now be like his uncle or his father. Yes, Aunt Gus. I'll take your money. It's the last decent thing I can do."

I shall always give Julia credit that never by so much as a hint or a snicker has she said: "I told you so." But then Julia has never been a small woman. However, let me say in my own justification that neither have I. George Millinder finally got rid of Oswald, but not until the latter's dramatic switch of international sympathies at the time of the Hitler-Stalin pact had aroused the suspicions whose seeds I had laid. It turned out later that the Millinder Foundation had made grants to fifteen Communist-dominated organizations, and that George's own sacred name was on the lists of directors of no less than five of them. The whole affair was very malodorous, and George's new public relations man had to work busily for two years to place it before the public eye "in its proper perspective." Everybody tried to act as if this campaign had succeeded. On George's seventy-fifth birthday, just after the war, he was toasted for his benefactions by the governor, the mayor and the cardinal at a large subscription dinner at the Waldorf-Astoria. But I am told that he was also mentioned in a recent speech by the junior senator from Wisconsin who is much in the news these days. Perhaps the ghost of Oswald has not been entirely laid.

Oswald himself has found it expedient to settle in Guatemala out of the reach of congressional committees. He claims that he has never been a member of the Communist Party, but he has also refused to deny it under oath, and that is enough for me. Willie disinherited him, leaving his share to little Julius, but Julia continues to support her prodigal on a scale that has allowed him to acquire a famous collection of Mayan sculpture. He writes me cheerful notes on my birthday and at Christmas and always urges me to come and visit him in the modern house that he has built. It might be amusing, but I'm afraid it's too late for me to give Oswald a second chance. At my age, some judgments must be final.

11

I HAVE VERY little to say about the period that elapsed between Oswald's departure for Guatemala and the year 1948 in which I write. My story, after all, is the story of my family, and following what they considered my blackmail of Julia, I ceased to see very much of the Willie Millinders. George's branch also tended to avoid me, for George, who could never admit that he had been wrong, saw in me only a horrid reminder of the business with Oswald. Cora, entirely absorbed in her Normandy farm, made no further trips across the Atlantic, and Ione was taken up in her great position as Mrs. Fay. Aunt Euphemia's daughters I had never got on with, and Aunt Polly's never forgave me for what they considered my unaccountable behavior in releasing Collier Haven from his pledge. And so it happened that I lost my vantage point as a family historian. Then there has been my arthritis which of recent years has caused me to withdraw almost entirely from social life. Indeed, when I consider my physical bulk and the number of my ailments, I realize that I must be grateful for the seventy-five years already accorded me and not look forward to becoming a nonagenarian like my two aunts.

My principal task has been to provide a normal home for my great-nephew, Julius. It has not been an easy one. A very young bachelor and a very old maid were never meant to live together in a very large house. Oddly enough the person who has been the greatest help has been Elsie Fales. Who would have conceived that a woman like Elsie would have been interested in the nephew of her first husband? Yet some good instinct made me write her that I hoped Julius would not grow up without knowing any of his father's family. Elsie's response was prompt and enthusiastic. She already had three Fales children of her own, one a boy just Julius' age, and she would be glad to take Julius for the whole summer. She stipulated the contribution that he was to make to her household expenses which though high (Elsie was not one to underestimate such matters) struck me as entirely fair. I jumped at the opportunity, and the summer visit to the Fales's became an established custom. Elsie had improved enormously when she had finally got what she wanted out of life, which was simply Townie Fales. She was and is as beautiful as ever (beautiful, now, even to me), and there was a competence in her handling of children, guests and animals that made her life seem an effortless blend of rustic and urban virtues. Her native conservatism has actually helped her to keep abreast of the times. Instinctively, she has always accepted the verdict of the majority, at times appearing almost to have inspired it. To hear her talk about the importance of summer jobs for college boys and cooking lessons for engaged girls, one would hardly imagine that she was ever a debutante in the spoiled era of the early twenties.

Julius immediately adored his first cousin, Lydig Junior, despite the nine years between them, and copies him to this day in his hobbies and mannerisms. They are astonishingly alike, both tall and dark-haired and both very serious-minded and inclined to be a bit deficient in humor. But they lack the romantic aura that my Lydig, at least in his youth, emitted; they seem made of more ordinary material. No doubt it is just as well. Lydig Junior was old enough to be a marine in the last war. As I write, he has a job in a law firm downtown where he works at least three nights a week. He is married, has two children, two cars, a house in New Canaan and lives like his neighbors. The fact that he spends less than a third of his income after taxes is generally known in his community and generally approved. Adherence to the normal is as vital to his generation as ostentation was to Mamma's. It is all a bit beyond me, but I can see that Julius is going to go the same way. He will be a freshman at Yale next year and has already decided to become a doctor. Last summer he worked in a laboratory though I offered him a trip to Europe. He even puts himself on an allowance out of his own income, and the allowance is carefully computed to be the average of what all the boys in his form at Chelton receive. Obviously none of Mamma's great-grandchildren, excepting the Conti descendants, will have any use for my money, most of which I plan to leave to the Mayan Institute for archeological work in both Americas. After all, I am a bit of a fossil myself.

As I read over these lines, I detect what strikes me as a rather unattractive note of bitterness. And, really, if I face the facts, why should there be? Did not my great-nephews have a better answer to the problem of the money than I ever had? What more painless and dignified death could I ask for the family name than that it should descend into the dust of uniformity from which it arose? There had been generations of unknown Millinders before Grandpa, going about their business, no doubt, in the streets of Hamburg, not differing from their neighbors in the smallest particular of their daily lives and probably not even wishing to. Into that grey sky had come the flashing streak of Grandpa's fortune and for some six or seven decades afterwards the Millinders were people to write about in the illustrated weeklies and to photograph for the Sunday papers. And now, without a protest, perhaps even with a gentle sigh of relief, they are taking their places once more in the highway of life with the eternal ebb and flow of commuting brothers. It is a sufficient comment on the contrariness of my own nature that as a young woman I should have detested the notoriety of the money and as an old one I should resent its eclipse. Of course, it may be simply that I have depended on it more than I have ever allowed myself to believe. The truth is bitter tonic, but it had best be swallowed. Had the glamour ever existed that I thought Lydig Jr. was renouncing? Had I ever really thought of Mamma's or Aunt Daisy's lives as other than pageants on wide lawns and in overgilded rooms? I sometimes think with discomfort that the uniformity that I deplore in young Lydig's life existed not only in the past before the making of the fortune, but also in those very glittering decades to which I have referred, and that my family were at all times simple, ordinary people, pursuing simple, ordinary tasks, who stood out from the crowd only in the imagination of those observers who fancied from reading the evening papers that tiaras and opera boxes made an organic difference. Perhaps that is my ultimate discovery of what the money meant, that it meant nothing at all, or, at any rate, very little. But I find such a conclusion oddly disagreeable. It makes me wonder if I should ever have bothered to write these pages at all. It makes me feel no better than a shopgirl who goes to the movies to see Joan Crawford play an heiress and to imagine herself throwing a diamond necklace from the stern of a yacht to satisfy a passing tantrum.

In any event, I have tried to tell the story as I see it today. It has caused me considerable pain to be as explicit as I have been. Now that I have completed the task, I shall allow myself to toss and turn for a while in the downy bed of more romantic concepts. Having done my duty, why should I not? Why should I not see Aunt Daisy as a small, stately, much beloved queen bowing solemnly to a loyal multitude from her balcony over Fifth Avenue? Or Mamma as a Renaissance princess whose worldly ambition was sublimated into a love of art? Or, if it pleases me, my Lydig as a young Lorenzo? Surely it is a harmless diversion for one of my years to return to the solace of Grandpa's gallery and see again Napoleon's stern, set features as he rides through the snow with Moscow burning behind him or Isabella the Catholic emptying her jewel caskets before a pleading and persuasive Columbus. Standing beneath them all, on top of the ottoman, is still, of course, the white captive, her hands tied to the post, her eyes fixed upon her captors with defiance and bewilderment. She has simply grown old, that is all.

Portrait
in
Brownstone

For Blake and Shiela Lawrence,

*with all my love and thanks for the long
summer visits to Lake Champlain
where this story was conceived
and much of it written.*

Contents

PART ONE
THE DENISONS
OF FIFTY-THIRD STREET

1

IDA: 1950

I HAD EVEN reached the point of wondering if Geraldine Brevoort's suicide, so long dreaded, might not prove in the event a relief, but like everything else about Geraldine, when it came, it came with a nasty twist. She
had plagued me living; now, apparently, she would plague me dead. In the
preceding weeks, night after night, she had called me on the telephone to
pour out her bile and her terrors, in maudlin, drunken rambling, to complain about God and the manager of her hotel, the rudeness of taxi drivers
and the magnitude of tips, and to express her undying resentment against
the fancied indifference or fancied jealously of her long-dead parents and
our long-dead uncles and aunts. If Derrick happened to be about, I would
go upstairs to the telephone in my bedroom. I was afraid that if he heard
her squawking cry: "I wish I were dead!" he might exclaim too loudly: "I
wish you were, too, Geraldine!" For it was Derrick's theory that Geraldine
was trying to torture me by insinuating that my home was built on sand,
my serenity (as she called it) on illusion, and that if I had attained any peace
of mind, it was only because I had never known ecstasy, only because I had
never *lived,* as she, Geraldine, had lived. And it was certainly true that
Geraldine, with her shabby past and her shabby secret, vacillated between
the inconsistent claims that I was rich because I had looted her happiness
and poor because I could never hope to share her lost youth. To her, I
would always be the little brown cousin who had worn her hand-me-downs
and still envied her the glamour of a debutante year in which no fewer than
eight men had proposed.

That last night it went on interminably. I stared into the mirror over my
desk as I offered the mechanical words of consolation and wondered if they
seemed as weary and bored as the apprehensive eyes that stared back at me
between the dark circles and the waves of grey hair that Geraldine liked to
describe as my "rocking-chair brigade."

"But, Geraldine, I *never* said I was any better than you, I never even
thought it, no, I didn't, dear . . . No, *listen* . . . I only said I minded your
drinking because it makes you ill and unhappy . . . No, I didn't say it was
immoral . . . I *didn't,* Geraldine, you're putting words in my mouth . . .
My dear, I know I've had an easy life, no one is more aware of it than I

. . . I'm *not* being smug . . . Look, dearie, why don't you let me come and spend the night with you?"

Of course I knew she would never consent. She might fool the nurse about her drinking, but she could never fool me. And it struck me, still talking, that there was something ignoble about the way I was always building up a record that would exonerate me on the ultimate day of disaster, like a quartermaster keeping a log that nobody would ever want to read.

"I know you have a nurse, Geraldine, but what's a nurse? . . . Of course I want you to live, dear, I want you to live for years and years . . . No, you're wrong, you still have wonderful looks . . . Minerva Denison was saying just the other day, if Geraldine would only take off twenty pounds she'd be as lovely as the day she came out."

Really, was there no end to pity, to family loyalty, to my childish habit of respectfulness for slightly older cousins? The lower Geraldine descended into the pit of drink and self-pity, the more sentimentally, it seemed, I deferred to her, until the stout painted creature with the whiskey breath who lived entombed in two little rooms full of bibelots and junk at the Algar, husbandless, childless, friendless, treated me with more condescension than she did the maid whom she paid to come in and drink with her! Here was the result of what Derrick called my fetish about the past. He complained that I attributed his success to Uncle Linn Tremain who had given him his start, a debt which, in Derrick's version of my credo, had been passed down, unamortized, from Uncle Linn to Geraldine, so that the cluttered little parlor at the Algar was now the chapel in which the orisons of our joint gratitude should be daily offered. Well, perhaps there was something in it. Perhaps I *had* been a fool.

"Then why don't you come here? . . . No, seriously, why don't you, Geraldine? . . . Don't be silly, of course Derrick wouldn't mind . . ."

Derrick loomed up in the doorway, holding a cigar. The dim light in the vestibule over his broad shoulders gave to his thick mound of grey hair a more than usually magisterial look.

"Derrick most certainly *would* mind," he called across the room. "Derrick will not have that woman in the house!"

I quickly covered the mouthpiece. "Derrick, hush! Do you want her to hear you?"

"I don't care! I will not have that woman in the house!"

"But she's ill! Desperately ill!"

"She has a nurse, hasn't she?"

"Not a very good one, I'm afraid."

"Then get her another."

"Derrick, how *can* I? At this hour?"

"I don't know, and I don't care. All I know is that as long as I'm living in this house, that woman is not going to come here. I promise you, Ida, I'm serious!"

I took his opposition so for granted that it shocked me suddenly to consider that I might have invited Geraldine only in reliance upon it. Since my sixtieth birthday, over a year before, my powers of self-analysis had uncomfortably sharpened. And I had so counted on an old age lulled by the slapping waves of fatuity! "Here I am, dear," I continued into the instrument. "I had to close the window. It was blowing in. Perhaps you're right. Perhaps it's better and more restful if you stay where you are and take a sleeping pill . . . No, darling, it has nothing to *do* with Derrick, he's at a bankers' dinner, anyway . . . Yes, of course I'm sure . . . Well, Geraldine, really how you *insinuate* things . . . No, I'm not cross . . . What?"

I listened for a moment until I realized that I was hearing the dial tone. Geraldine had hung up.

"I don't think you appreciate how ill she is!" I exclaimed, turning angrily on Derrick. "I've told you that we ought to commit her!"

"She's not that nutty."

"She complains that the hotel allows corpses to be stacked in the corridor!"

"That's only delirium," he retorted with a shrug. "Once you had her under lock and key, and off the booze, she'd calm right down and unspring herself. And then tell everyone you'd done it out of spite!"

"I don't care!" I protested miserably. "I only care what's good for Geraldine. She won't let me go to her, and you won't let her come here. The only thing to do, then, is get her to a hospital, and if she won't go, she must be committed!"

"I tell you, it won't work," he said decisively. "I think you'll have to take my opinion on that. I've talked to the lawyers, and you haven't. Geraldine has an expensive psychiatric nurse whom *I* pay for and who's supposed to know all about her case. That should be quite enough. And now I suggest you go to bed."

"But, Derrick, I don't trust that nurse!"

"Then get a new one," he said with a yawn. "*In* the morning. If you ask me, you're making a great deal of fuss about a querulous, selfish creature who has drunk herself into her present predicament. I'm sorry," he continued, turning at the door and raising his hand to quell further protest, "I have no patience with this modern, morbid preoccupation with the mentally ill. If you wish to wear yourself out for Geraldine, that's your prerogative. *I* prefer to keep my strength and energy for those who can still profit by it. Good *night*, my dear."

I sat up late that night, uneasy and foreboding. It gave me little relief to recall how often in the past I had had the same premonition. Dr. Valdez, Dorcas' psychiatrist, had told me that to apprehend a death was subconsciously to wish for it, but if such was the case, I had learned to live with my subconscious. All I could do for Geraldine was to let the same heavy hands of the past press upon my shoulders that pressed upon hers. The old brownstone house and I were the sole survivors on Fifty-third Street of that crowded, organized family childhood that she and I had so intimately shared. Derrick had always wanted to move uptown, but the compromise that we had reached, after he had started to make what he called "real money," was that if he would keep my family's house, I would give him carte blanche to build as he chose in the country. Even at that, he had cheated a bit, for when the old stoop began to crumble, he had taken it off and installed a front hall of grey limestone with a showy marble stairway that always embarrassed me. And, of course, I could not prevent his buying the house next door and cutting through doorways to his new library and study. But the rest of the house was much as it had been half a century before when Mother, breaking away from the stiff parlor tradition of an earlier New York, had managed, with surprisingly few dollars, to add a touch of French eighteenth century to the dark Victorian things.

Below in the hall I heard the front door close and, a minute later, the click of Hugo's evening shoes on those marble stairs. Ordinarily he took the elevator to the top floor which he had converted to his apartment, but when he saw the lights in the front window he would stop in to chat.

"Hello, Ma! What keeps *you* up?"

"I was just thinking."

"Good Lord! That bad?" He came over and kissed me on the cheek. He rarely kissed me except when I was sitting down, for he hated measuring his height against that of any woman even a fraction of an inch taller than himself. Hugo was by no means a small man, and a temper as dark as his hair and eyes more than compensated for any question of size, but he had always resented a fate that had made him shorter than his father. "You should have been at Aunt Irene's. No nonsense like that with her and Uncle Chris."

"I imagine not," I said with a faint smile. "Actually I was a bit worried about Cousin Geraldine." Hugo was the only one of my family who still cared in the least for Geraldine. She was at her best with him, because she loved to hear about the social world.

"Is she bad?"

"Oh, you know, the same. Except every day it seems a tiny bit worse. How long can it go on, do you think? How long can a person be terrified of dying and want to die and *not* die?"

Hugo straightened up at my tone. "See here, Ma, do you want me to go round and check on her?"

"Oh, no, darling, that's not necessary at all. There's nothing you could do. Besides, you need your sleep."

"Need my sleep?" He laughed, the old high explosive laugh of all my mother's family. "I'm thirty-five, I'll thank you to remember. Can't you ever face the fact that your darlings are grown up? Grown up? Hell, they're middle-aged. Do you realize Dorcas will be forty in two years?"

"Will she?" How could Dorcas be middle-aged before she had had her youth?

"And yet you never let any of us do anything for you. Not, I grant, that you'd get much. Dorcas thinks of nothing but *her* children. But try your bachelor son. Seriously, would you like me to go and sit with Cousin Geraldine? I can sleep on the sofa there."

"Oh, darling, no, she's got a nurse!"

"A reliable one?"

"Oh, perfectly reliable. Please, dearest, go to bed."

"I will, if you will."

I rose, and as we put out the lights, I reflected that however much I had always fussed over Geraldine, I wouldn't give her a single one of my child's hours of sleep. No, I whispered grimly as I started up the stairs, not even to save her life.

I slept deeply that night, and, as usual, without dreams. I did not even hear the telephone, and I was awakened at eight o'clock by Derrick, already dressed, standing at the end of my bed and calling my name. I always regained all of my senses at the moment of waking and took in immediately the gravity of his expression.

"What's happened?"

"We needn't worry any longer about commitment," he said in a tone too dry not to have been rehearsed. "Geraldine went out the window half an hour ago. She fell eight stories. The hotel just called."

I sat up sharply. "And the nurse?" I cried in agony. "Where in God's name was that nurse?"

His gaze never flinched. "The nurse was in the bathroom."

One thing that I had to admit about Derrick was that he always knew when to shut up. To have pretended the smallest concern about Geraldine would have been ignoble; to have apologized for steps not taken would have been to invite a bitter storm of reproach. For the years had taught him that I was not of those who are disarmed by surrender; I had, on the contrary, a tendency, born of my very lack of confidence, to rub things in. I got up and dressed in two minutes while he stood there, silent.

"Where are you going?" he demanded, as I started to the door.

"To the Algar, of course."

"Not till you've had breakfast. There's nothing you can do now. I've got the office on the job, and they'll have a lawyer and an undertaker there." Derrick was immediately easier as soon as he could identify anything with his office.

"There's no need!" I cried, on the verge of tears. "I can take care of everything!"

"Nonsense!" he retorted firmly. "There'll be all kinds of details you shouldn't be bothered with. Besides, according to the will at my lawyers', I'm Geraldine's executor."

"*You* are!" I exclaimed in astonishment. "*Your* lawyers have Geraldine's will?"

"They have *a* will," he said with a shrug. "It was executed years ago, after Freddy died. But until someone turns up with a later one, I shall at least make noises like an executor." He took a step towards me as if to grasp my hand, but then appeared to think better of it. "I know your heart is full of bitterness, Ida. But Geraldine is dead, and all that can wait. You and I have a job to do. Let's do it together."

I caught my breath and struggled with the impulse to shout at him. But what was the use? What was the use of gestures? I sighed at last and nodded. "Of course, you're right. It's disgusting of me to think of myself at a time like this. If you're the executor, you must do as you see fit. I don't suppose, though, that poor Geraldine left much to 'execute.'"

We went down together to the dining room where Hugo was waiting for us in pajamas and a kimono. He usually had breakfast in his own apartment, but he had come down when his father telephoned. He got up to kiss me, without waiting for me to sit, and for just a moment I clung to him.

"What ghastly news," he murmured. "Poor Ma."

"I'm all right, dear," I said quickly and took my seat. "It isn't so much Geraldine's death I grieve for. It's her life. Let's all have coffee. Nellie!" I called.

But Nellie was already there with the coffee urn, and we drank in silence. Derrick turned to his newspaper, and I saw Hugo eye him with disapproval. In moments of tension they always fought.

"Shall I go with Ma to the Algar?" Hugo asked.

"It won't be necessary, thank you. I'll take her."

Hugo continued to stare at his father's paper. "When? After you've finished the *Times?*"

"When I've finished my breakfast, thank you," Derrick retorted testily, unfolding his napkin and turning the front page of the paper. Sensing Hugo's eyes still on him, he looked up suddenly and snapped: "I can't do more than all the king's horses and all the king's men, you know. I can't put Geraldine together again, can I?"

"And I daresay you wouldn't if you could!"

Derrick met his son's angry eyes with a retorting glare. He was obviously relieved by the excuse to speak his mind. "It's quite true, I wouldn't. If ever I knew a useless human being, it was she. I can see nothing to be gained in false sentiment about her death."

"Nothing!" cried Hugo. "I quite agree, nothing! But you might at least recognize that Ma loved Cousin Geraldine. Don't let *her* see how you feel."

"Hugo, *please!*" I murmured, but my protest was lost in Derrick's answering roar: "I think I may be allowed to express my feelings in my own home! Everyone else does!"

"Do you insinuate that I stretch my privileges?" Hugo demanded, flaring up immediately. "Do you imply that I'm not welcome? It's very easy for me to find other lodgings, you know."

"Look, Hugo." Derrick paused now to regulate his exasperation and make it a more effective instrument of his antagonism. "You don't have to play that game with me. You know perfectly well that you're welcome here. You know also that, as far as I'm concerned, you may leave whenever you wish. Any issue that may exist on that subject is entirely between you and your mother. But I expect to do as I like in my own home. And I expect those who share it to accept that."

I imagined that if Hugo could have been sure of making the smallest dent in his father's feelings, he would have left. As it was, there was no point in his abandoning a free apartment.

"Darling," I said soothingly, "you can help me by not fighting with your father. I think we're all on edge."

Derrick and I went straight from the dining room to the waiting car where his faithful Hans, in tucking the rug over my knees, murmured some inarticulate words of sympathy. It touched me, for Hans, a former convict of whom Derrick, in his practical fashion, had made a slave by the simple expedient of employment, regarded himself as Derrick's chauffeur and only incidentally as mine, just as he regarded the big black waxed and shiny Cadillac as his master's exclusive property. Certainly, it was a point of view to which I had no objection. I hated the ostentation of the Cadillac.

We were met at the door of the Algar by the manager, a lawyer and a detective. Derrick always enjoyed the little hubbub that was apt to follow his arrivals in the big car.

"Why don't you go right up to Geraldine's rooms?" he asked me. "I can take care of things down here while you look through her desk. There may be a last note or a memo with funeral instructions."

"Not before I've seen her!" I exclaimed suddenly. I turned to the manager. "Where is she?"

"We've laid her on the day bed in the back office."

"Ida," Derrick protested, "please don't go in."

"Oh it's all right, Mr. Hartley," the manager assured him. "The head was not damaged at all."

"Take me to her!"

I followed the manager quickly to a dark little room in back and found myself standing by what was left of Geraldine. The body, broken by its fall, swollen by the stoutness of the last five drinking years, rose in a mound under an old brown blanket. Only the head was exposed and the dyed, braided golden hair. As so often is the case, Geraldine had regained in death something of her old beauty. I saw again in that long oval face, in those marble cheeks, in that delicate straight nose the magnificent luster of the Edwardian belle, and I remembered, with a sad, sick jealousy and agonized regret, how Geraldine had dominated our childhood world of cousins. I would have broken down had it not been for the manager's voice.

"I trust Mr. Hartley will look after the press," he was whining. "Naturally, he will care as much as I do that nothing be said about this."

"It is of not the slightest importance to me what the newspapers print," I said abruptly. "I'll go to Mrs. Brevoort's room now, thank you."

In Geraldine's apartment I closed the door firmly in his face. It was suddenly unbearable to have to share her death with any more humans to whom it meant nothing but its method. Alone in the little living room, at least, I was alone with a past that had loved her. Her father, who had been my Uncle Victor, Mother's favorite brother and the most charming of the Denisons, with his slanting eyelid and walking stick, smiled down from a portrait too large for the wall space, surrounded by the remnants of his little art collection: Vibert, Detailles, Walter Gay. Guarding the door to the bedroom was the big Indian elephant screen that had so fascinated me as a child. And everywhere, on the floor, on the sofa, on chairs, abounded the dolls that Geraldine had so passionately collected and clung to: big, floppy dolls in pajamas that nobody had seen since the 1920's, dolls in crinolines, dolls in dirndls, Raggedy Anns, eighteenth century marquises. Propped up on the back of the sofa and leaning against the wall was a huge pink cushion with the embroidered legend: "Don't worry, it never happens." I went over quickly to turn it and then sat on the sofa and allowed myself the bitter luxury of tears whose sincerity I even doubted myself.

I knew that Geraldine kept her papers in two drawers at the bottom of her desk. Into these she had thrown what she wanted to keep, helter-skelter, but as she had cleaned it out before her move to the Algar, I had now only a small bundle of old documents and the random accumulations of three years. The latter were quickly sifted: unpaid bills, addresses of drugstores that were not fussy about prescriptions, names of cleaning women who would gossip as well as clean, and copies of indignant letters about city smells and street noises to the *Herald Tribune*. The older papers were tied more neatly in a bundle: Geraldine's first divorce decree, the court papers of her legal squabble over Freddy Brevoort's trust, galleys of a slushy yarn about a rum runner and a debutante with green fingernails that Geraldine had written for a pulp magazine in the early twenties, and then, unexpectedly and touchingly, a letter that my mother had written her when Geraldine had left Talbot Keating. Geraldine had always been Mother's favorite niece, but Mother had understood her and, unlike myself, had known how to give advice without offending.

"We're all of us selfish," the long slanting handwriting warned Geraldine. "It's a Denison characteristic, and there's precious little we can do about it. But I find people don't mind so much if we're selfish and pleasant. It's being selfish and cross that they never forgive!"

I felt a stab of jealousy at the thought of how Mother would have loved to have had a daughter as beautiful as Geraldine. But would anything have been worth the aftermath? "When the tide goes out," Mother used to say of old age, "it's *your* beach that's left." Mother's tide had not gone out, for she had died too young, but I had my vision of what a clean, gleaming beach hers would have been. Poor Geraldine's, on the other hand, had been strewn with old bottles and seaweed and dead crabs and odd spiked things tossed from the deep, and . . . and the paper that I now spotted beneath Mother's note, bearing the letterhead of a law firm and a date in March of 1935, just fifteen years before.

Dear Mrs. Brevoort:

You have asked our opinion on the legal consequences of the following state of facts: Plaintiff, as a young woman, received a proposal of marriage from Defendant, which she declined because he had been paying marked attentions to her cousin. Defendant and Plaintiff's cousin were subsequently married, but some years later Defendant told Plaintiff that his marriage had been a mistake and that he was still and had always been in love with her. He promised to get a divorce and marry her if in the meanwhile she would become his mistress. Plaintiff, relying on his promise, entered into the proposed relationship. Defendant, however, never thereafter took any steps to obtain a divorce and at last told Plaintiff that he had never intended to do so. Does Plaintiff have any legal redress?

As a practical matter, Plaintiff does not. No action could be based on the promise of marriage which Plaintiff knew that Defendant was in no position to fulfill. There is, we suppose, a conceivable action in seduction, but Plaintiff's knowledge of Defendant's married state would make any recovery most unlikely. Undoubtedly advantage has been taken of an unfortunate woman, but it is one of those wrongs for which our law provides no effective remedy.

Even at such a moment, when all my childhood and early years seemed to shrink into the grotesque accumulation of that room, when the back of that absurd pillow with its admonition against worry seemed to grin at me in its base joy at my disillusionment, I was able to repudiate the "advantage" taken of that "unfortunate woman." I had known Geraldine for a hypocrite and an egotist, but *this!* I saw the room and its accumulations suddenly as anybody might have seen it, stripped of the associations in which the past had wrapped it for me. Now it was merely cluttered and shabby, and Uncle Victor's portrait a slick fashionable dated job, and Aunt Sophie's porcelain chipped and bad Victorian. But what was worst of all was that there seemed not only no taste but no principles, or at least no principles that weren't everybody's principles. I was suddenly abandoned in a wasteland of moral equality where tact and kindness and self-sacrifice and greed and lechery and simple selfishness were so many cactuses of the same size and barbs, and Geraldine and I were one at last—and nothing. Yet the only real surprise which that letter had contained for me was that she should have written it.

When I heard the door open and saw Derrick before me I did not bother to wipe away the tears. I simply stared at him reproachfully.

"I'm glad you're giving in to it," he said with conventional sympathy. "It's bad to dam things up."

"Oh, yes, I'm giving in to it."

"I don't suppose you've had a chance to see if there's another will?"

"There isn't," I said briefly.

"Then it's all yours."

"*What's* all mine?"

"This apartment. All these bibelots. The papers you're going through." He shrugged. "The whole damn estate. Of course, it's no fortune, but I figure, after taxes and everything, it ought to amount to some four hundred thousand dollars."

My first dizzy reaction was that it must have been a gesture of conscience on Geraldine's part. "But don't I have to share it?" I demanded. "Shouldn't it be divided equally among all the cousins?"

Derrick seemed amused. "I always count on you, Ida. You never let me down. You can convert a windfall into a duty the very minute you hear of it. Who but you could imagine that it was an obligation to turn over the money to a parcel of cousins who didn't give a damn about her?"

Another idea struck me. "Derrick, did you say you *knew* about this will?"

"Certainly. She told me about it the winter I took over her investments, just after Freddy Brevoort died. It seemed to me perfectly appropriate. You had been very kind to her, and she had no children of her own. Besides, I made most of that money for her."

"And was *that* why you wouldn't let me commit her?" I demanded, rising from my seat. "Because you thought she might get well again and be so angry she'd change her will?"

It was Derrick's particular pride that his face never betrayed him. He surveyed me now with a dispassionate stare and shrugged again. "I'm not so hard up that I have to play little tricks like that. I assumed that Geraldine had changed that will a dozen times."

Had he? I would never know. It was true that the money was not important to him, but the smallest sum would have been more important than Geraldine. I handed him her letter from the lawyer.

"Read that. I'm beginning to wonder if, between us, we didn't do rather a job on Geraldine."

But if Derrick had been able to face my first attack, there was nothing in my second to make him quail. When he had finished the letter, he tossed it back on the desk with a grunt.

"So she even went to a lawyer," he muttered. "I might have guessed it. Geraldine could never believe that the machinery of the state wasn't constructed especially for her own petty complaints."

"Is that all you have to say?"

His face showed a mild surprise, but that, too, was premeditated. "What more is there to say?"

"What about *me*?"

"But you knew all about it, Ida!"

"I didn't know that Geraldine intended to marry you!" I exclaimed passionately. "I didn't think it was you who had turned her down!"

I thought that I could make out for the first time a sincere astonishment on Derrick's features. "What *did* you think?"

"I thought she threw you out because she wouldn't take *my* husband!"

Derrick stared for a moment and then emitted a low whistle. "And you'd rather believe *that*? Rather than that I never wanted a divorce?"

"Yes!" I cried. "I'd rather believe that you and Geraldine were in love, and that she was big enough to give you up, than that you seduced her with a lie and that she plotted to take my husband! What decent woman wouldn't?"

Derrick sat down on the sofa and was quiet for several moments. Perhaps he was reflecting that in all the years of our marriage I had never spoken to him so violently. "So that's it," he said at last. "That's what you are. A decent woman."

"You find it out just when I discover that the term is meaningless!"

"And what does a decent woman do now? Leave me?"

"Of course I'm not going to leave you," I said, exasperated at his obtuseness. "Why should I leave you for something that happened fifteen years ago? I'm not such a sentimental fool. Not now, anyway. No, there's nothing you have to *do* about this or even think about it." I pointed to the letter on the table with a trembling hand. "I shall burn it, and as far as you're concerned, that will be the end of it. You can go on about your own life as if nothing at all had happened."

"And you?"

"Oh Derrick, what do you care? Leave me *be!*" I got up and walked to the open drawer and took out the last bundle of papers. "I have work to do."

"I want to know what all this means to you," he insisted stubbornly. "After all, I'm responsible, no matter how long ago it was. How do you know I can't help you?"

"Can you mend a broken past?" I demanded bitterly. "A broken past that never existed?"

"Why did it never exist?"

"Because it was only in my own silly mind." I threw down the bundle of letters and walked to the fireplace to pick a cigarette off the mantel. "Geraldine was right. She's always been right." I turned to him defiantly. "I've seen the world with the eyes of a child. Always. Mother and Uncle Victor and Aunt Dagmar and *all* the Denisons. What gods and goddesses they were to me! And how Geraldine always sneered at me and said that everybody was carrying on with everyone else, even her own father, and that Aunt Dagmar drank whiskey in her bedroom!" I gave a little helpless laugh at my own naïveté and at the seeming absurdity of bringing it all up after so many years. "I daresay they all did!"

"I very much doubt if your Aunt Dagmar drank whiskey in her bedroom," he observed judiciously. But then he appeared to consider. "At least she never showed it if she did."

"Oh, what does it matter, who cares? She's been dead these last twelve years!"

"*You* care!"

"Well, I'll get over it. It won't kill me."

"You make me wonder."

"Only it *does* seem to me," I went on, with a sudden resurgence of indignation, "that if Geraldine cared enough to want to marry you, you might have been a little kinder to her at the end!"

But Derrick simply shrugged as he rose. "She didn't want to marry *me*," he retorted quietly. "She wanted to marry *your* husband."

The door that he closed on me seemed to shut out more than the present. It shut out my own past and left me with Geraldine's. For a few terrible moments I thought it was going to stifle me, that those grotesque dolls would end by convincing me that truth lay in their placid leers or else drive me out the window after their defeated mistress. I had already reached the door, on my way to the lobby to call after Derrick, when I finally got hold of myself.

"No, no!" I whispered hoarsely. "I don't care if you *are* dead, Geraldine! Your whole life was rotten! And I'm still alive!"

It seemed for a moment that Uncle Victor might be going to wink from his portrait. But no, Uncle Victor also was dead. I picked up Geraldine's copy of my little printed pamphlet, *The Ancestors and Descendants of Wil-*

liam K. Denison and Dorcas Fuller, and, turning to the page which contained the dates of her birth and of her two marriages, I carefully inserted
the date of her death. The first trembling in the old jerry-built castle of my
evasions was over. It had shaken me badly. But now that the bricks were
tumbling and one great tower had disappeared in a roar of dust and masonry,
I felt, in the very core of my misery, a little stir of elation. I wanted to see
it all go. I wanted to rave and shout over the general ruin from a last tot-
tering turret until I, too, should fall into the wreckage and be buried in the
rubble with whatever stern lesson might have been turned up in the bricks
of that ancient past.

2

IDA: 1901

Aunt Dagmar Tremain dominated our childhood world on Fifty-third
Street, but behind Aunt Dagmar there was always Uncle Linn. We became
more conscious of him as we grew older and learned in what esteem our
parents held this tall, silent, sardonic, whiskered gentleman who was known
to be brilliant in finance and supposed to be brilliant in everything. He had
inherited the cultivation and independence of parents who had left an ante-
bellum New York for the Florence of William Wetmore Story and the Robert
Brownings. There Uncle Linn had lived as a young man, dabbling in painting and sculpture, and haunting the studios of those American artists who
created towering marble figures for monuments and painted pictures of
crowded and bloody historical scenes. It was typical of his prudence and
detachment that he should have destroyed every item of his own early work
and that he should have married his Italian mistress, not on the birth of his
daughter Livia, but only on the ultimate birth of a son. The poor gratified
creature's subsequent death (a Nunc Dimittis, as Mother used to call it)
had freed Uncle Linn to return with his small family to New York and to
the downtown world of stocks and bonds for which nature had all along
intended him. There he found himself and his fortune, and he was already
a rich man when his purchase of Grandpa Denison's little banking business
brought him to Brooklyn and to Aunt Dagmar.

It was a family legend, despite the Italian lady, that Aunt Dagmar was
the first and only passion of his life. Of course, when I was little, she was
already in her fifties and inclined to be plump, but I could still piece together
the beauty that must have dazzled Uncle Linn. It was a beauty that photographs never captured, the moist, shiny-eyed beauty of a nereid in pre-
Raphaelite painting with long, blown hair that somehow managed to be neat,

and skin of pinkest pearl. Although she was tall, like all her family, and magnificent in simple reds and blacks, she had the rather lovable inclination of a fussy generation for too many scarfs and lace handkerchiefs and lockets and frills. Aunt Dagmar's heart was as soft as her person, and I don't think anyone but her step-daughter Livia ever really disliked her.

When Uncle Linn met her, she had passed her thirtieth year and was serenely keeping house for a widowed father and those of his younger children who were still unmarried. He proposed to her on their second meeting, and, being refused, crossed the East River every Saturday afternoon for three months to call on her. Aunt Dagmar was bewildered by such persistence; she had resolved not to marry while her father lived, and suitors had long since stopped coming to the house. But Grandpa Denison had had one stroke and was determined to see her settled before his next, and Uncle Linn, aided and abetted by the united Denisons, at last, amid storms of tears, prevailed. The boat to Europe was nearly missed when Aunt Dagmar, a still sobbing bride, insisted upon a final visit to the family homestead.

The sobs continued. Even after the honeymoon and her establishment in the French Renaissance mansion with the pink façade and big grey pedimented windows that Uncle Linn built for her on Fifty-third Street between Fifth and Sixth Avenues, Aunt Dagmar pined for her native Brooklyn. Had she had children of her own, the homesickness might have passed, but she didn't. Uncle Linn's answer was to bring over her family one by one. First came Uncle Will Denison, the oldest brother, who was given a junior partnership in Tremain & Dodge and moved his wife and six children into a house two down from Aunt Dagmar's. Then Uncle Philip, the bachelor brother and auctioneer, took over a floor of the Tremains' house and lived there until his marriage to Mrs. Clyde enabled him to build an even larger one on the corner of Fifth. Third came Uncle Victor, the doctor and favorite brother, who established his family and practice in the street, and last of all, my mother, Lily, the adored "baby," who persuaded my father, Gerald Trask, to take a job in a trust company of which Uncle Linn was a director and move into the brownstone that Uncle Linn had bought to ensure Aunt Dagmar's sunlight. Small wonder that the street became known as "Denison Alley."

It must have been Uncle Linn's hope that if he ever rid Aunt Dagmar of her homesickness, her heart would turn more wholly to him. But she was one of those lovely, vexing creatures who never fully mature and whose primary affection is reserved for siblings. For a long time Uncle Linn watched with a bemused and tolerant eye while his wife reconstructed her adult nursery around him. It had the incidental advantage, of course, of providing a host of children with whom his own delicate and adored son, Charley, could play. Aunt Dagmar's love for Charley, indeed, almost compensated her husband for the other things that she failed to give him. But after Charley's death his stricken father began to see the Denisons with an increasingly critical eye. He was perfectly willing to smile at their jokes and go to their parties and even to foot their bills, but they bored him. To tell the truth, human beings bored him. Uncle Linn had had his brief fling with passion and lived on for such slight diversion as his business offered. With stocks and bonds, a daily game of whist at his club and here and there the purchase of a picture, he could just get by.

His in-laws were just the opposite. They never seemed to feel the need to get off into corners and hug things to themselves. Even a small desire for privacy they regarded as almost anti-social. "Tell your Aunt Dagmar, she'll be so amused," Mother was always saying to me, or "What a pretty dress, do run across the street and show it to Geraldine." To want to be alone was to be a "moper" and to break a cardinal rule, like gushing too much or whining too much or reading too much or praying too much. Excess was "sloppy," as I learned to my pain, for I was the sloppiest of the little band of cousins who bicycled in the Park and sat on the stoops in spring evenings, shouting and giggling back and forth. To me immoderation, however wicked to my uncles and aunts, contained the secret of all the delights of living. When Mother or Aunt Dagmar gave me a present, I wanted to hug them dramatically in return, and at the least bad news, or the death of anybody, I wanted to sob and sob. If I liked doing something, I wanted to go on doing it; I wanted to see Ellen Terry *every* Saturday matinee in *Cymbeline,* and I wanted to read Marion Crawford and Mrs. Humphrey Ward right through the night.

"Ida Trask," I can hear Mother saying, "don't you think you spend enough time in school without sitting all afternoon in this dark library? What are you reading? Tennyson? But all his most beautiful passages are about the out-of-doors! Aunt Sophie tells me that Geraldine is organizing a picnic supper in the Rambles. Why can't you think up things to do, like Geraldine?"

Alas, why not? Geraldine was the golden-haired darling of the block. All the grownups took an unreasoning pleasure in her sly, soft, flattering impertinence. Only to the juniors of her own sex did Geraldine allow peeps of a less lovable side of her nature and I, being closest to her age, had the privilege of an uninterrupted view. She was always pulling my pigtails or sneering at me because she had silk stockings or real pearls and I didn't, and once, at Aunt Dagmar's Christmas party, she went so far as to push a book off a table while I was reciting *Oenone* to make me forget my lines. When she needed me, on the other hand, she could turn me into a confidante as dedicated as any in French tragedy by the simple expedient of taking me up to her bedroom and letting me try on the dresses that the indulgent Uncle Victor was always buying her. These sessions were apt to end in my doing her homework, though she was in a class above me at Miss Irvin's School.

My bitterest lesson in the art of not being "sloppy" came partly through Geraldine and partly through the death of Queen Victoria. The sunset of that long and glorious reign had cast its dramatic glow across the wintry Atlantic to our awed breakfast table, and Mother and I had followed with an absorbed interest the bulletins of the royal decline.

"I wonder if we should cancel Dagmar's birthday party," Mother said to Father on the morning of the final one. He glanced up from his paper with a faint smile.

"I should think ex-colonies are exempt from court mourning."

I would have been shocked by the idea of even a family party on so tragic a day had it not occurred to me that it would be the perfect opportunity to recite Lord Tennyson's dedication to the *Idylls of the King* which I had just learned by heart. I quickly conceived the hushed, even tearful silence that would fall over the assembled family as I rang out:

Break not, O woman's heart, but still endure,
Break not, for thou art royal.

Oh! In a sudden, suffocating fit of emotion, I hurried through breakfast and joined Geraldine and Elly Denison to walk to school with Miss Brown, wondering how I could get through the day and reciting the opening lines over and over with moving lips. But at school something more awe-inspiring than even Queen Victoria's death awaited me.

Miss Irvin herself was in the front hall, our large, red, bespectacled deep-voiced headmistress whose twin passions were discipline and poetry. As we passed her to enter the assembly hall for morning prayers, she touched me on the shoulder.

"Miss Gilder tells me you've learned the dedication to the *Idylls*. Do you really know it, dear?"

"Oh, yes!"

"Do you think you could recite it at assembly? Before the whole school?"

"Oh, Miss Irvin! The whole *school?*"

"You needn't if you don't want. I can read it aloud. But I thought it would be so much nicer to have it recited."

"Oh, yes! Oh, yes please, I will!"

Miss Irvin nodded and gave me an approving smile, as if to show that we were now equals, and then led me down the aisle between the rows of seated girls to sit by her until the entire school was present. Then she rose.

"Girls, you have all heard the sad tidings about the Queen of England. She was a great sovereign and a great woman, and with her we have lost one of the most illustrious of our sex. I am now going to call upon Ida Trask to recite Lord Tennyson's dedication to the *Idylls of the King*. He dedicated them, as some of you know, to the memory of the Prince Consort, her beloved husband, whom she survived through four lonely decades."

How glad I have always been that I responded so promptly and so uncharacteristically to Miss Irvin's challenge! In a way, the whole rest of my life has been an anticlimax. For I never once faltered, not over a single word of that long dedication. It rang out loud and noble and clear, from the slow, mournful start:

These to His Memory—since he held them dear,
Perchance as finding there unconsciously
Some image of himself—I dedicate,
I dedicate, I consecrate with tears—
These Idylls . . .

to the organ peal of the final words of consolation to the royal widow:

The love of all thy sons encompass thee,
The love of all thy daughters cherish thee,
The love of all thy people comfort thee,
Till God's love set thee at his side again.

The big pale room of upturned faces ceased to have any relation to a school. It was like a sloping field of daisies that led my eyes away to a wild broad sea and across it to a grey, fog-enshrouded morning on the Solent with flags at half mast on the long line of misty ships and the muffled roll of drums. I, Ida Trask, was at one with this somber pageant of the death of kings. And I realized, with a perfect clarity, then and there, that it was only by the wings of poetry that I could be carried so far above the little world of all my cousins. In the respectful silence that followed my recitation I caught sight of Geraldine's face and saw that it was as awed as even I could have wished. Miss Irvin rose and cleared her throat.

"And now God's love *has* set her at his side again. Thank you, Ida."

All that morning I was listless and languid in my classes. I accepted the congratulations offered me with a weary little smile that I thought very effective. I was the great artist, exhausted by my performance and happier than I had ever been in my life.

The family were always very good about each other's accomplishments. That night, before the grownups' dinner at our house, when the children trooped into the parlor to offer their birthday greetings to Aunt Dagmar, each of my uncles and aunts congratulated me in the heartiest fashion. I was beginning to be afraid that I was preempting the attention that properly belonged to Aunt Dagmar when my father called for silence, and Geraldine opened the skits with a take-off of Maude Adams in *As You Like It*. Everyone found it terribly funny, but I knew that its only purpose was to show off Geraldine in tight pants. In the applause that followed, Mother came over to whisper to me.

"I have a birthday request from Aunt Dagmar. She would love it if you could recite 'Annabel Lee.'"

I gasped. Would they have asked Melba to sing "After the Ball"?

"Wouldn't she like the dedication? I'm all ready with it."

"It's just a bit long and sad for a birthday party, don't you think, darling? And 'Annabel Lee' is Aunt Dagmar's *favorite* poem."

"'Favorite' or 'only'?" I retorted under my breath and walked gloomily to the middle of the room to comply. I was so indignant and disappointed, however, that I forgot my lines in the middle and had to be rescued by Mother who cried: "That's enough now, dear! We're having a soufflé, and we've just got time for two more. Elly, will you sing us 'Loch Lomond'?"

I ran up to my room, burning with humiliation, and fell sobbing on my bed. Mother this time must have sensed something of my misery, for she came upstairs after dinner before her guests had gone. Standing in the doorway, seeming even taller in her white dress, she gazed down at my sullen features with a mild reproach. Mother was not in the least feminine or soft, like Aunt Dagmar; she had a handsome, firm, rather square face and a very erect figure. But those calm, clear grey eyes were surprisingly capable of pain.

"Darling, you're not in bed."

"I'm just going."

Mother came over and sat on the edge of the bed. "You think nobody appreciates you, I know. But if you could have heard all the nice things they were saying downstairs about your recitation in school, your ears would have burned. I was so proud!"

"No, you weren't!" I cried miserably. "All you want to do is laugh at the silly things Geraldine does!"

"That's only at parties. People *like* silly things at parties."

"Well, I hate parties!"

"Hate them all you want, dear, but you must learn about them. Then they can't hurt you. Because you're my bright Ida. Ten times as bright as Geraldine ever dreamed of being. And don't worry. In the long run brightness may get you further."

I sat up suddenly and flung my arms around her neck. I must have rumpled her evening dress, but Mother knew when demonstrations had to be allowed. "But *you* like parties!"

"So will you some day."

"Never!"

"Never's a long time. You'll see."

"Never!"

I clung to her as I felt her pull away. But I knew she had to go downstairs.

"Never!" I repeated for the third time.

And I never have.

3

IDA: 1903

Livia Tremain was the maverick of Fifty-third Street. In the first place, she was not a real cousin, being only Aunt Dagmar's stepdaughter, and then she was half Italian and a Catholic and went to Mass with the maids. She had lustrous black hair and large dark eyes and had been educated—insufficiently—in a convent in New Jersey. She was pretty, in a tough, pouting way that Aunt Dagmar was afraid would not last, and stupid, in a tough, pouting way that Aunt Dagmar was afraid would. She was never in the least congenial with her stepmother or with her stepmother's family and exhibited to the adults on our block a truculence that they found very exasperating. I heard Uncle Victor once telling Mother that if she had the name of an ancient Roman, she had the character of a "wop."

Yet they tried their best with her. She was included in every party and treated like a true if difficult Denison. They planned to give her a place in New York which she could never have had without them, for despite the fact that Livia, after her brother Charley's death, was Uncle Linn's only child and presumably an heiress, the rumors about her birth did little to recommend her to the society of that day. Mother and Aunt Dagmar might have overcome the prejudice had Livia cooperated with them, but Livia had no taste for cooperation. At sixteen she tried to elope with Uncle Linn's groom and at seventeen with the boy at the desk of the Southampton Beach Club. In the latter case they got to New York before they were apprehended, and the episode was duly reported in the public prints. This settled, once and for all, the question of Livia's social career, and at nineteen she found herself isolated in a world that she had never understood, living with a stepmother who bored her and a father whom she bored, with nothing better to do of an afternoon than loll about the old playroom at Uncle Victor's where Geraldine and I did our homework, popping postcards from Aunt Sophie's collection of European royalties into the magic lantern.

Geraldine and I, however, were young enough to be impressed by her, particularly Geraldine. She and Livia were opposites in many respects, one so blond and Anglo-Saxon and generally loved, and the other so dark and Mediterranean and generally disliked, prototypes, if you will, of the heroine and villainess of Victorian fiction, but in another, more basic respect they were very much alike. Livia was redeemed in Geraldine's eyes by the very thing that damned her in those of our parents.

"Do you ever hear from Eddy?" Geraldine asked her one afternoon, looking up from the page of *Colomba* that I was helping her to translate.

Livia did not even turn her eyes from the magic lantern. "Eddy?"

"You know, the boy at Southampton. Surely you haven't forgotten him already!" Geraldine's tone wavered between incredulity and admiration.

"I don't even know where he is."

"You mean he's not at the club any more?"

"Are you kidding? Trust my old man to see *he* got the sack."

Geraldine clapped her hands. "It must be thrilling to be the cause of someone's losing his job."

"Oh, Geraldine!" I reproved her. "How can you say anything so silly? It would be horrid, and you know it."

"*You!*" She whirled fiercely on me. "You only say that because nobody could ever lose a job over you!" She turned back to Livia. "But would you write Eddy if you knew where he was?"

"What would I write him about? Nothing goes on around here."

"You could tell him you were thinking about him."

"Oh, *thinking*." Livia's shrug seemed to evoke the instinct of generations of Italian lovers.

"You mean you don't even think about him?"

"No, I guess not."

"Don't you even think of the things you used to *do* with him?"

Livia turned at last from the magic lantern. "What do you mean by that?"

"I mean the things you did that night in the hotel before Uncle Linn caught you and brought you home!"

Livia frowned for a second, but then shrugged again and smiled pityingly. "Look, little girl, you're too young for that kind of talk."

"I am *not*! I'm fifteen and a whole year older than Ida, and, besides, my father's a doctor. Oh, Livia, *tell* me about you and Eddy!"

She ran across the room and sat by Livia and put an arm about her waist to coax her, and Livia smiled and kept shaking her head, but after a few minutes of this persuasion she leaned down suddenly and whispered something in Geraldine's ear which made her gasp and then burst into hysterical giggling. When she had recovered, Geraldine sent knowing glances in my direction, to tantalize me, but I had no wish to be enlightened. I knew there were two worlds, the dry, brisk daylight of my own parents and that darker, more rustling hemisphere of Livia's adventures, and if I hardly felt a member of either, at least the first was familiar. When Geraldine, irked by my seeming indifference, ran over and seized me by the shoulders to whisper something in my ear, Livia jumped up.

"Leave her be, Geraldine! She's too young!"

Geraldine, however, simply laughed shrilly and tried to force her lips into my ear. I had pushed her away and was covering my ears when Livia pulled us roughly apart.

"I said leave her be, Geraldine! Do you want to get me in trouble?"

"I'll thank you not to lay your big hands on me in *my* house!" Geraldine screamed in one of her sudden fits of temper. "I'll say what I want to whom I want when I want!"

"Not to Ida, you won't."

"Who's going to stop me?"

"I am!"

"*You*!" Geraldine was reckless in her fury. "Why your parents weren't even married when you were born!"

I gasped in horror, but Livia simply slapped her face and strode, with a last contemptuous shrug, from the room.

I had hoped that the scene would end Livia's visits to Uncle Victor's, but that slap must have satisfied her resentment, for the next day she turned up again as if nothing had happened. Geraldine, who had been terrified that her remark would be repeated to Uncle Linn, was only too willing to forget the episode. Besides, the Christmas holidays had started and her brother Scotty, who was crazy about Livia, was down from Yale, and Geraldine cared about Scotty as much as she could care for anyone. He was an amiable young man, very grave when he was grave, and very gay when he was gay, whom I worshiped in the dumb, besotted way of my fourteen years. The nicest thing about him was that he never snubbed me or his sister or tried to drag Livia away from us down to the parlor where they could be alone. He would sit in the playroom while Geraldine and I worked and laugh and make gibes at Livia to which she returned her flat retorts, accompanied by the sullen pout and repeated shrug that Mother had taught me to associate with housemaids and their followers.

"Why are you always peering into that old magic lantern?" Scotty asked her once. "Isn't it for children?"

"It may interest you to know that my *father* has a magic lantern which he's constantly looking through. It helps him to study paintings."

"Oh, I suppose it's all right for Uncle Linn. Great men have to relax with simple things. But why do you relax, Livy? Were you exhausted by your manicure this morning? Or your drive with Aunt Dagmar?"

"Pretty fresh, aren't you?" Livia said scornfully. "What do *you* do at Yale but sit around the Porcellian Club and drink whiskey and talk about girls?"

"The Porcellian Club's at Harvard, old dear."

"I'll thank you not to call me 'old dear.' Who cares where a silly boys' club is, anyway?"

"A lot of people care. Uncle Linn may not, but then he never went to college."

"No. He had to go to work to support all you Denisons!"

Scotty gave a hoot of laughter. "That's what happens to 'malefactors of great wealth'!"

"To *what?*"

And so it would go, while I listened, entranced. Scotty had very ordinary American blond good looks, but to a girl of my age he was simply dazzling. Father always said that Scotty's was a tragic type because his youth would last only as long as a butterfly's and that by twenty-five he would be heavy and pompous, and I admit that Father's prediction came true, but Scotty's shining eyes continued to appeal to women long after he had passed that fatal quarter-century mark. He was desperately sincere, desperately anxious to please his own fond but rather cynical father, desperately determined to make his mark and do all the right things in the right way. When one expected him to talk about Yale and football, one was surprised to be met with a long, confidential discourse about himself and his innermost problems. Scotty had few reticences, because he could not believe that his emotional tangles were not fascinating to everyone. In my case, at least, he made no error.

He was waiting at the bottom of our stoop one afternoon when I came out on my way to his family's.

"Tell me something, Ida," he said, tucking my arm under his. "Have you any notion what Livia thinks of me?"

"Oh, does Livia think?"

"Cut it out. I mean, does she like me?"

"I thought all the family liked each other."

"Shucks, Ida, you know what I mean!"

"I guess she likes you as well as she likes Dicky or Peter."

"No more than *that?*"

I relented as he squeezed my arm. "Perhaps a little."

"Don't you think a girl *could* like me?"

I blushed furiously. "Oh, I suppose."

"Could *you*, Ida?"

"How could I like you like that?" I cried in agony and mortification. "Aren't we cousins?"

"What difference does that make?"

"Oh!" Scandalized, I escaped from his grip and ran up the stoop at Uncle Victor's as his laugh rang out below.

Sometimes his bickering with Livia took a more serious turn, and they had bad quarrels. This worst of these occurred on a rainy afternoon when he and Livia and Geraldine and I were sitting as usual in the playroom. I had been looking in the magic lantern at a postcard of Florence, and Livia, after pushing me aside and squinting at it, asked me what it was.

"Why, it's the Duomo," I said, surprised.

"Duomo?" she repeated irritably. "But that just means cathedral. I can *see* it's a cathedral."

Scotty put his eye to the glass. "But Ida's quite right. It is the Duomo. That's what it's called."

"What Duomo?"

"Why the Duomo in Florence, of course! You ought to know *that*. Weren't you born there?"

Livia flushed and looked very cross. "I haven't been there since I was a child."

Scotty, however, could be very obtuse. "But everyone knows the Duomo in Florence. It's famous, like Notre Dame or St. Peter's!"

"Well, I guess I'm nobody then!" Livia exclaimed, flaring up. "And thank you so much, Mr. Scott Denison, for taking such pains to make it clear!"

"Oh, Livy. I say! I didn't mean to hurt your feelings!"

"Of course you didn't *mean* to. None of you *mean* to. Because you don't think I have any. You all look down on me because my mother was Italian!" Livia suddenly began to sob. "And I *hate* you all so!"

I was astonished that she did not slap him as well, the way she had slapped Geraldine. She simply continued to sob until Scotty, murmuring consolations, came over to put an arm around her heaving shoulders. My hand was suddenly jerked, and Geraldine pulled me out the door and turned on me with excited eyes.

"Can't you see they want to be alone?" she hissed. "Can't you tell when you're *de trop*?"

"You mean—you mean?" I gasped. "You mean they're *in love*?" Being "in love" to me was something quite different from being "crazy about" or being "attentive to." It was a grave, grown-up thing, even a painful thing, having little relation to what I had imagined to be going on between Scotty and Livia.

"Of course they're in love, you ninny! But I'll murder you if you tell anyone!"

I was far too removed from Scotty's sphere to resent Livia as a rival. Indeed, it was actually more exciting to think of my hero as being in love. But I still found Geraldine's vicarious excitement distasteful. If she had cared more about Livia or even her brother, I could have understood, but as it was, I was sure that what she really wanted was the thrill of conspiracy.

"Why can't I tell anyone?"

"Because the family would break it up. They'd say they're too young. And, besides, they all hate Livia."

"Oh, Geraldine! Hate?"

"You know they do. Because she likes boys. Can you imagine anything so stuffy?"

I wasn't sure. It seemed to me that there might be a lot of difference between liking boys and liking Scotty. But it was Geraldine's secret, and I was honor bound by our code not to repeat it without her permission. When she had exacted the necessary pledge, she told me more. It appeared that Livia and Scotty had been corresponding regularly while he was in New Haven and had done so through Geraldine.

"Why do they have to write?" I demanded. "Don't they see each other often enough? What do they have to say?"

"Oh, all kinds of lovey-dovey things. Can't you imagine?"

I could not imagine Livia saying lovey-dovey things. But surely there was no harm in their writing, and if the over-dramatic Geraldine could only be convinced of this, and in turn convince Livia, there would be no further need for secrecy and hence no need for me to feel uncomfortable about keeping it from the family. The opportunity to clear the whole thing up occurred unexpectedly one evening at Aunt Dagmar's, while she was reading aloud, as she did twice a week, to Geraldine and myself.

I always felt that Aunt Dagmar reading aloud to us would have made a charming subject for a Sargent painting. I saw it posed with Aunt Dagmar in her green velvet robe which blended with the deeper green of the huge stuffed sofa, one long white hand, thinned a bit by the artist, resting on a pillow while the other supported the book. She would be seen in profile, her best view, which brought out her exquisite aquiline nose and the fine rise of her light, greying hair, while Geraldine, with golden locks and mutely admiring eyes, would be staring up at her. But, best of all, I had fixed on a pose for myself that was bound to steal the canvas. I was to be sitting up straight in the middle of the sofa, all intense and listening, a small brown thing made interesting and perhaps even a touch sublime by her evident passion for the words being read. That day they were from *Sense and Sensibility*, which was as far as I had been able to drag my aunt and cousin up the steps of good literature. But it was better, anyway, than *Lorna Doone*, Aunt Dagmar's favorite, and in the chapter where Elinor Dashwood assumes, on discovering that Marianne has written a letter to Willoughby, that they must be engaged, I gave a little cry of surprise.

"Is it so terrible for a girl to write a letter to a man she's not engaged to?"

Aunt Dagmar paused to consider this. "I suppose it must have been, then."

"But not today?"

"No, I don't suppose it would be so bad today."

"Would it be all right for Livia, say, to write Scotty at Yale?"

"*Does* she?"

I squirmed at the sudden pain of Geraldine's pinch. "Oh, no, I don't say that!" I exclaimed hastily. "But just supposing?"

"Yes, I think it would be all right," Aunt Dagmar replied judiciously. "Provided she didn't write so many letters that it interfered with his work. Besides, they're cousins."

"Not really," I pointed out.

"No, but for all practical purposes."

"You mean they could get *married*?" I had to move quickly to avoid Geraldine's darting hand.

"Well, I don't know about marriage," Aunt Dagmar said, frowning, "but that's not something we have to worry about for a long time yet. Scotty's only a freshman." She glanced with sudden suspicion at Geraldine and then at me. "Isn't that so, girls?"

"Oh, of course!" I agreed. "I was just thinking that Livia is like Marianne. So impulsive. And Scotty is surely as handsome as Willoughby!"

"But Scotty's a *good* boy," Aunt Dagmar insisted gravely.

"And Ida's a ninny!" Geraldine exploded at last. "As silly as Marianne and as dull as Elinor!"

"Geraldine, my *dear*!" Aunt Dagmar was starting to talk on the odiousness of comparisons, particularly of Geraldine's, when she was interrupted by the arrival of Mother to take me home. They always had a few words to say to each other first, and Geraldine and I were sent out to the landing. There she turned on me furiously.

"You dirty sneak!" she started right off. "Now see what you've done!"

"I only wanted to find out if it was all right for Livia to write Scotty!" I protested. "And now you see it is! So we don't have to be secret about it any more."

"That's all *you* know!" Geraldine retorted. "You've roused all Aunt Dagmar's suspicions. She was pumping you, but, like an idiot, you couldn't see it. You'd have blabbed out everything if I hadn't pinched you!"

"Everything?"

"Well, you may as well know it: they *are* going to get married! Now do you see the importance of keeping your big mouth shut?"

I stared in consternation. "They are? Oh, Geraldine, shouldn't we tell?"

"If you do, I'll never speak to you again in my whole life!"

"But what if it's wrong . . .?"

"Wrong?" she interrupted me with a bitter sneer. "Wrong for you, you mean. Because you're jealous. You're jealous of Livia! You want Scotty all for your own dirty private dreams!"

I flushed and turned quickly away. Yet to be accused of a grown-up emotion like jealousy gave me a little throb of elation. For to be recognized as having a stake, however small, in Scotty—was that not to be recognized as a woman? Just for a moment I trembled at the excitement of my vision, just for a moment, before the great shadowy owl of shame at my own presumption glided down to overwhelm me. I turned back to Geraldine, resolved to do anything in expiation.

"All right," I said grimly. "I'll be quiet. You have my word."

Geraldine surveyed me appraisingly. "Will you help?"

"Try me and see."

"Tiptoe over to the door, then, and tell me what they're saying."

I hated to eavesdrop, particularly on Mother, but I had given my word, and I tiptoed, sick at heart, to the door.

"She's doing it out of revenge, you can be sure of that," I heard Mother say. "It's her obvious way to get back at us all. I don't say it's planned out. I say it's instinctive."

"But you're so suspicious, Lily. You've always been suspicious."

"And I've been right as many times as I've been wrong. You'll have to admit that!"

I heard Aunt Dagmar sigh and the scrape of Mother's chair on the floor as she rose. I hurried back to Geraldine.

"Well?"

"They were talking about some lady who's out for revenge. They weren't talking about Livia and Scotty at all."

"You're sure?"

"Oh, sure."

And I was. It never occurred to me that anyone of my generation, even one as much older as Livia, could be a subject of such adult concern. Geraldine, impressed that I had shown the courage to eavesdrop, revealed the next day that Livia and Scotty were planning to elope and, after a civil wedding, to come back and throw themselves on the generosity of their fathers.

"But what about Yale?" I protested, scandalized. "Will he be able to go back to Yale?"

"Would that be the end of the world? He can go to work for Uncle Linn and make oodles of money!"

I knew there was no point discussing it further with Geraldine, and I turned away from her in dumb dismay. My father and all Mother's brothers had been to Yale; it was a thing that happened to men, like shaving and going "downtown." Uncle Linn, of course, had not, but then Uncle Linn was a "great man," an exotic figure, like a President, to whom a log cabin or a charge up San Juan Hill were equally permissible. I felt the quickened heartbeat of my adventurousness, the nervous excitement of being suddenly allied with Geraldine and Livia against the family and Yale. But being allied with Geraldine and Livia also involved being allied with the smothered giggles, and smacking sounds that occurred behind the closed door if Livia and Scotty were left alone, and I flushed deeply at the thought of what my shame and humiliation would be if Mother's grey, reproachful eyes should ever be fixed on me with the knowledge of what I had concealed.

I couldn't sleep. I couldn't do my homework, much less Geraldine's. The remarkable power of the united adult world in our block was that it seemed to draw forth revelations without even soliciting them. Geraldine, for example, knew that I was wobbly, yet she still told me things. And I, while determined to honor my word, was still too wretched not to seek assurance, from the very persons from whom the secret was to be kept, that it need not be a secret at all.

My little brother, Christopher, had had a bad throat that week, and Mother had been too preoccupied to notice that I had something on my mind. But towards the weekend, when he was better, her normal perceptiveness returned. As she was putting place cards on the dining room table one evening, I followed her restlessly about.

"Mother, is it really so important for boys to go to college?"

"What sort of boys?"

"Oh, boys like Dicky and Peter Denison." I paused. "And Scotty."

"Well, if they want to get ahead in life, it is."

"But Uncle Linn never went to college, and *he* got ahead."

"Yes, that's perfectly true," Mother conceded, pausing to pick up two cards that evidently would not go together. "But those were different times. Besides, Uncle Linn lived in Italy, and that was almost as good as going to college."

"Why?"

"Because it has so many museums and picture galleries."

I considered her theory and rejected it. After all, she was not really meeting the point I wanted to make. To get ahead a young man was supposed to go to college and not to marry until he had graduated.

"But Uncle Linn got married in Italy, didn't he?"

"What has that to do with it?"

"Did *his* wife keep him from getting ahead?"

"No, she died before . . ." Mother stopped herself. She had spoken too fast, and now, of course, she would have to cover up. "I daresay she was very sweet, but not the kind of woman who would be a help to a man in New York. Of course, she was Italian."

"So is Livia!"

"Only half. Besides, Livia was brought up here."

"You mean Livia *wouldn't* keep a man from getting ahead?"

Mother gave me a brief glance. She was much too smart to think that any child on the block was unaware of the family attitude towards Livia, but she was not going to let me trick her into admitting it. That was the eternal game between grownups and children. But at least Mother knew it was a game and minded the rules. "Livia has a bit of growing up to do," she observed in a more judicial tone. "One of these days she's going to discover that life is a great deal easier for girls who try to make people like them."

"Then will she be able to help a man get ahead?"

"Then perhaps she will."

"Even a man who hasn't finished college?"

I remembered afterwards that Mother had stopped placing her cards and was gazing at the middle of the table. It should have been my warning. "A man?" she queried. "I thought we were talking about boys. What sort of a man?"

"Oh, a man or a boy, what's the difference?" I shrugged. "Like Uncle Victor or Scotty. Or even Father."

"You've mentioned Scotty twice now," Mother said sharply, turning to me abruptly and putting down her cards. "Is there something between Livia and Scotty that Aunt Dagmar ought to know about?"

"Oh, no, not at all, how can you *think* so?"

"Come with me, Ida." Mother took me down the hall into the parlor and closed the door so that no maid could hear. "It happens to be your misfortune that you're a very bad liar. Now tell me what this nonsense is all about."

"Oh, Mother, I can't!"

"You can't? What do you mean, you can't?"

"Because I gave my word of honor!"

"Your word of *honor*?" Mother's tall, indignant figure loomed over me, and I felt shriveled and shabby. "How could you give your word of honor not to tell Uncle Linn and Aunt Dagmar something that vitally concerns them? Or something that vitally concerns Uncle Victor and Aunt Sophie? What sort of honor is that?"

"*My* honor. And Geraldine's honor."

"Honor! When Aunt Dagmar gave us the very house we live in? Not to mention your pony and all those matinees at Ellen Terry."

"Oh, I know, know!" I wailed wretchedly.

"It's not, of course, that Aunt Dagmar *expects* anything in return," Mother continued remorselessly. "What she does, she does out of pure love and kindness. But don't you think we might at least *try* to do something for her in return? Don't you think we might help her in the difficult job of being a good stepmother? Must we all stand by and see two silly children like Livia and Scotty ruin their lives because Ida Trask has to hug her sacred 'honor' to her bosom?"

Even when I felt I was right, I could never stand up to Mother when she was angry. As it was, my collapse was total, physical as well as spiritual. I fell on the sofa and wept and told her everything, in a wonderful orgy of confession. I felt my breath coming back as the facts tumbled out before Mother's expressionless stare, and when I had completed the sorry tale there remained for me only to grovel in the ultimate humiliation of begging:

"You won't tell anyone I told?"

"Not if I can help it."

"You promise?"

"I don't have to promise, Ida. I said I wouldn't. But you can congratulate yourself that you've saved your cousin Scotty from blasting his career before it's even started."

"And what about Livia?"

"Livia?" Mother for the first time betrayed the full extent of her contempt. "Girls like Livia should be put away in homes!"

"Homes? Whose homes?"

"Well, not ours! But never mind about that. I've got to go and see Uncle Victor."

My family operated with speed in a crisis, and the very next day Scotty arrived from New Haven, and drama throbbed behind the closed curtains of Uncle Victor's house. Geraldine hurried over to tell me in awed tones of the great happenings; she enjoyed the climax of disrupted plans quite as much as she would ever have thrilled at their fruition. It seemed that Uncle Victor and Scotty had been closeted for two hours in the former's office, that Uncle Linn Tremain alone had been admitted, and he only for a brief visit. Geraldine had tried lo listen at the doorway and been discovered and banished by her horrified mother, but not before she had distinctly heard the sound of Scotty's sobbing. Across the street, Livia had been confined to her room and allowed to see nobody. Geraldine never once accused me of treason, as Mother had let it out that a friend of Scotty's at Yale, in a fit of conscientiousness, had divulged the secret to Uncle Victor. I had to bear my new and now seemingly intolerable load of remorse alone.

But worse was to come. The next day was Sunday, and as Mother and Father were lunching out, I was sent, in the usual way, to Uncle Victor's where I had to sit through a somber meal with Scotty and Geraldine and their parents. I found myself a bit embarrassed for Scotty, who made so little effort to conceal the ravages of his emotional crisis. His eyes were red and tearstained, and his shoulders from time to time shook with a dry sob. Decidedly, there was nothing stiff about his upper lip, but I reminded myself that Frenchmen, even as soldiers, were not ashamed to cry, and I would have indulged in the warmest fantasies of consoling him had I not been haunted by the terrible vision of what his feelings would have been had he known the identity of his betrayer.

Uncle Victor did not share my attempted tolerance for such emotionalism. He was obviously disgusted with his son, who, even to my admiring eyes, seemed crude and juvenile beside the long grey elegance of the paternal figure. After a particularly gulping sob Uncle Victor slapped the table.

"If you can't control yourself, please go to your room. What a spectacle for the girls."

"The girls know perfectly well how I feel!" Scotty exclaimed, glaring at his father with suddenly rekindled rebellion. "And why shouldn't they? Would you want to have them think I can give up Livy without a pang?"

"You might try at least not to be such a baby."

"Victor," Aunt Sophie protested. "Haven't you been hard enough on him for one day?"

"Daddy expects me to tear a girl out of my heart as easily as . . . well, as easily as I'd pluck a flower out of my buttonhole."

"That will be enough, Scott!" Uncle Victor's drooping eyelid fluttered in indignation. "You will forgive me if I fail to plumb the depths of an emotion that can express itself in such stale images. You may leave the table. But please remember you're taking the three o'clock for New Haven and that I want to see you in my office first."

Scotty stamped out of the room, and his mother quietly followed.

"Sophie!" Uncle Victor called sternly after her, but for once in her life she ignored him.

"Daddy, what did you *do* to him?" Geraldine demanded excitedly. "How did you ever make him give her up?"

I imagine that she and I owed the revelation that followed to Uncle Victor's irritation at the independence of his usually submissive spouse and his consequent need to justify himself, even to a jury of two young girls.

"I didn't *do* anything," he replied testily. "It was only necessary for Uncle Linn to convince your impetuous brother that his bride would be disinherited if she married him. As Scott is hardly in a position to support her himself, what could he do but give her up?"

"He could have quit college and taken a job!" Geraldine cried stoutly.

Uncle Victor's eyes rested on her for a quizzical moment. "Which is exactly what he offered to do," he replied with an ominous moderation of tone. "And that is what we discussed this morning. I told him that if he left Yale, *I* should disinherit him. Which would have meant, of course, that he would be asking Livia to starve with him. Your brother may have acted like an ass, Geraldine, but he's still a gentleman. He saw, of course, that he had to give her up. For her sake, if not his own."

"But what about her?" Geraldine cried. "What did she say?"

"Oh, she was all for taking her chances with Scott." Uncle Victor's shrug contained no hint of admiration at such a choice. "She was all for love or a world well lost. No doubt it's her warm Mediterranean blood."

"I think that's magnificent!"

"Do you? Do you, really?" Uncle Victor was icy. "Perhaps you will understand one day that all grownups can do for youth is to protect it from irrevocable decisions."

"But *you* could have supported them!"

"Support Scott and that . . .!" Uncle Victor stopped himself in time and flung down his napkin impatiently as he rose from the table. "Try not to be more of a goose, Geraldine, than God made you."

My last sight of Livia for decades was in the evening of that same Sunday when Mother sent me to Aunt Dagmar's to return the last R.W. Chambers novel which she had borrowed. Stride, the old butler, let me in, and I ran, as I always did, up the circular marble stairway with the low, pink steps, but I stopped abruptly on the landing when I heard Livia's voice from the parlor. She was shouting at the top of her lungs, and the raucous sound that throbbed in the air and hurled itself against the great tapestry of the marriage of the Emperor Maximilian was as shocking in that still, ordered house as the bursting of a sewer pipe. I made out that she was addressing her father.

"But I promise you one thing! As soon as I get my hands on any money of my own—and I will one day—I'll pay you back for every bloody cent you've ever spent on me. As for *your* money, you can keep it. I don't want it! You can give it to *her*. All I ask of either of you is that you send me away where I'll never see you again!"

I crept to the door and peered into the big, dark room. Aunt Dagmar was standing before the fireplace, looking into the fire. As I watched, she took the poker and moved one of the logs. Uncle Linn was sitting in a high-backed chair, his hands clasped to the arms, also looking into the fire. Neither seemed to be paying the least attention to the ranting, gesticulating maenad in the middle of the room. She might have been a singer who was being tried out for an evening party and whom they had already decided would not do. In my misery and pity I turned and fled down the stairs to the front door, thrusting the novel I had come to return in the hands of the silent but comprehending Stride.

After that terrible Sunday life resumed, at least for the non-guilt ridden, its normal course. Livia was sent off on a trip to Europe with Uncle Linn's sister, Miss Tremain, a sober, severe, dark-garbed figure from whom she ultimately escaped with the aid of her first husband, their Italian courier. Scotty went back to New Haven and was allowed no weekends in New York for a year. And I was left with my tortured doubts as to whether it was jealousy or spite or simple weakmindedness that had induced me for the first time to put my hand into the spinning wheel of life on our street and bring it, however briefly, to a halt. Nobody suspected my anguish. Mother had too little time for the immediate past to conceive what I was enduring. I knew of no outlet but confession and nobody to whom I could confess but Geraldine. One afternoon, when she had asked me up to her room to see a new dress, I grimly decided that my moment had come, only to discover that it had already passed.

"Geraldine," I began somberly, "I have something to tell you. Something that will make you despise me forever!"

"You don't like my dress?"

"No. It was I who told on Scotty."

"Mummy says I shouldn't wear gold because of my hair. But I think it's fun every now and then to overwhelm people. Don't you?"

"Geraldine!" I exclaimed. "Listen to me! I was the one who told about Livia and Scotty."

"And just like you, too," she said indifferently, holding the dress up to her neck and shoulders and gazing affectionately at the image in the mirror. "You always were the most filthy sneak."

"But you don't understand!" I was determined to reap my just punishment. "They'd be married now if it hadn't been for me."

Geraldine turned to stare at me for a moment. "Yes," she said, taking it in at last, "I suppose they might be. Well, that's one good turn you did. In spite of yourself!"

"A *good* turn?"

"Certainly. Don't gape so. It makes you look like a frog." Geraldine resumed her contemplation of herself. "Daddy was right about all that. Livia is common."

I bowed before the bleak finality of the term. We had all been brought up on the creed that Venus herself would have been impotent before it. "But mightn't she have learned?" I faltered.

"You can't learn not to be common," Geraldine retorted. "She'd have dragged Scotty down to her level." I recognized Uncle Victor's phrase. "And they'd never have had any money, either. Uncle Linn isn't the kind to forgive. Besides, he doesn't like Livia. After all, he wasn't even *married* when she was born."

And so I discovered that whichever way I turned, matters came out for the best. Or for what my family thought the best. Sometimes it seemed to me that they were the universe and I a passively observing atom with no power to affect what it observed. At other moments, with the raw egotism that underlies shyness, it occurred to me that I might have been the sole reality and the family, in fact the whole Fifty-third Street world, the simple product of my fancy. For if I had no power to affect, I could still be affected. If Scotty and Livia managed not to influence each other's lives, they both still influenced mine.

That neither, unlike myself, was really malleable was borne out by their subsequent histories. Had they married each other, briefly or not, it would have made little difference in their patterns. Scotty never finished Yale; he left in his junior year to marry into the chorus of *Daisy, Daisy,* and, after an expensive annulment, became a customer's man in Tremain & Dodge. He married twice more, once to a beautiful woman who was unfaithful to him and then to a plainer and richer one who was not. He became a famous figure on Long Island as perpetual president of the Glenville Golf and Tennis Club, which he managed with loving efficiency and at whose bar his widening figure was a symbol of cheer and hospitality until his death there of a stroke in his early fifties. Livia exceeded him in marriages. She became a wife four times, always in Europe, and her last husband was a German count who put her eye out in a fist fight. Uncle Linn left his money to Aunt Dagmar for life and then to Columbia, but the trust fund that he had earlier set up for Livia was enough to keep her in minor titles. I met her on the street shortly before Geraldine's death, almost half a century after the episode with Scotty, and I did not at first recognize her. She was dressed smartly in black and was very thin and elongated. Her hair was purple, and her nose had a large but elegant hook. She stopped and put a hand on my arm and murmured in a low, throaty tone: "Don't you know me, Ida? I'd know *you* anywhere."

"Livia!"

"I've been to the dogs since last we met, but I've come back. Could we lunch, dearie?"

We lunched, of course, and talked, as might have been expected, exclusively of the past. It fascinated me that Livia should have done with it just the opposite of what Geraldine had done. Where the latter, in her last years, had turned it over and over in her memory to detect new slights and injustices on which to blame the whole sad collapse of her present, Livia preferred to see it as a garden of lost innocence down whose ordered and brightly colored paths she delighted, as an old woman, to stroll. She talked of Aunt Dagmar and her father and Uncle Victor and Aunt Sophie and my parents as if they were characters in a big crowded, lovable, moralizing Victorian novel that one had adored reading in school. She made them seem even further back in the past than they actually had been; they stood up in her conversation as quaint and stiff as figures in daguerrotype. They were more loving, more kindly, more strict, more righteous, than their originals. Livia had had to construct in her fantasy a Fifty-third Street world from whose too tight embrace she, a bright, hopeless, fascinating, doomed maverick, had been compelled to flee. "I had my own little benighted wings," she told me in that voice of semi-cultivation that is often developed by a life of sin, "and I had to try to soar." It was her revenge on a world of Denisons to have turned it into a fairy tale.

4

IDA: 1904

THERE WAS ONLY one other person on my small horizon, besides Livia, who resisted the organizing influences of Fifty-third Street, and that was my father's mother, Grandma Trask. But where Livia had been unquestionably wicked, Grandma was unquestionably good, and it was therefore conceivable that one might attain a species of independence under her proud little banner, if only in the privilege of being able to take sides, on rare occasions, with a relative who was not related, at least by blood, to one's mother and who disagreed with her in every known particular. The trouble with Grandma, unfortunately, was that she never seemed to take notice of her would-be allies, particularly when they were girls of a rather gushing fifteen. She was a small, immaculate, formal woman with a high, lustrous, black wig and a face that was like a white mask of frozen features, without a single line or wrinkle. Everyone always said that she had been a great beauty, and I can imagine that those large, clear, still, blue eyes, however chilling to importunate grandchildren, must have been alluring to young officers in days of civil war. Mother and Father took me to see her every Sunday in the neat, still brownstone house on Brooklyn Heights where she lived with two maids and four cats, and although the cookies at tea had no icing and her anecdotes were repeated with the Sunday and season, like lessons in church, I was awed by the grave dignity which made her seem as "difficult" and "special" as I thought grownups should be. It was hard for me to believe that she had a weekday existence.

I have since understood that her special quality for me consisted more in what she was not than in what she was. She was *not* a Denison, and hence belonged to none of the cousins in Fifty-third Street. When she came to Aunt Dagmar's on Thanksgiving and Christmas in black lace with long pendant diamond earrings, walking in measured steps, a Chinese shawl, symbol of festivity, wrapped tightly about her trim little figure, her eyes fixed gravely in turn on each member of her daughter-in-law's large family, I felt as proud of her as if she had been some Oriental princess or dowager empress come to shed a patch of her glamour on her admiring granddaughter. I could not see that my cousins were laughing behind their hands at her wig or that poor Grandma's plain, literal turn of mind and total lack of humor insulated her from the other adults much as deafness isolates its victim from the cheer of a family board. All I could see was that my maternal aunts and uncles made a great fuss over her, and that some of that fuss seemed to contribute to my own puny stature. Geraldine might have long, braided hair and her brother Scotty a real pearl stickpin, but I was the only one to boast a Grandma Trask!

My pleasure in Grandma's rather stately appearances at Aunt Dagmar's was further enhanced by knowing, from Mother's and Father's conversation at home, that she had but a small opinion of Mother's relations. To Grandma, apparently, the Denisons were a pushing lot who had taken possession of her only son and dragged him from a Brooklyn that had been good enough for his parents. To that "unseemly scuttle across the East River" she ascribed each subsequent disaster, from Father's failure to do better in his trust company to the early failure of his liver. Mother used to say that Grandma condemned in the Denisons the very qualities of gaiety and openheartedness that she had distrusted but never dared to criticize in her own husband. Grandpa Trask, it seemed, by dying young, had become sanctified and was now mourned in the perennial black and evoked by the host of relics required by a Victorian tradition.

Mourning, however, to Grandma's generation, was too common to be always associated with gloom, and she led a brisk, busy life which included an annual trip to Europe with her old and good friends, the Jerome Robbinses. She and the Robbinses departed and returned each year, as closely as possible, on the same day. They went to London where they stayed at Brown's Hotel and to Paris where they stayed at the Vendôme, always in the same rooms. The only variety in their trips was in the different watering places which they visited in their long and ultimately vain effort to restore Mrs. Robbin's flagging health. The family joke used to be that Mr. Robbins had never seen Europe except with his back to the horse, as he always occupied the seat facing his wife and her devoted companion.

When Mrs. Robbins finally succumbed, early one spring, to the ailments that had so stubbornly resisted every spa, Grandma's trip to Europe was canceled for the first time since the Franco-Prussian War. All the next winter she grumbled about the inconvenience that her friend had caused her, and as another Europeless summer loomed, her plight seemed pitiable indeed.

"It seems such a shame," Mother said one night at supper when Father had just returned from a visit to Brooklyn. "Why on earth shouldn't your mother and Mr. Robbins go to Europe together as they always have?"

"But they are."

"They *are*?"

"Certainly." Father glanced at me for a second, and I thought he was about to wink. "As you say, why shouldn't they?"

"Well—" Mother's eye also fell on me, and she was silent, but it was the silence of deep reflection. "It's really only the boat, I suppose, that makes any matter. There's something about two at a table that looks so . . . so connubial."

"And think of those deck chairs, side by side," Father continued with a small smile. "And down in the hold, Vuitton trunk by Vuitton trunk."

"Ida," Mother said suddenly, "how should you like to go over with your grandmother this year? You could join us in Baden-Baden. Wouldn't it be fun to be on your own for a bit?"

"Oh, Mother!" I cried, breathless with excitement.

"Come now, Lily," my father protested, "if Mother needs a chaperon, we'll *all* go with her. I won't send a fifteen-year-old girl to do our job."

"Who said anything about a chaperon? I never heard anything so absurd. I simply thought it would be nice for your mother and Ida to have a chance to get to really know each other. Besides, your mother's not going till the end of June, and we're supposed to join the Herndons at Genoa on the eighteenth."

I could hardly believe anything so tremendous was going to occur, that something wouldn't happen to prevent it, such as Grandma's getting ill, or even dying, like poor Mrs. Robbins. There was not only the excitement of going abroad with Grandma, which held infinite possibilities in its sheer novelty, but there was the excitement of being left alone with Christopher and his nurse and the maids during the two weeks between Mother's and Father's sailing and Grandma's. It was one of the nicest things about Mother that she always understood and never resented such feelings.

"You must run the house so well," she told me, "that when Aunt Dagmar comes in the afternoon to check up, you can give her tea like a lady and have nothing to do but gossip!"

So occupied was I at home that it was not until the afternoon of my departure, when Aunt Dagmar took me down to the big, white, clean Cunarder to meet Grandma, that the full strangeness of the forthcoming trip burst upon me. Nobody had told me that Mother, in one of her economizing moments, had prevailed upon Grandma to share her cabin with me! When the whistle blew, and Aunt Dagmar left us, Grandma and I stared at each other suddenly like two children at a party who have been told to make friends.

"Come, Ida," she said at last in her flat tone, "we must go up on deck and wave goodbye to the Statue of Liberty."

Up in the air and the sudden sea breeze Mr. Robbins joined us in what I remember as a captain's cap (I don't know why he was entitled to it) and pumped my hand and let me look at the boats in the harbor through a huge black pair of binoculars. Later, at dinner, when I was allowed a glass of champagne, I began to feel, a bit giddily, that the trip might work out, after all. If it only hadn't been for sharing that cabin! I doubt if any bride ever approached the nuptial chamber with more apprehension than I approached Grandma's that night. Would I have to witness the dismantling of the famous wig? Or did she sleep in it? Once again it was Grandma who took the initiative. Poor woman, she must have dreaded that moment as much as I.

"You will get ready for bed first, Ida. In the bathroom. Take your things."

When I came out, I saw to my astonishment that Grandma, using a sheet and several towels with the dexterity of an accomplished seamstress, had hooked up a little tent that enshrouded her dressing table. She remained within its protective cover long after I had gone to bed, with only a muffled lamp, and I was beginning to wonder if she was going to sleep there, when the sheet was finally pulled back and Grandma emerged, like a sheik, in a big white cap and a billowing white wrapper, more clothed than when she had gone in. I sighed in relief and went to sleep. The trip had started well.

Mr. Robbins walked me around the deck in the morning and every morning thereafter. He was a short man with very short legs, a high bald dome and a long nose that gave him a rather intellectual appearance in contrast to his bright, natty clothes. He walked fast and talked briskly and wore a pince-nez with a flowing ribbon. He ran a streetcar company in New York and used to hold forth with great knowledge, but rather fatiguingly, about the transit problems of the city. He was the most impersonal man I have ever known; I doubt if there was much difference between his conversations with me and those with my grandmother or any other of his fellow passengers. I remember his telling an anecdote about the construction of the Third Avenue Elevated to a gentleman who simply walked away in the middle of it. Mr. Robbins, nothing daunted, perhaps not even noticing, completed the anecdote to the next gentleman who greeted him. Mother used to say that his habit of talking for his own benefit came from years of traveling with two women who never listened to him. But I was flattered to be treated as a grownup and considered boredom a perfectly reasonable price. Besides, Mr. Robbins bought me a small present every morning after our walk at the ship's store.

In the dining room we sat at a table for three, and at dinner Mr. Robbins would drink a great deal of champagne, very fast, throwing his head back as if he were gargling, which he said was the only way to drink it. He would then become rather disputatious and take evident pleasure in seeking to disillusion Grandma about the financial leaders of the era, in whose reputations for wisdom and generosity she had a persistent, peasantlike faith.

"Jim Herndon!" he would exclaim, naming the railroad executive whose yacht Mother and Father had boarded at Genoa. "Don't talk to me about Jim Herndon! I was a director of the Rhode Island Shore Line when he took over. Of course, he expected to find us a bunch of rubber stamps. Quite!" Here Mr. Robbins took another gulp of champagne. "Well, your friend Jay Robbins set him straight on that one. Oh, my yes! When I found what he was doing with our preferred stock, I said: 'Mr. Herndon, is it your intention to loot the company?' Well, he frowned and blustered like Jove, but when he learned that I was going to lay the minutes of the meeting before the Attorney General, I can tell you his voice became sweet as honey. "Perhaps you and I can have a little talk, Mr. Robbins.' 'Certainly, Mr. Herndon,' I said, 'we can have that little talk right here before the board. Unless you'd prefer to ask the Attorney General in now?' Well, you should have seen him back down. You should have heard his 'Yes, Mr. Robbins' and 'No, Mr. Robbins'! He knew when he had an honest man to deal with!"

"But you didn't remain on that board long, did you?" Grandma observed dryly.

"Of course I didn't!" Mr. Robbins retorted, banging down his glass on the table. "I tell you, Herndon wanted rubber stamps. He got rid of me as soon as he dared. But as long as I was on that board, he didn't loot that company, I can promise you that!"

"He probably had no intention of doing anything of the kind. You probably simply misunderstood him."

"Amelie!" Mr. Robbins retorted in high exasperation. "You don't know anything about business!"

"I may not know anything about business, but I think I know something about people. Mr. Herndon happens to be a friend of my son's. As a matter of fact, Gerald and Lily are guests on his yacht in the Mediterranean at this very moment. I hardly think that a son of mine would care to travel with a man who 'looted' companies."

"What does Gerald know about business? Gerald's a trust officer. In the crowd he and Lily play with, all that matters is how big a house a man has and how good a dinner he serves. What's it to them if he's a crook?"

"A *crook*, did you say? You insinuate that *my* son is on board the yacht of a crook?"

"If he's on Herndon's yacht, he is."

And so it went, back and forth, until Grandma made her stately withdrawal, after a single demitasse in the lounge. It was apparent even to me that they enjoyed these arguments. In the morning, meek once more, Mr. Robbins would mumble apologies for the champagne-incited rebellion of the previous night, and Grandma would nod, rather ungraciously, as if she had expected it all along. But I am afraid that she admired Mr. Herndon, whom she did not even know, more than she did Mr. Robbins. The latter was a small tycoon in an age of titans, and Grandma believed in titans.

It was unfortunate for Grandma that Florence Polhemus should have been on board. Miss Polhemus was the person she most respected in the world. She lived in Pierrepont Place in a square brownstone three-storied box with red velvet curtains looped over the windows so as almost to exclude the beautiful view of the East River. She had never married, according to legend, because of insanity in her family. She was very sweet, in a mechanical, repetitious way, and Mother always said that she was pretty, though it seemed to me an absurd term to use in relation to a woman past her seventieth year. Whenever I met Miss Polhemus at Grandma's, she told me that she, too, would have been an Ida, named for her mother, but for the circumstance of her birth in the capital of Tuscany where her father had been minister.

"Why does she always tell me the same thing?" I asked Grandma once.

"Because you always have the same name."

"But doesn't she remember she's told me before? She can't be very intelligent."

"You mustn't say that about Miss Polhemus," Grandma reproved me. "She has a million dollars."

How I remember Grandma's tone as she said that! For her there was no need of hypocrisy. When I think what pains Mother and all the Denisons took to emphasize the homely virtues of their rich friends and to praise the little-known acts of generosity and kindness for which they *really* loved them, I cannot but admire the simplicity of Grandma's attitude with its suggestion of an unsophisticated, unashamed early New York reverence for birth and property. The Polhemuses had outranked the Trasks in Brooklyn at the time of Grandma's marriage, and for her they always would. She would no more have considered herself the equal of her spinster friend because she had married and became a mother than would a matron of the court of Louis XV have presumed that her fecundity had placed her any nearer to the virgin daughters of France.

While making my tour of the deck with Mr. Robbins on the third morning out we encountered Miss Polhemus. She had evidently been ill, for it was her first appearance on deck, and her maid was tucking her into a chair. She stared at us blankly as we approached her chair and then gave a sudden little cry.

"Why, Jerome Robbins. I had no idea *you* were on board!"

"But I go every year on the *Mauritania*."

"You *did*. Of course, I know you *did*. But I didn't know you still do."

"That's my biography, Florence. I did, and I still do. And I shall continue, so help me, for the little time I may be spared."

I always minded when old people talked of the little time they had left. One of the things that I liked about Grandma was that she never did. Mr. Robbins and Miss Polhemus continued chatting for several minutes while I turned away to the railing. When she called me back, I thought she seemed flushed and excited.

"How is your grandmother, Ida?"

"Very well. Have you been seasick?"

"No, I have *not* been seasick," Miss Polhemus responded in a very definite tone. "I'm as old a sailor as your grandmother. Will you tell her that I shall wait upon her in her stateroom tonight if she is free?"

"Oh, I guess she's free now."

"I said tonight, my dear," Miss Polhemus insisted with a hint of mild correction. "I have no wish to intrude upon her while there are other calls on her time."

She nodded rather frostily to Mr. Robbins, but I did not know why until that night when I had gone to bed and Grandma received her visitor. They sat at the far end of the cabin, and spoke in hushed tones, but I could hear them distinctly.

"You must have been *so* upset when you discovered Jerome Robbins on the boat," Florence Polhemus began.

"Upset? Why should I have been upset?"

"Well, of course, nobody could think for a minute that you *arranged* it. I don't mean that. But in view of all the years that you and Carrie and he went abroad together—well, let us say it has an unfortunate appearance."

I remember distinctly that there was not even a hint of unpleasantness in Miss Polhemus' tone. There was an invincible sweetness about her, an unsurmountable attitude that one must, of course, agree with her, before which my poor grandmother could only crumble.

"How *does* it appear?"

"Surely, Amelie, you don't need an old maid to explain such things?"

"You mean that anyone could possibly think—!"

I shut my eyes quickly as both heads turned on the same impulse to make sure I was asleep.

"I have never considered what it is that people think," Miss Polhemus continued serenely. "I was brought up to believe that certain things looked badly and certain things looked well. *Why* they looked badly or well was never the point."

"You mean it's as bad for a woman my age to go to Europe with an old man as it would be for two young people?"

"Worse! A woman your age should know better!"

"Now, Florence, you're being absurd! Don't you know that after seventy there are things—?"

"Please, Amelie. I'd rather *not* know!"

"But, my dear, it's too ridiculous. I suppose I should be flattered!"

"*Amelie!*"

In the pause that followed, Miss Polhemus must have stared my grandmother down, for when she spoke again it was in an even sweeter, firmer tone.

"I came in tonight as a friend, as I'm sure you recognize. And I know you'll take my advice, as I would take yours. Isn't that the way things have always been between us?"

"I suppose so," Grandma answered sulkily. "But what can I do about it now? Get off in a lifeboat?"

"You should do nothing that would attract the least attention. But you and Jerome must not stay at the same hotel. And you must not allow him to handle your passport or to make the arrangements about your luggage. If he dines with you in Paris, you must have Ida with you. You must never travel on the same train, and you must return on different boats."

"But I'll have to rearrange everything!" Grandma protested with a wail.

"That, my dear, is a mere detail," Miss Polhemus said, rising.

When she had gone, I realized how much she had upset her friend. For Grandma had actually commenced her preparations for the removal of the famous wig without first erecting the protective tent! She brought out a small wooden stand, evidently to place it on, and two little silver brushes. I realized in sudden fascination and horror that there must be a whole nocturnal ceremony of brushing, adorning, perhaps even washing the wretched thing, and that it was to be my awe-inspiring privilege to be a witness. I closed my eyes just in time as Grandma turned sharply around to check on me again, and I did not reopen them until the dread business of dismantlement was already in process. Grandma, using all ten fingers, slowly raised the wig, held it for a second above her head to be sure that it was clear and then moved it to the stand and started to work on it busily with both little brushes. What appalled me most, as it had appalled the witnesses to the execution of Mary Stuart, was not to find that she had *no* hair, but to see instead the long, sad, thin, grey wisps. Grandma's profile seemed suddenly that of a very old and broken woman, an impression created not only by the grey wisps but by the unaccountable and dismal fact that she was weeping. Grandma was actually weeping! It was not that I thought of her as hard, but simply as a being with whom tears had no known relation. And now, like a child, she was weeping at the disruption of her plans, at the break in a pattern that was probably the only thing that made sense out of the chaos of her widowhood. I ached to run over and fling my arms about her, but I knew that she would never forgive me for seeing her so exposed. I could only lie there miserably and watch that sobbing figure brushing fiercely at the high pile of shiny black locks in front of her. And when she had finished and dabbed her eyes with the corner of a handkerchief, I found she had still another surprise in store for me. She put on a nightcap that had locks of sewn-in black curls along its border! Grandma was now ready for every contingency of marine disaster.

In the morning she seemed herself again, except that she was more preoccupied than usual at breakfast. When I was about to leave the table, she put her hand suddenly on my arm and asked me in a very grave tone: "Tell me something, Ida. Should you mind terribly spending three weeks in Paris before joining your mother and father in Baden-Baden?"

I hesitated unhappily. The novelty of being with Grandma had begun to wear off, and I was already homesick for my parents. But I remembered what Miss Polhemus had said about the value of my company to Grandma, and I hated to disappoint her.

"Oh, I don't know. What would I do in Paris?"

"It won't be very gay for you," Grandma conceded, "but you can learn a great deal about French history from Mr. Robbins. He's quite an expert, you know. And when we get back to New York . . . I'll give you . . ." Her words, after the pause, came in a rush: ". . . my little ruby bracelet that you used to admire. Do you remember it?"

"Oh, Grandma, no!"

Nothing could have convinced me more vividly of her desperate need than this sudden, shocking bribe. We faced each other with startled eyes, and when I recovered, I knew that our relationship was altered.

"I don't need a present, thank you, Grandma," I said a bit primly. "If Mother will let me, I'll be glad to stay."

"You're a good girl, Ida," she said with an immediate humility that made me wince. "Of course, I was silly about the bracelet."

That afternoon she had a long conference in the lounge with Mr. Robbins, which I could observe from the table where I was playing solitaire. They consulted papers and maps, and he seemed a good deal agitated and cleared his throat continuously. I learned afterwards that they were reorganizing their whole summer trip to conform to Miss Polhemus' specifications. Poor Mr. Robbins had to change his hotel in Paris, and the trips to Dinard and the château country were canceled. It was decided that they would spend their time in the French capital and see each other daily, but under certain definite conditions. And one of those conditions, undoubtedly the most stringent, was that *I* should always be present.

Paris in 1904! Who does not think of trim carriages in the leafy Bois and big, plumed hats and the blurry greens and whites of Renoir and of Yvette Guilbert and an elegance the more haunting in retrospect for being doomed? But I think of these things only with a conscious effort. The memory that is first conjured up is of the somber, paneled dining room in Grandma's hotel and the discreet clink of glasses and chink of silver as a dozen Americans ate silently and chewed long. Paris to me will always be a grey, damp city where old people talk—incomprehensibly—of love.

After only a few days in Paris the daily pattern asserted itself. Mr. Robbins would call at our hotel in the morning, and he and Grandma would chat for half an hour in the courtyard. Then Mr. Robbins would take me out for a walk. I would come back to the hotel to lunch alone with Grandma, and at three o'clock Mr. Robbins would call for us in a Victoria, and we would drive in the Bois, or sometimes on expeditions as far as Saint-Germain or Saint-Cloud. In the evening we all dined at the hotel, and Mr. Robbins always brought Grandma an orchid.

It was a slow life for a girl, but I was used to being alone with my elders, and it was a strong principle of the Denisons that the pleasures of children were incidental to the conveniences of adults. What I liked most (or, perhaps I should say, what bored me least) was the morning walk with Mr. Robbins. His hobby was Cardinal Richelieu, and his knowledge of seventeenth century Paris was copious and detailed. We spent a great deal of time poking about the Palais Royal, the Louvre and the old hotels of the Place des Vosges. I was reading and adoring *The Three Musketeers*. Richelieu to me was a fascinating villain in sweeping scarlet who was always tearing about Paris in a great rumbling coach, escorted by guards with red tunics and white crosses who were ambushed at every turn by the king's musketeers. There was little in common between my cardinal and Mr. Robbins' dry statesman who had established the first post office and the French Academy. In fact, at times it seemed to me that he was doing to Richelieu what adults did to everything, that he was changing him from a figure of glamour into one who had tried to strip history of what little glamour it possessed. But at least we were each interested in a man in red robes, and as we slowly paced the gardens of the Palais Royal, we had each our picture of him.

It was after one of these walks that Mr. Robbins gave me an envelope for Grandma. I handed it to her just before we went in to lunch, and she read it in the foyer. She seemed very upset during our meal and afterwards, before going back up to her room, she said: "You will tell Mr. Robbins, Ida, that I have a headache and cannot go out this afternoon. But I suggest that you go and give him a letter that I will leave at the desk."

Mr. Robbins drew up promptly at three o'clock in the Victoria. The project for that afternoon was the Cluny Museum. He seemed much put out about Grandma's headache and coughed nervously as he read the letter. He then made the first personal remark that I had ever heard him make prior to his consumption of the evening quota of champagne.

"Women!" he exclaimed. "Women! If there's a way of complicating a simple situation, trust a woman to find it!"

I was old enough to know that when adults made remarks like this, they

were not referring to family but to romantic relations. There was no implication that Mr. Robbins could not trust women like Mother or Aunt Dagmar. But there was a definite implication that Mr. Robbins could not trust
Grandma, and therefore their relationship had to be romantic.

"Have you put *your* faith in Grandma?"

"I've asked her to be my wife!" he exploded. "If that's not putting your
faith in woman, I'd like to know what is!"

"And she won't?"

"She doesn't believe in second marriages," he said gruffly, already regretting his indiscretion. "Of course, she's entitled to her point of view. I daresay
it does her credit. But, for myself, I could never see the point of eternal
mourning."

"Did Richelieu ever marry?"

"Of course not. He was a priest."

"Do you suppose that was why he was such a great man?"

Mr. Robbins slapped his hand on his knee. "By golly, it wouldn't surprise me in the least!"

As it turned out, the rejection of Mr. Robbins made little difference in
our daily round. He continued to drive out and to dine with us as if nothing had happened. Grandma and I were alone only at lunch, for she breakfasted in her room. These lunches were always the same. Grandma ordered
the table d'hôte and made me drink Perrier water instead of wine. But she
allowed me to select what I wanted from the pastry tray which almost made
up for it. My awe of her had been reduced by her proffered bribe of the
ruby bracelet, and the day after my discussion with Mr. Robbins, I asked
her bluntly: "Why don't you marry Mr. Robbins?"

Grandma was startled, but I could see at once that she was not as startled
as I had expected her to be.

"I don't know if that's a proper question for you to ask."

But I knew that she was only dodging me, and I repeated: "Why don't
you?"

"In the first place, it would not be loyal to your grandfather. He was a
very fine and good man."

"But how can you be loyal to someone who's dead?"

"He seems dead to you, Ida, because you never knew him."

"But he's still dead, isn't he?" I protested. "Hasn't he been dead for years
and years?"

"Years and years seem longer to some people than to others."

"If you died first, do you think he'd never have remarried?"

I saw by the grave way that she settled her blue eyes on me that I had
really startled her now. My indiscreet speculation had put a solid period to
our discussion, and I could never again get Grandma to revert to it.

I wrote my parents, who had finished their cruise and were now in Baden-
Baden for Father's cure, all about Grandma and Mr. Robbins, and my letter had a greater effect than I could have possibly foreseen. They agreed at
once that one of them should go to Paris and see that Grandma did not
jeopardize her happiness for an outdated scruple. Mother felt that as an

in-law she was less intimate with Grandma and could present the case more effectively, and Father, whom an attack of asthma had robbed of much of his energy, finally agreed. She gave neither Grandma nor myself any notice, but simply arrived one evening before dinner. I cried out with surprise and joy when I saw her tall figure in a dark traveling suit by the desk, and she turned, smiling, to take me in her arms. Mother was never one for public demonstrations, but she always knew when to make an exception.

She and Grandma, for all their differences, had a definite mutual respect. Grandma appreciated Mother's practical contributions to Father's business and social life, while Mother admired Grandma's independence as a widow and the way she was able to fill her life without appealing to the sympathies of a married son. But to her the limitations of Grandma's social and religious thinking were the limitations of a quaint and bygone era. Mother treated Grandma with the outward respect and inner amusement of a British admiral greeting an Indian rani. They formed an odd couple together in the ensuing hot July days: Grandma so small and black and dignified, a being indifferent to and unaffected by weather, and Mother, so tall and towering in white, with her veil tucked up under her big feathered hat and beads of perspiration on her brow and under her eyes. Nobody could be more impressive than Mother in the right clothes, at the right time. The long lines of the Edwardian dress and the wide-brimmed hats were perfectly adapted to her strong, straight figure, and with her easy gait and swinging parasol, with her loud, high laugh and fine boldness of demeanor she was a striking figure on any boulevard. But at the same time, perhaps from her very bigness, she seemed more affected by changes in weather and temperature than other women of her generation. When Mother cried "Brr!" and flung a scarf around a neck or "Whew!" and mopped a dripping brow, there was a naturalness in her gesture that made it an attractive contrast to her otherwise neat and ordered look. This note of the commonplace, or even sometimes of the faintly comic, was why she even looked well in the absurd black bathing suits and long stockings of the period. Grandma would not have appeared in one of them to save her life.

Our Paris routine continued the same, except that Mother now joined us on the afternoon excursions, full, as always, of comment and suggestions. But in the mornings, while I was out with Mr. Robbins, she had a series of long talks with Grandma. Much later she told me about them. Poor Grandma, it appeared, was suffering from an apprehension common to her generation; she was afraid of confronting Grandpa with Mr. Robbins in the next life. She visualized the encounter against a background of highly specific detail. She and Mr. Robbins would be walking uptown home after church on Sunday and would run smack into Grandpa. She told Mother that she was afraid that Grandpa would laugh at Mr. Robbins. It was probably just what he would have done.

"But have you never thought that *he* might have married again?" Mother interposed.

"He? Who's he?"

"Mr. Trask, of course."

"My dear Lily, surely you're not implying that your father-in-law could have been guilty of bigamy?"

"I don't mean that he married again *here*. Obviously, we know he couldn't have done that. I mean that he may have married again *there*."

Grandma became very grave at this. "I don't think it's right, Lily, to make fun of sacred things."

"Who's making fun of them? I'm perfectly serious. Why shouldn't Mr. Trask have married again in the next life? Why, for that matter, shouldn't he have married Mrs. Robbins?"

"Carrie Robbins was an invalid!"

"Ah, but not *there*."

"I must say, Lily, I had no idea you had this whimsical turn of mind. Of course, people don't marry in heaven!"

"You mean, there are no marriages there? I hate to think that."

"I mean there are no marriages *performed* there."

Mother now made her crushing point. "If there are no marriages performed there, it's because God doesn't permit them. And if He doesn't permit people to *get* married, why should He permit them to *be* married?"

"Then you and Gerald won't be married there?"

I imagine that Mother looked away at this. Though she never boasted about it, she regarded her own marriage as uniquely happy and not to be compared to others. "I'm sure that Gerald and I will be very good friends there," she said lightly. "At the least. But that's *your* point, Mrs. Trask, not mine. I believe that marrying *and* marriages exist there. Aren't all things possible in heaven?"

Grandma became very thoughtful, but she said no more on the subject that day. However, it came to be tacitly understood between them that the topic could be reopened each morning. After only two sessions Mother had led Grandma out of the thickets of her religious difficulties, and was clearing a quick path through the underbrush of practical considerations. Did Grandma want to know how Gerald would feel about her remarriage? Why, he was all for it! *For* it? Grandma really stared. Did Lily mean that he knew about it? That they had been discussing it?

"Why, ever since poor Mrs. Robbins died!" Mother exclaimed boldly. "Even before, if the truth be told. I know that sounds terrible, but it's the way we are. You may as well accept it."

"But I never discussed any such things about *my* mother," Grandma replied, deeply disturbed. "Not even with my own sisters. I never heard of such a thing!"

"Times have changed."

"Not for the better, I fear."

"But it's only because Gerald loves you, Mrs. Trask!" Mother protested with an opportune demonstration of feeling. "He loves you and wants you to be happy!"

One by one, Grandma's poor little objections, like gawky, conscripted farmers, were summoned up, drilled, reviewed and dismissed. There was no escape on the broad, clean parade ground of Mother's determination, where the least misstep sounded like the retort of a pistol. Grandma's final scruple was the simplest of all. She believed that it was a wife's absolute duty to leave all she had to her husband, and how could she leave the little pile of securities that she had salvaged from Grandpa's extravagance away from his own son and grandchildren?

"But, bless my soul, Mr. Robbins would never hear of it!" Mother exclaimed. "He's far too much of a gentleman. As a matter of fact, though I hate to mention it, if you married him, it would probably be to Gerald's advantage. After all, Mr. Robbins has no children of his own."

Everybody in the family always thought that Mother did a wonderful job that summer. Father used laughingly to describe it as the time when she made an "honest woman" of her mother-in-law. But I have often wondered if she didn't overdo it. She meant well, of course; she meant enormously well. She could not bear, sensible, practicable woman that she was, to see Grandma lose an innocent happiness for a handful of ridiculous scruples. But Mother, like all of her family, never made allowance for the power of her own personality. She took it too much for granted that no woman of Grandma's generation could be dominated by any woman of hers. She did not realize how much of her mother-in-law's seeming strength was simply reserve and dignity. Far from home and faced with a strange, bewildering problem, Grandma allowed herself to be taken in hand by her big, kindly, reassuring, fast-talking daughter-in-law. But I doubt very much if, left to herself in Brooklyn, she would ever have married again. Marriage to her meant Grandpa and love, and that had been over three decades before. All that she wanted from Mr. Robbins was the continuation of the schedule of bygone summers, lightly flavored with the atmosphere of an indefinitely protracted courtship. She liked her daily drive and her daily orchid and her daily argument over the bottle of champagne. She liked to talk about friends and relations to the waltzes of a three-piece orchestra at tea time. And it could even add to the delights of the situation if some of Mr. Robbins' old friends, as the romance prolonged itself, should see fit, sitting in their club windows, to describe her whisperingly as "cruel." Wasn't it all that Mr. Robbins really wanted, too?

But, no, they could not be allowed so little. The old have in common with children that if something is fun, it is bound to be stopped. Grandma and Mr. Robbins had to do the sound, sensible, up-to-date "Denison" thing. Miss Polhemus was much less demanding than Mother; she insisted only that they be proper. Mother insisted that they be happy. When Grandma had at last been induced to yield to the respectful importunity of Mr. Robbins, she was frightened by the burst of congratulation in the messages from relatives and friends. Aunt Dagmar cabled from Long Island, and Uncle Victor and Aunt Sophie came up from Dinard and Uncle Philip from the château country. The Denisons seemed to be claiming poor Grandma as one of their own. She became Mrs. Robbins in the private episcopal chapel of one of Mother's expatriate friends in the presence of her son and daughter-in-law, two of her daughter-in-law's brothers, a granddaughter and Miss

Polhemus, who wept copiously throughout the ceremony. Grandma wore a dark brown dress, which was as far as Mother could make her depart from her habitual black, and a round straw hat with yellow flowers. There was something faintly macabre about such a note of gaiety over her expression of sober resolution, and when she leaned down to kiss me at the chapel door, I wondered if her rather bleary, preoccupied eyes had even recognized me. I remember speculating if Mr. Robbins would now see her without her wig. Perhaps, poor woman, it was what she was speculating herself. Perhaps it was exactly what her second marriage meant to her.

But I feel sure now that Mr. Robbins never saw the wig removed. When they returned to New York and settled in his house in Manhattan, Grandma brought over a few favored pieces of furniture from Brooklyn and put them in her own bedroom. This became her private domain and her only one; the rest of the house she left as it had been in the days of the first Mrs. Robbins. It stands to this day, occupied by an antique dealer, and whenever I pass it, I think of Mother's description of Mr. Robbins as a man with one million, and of his house as a slice off the house of a man with many. For its narrow grey limestone façade, no more than twenty feet in width, is covered with grinning lions' head and balconies for flowerpots supported by squatting ladies, and topped with a giant dormer studded with bull's-eye windows. Nobody passing it today would believe that it had not been built by the most pushing parvenu. Yet I know how little the houses of that era sometimes expressed the souls of their occupants.

I tried at times in the ensuing years to recapture some of the intimacy that Grandma and I had enjoyed in Paris, but I never really succeeded. She had retreated to her old position as the rather stately head of her little family, and I was no longer especially favored. Perhaps she was embarrassed to consider all that I had seen and heard. But I often felt in the lower pitch of her voice when she addressed me and in the extra flicker of her smile in my direction when I took my leave that I at least reminded her of a period of very special emotion. When Mr. Robbins died, she gave me his notebook about Richelieu with a card on which she had written: "For dear Ida, in memory of happier days when she was *such* a comfort to her Grandma."

It was so like her to think of needing a "comfort" in "happier" days. Grandma never quite trusted happiness. Certainly there was very little of it in her second widowhood. Mr. Robbins left her the income of his whole estate, but stipulated that the principal should go to two of his nephews on her death. It was a handsome provision for a second wife, but nobody could persuade Grandma of that. She felt that he should have trusted her to leave his money back to his family. In a curious mood of retaliation, she cut her expenses to a minimum, remaining in the town house winter and summer with only one old servant, in order to save out of her Robbins income a small pile of money to leave to her Trask grandchildren. Perhaps it was thus that she tried to make up to Grandpa for her great and sole disloyalty. But the surname on her tombstone bears witness to this day that in the crisis of her later years she succumbed to the philosophy of Fifty-third Street. It seemed to me at my impressionable age that I could only follow suit.

PART TWO
THE COMING OF DERRICK

5

DERRICK: 1911

WHEN DERRICK HARTLEY came to New York in the fall of 1911, he was twenty-seven, and, having buried both his parents, was possessed of a small competence. He had graduated from Harvard and worked for five years in a Boston trust company before the final illnesses, in quick succession, of his father and mother, and the ensuing necessity of salvaging what he could of the family property, had brought him back to the village near Concord where he had been born. Now it was over; the little white house on the green, to which his father had moved on retirement from ecclesiastical duties, and all the china and furniture, a modest lot, had been sold, twin marble slabs erected in the cemetery plot and the past seemingly liquidated. Derrick had been fond of his parents, but he had never professed himself a man of intimacies or dependencies, and he kept one eye, and sometimes two, on the future. There were obvious advantages, from an unsentimental point of view, in facing it disencumbered. He prudently invested the small proceeds of his father's estate, made arrangements by correspondence to share the Tenth Street flat of a bachelor friend, ordered two suits from an expensive tailor and resigned his position, with many diplomatic expressions of good will, at the trust company. He was at last ready for Wall Street and Linnaeus Tremain.

He had not seen Mr. Tremain since he had been a boy at Shelby School and a friend of his son Charley, but he had never forgotten the cool, appraising, yet not unkindly eye with which that tall, trim, slowly moving gentleman had seemed to take in every boy, every building, every master, as if to put them up on some auction block in his mind where one felt sure they would fetch but a small sum. Derrick had sat with him on the porch of the parents' house all one Sunday afternoon and had been fascinated at how quickly and surely Charley's inert, cigar-smoking, lazily questioning father had laid bare the very heart of the institution.

"I approach everything in life as if I were going to buy it," Mr. Tremain had explained. "Both things spiritual and things material. It's a useful little habit that I recommend. Even God has His price, you know. It may be faith or prayer, rather than cash or credit, but it's still a price."

Derrick at home had been used to the daily, almost hourly deference to the distinction between flesh and spirit. It was exhilarating at last to hear it categorically denied. It seemed to him a very splendid thing to be, like Mr. Tremain, in absolute control of one's tiny corner of the universe, and

not a gangling, sheepishly smiling sentimentalist like his own father who
always had a cowlick in his hair and dandruff on the shoulders of his black
suit. It was the affliction of Derrick's life that the Reverend Hartley, whose
parish abutted on the grounds of Shelby, should have been asked, out of
the headmaster's courtesy and neighborly spirit, to preach at the school
chapel once a term. He was known to the boys as "Reverend Tug" because
of a sermon in which he had drawn a parallel between a Christian and a
tugboat. Were not both engaged in God's work of pushing others ahead?
Derrick knew, of course, that he owed his scholarship in Shelby, a church
school, to the proximity of his clerical parent, but he sometimes wondered
if it was worth it. Not until Mr. Tremain had told him that some of the
most successful men in the business world were sons of New England ministers did it occur to him that there might be an asset side to the "Reverend
Tug."

Charley, always a frail boy, had died of pneumonia the following year,
and there had been no occasion for Derrick to see the stricken Mr. Tremain
again. But that image of silent competence, so free of cant, had remained
in mind through the rest of school and college days, and, afterwards, at the
trust company, Derrick had always been alert to any reference to the New
York investment house of Tremain & Dodge. Though relatively small, its
reputation had penetrated to Boston, and Derrick often heard Linnaeus
Tremain spoken of as an "artist" among underwriters. Apparently he had
never been known to visit a plant or factory or to read any more about one
than its bare financial statement. No market crisis had been allowed to interrupt his trips in search of Italian primitives or even his late afternoon whist
at the Knickerbocker Club. A glance at the ticker tape seemed to tell him
all he needed; he could see a forest in every tree. As Derrick gradually put
the picture together, it became his fixed conviction that Tremain's was the
studio where he must learn his art.

When he sent in his card, on his first visit to Wall Street, after settling
himself in New York, he had scribbled on it: "I wonder if you remember
me from Shelby?" It came back with the message, "I remember you perfectly. Please wait," and wait he had to, for an hour. At last he was ushered
into a dark, rather small office with linen-fold paneling and three small brilliantly colored religious paintings with lights over them. Mr. Tremain did
not even look up. He was examining a stamp through a heavy magnifying
glass with a stout silver handle. Derrick interpreted the pose as favorable to
himself.

The old ham, he reflected, as he sat himself, uninvited, before the desk.
I bet he's been rehearsing it for the past hour.

Mr. Tremain looked as lean and gaunt as he had looked a dozen years
before, but his long, thick hair had turned a snowy white and his dark skin
was even browner. The clear, almost childish, light blue eyes over the aquiline nose now fixed their gaze on Derrick.

"Would you like to see a Laga Canal 'blue' issue of 1887?" he asked
abruptly. "I believe this is one of three specimens in existence."

Derrick rose to take the proffered glass and leaned over to squint at the
dusky profile of Queen Victoria. He knew nothing of stamps and was sure

that Mr. Tremain would be waspish if he pretended to. He simply nodded and resumed his seat.

"I've come to ask you for a job, sir."

"Presuming, no doubt, on your friendship with my dead boy?"

Derrick looked up in astonishment to catch the flash of hostility in those suddenly kindled eyes.

"I should have presumed before now had I been going to. I've been out of Harvard five years."

Mr. Tremain stared back at him for a moment and then nodded. Evidently he was satisfied, but Derrick, with a quick breath, vowed that *he*, at least, would not soon forget so wanton an insult.

"Tell me about yourself," the older man continued with a shrug. "I mean, the part after school. I remember that your father was a parson and that you had a scholarship. You were a prefect, too, weren't you? And then you went to Harvard?"

Derrick briefly described his career in Cambridge and at the trust company. "Of course, I realize it doesn't amount to much," he concluded with a candor that invited no rebuttal. "The only thing that might interest you is my resolution about working for your firm. It seems to be a case of Tremain or nobody."

Mr. Tremain looked critically down at his long white folded hands. "You mean if I don't give you a job, you won't go to work at all?"

"Not while my money holds out."

"Then I hope you are rich, Mr. Hartley. For I tell you frankly, I haven't an opening. And I may not have one for a year."

"I can wait a year."

"But I can't promise you one even then. I might die or retire. If you wait for me, you may wait till Doomsday."

"I guess that's my lookout."

Mr. Tremain's eyes narrowed in what might have been either surprise or irritation. It was difficult to tell. As Derrick had first surmised, he was a real ham.

"Would you mind explaining this remarkable compliment to me? If it is a compliment?"

"I want to learn about money from a man who knows about money without being impressed by it. Or by anyone who has it. I want to learn from a man who wouldn't hesitate to say: 'To hell with you!' to anyone he damn pleased. And just because he pleased!"

"Dear me. And you think *I'd* do that?"

"Look at the way you told *me* off."

"But, my dear Mr. Hartley, you happen to be a very unimportant young man."

"I won't always be."

"Perhaps not. But you are now. Do you think I'd walk down to 23 Wall Street and tell Pierpont Morgan to go to hell?"

"I think you'd be quite capable of it."

Mr. Tremain laughed cheerfully. "Well, I see your game, and I like it. You're trying to describe me as you think I want to see myself. And you're probably laughing up your sleeve at me all the time. Why not? It's perfectly fair. But what *I* must consider is that if I take you on, I'll never get rid of you. I can see you're the type that sticks. You'd expect to be a junior partner and then a senior partner. I daresay you'd wind up as my executor and liquidate my estate!"

"Why not?"

"Oh, come, Mr. Hartley, now you're overdoing it," the older man said dryly. "I don't like that. You may leave your name and address with my secretary, but I repeat: I have no openings, and I don't expect any."

Derrick was good to his word about seeking no other employment. When he left the office of Tremain & Dodge, he went uptown and made his plans for the waiting period. His friend Harry Prime, a gentle and amiable bachelor who worked for a small, quiet law firm of old name and diminishing status, was glad to continue the arrangement about his apartment, and Derrick set aside from his capital the goodly percentage of it which he estimated would be needed to defray the expenses of a year in New York. He then settled down to enjoy himself, for he knew that it was not in his nature to prepare for a job by reading economic tracts. He was a man who had to work altogether or play.

Fortunately, New York in 1911 was an amusing place for a bachelor to play. Society was still homogeneous, and Derrick found that his looks, his self-assurance and his Shelby and Harvard connections brought him invitations to a number of dinner parties and receptions. He and Harry would dress for the evening over a glass of sherry and stroll to a bar on Sixth Avenue where, standing under a monumental painting of a Roman banquet, they would eat oysters and drink a Martini cocktail. From there they would progress to one of those stately dinners where the excellence of the food and the variety of the wines, the profusion of scented flowers and the gleam of silver and gold over square yards of damask went far to make up—at least to young eyes which, as Derrick quite recognized, were still dazzled—for the general mediocrity of the conversation. He found that for a few weeks, or even months, he could be content to sip Moselle or champagne while the ladies on either side of him chattered across his white shirt about servants. He was free to indulge in fantasies that he was as rich as his host, with a centerpiece that had belonged to Napoleon and a Gainsborough duchess over the mantel. Afterwards, back in the apartment, he and Harry would discuss their host, and whether the money had been earned, married or inherited, over a glass of brandy. In the morning he would take long walks, or ride in the Park, and every afternoon he practiced billiards at the Harvard Club.

One night he found that his dinner partner was a large, vigorous, friendly woman called Mrs. Gerald Trask. She was the kind of woman who easily elicited confidences, and when he had told her about his ambitions for a job in Tremain & Dodge, he was startled to discover that she was the younger sister of Mrs. Tremain.

"I should think Linn could use a young man like you in his shop," she observed. "I know if anyone cared that much about working for *me*, I'd find a place for him."

"Of course, your brother-in-law can pick anyone he chooses."

"Not quite. And, besides, enthusiasm is a rare flower. I'll tell him you ought to be plucked."

"Will he take your advice?"

"I can't say. The poor man is singularly afflicted with sisters-in-law. But he and I are rather special. At worst, it will do you no harm."

It didn't. On the following Saturday afternoon, when Derrick was at the billiard table of the Harvard Club, surrounded by a silent, smoking group, he happened to make a brilliant shot, and there was a little burst of applause. As he turned to acknowledge it, he spotted Linnaeus Tremain, expressionless except for a grim wisp of a smile about the corners of his lips, standing at the edge of the group. At the end of his game Derrick went over to him.

"I understand that you live entirely for pleasure now," Mr. Tremain remarked gruffly, taking a tightly clenched cigar from between his teeth. "I hear you have become a society playboy."

"Whose fault is that?"

"My word, you *are* a bold one. But tell me, do you think you could analyze a financial statement as sharply as you made that last stroke?"

"If somebody would let me try."

"Well, I suppose 'somebody' mustn't be responsible for your continued idleness," Mr. Tremain said with a little grunt. "I shall expect you in the office on Monday morning. At half past eight."

It was a moment for jubilation, even for impertinence. "So Doomsday's here at last!" Derrick exclaimed with a little shout of laughter, and brandishing his cue, he returned to the billiard table.

As he had hoped and expected, he liked everything about Tremain & Dodge, from the great high-ceilinged front hall of yellowing marble, with its ponderous brass chandeliers and row of cashier's windows, to the comfortable paneled offices of the partners, the black oak conference room with its ticker tape machine on a malachite stand and the long gallery of whiskered portraits beneath which old grey-coated clerks, seated on stools at high tables, made entries in ledger books in an atmosphere of Victorian fidelity. Derrick worked exclusively for Mr. Tremain, as he had wanted, and the long hours interfered with his social life, but that had been a fill-in at best and easy to give up. All his attention was now absorbed by his job and the fascinating study of his new employer. Derrick had a feeling that Mr. Tremain's mind never wandered far from Wall Street. Whatever he was doing, whether presiding over a dinner table surrounded by his wife's guests and relations, or bargaining for a tryptich at Duveen's, or playing whist at the Knickerbocker Club and puffing silently at a long cigar, Derrick suspected that the back of his mind was a jigsaw puzzle of mergers and reorganizations and new ventures over which his subconscious or half-conscious self was always languidly presiding, in the relaxed but confident search of the right price. Compared to the brief ecstasy of such discoveries, his travels, his paintings, even his lovely wife were but shadows. Had Charley lived, it might have been otherwise, but Charley had not lived, and the greater part of his father's heart must have died with him.

Derrick, on the other hand, was no artist; he was interested in what the business would do for him. He wanted elementary things, like money and power. But he enjoyed the means quite as much as he expected to enjoy the ends, and his mind embraced affectionately each tool of his ambition, the small as well as the large. It was not only the work in the office that fascinated him; it was the office itself. Derrick loved to figure out the deficiencies of the file system and to calculate to the penny the cost of surplus office boys and stenographers.

"If we ever *do* make you a partner," Mr. Tremain would grumble whenever Derrick pointed out such things, "one of the conditions will be that you take over our housekeeping."

"How much longer do you think you can afford to wait?"

"A good bit longer than you think!"

Their relationship was pleasant, at times almost intimate, but curiously lacking in affection of any real depth. They needed each other too much and understood each other too well. Derrick knew that the older man's hardness was a front for a repressed sentimentality which was in turn a front for a deeper layer of hardness. What he wanted was another son, and he respected Derrick for eschewing the role at the same time that he deplored his being neither sufficiently mawkish nor sufficiently calculating to attempt it. Mr. Tremain had buried his only love, and Derrick did not believe that his would ever be born. It was a bond, but not an easy one.

On Sunday nights the Tremains had family supper in the big red French Renaissance house on Fifty-third Street, and Derrick was soon a regular guest. Mr. Tremain called it "family supper," but Derrick soon made out that the family was all his wife's. The Denisons talked very fast and ribbed each other and were always laughing, and the Sunday evenings were lively. There Derrick met again Mrs. Gerald Trask, who winked at him conspiratorially, and her handsome, affable brother, Dr. Victor Denison. He noted that Mr. Tremain was amused by his brothers-in-law, but evidently had no very high regard for their intellectual capacities, while they, although respecting his brains and success, clearly found him heavy going at a party. For Mr. Tremain usually said very little or else spoke at considerable length, both habits incompatible with the kind of breezy repartee in which his wife's family specialized. But Derrick began to suspect that the Denisons were capable of more design than he had first apprehended when he found himself for the third consecutive Sunday seated next to Ida Trask.

She was a junior at Barnard and passionately proud of the fact. To go to college, she told him straight off, she had had to overcome a formidable and united family opposition. Actually, as her mother had already explained to him, this opposition had amounted to little more than friendly scoffing. Mrs. Trask did not really disapprove of college for women, but she decidedly disapproved of bluestockings, and Ida's tendencies in this direction had to be watched. Derrick, listening now to Ida, agreed with her mother. He liked her large, worried, limpid brown eyes, the heart shape of her face and the fine, high line of her cheekbones. But he could not equally approve her general lack of gracefulness and the excitement and volubility of her conversation. She was in the throes of a reaction to what she regarded as her family's worldliness and complacency, and she loved to chatter of the abolition of slums and the raising of educational standards. She was much upset when she discovered that Derrick did not share her enthusiasms.

"But don't you *care* that there are people in Harlem who sleep twelve in a room?"

"Care? Of course I don't *care*. I deplore it, I condemn it, whatever you want, but I don't care. I don't enjoy my dinner tonight a whit the less because of it. Do *you*?"

"I think I do," she answered thoughtfully. "I think I really do."

"Well, it's wasted worry," he retorted. "It does nobody any good. I make a point of caring only about the things I'm responsible for. The things I can *do* something about."

"Everything else can go to rack and ruin?"

"I didn't say that. I can promise you that if I owned any buildings in Harlem, my tenants would *not* sleep twelve in a room."

"Only nine, I suppose."

"Now, Miss Trask, that's hardly fair. You penalize a man because he's honest. I'm a relative stranger in New York, working in a humble job. You come of an influential family with every sort of social connection. But what are *you* doing about Harlem? You're looking extremely pretty, in what I imagine to be a very expensive dress, eating your aunt's excellent dinner and posing as a friend of the masses!"

"But Aunt Dagmar *gave* me this dress!" she protested excitedly. "And can *I* help it if she has a good cook? And . . . and . . ." She paused in perplexity and then flushed as he burst out laughing. "And what's more, I think you're horrid!"

But he was quite satisfied that she did not. He could see that she wanted nothing better than a man to convert, and he deduced from the eagerness with which she went about it that the candidates had so far been few. In the short time that those things take he found himself regarded as Ida's property at her aunt's Sunday night suppers. She would jump up now, when he came in, to appropriate him and pick up the argument where they had left it the week before.

"I thought you'd be interested to know that I talked to Professor Stookey —he teaches American history—about your theories on how the railroads got their land. He doesn't agree with you at *all*. *He* says—and I believe he's one of the first men in his field—that being a pioneer is no excuse for being grabby. He says it would have been better if we'd taken more time developing our natural resources and done it in a more orderly way. After all, what was the hurry?"

"Hurry? *You* might have been in a hurry if you'd been in a stockade with Indians outside whooping for your scalp. And a mighty pretty scalp it would have made, if you'll allow me to say so."

"Don't shift the argument," she retorted in a tone that, for all its primness, betrayed a throb of pleasure. "And, by the way, Professor Stookey thinks we treated the Indians abominably. After all, whose land *was* it?"

"The buffaloes', if you come right down to it. From the way he talks, your Professor Stookey sounds like a socialist. I'd like to have seen *him* out there when the Wild West was being tamed. Him and his 'little more time' and his 'abominably treated' Indians."

"Professor Stookey is as much of a man as you are."

"Has he ever run a business? Has he ever hired labor? I'll bet not. Unless maybe he once sold cosmetics behind a counter. I'm sorry, Ida, but I hate that namby-pamby type of idealist. No wonder he ends up teaching girls!"

"*Well!* I suppose you think women shouldn't be educated, either."

"Not by the likes of Stookey. What do women want to know about railroads? What do your mother or your aunt know about them? Haven't they got on all right?"

"But Mother and Aunt Dagmar belong to a different generation."

"And a generation that has nothing to be ashamed of. I'd a damn sight rather have your mother with a rifle alongside me in that stockade then dear, mincing Mr. Stookey!"

"You're quite impossible."

Impossible or not, on the first Sunday when the Tremains were out of town, Derrick found himself invited to supper by Ida's parents. He even wondered if Mrs. Trask had not sent her sister to the country to provide her with the occasion for asking him. He was learning that the Denisons were capable of concerted action. But he still had no idea of declining the invitation. He was beginning to like Ida, despite her theories, which he was sure would pass with time; he certainly liked her mother, and as a lone bachelor he liked the family atmosphere in which the Tremains and Trasks and Denisons enveloped him. A man could be independent, after all, and still miss the reassurances of family life.

The Trasks, he discovered, lived in an ordinary five-story brownstone house with a high stoop, in the same street with Mrs. Trask's sister and brothers. They were obviously not rich, like the Tremains, but they lived very comfortably. Derrick guessed that Mrs. Trask had a flair for making a little money go a long way. Looking about the living room, he noted that she had created a rather expensive French eighteenth century atmosphere by the judicious use of a sofa, three good chairs, a tapestry, an ormolu mirror and a gilded clock. And she had been too smart to make the mistake of asking Derrick alone. There were six other guests, and he was not even seated next to Ida.

At dinner he discussed with his hostess the difference between a New England and a New York conscience. Mrs. Trask said that the New York woman had the more difficult time, for her conscience required her to be not only good but in fashion, which was a great strain. It was easy enough to be good, she maintained, in last year's hat. Derrick laughed and thought what a pity it was she had thrown herself away on her quiet, asthmatic husband who spent his evenings reading English history in the smooth, soothing prose of nineteenth century authors. What if she had married a man like her brother-in-law? Or himself!

After supper he took a seat by Ida in the living room and found her full of curiosity as to what he thought of her parents in the atmosphere of their own home. For all her indignation at what she called their "lack of social consciousness," she was obviously proud of them and accepted his polite comments as literal truths. Derrick admired the competence with which Mrs. Trask must have handled her gushing and at times explosive daughter. Clearly she gave her a good bit of rein, let her read and study what she wanted and laughed at her with a devastating good-nature, but she always knew when to pull her up. There had been, for example, the awful coincidence of Ida's initiation into the sorority, Kappa Kappa Gamma (described by her mother as "Wrapper, wrapper, pajama") which had fallen on the same night as her grandmother Robbins' birthday party. Ida, to whom election to the chapter had been the great event of a lifetime, had pleaded with tears for permission to absent herself from the family dinner. Her mother had been adament.

"I have no objection to your joining a sorority if you care that much," Mrs. Trask had told her. "But taking on new obligations and commitments does not mean that you can shake off old ones. Your grandmother's birthday was a fixed date before Barnard was even founded."

Ida's voice had still an edge of resentment as she told the story to Derrick that first evening at her family's.

"You can imagine what I went through!" she exclaimed. "Having to explain to the other girls that I was skipping my initiation because of Grandma's birthday!"

"Did they understand?"

"Well, they were very nice about it, I admit. But I don't think many of them came from the kind of family that takes birthdays quite so seriously."

"No? What *do* they take seriously?"

Ida looked up in surprise at this mocking tone. "Well, do you assume, if they don't take birthdays seriously, that they don't take *anything* seriously?"

"No, but I think gracious living requires attention to detail, and gracious living is a woman's job. Your mother knows you can't pull too many bricks out of that wall before it caves in."

"And Grandma's birthday party—or rather my presence at it—is such a vital brick?"

He shrugged. "It's a brick."

"You mean you actually *approve* of Mother's making me go?"

"Yes, I guess I do."

"And you'd do the same thing with a daughter of yours?" She dropped her eyes at a sudden sense of the boldness of such a reference.

"I would. Sororities are all very well, but they're hardly part of a grown-up world."

"Like birthday parties? What would you say if you had a son, and it was a question of his initiation at the Porcellian Club?"

"That's a different thing entirely."

"I *see*! You really believe in the double standard, don't you?"

"I make no secret of it."

Ida was very silent and thoughtful for several moments after this, but he was confident that he had lost no real stature in her estimate. He had no doubt that, except in the case of a few unnatural spinsters, all feminist chatter in women was a kind of parlor decoy to titillate and attract the opposite sex. He believed that women took up their cudgels only for the delight of flinging them down, that all they sought on the battlefield for equal rights was the ecstasy of surrender. Nor was there anything in Ida's subsequent conduct to shake his convictions. At the Tremains', the following Sunday night, she was more than usually proprietary in this respect, misquoting him loudly to support her side in argument with her Uncle Linn and strewing her conversation with such phrases as: "But Derrick says—" He took her twice in the course of the next two weeks to walk in the Park, and it became his regular practice to call at the Trasks on Saturday afternoons. Mr. Tremain spoke of this development, in a gruff voice, as they were leaving the office together one evening.

"You're seeing a good deal of Ida Trask."

"Is there any objection, sir?"

"Oh, no. So long as you realize that you may be raising expectations. My sister-in-law may have an easygoing manner, but when it comes to the point, she can be a very firm woman."

"I can well imagine it. Don't worry, sir. I shall not trifle with Ida's affections."

"Good." Mr. Tremain cleared his throat in relief. "Then that's all I need say. Except that she's a good girl, Ida. She's the best of the lot of them."

Derrick had appeared self-assured, even casual during this brief interchange, but his brows were knit when he parted company with Mr. Tremain at the door of their building, and he declined a lift in the Electric in order to walk. He knew perfectly clearly, as he strode up a dusky Broadway, that if he continued to see Ida after so straight a warning, it would be tantamount to a proposal of marriage. Mr. Tremain might have intervened more to warn a favorite employee than to gain a husband for a favorite niece, but the fact remained that he *had* intervened. Derrick, as the lawyers put it, was "on notice." But did he really mind? That was the only valid question. Wasn't Ida Trask as good a wife as he was apt to get? He had expected more time, it was true, to make up his mind, and he was a man who hated to be hurried, but Ida's virtues were incontestable. With the fulfillment of marriage all her silly ideas and half-baked notions could be expected to blow away, and with a bit of discipline and care about her dress and weight, she could easily become a very handsome woman. She was certainly intelligent and fundamentally clear minded, and the natural submissiveness of her female nature could be counted on to check her tendency to intellectual independence and provide the perfect complement to his own need for possession. For Derrick minced no words with himself; he wanted a woman who would be his property, spiritually as well as physically, and he knew the New York social scene already too well not to understand how few of such women it offered. Ida admired him and was perhaps already in love with him. He felt sure that she would not be fickle. Did he love her? Probably not, but when *had* he been in love, and how long did a man have to wait? She never bored him, even when she was being silly; that was the great thing. He liked the big friendly family setting of which she was a part and the social opportunities which its ramifications so abundantly offered. He liked the prospect of children, and Ida seemed strong and healthy. The only thing that she would not bring him was money, but was she not a niece of the man through whom he expected to make it?

At the Metropolitan Museum, the following Saturday afternoon, he found himself alone with Ida in the Egyptian room, staring up at the great pink seated figure of a pharaoh who stared bleakly back.

"That was my kind of civilization," he remarked. "Not even a hint of sentimentality."

"But they were always thinking about death."

He looked at her in faint surprise. "Is that sentimental?"

"It's egocentric, isn't it, which comes to the same thing. What is a pyramid but a monstrous valentine?"

"Sent by a man to himself?"

"Posthumously."

As they laughed, he felt a small twinge of jealousy at the sudden thought that she might, in some ways, be quite as clever as he.

"Now that you've destroyed the Egyptians for me," he said, a bit brusquely, "what will you put in their place?"

"Must it be something unsentimental?"

"By all means."

"But sentimentality isn't always bad! It may be just the lace frill around a genuine feeling. Or don't you believe in genuine feeling, either? Must we all be granite all the time?"

Her smile faded as she looked up at him, and her eyes for a second earnestly searched his. Then, abashed, she looked away and quickly shrugged. Derrick smiled, and taking her by the hand, turned her around.

"Does this answer your question?" And leaning forward, he kissed her on the lips.

She jumped away from him with a smothered "Oh!" and walked hastily to the next room where there were people. Stopping abruptly before a glass case of earthenware jars, she pointed to different specimens, and delivered, in a sudden inarticulate flow of words, an improvised lecture on Egyptian pottery. But despite her evident reluctance to discuss what had happened, it was easy to see that her agitation betokened a bursting happiness, and when he handed her into Mr. Tremain's Electric that was to take her home, she gave his hand a confiding little squeeze.

There was no Sunday supper the following night, for both the Tremains and Trasks had gone to Long Island for the weekend, but the next Tuesday he received a little blue note from Ida that fairly throbbed with the suppressed, seething excitement of the girl who knows that only formalities now stand between her and her ultimate happiness.

I can't be at Aunt Dagmar's next Sunday because Mother is sending me to Atlantic City with Grandma Robbins who has been ill and needs a change of air. But if you go, you'll meet my cousin, Geraldine Denison,

*and then, of course, you'll never even notice I'm not there. Don't have such
a divine time with her, however, that you forget to give just one little thought
to your poor lonely friend, treading the boardwalks by a cold grey Atlantic and dreaming of old Egypt and valentines!*

The "one little thought" that he devoted to Ida that Sunday night was
the reflection of how right she had been in predicting that he would have a
"divine time" with her cousin. For there was no question about it; Geraldine
Denison was the most beautiful woman he had seen in his life. She had a
golden, breath-taking, erupting beauty; she swooped upon the little family
party and upon her Aunt Dagmar with a rasping cry of love like a bird of
paradise. When Derrick had recovered from the shock of his first impression and could observe her more closely, he made out that her face was
thin and oval, her skin of a marble whiteness, her eyes, large like Ida's, but
grey, clear and restless, now evasive and now very direct, and that the
impression of gold was all from her marvelous hair, which she wore long
and straight, rising in front to a small pompadour. Geraldine, like all the
Denisons, was tall, but she moved with a grace that Ida never approached.
She managed to seem fragile when she was probably strong, helpless when
she was almost surely able to look out for herself. But where she differed
most strikingly from her aunts and cousin was in the obvious pleasure that
she took in her own femininity.

"I know I'm a terrible substitute for Ida," she murmured to Derrick at
supper, betraying, in her very first words, that she had been "warned off."
"Ida's so full of books and facts and figures. It's really quite frightening.
Everyone says I'm just a butterfly compared to her. But there you are." She
smiled in mock pity. "For one whole evening you'll have to put up with a
butterfly!"

"Why haven't I met you before? Where have they been keeping you?"

"Oh, I've been abroad. Aunt Dagmar gave me a trip to Paris for my birthday. You see, I'm like Amy in *Little Women*. I'm the niece who gets what
she wants."

"Did you get what you wanted in Paris?"

Her grey eyes seemed to debate the possible impertinence of this. "I don't
think I really wanted anything in Paris."

"What you wanted was here?"

"Oh, yes, there are lots of things I want here."

"What kinds of things?"

"Well, for example, I want to redecorate my room in beige, instead of
pink. And I want to have my aquamarines reset. And I want terribly to see
my portrait by Zorka in the exhibit for the hospital fund." She paused to
smile again. "You must understand that I'm entirely trivial. I'm not a bit
serious, like Ida."

That she should mention Ida a second time could only mean that she
was pointedly flirting. "You're serious about the things you want, anyway,"
he suggested. "So am I. And they're the only things worth being serious
about."

"That sounds frightfully immoral and rather like Oscar Wilde."

"Except that I mean it!" he exclaimed in a louder voice. "If you don't get what you want in this life, you're nothing. You're not even pitiable!" He flushed suddenly as he realized that he had spoken too violently, and now moderated his tone. "I'll bet you've figured out already who's going to give you each of those things you said you wanted."

"Well, perhaps I have," she mused. "I think Aunt Dagmar will give me my new bedroom."

"Because you came back from Europe when you were supposed to?"

She laughed good-naturedly. "Has Ida been talking? It's quite true, Aunt Dagmar didn't want me to stay any longer in Paris. Neither did Mummy and Daddy." She paused, and Derrick concluded that there must have been an adventurer, probably a penniless count. "And I imagine that Uncle Linn will take care of my aquamarines," she continued, gazing at him with widened, quizzical eyes. "And that leaves only the exhibition. But, everyone's already been, so I guess I must go by myself."

"Unless you go with me. Tomorrow afternoon."

"Why, Mr. Hartley! Don't you work?"

"Only when I'm not taking beautiful girls to see their portraits."

"Oh, shush! Of course I couldn't *think* of letting you." When she changed the subject and began to talk about his work in her uncle's firm, he knew that she meant to go with him, and he clenched his fists in excitement under the table. "Tell me," she was saying, in the mild, quizzical tone that young ladies reserved for the "serious" topic; "it always seems to me so unfair the way you bankers treat the poor little inventor. After all, when you stop to think of it, none of the great fortunes ever seem to go to the man who really thought the thing up, if you see what I mean?"

As he proceeded to explain the rewards that were necessary to induce men to risk their capital and the superior function of the investor to the inventor in modern society, he became gradually aware of disapproving glances around the table. Mrs. Tremain twice interrupted him with direct questions to Geraldine, and Dr. Victor Denison made several efforts to make the conversation general. Only Ida's mother betrayed nothing. Derrick smiled grimly and continued to address himself exclusively to the lovely creature on his right, but his throat was constricted with a sullen defiance. It was evident that the Denisons thought him good enough for Ida, but not good enough for Geraldine. Well, they would see!

After dinner, as the gentlemen joined the ladies, Derrick was crossing the living room towards Geraldine when he heard his name called by Mrs. Trask in a tone that he could hardly ignore. He turned and saw her pointing, with a smile that recognized, without mocking, his helplessness, to an empty chair beside her.

"Come, Derrick, you can't have Geraldine to yourself all evening. It's hardly gallant of you to make us older women fight for our rights."

"I had not imagined that this seat could be vacant," he replied with a smile that he hoped matched hers. "I didn't have the presumption to look."

"That's better," she said with a chuckle. "Much better. Good manners is the only rag between us and the apes. Let's keep it there."

It was only too clear that she meant to fix him at her side for the balance of the evening, and there was nothing that he could do about it but grumble to himself that such maneuvering must fail of its ultimate goal. Mrs. Trask would elicit from him neither apology nor recantation. For Derrick knew already, with a clarity unique even in his clear mind, that what had happened to him that night was something that had never happened to him in the twenty-seven years of his life. It was as if he had been playing up to that moment with a pack of cards from which the aces had been drawn. Now it was a different game. There was a bright glow within him that made the unuttered remonstrances of Ida's mother seem like snowflakes landing on a window, observed from within. Hard on Ida? Of course it was hard on Ida! But he clenched his fists in his lap again at the leaping idea that with Geraldine he could go to the top of the world!

Mrs. Trask must have taken in his attitude—perhaps she had observed those clenched fists—for she said, still smiling: "Geraldine is our Freia. When she's away, we all seem old. Like the gods in *Rheingold* behind that scrim."

"She's the most beautiful girl I've ever seen!" he said stoutly.

"My poor Ida!" Mrs. Trask exclaimed, raising her hands in a half-joking gesture of dismay. "It's always been that way. Geraldine dazzles all the men. If we go to Paris, Ida comes home with an album of post-cards and Geraldine with a proposal from a duke!"

"*Did* she have a proposal from a duke?"

"Oh, I guess he wasn't quite a duke. But he was better than those portraits in the Louvre which were all my Ida got." Mrs. Trask's grunt indicated that her own tastes were closer to her niece's. "However, duke or count or whatever, he was only an interlude for Geraldine. Everyone's been an interlude since Talbot Keating."

"Who is Talbot Keating?" But he knew about the Keatings, and, of course, she knew that he knew. He could measure his own ineligibility against the name alone.

"He's a very handsome, very rich but very idle young man who has wanted to marry Geraldine for the past two years. She thinks, and her parents agree with her, that he lacks a real purpose in life. That he needs more drive. So it was arranged that she should go abroad while he took a job in a bank. And after that they would see."

Derrick could not help admiring the speed and decisiveness with which Mrs. Trask's mind worked. Faced with a crisis, she promptly unsheathed the weapon of a family secret. She did not resent his being dazzled by Geraldine; she regarded it, on the contrary, as entirely natural. But that did not mean she had given up the fight.

"And what have they seen?" he demanded.

"I imagine it's still too soon to tell. But everyone seems to think that young Keating has done very well in the bank."

"Well?" Derrick repeated with a mild sneer. "For a whole month? Or even two? Then there's hope indeed!"

Mrs. Trask shrugged. "You know how it is. After all, you're not a boy. Very little is expected of the young Keatings of this world."

"And very much of the young Hartleys?"

"I don't think that's altogether fair," she came back at him with her first undisguised note of reprimand. "My brother-in-law gave you a job, and my whole family has welcomed you as a friend."

He flushed before that penetrating gaze. "I'm sorry," he murmured. "You've all been very kind. You especially."

"Because we *like* you, Derrick. It's as simple as that."

He rose when he saw Geraldine rise, bade good night abruptly to Mrs. Trask and crossed the room to take his leave of Mrs. Tremain. There was no better or even kinder way of letting Ida learn what had happened than by making it thus coarsely plain to her assembled family. He found Geraldine in the hall with her parents, and all four went out together. Dr. and Mrs. Denison lived just down the block, and Derrick was allowed to walk with Geraldine to their stoop. The time was brief, but it was long enough to ascertain that he might call at three the following afternoon and take her to the art gallery. She conveyed this information in a quick, low tone that would not carry to her parents, and he was faintly surprised that a girl of twenty-two should feel the need to be so furtive. Afterwards, as he strode the two miles down Fifth Avenue in the thickening drizzle, he laughed aloud to discover, at this late date, that his inner turmoil could make the damp, dark shop fronts a spring garden of riotous color. For his joy was more than the joy of the first stirrings of love; it was the joy of discovery that love, after all, was real and that the poets had been prompted by something more than their ambition to write memorable verse. Derrick was not dismayed by the late arrival in his life of the goddess who had so long slighted him; he was delighted, on the contrary, to meet the guest of honor, in whose coming after so long a wait, he had ceased to believe. For it was she, was it not, upon whom the ultimate success or failure of the party depended? Wasn't that the whole message of poetry? It was regrettable, certainly, that poor Ida should have to be hurt and his career in Tremain & Dodge jettisoned, but false starts were better soon corrected, and with Geraldine, the world could still one day be his.

6

DERRICK: 1912

No sooner had the maid at Dr. Denison's opened the front door the following afternoon than he heard the swish of Geraldine's skirt in the dark vestibule and caught the scent of her perfume. She just touched his hand and hurried down the stoop to the waiting hansom cab.

"You're very prompt," she said as they started off. "I like that in a man."

"I've been sitting at the bottom of that stoop all day."

"Really? And to think nobody saw you!"

"I wore different disguises. Sometimes I was a pigeon and sometimes an English sparrow."

"Come to think of it, there *was* a rather aggressive little sparrow around here this morning. He drove all the others away."

"I can't brook rivals."

"Are all the men downtown so fanciful? It gives me such a new idea of Uncle Linn's office."

"They're fanciful when they're in love."

She turned to him quickly, too quickly, her lips tightly pursed, her high brow contracted in a pouting frown. Fast as he had been, she was still ready for him.

"If you're going to be silly, Mr. Hartley, I'm going straight home."

"Do you call it being silly when a man's dead earnest?"

"I call that being silliest of all. You can be that way with Ida if you want. That's as it should be. But you and I are simply acquaintances—friendly acquaintances, I hope—who happen to be going together to an exhibition of pictures. Now—is that understood?"

"I tell you what's got to be understood, Geraldine," he retorted, emphasizing her Christian name which she had not yet asked him to use. "I'll tell you just once, and then we'll talk about the exhibition or anything else you want. I don't belong to Ida, and I don't intend to belong to Ida. I think you're the most beautiful and wonderful girl I've ever met, and I want to marry you. There! Now shall we talk about your portrait?"

Geraldine stared silently ahead for a moment. "I think we'd much better," she said, at last, but her voice trembled. "They say Zorka's made my neck too long."

"That's typical. There hasn't been a normal neck since Boldini."

"And, apparently, there's something wrong about the mouth. Isn't there always something wrong about the mouth? Oh, dear!" She plunged her hands petulantly into her muff. "You've got me all upset! Why can't we *get* there?"

"Don't worry. I promise to be good."

And he was. At the gallery they talked only about the pictures, briskly and artificially. The neck in Geraldine's portrait *was* too long, and the mouth a sullen red blob. It was a conventional painting of a society girl in a white ball dress, standing before a mantel. The only thing that struck Derrick about it was the faint hint of a lurking fear in the eyes, but the rest of the painting was so bad that he concluded that this must have been an accident rather than the effect of any subtlety or penetration on the artist's part. When they had made a single tour of the room, Geraldine asked to be taken home, and she slipped out of the hansom and darted up her family's stoop like Cinderella returning from her ball. But not, however, before he had extorted permission to call the following Sunday. He paid the cab and, once again, walked the two miles home, even more elated this time than the first. For he was convinced that he was making progress. If she had taken him up initially for the satisfaction of flirting with Ida's beau, she must have been aware by now that she was caught in a game of someone else's choosing.

On Sunday afternoon, as he walked down Fifty-third Street to the Victor Denisons', he was aware that Ida might have been watching him behind her window curtains, and he turned defiantly to scan the unexpressive tan front of the Trasks' house. He had not written to Ida, but it had not been from fear. To have apologized would have been to insult her. A gentleman could only assume—whatever he might suspect or even know to the contrary—that a kiss such as theirs in the Egyptian Room had meant as little to her as to him. There were certain crises when brave men and cowards had to behave in the same way.

Geraldine and her mother received him in the back parlor that had been furnished in Indian fashion with the relics of Dr. Denison's early traveling days. Gleaming scabbards and pieces of Oriental armor hung on the wall amid the heads of water buffalo and tigers, and the floor was strewn with shaggy bearskins. The chairs and settee were of dark, elaborately carved wood, like grotesque New England porch furniture, and two great painted screens showed various steps in the domestication of elephants. Over the mantel was the single Western motif in a portrait of Mrs. Denison by Madrazo, looking very solemn and long-nosed and holding a large red rose. Geraldine sat in one of the dark chairs by the tea table and dispensed hospitality with an easy, if somehow defiant, gracefulness, while her mother, looking strained and unhappy, talked about the weather. Nobody else was there, and nobody came.

"I wonder if your father wants his tea," Mrs. Denison speculated at last, and when Geraldine simply shrugged, she rose abruptly and left the room. No sooner was Derrick reseated than her daughter leaned stiffly back in an evidently premeditated pose of self-command.

"I think I should tell you that I asked Ida Trask to come in this afternoon. Unfortunately, she had another engagement."

"I thought you understood that references to Ida do not embarrass me."

"Because you're quite shameless!"

"On the contrary. I've been very much ashamed, but I have no intention of being ashamed forever. It isn't as if we'd been engaged."

"But you admit you made up to her?"

"I paid her some attention—yes."

"And the moment another girl came along, you dropped her flat!"

"The moment *you* came along."

"What assurances would *I* have that I wouldn't be treated the same way?"

"You'd have two. In the first place, you're a hundred times prettier than Ida."

"Poor Ida! Really!"

"And in the second, I love you." Geraldine shook her head in quick deprecation, but he went firmly on. "I never loved Ida, and I never told her that I did. We have no obligations to each other."

"But did you never kiss her?"

Derrick smiled. There were moments when Geraldine seemed the very portrait of feminine sophistication and others when she might have been fourteen. "If I had, do you think I'm the kind who'd tell?"

"And what does Ida think of all this?"

"I haven't the presumption to guess."

"I bet she's utterly wretched!" Geraldine exclaimed with a little wail. "It's all the most dismal mess!" She stamped her foot in sudden petulance under the tea table. "Why did I have to go to Aunt Dagmar's that night? Why did I have to meet you in the first place?"

"Because you were bored with Talbot Keating," he answered promptly. "Because you wanted to meet a man who would really care for you." He seized her hand suddenly and pressed it hard, and she stared at him with a paralyzed horror as if she realized that he was going to kiss her, there and then, under the horns of the water buffalo, and that he might not have finished before her father came in. He read this in her eyes and more, that she yearned now to have him do it and get it over with, to have him add the scandal of his presumption to the scandal of his inconstancy and confound them both in irredeemable sin. He leaned over, half rising from his chair, and then drew back as Dr. Denison appeared in the doorway.

"My dear Hartley, I'm delighted to see you," he murmured as he strolled in. "Geraldine, my dear, you know how I like my tea." He sat down and pulled up each trouser leg carefully, as affable and easy as his wife had been nervous and uncomfortable. He was as handsome, for a man in his midfifties, as was Geraldine for her own sex and age. He had thick grey curly hair and Geraldine's wide clear eyes in a long, smooth oval face. One eyelid drooped in a way that Derrick had heard was supposed to be fascinating to women. But he evidently intended to stay.

Geraldine busied herself with the tea things while the doctor embarked on a discussion of the great differences between Derrick's profession and his own. Yet the leisurely way in which he plunged his thumbs in the pockets of his grey vest, his little cough as he surveyed a well-shod foot, his air of faint but perennial amusement, suggested much more the exchange and the ticker tape than the angry reds and gleaming whites of the emergency ward.

"You financial boys have it all over us doctors. If one of you slips up, what happens? Some poor devil loses his money, isn't that about the gist of it? But when a doctor slips up—and even the best of us do, you know—it may be the same poor devil's life."

"But you have one great advantage," Derrick pointed out. "If the poor devil's dead, he can't complain."

"True! And you don't even give them ether when you take their money!" The doctor tilted his head back and opened his mouth as if to laugh, but no sound emerged. "Maybe it all evens up in the end. But there's another thing I envy about Wall Street as I get older, and that's the respect you pay to age. Take Linn Tremain, for example. I'll bet all of you young fellows downtown consider him a sort of financial Nestor."

"It's true, we do."

"Whereas I'm sure all the interns at St. Luke's refer to me as an exploded old quack."

Derrick laughed spontaneously at the probable accuracy of the doctor's idea. But at the same time it occurred to him that the man who could see this was no fool. "You forget a very simple thing, Doctor," he said. "In my field, if the old man is still around, he's probably rich. Opinions may vary about who's a good doctor, but a man who's made a fortune is always a good money-maker. What other criterion do we have?"

"Gracious me, is that what comes of working for Linn? So young and such a cynic!"

And so it went, back and forth, for half an hour, while Geraldine sat looking from one to the other with an apprehension that seemed to take both sides at once, until Derrick, realizing that he had been blocked by a major diplomat, rose to take his leave. But as he turned to Geraldine, the evident relief in her evasive eyes angered him, and he blurted out: "Will you ride with me tomorrow in the Park?"

He turned again, before she could answer, to her father, who was smiling cryptically. "I'm quite aware, Doctor, that I am not entirely welcome in this house. But it's absolutely vital for me to have a talk alone with your daughter. If she met me in Central Park, and if she left me there, would it be all right for us to ride for an hour?"

"A 'last ride together'?"

"In a fashion, yes."

Dr. Denison put his head back to execute again his soundless laugh. "My dear fellow, do you really think a girl Geraldine's age needs her father's permission to go riding with a young man in the Park? I should like to see the fix I'd be in in this house if I started laying down that law!"

Derrick swung immediately back to Geraldine. "How about it then? Tomorrow at three?"

She appealed in a worried glance to her father, but for what answer it was not clear. His only response was a faintly irritated shrug. "At three," she murmured and turned to the mantel as the good doctor, reverting again to the contrast between financial and medical men, escorted Derrick slowly to the door.

The next morning Derrick went to Mr. Tremain's office and told him the whole story. The latter listened silently, touching the tips of his fingers together, his lips pursed, his head slowly shaking.

"I won't say I haven't heard about it," he said at last. "You've got them all really down on you now."

"Mrs. Tremain's family?"

"Yes. And a formidable lot they can be, I assure you."

"I don't care a rap about them, sir. I only care about you. Are *you* down on me?"

Mr. Tremain squinted at the window for a silent moment. Then he faced Derrick again with a sterner stare. "What's between you and Ida?"

"A bit of tomfoolery. A kiss. That's all. I'm sorry about it, sir, but I can't go back to her now, feeling as I do. Would you want me to?"

"Oh, no! *No!*" Mr. Tremain hit the desk in sudden emphasis. "Poor Ida, she's had enough without that. Don't you dare quote me to any of the Denisons—they'd have my skin for it—but as long as this thing has happened, you may as well go after Geraldine and grab her if you can. She's not worth a quarter of Ida, but I'll admit she's a stunner. And if anyone can make anything out of her, it's probably you!"

Derrick never forgot that afternoon. He was not a man normally sensitive to nature, but the dark and light greens of Central Park under the pale sky of an early spring, the slowly prancing horses with their smartly cut tails and Geraldine in black riding clothes with a tall black hat, was always in later years to be re-evoked for him by a Constantin Guys or a Toulouse-Lautrec. Geraldine had never been more animated. She talked without stopping about Paris and parties and what the man at Cartier's had said about her aquamarines and how she didn't like Southampton because there was sand in everything. Derrick smiled at the thought of how it would have bored him had he not been in love; a drugged man can laugh at pain. And Geraldine was at her best with trivia. She faced the world, her world, with the bright eyes of a little girl before a mountain of ice cream and spun sugar. He could imagine her idea of a serious discussion—was it possible, did Derrick think (and here she undoubtedly would pucker her brow and stick her chin forward to indicate a bold candor), for a man and woman to be . . . just friends? And he began to realize, as their ride progressed, as his soul smoothed itself out, "a long cramped scroll" in the phrase of the Browning poem suggested by her father, that such was precisely the topic that she was now trying to introduce. Between him and his urgency she was piling up, with nervous, darting hands, a makeshift wall of parasols and hatboxes and gloves and tissue paper. What she planned to use for cement was Platonic love! With a shrug and a snort he swept the wall away.

"Of course, we're just avoiding the real topic."

"Oh. Derrick!" she pleaded, with panic in her eyes. "Don't! I'm having such a good time!"

"I know you are. And I'd be perfectly willing to have you go on talking as long as you want, if I thought I'd have another chance to see you. But *will* I?"

"See me? Of course you will. How ridiculous."

"It's not ridiculous!" he said, and the roughness of his tone made her immediately spur her horse forward. "Your parents are obviously determined to keep me away from you, and I'm equally determined that they shan't. If you'll agree to treat me as you would any other eligible beau—like Mr. Keating, for example—I'll agree to go on talking about friendship between the sexes as long as you like. But will you?"

She reined her horse in and faced him now with an expression of condescending reproach. "I don't know what you mean by an 'eligible beau,'" she retorted, "and I think it's highly impertinent of you to mention Talbot Keating's name."

"All I want to know is whether you'll go riding with me again next Sunday."

"I refuse to be pinned down like that. Really, Derrick, you're the limit!" As her horse moved into a trot she called back to him: "Why can't you be like other people?"

He kicked his horse to catch up with her. "Why can't I be treated like other people?"

"You are."

"Not by your father. Oh, I don't blame him, of course. I suppose it's only natural for him to look higher. You could marry a duke. Or even a millionaire." He laughed crudely, in sudden, sheer good spirits as he caught up with her. "Only I guess you'd have to marry the millionaire first!"

She pulled up to a walk, her eyes alive with anger. "I think you're perfectly horrid!" she cried. "What have I ever done to you that you should insult me?"

"I'm only admitting I'm no catch," he protested. "But just give me time. I'm going to make as much money as your Uncle Linn ever made. And *he* was the one who brought the Denison's over from Brooklyn!"

Geraldine opened her mouth for a moment, but then closed it and turned her gaze serenely to the tops of the trees by the bridle path. "I think you're the rudest man I've ever met," she said in a remote, reflective tone. "*And* the most mercenary."

"Why? Because I call a spade a spade?"

"No. Because you assume that my family are after a 'catch.' As a matter of fact, at the risk of spoiling you, I may as well admit that they agree with you. They think you *will* make as much money as Uncle Linn."

His heart bounded. "Then what's wrong with me?"

"You're Ida's beau." She turned to make a little mocking face at him. "Or should I say, Ida's 'eligible beau'?"

"But I'm not!"

"Oh, but you are. In Daddy's eyes. And in Aunt Dagmar's. And in Aunt Lily's. I assure you, I've been told, in no uncertain terms, to keep my hands off you!"

"But there's nothing between me and Ida!" he cried in exasperation. "Nothing at all!"

"Nothing? Do you call kissing nothing?"

"For pity's sake, is there *no* privacy in Fifty-third Street? Or do the Denisons have public confessional?"

"It's just like *The Mill On The Floss*," Geraldine continued in her maddening superior tone. "Only there Philip hadn't even kissed Lucy. Or if he had, George Eliot doesn't say so."

"So now we take our morals from George Eliot! An old drab who lived in open sin for twenty years!"

"She did not!" Geraldine exclaimed indignantly. "She and Mr. Lewes simply shared a home. It was very daring, of course, but basically I'm sure everything was all right."

"You can't really be so naïve as to think—!" But he stopped as he made out the lively interest beneath the stubbornness in her averted face. Obviously, she would be relieved and delighted to spend the rest of their ride discussing the nature of George Eliot's relationship with Lewes. "Look, Geraldine. If I were to give you up—"

"Give me up!" she retorted angrily. "What do you mean, give me up? Do you think you own me?"

"Give up pursuing you, then. Do you think if I did, I'd go back to Ida?"

"I'm sure I don't know, and I'm sure I don't care. The point is, I can't go riding again, or anywhere again, with a man who has been so markedly attentive to my own first cousin."

"Then you had no business leading me on in the first place!" he exclaimed hotly.

"Leading you on?"

"You know perfectly well what I mean!"

Tears of real anger welled up in her eyes. "I think you're the horridest man I've ever met. And if I did . . . flirt with you . . . just for a few minutes, it was wrong of me." She shook her head emphatically. "Very wrong of me."

"It was the best thing you ever did in your life!" he cried. "You saved Ida, and you saved me. And you saved yourself from Talbot Keating—that's what I'm going to prove to you."

"Never!"

"Are we both to miss everything because of Ida?"

"You kissed her, Derrick!"

"Oh, Geraldine, *really*," he groaned.

"You *did*!" She shook her head violently. "And Aunt Dagmar called me in and gave me such a bawling out as you never heard in your life. And so did Daddy. And Aunt Lily looked at me with those reproachful eyes of hers, which was even *worse*. They said I'd always had all the beaux, and now I had to take Ida's. They made me feel so *awful*. Oh, Derrick, you can't imagine. And I *promised* I wouldn't see you again!"

Derrick, watching that stubbornly shaking head, felt a sudden desperate bafflement. He could hardly believe that the hard swift vessel of his passion was going to founder on reefs of such obviously cardboard scenery, but something in the pit of his stomach warned him that so it might be.

"Geraldine," he pleaded, "listen to me. Listen to me this once. You are the only woman I've ever loved. The only one. What you and I could have together might make us different people. Real people. Happy people. I've had my glimpse of it now, and I know. You're surrounded by family who live by the morals you find in children's books: what you owe to Ida or Talbot Keating and who gave who his word. Don't you see you can't *live* that way? Or love that way?" He was addressing himself to the back of her head, but he knew by the rigidity of her posture that she was listening. It was the time to take his ultimate gamble. "I can't compete with any of them on Fifty-third Street. It's not my territory. And I can't compete with Talbot Keating in offering you possessions. But if you would come with me for an hour to my apartment, I could try to show you what love is."

She turned quickly around, her face very white and drawn. "Oh, Derrick," she murmured in a horrified tone. "Don't *say* things like that. Please!"

He rode up abreast of her. "I have to. I have to prove to you that you're a woman. As well as a niece and daughter."

"Oh, I'm a woman," she said softly in a different voice. "I promise you, Derrick, I'm a woman."

"Show me," he said, and stretched his hand across to her. She looked at him for a moment and then at his hand and then slowly reached out her own.

As he grasped her fingertips, the thing happened that changed his life. Or at least so it seemed at the time. Later, he was to speculate that it had simply caused Geraldine to do on impulse what she would have done anyway on reflection. Her horse shied to the left, and as she lost her balance and fell towards him, he caught her round the waist and lifted her from the saddle. So far, fate might have played into his hands, for there was an old if rather hackneyed note of romance in his gesture, and Geraldine was not impervious to such notes. But there was nothing out of Walter Scott in what happened next. His own horse shied, and Derrick, not an experienced rider at best and unused to his extra burden, tumbled with a screaming Geraldine to the mud of the bridle path. They both rose to face each other, with nothing damaged but Geraldine's coat and their relationship.

She turned away without a word and walked quickly down the bridle path towards the shed where they had leased the horses. The latter were already out of sight.

"Geraldine!" he called, hurrying after her. "Forgive me!"

She did not turn, and when he caught up, he saw that she was staring grimly ahead down the path, very pale and set. But when he tried to take her hand, she lashed at him suddenly with her riding crop and hissed the word "Beast!" She was evidently on the verge of hysteria, and there was nothing he could do but bow his head and pause to let her go ahead alone.

The oddest thing about the whole sorry business, he reflected later that night over many solitary brandies, was his own premonition, despite all that his reason told him, that his cause was hopeless. Of course Geraldine cared about him, and the objections of her family were trivial. How, then, was it not a situation where sex and boldness and youth were bound to prevail?

How could the domestic principles of Dr. Denison and his two sisters, like the pretty, cuddlesome bunny rabbits of Beatrix Potter, not scamper away before the first rumbling growl of the real world? Surely the clue had to lie in Geraldine herself and not in her paternal aunts. Derrick knew very little of nerves from his own, but his mother had been a prey to their disorders, and he had seen as a child how fear could paralyze any instinct, even that of self-preservation. Geraldine, he was sure, would have made love with the devil himself—unless Aunt Dagmar had classified the devil as "unattractive." Somehow, perhaps because of her own mother's quivering abdication as a parent and rumored solace in drugs, she had set herself limits of conduct, had staked out the area of permissible frolic with little replicas of those very bunny rabbits that had just come to mind. Perhaps she now gazed at him over her artificial border with eyes of tremulous distrust. If he could only get at her, if he could only fix her attention entirely on himself and away from her family for a few days or even hours, he was bound to prevail. But how could he get the time?

How indeed? In the next two weeks she was always "out" when he called at Fifty-third Street, nor would she even come to the telephone or answer his letters. Half crazed with anger and frustration, he found, for the first time, no relief in work. Mr. Tremain, who knew all, stopped by his desk one morning and placed a sympathetic hand on his shoulder.

"You'd better give it up, my boy. Young Keating's at the house every day now. Dagmar tells me the engagement is going to be announced next week. It's just as well to get the damn thing over with."

Derrick did not even look up until he heard the older man's sigh and retreating step. He had never been able to endure the least expression of sympathy from others. The following Saturday afternoon he climbed the stoop of the Victor Denisons' house, determined to stand in the doorway until they permitted him to see Geraldine or sent for the police. As he was about to ring the bell, however, the door opened, and Ida Trask came out. The little vestibule that contained their startled meeting was at once a tight, suffocating box of embarrassment.

"Hello, Derrick."

"Hello, Ida. You're looking well."

"Oh, I'm fine." Her voice was low, but unresentful. She moved to the outer door and then turned suddenly back, a hand on the knob. "Don't go in, Derrick," she pleaded. "For your own sake. Talbot Keating is there with his mother. It'll be so miserable for everyone."

He looked into her dark, troubled eyes and read there only kindness and solicitude. It struck him for the first time that, for all his attempts to be honest, he had not faced the magnitude of his unkindness to Ida. It was an immediate solace to him that she should see him in his present misery. "Thanks for the warning. I know it was kindly meant. But if one was born a mule, one must lead a mule's life."

Ida nodded quickly and hurried down the stoop without again turning back. Derrick watched until she had crossed the street, then shrugged ruefully and pressed the bell. The Irish girl who opened the door looked scared when she recognized him and blurted out that Miss Denison was not at home.

"Look, Bessie," he said in a firm tone, "I *know* Miss Denison's at home and that Mr. Keating is with her. I want you to be good enough to step into the living room and ask if she will come down and let me put her one question. Surely that's reasonable. Wouldn't you do as much for one of *your* young men?"

The girl hesitated and blushed and stammered out something about her instructions, but as Derrick simply stood there, staring at her, she finally turned and ran up the dark high straight stairway into the blackness of the landing. The murmur of voices which he could just hear from the upstairs living room ceased as she went in, and he next heard Dr. Denison's voice alone. A few moments later there was a step on the landing, a masculine step, and a handsome, but rather florid young man in tweeds came slowly down the stairs. As he approached, Derrick could make out that he was smiling, probably in embarrassment.

"I'm Talbot Keating," he announced, halfway down, and then had to proceed, rather foolishly, to the bottom in silence. He put out a hand that Derrick grasped briefly. "Geraldine thought I'd better see you. Look here, old man, I know this is hard on you. No one knows it better than I. But the thing is—well, Geraldine and I are engaged."

"Since when?"

Keating looked surprised at the sternness of his tone. "Well, officially, I guess only since yesterday. But there's been a kind of understanding for a year."

"Would you think me very presumptuous if I asked to have my dismissal from Geraldine herself?"

Keating's eyes avoided Derrick's stare. "Isn't that a bit rough on her?"

"I think she owes it to me. Just that and nothing more."

Keating shuffled his feet and then shrugged and went back up the stairs. Derrick could hear his voice in the living room followed by Geraldine's shrill "But I won't!" This in turn was followed by a buzz of family argument, and at last he heard her quick step and his name called from the landing.

"Derrick Hartley!"

He went to the bottom of the stairs and looked up. Her outline was tall and white and forbidding against the dark landing.

"Yes, Geraldine."

"I'm engaged to Talbot Keating! *Now* will you go?"

"Yes!" he shouted back up at her in a sudden explosion of wrath. "I'll go and I won't come back. And I'll always remember you didn't even have the guts to come down these stairs to dismiss the man you'd led on!"

As he strode back up Fifty-third Street to Fifth Avenue he felt a certain rude exhilaration that every Denison was probably watching his retreat from behind the shelter of second-floor curtains.

If Derrick had been unable to work while his fate was uncertain, this was no longer the case after it had been sealed. If it had seemed to him, for one long dazzling week, that his future might contain not only a partnership in Tremain & Dodge but marriage to the most beautiful girl in New York, one of these destinies, at least, was still open to him. For three months after his last visit to Fifty-third Street he worked downtown until midnight almost every night, relaxing only on Sundays and then only on walks. When he read in the newspaper of the wedding of Miss Geraldine Denison and Mr. Talbot Keating at Saint Thomas' and the brilliant reception which followed at Sherry's, he felt, with a relief that surprised him, that his heart could now come out of mourning. He started to go to parties again and to play billiards at the Harvard Club. Mr. Tremain never referred to the matter but once, when he asked gruffly if everything was now "all right." Derrick had simply nodded, and that had been that. But it was tacitly agreed between them that Derrick had better come no more to the family Sunday suppers.

The first member of the Denison family that he was to see again was Mrs. Trask. He was summoned to Mr. Tremain's office one day at noon to find Ida's mother sitting by her brother-in-law's desk. She seemed as cheerful and self-contained as ever, greeting Derrick as if no shadow had ever dimmed the pale sun of their friendship.

"Linn has been helping me with my little investments," she said. "We do it once a quarter, and I always feel that I'll get richer if I come downtown myself. I didn't want to leave without saying hello."

"I'm glad you didn't, Mrs. Trask."

"I'm not sure you deserve it, though. You never come to see us any more."

"You never ask me."

"Well, that's soon remedied. Come dine on Saturday, will you?"

"I shall be delighted."

There was no refusing a woman who was such a sport. She seemed to be saying: "I don't hold Geraldine against you. Any man could lose his head over Geraldine. But she's gone, and you and I are realists, and how about Ida? If she suited you once, can't she suit you again?" And couldn't she? He had miscalculated once, because he had not thought himself capable of the sudden flame of feeling that Geraldine had kindled. But could it be kindled again? Didn't he, at last, really know himself? And hadn't Mr. Tremain said that Ida was worth four of Geraldine?

On Saturday there were eight for dinner, and as on his first evening at the Trasks', Derrick was not seated by Ida. She looked flushed and uncomfortable and constantly avoided his glance. Had her mother not warned her that he was coming? Anything was possible with Mrs. Trask. After dinner he went to the living room ahead of the other men and walked deliberately to the corner where Ida had retreated with her needlepoint. She could hardly stop him from sitting beside her, but she leaned more closely over her work.

"I want to thank you for warning me that day at Geraldine's. You were right. It was miserable for all."

Ida's voice was very sad and low. "I'm sorry for the pain it must have caused you."

"That's all over now."

"Oh, yes, everything's over now."

"Everything?"

"Everything," she replied with quick emphasis, pulling her needle through the material. "We all get over our disappointments." She was still flushed, but she forced herself to go on. Evidently it was a point that had to be made. "I mean, you're not the only one," she explained.

"You mean that *you've* got over me."

"Please, Derrick." Her voice trembled. "Let's not go into the past."

"But if I want to? If Geraldine was only an insane infatuation?"

"Derrick!" She looked up now and glared at him fiercely. "What do you think of me? That I'm a tap to be turned off and on?" Her breath came in a gasp. "How can I make you understand that there can never be anything again between you and me? I can forgive you Geraldine. I could forgive any man Geraldine. The only thing I could never forgive would be your trying to come back to me!"

Across the room, as her words hung in the air between them, came the long high peal of her mother's laugh. Someone must have told a really good story, for Mrs. Trask was sitting with her head tilted way back and her shoulders were shaking. It seemed to fill the room, that laugh, like a cool, splashing stream, eddying about to clean out every corner of the dust and litter of hesitations and sensitivities, filling up every vacancy with its clean and bubbling demand, its despotic normality, and Derrick was surprised to feel the stirring of a regret, faintly kin to remorse, that the fine, pale candle of Ida's scruples was so sure to be doused by it.

PART THREE
IDA BETWEEN WORLDS

7

IDA: 1912

I WAS ALWAYS ashamed of the tremor of excitement with which my heart greeted any news of illness in the family. It was not that I really wanted anyone to be sick, but my relatives, when stricken, seemed less superior, and my assiduousness at the bedside, in contrast to the reluctant visitations of the others (for the Denisons had a horror of maladies), made up in my mind, at least in part, for the shyness and awkwardness which I stubbornly insisted that my family deplored in me. Never was this shame more burning than on a day when my poor father's increased apathy and lassitude were at last diagnosed as the symptoms of a virulent liver disease. My mother, so strong on other occasions, went almost to pieces at the news, and the tumult of her restlessness, of her hoarsely whispered telephone calls to doctors, of her ordering about of nurses, threatened to destroy the peace and quiet so necessary to the patient's unlikely recovery. When Aunt Dagmar suggested that I give up Barnard to help keep order at home, I was only too glad to comply with her wish. By hard work and sacrifice I might be able to make some reparation for having, even for a minute, considered Father's illness in the light of an interruption from another preoccupation. I could sublimate the sufferings of Ariadne to the tender ministrations of Florence Nightingale.

I speak, of course, with a detachment and insight acquired in later years, but even at the time I wondered if Mother's perfunctory acceptance of my sacrifice of college might not have sprung from her intuitive understanding of my mixed motives.

"When this is all over, and your father is well again, we'll take a trip to Europe," she promised me. "We might even charter a little yacht and do the Greek islands. That would be a lot better, wouldn't it, than hearing some old maid with a pince-nez lecture on Helen of Troy?"

I recognized Mother's picture of Barnard and made no comment. For I had every intention of ultimately enrolling myself among the academic old maids of her fantasy, and despite the mockery in her tone, I was moved by the idea of Helen's legendary beauty finding a state of preservation in the soft tones of a withered virgin lecturer. The only way that I had been able to reconcile myself to the horror of Derrick's desertion had been in cultivating the hope that the dismal chapter of love was now over for me and that the balm of a long grey institutional life might one day assuage any lingering pain. Who had I been to presume to look to such a man as Derrick? Did he not, in his male strength and egotism, belong to the kind of female that Geraldine represented, a Rossetti Guinevere of pale willowy weakness? I was deservedly crushed for my boldness by the armored heel whose very armor had attracted me. It was suitable that one who had shivered in pleasure before such ruthlessness should now shiver in pain. If I could only succeed in robing myself in the gown of learning and in spending a lifetime with beautiful and soul-lifting things, even under the shadow of the menacing male figure who had cast me aside but who had given me a kiss that I would always remember, might I not be seizing as much happiness as I had any right to expect?

But now it appeared that I might not be permitted even this. For, however humble an ambition, what was it but variation, and was not variation the very crime that Mother's family could always detect? And did it really matter, if one varied, whether one did so as a king or as a peasant, as a great actress or an old-maid dean? I felt in our house, and even in Uncle Victor's, that Derrick had been forgiven and that the family thought it only a matter of time before I would take him back. Their attitude was the harder to combat in that it was never expressed. Nobody asked me to see Derrick; nobody had the indelicacy to praise him to me. Everybody simply assumed that he could continue as a part of the Denison pattern of life, and how could that be unless he was incorporated into the family? I had thought that Father's illness might bring postponement. As it turned out, it brought acceleration.

My sickbed duties consisted largely in reading aloud. Father had an inexhaustible enthusiasm for nineteenth century fiction, and he preferred me to Mother as a reader because I did not keep stopping to fuss over his bed or medicine table or to close a window or to check up on a nurse. I read Jane Austen and Trollope by the hour while he lay silent and still, his large, dark sad eyes fixed on me and the book. He was heartbreakingly patient and cheerful. I think he minded dying only on Mother's account.

"Ida," he said quietly, on the afternoon that we finished *Ayala's Angel,* "I think it's time we had a little talk. I'm not much on little talks, but we can't altogether avoid them."

"You're not supposed to tire yourself," I protested, more in alarm for myself than for him. "Can't it wait till you're better?"

Father's smile was charming. "Oh, but when I'm better, we'll never do it! We'll talk about silly things. What have the healthy to do with facts?"

I clasped my hands on top of the closed novel. "We'll talk about anything you want."

"Let us start briefly with myself." He turned his head away and stared up at the ceiling as if to find his words there. "There will always be people who will tell you that I was dominated by your mother's family. If nobody else does, your grandmother will. And, of course, it's perfectly true. But I want you to remember that I chose it that way. Your mother's family are the kindest, fairest people in the world. If I had it to do over again, I'd do it the same way."

"But surely Grandma understands that!"

"No." His lips parted in a faint smile. "Grandma prefers independence to happiness any day, God bless her. Each to his taste. All I want you to understand, Ida, is that my life has been my own doing. For better *and* for worse. Perhaps I should have had the guts to get out of the trust business and go into teaching. Nobody tried to stop me. Certainly not your mother. But I preferred my little rut, and I bless those who made me happy in it. In life you can be a leader or you can be led. It doesn't make much difference which you choose, as long as you *do* choose. My life could have been a tragedy if I had decided that I was the victim of a family plot. I didn't."

"But you *are* a leader," I protested. "All the family look up to you and respect you."

"They respect me, of course. As I say, they are very fair. But that is enough about me. To come to *you*." He reached out a thin hand to put on mine. "You could be a leader, my dear."

"Oh, Father, me?"

"Yes," he insisted, "I'm quite serious. Everyone thinks you're like me, and that little Christopher's like your mother, but everyone's wrong. Chris is basically the conformist, and you . . . well, I can easily see you as a radical dean or a window-smashing suffragette."

"You're making fun of me!"

"No. It would simply be a matter of making you mad enough. But you could also be passive. Oh, yes, I see that, too. If you married Derrick, for example, *he* would always be the leader."

"I'll never marry Derrick!"

"What is the use of unilateral resolutions?" His tone was dry, and he closed his eyes. I saw that my violence had tired him, and was silent. "They can always be revoked, anyway. I'm not suggesting that you marry Derrick. I'm suggesting that if you did, he would be the leader. But there's nothing wrong in that. It's just as good a life to be Mrs. Derrick Hartley as to be a radical professor. The only thing to remember is that it's *your* choice. My worry about you, Ida, is that you might slide into it. Into being passive. Or even into being active. Without knowing that you were committed."

"Do you think I *should* marry Derrick?"

Father closed his eyes again in protest against such a rejection of all subtlety. "I think you should recognize there's no reason you shouldn't."

Which was all I could get out of him. Father, even when well, detested the didactic and rehearsed ahead of time his rare bits of advice to reduce them to the fewest possible words. Now, too, a little stir in the corridor betokened the daily visit of Grandma Robbins. She always paused for a moment on the threshold to apprehend with one quick, bird-like glance if her only child was still alive and then moved with a rapid rustling of black skirts to the bedside. She was so totally intent upon Father that she did not even nod to me, and, putting down the Trollope, I silently left the room. I found Mother in the corridor where she always hovered during Grandma's visits, not wishing to tire Father with the presence of two women at once, but always at her post to be able to drag off her mother-in-law at the first hint of fatigue in the patient's voice.

"You have a visitor downstairs," she told me, and I was glad for the darkness of the corridor. "Put on a dash of powder before you go down. You look done in, dear. I told him you were reading to your father, but he said he'd wait. He's been in the living room half an hour."

"Oh, Mother, is it Derrick? Why didn't you tell him to go?"

"Because he didn't come to see *me*. Do you want me to pick your friends for you? Is that my Barnard girl?"

"Must I go down?"

"Of course you must! If you don't want him to come to the house, tell him so yourself!"

"You know I wouldn't dare," I murmured resentfully, and hurried down the stairs to get it over with.

Derrick and I sat in the living room amid the peculiar hush that sickness gives to a dark house. Yet he appeared to feel no constraint; he talked about himself and his business and how clever Uncle Linn was and even about Galli-Curci and her mad scene in *Lucia*. I sighed with relief as irrelevancy succeeded irrelevancy. Yet I could hardly bring myself to comment except in monosyllables. My world had shrunk to the sickbed upstairs and to my shame at my preoccupation with Derrick. I longed for him to go away and leave me to the lesser discomfort of missing him.

"Don't you think it's rather artificial to go on like this? When we're both thinking the same thing?"

"But I *want* to be artificial!" I protested in alarm. "Artificiality is an art."

"And one you've been taught by masters."

"I don't suppose that's a compliment, but I shall take it as one."

"Why do we have to be so stiff, Ida? Here you are, and here I am. I feel about you exactly as I did that day in the museum, and I believe you feel the same way about me." I made a gesture of protest, but he went straight on. "If there's such a thing as common sense, why shouldn't we be married?"

"You never asked me!"

"But you knew I was going to!" he insisted boldly. "I was just about to when Geraldine hit me. And if you were really fair, you'd admit that was your fault. Who went off to visit Granny and left me in a house with measles?"

"Measles?" In spite of everything I smiled. "Is that what you call poor Geraldine now?"

"What else? She gives a high fever, but she can't be caught twice. If you had a business mind, you'd see that I was a more valuable property after Geraldine than before."

"I'm not worried about your value, Derrick. I'm sure it's very high."

"Then you'd better marry me."

"Before another Geraldine catches you?"

"No, I tell you, I'm immune. You'd better marry me before some Geraldine in striped trousers and a bowler hat catches *you*."

"Oh, me." I shrugged at the absurdity of his idea. "I, too, am immune." I managed to look at him steadily for a moment. "Because, you see, you were *my* measles."

He laughed loudly, and the noise seemed to rattle the whole still house. "But you don't have to get over *me*!"

"Ah, but I do," I said gravely, shaking my head. "It's just exactly what I do have to do."

"Why, for pity's sake?"

"Because you don't love me."

Derrick rose and paced up and down the living room rug. When at the furthest end from me, he turned suddenly, like a cross-examining lawyer. "Why do you think I want to marry you? Surely not for your money?"

"Nor for my beauty," I answered meekly. "I'm afraid you only want to marry me for my family."

"My dear girl, you're absolutely out of your mind! A man doesn't marry to acquire in-laws. If anything, that's what keeps him a bachelor."

He seemed so burstingly alive, so noisily alive at just that moment, in contrast to the approaching death upstairs, that I clenched my fists in a sudden agony of wretchedness. How could I talk about my family when it was disintegrating on the floor above? Surely he was right, and I was out of my mind to think that any young man could want a family that consisted of a dying man, a distracted wife, a moody, muddled girl and a small boy!

"Why do you want me, then?" I asked with a stifled sob.

"Because you suit me."

"Is *that* love?"

"You may well ask." He shrugged philosophically. "Is your suiting me love or was measles love? What I feel for you, Ida, is much pleasanter and deeper and more lasting."

"I'd rather be measles!" I cried in petulance. "What girl wouldn't? Please, Derrick, go now. I can't stand any more of this!"

He came over to take my hand. "I'll go, of course," he said quietly. "And when I come back, don't worry. I shan't be importunate. I'm not a man to beg. But I can talk about the weather and the high events of Fifty-third Street as long as the most garrulous of the Denisons!"

I was hot and ashamed, when he had gone, to find that, like the heroine of *Pride and Prejudice,* which I had read the week before to Father, I was regretting already that my rejected suitor so obviously meant his words about refusing to beg.

In the next weeks Father grew weaker and weaker, and finally there was no further question of reading aloud. Mother would hardly leave his room now, and the household chores and the visitors were turned over to me. I would not have gone out at all except that Aunt Dagmar insisted that I drive with her in the afternoons. None of the family forgot about youth, even in the presence of death, and Father's illness was considered in the light of its ultimate effect on everyone, including myself. Aunt Dagmar had a very good idea that filial grief was not the sole cause of my apathy, and those afternoon drives were designed to shake me out of my morbidness.

Even the automobile assisted her plans. Aunt Dagmar's Brewster, with its tiny round engine and huge roundish wicker body, its cushions and tassels, reminded me of a luxurious Easter egg basket in the window of a Fifth Avenue shop. Perched inside like a big handsome nesting bird, a picture of ease and indolence, its owner would deliver her sprightly lectures of practical advice. Aunt Dagmar, more dependent on servants than any woman I have ever known, who could be induced to walk a block a day only under the most peremptory orders of her doctor, yet maintained successfully in our tolerant family her reputation for vigor and energy.

"I'm going to give you a tip, my dear," she told me on the terrible day when the doctors had withdrawn our last hope. She reached for my hand with her two black-gloved ones and brought it over to her lap. "It's never too soon to face the fact that your position in the world has changed."

"Oh, I know," I murmured. "We shall be very poor. Mother may have to sell the house."

"What do you think *I'm* for?" Aunt Dagmar demanded irritably. "There'll be no selling of houses while I'm around. I'm not talking about a vulgar, useful thing like money. I'm talking about your *position* in the world. You're not a *jeune fille* any more, my dear. You've got to help your mother now. You've got to take over, until she pulls herself together. You've got to run your little family."

"I'll do my best."

"Of course you will. You're a good girl, and you always have been. As your Uncle Linn says (though don't spread it about) you're the best of the lot."

Compliments from Aunt Dagmar, however exciting, always filled me with a bottomless sense of my inadequacy. "If I can ever be a tenth of what Mother is, I'll be happy."

"You can be more than that, my dear, if you have the help *she* had." She paused significantly. "If you have the help of a good, strong man."

"Oh, Aunt Dagmar!"

"Now hush up, till I've finished. I know you're not going to like it, but I want you to hear me out. Derrick Hartley has the respect and affection of all the family. He lost his head over Geraldine, and he behaved badly. No one denies that. But he took his disappointment like a man, and I think he's learned his lesson. He's hard working, he's bright, and your Uncle Linn and I, in spite of everything, think that he's fundamentally steady and dependable. I haven't much doubt that one day he'll be a partner in the firm. Maybe even the senior partner. He's not a young man to be easily stopped."

"But I don't want to marry a man just because he's not easily stopped!"

"Will you be quiet?" Aunt Dagmar raised her voice severely. "Nobody's asking you to. All I'm suggesting is that if you're turning him down because of Geraldine, you're a ninny."

"But he loved her, Aunt Dagmar! He still does!"

"Men are inconstant creatures, Ida. I *know*. But they're also creatures of habit. If Derrick wants to marry, Derrick will settle down. Now, if you don't care about him, that's another thing. But *if* you care about him and let your pride—your vanity, I should say—deprive you of a good husband, and your mother and little Christopher of a man to take care of them, you're worse than a ninny. You're downright irresponsible!"

"Oh, Aunt Dagmar, *please!*"

"I know it hurts, my dear, but it's my duty. Your happiness may be at stake. Now answer me one question. I needn't say honestly, for you've always been, if anything, too honest. Do you love Derrick?"

"You know I love him!" I wailed bitterly. "Everyone in Fifty-third Street knows I love him!"

"Then may I tell him not to despair?"

"Oh, despair. He won't do any despairing. He's probably out riding with Ellie Denison now."

"He's doing no such thing! He's sitting right in my living room, waiting for me to come back and tell him if there's any hope!"

At this I started to weep, and Aunt Dagmar wisely dropped the subject. But she knew, and I knew, that the decision had been made. I loved him, and I had not positively asserted that he had no hope. In such matters silence has always been properly taken for assent. How could I stand out against my whole family, with their shining panoply of common sense, as well as my own somber, preoccupying love? I knew, even then, that my red danger signal was in the simple fact that I loved Derrick most when he loved me least, but with no one to help me, how was I to persuade Aunt Dagmar of anything that would have struck her as so foolish? Father would have known and understood, but would he have counseled me to act on instinct? When had he so acted himself?

Aunt Dagmar promised me that I should have all the time I wanted, but I knew that I would not get it. I knew that she would speak to Derrick that afternoon, and Derrick was not one to wait. He had the consideration, however, to let a week go by before he called. Consideration? Or was it cleverness? At the end of that week I was beginning to be sick at heart that he might have changed his mind again. Or that he might not come before Father died.

When he came, I went down to meet him in the old back parlor, and he walked across the room to take me in his arms.

"You're a great one for regretting things, Ida, but you're never going to regret this."

We knew Father had only a day to live, and I see the scene now as a Victorian engraving. But it was hardly Victorian, at such a moment, for me to kiss Derrick as desperately as I kissed him. It may, however, have been Victorian of him to assume the demeanor of gravity that he did, as if to avoid the insincerity of announcing his small flame as a bonfire. The Victorian novel usually ended in the embrace to which I clung, and that, no doubt, is the reason that I, like Father, have always so loved Victorian fiction. But in taking Derrick as I took him, in full knowledge of my passion and his coolness, I was surely being as crafty as he. If he owed me anything for what he had done to me, I had wiped the slate clean.

8

IDA: 1922

My brother, Christopher Trask, was living in the old family brownstone with me and Derrick in the winter when Derrick, who had been hitherto a most indifferent father, first began to take any real notice of our daughter Dorcas. Indeed, Christopher was the first to point this out to me, as he pointed out many things that year. Too little was happening in his life, and too much in mine, and he did not miss one of my minor catastrophes.

"I have the feeling," he told me, "that the destinies of Tremain, Hartley and Dodge are being controlled by a prim little girl of nine on her morning walk to school with Daddy."

"You think they talk about business?"

"I think *he* does," Christopher replied. "I've walked behind them on my way to the subway. Derrick's lips are always moving, and he gesticulates with his left arm in that jerky way of his when he's making financial decisions."

"And what does Dorcas do?"

"Oh, she nods. Very wisely, the little minx."

"But I think that's rather cute, don't you?"

Christopher shrugged. "I wonder if I really believe in the American legend that successful fathers naturally adore their daughters. Isn't it a question of default?"

"By their wives, you mean?"

"Well, hardly by their brothers-in-law."

It was not like Christopher to be so biting, nor was he with anyone else. But Mother was dead, and he was much alone, and it was only natural that an older sister, who exasperated him by her very failure to play the maternal role which he would have passionately resented her least attempt to play, should bear the brunt of his inner dissatisfactions. I was glad, anyway, to be of that much use to him, for Christopher had used up too much of himself in his desperate effort to enlist in the war. He had been first under age and then underweight, and he had succeeded in getting to France only as an ambulance driver and then at the very end of hostilities. Mother's death, the day after the Armistice, had intensified his sense of anticlimax to an almost unbearable degree. He had not wanted to return to a New York that would have made him feel too desolately an orphan and had remained in Paris for two years, conscientiously cultivating the young artists and writers who came to be known as the lost generation. But Christopher, despite an unpublished novel and some dabbling in cubist painting, never became a true member of the left bank. His candor had too little egotism; it was the candor of good manners and not of self-revelation. And for all his Denison charm and thin, dark, tense good looks, he was, like all my family, basically reserved. He must have stood apart as Uncle Linn had stood apart in Florence half a century before. And then, too, he dressed too well to be ever quite lost. Wall and Fifty-third Streets were waiting for him.

When he returned he went straight into Tremain, Hartley and Dodge, as Uncle Linn's firm had been renamed on his death, and came to live with us in the old house that he and I now jointly owned. The arrangement had been meant to be temporary, but it had extended itself for a year, partly, I fear, because Christopher, for all his exasperation with my nerves and messiness, sensed how much I needed him and was too kind to push me off. Derrick was constantly away on business, in spirit as well as body, and his hours were late, and I clung to my unattached younger brother to throw before the sardonic but basically sympathetic court of his judgment the little problems of my days and nights. Besides, he was wonderful with the children, buying them presents and taking them to the circus and zoo. He seemed to understand Dorcas' damp, steamy moodiness and little Hugo's violent fits of temper which so terrified me, and he never, like Derrick, showed the least preference between them, even when they fought over him and demanded his opinion in favor of one or the other. He was faithful, too, in his calls on Aunt Dagmar, the inconsolable widow whom only he could console, and on all the aunts and uncles in the block. In fact, Uncle Victor, who, more than anyone, had filled Father's place in my life, warned me that the family were taking advantage of Christopher.

"That's the devil of being the youngest of a generation. Chris was too little to get the good of Dagmar and the rest of us when we were at our best. And now that we're beginning to be querulous old crocks who want attention, he's the only one who isn't married and can't get away."

I knew that Uncle Victor was right, for I had seen the trapped look in Christopher's eye at the Sunday night suppers that Uncle Victor had taken over during Aunt Dagmar's mourning. I knew that it pained him not to be a more real part of life in the old house where our adoring mother had once made him the central figure. He suffered from the young veteran's loneliness and inertia, and it was clearly my job to take Mother's place and push him, as she would have done, out of a nest that was filling with my own noisy brood. But I kept postponing the decision. I would say to myself: "Any day now, he'll meet the right girl," or "How do I know that he won't be moved to the Boston office?" I tried to persuade myself that it was not worth his while to leave me for the real reason that I wanted a buffer between myself and Derrick.

It was the critical year of our marriage. It had taken me a decade to learn that I could never change Derrick, and now that I had learned it, I was afraid, not of what he, but of what *I* might do. His self-sufficiency had had the effect of encasing my feeling for him in a cold-storage cellar where all of its strength but not all of its sweetness had been perpetuated. I no longer liked many of my thoughts about Derrick. I did not like, for example, my habit of dwelling on his refusal to take any part in the war. He had claimed his family as dependents and had told me blandly that he could do more good in Wall Street than in a trench. Perhaps this was so. I am certain, anyway, that he believed it. Derrick was no coward. But why should *I* have minded, unless I had minded his not taking his chances with Christopher and the other men? And if I had wanted him to do that, was it not possible that I wanted him to be killed? There was a thought to ruin a night's sleep for one of my masochistic disposition. Also, I disliked my growing tendency to note and remember Derrick at his least becoming moments, as when he bowed from the waist to a rich banker's wife or when he tried to impress my uncles with how much better Uncle Linn's firm was being managed than in the old days. I shrank increasingly into silence as I recognized my own inclination to cry out against his beliefs. For once I had started, how did I know where I might end?

The crisis came when he fired Scotty Denison. Scotty's first two marriages had collapsed, and he had not yet met Minerva, who was to save him. Uncle Victor had decided that a job in the Tremain firm might help to keep him off the bottle, and pressure had been successfully placed on Derrick. But the latter had warned the family that Scotty's job would not survive the first evidence of his drinking in office hours, and he was good to his word. I heard of it only when Scotty called to entreat my intervention.

It was painful, no doubt, for Scotty to have to go begging to a younger female cousin, and one who had followed him about in his childhood with adoring eyes, but it was still more painful for me to have him do it. And my pain continued, too, after his had worn off, for, taking in my discomfort, his confidence returned, and some of the old, gay, boyish, cheerfully condescending Scotty began to peep out from behind the round red contours of the pompous, middle-aged failure.

"I know I don't come up to Derrick's lights, but we can't all be Derricks, can we?" he protested. Seeing my nod, he ventured a wink. "What sort of a world would it be if we were? A pretty cutthroat affair, I wager. I don't mean that Derrick isn't doing a splendid job, but how did my having a nip at lunchtime hurt him?"

"I'm sure we can fix it somehow."

I resolved to speak to Derrick that night while he was dressing for dinner. It was unfortunate that it should have been for a dinner given by a customer that I had declined at the last moment because of Hugo's croup. He was an undersized child, and his coughing that winter had been very violent, and I hated to leave him even with the most competent nurse. But I should have anticipated that Derrick's anger at my maternal agitation (which he always construed as a rejection of himself) would preclude the least chance of my receiving a sympathetic ear.

He was in his dressing room, in black trousers and undershirt, shaving before his full-length, mahogany-framed mirror. Dorcas, with the plump, demure look that she adopted now when under her father's aegis, was intently engaged in putting the pearl studs in his stiff shirt front.

"I can imagine what's on *your* mind," Derrick said without turning, and the smile whose edge I could make out in the mirror was his stubborn smile. "I can guess who came to weep on whose shoulder this afternoon."

"Oh, Derrick, he was *so* pathetic."

"Let him be pathetic at his own expense, then. Not at mine."

"Couldn't you give him some position where he'd be harmless?"

"I could make him a messenger." He turned abruptly when he caught the reflection of my impatient shrug. "No, I'm serious, Ida. We have messengers older than Scotty. Or I could put him in the mail room or even on the night switchboard. It would keep him out of trouble."

"I mean something dignified."

"We don't have 'dignified' jobs," Derrick retorted flatly, turning back to the mirror. "Not the way I've set up the office. We have responsible jobs and menial jobs, and they don't mix. I refuse to give Scotty the least opportunity to bring discredit on us. Now if it's a handout he wants, I'm willing to consider that."

"He'd never take it!"

"Then he's most unreasonable. He's too proud to work and too proud for charity. I'm afraid he's too proud for me."

"You make things so black and white. All he wants is to be tided over for a bit. The firm used to do that kind of thing all the time. I remember how Uncle Linn would . . ."

"My dear," Derrick interrupted dryly as he sharpened his blade against the strap, "you never really knew your Uncle Linn. You only knew the family legend of him."

I was turning to the door, my lips closed tightly to avoid any open expression of resentment in front of Dorcas, when I heard her exclaim: "Cousin Scotty's a drunk! Isn't that so, Daddy?"

"Go to your room, Dorcas!" I cried in a tone that I had never used to her before. "Go and do your homework. And I never, never want to hear you talking like that again!"

"But this is my time with Daddy!" she protested, shocked and frightened. When I turned back, she reached out to take hold of the suspenders hanging from Derrick's waist.

"Do what your mother says, Dorcas," Derrick said gruffly, and she ran to the door, pausing at the threshold to ask, in a timorous voice: "Mummy, are you sick?"

"Go ahead, Dorcas," her father said.

Alone with Derrick, I crumpled in a chair and gave myself up to a bit of weeping. He gazed at me silently a minute and then shrugged and continued to shave.

"Do you know something, Ida? You've never heard of feminine guile. You've been brought up in a family where the women get their way by raising their voices. It doesn't happen to work with me. But do you know what might?" I shook my head sullenly. "If, when I came home after a hard day's work, you didn't start wailing about Scotty's job. If instead you put on your best dress and went out to dinner and made me proud of you. And then, on the way home, if you put your head on my shoulder and shed a little tear about Scotty and said you understood my position, but wasn't it a pity . . . Well, who knows what might not happen?"

I suppose that was my chance. I wiped my eyes and blew my nose and even considered it. "I don't really think I'm the geisha type."

"That's just it! You think if you ask for something, you're being a whore. That's all you learned at Barnard. A lot of claptrap about women's rights!"

But he was wrong. Utterly wrong. I would have been willing to play the geisha had I only known how. It was the fear of being ridiculous that prevented me, or, worse than ridiculous, presumptuous. The Geraldines of this world could be geishas, not the Idas.

"I didn't really want you to do it for *me*," I said sadly as I got up again to leave. "I wanted you to do it for Scotty. Or for the family."

"And do you think I've done nothing for them?" he demanded, angry again. "Who's kept the firm together? Well, if my wife won't recognize it, at least my partners will. Have a look at *that*." He took from his bureau and handed me an engraved letterhead which announced in big block type the names: "Hartley and Dodge." I stared for a moment before I realized what it meant.

"But where's Uncle Linn's name?"

"We've taken it out. The firm has decided not to carry the names of deceased partners." As he looked at me now, with a first faint furtiveness, I realized, in a thrill of temper, that even he was nervous. He had not known before how to break this to me and had taken a quick advantage of his own impatience. "Besides, Hartley and Dodge is shorter and easier to remember."

"To *remember*," I exclaimed, as the full outrage of what he was doing filled my consciousness. "What have you to do with memory? Have you asked Aunt Dagmar about this?"

"Of course I haven't asked Aunt Dagmar! What business is it of Aunt Dagmar's? Honestly, Ida, your disloyalty is positively psychopathic. You'd rather see the name of a dead uncle on the door than a living husband's!"

"It's not a question of my loyalty to you," I insisted, humiliated to find the tears again in my eyes. "It's a question of *our* loyalty to Uncle Linn who gave you your start. Who made you what you are today!"

"Your ignorance of the business world is exceeded only by your ignorance of your family's role in it," he retorted coldly. "Obviously, there's no point in our continuing this discussion."

The following day I spent in an agony of apprehension, for Aunt Dagmar, despite the note of entreaty in my voice on the telephone, would not see me until the late afternoon. She had changed greatly since Uncle Linn's death, to which she had reacted with a querulous resentment. She seemed to feel that a providence which had denied her children owed her the reparation of preserving her husband at least to his ninetieth year. She stayed home all the time now, receiving visitors with a rather peevish air and making lists of relatives who might wish a pair of Uncle Linn's cufflinks, or a drawing, or even a page of his stamp book. It exasperated her that Derrick, her co-executor, paid so little attention to these details.

"It doesn't surprise me in the least," she said, when I had stammered out my news. "I only marvel that he didn't do it the day of the funeral. Linn always said he'd end by swallowing us up."

"Aunt Dagmar, I'm so sorry."

"Sorry!" she exclaimed fretfully. "He was your choice, wasn't he?"

"I sometimes wonder," I murmured dismally. "You were all so for him."

When Uncle Victor came in from next door, for his daily call, she told him my news while I hung my head.

"Oh, I say, Dagmar, that's too bad!" he exclaimed. "The man was never quite a gentleman." Then he took in my stricken countenance. "Forgive me, Ida, that slipped out. Derrick is a brilliant man, I know, but he goes a bit far at times. He's young, of course. You should learn to curb him. That's a woman's job."

This was too much. I got up, one hand on my lips and hurried from the room. Aunt Dagmar called after me, with contrition in her voice now, but I did not heed her. When I got home, I went upstairs to my little green living room and shut myself in. There, at last, I could give in to my misery. For the shadowy, secret thing which I had always dreaded without making out all of its contours in the misty corners of my fantasy had finally happened, and there was none of the relief of despair in its happening, but only further terror. I had destroyed Fifty-third Street. I had destroyed the family. It had been in the cards that I would do it; everyone, even Geraldine, had always suspected me of being the agent of dissenting forces. Poor Mother, with her sad, hurt eyes, had known that she had produced a Trojan horse. And Derrick had promptly seen that *I* was his way in. Well, Derrick would have my help and sanction no longer. The family could choose between him and me, and if they chose him, which I felt sure, in their own perverse fashion, that they would, I could retire like Scotty, and Livia of old, into the limbo of those who were unable, and in the end unwilling, to keep up the eternal Denison appearances.

Christopher came home before Derrick, and it was he who discovered me in my state of disheveled collapse.

"Hello!" he exclaimed. "You look as if you'd run through Hell with your hat off."

"Oh, Chris, have you heard? About changing the firm name?"

"Congratulations, Mrs. Hartley!"

"Don't make fun of me," I wailed. "Doesn't it shock you?"

"Shock me? Why should it? I don't like it, I confess. I'm a bit of a stickler for the old things, and Uncle Linn was very good to me. But Derrick's right. Let the dead bury the dead."

"You don't really believe that! You're just saying it because you're afraid I'll do something crazy. Well, you're right. I'm going to leave him."

Christopher came over and sat down on the sofa, leaning forward towards me, his knees tight together and his hands clasped over them. He was still smiling, but the sarcasm had gone from his voice, if not his words. "If you're talking about divorce, you'd better get a first-class lawyer. Your grounds seem a bit wobbly to me."

"Please be serious!"

"But I am. I doubt if any court would give you a penny of alimony or custody of the children. Though I suppose Derrick might let you take Hugo."

"But I don't want alimony!" I moaned. "Let him keep the children and the house and everything. I'm no good to anybody. I may as well crawl into some little hole and die."

Christopher stared for some moments at the carpet as if he were looking for something and then shook his head regretfully. "Poor Ida. She's so far down in that old bog of self-pity I don't know if we can still get her out." He jumped suddenly to his feet and pretended to be pulling someone from an imagined swamp in the middle of the floor. It was infuriating, it was absurd, but it was the best possible treatment for me, this elaborate panto-mime before which it was impossible to sustain any mood more harmful than irritation. At last he simulated a recovery of the body and shook his head again dubiously. "Pretty far gone, I'm afraid. But we'll see what a drop of whiskey can do."

I sat morosely on the sofa until he returned with a flask and two small glasses. After one of these I was sufficiently revived to tell him about Aunt Dagmar and Uncle Victor.

"But don't you see they're getting older?" he pointed out. "They don't see things the way they used to. They take themselves more seriously. They take themselves almost as seriously as *you* take them. What is Derrick, after all, but an up-to-date Denison? If Mother were alive, wouldn't she give you the dickens for pulling a scene like this!"

"Then is honor to go for nothing?" I demanded bleakly. "Is tradition and family feeling to go for nothing? Is gratitude to go for nothing?"

"Are marriage vows to go for nothing?" he came back at me. "Are mater-nal duties to go for nothing?"

I brooded over this, reflecting sourly that I was no longer in a position to answer back with the privilege of an older sister. "You think Mother would have expected me to take this lying down?"

"I think she would have expected you to take it. I doubt very much if she would have recommended the posture."

"And you? How will you take it?"

"That, my dear Ida, is my affair. It so happens that I am not wedded to Derrick."

I had another few sips of whiskey, and when Derrick came home I was quite calm. I even went to the dinner party given by Mr. Dodge to cele-brate the firm's change of name, and I confess that I was not displeased by the embarrassment which my silent, unexpected and rather grim presence caused my husband and the others. But there was no disguising my capitu-lation. That day was the most important in my life, at least until the day, twenty-eight years later, when Geraldine went out the window of her hotel. Father had told me that I could be a leader or be led, but that it was vital that I should choose. I had not chosen until that night, but I chose then.

One thing, however, happened to cheer me in my new passivity and make me less somber in the months that followed my talk with Christopher, and that was his resignation from Hartley and Dodge. He told Derrick that he had borrowed the money from Aunt Dagmar to purchase a stock exchange seat and start his own firm, and he told me that the time had come when he had to be on his own, clear of the family. I have no doubt that both reasons were valid, and, indeed, he moved to an apartment the very next month, selling his half of our house to Derrick. But I have never had the smallest doubt that the real reason for his leaving was his disgust at Derrick's treatment of the shade of Uncle Linn. It was like Christopher to make no open protest. "If somebody can't see a point of honor, there's no point explaining it," he had always said. He has led his life ever since in his own neat, brisk, successful fashion, more disciplined than I ever dreamed of being, both in big things and in small. Even now he will stop his car to rub a bird stain off the hood, and he still brings an extra shirt to his office to put on after lunch, but the good side of this particularity is that his kindness and his decency are always scrubbed and ready for use. It has been my consolation through the years that he sees Derrick with my eyes. For thus I have always had the sense of an inarticulate ally. If Christopher and I have learned to act like Denisons, we both still feel as Trasks.

9

IDA: 1950

I DID NOT ask any of the men of my immediate family, after Geraldine's funeral services, to go to the interment in the Denison plot in Brooklyn, but when Dorcas, conspicuously large and tweedy in the sober little group that had gathered on the church steps, plucked my elbow and asked in that voice that she never bothered to modulate if it was all right "now" for her to go back to the country, I felt that I could no longer postpone the little lecture which I had been preparing for her.

"I won't keep you more than an hour. I'd like you to go with Cousin Minerva in her car and then come back with me."

"But Daddy's not going," she protested in surprise.

"Neither is Mark." Dorcas' husband had already left with Derrick for a downtown world removed from the irrelevancy of death. "They leave the mourning to us."

"But I should get back to the girls."

"Why?"

"I told Lucy I'd go to see her basketball team play."

"Well, you'll have to be a little late, that's all."

I walked to the first of the hired limousines which was to take me and Christopher, leaving her no decent alternative but to go with Minerva Denison, who, standing beside us, had heard my directions. But I was not fooling myself. I knew that it was going to be difficult to scrub off the effect of the years in which I had given in to Dorcas. The soaked hull of our relationship was covered with the barnacles of all that she had taken for granted. I had let her believe that Mark and life with Mark and children

by Mark were her sole duties. I was only now, in my new thinking since
Geraldine's death, beginning to see how insulting my sense of her limitations had been.

Christopher and I, in the car, plunged as always, when alone together,
into the past.

"I keep going back in my mind to that winter when Derrick and I first
met," I told him. "The winter, too, when he first met Geraldine. Do you
think she'd have had a happier life with him?"

"Well, she couldn't have had a much worse one, that's for sure."

"What about him? Would he have been happier?"

Christopher smiled, recoiling instinctively at my tone of self-indictment.
"She might have done a better job with his social life. At least until she
started drinking. She might have charmed all those butter-and-egg men."

"*I* tried."

"Oh, Ida!" He burst out laughing and slapped a hand on his knee. "I
remember you at those dinners. Vaguely sweet. With a remote smile. Like
a cultivated Greek slave at a Roman banquet. It must have been pretty hard
for Derrick to bear."

The car stopped for a red light, and ahead of us I could see the hearse
growing smaller down the long street until it turned the corner.

"You blame *me*, then," I said morosely. "For everything."

"I don't know what you mean by everything. I blame Derrick for being
hard. You were never hard, Ida."

It was a small tribute, but it helped to mollify me. Christopher looked
more and more like Father as he grew older, with the same gentle brown
eyes, the same clear skin and fine features. But, unlike Father, his hands were
always on the move, to tighten his tie, to straighten a hair, to scratch the
corners of his chin, to gesticulate. He had made a fortune in his brokerage
firm; he had married a beautiful and much photographed woman, and at
fifty he was still a competent polo player. He had taken the advice that Father
had offered me and chosen to be a leader. But he was still a Trask who by
force of will had turned himself into a Denison. And how could that be,
when the essence of being a Denison was precisely that one didn't try?

"Hard?" I queried. "Do you think Derrick is really hard?" I paused to
consider it. "Perhaps he was, to Geraldine."

"Wasn't that Greek meeting Greek?"

"I don't mean *then*. I mean years later, when they had their affair."

Christopher's mouth fell open. "Oh, you knew?"

"Of course I knew. Even shutting my eyes as tightly as I could, I knew."

He closed his lips the way Mother used to when something distasteful
was mentioned. "*De mortuis* and all that, but let's face it, Ida. She was a
pretty bad girl. And as for Derrick . . . well, it was long ago. Best forget it."
He rubbed his hands together in the Denison gesture of dismissal that applied
to the awkward, the unpleasant and the inevitable. And how better could
one do than dismiss them? I felt perverse and ashamed.

"But it was much worse than just knowing about it!" I exclaimed. "I
encouraged it. I thought it was my punishment for marrying Derrick when
he was still in love with her. Do you know, I even helped her decorate the

apartment where they used to meet? With Mother's things! Can you imagine what Mother would have thought?"

Christopher at this gave a real whoop of laughter. "But she'd have absolutely adored it!" he cried. "Did you really? Poor Ida, how *like* you."

"How sloppy, you mean?"

He threw up his hands. "But the very cream of sloppiness! Mother would have treasured it!"

"Sloppier than adultery?"

"Oh, no." He frowned, serious again. "But then Geraldine was always fundamentally the sloppiest of us all. Even Mother, who had a weakness for her, knew that."

It was absurd, but Christopher's judgment came to me as if from another world, as if Mother and Aunt Dagmar had sent me a message of cheer. "Did you really think, poor foolish Ida," they seemed to be asking, "that we didn't know how hard you tried? Could you honestly have thought that we didn't see through Geraldine?"

"It's sloppy, you know," Christopher warned me, when we turned in the gate of the cemetery, "to be always worried about being sloppy."

As we walked behind the coffin to the Denison plot where my grandparents lay under a brown obelisk and Aunt Dagmar under a brooding angel and Father and Mother under their simple twin grey slabs, I slipped my arm under Christopher's and was comforted by his answering squeeze. To the dead, at least, I had done my duty. I could face those tombstones and whisper with courage, even with presumption, so long as Christopher was beside me: "I *was* a good daughter. I *was* a good niece." The realization that my failures were all with the living made of the graveyard a preface and not an epilogue.

"He cometh up, and is cut down, like a flower . . . In the midst of life we are in death."

My prayers were for Geraldine, but my tears, as I stood through the rest of the brief service, were for Mother and the thought of what she would have done with the years that Geraldine had wasted. She would have helped me to bear my disappointment at Derrick's disappointment in me. She would have taught me to realize that my refusal to become the woman he wanted was due as much to stubbornness as to pride. She would have kept me from transmuting the mere tastes of my forebears into moral principles. She would have driven into my stubborn mind that Derrick had not chosen me for my emotional depths or even for my intellectual heights, but because he wanted a partner to bear his children and to grace his triumphs. Without Mother I had stood apart, to preserve my honor, a shabby old rag clutched in two desperate fists, exposing Dorcas to his possessiveness and Hugo to his misunderstanding. There seemed, at that moment, little enough to choose between Geraldine and me.

But Geraldine was dead; what remained of her was being lowered into the earth by four men before my eyes. I turned away with Christopher and looked up, as we walked, at the cloudless grey sky of that warm winter day.

"Well, that's that," I said. "Whether I did too little or too much, and no matter what my motive, that's that."

"Are you exorcizing her?"

"No, I'm learning to live with her."

"You're just in time. Ghosts are the hardest to live with."

Going back, I sent Christopher with Minerva and took Dorcas with me. I glanced sideways at her as she stared moodily out the window of the car. She was still resentful that I had made her take a morning from her children.

"Is it true that Cousin Geraldine left you all her swag?" she asked without turning.

"Yes. What do you think I should do with it?"

"Well, I suppose it makes sense to get it over to the grandchildren as soon as possible. There's no point just giving it to Uncle Sam in estate taxes."

I considered the different strands of rudeness that went into her advice. Not only did Dorcas take for granted that I existed only to assist her children; she assumed that I had little time to exist.

"If Geraldine had wanted to leave her money to your children, presumably she would have done so. She left it to *me*."

Dorcas glanced at me briefly as if to determine whether this was a poor joke. "Of course, you may do as you like with it," she said, throwing her cigarette out the window. "Only why ask me, then?"

"Because I thought you might suggest something that was fun."

"Fun? Well, wouldn't it be fun to do something for my poor girls? Daddy's interested in nobody but little Derrick."

"He didn't always prefer boys."

"Well, he's getting old, Ma, let's face it. Mark says he's becoming bogged down with details. You ought to get him to take more time off."

"Ought? Why ought I to? Why should I concern myself with what happens at the office?"

"Well, of course, if you're going to take *that* attitude, I don't suppose anything matters." Dorcas shrugged and turned to stare again out the window.

"Oh, but I think some things *do* matter," I insisted. "I think, for example, loyalty matters."

"Loyalty to whom?"

"To one's father."

Dorcas turned back quickly with angry eyes. "What about to one's husband?"

"Mark owes the same loyalty that you owe. To your father."

She had become so accustomed through the years to my accepting, at least by silence, her own values that my smallest independence of judgment now struck her as treachery. "Isn't it for Daddy's good to keep him from wrecking his own firm?"

"You exaggerate. He's not wrecking it. And even if he were, it would not be your place—or Mark's—to stop him."

Dorcas gave a little cry of outrage. "You think I'm undutiful? Is that it?"

"I think you may not realize how much your father, as he gets older, is going to need you."

"Why won't he have you?"

"Because I've failed him," I said simply, "and you haven't. *Yet.*"

I was surprised to see something like fear creep over her face. "How have you failed him?" she demanded.

"Oh, in many ways. More even than I know. He's a lonely man, dear. And he's built too much of his life around you."

"But I never asked him to!" she cried in a sudden fit of excitement. "I never wanted him to! As a child, I never suggested he take me on those fishing trips, with all those men. And do you think it was fun, at dances, when I wanted a boy to take me home, to find Daddy waiting for me, at the foot of the stairs, smoking his eternal cigar?"

Her cheeks were now mottled with indignation, and her bosom heaved. Emotion had never been becoming to Dorcas.

"I know you never asked for your father's affection," I assured her. "And I can well imagine that you didn't want it. But, after all, you accepted it. As you have accepted all the benefits that flowed from it."

"What benefits?"

"All kinds of money that Hugo has never seen. Not to speak of Mark's partnership in the firm."

"Mark made that on his own!"

"He might have. But the fact remains that your father put up his capital. The fact remains that your father has groomed him to be his successor."

"If Daddy ever retires. But *will* he?"

"If Daddy chooses not to retire, that's Daddy's affair," I reproved her in a more severe tone. "You have got into the habit, my dear, of blaming everything on Daddy. Maybe he deserves it. But his deserving it has nothing whatever to do with your duty to him. That may not seem fair, but since when has life been fair? Daddy is *your* responsibility."

I was prepared for anything but what happened now. I was prepared to have Dorcas rap on the glass and tell the driver to stop and let her out. I was prepared to have her excoriate me and bring up childhood injuries to thrust in my face. I was even prepared to have her retreat haughtily, as she had done as a little girl, behind the high barrier of her exclusive intimacy with Derrick and tell me that I did not understand him. But I was decidedly not prepared to have her burst into hysterical tears and continue sobbing for the rest of our drive. When I tried to talk to her, she simply shook her head, and when I tried to put my hand on hers, she huddled away from me into her corner and sobbed even louder. I would not have minded had I thought it was merely her old resentment. But it struck me oddly that Dorcas was not thinking of me at all. Something that I had said about her father seemed to have aggravated a wound that had already been festering. It was too bad—if it *was* too bad. But it was going to take more than Dorcas' sobs, to which the years had accustomed me, to drive me back to my role of silent watcher.

PART FOUR
DORCAS' MEN

10

DORCAS: 1934

Dorcas decided, after her graduation from Barnard, that it was time for what her father called a "stocktaking." She had a favorite vision of herself as too young and too helpless for such assessments, as a quivering furry creature crouched in the palm of some vast protective hand, but she knew perfectly well that such fantasies were for her private amusement and not for getting ahead in the bleak world of fact. For the latter, alas, a quite unamusing detachment was needed, and when she had finally induced herself to step back and take that stock, she had had to conclude regretfully that her principal assets seemed to be a clear mind and robust health. Her father, in transmitting to her his natural endowments, had, in his usual fashion, overdone the job. With his health he had given her too much of his figure; she was too tall, too long strided, too broad in the shoulders and hips, too reminiscent of one of those exercising blond fräuleins in a Nazi poster. And with her good slice of the paternal mind, she had also been burdened with a slice of the paternal temper which took the unlovely form of bursting into tears when her feelings were hurt or even stamping her feet on the floor. It was her particular grievance against her brother Hugo that he refused to regard these fits as involuntary.

"You think they're attractive," he insisted. "Basically, you think they're feminine and rather appealing."

"I do not!"

"Oh, but you *do*." Hugo loved to analyze her coolly, with small, glinting, sibling eyes. "You want to seem volatile and romantic, when really you're just as mean and calculating as Daddy."

"You judge everybody by yourself!"

"Ah, but I have *other* qualities. A sense of humor, for example. And a lively imagination. The imagination to see that you're going the wrong way about getting what you want."

"And what, may I ask, do you assume I want?"

"A great big hairy man!" His raucous laugh cut short her gasp of protest. "Oh, please don't deny it. Spare me that. But can't you see that your error is in assuming there's only *one* way to be feminine? Nature made you big and strong, and you try to be small and messy."

"I'm no messier than you are. I peeked into *your* room this morning!"

"Just like you to be spying on me. The poor fellow you finally catch had better come to me for a tip-off. *I* could tell him how much aggression lies under those layers of would-be passivity."

"I imagine I could prove of equal help to the future Mrs. Hugo Hartley."

"I'll bring her to you!" he exclaimed in glee. "I'll be glad to! If she won't have me, knowing the worst, I don't want her!"

Hugo's razor sharpness in family arguments made him respected, not only by their mother and Dorcas, but by their father. For with Hugo none of them had any assurance of a basic family affection to blunt his wit. He probably cared about Ida, in his own sardonic way, but it was perfectly possible that the pains which Dorcas had seen him take in the selection of his mother's Christmas and birthday presents had been for the real purpose of bolstering their alliance against Daddy. Dorcas had taken freshman psychology at Barnard and understood the division of her family into rival pairs of father-daughter and mother-son. But the peculiar feature of the Hartleys was that her father had lacked the patience or tact, upon the ultimate awakening of his latent interest in Hugo, to overcome the latter's prickliness. Hugo had little use for Johnny-come-latelies, and the father who had been too busy to accept the offer of a favorite toy or teddy bear was not to enjoy, on mere demand, the confidences of the college man. The resulting constraint between him and Derrick had settled the mantle of paternal affection more heavily upon Dorcas' shoulders, and she had taken to repeating every night her resolution that she would not be "Daddy's girl" all her life.

For there was no point denying to herself that Hugo had placed his icy fingertip on the very palpitating pulse of her greatest problem. She had failed, at least so far, with other men. She had an unfortunate inclination to seem either eager or hostile. If a man attracted her, she either made too much of him, with many exclamatory interruptions, head shakes and sudden, pointless laughs, or made too much of herself by being disputatious or even contradictory. Sometimes, disgusted with her two extremes, she would relapse into daydreams and waste valuable time at parties in fantasies of movie stars when there were attractive men right at hand. She had always been the kind of girl whom other girls introduced to their brothers, and now she saw herself in danger of becoming the kind whose married friends ask to supper without providing a beau. The first casualty of her stocktaking was her plan to go to graduate school. She decided that she had wasted enough time on the art and literature of dead days. She would take advantage of the shorthand and typing that she had learned in the summers and become a secretary.

Her father had no objections; in fact, he seemed relieved that she was giving up the idea of a master's degree in the fine arts. He believed that women, if not wives and mothers, should occupy useful, subordinate positions in the business world. But Dorcas' trouble came when she announced at dinner that she planned to look for a job in a publishing house.

"I had hoped that you might consult me first," he said in the slow, deliberate tone that marked his swelling irritation. "I was thinking of offering you a job in the office. I thought it might amuse you to be our receptionist for a while."

Dorcas breathed quickly and smiled in what she hoped was a disarming manner. Anything connected with the office was the highest imaginable honor. "I'm sorry, Daddy, but wouldn't you rather have me go into something that has a future for women? After all, you couldn't very well expect me to be a partner in Hartley and Dodge, could you?"

"You might be some day. A limited partner."

"I'm sure it would have to be very limited!"

"You don't understand me, Dorcas," he said, clearing his throat testily. "If I should die and leave you an interest in the firm, you would become what is called a limited partner. It would do you no harm in the meanwhile to learn something about business."

Dorcas knew that the moment had come to get up and give him a kiss. Of course Hugo would be nasty about it, and call her a hypocrite, but she had to learn not to mind Hugo. After all, did the fact that one saw the fitness of one's gestures make them any less sincere? As she leaned down to kiss her father's leathery cheek, she gave her brother a defiant glance. "I can't bear it when you talk about dying, Daddy. All that won't happen for ages and ages, when I'm an old woman. It has nothing to do with the kind of job I take now." She went back to her seat and smiled down the table at him.

"'What shall Cordelia do? Love and be silent,'" Hugo quoted mockingly.

"A lot of girls take jobs for the chance of meeting young men," her father continued in a mollified tone, and she saw Hugo wink at their mother. "I don't know what part that may play in your plans—I can't imagine why it should play any—but if it does, there's a much better chance of meeting a worth-while fellow in my shop than in any publishing house."

"Why do you say that?"

"Because the young men who go into publishing are men who can't stand competition. If you can call them men at all. Poor creatures who haven't the guts to live in an attic and write. So they 'publish.'" Her father made a grimace as he uttered the word. "With a small salary to amplify a small trust fund they live delicately in a world of 'nice things.'"

"But if Dorcas came downtown, Daddy, how could you be sure she'd go for the right young man?" Hugo intervened. "How do you know she wouldn't fall for an elevator boy or a pink, pimply file clerk?"

"I think you're both horrid!" Dorcas protested angrily. "You can't believe a girl has anything in her mind but getting married. I want a job that's *interesting*. Isn't it better to read manuscripts by people who may one day be famous authors than take dictation about stocks and bonds?"

"If you want to read, there's always the Public library," her father retorted. "Better than these modern novels about sex in Chinatown."

"That's not the point, Derrick." Ida came unexpectedly to her daughter's aid. "Dorcas wants to be connected with a living organization. It's not just books. It's publishing. I wish I'd done something like that myself at her age."

Dorcas always felt disloyal to her father in accepting her mother's assistance, but she was in no position now to reject allies, so she gave Ida a grateful look and stared uneasily into her plate. Derrick continued to grumble about the cheap standards of the publishing world, but his grumbling took a general form, and she knew that the individual issue, for the moment, was closed.

The next two weeks were devoted to job hunting. She was determined to use neither letters nor references, but simply to make the rounds of the publishing houses. She had two offers, but at a very low salary, and it was not until she called at the Brandon Press on Madison Avenue that she found what she was looking for. This company, as she had learned from her talks at other houses, was owned by Jack Brandon, a steel heir who had started it with the rich liberal's proclamations that its future standard would be quality alone, but since then he had lost interest, and it had settled back into the routine of general publishing, that broad, grey sea of humdrum emotion on which gleamed the occasional atoll of a thoughtful book. But there was money in the firm, and the young editors had a reputation for being eager and able, and fourteen days had taught Dorcas that this was all one could expect.

Her interview with Mr. Robin Granberry did not start well. He seemed more concerned with what he could tell her about herself than with any information that she had to offer. In fact, as he hardly allowed her to say a word, she could only stare at his long, lanky body and long lanky hands, at the black suit that needed pressing and the brown sweater with its large stain in front. He had thick black hair that fell across his forehead and a face, long like his body, with a sensitive white skin that bore the red welts of careless shaving habits. But he had beautiful eyes. Dorcas decided that one might forgive a disorganized appearance for such a pair of dark, restless, worried eyes. Like a deer's, she thought and immediately regretted the phrase as if those now jeering eyes would pounce on it and tear it out of her mind.

"You don't have to tell me what you want," he was saying in a tone unpleasantly like Hugo's. "I'll tell *you*." She was struck by how much he had to be doing as he talked, pulling his hair, rubbing an itching elbow on the table, turning his swivel chair. "You're an English major, and you *adore* Herman Melville. You fancy yourself picking a new *Moby Dick* out of the scrap basket where some Philistine editor has flung it. You take it to Mr. Brandon who promptly gives you *my* job. Then Melville comes to town and falls madly in love with you, but you won't let him leave his wife, so he commits suicide, and you win the Pulitzer prize by publishing his love letters. Isn't that the gist of it?"

Dorcas was flustered, but she reminded herself that that was just what men like Mr. Granberry wanted. She felt that her father would have been proud of her answer: "I can type and take shorthand, Mr. Granberry. Try me!"

"You can. Of course you *can*. But *will* you? That's the point. Or every time I give you a letter, will you gaze at me with eyes of soulful reproach because it's not a page of *Omoo*?"

"Well, is it wrong for a girl to want to make something of her job?" Dorcas exclaimed. Hearing herself go so far, she surrendered to the balance of her temper. "I suppose you're the kind of man who thinks a stenographer should always stay a stenographer! That menials should know their place!"

"On the contrary," he said, taken aback. "I consider myself an advanced liberal. Rather on the pink side, if anything. I simply consider that stenographers should be stenographers *while* they're stenographers. Forgive me if

I have my doubts as to whether you'd be content with such humble fare."
He paused now to study her application card. "I see that you attended Miss
Irvin's School and that your father is the Hartley of Hartley and Dodge.
Are you sure you wouldn't be more comfortable in a stock-exchange seat?"

"Look, Mr. Granberry. Either try me out or let me go."

He studied her for a moment and then smiled in grudging approval. "I
like that upper class quiver of your nostrils. Perhaps, after all, you might
give us a needed tone. Could you start tomorrow?"

Dorcas in the weeks that followed decided that she had every reason to
congratulate herself. She acted as secretary for Mr. Granberry and another
young editor and had been promised an early opportunity to try her hand
at jacket blurbs and press releases. She found that she could type as well as
anyone else in the firm and that her services were in great demand whenever she had free time. Only the office itself disappointed her. The great
two-storied room where she worked, with its huddled center group of typewriter desks and its lawn of an emerald rug, surrounded on three sides by
the glassed-in cubicles of the junior editors and on the fourth by a gigantic
bookcase rising to the ceiling and packed with dust jacketed volumes, had
no relation to the publishing house of her fancies with its quiet, dignified
aspect of considered disorder. She could not imagine, for example, Charlotte Brontë or Thackeray coming to the offices of the Brandon Press. And
if they had, would anyone have recognized them? A classic, in the eyes of
her fellow workers, could go no further back than Joyce.

Granberry, himself, as if to rectify the unseemly intimacy of their initial
dispute, made every effort to treat her formally. He would barely look up
when she came in for the morning's dictation and would throw her the
opening lines of his first letter without so much as a word of greeting. He
obviously meant to appear too absorbed in thought to be aware of the very
existence, much less the sex, of his amanuensis. But at the same time he
was incapable of resisting the urge to show off; he had always to interpo-
late, to explain to Dorcas, respectfully waiting, pad in hand, the role that *he*
had played in the negotiations leading to this very letter, to fill in the background that she might comprehend how beautifully his scheme fitted the
facts and, incidentally, how vividly he could describe the characters involved.
Robin Granberry wanted approval—from the Brandon Press, from its shareholders and authors, even from Dorcas Hartley. She understood, as she
watched him strut about his little office, declaiming his correspondence, or
slumping in his chair, a leg dangled over the arm, that he was a man who
could never have enough applause.

"I guess you really told them off that time, Mr. Granberry!" she learned
to exclaim, or: "I'd love to see their faces when they get *that* letter!"

And Granberry would shrug and turn away as if he had barely heard, as
if her excited comments were of no more significance than the jingle of her
charm bracelet as she whipped over a page in her dictation book. But that
he paid her more attention than his demeanor admitted was proved, after
she had been working there only a month, when he casually handed her a
pile of manuscript, some chapters from Ely Bliss's work in progress. Bliss
was a wordy, nostalgic young novelist of Iowa farm life, who was then en-

joying a phenomenal vogue. Dorcas had heard in the office that Granberry owed his editorship to his Swarthmore friendship with Bliss, and she was intensely flattered that her opinion should be sought. She took the manuscript home and read every word of it that night, staying up late to rehearse aloud her detailed report to Granberry. But when she appeared, pale and excited, in the doorway of his office the next morning, he simply scowled.

"No dictation just now, Dorcas," he grumbled. "I've got one sweet bitch of a hangover. I was out with Bliss last night."

"So was I!"

"You were?" His face looked utterly blank. "My God, I must not remember anything."

"Oh, I don't mean *really*. I mean I was reading the book."

"What book?"

Nothing, however, was going to deter her. Sitting down, uninvited, before his desk, she started off on her piece: "I think Mr. Bliss writes with great beauty of style. Sometimes I feel that the length of his descriptions impedes the reader who is primarily fascinated with the story. On the other hand, it is very difficult to know where to cut."

"Cut! Did I ask you to cut?"

"You asked for my opinion, Mr. Granberry. I think I would cut in the love scenes. Why, when there are so many beautiful things in the world, is it necessary for Mr. Bliss to emphasize the sordid side of sex?"

"Because that's precisely the beautiful side!"

"Oh, Mr. Granberry! You can't believe that!"

He uttered a groan and covered his face with his hands. "Please, *please*! It's a bit early in the morning to face Kate Greenaway hand in hand with Mrs. Humphrey Ward! Has it never struck you, my dear Miss Hartley, that there might be *some* things you hadn't experienced? *Some* things Mummy didn't tell you?" He looked up at her now with a sudden irate resentment. "And who the hell do you think *you* are to set yourself up as the arbiter of what is beautiful and what is sordid? To me the really sordid things are probably just the ones you like! Moonlight and handholding and soul kisses. Ugh!"

Dorcas closed her lips tightly, for she felt them trembling. "If you have such a low opinion of my critical faculty, I wonder why you thought me worthy of even peeking into the sacred pages of Ely Bliss."

"Because, God help us, it's women like you who make up the reading public!"

She strode out of his office and back to her typewriter. She worked very busily and inaccurately all that morning, and by noon she had decided to resign. It was hardly fitting that she should stay a day longer after being so grossly insulted. It was certainly hard that what should have been her proudest moment, the delivery of her first report, should have turned instead into her bitterest humiliation, but it was not her fault if the publishing world was full of brutes. She was still banging furiously at the keys when she felt the final impudence of a hand on her shoulder and whirled around to face Granberry.

"Will you kindly keep your hands to yourself!"

There was instant silence from the adjoining machines as the other girls delightedly stopped to listen.

"I was simply trying to attract your attention," he replied, unruffled. "I spoke to you twice, but you didn't hear me. Would you be good enough to let me take you out to lunch and apologize for my very bad manners?"

She nodded quickly, but made no attempt to speak. It was quite bad enough that her eyes were already full of tears.

"Shall we say twelve-thirty?" he continued in the same tone, and when she simply nodded again, staring straight ahead, he turned back to his office with a little shrug and a smile for the benefit of his approving audience.

At lunch in the booth of a Third Avenue bar, over sandwiches and beer, he explained himself, on the whole, very graciously.

"We must learn a mutual tolerance, Dorcas. I don't want you to get huffy and quit. You're too good a worker, and you've got too good a brain, if a bit encumbered with minor prejudices. There's a place for you at Brandon, and I don't mean just as a secretary. You could be a copy editor. You could be in charge of dust jackets. You might even ultimately run our publicity. Only don't *ever* get the idea you could work with authors. It's not your line."

Dorcas, mollified by his tone and warmed by the unaccustomed midday beer, was easily resigned to the diminution of her prospects. "Why couldn't I?" she asked mildly. "What's wrong with me?"

"As a businesswoman, nothing. As an editor everything. You don't have the first notion of why a man like Ely Bliss sits down at a typewriter to pound out his little fantasies of guilt and hate and yearning. And why should you? Leave the job of handholding to the frustrated writers, like myself. The woods are full of them. What this firm really needs is a good housekeeper. Why shouldn't it be Dorcas Hartley?"

It was not exactly what she had dreamed of as a publishing career, but what had she really wanted of Brandon but the chance to meet men, and who but a man, a brilliant man, however erratic, however uncreased his trousers and sour his moods, was taking the trouble, right then and there, to offer her his friendship?

"I'll try," she murmured docilely. "I'll try to learn to be a housekeeper."

The following Monday a new arrangement was proposed by the office manager whereby Dorcas would work full time for Granberry, as his assistant and secretary, and before the day was out her life was entirely altered. The telephone was to be her medium and not the typewriter; she was to call hotel and magazines and radio stations; she was to organize cocktail parties and lunches; she was to plan the visits of out-of-town authors, and above all she was to guard Robin Granberry's calendar and see that he kept his appointments.

He needed her badly; that she found out right away. She did not comprehend, indeed, how he had previously managed without her, either in his business or his private life. For she even had to compose his letters to his old mother and warn him when he had asked two girls for dinner on the same evening. He treated her as a friendly if sardonic lieutenant might treat an efficient if sometimes officious sergeant: democratically, companionably, affably, at times waspishly. But there was always the lieutenant's bar between them. However much Dorcas tried to see their relationship in the light of Jane Eyre and Mr. Rochester, she had to admit that there seemed little future with a man who asked her to his apartment to cook his supper when another girl had stood him up and who addressed her as "Hartley."

"What is Mr. Granberry *like?*" her mother was always asking.

"He's handsome when he's not being ugly. And bright when he's not being stupid. And divinely agreeable when he's not being rude as hell!"

"He sounds interesting."

"Don't worry, Mummy. He's madly in love for the moment with a neurotic poetress called Vera Stiles."

"Is she attractive?"

"How does one tell? She wears her hair in her face."

What she omitted to tell her mother was that when Robin was nice to her, he was nice in a way that she had never experienced before. He might expect her to take Vera's place and cook his supper at the last moment, but if the supper was good—and Dorcas blessed the paternal creed of self-sufficiency which had made her adept in the kitchen—he would light a cigar, pour a glass of brandy, sprawl on the day bed and begin to ask questions about herself and her family. His curiosity seemed inexhaustible; he explained it as the craving for fact of a frustrated writer. It had never occurred to Dorcas that another human being would listen to her, *really* listen. She was inured to the glazed eye of the girl friend that lit up only in anticipation of the story to be belted back in return for the story that one was telling. But Robin wanted to know everything about her and her mother and father and brother and even about her great-uncles and aunts. He loved what he called the "Denison Saga" and claimed that it was perfect material for a novel, far better than his own bleak boyhood in Syracuse that he had been "working up" on weekends for the past two years.

"My novel is about my father," he told her, "but I'm not sure I wouldn't do better with yours. I like the whole idea of his relationship with the Denisons. The merger of two different types of social climber."

Dorcas was torn between her delight at his candor and her sense of outrage at what he said. It was thrilling to hear anyone speak so disparagingly about a father of whom she had so long stood in awe, but such thrills were followed by pangs of guilt and remorse. One by one her inhibitions gave way before the beaver jaws of Robin's conversational habits, and she began to be afraid that her moral standards would be eroded along with her prejudices. For to Robin nothing about himself and certainly nothing about herself seemed immune from analysis or jokes. He took a perverse joy in assuming that she could not be shocked.

"In families like yours," he told her, "the daughter is always proud of her father's attention. It proves that she has filled the void left by her mother. For Mummy, of course, always seems to her a frigid failure. To Hugo, on the other hand, Mummy's frigidity is the symbol of Mummy's honor. It proves that she has never been willingly violated. What you each want, basically, is a virgin parent of the opposite sex."

But there were times when his mood was sour, and he was simply abusive. He would watch her with a little smile as if he were seeing how much he could make her take. And finally, one night, when she was tired and angry, and full of a dull depression at the cerebral quality of their relationship, she got up immediately after supper to take her leave.

"Where on earth do you think you're going?" he demanded.

"To the movies."

"The movies? Who said we were going to the movies?"

"We're not. I have a date."

"A *what*?" He fell back on the sofa with his arms over his head. "I never expected to hear a graduate of Miss Irvin's School use *that* term! With whom, may I ask, do you have this 'date'?"

"No, you may not ask. You know too much about me already. I have to keep some little private corner for myself."

"And that little private corner is the real, true, pulsating you, isn't it, Hartley?" he cried mockingly, jumping up and catching her hand. "Is that what you're trying to tell me?"

"It's none of your business and don't call me Hartley!" She shook herself loose from his grip and went to the door. "And you can do the dishes yourself for once. *If* you know how!"

He hurried over to place himself between her and the door. "I hate people who brood over their grudges and then suddenly explode! Why can't you give a guy a little warning? Why can't you say: 'Look, Granberry, you egocentric heel, do you think a girl has nothing better to do than cook your supper and listen to you jaw?' How was *I* to know that all this time you've been *seething*?"

"But I haven't!"

"Of course you have! And I was an ass not to see it. What does a girl your age want with good talk? She wants corsages and movies and 'dates'!"

Dorcas tried desperately to reassemble the remnants of her dignity. "I like to be made to feel like a woman once in a while," she protested. "Maybe it's silly, but girls *are* silly. At least, most of us are. Of course, I can't speak for your neurotic poetress. But I'll bet you never made *her* clean dishes. I'll bet she never has! And I'll bet her apartment's a pigsty."

Robin, with a suddenly judicial air, considered the violence of her conclusion and then shook his head. "You're wrong there. Vera's neatness is her only discipline. But come back and sit down. Just for a moment. I won't keep you from your little date." He took her by the hand and led her firmly back to the sofa. "Now tell me what I must do to make it all up. Of course, it's fun to nurse a grudge, but a generous nature should scorn that kind of fun. Do you have a generous nature, Hartley? I mean, Dorcas?"

"Well, I try."

"Then stipulate my penance. Shall I stand in a hair shirt on the snow-piled steps of Canossa?"

She was about to dismiss it all as another of his jokes when a better idea, suggested by his image of the penitent emperor, occurred to her. "You can come to a family supper!" she exclaimed in excitement. "That's it! You can meet my mother and father. You're always asking about them, but you've never met them!"

"Exactly. It's like a James novel. I make them out entirely from your point of view."

"But that's not fair to them!"

"It's probably fairer than you think. You see, I regard myself as a trained reader. I make allowance for your astigmatism."

"But life isn't a novel!" she protested.

"No, but we can try to make it one, can't we?"

She paused, baffled, unable to believe that he was as suddenly serious as he looked. "Anyway, it's your penance," she insisted. "To come to family supper on a night of my choosing. I'll let you know tomorrow. You'll be bored, but that's part of the penance. Do you agree?"

"I believe it's an error of style to change in a novel from the third to the first person. There's no telling what crudities may ensue. But, of course, if it's my penance, I must submit."

When she left his apartment, she sat alone through two hours of a neighborhood movie that she detested in order to be ready in the morning for any cross-examination about her "movie date." But he never mentioned it. He always seemed to sense intuitively when she was ready for him.

They were just four at dinner on Friday, and Dorcas' father maintained a silence that she could only interpret as ominous, while her mother kept up a little splashing rivulet of comment on books and publishing firms and whether Robin believed there were any "really great" authors still writing. Dorcas was surprised at how politely he answered. Looking about the dining room that she had accepted from her childhood as a handsome room, she saw it as she imagined that Robin must see it, and wondered for the first time if her mother had any taste at all. Had she not simply left the things as Grandma Trask had left them: the dark Piranesi prints of Roman domes and colonnades, the high-backed, Italian chairs, the imitation Sheraton sideboard with its overload of silver plates and candelabra? Was it not all too crowded, too self-consciously stately? Surely her grandmother, with her reputation for style, had filled it with flowers, painted the walls a lighter color, done *something*? It came upon Dorcas, with a flash of pride at her new perspicacity, that her mother lived in the house more as a daughter than as a wife, and she wanted to finish dinner so she could tell Robin. But now her father had entered the conversation, and her heart fell at the instant prospect of trouble.

"Hitler's still living, and he's written a great book. At least, some eighty million people would *call* it great."

"Does that make it so?" Robin's tone was suspiciously mild.

"Well, I suppose 'great' is a pretty vague term, but it's certainly a book that's had an impact on history. You can't deny that."

"I wouldn't try. But surely the ravings of a lunatic can hardly qualify as literature."

"A pretty smart lunatic, I'd say."

Robin's little smile hardened into something closer to a sneer. "Tell me, Mr. Hartley," he pursued in the same mild tone, "I've heard that men in the financial world are divided in their views on Hitler. Is it really so? Is it possible that a sane man could regard him as anything but evil incarnate?"

"Evil incarnate is a pretty fancy phrase," Derrick retorted. "I don't go in for fancy phrases myself. I'm not a publisher. Hitler's a rabble rouser and a fanatic, of course. And I don't propose to defend his conduct towards the Jews. But as a businessman I'm trained to view things in terms of their alternatives. The alternative to Hitler was communism."

"Which you think is worse?"

"Which I think is a hell of a lot worse, Mr. Granberry," Derrick emphasized severely, turning his full glassy stare on Robin. "I know your generation likes to flirt with communism, but you'll find out one day that Stalin's gang of thugs make Adolf Hitler and Co. look like the Colonial Dames!"

"I'll still take the thugs!" Robin exclaimed with a shrill burst of laughter, and Dorcas realized that the roughness of her father's tone had removed the pretense of manners between them.

"At least, Daddy, the communists have an ideal," she protested hastily. "Just because that ideal hasn't always been lived up to doesn't mean it has ceased to exist. But Hitler has no ideal. It's all just hysteria and hypnosis and silly saluting."

Her intervention, however, seemed only to make her father unreasonably angry. "I'm glad you find Stalin's slaughter of ten million peasants a mere matter of not living up to an ideal!" he exclaimed heatedly. "I'm glad you prefer it to saluting. I suppose it's old-fashioned of me to place a somewhat higher value on human life."

"Human but not Jewish!" Robin cried. "Isn't Hitler's treatment of the Jews merely something you don't 'propose to defend'!"

"I'll choose my own words in my own home, young man!"

"Derrick, my *dear*!" Ida intervened hastily, for Robin had flung down his napkin and seemed about to get up. "Mr. Granberry, I beg of you, please let's talk of something else. Isn't it bad enough to have all Europe about to explode without blowing up ourselves? Derrick, you hate communism and dislike Nazism. Mr. Granberry, I suspect, dislikes communism—at least the way it's produced in Russia—and hates Nazism. Is there really so big an issue between you? Now, I'd like to know who Mr. Granberry considers the greatest novelist: Ellen Glasgow or Willa Cather? Or perhaps you consider neither great?"

Dorcas had to admire the way her mother forced the answers out of Robin and kept her topic in tepid discussion until Nellie came in to announce that Mr. Hartley was wanted on the telephone. Once out of the room, Derrick never returned, and when dinner was over, and they were crossing the hall to the living room, Robin stopped and abruptly bade his hostess good night. Dorcas followed his swiftly retreating figure down the stairway into the front hall.

"Robin! What are you *doing*?"

He did not even turn. "I was asked for dinner, and I've *had* my dinner."

"But you can't just eat and run!"

He turned so suddenly that she collided with him. "Would it be better if I stayed and gave your father another chance to insult me?"

She paused, wretched. "Where are you going?"

"To have a drink. As a matter of fact, I'll probably have several drinks."

"Don't you think *I* need one?"

"Come along then!"

In the taxi he reached over and took her purse from which he calmly removed the little wad of bills. After counting it carefully, he nodded and gave the address to the waiting driver.

"Twenty-five dollars. We can afford LaRue."

She was careful not to reveal how much she minded. Of course, he would simply tell her that she was "bourgeois" and sneer at her middle class rules, and she was determined that she was not going to spoil anything more that night. But it surprised her that her father's principles should be so tenacious in their grip. She tried to shake off her feeling about the money in the exuberance of her enthusiasm over everything else: the corner table, the gay, crowded room, the familiar music.

"I love LaRue. And nobody ever takes me any more!"

"All you have to do is pay the bill."

"Oh, please, Robin, who cares about the bill?"

"*You* do. It's written all over you."

"Well, for heaven's sake, who's talking about it? Oh, look, here comes our waiter. Do you think I could have a stinger? Please?"

Robin, however, was moody all evening. He drank a great deal of whiskey and made venomous remarks about the girls on the dance floor, speculating on which ones had been to Miss Irvin's and what their relationship was with their partners. He refused to dance even once, for all Dorcas' urging.

"All right," she said at last wearily. "Let's have it out. Let's get it over with."

"What?"

"What you think of Daddy."

He drummed his fingers on the table and whistled, out of tune, to the music. "Do you want it straight?"

"Do you ever serve it otherwise?"

"Very well." He moistened his lips. "I don't think I mind so much his being a dyed-in-the-wool fascist. I expected that from the business milieu in which he lives. What I really mind is that he isn't content just to blow off steam like the other old dodos. He really *cares* about destroying the opposition. He's a tyrant of the ancient Tartar type. He's not really cruel; he just happens to like chewing bones."

Dorcas managed a nervous laugh. "Well, there! That wasn't so bad, was it?"

"For you or for me?"

"Oh, for me, of course. I'm sure you enjoyed it immensely."

"Didn't *you*? We all love to hear nasty things about our parents. It makes our imaginary debt to them seem smaller."

"Must you be psychological about everything? I'm simply trying to be objective about Daddy. He is rather a tyrant, of course. He likes to have things his own way. But aren't many men like that?"

"Not in America. It must be terribly hard on your poor mother to be the only dominated wife in the Park Club!"

"Don't take Mummy for granted. She's not as dominated as you think."

"She hasn't totally surrendered, if that's what you mean. There are still little oases to which she flees. Women's groups and gentle gossip and charitable works. Harmless little copses of fatuity where the monster cannot penetrate. Yes, I caught a kind of hunted gleam in her eye when she looked at me. Some dim awareness that she was once a woman."

"That *you* brought out in her?"

"Why not? I'm a man, aren't I? You don't have to chew bones to be a man. Whatever your father may think."

"Do you imply that Mummy was *flirting* with you?"

"Basically, yes. Why do girls always think of their mothers as sexless?"

Dorcas felt tired and depressed. She might have been willing to have her parents ridiculed had Robin not lumped her with them. If he had ridden up to the family threshold, bearing the smallest resemblance to a Lochinvar, on anything remotely resembling a white charger, no matter how spavined and broken-winded, had he declared, or even so much as hinted: "Your parents may be illusions, but *I* shall be your reality!" how gladly she would have clambered on that steed, and even Hugo's mocking laugh would have meant nothing as they galloped off. But no, he appraised and sneered and shrugged and then left her with her family. He had not even once commented that night on the house or on the dinner, nor had his eye distinguished so much as a picture on the wall or a carpet on the floor to laugh at or to praise. Usually he noticed such things, but evidently her home was a bourgeois blur of vulgar values. There was nothing in it to hate and surely nothing to love.

"I suppose my family's very dull," she said despondently. "It's hard for me to see it because I'm dull, too."

"Now don't take *that* attitude," he cried in disgust. "Fight back! You shouldn't allow anyone to say the things I've said about your parents. You ought to tell me I'm a pipsqueak hack editor who's eaten up with envy of your father's dough. Which, incidentally, I am. And then you ought to demand the money I took out of your pocketbook and march out of here, leaving me to wash dishes to pay the bill. If you're born a lady, *be* a lady, for God's sake!"

It was simply too much, and Dorcas solved all her problems by bursting into tears.

"What a horrible day!" she wailed. "Everything I do seems to be wrong. I don't *want* my money back! I only want a dollar so I can get home!"

Robin, visibly appalled for once, signaled the waiter frantically for the check, and in the minutes that elapsed before it came, alternately consoled and chided her, distracted by the widening circle of attention that surrounded them. But Dorcas, refusing to acknowledge anything he said, whether desperate entreaty or fiercely whispered abuse, simply continued to stare down at the table and violently sob. In the taxi she pushed him roughly aside when he tried, as a last resort, to give her a peck of a kiss on the cheek, and dashed into her family's house on arrival without even turning to bid him good night. It had all been rather terrible, she decided, climbing the stairs, but it had been a greater scene than she had thought herself capable of. In bed, lulled alternately with feelings of shame and pride, she went soon to sleep.

When she arrived in the morning at the office, she was fully determined to go straight home if Robin so much as mentioned the events of the previous evening. But he didn't. With a subtlety (if such it was) that surprised as much as it relieved her, he was very dry and businesslike and even, towards the end of the day, took occasion to pick her filing system to pieces. It was a lecture, he warned her sharply, that was long overdue. After this their friendship was renewed, but not quite on the old basis. He never addressed her now except by her Christian name, and when he asked her to dinner, it was to take her to a restaurant and not to a meal cooked by herself. He never referred to Vera Stiles or to any of his other girls, and their relationship, losing its resemblance to that of lieutenant and sergeant, began to assume the proportions of a marriage where the husband respects, if he no longer loves, the wife. Yet Dorcas drew a bleak encouragement from the fact that their principal topic of conversation had shifted from her family to himself.

He talked a great deal now about his unhappy childhood in Syracuse. "At least," he would say, "I have *that* qualification to be a twentieth century novelist." His father had left his mother, one of those sweet, passive creatures who invite abuse and betrayal, and gone to New York for a life of dissipation which had ended in a violent death. Robin at the age of seventeen had been able to collect the life insurance that put him through college only by giving half of it to his father's mistress who had threatened to inform the company that the insured had died a suicide. When Dorcas let it be seen that she was shocked, he showed the quick temper of a bad conscience.

"It's all very well for *you* to take a high moral stand. You can afford it. The only chance I had to go to college was to get my hands on that money. My father owed it to me. He'd never paid a penny to support me or Mother."

"I quite agree that your father owed it to you. But it wasn't his money. It was the insurance company's."

"As I say, you can afford these subtle distinctions. I couldn't!"

"I don't see anything subtle about that. You were telling a lie to the insurance company!" She was sorry as soon as she had said it. It was her old habit of blurting things out. She was so used to the whiplash of his tongue that she had forgotten how little experience he had had with hers.

"Lie!" he retorted, furious. "How do you know it was a lie? How do you know that my father hadn't died by accident and that *she* was lying? How do you know she hadn't pushed him out that window?"

Dorcas had on the tip of her tongue to say: "All the more reason not to pay her for it," but she checked the utterance. The unwonted exercise of such self-restraint gave her an instant, exhilarating sense of maturity. So *that* was how it was done! If one loved a man, one learned to deceive and flatter. Love? *Was* it love? She was on a giddy peak surrounded by grey abysses of hysterical laughter.

"How stupid of me!" she cried. "Of course! She was only trying to cheat you out of your rights! You paid her not to lie. As a matter of fact, you saved her from committing a crime."

Robin looked startled for a moment, and then suspicious, but he ended by greedily accepting her reassurance and piling her new theory, a wobbling boulder, on top of the jerry-built structure of his contrived excuses. Dorcas felt superior to him for the first time, but it was not a superiority that tarnished her image of Robin the man. It was simply that she knew she was experiencing for the first time the superiority that every woman feels when she learns to deal with the masculine moral need to have his cake and eat it. As Robin went on to describe to her the novel that he was writing about his father, she reflected that, if published, it might make painful reading for his mother. But this, too, called for silence. What, after all, did she care for Mrs. Granberry? Was she any more real to Dorcas than the mistress who had swindled the insurance company? The point to remember was that she and Robin were suddenly coming close. At least, he was coming close to *her*, and was that not closeness?

The crisis that was to bring them together at last, however, came over Ely Bliss's defection from the Brandon Press. Dorcas and Robin had twice dined with him in restaurants, and she had observed with a silent distrust the author's almost hysterical egocentricity. At neither dinner had he addressed more than a few words to her; he had simply poured forth to an abjectly attentive, sympathetically smiling Robin the hour-to-hour grievances of his daily round: the flutter of his heart, the ache in a tooth, a neighbor's loud radio, a wrong telephone number, a laundry's "emasculation" of his shirts and the idiocy of critics who insisted on comparing him to Thomas Wolfe. When she had protested to Robin afterwards that Ely Bliss seemed eaten up with self-pity, he had merely retorted: "But that's what makes great literature. Except when it's translated into fiction, we call it compassion."

But what he utterly failed to see, and what Dorcas intuitively understood, was that a man like Bliss was incapable of even a transient loyalty. He existed to distrust. When the contract for his new novel, of which Dorcas had read the extract, was being prepared, Robin told her that Bliss had objected to the option clause.

"Shall I strike it?" she asked.

"Certainly not. We can't afford to let these purveyors of sexual fantasy put *everything* over on us. From time to time it pays to pull them up a bit."

Dorcas smiled at the contrast between the gently smiling Robin of the dinners with Bliss and the peremptory editor before her now. "But you've always said these options are worthless," she pointed out. "Nobody tries to hold an author to one. Why isn't this a cheap way to oblige him?"

"It's true they're hard to enforce legally. An author can always dig out some juvenilia and throw it at you as his 'next book.' But they do constitute a moral obligation, and that means something in the publishing world. However much your father might sneer at the idea!"

"*I* can't help sneering at the idea of Ely Bliss recognizing any moral obligation."

"You just have it in for him because he pays no attention to you. So like a woman!"

Dorcas, adhering to her new discipline, finished typing the contract without further comment and mailed it to Bliss. But her worst misgivings were justified a week later when she was awakened by her mother at midnight to say that Robin Granberry was on the telephone and insisted on speaking to her.

"I'm afraid he's not quite sober, my dear."

Dorcas brushed past her and ran down the corridor to the telephone.

"What is it, Robin?"

"It's that bastard, Ely," the high unsteady voice came over the line to her. "Do you know what the son-of-a-bitch has done? He signed up with Doubleday!"

"Oh, Robin," she murmured. "Are you at home? I'll be right down."

She refused to listen to her protesting mother as she dressed; she simply kept repeating that her friend was in trouble, and that she had to go to him. She ignored Ida's ultimate threat to arouse her father and fled down the stairs into the street. As she stood in the icy night air under a street lamp and frantically hailed a taxi, she murmured to herself: "God forgive me, but it's the happiest day of my life!"

Robin was alone and more than half intoxicated, and told her morosely to go home and mind her own business, but when she refused and continued to sit placidly on the sofa, he sulkily poured her a drink that was much too strong and began to sob. She listened sympathetically as he moaned that he was bound to lose his job at Brandon and that he had never had a proper break in his life.

"Nonsense!" she exclaimed briskly at her first opportunity. "Nobody at Brandon thinks as much of Ely Bliss as you do. They'll be sorry to lose him, of course, but losing writers is an everyday affair. How many times have you told *me* that?"

"But not Ely," he muttered, shaking his head. "There's only one Ely."

At last she divined that what he wanted was not encouragement but consolation. He wanted to twist and writhe on the luxurious bed of his new agony, to relish every turn of his rack, to glory in the unrivaled magnitude of his wretchedness. Dorcas changed her method, and listened with moistened eyes, when she was not pouring drinks, to his catalogue of the abominable perfidies of Ely Bliss. She then heard a new Robin's complaints against his mother, his deceased father, Syracuse, Swarthmore, the Brandon Press, her own parents, and, at last, rather flatteringly, herself. He ended by drunkenly accusing her of being a Philistine, a slyboots, a hypocrite and a designing bitch.

"You even got me drunk," was his final retort, "so you can go to bed with me."

After this he became silent and sleepy, and Dorcas helped him to remove his coat and trousers and to lie down on the bed. She then lay beside him and took his head in her arms, and so they spent the night.

When she awoke in the morning, he was no longer beside her, but she heard him moving in the bathroom and in a few minutes he came in, cleaned and shaved and wearing a new grey suit that she had not seen before. He looked as oddly spruced up as a schoolboy for Sunday chapel and quite as cantankerous.

"I suppose you think I have to marry you now."

Dorcas felt only a surge of hilarity, of sudden, irrepressible gaiety. "Do you think Daddy's waiting in the street with a shotgun? Oh, *do* look and see!"

"Well, if he thinks he can buy you a husband or even scare me into it, he has another think coming!"

"You don't understand my father," she said, sitting up suddenly and getting out of bed. She walked to the bureau and straightened her blouse and dress. "Will you *look* at me!" She took his comb and pulled it through her rumpled hair. "He wouldn't waste a dollar on you, much less a bullet. Even if I were pregnant, which, under the circumstances, would be odd. And if I *did* marry you, in spite of everything, he'd never give you a penny. Never! He's quite remorseless."

When she turned around, she saw that the trapped look had gone from his face and that he was staring at her with tensely searching eyes.

"Do you mean that?"

"Certainly I mean it. If that's not fair warning, I guess a girl's never given it."

"But do you promise me, Dorcas Hartley, that if you married me, you would turn your back on your father's money?" She had never seen his eyes so glittering. "Do you promise me," he continued, in the same desperately serious tone, "that you would be *my* wife? That you would aid and comfort and console me?"

Some instinct told her not to be as serious as he. "Didn't I last night?"

"But would you *always?*"

"Always is a long time."

"Would you for a long time, then? Would you for ten years?"

"Is that all you think you'd need of me?"

"Dorcas!" he cried, taking a step towards her. "Will you marry me?"

It was part of the fantastic exhilaration of the moment that she should then discover that her mind saw clearly in a crisis. To have accepted him now would have been to put him in a panic before the day was over. She raised her hand forbiddingly, but she kept her tone gay.

"This is hardly the time or the place for a proposal," she warned him. "You'd only say again that I'd trapped you into it. And please get one thing absolutely straight. I don't want a husband who feels even the tiniest obligation to marry me. Nothing happened last night, but it wouldn't make any difference if it had. You are free, Robin. Absolutely free!"

His eyes dimmed with what she hoped was disappointment, and he laughed in his old sarcastic way. "My God, you're a clever woman, Dorcas. A chip off the old block!"

"I won't try to have the last word with you," she retorted. "I know I'd be bound to fail. All I can do is tell you where I stand." She turned to the door. "And now I think I'd better go home and change. I'll see you at the office."

"Mind you're not late!" he shouted after her down the hall. "It would be very bad taste for you to presume on whatever happened—or didn't happen—last night."

Her exhilaration persisted in the taxi, and the cold, thin, granite-bitten winter air on her cheeks, the grey, slowly moving restlessness of early morning streets, the sexlessness of the huge waking city so oddly in contrast to the sticky warmth of her own body and unchanged clothes, all of these things, together with her sense of the enormity of having been out all night and her unexpected indifference to what her parents might say, united to press down upon the happiness in her heart and to delineate and make more explicit every nob and bump of which it was composed. Robin had slept in her arms, and Robin had proposed to her! Whatever regrets, even horrors, should assail him now, he had made up with a few words for all his months of ungallant behavior.

The front door in Fifty-third Street opened before she could fit her key in the lock, and there stood Ida, in her nightgown and pale flannel wrapper, worn and tired.

"Mummy! You haven't been to bed!"

"Of course I have," Ida murmured, closing the door behind her. "I just happened to wake up early and went to your room to see if you were in. When I found you weren't, I came down to see if you'd left a note. That's all, darling. Really."

"Oh, Mummy, what a fib! You were afraid the maids would see me, and you've been sitting here all night. How ridiculous!"

Dorcas sat down on the little pink marble bench under the stairway by the big green plant. She felt elated, indignant, superior—and pitying.

"Is Mr. Granberry—feeling better?"

"Mr. Granberry's feeling fine!" She knew the misinterpretation that her mother would place on her note of triumph, but she was still irritated by the deepening dismay on Ida's countenance. "Really, Mummy, there's no point going on as if I were a fallen woman! Or as if Daddy were going to turn me out in the snow. I'm over twenty-one, and I know what I'm doing. It's not like when you were a girl. Today a woman can *be* a woman."

But Ida seemed quite unconcerned with the implication as to what *she* was. "Are you going to marry Mr. Granberry?"

"It's not impossible," Dorcas replied with a shrug. "But if I do, it won't be because of last night."

"I think being married to him might make an interesting life."

Dorcas' pride shivered into splinters on the unexpected pavement of such ready acceptance. It was as if she heard already the faint strains of an organ in the dusky hallway, and she jumped up, feeling panic in knowing what Robin's panic would have been.

"Oh, come, Mummy, one thing at a time!"

"Just remember, my child. If you want to marry Robin, there's no reason we can't work it out."

Dorcas' tears of mingled gratitude and exasperation were checked by her father's step on the stairway. He was wearing the red velvet dressing gown with the yellow brocaded tassels that gave him the air of a doge.

"What does this mean, Dorcas? What do you think you're doing, coming home at this hour? Have you been all night at that man's apartment? It's a disgrace, that's what it is. A dismal disgrace. In my day no decent woman would have ever spoken to you again!"

"Derrick!" cried Ida. "Please. Someone will hear you."

"Let them. A fat lot Dorcas cares what people think."

"Aren't you taking rather a lot for granted, Daddy?" Dorcas demanded indignantly.

"I'm only drawing the conclusions that any father would draw," he retorted coldly. "But that's where the resemblance to other fathers ceases. Another father might disown you if you didn't marry Granberry. I shall disown you if you do."

Dorcas found at once that she was trembling all over. For it was suddenly terrible that her father was not concerned with what might or might not have happened in Robin's apartment. He brushed it aside, as he brushed aside anything that could be encompassed in the limits of a single hour or day, and went directly to what he considered the only issue. "I'm very sorry about that, Daddy," she cried in a harsh voice that sounded new and strange to her. "But I'll have to take the consequences. Robin and I are engaged."

"You damn little fool!" he shouted. "Can't you see he's nothing but a cheap neurotic who wants to live off you? Can't you see you're taking on the support of a moral infant?"

"Robin will never touch your money."

"If he won't touch it, it's because he's afraid of it. And if he's afraid of it, that's worse. My God!" He stamped his foot with a disgust so obviously genuine that her heart sank. For the curtain that seemed to be crashing between them was no longer the mere curtain of parental admonitions and attitudes. She grasped suddenly that her father was quite capable of drowning his love of her in the boiling sea of his hatred of Robin, and with this new concept came a weary sense of abandonment. For where in all of this crazy scene was Robin?

"When I think of what fathers go through," he continued, striking his forehead. "And what for? To hand the product of twenty-two years' labor over to a fuzzy-minded radical who despises her family for every decent thing they stand for. Well, let him despise my money all he wants. He sure as hell isn't going to see a penny of it!"

"We'll never ask! Not if you come and beg us!"

Her father turned and walked quickly back up the stairs. As she stared irately after him, she felt her mother's hands on her shoulders.

"Darling, don't worry. I *promise* you he'll come around!"

"But I don't *want* him to!" Dorcas hissed fiercely and ran into the kitchen and up the back stairs to her room.

Robin did not come to the office till noon and then he went directly to her desk.

"Was it awful?" he whispered.

"Awful?" She looked up calmly. "No. But if I want to be a good girl and please Daddy, I won't ever see you again."

"And what do you want to be?"

"That depends on what *you* want."

"Let's get out of here."

She followed him to the drinking fountain in the vestibule.

"The reason I'm late," he said hurriedly, "is that I've been looking up marriage requirements. We could be married in forty-eight hours in the Municipal Building. Are you willing to tell your family to go to hell?"

She looked carefully into those brown, furtive eyes and decided that they gleamed with a new intensity and resolution.

"Am I to do all that," she asked gravely, "for a man who's never even told me that he loves me?"

"Yes!" he cried with his high peal of laughter. "It's the last stand of an old bachelor! No mush!"

"No mush," she said, shaking her head ruefully. "Very well, no mush. But you must let me tell you that I love *you*. I have to do that if I'm going to marry you."

And, oddly enough, as he kissed her gently and briefly on the lips in that corridor that was so rarely and luckily empty, as he squeezed her hand and smiled, as he started, crudely and verbosely, to hold forth on licenses and medical requirements, she felt, with tears of uncertain happiness, that the person to whom she had been unfair was not Robin, and certainly not her outrageous father, but Ida, the neglected Ida, who had had the heart and the simple kindness to wish her an interesting life.

11

DORCAS: 1935

AFTER A WEEK of constrained honeymoon in Virginia, where Robin displayed a great deal of temperament and Dorcas an equal share of passivity, they came back to New York and to his apartment. He flatly objected to her making any changes in it, but here Dorcas became insistent and, with her mother's help, she ultimately persuaded him to allow her to introduce a degree of color and comfort into the bleak decor of his two rooms. For Ida, by refusing to acknowledge a break, had managed to gap it, and, by treating Robin as a welcome son-in-law, had ended by making a friend of him. Derrick, however, continued adamant, and Dorcas never went to Fifty-third Street. She would have more resented his attitude had it not been for her mother's assurance that it was bound to change, an assurance, however, that was by no means altogether comforting. It gave her the pressed feeling that she had to build her happiness on a firm foundation before her father should intervene to knock it down. Such an attitude might have struck her as uncomplimentary to her own husband, had she not already understood that one could love a man without deeming him a match for one's father. Dorcas was proud even of the proprietary aspect of her conjugal love. At last she had something of her own.

In many ways he was an outrageous husband. He snapped at her and criticized her and left her alone when he wanted to dine with his authors. He made her quit her job and then complained about the loss of her salary. He was rude about her "banal chatter" at cocktail parties and disgusted when she said nothing. He never stopped to consider her mood when he wanted to make love, and he scoffed at her "spoiled" upbringing without acknowledging her efficiency as a cook and housekeeper. But he accepted her. That was the great and redeeming fact. He accepted her, as a now integral part of his existence, as someone who had come to stay. Beneath all his grumbling and abuse she thought she could dimly make out an undercurrent of relief that he had, at last, pulled it off, that he was, and never again could not be, a married man. And when he complained about the loss of a freedom that she did so little to curtail, she was subtle enough to perceive that his sense of confinement grew more from his gradual comprehension of her permanence than from any desire to be rid of her. This comprehension alone might be enough to build a marriage on. Dorcas, the wife, and Dorcas, the defiant daughter, were full of new confidence. If she was submissive to Robin, she was already aware that it was a voluntary submission.

When his mother came down from Syracuse to meet her, she was agreeably surprised to find her a dowdy, affectionate, talkative, dear little woman, with opinions as Philistine as any which Robin derided in her own parents, and she made the discovery that formidable persons do not always have formidable relatives. Robin interpreted her enthusiasm correctly.

"I should have kept Mother hidden," he told her afterwards. "If a husband is to be respected, his wife should never know there's another woman in him."

"Even when it's such a nice one?"

"No!" He raised a clenched fist above his head. "He should be a god!"

"But, darling, you *are*."

He gave her the little mocking smile that accompanied his moods of acutest perception. "You're really becoming a damnably clever woman. You're learning to manipulate me like clay. Or at least you think you are. But don't be too sure that I haven't a hand on that potter's wheel. How do you know it isn't my super-subtlety to be shaping you into a shaper of me?"

"I don't."

"Married life is a kind of masquerade, isn't it? As long as I pretend to be strong and you to be weak, it's just as good as if I *were* strong and you *were* weak."

"But I *am* weak," she insisted with sudden vehemence. "I lean on you. I depend on you."

"In a way." The expression in his eyes became curiously sad. "You're what I might call an aggressive dependent. If I fell, it would be with your weight upon me. But I should be crushed in the process, and you'd get up and dust yourself off and find another man."

"Never!"

"Oh, Dorcas, my *dear*!" He shook his head and raised a finger to his lips. "What a word to use! You forget, I have the clairvoyance of a failure."

"You're not a failure!"

"I'm afraid your conversation has degenerated into a series of passionate denials. Never try to make feeling do the job of sincerity. It makes for a fearful din."

She knew that he hated to be taken too seriously, and she did not now pursue the subject. Such discretion had been attained only after repeated efforts. She was learning that the world to Robin was only fascinating if half revealed. He wanted always to pause before a half-closed door, to dangle a question mark, to play with a supposition. Her habit of flinging doors open and throwing up sashes was acutely distasteful to him. If she had to move at all in the house of his imagination, she was learning to do it on tiptoe.

She was learning, indeed, so fast that at the end of two months of marriage she was beginning to believe that hers might be a happy one. But this dawning conviction was cut short by another discovery. She was pregnant. Even in the mixed shock of first realization she did not fool herself that Robin would be pleased. They had planned not to have a child for two years, and she now wondered if he would want one even then. But she was not prepared for the full violence of his reaction. He raged up and down the room, repeating over and over in a high, dry, distracted tone: "Of course, we can't afford it. We'll have to move. We'll have to get a new apartment, and where do you think the money's coming from? Your father? You know I'd go on relief before taking a penny from your father."

"We could get it from Mummy."

"How like a woman!" he jeered. "To judge the degree of larceny by the pocket you pick from."

"But it's different," she protested miserably. "It really *is*. Mummy has money that she inherited. It has nothing to *do* with Daddy."

"I refuse to go into that kind of middle class logic-chopping. It's the butchery of every moral standard."

"I wouldn't take any money if it was for *us*," she said, with tears in her eyes. "But it's for the baby. What has the poor baby ever done to Mummy or she to it?"

He stared at her with wildly exasperated eyes. Just because it was so eminently the moment for him to kiss and reassure her, of course he wouldn't. She sighed and turned away as he continued to rant.

"I'll bet it wasn't an accident at all! I'll bet you *planned* it. You're all alike. You *pretend* you want to look up to a man. You pretend you want a lord and master. But all you really want is a stud. So you can fill your home with squawking progeny that will shout him down!"

She knew that he was feeling sorry already for his unkindness; she could sense the self-punishment in the very shrillness of his tone. She even recognized that he wanted to apologize and to tell her that he would not mind the baby so much, after all. But it was a case where the deed was everything, the feeling nothing. Instead of welcoming her baby, he had babbled petulantly against the laws of nature. For the first time, she saw him as just a bit ridiculous. She loved him, of course, but she had judged him. And she knew it.

"I can manage in this apartment," she said dryly. "It will all be much easier than you think. You'll see."

At least he had not suggested an abortion. It was something. And two nights later, when she had got up from bed to be sick, he propped himself up on one elbow and called into the bathroom: "If you really want a new apartment, I don't mind borrowing the money from your mother." He laughed a bit wildly. "I suppose I can be big about something!"

His grudging attitude accelerated the inevitable reconciliation with her father. Had he been nicer about the baby, she would have been less undone by Derrick's congratulations. The morning after Robin's offer about the apartment, Dorcas called to repeat it to her mother. Two minutes after their talk was over, the telephone rang.

"Dorcas, this is Daddy. Please don't hang up. I'm so *proud* about the baby!"

"Oh, Daddy, darling! *Are* you?"

"If you're a generous girl, you'll forgive me. And the best way to forgive me is to let me make you a present of the new apartment. To hell with this idea of a loan. Tell Robin I'll buy the apartment in *his* name. Will that make it easier?"

"Oh, Daddy, what a beautiful idea!"

"And, darling, I can't wait for my first grandchild. I have a funny feeling it's going to be a boy. Do you know what? I think a grandfather is what I was always meant to be! I've made my mistakes with Hugo, but I'm not going to make them with this fellow. I promise!"

"Oh, Daddy. I'm going to cry. Goodbye!"

When Robin came home that night, she had worked herself into what she hoped was a state of near hysteria.

"You don't want the baby!" she shrieked at him. "You don't want the baby, and you don't want me! I'm going home to Mummy and Daddy, and I'm going to have my baby there, and I'm going to call it Derrick Hartley!"

"Even if it's a girl?"

"Even if it's a girl!"

Robin put his briefcase on the desk and pretended to look over the morning mail. She stared at his back, breathing in sobs. When he turned, he had a rather grim smile.

"If you're making a scene because there's something you want, why not tell me? Isn't it simpler?"

"I'm going home!"

"If you've made up your mind, why make a scene?"

"Because I *want* to make a scene! Because I want you to know what a selfish brute I think you are!"

She stamped her foot in a rage that was only half simulated and started to hit the table by the sofa with both fists. Robin came over at last and caught her hands. His smile was gone, and he looked tense and tired.

"Stop that!" he cried. "Do you want to have a miscarriage?"

"Yes!"

"Stop it, you fool!"

She pretended to give in to his strength and threw herself down on the sofa to weep.

"All right," he said wearily, "what is it?"

"What is what?"

"What am I to do to make up? Haven't I promised to let you have the new apartment? What else must I do?"

She opened an eye to consider his chastened look. "You can help me make our peace with Daddy." When he said nothing, she instantly sat up. "He promised to put the apartment in *your* name. I think the least you can do is thank him for it!"

"So that's it." He shook his head with a dry bitterness and turned again to the morning letters. "I might have guessed. Very well, Dorcas. I shall make my peace with your father. And I'll do it handsomely, never fear." There was a slight tremble in his voice. "But I'm afraid I'll always remember that you made me do it."

"That I *asked* you to do it!" she corrected him passionately. "And why not? Daddy's *proud* I'm having a baby!"

After a week at the hospital Dorcas brought her nine-pound son, Derrick, and a nurse to stay with her parents in Fifty-third Street. Absorbed with her baby, she had allowed herself to be persuaded by the arguments that he would be better looked after, that there was more room for the nurse, that it would be easier for Robin who would not be awakened by the baby's feeding. And Robin himself had added his voice to her family's; he seemed to get on with everyone now. He had been so jubilant over the birth of a boy that he and Derrick had actually danced a jig together in the hospital corridor. Dorcas, hearing of this, had closed her eyes in sleepy content and wondered if her family troubles were over.

But, of course, she knew all the time that they had just begun. The period in the hospital had been a period of suspended hostilities, a doped, blessed, euphoric time, that she knew, nonetheless, was euphoric. The smiling, cooing masks at the bedside were bound to come off, in due course, and she would see again the worn, familiar faces of apprehension and jealousy. But there was still a difference, a wonderful difference from other times, and that was in the presence of the damp, red, heavy, sucking and screaming bundle that would grow up to be an ally and protect her from the aggressive loves of spouse and parent. Dorcas was conscious of the survival of her objectivity even in her moments of most intense maternal satisfaction. Watching Robin's eyes while she fed his son, she was perfectly aware that the sight was distasteful to him. He had wanted to be a husband, and he had, at the last, wanted to be a father, and now, by God, he had pulled off both jobs. He had shown the world the master sketch, and the details could be filled in by students.

She was much more painfully conscious of this attitude when she had moved to Fifty-third Street. He called in the evenings after work, but he barely stayed a half hour. The house bored him, her family bored him, the talk about the baby bored him and, worst of all, *she* bored him. For at home in the months of her pregnancy he had never had to make conversation with her; he had simply talked about himself and his day while she worked on baby clothes. Now, seated stiffly in a chair by the bed in a room which they had never shared, he seemed to find nothing to say. He could hardly wait to get back to the alcoholic ease of his renewed bachelor evenings.

"Tomorrow they're letting me get up for dinner," she told him one night as he was leaving. "I hope you'll stay. You can go right afterwards."

"But I'm dining at the Jack Brandons'!"

The mention of his employer's name was intended, of course, to arrest all further protest. But Dorcas was not at all sure that he was really dining at the Brandons'.

"Oh, they'll understand. My *first* night down. They've had babies."

"Of course I realize my career's of precious little importance to the Hartley family," he said bitingly. "But however poor a thing, it's still mine own."

"You *know* how important your career is to me!" she exclaimed, the quick tears in her eyes. "But I'm sure Mr. Brandon wouldn't expect you to go under the circumstances. He probably only asked you because he thought you were lonely. May I call him up and ask him?"

"Certainly not!" Robin cried, jumping to his feet. "I'll do it myself, thank you. Since it means so much to you!"

"No, no," she wailed, shaking her head in misery. "Not if you feel that way. I'll *hate* it that way!"

"It's all decided," he said coldly. "I shall be here tomorrow at seven."

Dorcas felt very low that night after he had gone. She knew that what he could least endure was the sense that he might be missing a good time. To have to sit in one place and think of a party in another raised emotions in him akin to panic. Yet it was equally true that if he went to the party, he soon tired of it. He tired of everything in possession; things lost their value with their change of title. He had wanted her to belong to him entirely, to give up her family for his sake, and once she had done so, he had thought her a poor fool. For if, fundamentally, he set a low price on himself, what price could he set on his belongings? As for the Hartley money and position, he had seen in them, with his peculiar combination of resentment and quick boredom, only the chance to make one of those splendid gestures of which he believed the good life to be made up: the gesture of contemptuous renunciation. But gestures, even splendid ones, became a bore, and it occurred to Dorcas that her husband might have already tired of renunciation.

That night she lay awake for a long time, thinking, and in the morning, early, she put on her wrapper and went down to the dining room. Her unexpected appearance had just the effect on her father that she desired.

"Dorcas, good heavens, is anything wrong?"

"Nothing at all." She sat beside him and reached for the silver bell. "I've come to have breakfast with you. There's something I want to discuss."

The paternal gaze blurred as she opened her subject, and she sensed the re-emergence of the senior partner. She was determined, however, to be as stubborn as he. If he had a daughter, she had a son; it made them equals. She could never win an argument with Robin, but she knew that in scenes she was apt to prevail. With her father she sensed that just the opposite might be true.

"You're always telling me that some day I'll be a limited partner in your firm. That some day I'll have this or that. But 'some day' means very little to me. I've got a husband who's full of talent that he has no time to use. You once told me that publishers were people who didn't have the guts to live in attics and write. Well, Robin might have done that, if it hadn't been for me and little Derrick."

"But you and little Derrick were responsibilities that he assumed. He knew what he was doing!"

"Daddy, that's just talk, and you know it. One doesn't 'assume' a responsibility like marriage. I wanted to marry Robin, and I pulled it off." She gave a dry little laugh that surprised them both and perhaps even shocked him. "The poor boy didn't have a chance."

"That isn't the way *I* got married."

"I know it isn't. But it *might* have been. If Cousin Geraldine had been let alone." She stared at him boldly, though with a pounding pulse, and, for once, he looked away. "Things have happened to Robin, and they've happened because of me. It won't take much money to set them straight, and I want you to give it to me. I know all your opinions about in-laws and grown up children, and I don't give a hoot. I need the money, and I'm asking you for it."

How easy it was! She could hardly believe it, and in the exultation of the moment she almost forgot her objective. But Derrick did not. He stared back at her so long that she began to wonder if those hard gray eyes were taking her in at all. Was he calculating the amount? Whatever it was, it could hardly matter to his exchequer. Only to his conscience. And then she felt a small damp chill near her heart that he should be thinking so hard.

"All right," he agreed suddenly. "If you will let me do it my own way."

"How will that be?"

"You'll see tonight. Didn't you say Robin was coming for dinner?"

She underwent a violent reaction that night when Robin appeared in her room as she was getting dressed, smiling and armed with a huge bunch of red roses. He made such a fuss over her and the baby that she burst into tears.

"No matter what I do," he protested, "I seem to get a liquid reaction."

"Oh, Robin!" she murmured and flung her arms around his neck.

Dinner was gay, even a bit hysterical. Although they were only four, and Ida drank scarcely more than a sip, Derrick opened two bottles of champagne. He toasted the baby; he toasted Dorcas; he even toasted his son-in-law.

"I have a confession to make," he announced in his easiest, most friendly tone. "I'm beginning to see that certain ideas of mine may have been too rigid. Life has a funny way of getting back at people whose ideas are too rigid. It has a way of tripping them up."

Robin finished his glass and held it out to the bottle which his father-in-law reached over to him. "And that's happened to you, sir?" he asked politely.

"Exactly. It happened to me. Tell me, Robin, is it true you're writing a novel?"

"Oh, when I find the time. Of course, it's just a weekend proposition."

"Of course. And one of these days Mr. Hitler is going to start a war, whether he means to or not, and sure as shooting, we're going to find ourselves in it. Which will mean further delays for your book. And by the time it's all over and you're out of the service, who can tell? You may have lost the inclination. That book may never get written."

"I imagine the cause of literature will survive," Robin said pleasantly.

"But it might not," Derrick insisted soberly. "It might not. And what really bothers me is that here we are, a family at last united and happy, with enough money to allow us all to pursue our serious goals. If you, Robin, a brilliant young publisher who has proved a dozen times over that he can support his family, are not to be allowed to finish what might be an important work of fiction because of *my* scruples, or because of *your* scruples about my scruples, I think we are both very much to be blamed."

Robin put down his glass abruptly. "How do you mean, sir?"

"Well, damn it all," exclaimed Derrick, hitting the table with his knuckles, "I simply mean that you should resign from the Brandon Press and do me the courtesy of letting me pay your salary until such time as you have completed your novel!"

Robin fixed his gaze on Dorcas, and she saw, with a suddenly sinking heart, how interested he was. For it all now seemed too easy, too pat to her. There was something shocking about the speed with which her father cleared away the underbrush that had kept her from him. As he moved closer, in long, easy strides, with that swinging scythe, she had a sudden, terrible sense of what might have been concealed in that torn, tossed underbrush.

"It's certainly a handsome offer," Robin murmured. "What do you think, Dorcas?"

"Well, I think your career as a publisher is important, too," she answered and saw his eyes instantly darken with dissatisfaction.

"We can always go back to publishing," her father remarked with a little grunt, eying her suspiciously. "Particularly if we're prepared to make a small investment in the firm. But now that we've finished dinner, I suggest that the gentlemen withdraw to my study and continue the discussion over a brandy and a cigar."

Upstairs in the living room Dorcas appealed to her mother as the latter turned to her needlepoint.

"What would *you* do, Mummy?"

"Well, it's really Robin's decision, isn't it?"

Dorcas reflected despondently that no woman married so long to her father could be expected even to imagine a man who did not make his own decisions about his own career.

"The trouble is it was my original idea," she confessed. "And now I've got cold feet. Daddy has such a way of taking things over. I stuck out a finger, and my whole arm's gone."

"But is it really such a vital decision? Don't we give too much weight to these money matters? The more I think about it, the more it seems to me that Aunt Dagmar had the right attitude. The only thing to do with money is to make yourself comfortable."

"But Aunt Dagmar's money was her husband's not her father's."

"I doubt if Aunt Dagmar would have cared whose it was."

"But I do! It's the difference in the generations."

When Robin and Derrick joined them, the former was smoking a big cigar and walking with a slightly unsteady step. Both, however, were smiling, and a pact had evidently been selected. Robin wanted to say good night immediately, but Dorcas insisted that he go with her upstairs to see the baby. In her bedroom she closed the door quickly and turned to him.

"It's all agreed, then?"

His eyes immediately hardened. "Do you object?"

"Only to the speed of the whole thing."

"You have no faith in my novel," he said with sudden petulance. "You never have had."

"I confess I distrust my father's sudden faith in it."

"What do you think he's trying to accomplish?"

"I wish I knew."

"Dorcas, my dear, this is absurd." He smiled and came over to put his hands on her shoulders. "You're so overwrought you can't even appreciate the poor man's simple gesture of generosity. Why, just because he was once a Philistine, must we condemn him to be one forever? Everyone knows that having a baby knocks your judgment out of whack. In your case it's revived all your old suspicions of your father. Perhaps I made a mistake in letting you come here. Perhaps you should have come straight home. Anyway, when we get into our new apartment, everything will be all right."

Dorcas allowed herself to be consoled and decided that all might still be for the best. After all, her father and Robin were at last agreed about something. She turned her energies to the search for an apartment and, as soon as she was well enough, spent long pleasant mornings with her mother, looking over the market. She finally found what she wanted on Gracie Square, with Carl Schurz Park nearby for little Derrick and a big nursery with a gay wallpaper of rabbits and elephants that had a beautiful view over the East River. She was so happy about it that she wondered if there might not be more in Aunt Dagmar's formula than she had supposed. Perhaps all she had to do in making decisions was to substitute her baby for herself. If she could just succeed in making little Derrick really "comfortable," how much did her doubts and fretting matter?

Robin rented a room on Third Avenue in which to do his writing. He said that he could never write at home with a baby and the telephone, and he added the comment that the atmosphere of Gracie Square was too rich for his muse. He left the apartment at ten and sometimes did not return until late at night. The subject of his novel was his father's life and suicide, and there were to be several chapters about the son's dilemma over the insurance policy. Dorcas thought it sounded like promising material, but after the first month it became apparent that it was not going well.

"Why don't you just grit your teeth and write it all out, so many pages a day, until it's finished?" she asked on a morning when he seemed particularly despondent. "I know it might all be very bad, but at least you'd have something to work on and revise."

"Do you think writing a novel is like writing a prospectus for stocks and bonds?" he cried indignantly. "I declare, you're a worse Philistine than your father!"

"I thought we'd ceased to regard him as one."

"Then you've taken his place!" Robin arose from the breakfast table to stare down on the turbulent grey of the East River. "I might have known! A few weeks on Gracie Square, and you revert to basic type. The lady bountiful who despises modern fiction but wanted a 'lit'ry' man for a husband!" He threw up his hands as he warmed to his argument. "Imagine my having been fooled for a minute! My simple role was to give you the opportunity for a divine row with Daddy. And then to provide you with a child whom you could name after him and have an equally divine reconciliation. Finis, Robin! Your time to bow out, boy!"

"Why don't you put that idea in a novel? It might make quite a good twist."

"Don't think I *won't*!"

"Well, at least, you can't say I haven't afforded you inspiration." Dorcas glanced at the clock. "I have to take Derrick out. Aren't you going to work today?"

"Are you now the overseer of your father's fortune?" he demanded furiously. "Are you afraid he isn't getting his money's worth out of the poor hack writer? Shall I put up a time clock? Or bring you the sheets each night for your inspection?"

"I only thought it might help you to talk it over," she said with a shrug. "If you want me to shut up, I'll shut up."

"Nothing helps me! Not even the panacea of your proposed silence!"

Robin became moodier and moodier. Invitations for week-ends, which he would never have previously accepted, he now grabbed at eagerly, and if Dorcas could not leave the baby, he would go alone. He had to have a "change"; he had to "discuss the book" with somebody; he had to have "another look" at Westport or Sharon or wherever it was, because of a chapter that was now to be set there. Every sudden whim that struck his fancy, the yearning for a movie in the middle of the day or a night club in the middle of the night, had to be promptly gratified and then justified as the search for raw material. Dorcas tried for a while to keep up with his nervous activities, but the baby, whom she breast-fed for five months, had a first lien on her time, and when that was over, Robin had already adapted himself to his semi-bachelor life and showed little disposition to share it. It was better for his "creative thinking," he explained, if he spent a certain amount of time by himself. But "by himself," Dorcas ruefully concluded, seemed simply to mean without her.

There was heartache, of course; there were long, low dismal mornings, in which she sadly, and more and more resentfully, pieced together the self-ishness that made up the pattern of his conduct to her, but little Derrick continued to compensate. He was a fat, strong, laughing child, with a comic resemblance to his grandfather, and he accepted greedily all the maternal attention that his own father spurned. Dorcas had hired a nurse, that she might have more time to spend with Robin, but when he failed to avail himself of it, she dismissed her and took over the care of Derrick herself. When Robin remarked that she was becoming a domestic drudge, they had their first real words on the subject.

"What else have you left me to be?" she exclaimed in sudden, blazing indignation. "Do you care anything for my opinions or even my company? What do you *expect* me to do with my time?"

"You might read," he said sheepishly. "Think of all the things you could read. You're always complaining that my literary friends won't talk to you. Well, catch up with them!"

"But I don't want to! Why should I read a lot of trash so as to talk to *your* friends instead of looking after my own child?"

His look of abashment took in the angry mother in the once submissive wife. "I thought you might want to help me out."

"Help you out? When you won't even let me type your manuscript!"

He made no answer to this, and she felt an immediate compunction at so easy a victory. For it occurred to her that she might have jabbed a knife in the tenderest of his wounds. Perhaps the reason that he gave her no manuscript was that there was no manuscript to give.

But she had to get on with her own life. She would have shared a garret with Robin had he asked her; she would have turned her back on her father and his money had he merely solicited the gesture. But it was only too clear that the primary function of her father in Robin's mind was to serve as a target for his cruder jokes, and this was just as true after he had taken his money as before. Robin had simply changed his attitude from one that held money to be corrupting to one that held it to be unimportant. *He* could be above it, but she, apparently in his philosophy, could not. He continued to taunt her with the elevation of their standard of living, telling her that she could no more escape her background than a fly from sticky paper. Very well, she decided wearily. She would accept her background. She would no longer kick against the pricks. It slightly soothed her injured feelings to suspect that in the long run young Derrick would prefer the Hartley to the Granberry way of living.

Robin was startled when she announced that she had accepted her father's offer of the guest cottage at Oyster Bay for the summer.

"You don't expect me to commute, I hope?"

"Why should you commute? You'll have your own study there. Or, if you prefer, you can work in the big house. There's a room on the third floor with a beautiful view of the bay where you'd never be disturbed."

"Do you really think I could connect a single subject, verb and predicate on *that* gold coast? Why the very air would disintegrate any idea except a few old chestnuts already used by Scott Fitzgerald!"

"Stay in town, then," she said, a bit curtly. "But you surely don't expect me to keep the baby in the broiling city because of your theories about the air on Long Island?"

"*Other* babies, I believe, spend the summer in town. I've even heard on good authority that some of them survive."

Dorcas, as a mother, scorned to answer this. "You'll come on weekends?"

"I'll have to see how things go with the book."

She found, when she was settled in the cottage with her old nurse, Margaret, who had come over from the big house to help with the baby, that she had a sense of tranquility tempered with relief. Was this how Robin felt when he was away from *her*? The little white cottage was clean and fresh and full of gay chintz; it had a modern kitchen, and Margaret was both consoling and efficient. Dorcas had quiet dinners every night with her parents and spent long, lazy days sitting on the lawn by the Sound, watching the sea gulls and the sailboats and rocking the baby carriage. It was peace, a rather inert peace, to be sure, but still peace. And the whole big shimmering place, her father's pride and joy, with its broad, close-cut lawns and its tall, gabled, slate-roofed manor house of purple brick, so evocative to her of stately colonial days on the James River, had always been dear to her heart.

But her sultry idyl was shattered one afternoon by the arrival of a haggard Robin who announced that he had burned his manuscript. Dorcas took him down to the beach where he could lie on the sand and shake and moan while she made little noises of consolation and poured him an occasional drink from a thermos. By evening he was quiet and seemingly resigned, and he even agreed to go to the big house for dinner. She told her mother on the telephone what had happened and warned her not to refer to it, nor did she, but her father, in the middle of what till then had seemed a pointless lecture about business, suddenly gave it a personal application.

"You know, Robin, I think I could make an investor of you. I really do. I think you have the nose for a good thing."

"*Me?*"

"Yes, it's hard to explain, but one has a feeling about these things. I'm not suggesting you give up your writing, or anything like that, but don't you ever get what they call 'writer's block'?"

"Do I! With me it's chronic!"

"Well, next time you feel an attack coming on, how about warming a desk in my office till it goes away? A bright fellow like you could pick things up fast. And who knows? You might even find you liked it. After all, you could be a weekend writer with me as well as with a publisher."

Robin stared at his father-in-law with wide semi-hypnotized eyes.

"You mean you want *me* in Hartley and Dodge?"

"Why not? Life isn't as tightly pigeonholed as you writers seem to think. You'd be surprised how much creative imagination you'd find downtown. Besides, some day that boy of yours is going to have a slice of my business, and I'd like to think you'd be able to help him with it."

To Dorcas her husband's expression had changed from wonderment to something closer to awe. Who, it appeared to ask, was this man who had so sublime a disregard for every principle as well as every prejudice? All of Robin's poor little artistic credo, his do's and don't's, seemed to run off like dirty water over the glazed steel of Derrick's basin.

"Do you think I might start tomorrow, sir?" he asked in a hushed tone.

"By God, you can start tonight!" Derrick exclaimed heartily. "You can come into my study, and I'll tell you about a little oil project we're thinking of going into."

When Robin and Dorcas returned to the cottage, he was silent and subdued, beneath an air of mild exhilaration that was only partly due to Derrick's brandy.

"I told you about the air down here!" he exclaimed. "It's made me a banker in eight hours time!"

"But, darling, it's only temporary," she said soothingly. "Just until you get started on your next novel. I think it's a wonderful idea. It'll take your mind off the old book and give you material for a new one."

"Temporary!" he cried, with a rather screechy laugh. "As if anything about your father could be called temporary!"

He refused to discuss it further, and the next morning he went into the city with Derrick on the early train. For two weeks he commuted regularly, an odd, deflated, silent Robin who drank five martinis before supper and went to bed directly afterwards. He behaved with a new respect towards her father, but with Dorcas herself he was increasingly moody and sour. He was now given to murmuring quotations from T.S. Eliot that were apparently relevant to his commute: "A crowd flowed over London Bridge, so many, I had not thought Death had undone so many." In less literary moments he uttered dark hints about zombies and the "living death." He refused to tell her anything about what he did in the office, but she gathered from her father that he was supposed to be occupied in reading statistical reports of electric companies. Whatever happened, she reflected with a dry discouragement, it was bound to be blamed on her, whether the failure of his novel or the failure of his job.

After the second week he telephoned from the office that the weather was too hot for commuting and that he was going to stay in town. She expected him for the weekend, but he did not come. The following week he telephoned only once, to complain about the laundry, and the week after, her father reported that he had failed to appear in the office at all. Dorcas simply shrugged, without even attempting an explanation, and her father, in his usual fashion, dropped the subject. But three days later he called at the cottage on his way home from the station, looking very grave.

"It should interest you to learn that your husband has spent the last two nights in the apartment of one Vera Stiles."

"How do you know?" she asked in a dead voice.

"I've had a detective on him for the past ten days."

Her head was spinning, but she could still accept it. "I suppose I'm not surprised. What do you think I should do?"

"I think you should divorce him."

She was intrigued by the distant roaring in her ears. "Isn't that rather drastic?"

"Strike now, child. The man's no good. He never has been. God knows, I've tried to see things his way, but what's the use? He's rotten through and through!" He slapped the table with the palm of his hand as his argument gained its crisis. "We've got to move and move fast. I want you to see a man called Mark Jesmond. For my money, he's the smartest young lawyer in town. Frankly, I'm trying to get him out of his firm into my business, but that's neither here nor there. Will you see him?"

"I don't know."

"Will you just see him? That's all I ask."

"I don't know!" She jumped to her feet with a little cry of delayed agony. "I've got to see Robin first!"

She found him, the next morning at noon, in their apartment. He had not shaved and was still in his pajamas, reading a newspaper. He did not even get up as she came in, and his smile combined resentment with hostility.

"I can see you know 'all,' as they say."

As she stared down at him, her whole body trembled with what she felt now must be dislike. For what else could it be? Could the wildest sentimentalist have still called it love? "I know a lot. What I'd like to know is what you want. What you plan."

"Why don't you ask your father?" he demanded sneeringly. "Doesn't he make all the plans for you and me? Isn't it his Gilbert and Sullivan detective that I see at restaurants, hiding behind a false beard?"

"Can't we leave Daddy out of it for once? Can't we discuss this thing as it concerns *us* and us alone?"

"Of course not!" he cried, jumping to his feet. "How can we leave out God?" He slapped his forehead and strode to the mantelpiece, turning to face her in a rather stagy pose. "From the very beginning he has plotted to destroy me. Oh, I may be a sniveling, self-pitying failure, but there are still things I can see. For all my faults, I'm bright. I'm as bright as your father, even! I can see that he was smart enough to anticipate that, living on *his* money, I'd never be able to finish my novel. He knew that his greenbacks, like faithful little soldiers, could be counted on to do *that* job!"

"Why are you so sure it was his money?" she interrupted. "Can nothing ever be *your* fault? How do you even know you were cut out to be a writer? Maybe you weren't. There are other things in life, after all."

"That's right!" he shrieked, with a savage glee. "Be a good wolf cub and join Daddy. Tear me in pieces! How do I know you weren't in it with him from the beginning?"

"In *what*, for God's sake?"

"In the whole business of degrading me. Of course, once he'd killed my novel, the rest of the job was easy. All he had to do was turn me into a poor zombie of a commuter, so you could see me in Daddy's office, Daddy's office that I'd sneered at. He *knew* you had only married me to irritate him. All he had to do to crush your silly rebellion was to *approve* of me. My God, if ever a man was castrated, you see him now before you!"

Dorcas surveyed him with a new detachment despite the dead weight in her heart. She was even able to reflect on the points of possible truth in his crazy picture. But what did truth or falsehood, guilt or innocence, matter once a thing was over? There remained the obsequies, a decent period of mourning and then—and then a life with little Derrick.

"It must be my poor consolation," she said as she crossed the room to the telephone, "that Daddy and I continue to provide your imagination with such excellent literary material. Perhaps there will be a new book, after all." She dialed her father's number and gazed down at the river as she waited. "Mr. Hartley, please. His daughter calling." She sent a dry, cold stare across the room to Robin as she heard her father's voice. "Oh, Daddy? I think I'd like to see Mr. Jesmond after all. Could you arrange an appointment? Oh, he's with you now? Can I come down? How perfect."

The white walls of her father's square office gave out a gleam like his own burgeoning assurance. Three landscapes: a green field, a riverbank and cattle in pasture, executed with the mirror accuracy of the Barbizon school, testified to their owner's clear flat view of the universe, New York Harbor, spread out in the wide south window, blue and grey and smoky, might have been done by an intruding impressionist. Mark Jesmond sat at the gilded Directoire table that her father used for a desk and scratched his cheek. He was a man of rather less than medium size, with tousled brown hair and grey slanty eyes, who wore a combination of a rumpled old tweed coat and grey flannels that Dorcas had never expected to see on Wall Street. It went with his restlessness, his boyish rustic, snub-nosed face, his air of a farm boy who had stumbled into Wall Street from the hills of New Hampshire to beat the toughest traders at their own game. For that was it, she decided as she eyed him apprehensively and told her tale. He was tough. He specialized in toughness. There was a dull gleam in those grey eyes that might have come from metal. Small wonder that her father liked him.

"So there we are," she finished with a deprecatory shrug. "I suppose the question is, what next?"

He put both hands over his face in a somewhat disconcerting gesture and dragged them slowly down, revealing first the long eyelashes now comically slanted, then the pulled skin of his eyelids and cheeks. "The first thing is to change the lock in your apartment. Mr. Granberry's clothes can be packed and left in the lobby. Don't worry. I'll take care of the details."

"But the apartment's his."

"No, it's not. Fortunately, that plan was never carried out. It stands in your name."

"But where will Robin go?"

"That's his affair. Let him go to that woman's. Why should you give him a home?"

Dorcas nodded slowly. "And after that?"

"I suggest we file the complaint for divorce tomorrow, naming Vera Stiles as co-respondent. There need be no publicity unless Mr. Granberry fights us. But I doubt if he will. We won't ask for any alimony. Simply for sole and absolute custody of the child."

"Oh, but I'd want Derrick to know his father!" she protested.

"That will be up to you," Mr. Jesmond said briskly, rubbing the tip of his nose with the palm of his hand. "My job is to see that you hold the big trumps. After that you can play your hand as you wish."

"But don't most people go to Reno or Mexico?"

"Most people don't get valid divorces. Your father wants you to have a binding decree here in New York, with unquestioned control of your child. All that we ask of Mr. Granberry is that he remove himself from the family picture. Neither his wife nor his child need ever cost him a penny."

And Dorcas, watching those eyes, knew that it would be so. She was in her father's hands, the firm, dexterous hands of a master surgeon. Indeed, the whole procedure was rather like an operation. All she had to do was submit and lie back to be anesthetized.

"You mean I won't even have to *see* Robin again?"

"Why should you go through any more pain? It seems to me you've suffered enough from him."

She knew that it was cowardly not to see Robin and discuss it with him, but she didn't care. The luxury of a future without scenes was irresistible. She decided to obey her father and Mr. Jesmond in every instance, and went back to Oyster Bay where she and little Derrick moved into the big house and where a detective watched, night and day, to be sure that poor Robin made no move to steal, or even to see his child, or to harangue his wife with useless but painful complaints. Dorcas never answered the telephone herself, and the servants were told to hang up if Mr. Granberry called. Two envelopes, addressed to her in his handwriting, were returned unopened with a typewritten note that all communications should be made through Mr. Jesmond. It turned out later that Robin had offered to give up his son if an out-of-state divorce could be arranged and Vera Stiles's name left out of the proceeding, but Derrick was inexorable. A New York divorce was necessary, and a New York divorce was obtained. In the end Robin failed to appear, and Dorcas' petition was granted in full.

During the suit Mark Jesmond made several trips to Oyster Bay to confer with his client. He seemed, each time, disposed to linger when his brief business was over, and Dorcas took him once for a stroll around the place and once to the beach for a swim. He proved to have a surprising enthusiasm for the out-of-doors, and in the Sound he swam out so far from the raft that she became nervous and called him back. He talked incessantly, about himself and his ambitions, scratching his head and his sides as he did so, and he made as many disarming references to his poor childhood on a farm in New Hampshire as he did clumsy ones to the important people whom he knew. He was an odd blend of naïveté and worldliness, with a sturdy, down-to-earth farm boy's charm and the hard, dry eye of an old tycoon. He evidently sensed the uniqueness of his own mixture, for he constantly played it up. On the day that he brought her the final decree, they had cocktails on the terrace, and he toasted her new liberty.

"I hope it doesn't mean that you're going to be free of me," he added, and, astonishingly enough, he winked.

"Oh, no, we're old friends now."

"I think we are." And, even more startlingly, he reached over to put his hand on her knee. It was only for a moment, but it was a moment that paralyzed her. Before she had recovered herself, the hand was gone, and he was looking over the Sound and whistling a tune. Then he finished his drink in a gulp and got up suddenly to hit a croquet ball through the first two wickets on the lawn. She was grateful that his attention was distracted from her, for she was trembling in every limb. How could it be that this small, tense man, this cold and chattering egotist, with one crude, perhaps haphazard gesture, had aroused her lust as Robin had not done in the whole course of their marriage? For why else was she trembling, she asked herself in a sudden giddy twinge of shame? Why, except that she wanted Jesmond, wanted him as she had never dreamed she could want a man before? And all in two minutes! The screen door banged behind her, and she gasped with relief as her father came out on the terrace.

"Mark says it's all over, Daddy!" she cried, running over to kiss him. "I'm so glad. And so grateful to you for arranging everything!"

And she flung her arms tightly around his neck and burst into tears. Her father held her closely and murmured consoling things. He and Mark, of course, would find it entirely natural that she should be caught at such a moment in the backwash of an old emotion. But how could they know that she was weeping for the unhappy Robin who had been caught up in the net of his own weakness and cast out of it again by two remorseless fisherman to die a gasping death on the beach? How could they know that she trembled with remorse at her own passivity, at her own surrender to the first show of force, at her own itching need to cringe, like a dog, before the boy master with a whip? Robin, yes, she knew what a poor thing Robin was, but what chance had he had in the hands of as poor a thing as she?

PART FIVE
GERALDINE'S RETURN

12

GERALDINE: 1935

W HEN FREDDY BREVOORT died of a throat cancer, only a little past his fiftieth year, he left Geraldine a childless widow and, what was worse, a poor one. The trust fund which had maintained them both so comfortably in Paris and in Cannes, in two small tidy flats, with an Hispano-Suiza town car for Geraldine and a Bugatti racer for Freddy, went back, "in default of issue," as the latter's inconsiderate grandfather had phrased it, to Freddy's three sisters who, although all married to men of means, had shown a selfish indisposition to waive their rights. Geraldine succeeded only in drying up whatever impulses of generosity might have otherwise lingered in her family-in-law by suing them on the grounds that she had been defrauded of her widow's share. And so again she found herself without a rudder in a sea churned up by the malevolence of relatives, just as it had happened ten years before when Talbot Keating had discovered her diary and used it in their divorce proceedings to dodge a man's proper burden of alimony. It was Freddy, big and red and obtuse, yet so gentle at heart, who had then rescued her from gin and melancholia and taught her that the secret of idleness lay in routine. The decade of her marriage to him had been her one decade of peace. In a France which had then been the haven of irregulars, she and Freddy had maintained a regular schedule where newspapers, naps, drives, movies, cocktails and lovemaking had lapped against the beach of their calm-like small, gentle, slapping waves. In the squall of tears and fruitless litigation that had followed the last horrible months of Freddy's illness, she had felt abandoned by all, by her dead parents, by her emptily cheerful brother, by his rich, hard, distrustful wife. She was already half intoxicated on the night when Ida's cable arrived, but not so much so that she failed to see in it her only salvation.

Hope you will come to us for the winter. Derrick arranging transportation and all details with Morgan's. Insist you worry about nothing.

And a scant ten days later she had been settled in the Hartley's guest room on Fifty-third Street, coddled and crooned over by an Ida more suited to the role of nurse than to any other in which she had yet seen her. Lying in the big mahogany bed and gazing at the sentimental eighteenth century prints of "L'Enfant Egaré" and "L'Enfant Retrouvé" which Aunt Lily Trask had picked up at some long distant auction, she felt lulled by a past that had once seemed to her so strict, even censorious, and that now bore the lineaments of some

stern old governess, visited in retirement, and found, after all, to be sweet and
dim-eyed and even rather clutchingly affectionate. There were meals, too, as
regular as Freddy would have wanted, and afternoon drives in the Park and up
Riverside Drive in a green, soft-springed limousine, and visits at teatime to
relatives and family friends. She and Ida talked by the hour of their childhood,
populating the street with ghosts, and she found that nostalgia, like faith, *could*
be cultivated and that it was pleasant to look back over the years to a girlhood
that seemed to have some of the innocence and goodness and subdued melancholy of an American primitive.

But Ida was not Freddy, after all. As he had been essentially calm, so was
her cousin essentially nervous, and Ida's nervousness had been bound ultimately to infect the peace of this new retreat. Geraldine was first irked by
the atmosphere of ceaseless supervision. Ida, who obviously considered her
an alcoholic, deeply disapproved of her habit of bedroom drinking. She even
disapproved of Geraldine's modest little efforts to make her bedchamber a
more feminine abode, with a pink-skirted vanity table and a bevy of big floppy
dolls with parasols and crinolines. But how in the name of thunder was a
lady expected to live surrounded by dark mahogany? There was even a shaving mirror on a mahogany stand in the bathroom and photographs of fraternity groups from Uncle Gerald's class at Yale! And would it have ever
occurred to Ida that a guest might like bath salts, and something more exotic
than Ivory soap? It was obviously a perverse fate that had wasted a fortune
on her cousin and left herself so poor.

Their first sharp words, however, were not occasioned by interior decoration but by Hugo. He was a short, bright, waspish black-haired young
man, with glittering eyes in a frog-shaped face, who went to Yale, probably
because his father had gone to Harvard, and came down to New York every
weekend. Geraldine enjoyed asking him about his girls and his parties and
telling him of the stormy years of her marriage to Talbot Keating. He would
knock at her door when he came in at night, and if she was still awake,
reading a detective story, as she usually was, he would bring her a nightcap.
It was one of these sessions that Ida interrupted, appearing in the doorway
in her nightgown, a pale moon of disapproval.

"Hugo, hadn't you better go to bed? You know you have to go back to
New Haven early in the morning."

"I thought I'd sit up till traintime, Ma," he replied easily. "Can I get
you a drink? Cousin Geraldine and I were talking about Paris after the war.
Did you know she knew Hemingway?"

But Ida did not seem to hear his questions. "Hugo, please go to bed!"

"Don't you think I'm getting a bit long in the tooth to be sent off that
way?"

"Hugo, *please*!"

When he saw his mother's tears, Hugo rose immediately, made a little
bow to Geraldine, winked and left the room without a word.

"What a fool you are to treat him that way!" Geraldine burst out in a
voice whose anger startled herself. "Do you want to make him despise you?"

"I don't want him to see you drinking when I've told him you're not
meant to."

"Really, Ida, you're a period piece! That boy knows far more about life already than you ever will."

"That's just what I'm afraid of. He knows too much about things that won't make him happy."

"Who are you to be the judge of that?"

"Well, have they made *you* happy?"

"I've had a lot of hard luck. We're not all blessed with your good fortune."

"Hard luck?" Ida's query had a scorn that only the late hour and maternal concern could have elicited from her. "You haven't had *that* much hard luck."

"I suppose it wasn't hard luck to lose my husband from cancer!" Geraldine cried angrily. "I suppose it wasn't hard luck to have his sisters steal my money!"

"It was *their* money," Ida retorted. "It was as much their money as if their grandfather had willed it to them directly."

"If you have nothing better to do than make yourself disagreeable, why don't you go to bed?"

Ida left, like Hugo, without another word, and the next morning at breakfast she was her consoling, solicitous self again. But there was a difference, from then on, in their relationship. Geraldine could not forgive her attitude about Freddy's sisters. This seemed to her a basic issue in the question of whether or not a person really cared about her. Even Derrick, who was surely a hard enough man of business, had taken a less dogmatic position. He, at least, had shaken his head and agreed that she had been badly used.

Derrick, indeed, had been perfect. There had been nothing in his grave, courteous, sustained air of hospitality or in the continuing sympathy of his questions about her health and spirits to suggest the least lingering resentment of his treatment at her hands two and a half decades before. And to make matters even better, the occasional gleam in his fixed stare gave play to the exciting suspicion that her old attraction for him might not be entirely dead.

He took over her tangled affairs and quickly unraveled them. His only requirement was that their business discussions be held in his office. She chose to read into this the natural desire of a self-made man to be seen in his glory by the woman who had spurned him when poor, and she understood and sympathized. Besides, she loved the air of moneyed masculinity of the vast new offices of Hartley and Dodge on Broad Street. Derrick had hired a decorator, but it was easy to see that he had not given her a free hand. The entrance hall had the green walls, the Sheraton armchairs and the dark Dutch landscapes with ruminating cows that were coming into fashion for investment houses, but Geraldine thought she could make out Derrick's influence in the wide, white chaste corridors and the heavy bronze plaques that bore the names of the partners by their doors. Each time he summoned her at noon, talked to her gravely for twenty minutes and then took her to India House for lunch.

"The thing about money," he warned her when she spoke of Freddy's trust, "is to know when you're licked. The greatest disasters come in trying to retrieve losses. My lawyers advise me that you will not prevail against

Freddy's sisters. So be it. Let us concentrate on making you comfortable with what you have left."

"But can you? It's so little."

"That's *my* problem."

"Oh, Derrick, how can I ever thank you?"

"By having lunch with me once in a while. Like this."

She blushed, she hoped, prettily. "I don't know if you ever read Edith Wharton. Ida and I used to love *The House of Mirth*. The heroine lets a married man speculate for her, and then he demands a reward that she has not anticipated." She laughed, a bit nervously, to make light of her reference. "She finds herself hopelessly compromised. Of course those were pre-historic days."

"But was he speculating with *her* money? Or with his own and pretending it was hers?"

"I don't remember. Does it matter?"

"Of course it matters. When a man speculates with a lady customer's money, the relationship is entirely professional. There can be no question of compromising her."

"Forgive me. I was being silly."

The smile that he gave her was enigmatic, and she even decided that it might ultimately be necessary to be more guarded in her talk. Yet the weeks passed, and Derrick said nothing that he could not have said in the presence of Ida. When the latter went off to Stonington for a weekend on an errand for old Aunt Dagmar, and Derrick suggested that he and she dine out at a new French restaurant, it seemed like the most natural thing in the world. As she sniffed her plate of steaming mussels in an alcove paneled after Fragonard, she reflected how little it really took to make her contented.

"What is Ida doing in Stonington?" she asked.

"She goes up regularly to inspect the old Denison house there. Aunt Dagmar has an obsession about the caretaker being a drunk."

"But Aunt Dagmar's half ga-ga!"

"Her word is still law to Ida."

"Ida is wonderful," she mused. "I wish I had her sense of family responsibility."

"No, you don't." Derrick's reply was unexpectedly curt. "You've always laughed at Ida and her sense of responsibility."

"*Derrick!*"

"Well, haven't you?"

"Certainly not. Ida is made out of different material than I am, that's all."

"Material you laugh at, that's just the point."

"Derrick, what are you driving at?"

"Simply this. I've been surrounded for years by an attitude of false admiration and false pity for Ida. I've come to believe it's a way people have of saying they don't like *me*. But I want *you* to like me, Geraldine."

"I do like you. I like you very much."

"You know what I mean."

She felt a little shiver as she glanced at those fixed grey eyes. He was so extraordinarily immobile, like an ivory Buddha.

"I wonder if you really appreciate Ida," she murmured.

"Of course I appreciate Ida. In fact, you might say she's my hobby. Ida fascinates me. I've never been able to make the least dent in the wall of her preconceptions."

"Perhaps you haven't really tried."

"Perhaps not. But if I had, one or the other of us might have been smashed. And I'm not at all sure it would have been Ida."

"You always think in terms of smashing things, Derrick. It's hardly the way with women."

"You mean I've frustrated Ida? Very likely. But she's been frustrated a long time. She must be used to it by now."

"A woman never gets used to it!"

"*You* wouldn't," he retorted, and an almost playful note crept into his flat voice. "But then you're not Ida. You haven't forgotten you're a woman. Men to Ida are basically irrelevancies. As long as she had her old house on Fifty-third Street and enough money for her charities, she'd never notice if I was gone. She could run errands for her old aunts until the last of them was laid away, and then be Aunt Dagmar herself."

"You surely don't mean, Derrick, that you're thinking of *leaving* Ida?"

"That depends entirely on you."

There was no mistaking him this time. It was going to be a giddy evening. "Upon *me*?" she gasped. "You mean, upon my advice? Well, surely, you don't think I'm going to advise you to leave poor Ida now, after all these years . . ."

"Look, Geraldine," he interrupted brusquely, "let you and me understand each other. In case we don't already. I've never forgotten you, and I think it unlikely, at my age, that I ever shall. I've turned the half-century mark. Some people call it the dangerous age. I call it the age of resolution."

The waiter was again hovering, and as he discussed the sauce with Derrick, who was a methodical and painstaking gourmet, she had a few moments to catch her breath. She found it exciting to suppose him a man who would not anticipate his physical possession of a woman by so much as a pat of her hand. A man who could break off a proposition to give a waiter minute instructions. She remembered *Wuthering Heights* from her days at Miss Irvin's and how she and Ida had thrilled at the hardness of Heathcliff.

"I said it was the age of resolution," he repeated as the waiter went off. "Don't you think it can be that?"

"What must we resolve?"

"We?" He smiled for the first time, a smile that had the same faint mockery as his expression. "Do I take it that my feelings are reciprocated?"

"Well . . . really, Derrick . . . I hardly know what to say . . ." She took happy refuge in a little sob. "My poor Freddy hasn't been dead two months."

"I knew you *years* before Freddy. I have the prior claim."

"Claim?" she cried indignantly. "How can you talk about claims? A married man?"

"I may not always be that."

"You don't mean you'd ever actually divorce Ida!"

"No, but Ida might divorce me."

"Do you really think she would?"

"She's not the kind to hang on to a man. She's much too proud."

"Poor Ida!"

"Yes, poor Ida. But her real humiliation took place twenty-four years ago. You ought to know about *that*."

"It wasn't my fault!"

"Let us agree now, once and for all," he said in a sharper tone, "that everything that has happened or that is going to happen is *my* fault. Let it all be on my shoulders. They're broad enough. You are in no way to blame." He paused, as if silence would ratify. She was silent. "After Ida's former humiliation, the present will seem light enough. She is older, and she lives in a more understanding world. Besides, she will have the sympathy of the whole Denison clan. A throbbing sense of injustice and a generous financial settlement can do worlds for a woman in that position."

"What a cynic you are!"

"I take the world as I find it. But let us come to your part in the matter."

"Mine?" she asked in surprise. "But I have none!"

"I beg your pardon. You have no blame, for that is mine. But you have a part. If I do all this for you, what will you do for me?"

"I cannot be committed," she replied in what she hoped was a tone that combined dignity with the least hint of disappointment. "How can you expect me to be disloyal to Ida? I wasn't before, and I won't be now. All I can say is that if you and Ida should ever decide to part, if you should ever find yourself a free man, I might—I just *might*, mind you—be willing to pick up this conversation where now, I'm afraid, we must drop it. Is that fair?"

Derrick's laugh was now frankly mocking. "I'm afraid it's not! As I say, I'll take the blame, but I won't take everything. Suppose you squint for a moment at your own position. You are a widow of extravagant habits and inadequate means. You're still a beautiful woman, but you're forty-six years old . . ."

"Derrick! You churl!"

"Ida's little family book, my dear, is full of dates. Let us stick to the facts. You expect me, a man of property and family and of the best reputation, to incur the ignominy of the world on the mere chance that you will eye me with favor amid the smoke of my burnt bridges. No, Geraldine, life is not like that. I should have thought you would have learned by now."

"What must I do?"

"You must give me some tangible evidence that you are not indifferent."

She turned away from that maddeningly level voice, hoping that her pallor would not tell him the full story of her shock. It was degrading, surely, to be titillated by so matter-of-fact a treatment of things that should be romantic or nothing. "I suppose I can imagine what that evidence is," she muttered.

"I suppose you can. I own a brownstone on Sixty-third Street—the second and third floors have been converted into a duplex apartment that is now vacant. It will be yours, decorated as fancily as you wish, complete with cook and maid."

She played for time, fussing with a cigarette and with his gold lighter. "And a key for you, I suppose?"

"No. I would take my chances that you would open when I rang."

"My dear Derrick, there are words for ladies who live in apartments paid for by men!"

"Words!" He grunted. "How women love them! I am simply trying to be honest with you. I will see to it that your capital is doubled, if not tripled. You will have a beautiful apartment, and everyone will say you were lucky on the market. Even Ida will be glad for you. Must all this be refused because Derrick Hartley, your investment counsel and cousin-in-law, occasionally calls to discuss the market at the cocktail hour?"

"Is that *all* he calls for?"

"In the eyes of the world, that will be all."

"And what if I say no?"

"Then our little idyl is over before it has begun."

She turned quickly and read conviction in his slowly repeated nod. "I suppose it wouldn't be so wicked if we got married later," she said doubtfully. "After you and Ida were divorced."

"I've told you. The wickedness will all be mine."

She sighed deeply. "Would you do me a favor?" she asked. "Could we say no more about it tonight?"

"I think we've said too much already. Let us enjoy our dinner. Will you allow me to order a bottle of champagne?"

"To celebrate? Certainly not!"

"To forget."

"What? My conscience?"

"No. Your approaching birthday."

"Damn you!" she cried with a burst of laughter. "And damn Ida's little book!"

She had to admit that he behaved handsomely for the rest of the evening. Not once, directly or indirectly, did he return to his proposition, and when he took her back to the house, he bade her good night at the door of her room in so perfectly a formal manner that, even in Ida's absence, she felt no need to lock her door. So many men would have fatuously supposed that any woman would have been secretly mortified, under the circumstances, had no attempt to open it been made! One of the enticing things about Derrick was that he was so obviously interested only in ultimate favors. To him there were no preliminaries. In love as in his business, he was a man who went straight to the point.

And what, she asked herself that night, when her lights were out, was the point of not coming to the point? Was it *her* duty to save a marriage that Ida seemed to care so little about? Were not the children grown up? And didn't Derrick have money enough for *everybody*? It was all very well to talk of family obligations, but who felt obligated to *her*? Had obligations kept Freddy's money from going to his sisters who didn't need it? Would obligations look after his widow?

"Derrick is perfectly right," she murmured to herself. "Ida doesn't *care*. She's never cared about anything, and life has filled her lap to overflowing.

With all the things it has denied *me*: children, money, security. Why should I always be left out? Why should I have to drag myself about to cheap watering places, smiling at old widowers with gummy eyes? Or else begging a pittance from Scotty's rich wife? And probably being refused! No, if Ida can't hang on to her possessions, if they keep just tumbling out of her lap, how can she expect people not to pick them up? And if *I* don't, someone else will! Because Derrick is wrong. He *is* at the dangerous age. And I could probably get more money out of him for Ida than Ida could herself!"

But Ida's reproachful eyes still remained in her fitful fancy until, exhausted and gently weeping, she fell asleep.

The next morning before lunch she went across the street to call on Aunt Dagmar. Aunt Dagmar was in her middle eighties and had begun to fail in the past year, but her position as head of the family had never passed to another. She continued to live in Uncle Linn's French Renaissance house. His will had provided that it should go, on her death, with the rest of his estate, to Columbia University. In this way, he had claimed, she would be rich but unpestered by relatives. Now she sat every morning, apparently contented, in her chair by the big stone fireplace surrounded by the newest books that she never looked at and the embroidery that she never picked up. Wrinkled and brown, with hair as white as drawing paper, she had still some remnants of her ancient beauty.

"Aunt Dagmar," Geraldine began, coming straight to the point, "do you remember when you and Daddy made me give up Derrick? Because he was Ida's beau?"

"Derrick who?"

"Derrick Hartley."

"Oh, *Derrick*. Of course I remember. But, my dear, he'd even been kissing poor Ida. Right in the Metropolitan Museum, where anybody might have seen them!"

"And where anybody who hadn't was told by Ida!" Geraldine murmured, but Aunt Dagmar did not hear. "Tell me frankly," she continued, "do you think it has worked out for the best?"

"You mean Derrick and Ida?"

"Yes."

"Well, I suppose it has. I doubt very much if *you'd* have made him happy."

The old were certainly unexpected. It had never occurred to her that Aunt Dagmar would have viewed the question from Derrick's point of view. "Why not?"

"Because it's an art to be happily married to a selfish man. I know something about that."

"Is it an art that Ida possesses?"

Aunt Dagmar considered this. "I think in her own way, she may."

"But did you know at the time he was selfish?"

"I don't remember what we knew at the time. Why does it matter?"

"Because I find myself wondering if I was right to give in to you. Nothing has worked out in my life, and everything has in Ida's."

"But he kissed her in the Metropolitan Museum! Right where anyone could see them!" Aunt Dagmar paused, trying to remember something. "I believe it was in the Egyptian Room."

Geraldine sighed with exasperation. "It seems to me I had as good a chance as Ida to make him happy. *Then.*"

"But, darling, Derrick could never have been happy without children. A rich man without heirs is like an unmilked cow. I know something about that, too. Of course your Uncle Linn had Livia, but she was worse than nothing."

"But Derrick couldn't have *known* that I wouldn't have children!"

"But you didn't, did you?"

Geraldine gave it up with another sigh and let the conversation revert to Aunt Dagmar's more usual topics: the finding of a new kitchen maid, the destruction of the house across the way, what Uncle Linn might have thought of Franklin Roosevelt. She reflected ruefully how untrue it was that the old lived in the past. They lived in the immediate present, the minute-to-minute present, except when they retreated for a stately recess into a fictional past. As for the past where Derrick had first proposed to her, that quiet brownstone past, with its fussiness and its quibbling and its love, how was it possible to bring *that* back? And why, really, should she want to? Was it not better to forget it altogether with its emotional tangle of stultifying family duties? Had it not forgotten itself? Where were the Denisons of Fifty-third Street, she wondered as she came out to the sunlight through Aunt Dagmar's heavy grilled doors. Uncle Philip's house at the corner was gone. A jewelry store occupied its site. Uncle Willie's had made way for a parking lot, and her father's was a night club, or perhaps worse. Everything in New York reminded one of the prevalent dust to which, almost immediately, it seemed, one was condemned to return. If one didn't seize that day, a contractor would.

She found Ida in the front hall, back from Stonington in a rather buoyant mood.

"You've been to see Aunt Dagmar. How sweet of you."

"Well, after all, she's my aunt too."

"I'm sorry, dear. I suppose I do get a bit possessive about her, living just across the street. Suppose I take you out for lunch? Would that be fun?"

Of course it would not have occurred to Ida, had she enjoyed double Derrick's income, to take her anywhere but the Park Club. Who but a benighted woman would not be content with a vegetable salad and lemon ice, consumed in the company of ladies, half of whose faces and all of whose names were familiar? The whoop-whoop of female laughter rose through smoke to a lofty ceiling decorated with tropical birds. Geraldine, glancing restlessly about, saw two classmates from Miss Irvin's. They nodded and waved, and she wondered, from the way their heads drew together, what horrors they must be saying of her. It was curious that even the girls who had been "fast" at school seemed now as settled as Ida. It was as if the New York female world had drawn together in a single dreary lump of uniformity to scorn Geraldine as a lonely maverick. Well, scorn, she would like to remind the members of the Park Club, could be a two-way street!

Her mood was not improved by having Ida, twice during their meal, rise from her seat to visit other tables.

"You're always talking about the way things *used* to be done," Geraldine observed crossly, the second time that she returned. "Surely, you know that table hopping is considered bad form."

"But I had to say a word to old Mrs. Kay about Annie's engagement. And to tell Miss Street and Cousin Ella Rhodes that our meeting at St. Luke's has been postponed."

"None of them seem to come to you."

"But, Geraldine, they're *older*."

"We're all still at school, aren't we? With old girls and new girls and medals and crushes. What is this very dining room but an extension of Miss Irvin's? And why should any group of women want to extend Miss Irvin's unless they've lost all hope?"

"Hope for what?"

"Why, for men, of course!"

"Geraldine, you're too absurd. At *our* age?"

"Of course at our age! That's just what I mean!" But the sharpness of her resentment was suddenly blunted by the notion that Ida's indifference might work to her own advantage. "How young do you start working on them?" she asked. "Is Dorcas a member?"

"No. But I think when her divorce is final, she may want to join. I doubt if poor Dorcas is going to be interested in seeing any men for a long time. She's been through a bit of hell, you know."

"Of course I know. Are you forgetting what I went through with Talbot?"

"Don't you think it's worse when there's a child?"

"Not when the child's a baby, like Dorcas'."

"I wonder if it matters how young or old the child is."

"Really, Ida! Suppose it's grown up!"

"Sometimes that only makes it worse. If Derrick and I were ever divorced, for example, it might completely disillusion Hugo. You can't tell. It might set him permanently against marriage. Of course it's purely hypothetical, but that's the reason, no matter what Derrick did, I could never divorce him."

Geraldine, looking suddenly up at the ceiling, thought that she was going to scream like one of the tropical birds. Could anybody have imagined such perverseness?

"It's only mothers who count, isn't it!" she exclaimed shrilly. "We poor sterile creatures can marry and divorce at will! I suppose you and Aunt Dagmar wonder why we bother with such technicalities? Why we don't simply flit from mate to mate and not intrude on the majesty of the law?"

"Geraldine, my dear, don't be a goose!"

Anger now convulsed her. If Ida wanted a fight for her husband, woman to woman, that was one thing. But to be frustrated, after all she had suffered, by one of Ida's dowdy, Park Club principles was too much to be borne. Was it possible that they had conspired to ruin her, this old-maid matron and her money-grubbing husband? Was *that* the revenge of Fifty-third Street?

"You've always resented me, Ida, and you still do! You resented me as a girl because I was prettier and had more friends and Aunt Dagmar preferred me! You resented her giving me my coming-out ball while you only had that dreary tea!"

"Darling!" Ida exclaimed, laughing in sheer surprise. "I adored your ball! I always admired you, and at times I envied you, but I never resented you. If I'd resented you, I wouldn't have asked you to come to me this winter."

"You only wanted to play Lady Bountiful!" Geraldine insisted with childish spite. "You wanted to have me, poor and bereft, dependent on your generosity!"

"I'm sorry if I made you feel that way," Ida said in a graver tone.

"And Derrick! You can't pretend you didn't resent my taking Derrick from you!"

"Taking Derrick!" Ida's eyes were limpid with shocked surprise. "But, my dear, do you think I can ever forget that it's exactly to your unselfishness that I owe my husband and children?"

Geraldine pulled a handkerchief from her bag and dabbed frantically at her eyes.

"There, dear," Ida continued soothingly. "I think it may do us both good to have a bit of a blow-up once in a while."

"Ida, please leave me," Geraldine murmured. "Just let me sit here alone a minute, will you?"

When Ida had gone, after hovering nervously about the doorway to look back at her, Geraldine took several long breaths until her incipient sobs were under control. She strove to keep her mind fixed on the one desperate resolution that would save her from being smothered in the stifling down of Ida's commiseration and Ida's principles. If she was to live, there was only one way for her, Geraldine, to live.

Outside the Park Club she walked to Madison Avenue and found a telephone booth. If Derrick were in, that was the answer. If Derrick were out . . . well, she shuddered to think. He was in.

"I've decided I'd like to see that apartment," she gasped, and leaned back against the wall of the booth, half in a faint, as she heard him telling her when and where to meet him.

The affair, like everything else in her life, including her brief conversion to the Catholic Church, turned out to be something of a disappointment. It was not that she found Derrick, after her first flurry of embarrassment at the abrupt change in their relations, an incompetent or clumsy lover. Far from it. He was deliberate, vigorous and forceful, just as much so as she had anticipated. But he was not romantic. In fact he seemed to go out of his way to be *un*romantic. He seemed to regard her nakedness more with the clinical eye of a doctor in a consulting room than with the rapture of a man who had been starving two decades for so privileged a sight. The good fortune that, after so long a period, had translated the Beatrice of his dreams to the Beatrice of his bed he took as much for granted as the good fortune which had brought him his Wall Street partnership and his membership in many clubs. It was hardly agreeable to Geraldine to feel like a piece of cheese which had fallen into the jaws of a patiently waiting fox or like another share of stock in the bursting Hartley portfolio. Nor was it agreeable for her to suspect, from the regular pattern of their meetings, that his interest was predominantly, if not exclusively, physical. He would never linger beside her after making love, but would get up briskly and dress and go to the bar table to mix a drink. In the desultory conversation that followed their brief moments of intimacy, he was apt to talk, rather boringly, about his daughter's divorce.

"The poor kid got herself off to a terrible start, but there's one blessing to the loose age we live in. At least, she can have a new try. If she could only get interested in Mark Jesmond, I'd feel the whole wretched business might have been worth it."

"But don't you see, that's just her trouble?" she asked, exasperated, as she tied the cords of her dressing gown. "You expect her to do what *you* want. The poor girl has to make her own choice."

"Robin Granberry was her choice."

"Was he? I wonder. Maybe she picked him out of sheer reaction. Maybe you were as much the cause of Robin Granberry as you'll ever be of Mark Jesmond."

"I think I ought to know something about my own daughter!"

"I think you ought," she retorted, irked at the impression which he conveyed that she was not fit to speak of anyone as pure as Dorcas. "You seem to forget that I've been through the same thing myself. I, too, believe it or not, was once a disillusioned girl."

But at once he changed the subject. It was impossible not to notice that he always did so whenever she was about to speak of her divorce from Talbot Keating. Did he think that the topic might lead to the question of his own from Ida? She dared not ask, for the simple reason that she had no weapon left in the event of hostilities. She had delivered herself into the hands as well as the arms of this calculating man, and she shivered at the consequences of her rashness. If it had been foolish to imagine him a Heathcliff, it had been idiotic to imagine herself a Cathy. How could she have forgotten the fate of unhappy Isabella?

"I must be getting back," he said, rising as he finished his drink. "Ida's having people for dinner."

"Ida? Since when has Ida had people for dinner? You mean you're entertaining for the greater glory of Hartley and Dodge."

"Not tonight. This is family night. All cousins."

"Cousins?" she asked querulously. "And what about little Geraldine? Is *she* no longer a cousin?"

"Ida wanted you," he said calmly, lighting the cigar that he always carried in the street, "but I talked her out of it. I know how those things bore you."

What could she say? That boredom was better than loneliness? He never expected her to be lonely. So long as she was ready to make love on the two weekday evenings when he called, after office hours, entering the building through the back yard by crossing from another of his properties, she was perfectly free to do as she liked, even to go out with other men. Derrick was evidently not interested in the exclusive possession of what he briefly but regularly needed. His attitude hardly augured matrimonial intent.

When she really stopped to think of it, her only true pleasure in the affair lay in decorating the apartment, and even that was almost spoiled by Ida who insisted on helping her and on ransacking the family warehouse to furnish what the tabloids would have described (had she or they only known) as her husband's "lovenest." Geraldine consoled herself by reasoning that it was only a matter of time before Ida would have to face the facts and that it might help them both to behave in a civilized fashion at the crisis if they had kept up their intimacy to the last possible moment. And so together they picked out of storage old Denison pieces and Barbizon paintings and boxes of Waterford glass and went shopping for rugs and curtains and fought over colors and in particular over Geraldine's craze for mirrors, mirrors on screens, mirrors as table tops, smoked mirror panels in the bedroom, and for large, floppy dolls.

"But, darling, only tarts buy them," Ida protested.

Geraldine was always scrutinizing her cousin for the least sign of matrimonial discontent, but Ida struck her as almost smug in her matronly security. At last, Geraldine began to feel the approaches of panic. She wrote a letter to the lawyers who had handled her abortive case against Freddy's sisters, putting her situation as if it had happened to a friend and asking what legal redress, if any, existed. She had to wait for two weeks before she got their laconic reply, and then she blushed with shame and disappointment as she read between the lines of that cynical, pompous epistle how easily its author must have guessed the identity of her "friend."

"Don't you hate lawyers?" she asked Ida at lunch. "They dry-clean the romance out of life."

"Only if you send things to them."

"You mean you never would?"

"Not my life, anyway. They'll have to be satisfied with my death. That I leave them gladly. As a matter of fact, I'm taking care of it this afternoon."

"What on earth do you mean?"

"I'm going down to sign a new will."

"To disinherit somebody?"

"Not quite. Derrick and I are going abroad. He has a passion for making final arrangements before any trip. It makes for a rather gloomy start."

"Oh?" Geraldine's voice was low and flat. "I didn't know you were going abroad."

"Neither did I. Till yesterday. Wouldn't you like to come with us?"

Geraldine had fully intended to have it out with Derrick before there should be any intimacies that day, but there was something in his expression (no different, it was true, from other days) as he stood at the door when she opened it, coat on arm, hat in hand, that precluded discussion. He went straight to the bedroom after his usual brief, gruff salutation, and she found herself once more submitting to him with tears of resentment that the question of her readiness, or even her pleasure, should so little exist for him. Afterwards, as he mixed the cocktails by the big gilt bar table that he had bought on her birthday, he did not even notice the remnant of her tears.

"I lunched with Ida today."

"Oh, did you?"

"She says you're planning to go to Europe. I was grateful for the information."

"In the early fall," he confirmed casually. "As you know, we've been worried about Dorcas. We thought it might be a good idea to take her to France after the divorce. She's awfully broken up, poor kid."

"I've heard all about it. Several times, thank you."

Derrick frowned at the implications of her tone. "She's been through hell," he emphasized gravely as he crossed the room to bring her her glass.

"Oh, hell, really! How you and Ida go on about it! Nothing has happened to Dorcas that she won't get used to. I know I did. And what about *my* summer?"

"Why not come along with us? Ida'd love it."

"And carry on under her very nose?"

Derrick laughed easily. "I might give you the summer off."

The summer off! Her temples throbbed, and her mouth, even after a quick sip of her drink, felt dry and rough. "Derrick!" she exclaimed. "When are you going to tell Ida?"

"Tell her what?"

"That you want a divorce! Or shall I do it?"

His face was suddenly grim as he stared back. "I wouldn't do that if I were you."

She rose from her seat in accordance with what she felt should be the dignity of the impending scene. "I think it's time you told me, Derrick, whether you have any intention of going through with what I understood you to promise."

His grimness faded when he pursed his lips and put his hands behind his back, as if she had simply asked him a tricky question. "You must remember that Ida and I have been married a quarter of a century. One doesn't snap such old ties lightly."

"Lightly!" she cried. "When did we ever suggest that it be done lightly? The question I'm putting is, will it be done at all?"

Again he hesitated, and then, suddenly, his hands reappeared from behind his back. She saw at once that the fists were clenched. "No!"

"Thank you! And now will you please tell me one more thing. Did you *ever* intend to ask Ida for a divorce?"

"Never!"

She stepped back under the double impact of his defiance, as if he had pushed her in the chest. Taking a deep breath, she just managed to keep up her high, deliberate tone. "Then you *admit* you seduced me under a false promise of marriage?"

Derrick turned to the bar table with a careless shrug. As far as he was concerned, the scene was evidently over. "Isn't it a bit idiotic at your age to talk about seduction?"

The last of her dignity vanished with her wild burst of temper. "No!"

she almost shrieked. "I *was* seduced. It was your revenge for what happened before you and Ida were married. You've been plotting ever since to make a whore out of me. To make a whore out of your wife's own cousin!"

"The day you became a whore was the day you married Talbot Keating."

"I loved Talbot!"

"The hell you did! You wouldn't know how to love. You sold yourself to him, and you've been selling yourself ever since. The only difference between me and the other men is that I don't pretend."

Now that the worst had come, now that hopes which had barely been hopes were shattered, now that a word had been used which she had dreaded all her life, she was surprised at her own fortitude. The only thing that seemed to matter was not her future, but her past. She drew herself up as she determined, whatever her disadvantage, to put in his place this churlish creature whom Uncle Linn had so rashly introduced into the family.

"There's another difference between you and the 'other men,' as you are crude enough to describe them. The others were gentlemen."

He opened his mouth as if to make a scornful rejoinder, but then paused and shook his head. When he spoke, there was even a hint of affection in his tone. "I grant I'm no gentleman. I don't pretend to be one. But that can make life so much simpler. You'll see. You and I should get on much better after this little blow-up."

"You can't, surely, mean that after what you've called me tonight, you actually still expect . . . ?"

"Wait a second, wait a second," he interrupted brusquely, "who called you what? *You* were the one who introduced that five-letter word. I have no use for labels. I'm too busy with the facts. And suppose you pause a minute and look at them. Ida and her whole family are coddling you as an inconsolable widow. I'm paying your bills and investing your money. Do you realize I've doubled it already? And what's more, there are no strings attached. You can see anyone you like. You can marry, if you want. Your reputation is at least as good as it was before I came into the picture. If ever a girl had her cake and ate it, it's you. Think twice, Geraldine, before you throw *me* over. You'll never duplicate a berth like the one you've got."

"It's charming of you to point out your generosity," she retorted icily. "But what does it amount to when it's based on a lie?"

"What lie?"

"The lie that you would marry me!"

Derrick threw his hands in the air. "For pity's sake, don't be so childish! Is adultery that ends in divorce any holier than adultery that doesn't? And, anyway, you don't really want to marry me. All you want is security. Why not? I understand that. My point is precisely that you're getting it. If you'll just go on the way we've been going, I'll triple your capital in a year!"

"Is this another proposition?"

"There you go, with your labels again! I know plenty of women, just as well born as you, who wouldn't mind listening to such a proposition."

"Would Ida?"

"Ida's different. You know about Ida."

"Well, I'm Ida's cousin! That's something you've never understood about me. Or perhaps about her, either. We were brought up under a code, and there are some things we just don't do. Perhaps the distinction between what is and what is not allowed is sometimes subtle, but it's always there. I wouldn't expect you, an outsider, to understand." Rising, she walked, with proud steps, to the door. She picked up his grey hat and dark blue overcoat and reached them towards him. "Good day, Mr. Hartley!"

"For good?"

"For good."

His smile was nasty now. "You seem to forget whose house this is."

"That would not be possible," she retorted, "with you here to remind me. You've always been the little boy from the small town with your nose pressed to the window of the great world. And no matter how much money you make, you'll always be that pushing little boy."

"The pushing little boy you tried to marry!"

Angrily she threw his coat and hat to the floor at his feet. "You're as common as dirt!" she retorted. "And you always will be. Common in your manners and common in your lovemaking!"

Derrick stopped to gather his belongings. "You're a fool, Geraldine," he said with a rueful shake of his head. "It may be true there was some revenge in what I did to you. You hurt me badly, years ago. But you can't see that what I did hasn't hurt you. Just the way you can't see that a great deal of real desire may be mixed up with that revenge. I suppose the only unique thing about you is that you've made a fool of yourself twice with the same man."

She flung herself back on the sofa when he had gone and sobbed for a quarter of an hour. Then, bored by her solitude and the sound of her own grief, she rose and spent an equal time at her dressing table, repairing the damage. It was gratifying, at least, to feel that the still beautiful face that stared back at her was once more the face of a Denison, a Denison of whom all the others could be proud. Then as she rose and surveyed her apartment, her eyes clouded at the prospect of having to leave it, and she felt a clutch of the old terror at the idea that honor might obligate her to give back the money he had made. But a moment later she tossed her head. Why should she? Was the money not hers? Legally *and* morally? Had he not said so himself? Were there to be no limits on the reparations demanded of a poor widow? Would even Ida ask them of her? Fortunately, she could never discuss it with Ida. And going back to her living room she sat on the sofa, a floppy doll tucked under each arm, and consulted her address book. Whom could she call at this hour, of all Freddy's friends who had said: "Let me know, Geraldine, when you're feeling better and have an evening free"? Some of them had meant, with their wives; some, perhaps, had not. She was reaching for the telephone, but she decided that she would first see if the martinis left in Derrick's silver pitcher were too watery. She needed to celebrate the restoration of the family honor.

13

IDA: 1936

IT HAD NOT taken me long to find out about Derrick and Geraldine; the latter had been too anxious for my enlightenment. I suppose it would have destroyed half her satisfaction in the affair had she been unable to throw it in the face of the younger cousin who had had the temerity to get all the things in life that Geraldine, now that it was too late, thought she had always wanted. And so it was impossible for her, even supposing that it was subconscious, not to bracket Derrick's name with each expenditure of new money in such a way as to drive my poor self-respecting little doubts out into the snowstorm of truth. She showed some of the cockiness that she had shown in the winter when she had first taken Derrick away from me, a cockiness that gleamed steadily, then as now, from behind the shabby old careless bead curtain of her perfunctory shame. I, too, was ashamed, but of minding her malevolence more than I minded Derrick's infidelity.

The muddy waters of my emotions were at their muddiest when the affair was broken off, for I found the end more distressing than the beginning. I had suspected from the increased acerbity of Geraldine's references to Derrick that a breach might have occurred, but I was not sure until the day when she poutingly told me that she had no summer plans.

"How about coming to Europe?" I asked her.

"You mean with you and Derrick?"

"Well, it wouldn't have to be with us. We could all meet in Paris."

"Do you think that would be wise?" Geraldine allowed a dreamy look to cloud her eyes as she stared over the tables in the Park Club dining room. "Paris, the city of love?"

"You mean, it would remind you too much of Freddy?"

Her cloudy gaze was faintly pierced by irritation. "The three of us in Paris? Surely, Ida, you've heard about two being company?"

This, I felt, was a cruder reference to the affair than my dignity, or what was left of it, could permit. "I'm sure I don't have to worry about that kind of thing with *you*."

"Every woman has to worry about every other woman," Geraldine murmured, in the irritating drone that she used for her worldy-wise clichés. "You must never forget what happened the winter that Derrick and I first met."

"But that's ancient history, Geraldine!"

"The embers might be lying around still." She surprised me by placing her long white hand on mine. "Best not risk it, dear. Because if there's one thing I'm clear about in my mind and heart, it's that I could never hurt you. Never, never!"

I knew the note in Geraldine's voice when she was trying to be sincere. And if she had convinced herself that she could never hurt me, it could only mean that the affair was off, and if it was off, was I to be in the position, once again in my life, of owing Derrick to her? I didn't like it. I didn't like it at all. My ancient feeling of guilt at having come between the archetypes of male and female, at having prevented what had then seemed to me so innately fitting a union, returned in force, and I had to evoke in my fancy the loudest bray of the Denison laughter to avoid the pitfall of trying to induce my husband's mistress to return to him. I saw now in this unexpected twist of my perverse disposition the traps of Trask sentimentality and that it was possible, by dwelling too morbidly on imagined guilt, to play the pander in one's own home. There had been more, evidently, then just a sense of appearances behind the philosophy of my mother's family. There had been a deeper sense of human dignity than I appeared instinctively to possess.

I had pulled myself together, however, by the time we sailed on the *Paris* and was able to accept with a degree of equanimity the new attentions of a Derrick who seemed determined to make up for anything that I might have suspected. He walked on deck with me in the mornings instead of reading his financial reports, and at table he was full of breezy suggestions about wines and special dishes. It was as well that one of us should make a noise, for Dorcas, from the moment of our sailing, had sunk into an unexplained depression and now would hardly speak to us, sitting all day in her deck chair, staring at the sea and quitting our table abruptly after a few spoonfuls of one course. For once in her life, she was particularly resentful of her father, whom she seemed now to blame for all the misery of her divorce, and he made things no better by his jovial espousal of the suit of Mark Jesmond, who had left the law to become his right-hand man at Hartley and Dodge and who was now the rather grudgingly accepted beau of the boss's daughter. Dorcas criticized Mark incessantly, before and behind his back, but she still went out with him. I could not decide whether her current moodiness arose from regrets over Robin or indecision over Mark, and I thought it wisest, unlike her father, not to prod her. One morning, however, she brought the subject up herself.

"I'm so worried about Robin," she said, her eyes fixed on a lively sea. "I can't seem to picture how he'll get on alone. He's so helpless, really. How do I know he won't drink himself to death? Or worse?"

"People like Robin have more resilience than you think. Just when you've given them up, they come bouncing back."

"You mean Robin will come bouncing back?"

"Well, not to you," I assured her. "But I wouldn't worry about his killing himself. When I last saw him he was cheerfully planning to be married to that Miss Stiles."

"When *you* last saw him?"

"Yes. I went to see him in his hotel. I had some of your misgivings about what he might do. Fortunately, he made me feel like a fool. He was totally merry and gay. And the next day I sent him a check for a thousand dollars as a wedding present."

"*Mother!*"

"Well, why not? I always liked Robin, and of course he was utterly broke."

"Did you tell Father?"

"No, and don't you, either. I did it with my own money."

"Did you think Robin had *any* chance of being happy with that woman?"

"No. I doubt if Robin could be happy with anyone. But I wanted to see him off to a good start."

"Because I treated him so badly?"

"No, dear. Because I liked him."

I left her to brood, her relief at learning that Robin was not suicidal understandably soured by the insulting speed of his recovery, and her mind now free to concentrate on the more interesting question of Mark. However little I welcomed the idea of a rapid second marriage for Dorcas, it was beginning to be evident even to me that she was a woman who would find it difficult to exist for long without a husband. She was more sullen than usual that night with her father, and early the next morning, when we were entering the Solent, I suggested that he disembark in Southampton and do his business in London while we went on to Paris.

"There's no point trying to shake her out of this mood," I warned him. "She'll come around in time. For the moment she has to have a scapegoat, and it might just as well be you. Lord knows, I've had *my* share of it!"

The hotel into which Dorcas and I moved the next day was near the Vendôme where I had stayed more than thirty years before with Grandma, and there was nothing about our situation to make Paris seem less hard and grey than it had seemed to me then. Yet this time, despite everything, I loved it. I had traveled very little in my married life because Derrick, who had to travel continually for business, preferred to spend his vacations at home. I had lived a New York woman's existence of charitable committees, lunching daily at the Park Club with friends whom I had known since school. We met in groups to discuss books and philosophy and current events; we lunched on Thursdays in French and on odd Mondays to learn Italian. It was a life that has been lampooned in a million cartoons, but it had been comfortably full, pleasantly monotonous, and my consolation was that I wondered if the cartoonists in the jungle of their own lives had had so many glimpses of that rare bird, content. But to be in Paris, with an open car and driver, with no friends or duties, and with long days in which to see the history of France expressed in its monuments, was at least to know that the bird had once been there. I remembered old Mr. Robbins and his cult of Richelieu and reflected wistfully how close the years had brought us.

Dorcas was at first my somber companion on daily excursions to Versailles, to Fontainebleau, to Chartres, but in a week's time she protested that she had had enough and wanted to look up some friends from the Brandon Press who had established a short story magazine in Paris. After that I saw her only at breakfast and sometimes at dinner. Fortunately, Hugo turned up at our hotel on his way to join college friends for a bicycle tour of Germany.

He was appalled at my solitary schedule and took me out to dinner at Maxim's to protest.

"Two women can't live in Paris together. It's a crime! I don't care how down Dorcas feels. Send her over to London to mope with Daddy, and let's you and me take a trip together. I can join my pals later. Hell, I see them all winter in New Haven."

"Darling, I'd be your ball and chain."

"Not so. I'd like to see you on your own for once. I'd like to see you *live*."

"What would I have to do to live?"

"Well, you wouldn't have to make eyes at a gondolier. Or go to the Beaux-Arts Ball in a fig leaf!"

"Hugo!"

"Isn't that what you think people mean by living? All you old girls at the Park Club? I just want you to go on a motor trip. With me. No big car. No chauffeur. No plans. We'd stay at each place as long as we damn pleased and no longer."

"Your father's spoiled me for that," I said, shaking my head. "I'd be lost without a timetable."

"Oh, Ma," he said disgustedly, "you never have any fun, and it's getting later all the time."

Hugo, unlike his father and sister, had never taken me for granted. I was always a person to him as well as just "Mother," pronounced in a tone of understandable protest. Hugo deplored me, criticized me, shouted at me and even at times hurt my feelings, but there was always juice in our relationship. It was not unlike the relationship that I had had with Christopher, except that Christopher had been gentler than Hugo and had cared about me less. Hugo cared about very few people, but I think I had a fixed if narrow bench in the hallway of his suspicious heart. As for my own heart, well, it was absurdly full of Hugo. I was always watching myself to be sure that I would not embarrass or oppress him with the abundance of my feeling. I was even terrified that he would persuade me to let him ruin his summer, and I was actually relieved when he was safely on his way to Germany.

I had reason to question the true identity of Dorcas' publishing friends on the day when I came back to the hotel at lunchtime, having expected to be gone until evening, and found Mark Jesmond sprawled on a sofa in the lobby. Even abroad he wore the brown coat and grey flannels which, with his rumpled hair and shrewd, grinning boyish face, wizened a bit as such faces become after the age of thirty, seemed to have as little reference to France as the morning mail at Morgan's.

"What a pleasant surprise, Mr. Jesmond," I greeted him. "Have you come over on business for Derrick?"

"Well, that's the usual excuse isn't it?"

"I hope you don't let him hear you say that."

"Oh, I think I can count on Derrick to forgive my real motive."

He looked at me in rather roguish manner as he threw off his employer's Christian name, and I inferred that he wanted me to go on.

"What is your real motive?"

"To marry your daughter!" he boomed at me suddenly, with a brazen grin.

I studied that grin carefully and noted how little humor there was in it. "That *is* a surprise," I said calmly. "Whether pleasant or unpleasant remains to be seen. You implied that my husband knows?"

"Oh, yes, I have *his* blessing."

"And Dorcas'?"

"Well, she wasn't exactly averse to the idea in New York," he said with another grin. "But I don't know about Paris. What's been going on over here?"

"Mr. Jesmond," I said sternly, to reprove his note of accusation, "may I ask if you're interested in *my* blessing?"

"Very much so. As many as I can get!"

"Then will you tell me why you think you can make my daughter happy?"

"Here and now?"

"Where better?"

"Because I'm not a weakling, like Granberry. Because I know where I'm going and where I want to take her!"

"You don't make it sound like a very attractive courtship," I observed. "At least not to my old-fashioned ears. But that's your and Dorcas' affair, not mine. I'm only interested that you're ashamed to tell me that you love her."

He flushed a mottled red and looked down at shoes which needed shining. "You're right, Mrs. Hartley. I'm an egregious ass. Of course I love her. I love her with everything I've got."

When he looked up and smiled, without grinning this time, it was a great improvement. "Thank you, Mr. Jesmond. I think we may get on. Yet."

At this point Dorcas walked out of the elevator and stopped abruptly as she saw us. Her mouth dropped open and then slowly closed, and the stare which she shifted from me to Mark changed from surprise to hostility.

"Well?"

"Your mother and I have been having a little chat," Mark explained. "I've been trying to win her over to our point of view."

"*Our*? I'm sure I don't know what you mean." She turned to place an unexpectedly protecting hand on my elbow. "Shall we go in to lunch, Mummy?"

"Wouldn't Mr. Jesmond like to join us?"

"No doubt. But I don't feel like joining Mr. Jesmond."

Mark simply grinned again. "I'm sure it's not your fault she's such a spoiled brat, Mrs. Hartley. She must have learned her bad manners with that long-haired literary crowd." He winked at Dorcas. "Goodbye, honey. I'll see you at drink time. Only try to be in a better mood, will you?"

Dorcas and I both stared after that jauntily departing figure, and when our eyes met, we looked away with the same impulse of embarrassment. It was as if her silence had been a consent to some intimate, almost unseemly gesture, which she would have liked to have hidden, but no longer quite dared to repudiate. Our constraint continued in the quiet hotel dining room.

"What I fail to understand is why you didn't tell me he was here," I said at last. "Have I ever in the least objected to your seeing him?"

"I didn't want you to be bothered."

"Bothered? But, my child, what do you think I came to Paris for, except you?"

"I know, Mummy, you've been a darling, but I can't talk to you about Mark."

"Can you to Daddy?"

"No." Her sullen shipboard look returned at the mention of her father. "Daddy's too much like him. Marrying Mark would be like marrying Daddy."

"Would that be so terrible?"

"Oh, Mummy, please!" Her voice rose with an edge of pain. "I don't want to hurt you. That's why it's all so difficult. Ever since my divorce I've seen Daddy with different eyes. I've seen what he's done to *you*. I don't want that. Would you want it for me?"

Dorcas' adoration of her father, however irritating, was far less painful than her disillusionment with him. It is never agreeable to seem pathetic to one's own child. "Have you considered that you might do better with a man like Daddy than I did?"

"You mean because I'd fight him?"

"No. Because you might believe in him."

She reacted to this with unexpected humility. "You think I'm so stupid?"

"Belief isn't a matter of intellect. There's nothing clever about *not* believing in a man like Mark."

She shook her head and sighed broodingly. "Perhaps. If that were all. But there's something else."

"About Mark?"

"About me. You'd never understand."

When I said nothing, but simply waited, Dorcas gazed about the high dark-paneled dining room and the silently chewing, elderly couples. "Well, we're in Paris, aren't we?" she said with a bitter laugh. "Maybe it's the place for such explanations. The thing, if you *must* know, is that my feelings for Mark isn't the kind to build a marriage on. It's too physical."

"Do you think mine for your father wasn't?"

She appeared to consider this apparently novel idea before rejecting it as irrelevant. "But Daddy was big and strong and handsome, and Mark is— well, to begin with he's smaller than I am. And he's funny-looking."

I began at last to sense how truly miserable she was. Dorcas had inherited all of my grandmother's capacity for sterile suffering. She had her father's literalness as well, but none of his toughness. When she turned her gaze impatiently to the window opening on the small graveled courtyard, I realized that I could not evade with any honesty the elementary fact that this perverse, proud, somber, stubborn creature was my daughter and was appealing to me. Appealing to me for the first time in her life. "Mark must be almost as near my age as he is yours," I suggested. "Which is why I can understand his attraction for you. He's very much a man, and that's not a quality one measures in biceps or toothy smiles."

"You mean *you* feel it?"

"Certainly I feel it."

There was jealousy as well as incredulity in her stare. "You mean you're *attracted* to Mark?"

"Well, I don't know if we need go as far as that. But I can understand *your* being attracted. He's a very attractive man."

Reassured but still gloomy, she debated the consequences of this. "He says be wants his answer this week."

"Why so soon?"

"He says if I won't marry him in Paris, I won't marry him anywhere."

"That's absurd."

"But if he means it, Mummy!" I was shocked by the way in which her eyes suddenly flooded with fear. "If he means it, and I lose him!"

"Darling, he can't mean it!" I shivered at the inward twist of my compassion with my exasperation. "Why are you so sure that you're not simply in love with Mark in the most ordinary, old-fashioned way?"

"I'm *not* sure," she exclaimed in what was almost a wail. "Was I in love with Robin? I thought so at the time, and look what a mess I made!"

"This strikes me as a much stronger thing."

"But how does one tell?"

I concentrated carefully on placing a tiny piece of butter on my Melba toast. "By going away with him."

Dorcas stared at me now with something like awe. "Going away with him?"

"For a few days. Nobody need know. Go to some little beach in Spain."

"*Mother!*"

"Well, I thought your generation was supposed to be so liberated."

"But not *yours!*"

"Must I remind you of the night you spent in Robin Granberry's apartment and flung in my face?"

"But we didn't *do* anything!"

At another time I could have laughed at her shocked expression. "Well, it's a pity you didn't. The only way you're ever going to make up your mind about Mark, whether you marry him or not, is by living with him. And if that shocks you, all I can say is that you're very easily shocked!"

"It shocks me coming from you," she insisted. "I can't imagine you doing such a thing with Daddy. Would you have?"

"Those were different days."

"Would you today?"

"In your position, I might."

"But, Mummy, I had no *idea* you were so immoral!"

"We live and learn."

An instinct told me that the only course was a fixed one, that apology or sustained defense might be equally fatal. I had taken from Dorcas her childhood image of me, and it was important that I should not hide it or even hold it too tightly, but that I should simply leave it quietly beside us on the table until she saw that it was only a doll with a painted smile and a body stuffed with straw. I finished my meal in silence as she brooded, feeling very Gallic and unlike myself. I remembered what Paris had done to Grandma.

What in the name of all the household gods of Fifty-third Street was it doing to me?

Dorcas did not accompany me that afternoon to Compiegne, and when I returned I found her writing at a desk in the lobby, a small suitcase standing by her feet. She jumped up when she saw me and put an arm about my shoulders and held her cheek against mine.

"I was trying to slip out before you got back, you wicked old thing," she murmured. "I was writing you a note. Try to keep Daddy from running all over France with a shotgun, will you?"

Which turned out to be not so easy to do. Derrick came over from London two days later and was furious when I told him what had happened. He strode up and down the little sitting room, seeming absurdly loud and Yankee against the grey panels, denouncing Dorcas as a loose woman and myself as an unprincipled sentimentalist. Only when he said he would fire Mark did I intervene.

"I wonder why you think you're in a position to lecture me as if you were Cotton Mather. I would have thought that recent events might have disqualified you."

The most attractive thing about Derrick was his instant ability to face a loss of advantage. He ceased his pacing and actually smiled. "Did Geraldine tell you?"

"That is something that you and I are never going to discuss," I retorted firmly as I rose to answer the buzz of the hall door. "Silence is our only possible salvation." The page in the hallway handed me a telegram. It was postmarked from Santander in Spain and read: "Mark and I married today. Returning Paris Monday. Can we dine gala? Beg Daddy forgive moodiness boat. Madly happy and love to all. Dorcas."

I handed it silently to Derrick and watched his face light up. "By God, Ida, I hand it to you. You've really done it this time!"

"But what? Isn't that the question?"

"You've given her a second life, that's all! After she made hash of her first one."

"I wonder." I took the telegram and ruefully studied its text. "I wish it had taken her a little more than forty-eight hours to rush to the sanctity of law. I'm afraid she's aghast already at her own daring in going off with him. The next step will be for her to forget that she ever did." Seeing Derrick's impatient frown, I shrugged. "As her father has forgotten already."

When Dorcas and Mark, exuberant, and Derrick, glowing, were ready to sail for home, I surprised them all by saying that I was planning to spend a few weeks with my cousin, Elly Denison, Uncle Will's daughter, who had married an Irishman. They protested, but not too much, and in less than a week's time I found myself settled in an old grey shabby Georgian house in Galway where time seemed the only luxury. Elly was big and cheerful, like the other Denisons, and her tweeds and red cheeks and blown grey hair went well with the Anglo-Irish hunting set of which she and her husband and six children were devoted members, but her particular asset to me at this juncture of my life was her impersonality. She would stride into my bedroom early in riding clothes, ask if I had everything I needed, and then I wouldn't see her again until dinner.

It was perfect. I would take her dogs out to stroll for hours on the windy moors until the early fall mists drove me in to the fire in the big library. I allowed the bleak, treeless, dune-green, hilly coast of County Galway to enter into my being until it seemed to me, when I strolled along the bluffs and listened to the roar of the Atlantic, that I had traveled as far as it was possible for a human to travel, at least from the brown gridiron city of my childhood, and was perched now upon the very border of the known world. I wanted to think that I was merging with the countryside like an old woman in black, sitting outside a white thatched cottage and chewing a pipe, but I could never quite fool myself. All that was really happening to me was the self-indulgence of detachment. Detachment from my little curriculum of self-appointed tasks. In the evenings now, when Elly and I chatted about the past, Fifty-third Street seemed as unreal and as quaintly entertaining as a novel by Jane Austen. Only when she made a bitter reference to Geraldine, whom she had always detested, was it again the street of my education, seen now with more perceptive eyes.

"She behaved like a bitch to you over Derrick—you can't deny that."

I shuddered to think what Elly, who was referring to the events of 1912, would have thought of the events of the preceding spring. She would never have understood that, according to my old, misleading lights, Derrick and Geraldine, by their affair, had given me back the freedom of which they had robbed me, years before, when she had rejected him. They had relieved me of the burden of obligation which I had so long and so uneasily carried, with the result that I had not been truly conscious of the wrong which their affair had done me until they had given it up. It was Derrick's attitude of fumbling apology on board the *Paris* that had made me see him for the first time as less than cold and self-absorbed, as less than a man who put a large career ahead of nation and family, but as actually shabby, as a mere small lying creature whimpering for his wife's forgiveness for a sin that he had been frustrated from committing. And Dorcas, by having been his pupil, had suffered in similar, if not in equal fashion, according to my now sterner estimates. I could stay with them and help them and be, indeed for the first time, an active agent in their lives, but in doing so I was descending from an elevation whose pinnacle, looming above me in the dissolving mist of my preconceptions, had an outline perilously similar to the lofty peak which I now identified with contempt. It might have been this very peak that I was fleeing on the moors of Galway. If I dared not look over my shoulder it was probably that I feared the fate of Lot's wife.

How long I might have stayed in Ireland without Hugo's cable I do not know. "Are you never coming home? Please remit explanation attraction Galway, Connemara. Park Club and I concerned your protracted stay."

I sailed from Cobh, and a week later I was seated on a trunk on a cold pier, listening to Hugo while we waited for customs. Derrick was in Chicago with the Jesmonds for a convention of investment bankers, and Hugo had journeyed down from New Haven to meet me.

"Cousin Geraldine was coming, too, but when I called to pick her up, she was in no shape to make it."

"Oh, darling, has she been drinking again?"

"Unless it was an excuse not to come. In which case I must admit it was a pretty good act."

"It seems so drab to come back to all that," I said with a sigh. "You'd have loved Ireland."

"Nobody drinks there, I suppose."

I asked him about Dorcas.

"Oh, she's blooming!" he exclaimed with a cheerful, if malicious laugh. "It's Mark this and Mark that, and have you *heard* what Mark's doing, and, Daddy, *when* are you going to make Mark a partner?"

"But doesn't Daddy want to make Mark a partner?"

"Oh, sure, but in his own good time. Women like Dorcas are terrors. When they finally get hold of a man who can satisfy them, they'll cut up the rest of us into patches to darn his socks!"

"You're crude."

"But accurate. What did you think you were up to in Paris? Forging a weapon against Daddy out of his own protégé?"

"You're being perfectly absurd," I protested. "Your father was all for that marriage from the beginning."

"Because he didn't *know*."

"Know what?"

"What it would do to Dorcas!" Hugo exclaimed gleefully. "But *you* did. I've always suspected that was a bit of a fiend behind that docile matronly brow. What are your plans for me? Had I better start running now?"

"Oh, darling, all I want is for you to be happy," I murmured, looking disconsolately down the long line of trunks that seemed to shiver in the cold grey of the wharf. It had been cold in Galway, but that had not been the grimey fall coldness that hangs about man-made things in a Manhattan out-of-doors.

"Well, keep your fine Italian hand off Hugo," he warned me. "Hugo's doing fine!"

And so perhaps he was. But why then had I come home? The brief flurry of activity that had followed the end of Geraldine's and Derrick's affair was now ended, and I faced, with a rueful sense of anticlimax, the resumption of my old life. Dorcas had returned, on a more solid basis, I hoped, to the preoccupations of matrimony, and Derrick had returned, after what I guessed to be a final diversion, to the joys of money-making. Hugo had his own bright eyes and his own bright future, and nobody needed me. Nobody, apparently, but Geraldine, and Geraldine I had little enough wish to help.

Yet I helped her, or at least I went through the motions. Geraldine, I often speculated in the years that followed, seemed to have been born to prove to my only too credulous soul how little we can do for other human beings. I sat with her; I laughed with her; I reminisced with her; I agreed with her. I did everything but drink with her, and that, in the last analysis, was the only thing she really wanted of me. Geraldine hated me, and for the next fourteen years I presented a bland, fatuous, smiling target for her hate.

As she grew worse, she took less and less pains to conceal her antagonism, and yet she clung to me, for she had alienated all the rest of the family. She could never descant enough on the injustice of life that had brought me so much and her so little. She remained to the end the little girl who has come down with a bright face and bright flowing hair to find in her Christmas stocking a switch and a book of sermons while mine was crammed with packages that I dared not open. To me she presented the constant illusion of an opportunity to make up at least to one Denison what I had failed to give the others, and the reminder, equally constant, that it *was* an illusion. It accorded with my sense of justice that I should have to wait until her death for the cloudy release of being a survivor.

PART SIX
HUGO IN LOVE

14

HUGO: 1950

HUGO'S APARTMENT, ON the top floor of his parents' house, was a store-house of the treasures which a shrewd eye in the auction business had enabled him to pick up. Indeed, the only thing in common between the Japanese screen, the Italian primitive triptych, the Greek head and the giant Dresden porcelain boar was that they had been purchased by a man whose love of bargains encompassed no corresponding need of harmony. Hugo let his acquisitions speak for themselves, furnishing his rooms with the odds and ends for which his parents had no further use below. What the odds and ends looked like hardly mattered, for he never entertained there. When he had to make a bachelor's token return for the quantities of hospitality that were lavished upon him, he did so at the Knickerbocker Club or at the Pavillon, and was always careful to include at least one customer of the Denison-Adler Gallery to ensure the tax deductibility of his check. As he lived at home and entertained on the nation, his salary was available for art and for clothes.

He could have gone back, after V-J Day, to Hartley and Dodge, where he had made a brief start in 1940, accepting his father's offer of employment with the careless shrug of one who knew that war was coming. But after four years of destroyer duty in the Pacific, years that had given him, for the first time in his life, though he would never admit it, the sense of a job well done, he found the New York scene, and particularly his father, so absurdly unaltered, so ludicrously unaffected by those thousands of drowned bodies in the Pacific, as to repel him. He was already thirty in 1945 and knew what he wanted, or thought he did: elegance and order and small talk and women and *no* commitments. He wanted to do little things well, but he wanted everyone to know that he could have done the big things well, too. Indeed, he wanted the people who did the big things to recognize that his own choice was a pointed reflection on theirs. Hugo had become even pricklier with the years. He was always suspecting the men at his dinner parties of sneering, as he was sure his father did, at his job in an auction gallery. What difference, he would snarl to himself, did it make to *them* that Denison-Adler, after a long period of eclipse, was regaining its old position among the galleries of the city? Did it not deal in paintings and bric-à-brac and old furniture, women's matters? Was that a field for men, like oil and steel and zinc and celluloid?

It was his habit in the morning, before going to work, to stop for a minute, two floors below, and chat with his mother. Ida was at her best at that hour, before the anxieties of the day had settled upon her. Sitting in bed in her wrapper, sipping coffee, her lap full of letters and newspaper, she was least feminine in a setting where another woman might have been most. But it was before she had put on her clothes and her powder and neuroses that Ida's intelligence and curiosity, both qualities essentially neuter, were allowed to function at will. With the long brown cheeks and haggard eye of the early waker, she looked almost gaunt in her inappropriate pink.

"How was your dinner party?" Her question was safe. He had always been to one.

"They talked the wrong way," Hugo reported briefly. "I ate most of my meal in silence between two female backs."

"You seem to have a bit of trouble with that. Maybe you scare your dinner partners off."

"I *think* I know how to talk."

"That's just it. You talk too well. Ladies at dinner parties distrust men who talk too well."

"You suggest, then, that I become a bore?"

"Or stop going out so much."

Decidedly, he reflected, she had become tarter since Cousin Geraldine's death. In the perpetual tug-of-war of their relationship, it bored him when she agreed with him and irked him when she did not. "What do you expect a lonely bachelor to do with his evenings?"

"You might take a course." She went so far as to hand him, from the pile of her mail, a list of lectures at the Metropolitan Museum. "Was Mrs. Tyson at your party?"

His hand was raised to throw the pamphlet back on her bed, but surprise made him pause and scan it. "Why do you ask?"

"She's been mentioned as a trustee for Miss Irvin's School. I was wondering what you thought of her."

"What *I* thought? Isn't Grinnell Tyson one of Daddy's partners?"

"Yes, but there are so many of them now. I barely know her. I thought she was a friend of yours."

Hugo pondered the question of Miss Irvin's School. He knew that he would never make headway against his mother's loyalty to women's groups. It was on such, after all, that the basic defense of her life had been erected. But how in her wildest dreams could she imagine Kitty that type? "Isn't all that school board business just compensation for frustrated women?"

Ida did not even do his attack the honor of looking up from her newspaper. "How like you to assume that if a woman accomplishes anything, she's only filling a void left by a man."

"Well, *isn't* she?"

"Naturally." She turned a page and shrugged. "If she were happy, she'd stay at home and do her fingernails. Isn't that your picture of us?"

"It's my picture of Kitty Tyson."

"Really? But I gathered from your father that she was rather pathetic. That Grinnell was something less than a faithful husband."

"Maybe she's something less than a faithful wife." He watched her out of the corner of his eye as he said this, but she was inscrutable.

"Then, of course, she won't do for our board. I'm sorry. I hadn't heard she was that kind of woman."

"Oh, Ma! Do you still believe in different kinds of women?"

"I believe in decent ones."

"Decent or inhibited?"

"What does it matter what I call them? You know perfectly well what I mean."

Hugo had learned from a psychiatrist whom he had consulted after the war that it was a common delusion of the libertine to regard every woman as loose except his own mother. But what about the mother's delusions? Was it not rather bewildering for the libertine if she had for her own sex her son's delusion about *her*?

"I'd better be getting to the office," he muttered.

"Are you doing anything Friday night?"

He hesitated. She was always trying to tie him up for her dinner parties which she always weighted down with relatives. "It so happens that these very Tysons want me for the Nurses' Aid Ball."

Ida's face continued elaborately expressionless. "You're committed, then?"

"Not if I don't choose."

"Minerva Denison's taken a table and wants you desperately. It's an older group, but Alfreda will be there. She's really a most attractive girl."

"Oh, the girls *you* find attractive!" he moaned. Yet he considered it. Minerva Denison was old and ugly, but she was also rich and gay. She and her young daughter followed the world of fashion from Palm Beach to Bar Harbor and lived in large hotels. The childish fallacy that such people were glamorous, though long recognized for a fallacy, still stuck in the top of his mind.

"I'd really appreciate it if you would," his mother pursued. "Minerva's always asking me to do things, and I can never get your father to go."

"I object to being used to pay off your social obligations, but I suppose I might have a whack at it. How old is the girl?"

"Twenty-one. And really such a darling."

"A bit young for me, isn't she?"

"Just the right age. And only a second cousin."

"Poor Ma!" he exclaimed as he got up, "what a pity we're not French. You and Cousin Minerva would have worked it all out in advance. The dowry and the date of the wedding and even where Alfreda and I would go on our honeymoon." He paused as the idea struck him. "Or *have* you?"

"You're perfectly ridiculous," she retorted in a tone of such complacency that he began, quite seriously, to wonder what she *had* done.

The Denison-Adler Gallery was housed in the same building that had housed it since 1892, when Hugo's great-uncle, Philip Denison, and Herman Adler, a Swiss art dealer, had founded it with a loan from Linnaeus Tremain. It was a large, grim, brown cube, with a few small half-circle windows, vaguely inspired by the Palazzo Strozzi in Florence, and it stood just off Lexington Avenue on Fifty-seventh Street. A modern structure was needed, and a site farther uptown, if the present prosperity of the business was to continue, but control had long passed to a handful of penurious Swiss stockholders, and the Denison shares, sentimentally retained by members of the family in memory of Uncle Philip, was not sufficient or sufficiently organized to permit Hugo to force his will upon the firm. The Adlers regarded him with mute admiration and mute fear. Since he had come to the gallery five years before, he had worked successfully in every department, preparing accounts and catalogues and even swinging the gavel on auction days, but more recently it had been inevitable for the management to use him, with his connections and his aggressive good manners, in the front office to deal with a clientele which included so many of his friends. How long, the Adlers wondered, could they hold him and still hold control?

Hugo enjoyed their concern. He had no ambition to run the business; he had picked it because he had a start there, because it irritated his father to see him an auctioneer, because the hours were regular and because he enjoyed seeing and handling beautiful things. He despised the slow, cautious, fat Herman Adler III and loved to make scenes in his office, demanding new policies and higher pay, and allowing himself, after much bluster, to be bought off by a small concession or a bonus or even by the opportunity to pick up a bargain from an estate before the auction inventory was completed. But his greatest pleasure in the business was in the display rooms with their changing shows, and no morning passed that he did not stroll through them, catalogue in hand, to check the descriptions and arrangement.

Only an hour after his talk with Ida, as he was making his first round, he caught sight of the graceful, diminutive figure of Kitty Tyson bending over a glass case in the book and manuscript room. She was hatless, and her hands were plunged in the pockets of her black, flare-skirted coat. It always amused him that a woman who dressed with such art could seem as careless as a college girl, unless, of course, that was precisely the goal of her art. Kitty with her small black ring curls and her large beseeching blue eyes, her little upturned nose and her air of wistfulness, was always in danger of seeming as cute as her name. Yet she could dispel the impression, just as it was hardening to a judgment, with a quick, cagey glance that opened vistas into her understanding of people's misunderstanding of her. Kitty cajoled a world to make it forgive her for being more than she appeared.

"I never think that beautiful ladies and old books go together," he said as he moved up behind her. "Like Dorothea in *Middlemarch*. Or don't you know *Middlemarch*?"

It was their game, on meeting, to start each conversation as strangers.

"I was supposed to read it at school, but I don't think I ever did," she replied, without turning around. "Anyway, I don't want a book. I want a picture. A beautiful, beautiful picture."

"You mean you want to *bid* on a picture. This isn't a shop, you know."

She turned now and nodded submissively. "I mean I'd like to bid on a picture."

"What kind of a beautiful, beautiful picture?"

"How do I know till I see it?"

"Well, come find it, then. You're in luck. We've just hung the Whitlock pictures. Collector's 'musts.' Monet, Piscasso, Vuillard, Walter Kuhn, Braque, Rouault, Matisse, and Dufy. The very pick of the fashion!"

He led her into the main gallery where a dozen persons were studying the Whitlock collection and took her up to a tiny smudge of canvas in a large gilded frame, a blurry rose by Renoir. "Just the thing for the little table by your favorite armchair. A shaving from the floor of the master's studio. A scraping from the palette of genius."

Kitty moved closer to squint at it. "One forgets how badly they could paint when they wanted to." He followed her as she toured the room, pausing longest before the Vuillard.

"Well, of course, that's a beauty, but the rest . . ." She shrugged. "Tell me, was it a banker's collection?"

"How did you know?"

"Because there's one of everything. What Grinnell would call a diversified portfolio. But he must have been stingy. He got all the bad ones, didn't he? Poor man," she mused, looking about in final review. "I wonder if he had any fun with it. Or did he do it all with an agent? What would he have bought fifty years ago?"

"Fake Rembrandts and bad Lawrences."

"And fifty years before that?"

"Oh, then, he might have had fun. With Landseer dogs and stags and Alma Tademas and seraglio scenes. Before taste was king. As a matter of fact, we have a rather fine Landseer that just came in. Would you like to see it?"

"Tomorrow. I only dropped in to see if you'd made up your mind about Friday night."

"Oh, yes, I'm sorry. I promised Ma I'd go to Minerva Denison's."

There was a pause as she fitted the name into the puzzle of his family. "That's, Mrs. Scott Denison, isn't it? A widow? A cousin?"

"Not close. But you know how Mother is about family."

"Ah, yes. And there's a daughter, too. Surely, there's a daughter?"

"There is, apparently, a daughter."

"Apparently." Her tone gently mocked him as she moved back along the wall and paused, with the faintest air of conjecture, before an angry factory by Leger. "And you had told me that you might have to go to Chicago."

"Well, it seems I don't."

"Then Mrs. Denison's invitation came *after* mine?"

"Oh, come now, Kitty, don't go on about it. It was a very little thing for Mother to ask."

"To give up my dinner? Thank you."

Hugo stared in surprise. The essence of Kitty, the very *point* of Kitty, was precisely that she never acted this way. "What's come over you?"

"Does it never occur to you that there may be limits to my enjoyment of being taken for granted?"

"But why suddenly make an issue of old Minerva?"

"Your mother's made it, not I." She turned around with a new look of stubbornness in those usually docile blue eyes. "It was *she* who made you give up my dinner. And with malice aforethought!"

"Kitty, you're being ridiculous!"

"I'm not!" she insisted with a sudden, tight little passion. "I *know* about mothers. I'm sorry, Hugo, but I don't like them. I didn't even like my own. Your mother wants you to marry that Denison girl. She's plotted it all out, and she'll succeed, too!"

There was nothing to do with so unprecedented an outburst but to treat it lightly. "It can hardly be malice," he said with a shrug. "Only this morning Ma was talking about you for her school board."

"Exactly! That will be my consolation prize. Oh, she's deep, I tell you." Suddenly she was pleading with him, her hand lightly on his arm. "Please give up Mrs. Denison's dinner for me, Hugo. Will you?"

"But it's all so absurd!"

"I've never asked you to give up anything before!"

"Well, of course, if you insist," he said angrily. "But I think it's most unreasonable of you. And selfish!"

"Thank you, darling," she interrupted in a quick whisper. "I *do* insist. Thanks a million. And now I'll go and let you work."

Before he could stop her, she had crossed the gallery and was out the door without even turning to nod good-bye. He cursed to himself at the thought that his mother would have already telephoned his acceptance to Minerva Denison. Women!

Their affair was nearing the end of its first year, and his ardor was considerably dimmed. Yet he was fair enough to admit that it might have been dimmed by her having been so exactly what he had thought he wanted. He had visualized a mistress beautiful, well dressed and widely admired, who would send him covert understanding glances across the drawing rooms where they would meet, who would lunch or dine with him, on selected occasions, in quiet, out-of-the-way places and who would come, veiled and silent, to a secret rendezvous. He had wanted, in other words, mystery, efficiency, ease and tact, all of which Kitty had been able to provide, and without experience, too, for he had believed her when she told him that he was her first lover. But in becoming his dream girl, she had condemned herself to the insubstantiality of a dream.

Oh, yes, she loved him. There was no minimizing that. But how long did a man have to be grateful for being loved? And was she not proving at last—she, whose chief virtue had been that she was always different from other women—the banality of the ages, that love *had* to become exclusive? Was it not the real Kitty he had just seen, and was not the self-effacing creature of the past year an artifice? Life was crammed with the inevitability of being possessed, hugged, stifled, and what but that had just happened to him in his own place of work, early, on a business morning? It was intolerable, as intolerable as Grinnell Tyson's friendly handshake and condescending offer of brandy and cigars, the little gestures of the older adulterer who hopes to prevent the younger from tiring of what has so long tired him. It was essential that Kitty should learn, if she wished to continue their present arrangement, that a lover must have at least the freedom of a spouse!

Minerva Denison's dinner was hilarious from the start, as warm and crackling as the fire under her massive marble *empire* mantel. She was a woman who understood the importance of cheerful beginnings. She lived in a crisp new apartment hotel with a crisp new living room, all white and yellow, with dark, seventeenth century canvases of flowers and dead game hung between French windows overlooking a dusky, winking Central Park. Minerva was one of those rare women who entertained well without fussing. She might have had her chairs rejoined and her rugs cleaned every winter, but she would not even turn her pink head or gaunt frame at the sound of a broken glass.

"Now, here's a good boy who's not ashamed to come on time!" she cried, extending two long brown arms to greet Hugo. "Bless me, dearie, if I don't see Denison written all over you. I'll bet you like parties and girls and horse races. Give me a kiss, honey. We're close enough kin for that. And then go over and talk to my little girl. She's been dying to meet you."

Alfreda was not big and bony like her mother, but she had the same outward manifestations of enthusiasm and energy. She was basically a rather plain girl, with a long Modigliani face and a small hooked nose, with a bit of twisted mouth and an oval chin, but everything that could be done to improve her looks had been done. She had the brightest teeth and the most beautifully waved blond hair that Hugo had ever seen, and her small, lively tan eyes popped at him from under arched, plucked brows. She seemed not only ready to laugh, but to be laughed *at*.

"Do you like my new dress, Hugo?" she began at once. "It cost a fortune, and I'm wearing it just for you. Because I'm too lucky for words to have a handsome cousin who's kind enough to take me to a dance and introduce me to everybody. You will, won't you? Mummy tells me there's nobody you don't know."

"Well, I didn't know *you*. So you see what a poor crumb I am."

"Ah, but you know me *now*. Or you will." She led him to a corner and a sofa that would hold only two. "Let me start by telling you about myself. I take courses at Columbia. Serious ones, too. I do best with precise subjects, like dates and figures and where things are. I'm an only child and I've probably spent too much time in Europe. I love parties and people, but I'm bored with boys my own age."

"You prefer old men like me."

"You're not old; you're thirty-five," she retorted promptly. "I looked you up in Cousin Ida's family book. I consider that the perfect age for a man. I shouldn't dream of marrying anyone who was a day younger. But don't worry. I won't try to marry you. Mummy tells me you're madly in love with that beautiful Mrs. Tyson, and I think it couldn't be more romantic. I'll just have to think of you as an older brother."

"Mrs. Tyson?" Hugo queried: "What Mrs. Tyson? Surely not the one who's married to a partner of Daddy's and has two girls in boarding school?"

He understood from her baffled look why she did badly in the more speculative subjects. "I mean Mrs. Grinnell Tyson," she complained in the tone of one who at a store counter spots a defect and wants her money back. "Isn't she the one? Mummy seemed so sure." As he shook his head slowly, with the air of a man groping for a clue, she had a happy inspiration. "Oh, I see! You're shielding her. I think that's so gallant! Anyway, I don't think of her as old, any more than I do you. You see, my mother was over forty when I was born. It gives one a different point of view."

"Do you intend to wait for the same period before embarking on family responsibilities?"

Again he had pulled her up too short. "Now, why do you ask that?"

"Because if you and I were to marry, it would mean that I couldn't become a father until my fifty-fifth year."

"But I could never marry *you*!" she exclaimed, as astonished as if he had made a serious proposal.

"Why not?"

"Oh, oodles of reasons. We're cousins, in the first place, and then you're in love with Mrs. Tyson, and, anyway, it isn't my idea at all. I've figured everything out. You're to be a perfectly divine friend, and it would spoil everything if we married."

"I don't know," he protested, a bit piqued by her air of conviction. "I might be a perfectly satisfactory husband."

"Oh, no, no, no!" She shook her head emphatically. "You're not the type at all. Not at all!"

"What is the type?"

"You won't laugh?"

"Cross my heart and hope to die."

She eyed him suspiciously as he moved a finger diagonally across his shirt front. "Well, he wouldn't have to be in law or business or anything like that. As a matter of fact, he wouldn't even have to make money. I figure I have enough for two."

"How gratifying. For him."

"Now don't be sarcastic. I'm simply trying to be truthful. Don't you think it's more fun when people are truthful?"

"By all means. Please go on. You still haven't told me your type of man. All I know is that he can be poor."

"Well, I'd want him to be in public life. Not necessarily in elective politics. He could be a career man."

"In the Bureau of Weight's and Measures, for example?"

She giggled. "Well, of course, what I'd really like is to have him in the State Department."

"As Secretary?"

"Now you *are* laughing at me. No, if I thought he had a future, he could be the lowest of the low. There! I've told you my ambition, and I'm sure you think me a total ass."

"Oh, no. I think you're honest. Which is a million times rarer. Which perhaps even justifies you. But tell me: is that why you want an older man? So you can be sure he's already launched in the right direction?"

"That's it. The young are so risky."

"But they can always be shed."

"Oh, I shall never divorce." Her gravity now struck a deeper note. "I'm like Mummy, a one-man woman. That's why the choice is so terribly important."

It was peculiar how quickly her candor effaced the crasser aspects of her silliness. She made him think of a brilliantly plumaged tropical bird, exotic despite a plain, quaint, honest face. She was intense, literal and probably dull. But he also suspected that if the man of her ultimate choice fell short of her goal, she would be a good sport about it.

At the ball he was unreasonably irked by the perfect discipline that kept Kitty from casting even a glance in his direction as he danced with Alfreda. He wanted her to see that he was not in the least apologetic.

"I see your beautiful Mrs. Tyson," Alfreda observed. "I'm sure she's disconsolate. Why not pop me back at the table and go join her?"

"I'm quite happy, thank you."

"Faithless man! But, then, of course, that's what everyone says about you. I suppose you're aware that you have an absolutely foul reputation?"

"But I'm a lamb, Alfreda! An absolute lamb!"

"It's not true, then, that Mrs. Tyson is disconsolate?"

"Oh, that's all over and done with."

"Goodness me, did anyone hear a cock crow?"

Just then they were cut in on, and as Hugo watched her move across the floor with her new partner, fitting herself neatly but somehow not provocatively into his embrace, he saw that she was talking again, and with the same awkward animation. It gave him the feeling that he and Alfreda and this other man were automatic figures, turning around and around on top of a music box. But this feeling changed in degree as he continued to watch them, from amusement to irritation and finally to something closer to actual anger. It might seem absurd to be angry that a girl whom he had just met should be as attentive to one partner as another, but Hugo was too old a hand in the business of women to waste time repining about such absurdities. They meant one thing, and one thing only, and although he was startled at such immediate evidence of sexual attraction to that bobbing figure across the room, he knew the futility of denying it. It then occurred to him that everyone had taken this girl with the utmost seriousness from the beginning, his mother with her arcane hints, Kitty with her unprecedented accusations and even old Minerva with the warmth of her initial greeting. Were they, as women, acting out their ancient, predetermined roles, his mother, a silent robed figure walking in from the wings and pushing a young bride before her, and his mistress, in the back of the set, drowning herself like a perverse lemming in a jealousy which she knew to be fatal to his affection? Or was it rather *he* who had set them all in motion? Did they sense, by some female instinct, that he had reached the mating point, a jaded Victorian bachelor, complete with opera cape and opera girl, ready at last to retire to his county with a well-endowed virgin whose pertness must be no stain on her purity? But how fatuous could a man be? Shaking his head to dispel such foolish thoughts, he crossed the floor to cut back on Alfreda.

"Even *I* know you ought not to cut back on the man who's cut in on you," she protested.

"Those are debutante rules. You're not a debutante any more."

"Thanks for rubbing it in! It happens that I was having a most interesting talk with that gentleman."

"He's a dope. Forget him."

"Forget him? Dearie, he's one of Mummy's guests, I—"

Again Hugo felt a hand on his shoulder, and he turned angrily to find Teddy Allen, with a constrained grin, and Kitty Tyson, at his side.

"Look, old man," Allen was saying, "Kitty suggests we do what used to be known as a double-cut. It's the only way I'll get a chance to have a word with my old friend, Alfreda. I have to catch the midnight to Washington."

Allen was a bachelor of Hugo's years, in the State Department but attached to the United Nations. They were "extra men" on the lists of the same hostesses, and Hugo detested him on the mere suspicion of a tendency, among their common acquaintance, to bracket them. He turned abruptly to Alfreda.

"Do you know this man?"

"Oh, but of course!" she exclaimed with a startled laugh. "Where would Mummy and I have been, the winter we spent in Washington, without Teddy?" She smiled at Allen. "You see, I've grown up since."

"Flowered, my dear, flowered."

As they moved off together over the floor, Hugo stamped his foot. "Flowered! What a filthy term!" He spun around on Kitty. "What the hell made you do that?"

But even such roughness could not disturb her self-possession in a public room. Her eyes expressed nothing but sheer surprise. "Why I thought, poor man, that your duty dance with your little cousin had gone on quite long enough!"

"How kind of you. But it so happens that it wasn't a duty dance at all. It so happens that I *like* dancing with my cousin!"

She turned her gaze to Alfreda and Allen who were talking, both at once, with great liveliness.

"At least, *she* doesn't seem to mind."

For a moment he was so angry that he considered walking off and leaving her. But in the next moment he realized that there might never again be a better chance to make his position clear, and taking her firmly by the elbow he guided her back to her table, now deserted by her guests on the dance floor. They sat in a rather severe silence while *he* drained off half of somebody's champagne glass.

"I want to be very serious," he began. "There's a matter I've been meaning to discuss with you for some time."

"It must be terribly important to make you look so grim. And to need so much of poor Teddy's champagne."

"Ugh! You mean this was *his* glass! You asked *him* to your dinner?"

"He was kind enough to fill *your* place at the last minute."

But her reproach was simple evidence that she, too, considered Allen as his logical substitute, and he became still angrier. "Look here, Kitty, I want you to get one thing straight. I'm not going to be at your beck and call. There's no point in our relationship if it's going to be as tight as a marriage."

Her eyes expressed only a vague wonderment, perhaps as to what marriage he was referring. "Have I ever claimed it should be?"

"So if I want to dance with Alfreda Denison," he pursued, "or go out to dinner with Alfreda Denison, I must feel absolutely at liberty to do so."

"As indeed you are."

For just a moment he felt deflated, but then he reflected that her tolerance was only a woman's ruse. "Well, so long as it's perfectly plain," he concluded with a shrug.

"It seems to me," she retorted, with an at last quickening resentment, "that you've been doing exactly that ever since we met. The only difference is that now you throw it in my face."

"Is frankness throwing it in your face? Is simple honesty throwing it in your face?"

"Hardly," she said dryly. "As you will see when I show you what those qualities really are. Let us *be* frank, Hugo. Let us *be* honest." She glanced at his glass and then at her own which she had placed face downward. "Do you mind if I have a sip of your champagne? Or of Teddy's? Whosoever it is?"

Hugo watched, with a first pang of contrition, as she touched her lips to the rim of the glass. He had never seen her need even a sip before.

"I want to tell you," she continued in a graver tone, "that you're as free as you could possibly wish."

"Meaning what?"

"Meaning that you're free to see Alfreda and dance with Alfreda . . . and marry Alfreda, if you like."

"Aren't you making rather an issue of it?"

"Weren't *you*?"

"But marrying her! Why must women always go to such extremes? If you will recall my exact words, I was merely trying to point out . . ."

"Don't play the lawyer with me, Hugo," she interrupted with sudden impatience. "I can read all that small print. And I'm perfectly aware that your sudden interest in this new cousin means that you're bored with me. Or is that throwing things in *your* face?"

"You don't think you're taking a rather extreme position over a rather small matter?"

"Perhaps. But then my life has been made up of small matters."

"Thanks!"

"And now don't play the injured and scornful lover!" she exclaimed bitterly. "Spare me that, too. We both know perfectly well what you want. To keep me on ice while you roam the field. But I won't be shared, Hugo! I won't be a handy odalisque during the dry courtship of an immaculate cousin. You're not the only one with pride!"

Hugo began to realize at last, from the new note of passion in her tone, all that he might be giving up. And then he saw, in a sudden, brilliant, horrible flash, that Alfreda was precisely everything he *didn't* want. Was it not the worst of man's perversity that he should know himself perverse? He leaned forward with a sigh, his elbows on the table.

"Honestly, Kitty, I don't know *what* I want."

"That's because I'm behaving so well. It's really rather bitchy of me. It's kinder, in the long run, to make scenes."

"You spoil me."

"I always have. But when I think what you'll go through with that little cousin of yours, I can almost find it in my heart to be sorry for you. *She* won't spoil you. There." She spread her fingers on the tablecloth and contemplated her scarlet nails. "I *have* been bitchy, after all."

Even in the fall of his spirits he was conscious of a small, blurred resentment that she would have so turned the tables on him. "You almost convince me that you have," he said with an irritated shrug. "What else can I say?"

"You said once that women never knew how to end things. I've always been determined, when the time came, that I would prove you wrong. I shall go home now. I'll tell Grinnell I have a headache, and I'll have a good cry, which should make me feel much better. Don't come to see me until I write you. When I have myself quite under control, I'll ask you to dinner. And then, perhaps, we may learn the hardest thing of all. How to be friends."

The music had stopped, and the dancers were returning to their tables. He saw Grinnell Tyson and a lady in blue coming across the floor towards them. He stood up.

"Kitty, do you know something? Do you know you're a rather great woman?"

"Don't be sentimental, Hugo!" she said sharply as she turned away from him. "Don't spoil a perfect record!"

15

HUGO: 1950

He was free now to devote all his time to Alfreda, which he did in a flurry of attentiveness, as if the very magnitude of Kitty's sacrifice required that not the least portion of it be wasted. He wrote Kitty that he looked forward to embracing her wise and kind offer of friendship and would telephone her when a "decent interval" had elapsed. He then proceeded to put her completely out of mind. Life with Alfreda was silly and crowded, but it was as hectic as it had promised. She and her mother loved to see large numbers of people and to do large numbers of things, largely, it appeared, for the pleasure of discussing them afterwards with the faithful clique that foregathered daily at the cocktail hour. Hugo was amused by the enthusiasm sustained by mother and daughter over matters which, according to universal experience, were supposed to pall. It was unthinkable that anything should ever spot the silks and satins of their apartment or disarrange the little row of Minerva's pink brow curls. Old age was never mentioned in their living room, and sickness rarely. Decay, like dust, was banished from the premises.

"What's the point of having people in for cocktails *every* day?" he asked Alfreda once. "Do you really think it will bring you nearer your goal?"

"You mean my diplomat?" She was not in the least abashed by the crudeness of his reference. She had given him his chance to label her as silly, and when he had not done so, she had taken for granted that he accepted her in every particular. She had a way, he was beginning to see, of creating allies by her very faith in them. "Why not? How does one meet people except at parties? That's how I met Teddy Allen. And that's how I met you!"

He laughed scornfully. "You're barking up the wrong tree with Teddy Allen. He'll be lucky if he ever gets further than Protocol."

"Now why are you so sure of that?"

"Because, my dear, I've made a study of the ladder of fame."

"You don't seem very interested in your own rung on it."

"Is that a dirty crack?"

"Oh dearie, of course not!" she exclaimed, abashed by the sudden flare of his hostility. "I just meant that you didn't seem to have that *kind* of ambition. Why should you? It's perfectly fine to be taken up with the sale of beautiful things. Honestly, I mean it!"

Hugo looked at her suspiciously. He was not a bit sure that she cared about beautiful things. She lacked the smallest inclination for the abstract or philosophic. Her alert eye went straight from the general design to the specific detail, as her mind raced to the nearest pigeonhole. "I get it!" was the phrase most often on her lips. She seemed bent on reducing the wilderness of observed phenomena to an ordered garden with white labels tied to the stem of every flower. But once defined there was an end to a subject; Alfreda was ready and eager to move on to the next. She saw no point in dallying, in turning things over, in pondering their implications. Nor, in truth, did Hugo, but the exaggeration in her of his own intellectual bad habits made him uneasily aware of the toll of their kind of bright, picking mentality. And it exasperated him that everything he tried to teach her was immediately drawn through the tight sieve of her preconceptions, so that only what she had already believed remained.

"Let's have another bottle of wine and skip the silly party," he suggested one night at a restaurant where they were dining before a reception at Irene Trask's. "I have it on the best authority there won't be even a consul there."

"But I *want* to go to the silly party."

"Doesn't the law of diminishing returns exist for you?"

Her glance seemed to deplore the irrelevance of his male habit of speculation. "Not till I've got what I want!"

He was careful not to betray the effects of her still growing physical attraction for him, except for an occasional gesture, confident but at the same time ambiguous. He would reach over to take her hand in his, in parody of an uncle, when he lectured her about her hasty enthusiasms for people or her bad taste in art, and if he helped her into a cape or a fur piece, he would allow his fingers to linger a moment about her shoulders. He knew that there could be no question of anything but marriage with such a girl—she *thought* only in terms of marriage—and he was still a great distance from any such commitment. She accepted his gestures, but seemed to regard them as mere manifestations of the type of demonstrative friendship that her little group espoused. So far as Hugo could make out, the bright hard sun of female influence on her life had yet to be darkened by a male cloud.

In the taxi that night, taking her home from the Trasks' reception, he tried to reassert the crumbling illusion of his authority with a kiss.

"Aren't you rather stretching your role of guide and mentor?" she demanded, moving promptly to the far end of the seat.

"Oh, hell, what's a little kiss. A good-night kiss? You'd probably give as much to any crummy sophomore."

"I don't happen to go out with crummy sophomores, thank you."

"Well, aren't we cousins? Doesn't a cousin rate a cousinly kiss?"

"Very well. I'll give you a proper cousinly kiss when I get out of the cab."

Which she did. As they drew up at the entrance of her hotel, she moved quickly over to give him a dry peck on the cheek. Before he could catch her in his arms, however, she was out of the taxi and greeting the old doorman with the mannered graciousness of an English princess visiting a settlement house. He had to admit that she knew how to keep her pigeonholes straight.

But the little scene in the taxi, however inconsequential at the moment, was, only a few hours later, to change his life. Back in his apartment he lay restlessly awake until the early morning and finally got up to smoke cigarettes by his open window and to conclude in disgust that the oldest and tritest and stupidest thing in the world, love, romantic love, *valentine* love, had finally happened to Hugo Hartley. And *when* had it happened? Why, precisely when his favorite novelist, Proust, would have predicted it: at the exact moment when it had struck him that Alfreda's feelings for him were those of a devoted cousin and nothing more! This shattering perception had made him the instant prey of a host of violent fantasies about a girl who had neither looks nor charm nor genuine intelligence, a girl who was fundamentally a goose, and a stubborn, calculating goose at that! O omniscient Proust! O master psychologist! What did she have but youth, ordinary, smooth-skinned, fungible youth? It was only, he knew, because he was losing his own that he valued this commonplace and semi-precious jewel above all the treasures of Kitty Tyson. But what good did knowing do? Was he any less enslaved? Was he any less agog than a child in a trinket shop? And what would Alfreda extort in return for her bauble of youth? What but a lifetime of service!

"All right!" he cried angrily out the window. "I'll marry her, by God! And *then* we'll see!"

He laughed wryly at the picture of what his mother's pleasure would be if his words were carried down to her bedroom window. Then he went to bed and slept.

When he awoke he jumped up as if the day might not be long enough for all he had to do. For he was perfectly clear all over again that he *did* want to marry Alfreda. Why not? Was he the first man who had fallen in love with a woman who was his intellectual inferior? What woman, after all, was *not*? The point was simply that he wanted her, and what was that but the basis of marriage? Would she have him? Oh, yes. In time. She was a girl to distinguish carefully between a proposal and a pass in a taxi. And, after all, how many proposals did a plain, silly girl, even a rich one, get? But he was determined about one thing. There would be no further display of emotion on his part until she had evinced some on hers. It did not have to be much, a lingering look, an enigmatic smile, a hint of pressure on the hand, anything that would pull the scantiest veil of sex over her bold, neuter conception of their friendship. His pride, his dignity, his very success required at least so much. He would be assiduous, he would be constant, but he would be scrupulously correct. He would confine himself to her silly circle; he would be Swann among the Verdurins. And, touched by the picture of a man of his parts torn from his own fascinating world by passion, he took a pad and pencil and drew up a program before breakfast.

In the following weeks he carried it out to the letter. He divided his social engagements into those where he might expect to meet Alfreda and those where he might not. All of the latter he ruthlessly canceled. New invitations he treated in the same fashion, except that he did not scruple to inquire of a hostess in the first category: "By the way, you don't happen to be asking Alfreda Denison, do you?" One or two of them took umbrage—his aunt, Irene Trask, went so far as to remind him that she did not keep a disorderly house—but the others were amused and usually invited Alfreda. At the least hint of romance the toughest of the old girls became misty-eyed.

He never deviated from his cardinal rule of conducting himself with absolute circumspection towards Alfreda herself. He knew by the apprehensive look in her eye when she found him next to her at dinner that she had been advised by her friends of his now assiduous pursuit. He would then hope, by confining himself to a polite discussion of any matters in which she showed an interest, to substitute bewilderment, or, better yet, disappointment, in the place of constraint. To act the lover, in other words, to every eye but her own, seemed to him the surest way of bringing her to terms. But he found to his disgust that she parried subtlety with bluntness.

"I never thought you and I were going to have such a pleasant friendship," she told him one night, "after that awkward little business in the taxi."

"Pray don't mention it."

"Why not?"

Why not indeed? He swore under his breath. "Because I made a fool of myself. It's a thing that happens to old bachelors. We grow too cynical. And too conceited."

"You mean you've gotten over it? I'm *so* glad! It isn't true, you know, that all girls like to be pawed."

"I mean," he said, with as much dignity as her choice of verb had left him, "that, whatever my feelings, they are now under control."

"That must be such a relief to Mrs. Tyson."

"I told you that was all over and done with."

"Ah, but *is* it? You implied as much when I first met you, and that same night I saw you across the room having the longest heart-to-heart with her!"

Hugo gazed into those round, tan, startled eyes, so bright now with curiosity, and at those small, scarlet pursed lips, so tensely ready to burst open in either dismay or laughter, he could never be certain which. Surely it was encouraging that she should speak of Kitty Tyson and that she should have watched him that closely. According to Proust, his own ardor should now be abated. Yet he did not find it so. He closed his teeth gently on the tip of his tongue as a dark fantasy of possession filled his mind, of gripping those twitching white shoulders until she screamed.

"That was the end," he said in a low, sad tone. "That was when I broke it to her."

"Broke *what?*"

"That it was no longer possible for me to offer her my exclusive devotion."

"And you waited to tell her at a party? Where she couldn't make a scene? I think that's the meanest thing I ever heard!"

In his fantasy Hugo moved that grip from her shoulders to her throat. "Kitty doesn't make scenes."

"The more fool she! How else are we poor women to protect ourselves? And who, do I dare ask, is to share that devotion no longer exclusively offered to Mrs. Tyson? What great lady is next on the list?"

Hugo was too astonished to speak. Was it possible that this entire campaign had simply gone unnoticed? In her absurd determination to treat him as an older brother, had she been able to blind herself to everything but that pass in the taxicab? It seemed incredible, but he reminded himself that women like Alfreda *were* incredible.

"I'll thank you to leave my private life alone!" he snapped.

"Oh, honey, I'm sorry! I thought you wouldn't mind a little tease. Don't you realize that girls like myself are absolutely *fascinated* by that kind of thing? It's all so wicked and wonderful!"

"I suggest we change the subject," he retorted coldly, "and discuss whether you'd look better in your green satin or your red crepe de Chine at the Boys' Club Ball."

"Oh, which do you think?"

But if her independence of mind and professed ignorance of the state of his emotions was galling to him, her loyalty was worse. It seemed to him now the same that she might have shown to some soft, sad, grey former instructress, an aging mademoiselle, taken once a winter to the matinee of a visiting French company. It never crossed her mind that he, any more than the mademoiselle, might lose interest in her dresses and parties. It was particularly humiliating for him to discover, when he asked her now to dine, that she wanted to join friends afterwards, or go to a party, or even a movie. She would put it tactfully that she did not want to waste one of his evenings, but he suspected that it was not the waste of his that most concerned her.

One Monday, when he telephoned to arrange to meet her during the week, he found all her evenings gone.

"What about Friday?" he asked peevishly. "I thought you told me you were going to be in Friday."

"Well, that's just it, dearie, I am. I promised Mums I'd stay home. Even *she* thinks I go out too much!"

"But a quiet dinner with your old coz isn't really going out. We can have cocktails with 'Mums' first."

"I *promised* her, Hugo."

"Oh, damn your promises!" Everything in his little office, the pale early spring sunlight through the window, the smudged grey of the walls, even the redeeming Ingres drawing over his desk, seemed of an equal vapidity. He had to be shored up in this tight little box of commercial nothingness while *she* could go anywhere! And yet her going anywhere was as stupid as his staying in his box. Hers was merely the larger one into which his, in Japanese style, neatly fitted. What a life! "Damn it all, Alfreda, if you don't want to see me, you only have to say so! I'm not the intruding type, you know!"

"Oh, honey, how can you even think it? You're my friend of friends!"

"I'm not so old I can be treated like an uncle," he grumbled.

"An uncle! But you're my wolf of wolves! The most adorable extra man in town! I tell you what. Come dine with Mummy and me on Friday. She'd love that. And maybe you and I can slip out afterwards and go to the movies."

He had to be content with this and mollified by what he hoped was the sincerity of her tone. He had to go on dreaming of a future where he might have the privilege of knocking into her stubborn head the simple idea that her delights would be provided by him and him alone. For he had not given up hope that Alfreda would ultimately regard the conquest of so confirmed a bachelor as the crowning achievement of her silly social career and one that might appropriately mark her retirement.

It came as a shock, therefore, on Friday night to discover that Minerva Denison, who he had imagined himself rescuing from a solitary widow's supper, was giving instead a dinner party of her own noisy group. He found himself seated between two old girls who gossiped across him as if his masculine charm were nothing but a clothesline. Moodily he drained his glass of wine and contemplated the melancholy picture of his degradation. Perhaps it was beginning to be a bit too much like *Swann's Way*.

After dinner, when the gentlemen joined the ladies, he went promptly to Alfreda's side.

"I want to play backgammon," he insisted. "Over there in that corner. And I won't take 'no' for an answer."

"Honey, it's not friendly. Mummy expects us to help out."

"I *have* helped out. I've been a bowl of milk for two old tabbies, and I'm lapped dry."

She stared at him for a second and then uttered a cry of laughter. "You poor sweet! I guess you have earned it. Come along."

They sat in the corner before a table whose ivory surface was shaped as a board and arranged the red and black disks. But Alfreda, for once, was more interested in talking. About to throw her dice, she put down the cup.

"Shall I tell you something really exciting? Can you be discreet?"

He slapped one of the disks on top of another in a quick gesture of apprehension. "*Now* what?"

"It's possible—mind you, *just* possible—that I may be on the track of my man."

In the instant crash of his spirits there was no chance to dissemble. "Your Secretary of State?" he asked sharply.

She giggled. "Well, just possibly."

"Who?"

"Teddy Allen."

For a moment he was so angry that speech was impossible. He simply sat and glared at her. Then he swallowed and moistened his lips and at last began, in a low, hissing tone: "That mildewed old faggot? If you're going to pick a failure, at least pick a man. Women like you are fantastic. Absolutely fantastic. It's not only that you can't spot a winner. You can't even spot someone who'll be good in bed. Or don't you care about vulgar things like that? Don't you care about anything but Georgetown cocktail parties. *God!*"

Alfreda looked at him with a petrified expression in which horror and amusement were equally mixed. "Are you out of your mind?"

"Everyone seems crazy to the mad!" he exclaimed in a louder voice. "I never heard of such a thing! And does your silly old mother approve?"

"Everyone seems silly to you tonight," she retorted angrily. "Please keep your voice down, or I'll go back to the others. And now to your wild accusations. How dare you call Teddy a pansy? You know it's the grossest libel."

"Why hasn't he ever married?"

"Why haven't *you?*"

"Because I like too many women. Not too few."

"I could name two women with whom I happen to know he's had affairs."

"Bully for Teddy boy! What an old stud!"

"Will you be quiet!" She glanced quickly in her mother's direction. "Will you admit you have no reasonable grounds for calling him a pansy? Come, Hugo. Be fair!"

"Well, if he's not, he might as well be. He *looks* like one."

"He does *not.* To me, anyway. And I have it on reliable authority he's about to be made First Secretary in Rome. He'll be an ambassador at forty."

"On your money!"

"Hugo, you're way out of bounds tonight! Teddy has more money than I do."

"Oh, who *cares?* If you wanted somebody young and handsome, I could put up with it, but if you expect me to stand by and watch while you set your cap at that mangy old epicene . . ."

"Hugo!"

"My God, you'd do a thousand times better with me!"

"With *you!*" She sat up straight and caught her fingers to her mouth.

"Yes, me! Why not me? At least I love you!"

"*Hugo!*" There was no misinterpreting the astonishment in her eyes. "Honey, do you know what you're saying? Are you drunk?"

"Of course I'm not drunk," he retorted, furious. "What's so strange about my loving you? And how could you miss it, you silly ass! Why do you think I've been calling you up every day? Why do you think I keep coming to lousy parties like this one? Do you think I'd be seen dead with these old crows if you hadn't turned me into a pail of slop?"

"Oh, Hugo, Hugo." She refused to meet his eyes, but stared down at the board and ruefully shook her head.

"What's wrong? Am I so ridiculous?"

"Oh, it's not that. Darling, I'm sure you'll make some girl the most divine husband in the world." She leaned over the table to put her hand pleadingly on his. "Only, honey, I haven't thought of you that way. It's all too sudden. I can't just turn myself inside out."

"You could if you wanted to!"

"Ah, but that's just it! I *don't* want to. I don't want to at all! I could never let myself fall in love with a man like you. What's discipline for?"

"A man like me? What do you mean, a man like me?"

"Well, sweetie, you're absolutely charming and the best friend in the world and all full of know-how about people and things—you really *are*—but, honey, you're like a beautiful dessert of ice cream and spun sugar, you'd never do for every day."

"What's wrong with ice cream and spun sugar every day?"

"Darling, it just wouldn't *do*." She hesitated. "Shall I be frank?"

"By all means."

"Well, honey, let's face it, you haven't one tiny scrap of ambition, and I'm riddled with it. We'd be the most ghastly couple. You'd be perfectly content to go on forever in that auction gallery as long as you could go to all your parties."

"You accuse *me* of caring about parties!"

"Pots just *will* call kettles black, won't they? But I look upon parties as a means. To you they're an end. You'd be willing to play second fiddle to a bunch of Swiss art dealers for the rest of your life, if you could put on a black tie every night and be charming."

It was shocking and detestable to find that he had been judged by the very jury that he had thought he was charging. "So that's it!" he cried bitterly. "I'm not good enough! I'm not even as good as Ted Allen!"

"Dearie, you make me sound so brutal, but what can I say? I know what I am and what I want. At least that way I don't hurt anybody. As a couple, we'd be ridiculous. Which doesn't mean for a minute that you're not the sweetest, darlingest friend in the whole wide world . . ."

"Oh, shut up!"

He got up and strode to the hall. He did not even stop to bid good night to Minerva who was staring after him. Alfreda followed him, pleading.

"Hugo, please!"

"Good night!"

They stood in the foyer, stupidly side by side, before closed doors, waiting for the elevator.

"I can't bear to have you leave this way!" she wailed.

The doors at last opened.

"Good night, Mrs. Secretary," he growled as he almost leaped into the elevator.

On Saturday morning he was too tired and disconsolate to plan his usual game of squash at the Racquet Club, or a ride in the Park, or even a visit to a rival gallery. He could not face the prospect of his father at the breakfast table, so he boiled an egg and brewed coffee in his own kitchen and then dressed and went down to see his mother. But she was about to go out.

"You look tired, dear."

"Don't say that!" he snapped. "It makes me feel worse. Where are you going?"

"I'm taking the dogs to the Park." She had a small dachshund and a large, very old, half-blind bulldog that she took out every morning.

"Can I come along?"

"Of course. But won't it be rather dull for you?"

"I'll be the judge of that."

There was just a touch of early spring in the air. The grass was damp and brown, but with a hope of green, and the sky was a mild, apprehensive grey. The paths were full of muddy puddles where here and there a sparrow splashed. Hugo's head ached from the whiskey of the night before, and he felt low and heavy and wanted to weep. How ridiculous! When had he last wept? Could he even remember?

"How are Alfreda and her mother? Have you seen them lately?"

He repressed a shudder of irritation. But what else, after all, had he wanted to discuss? "Alfreda is very well," he answered in precise, sneering syllables. "She thinks she may at last be on the trail of a man who will satisfy her inordinate ambition. A statesman who will be a proper host at her parties and still find a few spare moments to guide his nation through an atomic era."

"You don't mean she's engaged!"

"No. I mean that her eye has alighted on the man whom she may ultimately dignify with her choice."

It was like Ida not even to ask who the man was. "I had so hoped it might be you," she said sadly.

"Me!" He laughed shrilly. "A poor little art peddler! For the great Miss Denison! Surely, Ma, you forget yourself."

"Is that *her* idea? That you're not good enough?"

"That I lack ambition."

"She's quite right. You do."

Her matter-of-fact tone gave a sharper sting to the words. Hugo came to an immediate halt, and Ida was several paces ahead when he cried: "Ma! You too!"

She paused and pulled back the old bulldog which was trying to drink out of a mud puddle. "You've led a worldly life with worldly people," she pointed out. "You've even sneered at those who didn't. Why should you complain now if Alfreda has the standards of your set? At least she's honest."

"You defend her! *You!*"

"I don't defend her. I try to explain her. Why shouldn't she have a pre-conception of the kind of husband she wants? And if you care about her, why shouldn't you go a little way to meet her?"

"I?" he almost shouted. "You expect me to give up my business career and beg an allowance from Daddy while I try to shoehorn myself into the State Department? And all for a snotty little girl who sees life as a series of canape trays? No, thank you!"

"She wouldn't require all that. You don't understand women. No, you don't, darling, for all your conquests. If you became head of your gallery, or even a vice-president, I'm sure it would do the trick. It's only the idea of your not caring that she really minds. And why shouldn't you care? You could easily get ahead if you wanted. You might even . . ."

"You too!"

"Why too?"

"You agree with Alfreda! You think I'm a lazy bum!"

"That's ridiculous, Hugo."

"It's true!" he cried passionately. "I thought *you*, at least, were different. But you're as bad as Daddy and Dorcas. You think I'm nothing but a society butterfly!"

"Darling, you're being totally unreasonable."

"And, by God, none of you have any idea what it *takes* to be a society butterfly! I'd like to see Daddy try it! But why do I talk to you? What matters in your philosophy but for the men to get ahead and the women to raise babies? Talk and art and love and music and beauty and everything that gives life the least point count for nothing! *Nothing*! Well, I'm through with the lot of you! I'll go my own way from now on, thank you very much!"

"When have you not?"

"Can't you see I'm serious?" he demanded furiously. "How can you go on making fun of me? I don't know what's come over you, Ma. Ever since Cousin Geraldine jumped out that window, you just don't seem to have given a damn about anything. Good day!"

He was walking rapidly away when he heard her call "Hugo!" and turned. She was smiling!

"Thanks for walking with me."

He did not deign to reply, but strode on hurriedly until he was out of the Park. His holidays were always so carefully organized with exercise, reading, dressing, calling, shopping, writing in his journal, or even thinking, that when he found himself at once without engagements and without a purpose, he felt so empty and restless that it was impossible to remain in one place. The props on which he had bolstered his life were numerous but interdependent, and not one could be pulled out without shaking the balance of the whole structure. If Alfreda despised him, then everyone must despise him, including his ungrateful mother whose champion he had always considered himself. And was he not worthy of being despised, a foolish gadabout, a dealer in trinkets, with a collection that, in the last analysis, was nothing but a pile of junk? Even his prize, the Watteau drawing—what was that but a thin little sketch dependent on the luster of its supposed creator's name? He would sell the works and go to Paris and sit in a café, or to Majorca and sit on a beach, or maybe to the Orient. In the meanwhile he went to three movies, staying a half hour at each, and visited the observation tower of the Empire State Building and the zoo. In the middle of the afternoon he made a long visit to the bar of the Knickerbocker Club, and it was not until five that he arrived at Kitty Tyson's.

She was alone with a tea tray and expecting nobody. It was one of those perfect coincidences that he always claimed never happened in New York. Grinnell had gone to his brother's in New Jersey for the weekend. Hugo thought he had never seen her looking so beautiful. There was a dignity and serenity to her green-velveted, late afternoon loveliness that made the ambitions of Alfreda seem shrill and childish in retrospect. Secretary of State indeed!

"I'm glad you came," she said as he sipped his tea. "I'm glad you didn't wait till I sent for you."

"Should I have?"

"Don't you remember? But never mind, of course you don't. The thing is that I'm just beginning to realize how much I shall need friends."

"Has something happened?"

She gazed into the fireplace. "Grinnell has asked me to give him a divorce."

He held his breath. "Because of . . . us?"

"Oh, no. Not in the least." She shook her head a bit ruefully at the mere idea. "He wants to marry his Olive, that's all. At long last. He was very nice about it, really. The settlement he offered was quite handsome. I get this house and the children and an income for life. Even if I remarry."

"It's the least he could do."

"Ah, no, Hugo, be fair. Give the devil his due. It's hard for Grinnell to part with money."

"Then what are you waiting for? Grab it!"

"But that's just it. What you once said to me. That we women can never make an end of things. The moment Grinnell made up his mind to go, everything in me reached out to pull him back. It wasn't love. I doubt if it was even habit. It was just a basic, atavistic fear of losing my man."

"You'll be all right. You're young enough and pretty enough and rich enough. You'll see."

"Will I?" She shook her head. "I've always taken it for granted that people would ask me to their parties. Now I shall learn what it is to be a single woman. I can hear those voices on the telephone already: 'Oh, Kitty, darling, I'm *so* sorry, but could we put you off for the eleventh? Johnny Jones has given out. Thanks, darling, I *knew* you'd understand.' I'll have to learn to be nice to all the right pansies unless I want to sit home, night after night, and eventually be an object of pity to my daughters when *they* start going out. Oscar Wilde said that to be in society was simply a bore, and to be out of it, simply a tragedy. I used to think that such a silly saying, and now it seems to me an eternal verity!"

As Hugo gazed about the soft, familiar room, with its harmonious blend of Chinese objects, of dragons and bird panels and silver junks, against the chaste dignity of English things, as if the trade of the eighteenth century had been the gentle accomplishment of gentle decorators, without guns or storms or opium, he reflected that the world that Kitty had made was better than that of many who sneered at it. He began to speculate that if the room was an appropriate setting for a Mrs. Tyson, it might be even more appropriate for a Mrs. Hartley, a serene, loving, satisfied Mrs. Hartley, always grateful to her husband, with two pretty girls in matching dresses, affectionate, respectful, a ready-made family, with contagious diseases and adolescent tantrums behind them. Why was that not a picture of which any man might be proud? He rose and walked to the window and looked at the little yard with its neat gravel and pink marble fountain and benches. It would be ideal for cocktails later in the spring. And then he turned to the big, Renoir-inspired portrait over the mantel of Kitty and her daughters, with black eyes and pale faces and furs and flounces, at which he had so often laughed, and imagined himself in a velvet evening jacket with embroidered dippers, raising a glass of brandy as he pointed out its defects in the humorous but proprietary tone to a friend, to Minerva Denison, to his mother. And Kitty, after all, might still have a child.

"I wonder if it'll be as bad as you think," he said.

"Oh, yes. The best I can hope will be to be asked occasionally to the Hugo Hartleys'. When Alfreda's having one of her larger dinners."

He winced. "Alfreda's after bigger game than I. Her husband will have to be a famous diplomat."

"So? Poor man."

"You mean because he'll be married to Alfreda?"

"No. Because she'll always compare him to you."

"What a romantic you are, Kitty. Why do you assume that Alfreda's in love with me?"

"Aren't we all?"

He walked now to the bar table and poured himself a drink of straight, warm bourbon. He took a long sip before he turned to her. "Do you think I'd make a good husband?"

She returned his gaze without flinching. "Not very."

"Why not?"

"You'd be cross and fussy and dictatorial."

He threw back his head with a peal of laughter. "Oh, you're shrewd, you're shrewd! How do you manage it?"

"What?"

"Never to be eager. Never to be stupid. Never to be vulgar or egotistical. Go on, please go on. I promise you, it's working!"

She said nothing and sat motionless, but for the first time in their relationship he noticed something like a glitter in those blue eyes. He walked over to sit on the sofa and place a hand on her knee.

"Do you think you could put up with a husband who was cross and fussy and dictatorial?"

It was her turn to laugh. Her laugh was not a peal, as his had been, but there was a hint of abandon in it. "God knows I'm used to it!"

"That's right," he murmured as he leaned over to kiss her. "That's it. Keep it light. Keep it light."

Upstairs in her room, half an hour later, Hugo was aggressive, almost violent, in his lovemaking. He did not scruple to imagine himself in Alfreda's arms, taking his revenge for her foolish preference. The passionate response of his actual partner he translated in terms of Alfreda's reluctant surrender to his rape. But later yet, in his own apartment, the memory of Kitty's love and the healing balm of her dependence comforted him and stayed with him until he fell asleep.

It was not until he awoke in the early morning that he was aware that the leaden feeling about his temples was not a hangover but depression. He rose from his bed and went to the window to look down on the grey deserted street which in the foggy morning struck him suddenly as an Utrillo, a painter whose work he had never liked. As the events of the previous evening began to march through his mind, at first with a slow, halting, muffled tread and then, suddenly, with a cacophonous blare of trumpets, he realized to what a pass his absurdities had brought him.

"Hugo Hartley!" he cried aloud. "You may as well pitch yourself out the window like Cousin Geraldine!"

The sound of his voice roused him to a completer consciousness, and he laughed bitterly. It served him right! The whole damn thing served him right! Had not Swann married Odette only after he had *ceased* to love her? And after all of Hugo Hartley's vaunted independence, all of his boasts and sneers, had he not been driven into making a fool of himself by a silly girl who preferred an ass like Allen? Get out of his proposal? Of course he could get out of it! But it would be just exactly his ironical and appropriate punishment that for once in his stupid life he could be a gentleman!

PART SEVEN
THE EMERGENCE OF IDA

16

IDA: 1950

I HAD ALWAYS admired Minerva Denison. I suppose it is elementary that we admire those who least resemble us, and she struck me as my opposite in every significant respect. She stood up to life and beat at it, as one might beat at a rug. It was hard for her to keep her hands off things; she always felt compelled to give people, as well as situations, a remedial tweak or a twist. The appearance of life was never so good that she thought she could not improve on it, and improve on it she usually did. For Minerva, despite her beautifully waved pink hair, or blue hair, or even, at times, green hair, despite the studied elegance of her apartment, despite her passion for parties and night clubs, was a mound of horse sense. The large brown, round face, in which the tiny features and small piercing eyes were almost lost, and the large round figure, more compatible with one's idea of a cook or mammy than a lady of fashion, were more expressive of her real character than the cosmetics and silks with which she sought to disguise them. Minerva was a common enough phenomenon among American women. In parlor comedy she is usually depicted as having a heart of gold and a genius for the practical solution of the love problems of younger characters. In actual life she had . . . well, a *fairly* golden heart.

She had certainly adored my cousin Scotty. He had been the only human being, besides the tax collector, who had ever managed to separate her from a substantial portion of her fortune. The self-made woman of her era (and Minerva, although born an heiress, had tripled her inheritance) was impregnable except, in middle life, to sex. In the first year of her marriage she had allowed Scotty to throw away a quarter of her capital on an Arizona ranch. But that could only happen once. Thereafter she snapped shut her pocketbook and doled out to him a liberal allowance for clothes and clubs and sporting cars, reducing it in the periods when he was drinking too much. But she was shrewd enough to exercise her conjugal control in a way that Scotty never resented. One doesn't, after all, resent a nurse, particularly, a strong, devoted, sensible sharp-tongued nurse. Scotty, under her care, lived several years longer than he had any right to expect, and Alfreda was brought up unaware of her father's failings. It was a tricky job, but Minerva pulled it off.

I think she liked me from the beginning, perhaps because she knew that as a girl I had had a crush on Scotty. Geraldine, I am sure, must have taken pleasure in telling her so, not guessing that Minerva was the kind of woman who wanted other women to love her husband. At any rate, she liked me and none of the other Denisons. One might have thought that, being so gregarious and party-loving herself, she would have found them congenial, and so, at an earlier date, she might, but at the time of her marriage to Scotty, Aunt Dagmar's generation was mostly dead, and the survivors found Minerva plain and what Uncle Victor called "dumpy." Her actions had style, but not her appearance, and the Denisons cared a great deal for appearance. I, of course, did not, and she and I were immediately at ease with each other. I never criticized her; I never expected things of her, and it never bored me to dine with her and Scotty when the latter was tight. Better yet, I always struck her as being exceptionally in need of good advice and never took it, which meant that through the years we had an unfailing topic of conversation. Ultimately, I think I came to represent to Minerva the only family, outside of Alfreda, that she really had. With me she came as near as she probably ever came to relaxing the elaborate façade of her seeming good humor. With me she could enjoy the luxury of being cross.

She was very grumpy the day she told me the news I had been dreading. Minerva believed that misfortune was apt to be one's own fault and that one should be scolded for it. She had asked me to come to lunch ahead of her other guests, to have time to reprimand me.

"What's all this I hear about Hugo?" she began straight off when the maid had given her a very pale martini and me a glass of sherry.

"You must tell me."

"Oh, Ida, haven't you *heard*? Where do you live, anyway? He's going to marry Kitty Tyson. Everyone's talking about it."

I was grateful for Derrick's example, through the years, in maintaining a mask of calm. "I thought she already had a husband."

"Well, so she has. But she won't when the lawyers get through. It's only a question of how much Grinnell will have to give her."

"Those questions can be very serious ones to Derrick's partners."

"Really, Ida, how can you take it so glibly? Don't you *care* who Hugo marries?"

"Of course I care. I was just wondering why *you* did."

"Well, after all, aren't we family?"

"I mean, why do you object to Mrs. Tyson? She's rich and beautiful and what they call well born. Aren't those the qualities that your group admires?"

"What has my group to do with it? I'm thinking of you. Do you want an old bag of used goods for your favorite child? And don't tell me he isn't your favorite child. I *know*."

"Ah, well." I shrugged, hoping that my features were still inscrutable, however fevered my mind. My first impulse was to take Minerva into my confidence and talk the whole thing out. But that was the way I had always behaved. Chat, chat, the eternal chat, the cozy confidence with the understanding friend that made even disaster a staple for future exchanges. The negation of life that came from reducing it to the grade of a mere topic, an undulation in the atmosphere between two human beings who might cease to recognize each other without the bond of anecdote. As if talk could save me! I felt suddenly as if I had picked up thirteen cards at a table of experts and had to do my thinking while I arranged my hand. "What can a mother do?"

"Plenty. If Alfreda were going to make such an ass of herself . . ."

"But Alfreda's a girl."

"What difference does that make? I tell you, Ida, you have a whole arsenal of weapons that you've never even peeked into. Well, *peek!* Reach in, dearie, and fight for your life!"

Fortunately, the next of her lunch guests now arrived, and in ten more minutes there were as many ladies gathered in Minerva's living room. Her friends were always polite, but I knew how little congenial they found me. I had no interest in facials or hair, or in resetting jewelry, and I could not join in the violent shrieks of laughter that punctuated their gossip. Yet, being worldly women, they had a certain respect for the social position I *might* have had. "Now if *I* were Mrs. Derrick Hartley," I could read in their curious, appraising stares, "I wouldn't wear that dull black suit or those seed pearls, and I'd certainly do something about my grey hair. And I wonder if I shouldn't find better places to lunch than Minerva Denison's!" They left me to myself, on the outskirts of their circle, and that day, at least, it gave me a blessed opportunity to think. For I was beginning to make out that the reason Minerva was so upset was precisely that she, like myself, wanted Hugo to marry Alfreda. It was obvious, when one stopped to consider it. Hugo was older and experienced, and Alfreda needed an older and experienced man. He was bright and talented and able to hold his own in any world—all qualities dear to Minerva's heart. And then, too, there was Derrick's fortune. In the past I would not have hesitated to entrust my case to Minerva. I would have proceeded timidly into the thicket of maternal intrusion on the lives of others behind her broad back and stoutly wielded machete. But now I paused. If *two* mothers were in favor of a match, and one as unsubtle as Minerva, what chance had they with game as slippery as Hugo?

I took a big sip of sherry as I saw Alfreda come into the room and then beckoned to her.

"Cousin Ida, what fun!" she exclaimed in her animated style. "I came down early from Columbia because Mummy said you might be here. I'm so glad!"

I scrutinized her carefully. Why should I, who never gambled, have been so sure that there was sense and character behind her manner? Was it simply that she was my mother's great-niece? I told myself again that Hugo loved her. If I lost sight of that, I was lost.

"My dear, how sweet of you. But then Minerva's cook can't be matched on Morningside Heights."

"Ah, but I'm on a diet."

"You, Alfreda? You're too thin now!"

"One's never too thin."

"Now you sound like my Hugo," I ventured. "He's impossible about women. Heels can never be too high or eyebrows too plucked or waists too narrow."

"While *he,* of course, has a man's disposition to eat what he wants and do what he likes!" There was a distinct vibration of resentment in Alfreda's banter. "By the way, how is dear Hugo?"

"I thought you could tell *me*. *You* can imagine how much an old mother knows of that world."

"Or a young cousin."

"But you and Hugo have so many friends in common!"

"Mrs. Tyson doesn't happen to be one of them."

"Oh, Mrs. Tyson." I shrugged, with what I hoped was a brave show of carelessness, and even tried a French phrase. "*Que voulez-vous?* A man on the rebound is always going to make a fool of himself. I don't take Mrs. Tyson seriously."

"You don't?" Alfreda, usually so restless, seemed quite rigid with astonishment. "I imagine she'd be very sorry indeed to hear *that*. But who, pray, is Hugo rebounding from?"

"Who do you think?"

"Surely you don't mean *me!*"

"Who else?"

"Oh, Cousin Ida!" Alfreda's startled eyes seemed about to fill with tears, and I felt at once that I had been right in all my estimates. "Now, you're going to make me feel badly!"

"Why should you feel badly?" I demanded. "On the contrary, you should feel very proud. In fifteen years of playing the field Hugo's never once fallen in love. Never once! And now he's in up to his neck, and it serves him jolly well right. I've warned him again and again that one day a smart girl would come along who'd have the sense to turn him down flat. As a revenge for all of her sex! Well, now it's happened, and I'm delighted. It'll be the making of him!"

Alfreda's blankness was all that I could have asked. Surprise and concentration had drained everything else out of her thin, pale face. "Then you really think he won't marry Mrs. Tyson?"

"Never! He may be off his head, but not that far off. He'll take it out in other ways. I shouldn't be surprised if it made him president of his company. Oh, he's lazy, my Hugo, but he can work when he wants. And, of course, he's bright. He'll have the greatest auction gallery in the country one day, and it will all be thanks to you!"

If Minerva had been waiting for my signal she could hardly have announced lunch more opportunely. I smiled brightly and pleasantly at Alfreda, as though our little discussion had been quite completed, and rose to go into the dining room. At lunch, I talked with unwonted animation and even joined in the general discussion about Minerva's new masseur. But I observed out of the corner of my eye that Alfreda was pensive, and I resolved to telephone Mrs. Tyson immediately after lunch. There was no telling how long I would have strength to sustain my chosen role.

When I followed the pretty, polite little maid upstairs to the living room and found myself alone with Hugo's mistress (for so, in my perhaps old-fashioned way, I thought of her), it was all suddenly more difficult than I had expected. The room was even more perfect than I had feared, and Mrs. Tyson, seated before the Georgian tea service in a black Chinese robe with embroidered scarlet egrets, her small, deft fingers at work, turning on the flame, pouring hot water into the pitcher, picking up the sugar tongs, might have been the smiling, gentle, implacable favorite concubine, momentarily soothing the old, discarded wife. I wondered uncomfortably if what I had always considered as merely silly and kittenish was not essentially feminine. Or, essentially—and to use a word I never used—sexy. If we were going to battle over *that*, it seemed that the weapons must all be hers.

"I don't know how to begin," I murmured. "I seem to be nothing but nerves."

"Oh, so am *I!* I'm so glad we both admit it. How do you like your tea?"

I watched as she poured my cup and saw that she was not putting on her nervousness. She was clearly glad to have something to do with her hands.

"It's the second act of *Traviata*, isn't it?" she continued, her eyes and hands still busy. "Except this time it's the tenor's mother who's come. His father, no doubt, is too busy. Or perhaps doesn't even know. Or very much care." She looked up at last with a small rueful smile. "Of course you want me to give him up."

"I want you to give each other up."

"Thank you!" she exclaimed, with the faintest hint of mockery in her tone. She was not, after all, to be obsequious. "But I don't signify. Hugo is all that matters to you. How could it be otherwise?"

"You must matter to yourself, my dear."

"Or learn to," she agreed, nodding. She was silent a moment as she stirred her tea. "Yes, perhaps I must." She glanced at me now with a sudden, shy curiosity. "You know, Mrs. Hartley, what my first instinct was when you telephoned? To try to charm you. To try to win you over. That's why I put on this Chinese robe. I wanted to seem so cute and homey, with my tea set, and my little fire. But now that you're here, and I look at you, I begin to see things more clearly. If Hugo and I marry, you'll never forgive me, will you? And if we don't—well, I suppose I'll never forgive you? So there we are. We're doomed to be enemies. Its a pity, isn't it? Because otherwise I think we could be such friends!"

"We can still try to understand each other."

"Oh, I guess we'll do that." Her shyness was gone already, and there was a little girl's stubbornness in her sudden pout. "So long as you see, from *my* point of view, that nothing matters but Hugo's wanting to marry me. It's the only thing I've ever really cared about in my life." She closed her eyes, as if to shut me out, before repeating slowly: "The only thing!"

"But it's not true."

She stared. "What isn't?"

"That Hugo wants to marry you."

She regarded me for a moment with eyes that were half frightened, half quizzical. "I wouldn't have thought you could hit so hard," she breathed. "But he's asked me, you know."

"Yes, but . . ."

"There's no but!" she cried, almost in panic. "He's asked me to be his wife! Why should I listen to you? If he doesn't want to go through with it, all he has to do is to come and tell me. Why not? What rights do *I* have? He doesn't even have to come. All he has to do is stay away."

"Ah, my dear, isn't that just the reason that he won't? That you have no rights? Isn't that just what gives him his obligations?"

Her face clouded over. "You don't know Hugo."

"One of us doesn't."

"Well, I won't fence with you," she replied, turning away as if suddenly weary of it. "I'm sure you're too smart for me. Like Hugo. But I can't give him up. If he gives *me* up, that's that. But if, after my divorce, he comes to this house and says: 'Kitty, shall we go down to City Hall and get married?' I'm going. That's all there is to it, Mrs. Hartley. I'm going. It's ridiculous for you and me to pretend otherwise. You know I'm going!"

"You think, then, you can make him happy?"

"Hugo has taught me that women in love don't care about making men happy. Perhaps he's right. Perhaps they care only about possession. But I *think* I care about Hugo's happiness. And why shouldn't I add to it? Am I such a horror?"

Even at that moment, and even feeling as I felt, I was intensely aware of her charm. She was, indeed, a rare creature. Yet she was right. What did I care about rare creatures?

"Do you think he can be happy without children?"

She did not move, but her voice dropped to a whisper. "What makes you assume he won't have any?"

"I assume that, if it had been possible, you would have had more than two. Everyone knows how much Grinnell wanted a son. Isn't that the reason he's going to marry Mrs. Taylor?"

Mrs. Tyson had turned very white. "You don't pull your punches, do you?" she murmured. "But it may be different with Hugo. Yes!" she exclaimed, turning on me with glittering eyes. "With Hugo it may well be very different!"

I was silent. I found it very distasteful to have her physical life with Hugo flung in my face, but I had certainly provoked it. Staring into the fire, I thought hard, as hard as I had at Minerva's. I had come armed with the weapons of reason only to blunt them against a wall of passion. But Minerva was right. I had barely begun to turn over the contents of my arsenal. And then, of a sudden, I heard myself talking, and I moved into the light-filled circle before the black pit exposed by parted curtains. It was no doubt significant that in starting, as I thought, to "live," my first metaphor should have been of a stage.

"I shall not ask you to give him up, then," I was saying. "That, manifestly, would be absurd. I shall simply ask you to give me a little time."

"But Mrs. Hartley, time is precious!" she protested. "Time is on your side! How can you ask *me* for it?"

"A very little time. Only a month. You must be very unsure of yourself if you won't give me a month."

"Every woman's unsure of herself," she retorted. "And why should you need a month? You have a month. More, probably. I can't go to Mexico until Grinnell's signed the separation agreement."

"But mightn't he sign it any day?"

She shrugged impatiently. "I suppose it's possible. I don't know."

"And if he signed it today," I pursued, "couldn't you go to Mexico to-morrow? Couldn't you be divorced the day after?"

"But it's so unlikely! If you *knew* how slow Grinnell was about money matters!"

"But it's still possible," I insisted. "That's why I want you to promise me to wait a month before you go."

"But *why?*"

"That's my affair."

"I mean, why should I do it for *you?*"

"Not for me. For the sake of our future relationship. I promise you, Mrs. Tyson, that if you do this for me, I will be a good mother-in-law to you. If you and Hugo marry."

"*If!*" She stood up now and raised her hands awkwardly to her temples. She was evidently so unused to physical demonstrations that she had no accustomed gestures. She was clumsy, pathetic, like a walking doll with a broken spring. "But you obviously have some ghastly plot. Why should I help you? Why should I give you the rope to hang me with? No!"

"One month. Only one." I, too, was standing.

"No, I'm sorry, *no!*"

"Then I must insist." My heart beat furiously as I delivered my ultima-tum. "Otherwise Derrick will have to ask Grinnell not to sign your separa-tion agreement for a month." I paused. "Under penalty of his withdrawing from the firm."

She turned away, her hands clasped in despair, and walked slowly to the window. "What can I do?"

I watched her remorsefully. For the first time she struck me as having some resemblance to myself. My old self. For I, too, in earlier days, might have been naïve enough to believe that a woman having the power of which I had boasted would have been content to ask for so little. How easy, after all, it had proved to shoot my dart between the ribs of that beautiful frame. And what a peculiar and horrid feeling it was to be for once on the side of the strong, of the Derricks of this world! Particularly when one's strength was a lie. For Derrick, I knew, would never have endangered his relation-ship with the least of his partners to get me my month. I had become, like him, a monster.

"A month, then," I said as briskly as I could. "May I trust you for a month? May I have your word?"

"The word of one gagged and bound?"

"Please."

Her back quivered impatiently. "You have it, then."

"Goodbye, Mrs. Tyson."

"I suppose you don't want me to tell Hugo?"

I paused, but I was ready for this. "You must follow your own judgment on that. *After* you have decided which of us it would help most if you do."

In the same excited mood in which I had left Minerva's lunch I went directly from Mrs. Tyson's to a telephone booth where I called Mark Jesmond. He was in conference, but his secretary got him out.

"I want to see you," I said abruptly. "And I don't want Derrick to know about it. It's a question of investing my money. May I come downtown?"

"I'll come up. Shall I go to the house?"

I glanced at my watch. It was late, and Derrick might come in while he was there. "No, could you meet me at the Park Club? I'll only keep you a minute."

I had always had a curious relationship with Mark. He had been quick to make out, in the early days of his courtship of Dorcas, that I counted for nothing where Derrick or Derrick's firm was concerned. He was, however, a suspicious person, and he had been troubled by what he considered the potential behind my passive disposition. He had taken in that I was not dumb. Mark, like all people of undeveloped heart, had to have a scheme to govern every relationship in life. With me it resulted in an attitude of elaborate respect that sometimes bordered on the sarcastic and that was in noticeable contrast to the casual treatment that I received at the hands of his wife. But as the years passed, and as Mark never observed the smallest attempt on my part to unseat him as Derrick's major domo, and as he had many occasions to appreciate my help in smoothing over Dorcas' emotional crises, he began to relax and even, ultimately, to enjoy my company. Mark had been so violently competitive all his life, so sure that the world would yield him nothing that he did not snatch, that it must have been oddly soothing, for a change, to discuss his fears and hopes with a detached but listening woman who accepted him without being fooled. Indeed, there were moments when I suspected that Mark credited me with plumbing his nature to the depths and of being as great a cynic as himself. Such moments were signalized by what I interpreted as a conspiratorial wink.

But there was no time for his demiconfidences that afternoon in the stiff, still little parlor at my club where I received him. We sat in a corner in two high-backed chairs, and Mark, who loved to sprawl and slump and who hated a female atmosphere, seemed as tense and briefly motionless as a ruffled bird.

"It's about my Denison-Adler shares," I began. "I've come to a decision."

"You want to sell them?" He nodded his own affirmative answer. "Good. I've always said they were a poor investment. It's the kind of business where you must either control or get out. I know you've had sentimental reasons for hanging on to them, but sentiment is a poor businessman."

I waited until he had finished. "You said control or get out. I think that's good advice. I want to control. Oh, not just me, of course. All the Denisons together."

Mark rubbed his mouth and chin with the palm of his hand, a sign of cogitation. Like Derrick, he hated to betray surprise. "Have you had a tip?"

"Let's put it that I have. Do you know how to go about picking up the necessary stock?"

"Part of my job, part of my job. To know every company in your portfolio." I knew, however, that Mark would have said this even had he never considered Denison-Adler before. "As a matter of fact, one of the Adlers, Leonie, just died. Yes, we might pick it up. Let's see, how much would we need? There are about nine thousand outstanding shares, is that it?"

That was the thing about Mark. When you most thought he was bluffing, it turned out that he wasn't. "Ten," I replied, for I had already reviewed the matter with Christopher. "As you know, I have twelve hundred shares. My brother Christopher has two thousand. He's only kept them because of Hugo and because I've asked him to. Minerva Denison has another five hundred. Hugo has three hundred. I figure that, between us, we only need another thousand for control."

Mark made some jottings on the back of his newspaper. "That seems to be it. But, of course, the moment you start buying, you'll drive the price up."

"Can't I do it in a broker's name?"

"Of course. But even so, in a small company, the least activity in the market will tip off the management. It may cost you a packet of dough before you're through."

"What do you call a packet of dough?"

Mark scratched his head and made more doodles on his paper. "Hard to say. It depends what resistance we run into. But I know a bit about the company. I doubt if the stock would more than double. But at that it would cost you two hundred and fifty grand."

"Very well. Two hundred and fifty."

"Mrs. Hartley! May I ask what you propose to use for money?"

"You can sell what I have that's not in trust and borrow the rest. Against my inheritance from Geraldine."

"Aren't you plunging rather deeply?"

"Suppose I am. I know what I'm doing. You needn't worry. I've thought it all out."

"But, Mrs. Hartley, I *must* worry. Please remember that I'm not only your son-in-law, but your financial adviser."

"Yes, and I respect your financial advice. Extremely. But, you see, today, I'm not asking for it."

Mark smiled the fixed little smile that he reserved for combat. "Even so, it's my duty to warn you that this may be a rash step."

"I can always go to my brother."

His smile widened instantly to a grin. "In other words, I must put up or shut up? Is that it, Mrs. Hartley?"

"Well, I'd never express it so rudely. But I'm absolutely determined to do this thing. And I've come to you because nobody would be smarter about picking up the shares for me. But if you won't do it, I shall have to go to others, that's all."

Mark now laughed and, leaning over the table, scratched the top of his head with all ten fingers. It was a most unattractive gesture.

"If it's possible to get your stock," he exclaimed, looking up, "I'll get it for you. But don't blame me if you're sold out on your own auction block! With Hugo at the gavel!"

Mark was good to his word. When he gave in, he gave in gracefully, for he correctly assessed that my determination was something new and serious. In the following two weeks he telephoned me every morning to report his progress. He had started off with a great coup, having picked up three hundred shares from the Leonie Adler estate at considerably less than true value, but immediately afterwards the market stiffened, and soon it appeared that control of the gallery was going to cost every penny that he had antici- pated. In addition, he had to communicate with Minerva and my brother to be sure that they did not dump their shares. I became so nervous that I could no longer concentrate on anything. All of the capital of my resolu- tion seemed to have been expended in a single afternoon. I accepted any chance invitation for cocktails in order to avoid meeting Hugo at home. I was in terror that he would cross-examine me about Mrs. Tyson or Alfreda before I should be in a position to confront him with my plan. I do not know what might have happened had he not been sent at just this time on a business trip to Boston. Never would I have believed it possible that I should have contemplated with such satisfaction the departure of my favor- ite child.

On the night of his return, a week later, he dined with Derrick and me. He rarely so honored us, for his social calendar was very full, and family evenings were apt to be constrained. Derrick always tried to prove that he was not an indifferent parent by pushing the conversation into the field of galleries and pictures, and Hugo, sensing immediately the basic contempt under his father's casually expressed curiosity, inevitably bristled. That night, however, Derrick at least forbore till dessert.

"I see Archie Sturtevant is dead. He had quite a few old masters, didn't he? I suppose you'll be picking them up now and selling them at triple value to some fool Greek."

"Fakes," Hugo said briefly without looking up from his plate. "The lot of them. I know the collection."

"You mean, you've dined there?"

"You ought to know by now, Father, there are very few houses where I haven't dined."

"I never see how you return your obligations."

"I don't regard the Sturtevants as an obligation," Hugo retorted loftily. "If it is, I discharge it by going there."

"And by calling their pictures fakes?"

"Well, if they are, they are. That's a matter of principle. I quite realize that stockbrokers are more moral than other people, but we dealers have our little game, too. And little games have little rules."

"I wasn't casting aspersions on dealers, Hugo."

"Of course you were. You always are. But it's quite all right. You needn't worry about *my* feelings. I have learned to be stoical before the rumble of paternal anathemas."

"You take me for granted," Derrick protested, irked. "That's one of the reasons I'm the way I am. You *all* take me for granted."

"And what's wrong with the way you are?" Hugo looked from Derrick to me with an air of bright surprise. "I *like* the way you are. You and I regard each other from the top of fortified turrets. We're both well defended, so we don't fear a sortie. Occasionally, under a flag of truce, we talk. It's as much as most fathers and sons can say. What I respect about you is that you've never pretended we had more than that."

I thought that Derrick would lose his temper at this, but I underrated him. It was even possible that he took Hugo's analysis as a compliment. He simply grunted and returned to the original subject.

"Does it matter if the pictures are fakes," he continued, "so long as they're beautiful to look at?"

"My dear father, surely you know that authenticity is everything today?"

"Do you mean that if you had the choice of a bad Renoir or a beautiful attribution . . .?"

"I'd take the bad Renoir," Hugo interrupted briskly. "Certainly. I'm a dealer."

"Then I suppose you went into the right business. We won't have to worry when your shareholders elect you president."

"You needn't be so sarcastic. I *may* be president one day."

"I'm not in the least sarcastic. I shall be extremely surprised if you're not elected at the next annual meeting."

"And what do you mean by *that?*"

"Simply that at the rate your mother's been picking up stock, she should be in a position by then to elect you."

So there it was. Mark had betrayed me. Had I really believed that he wouldn't? But as the atmosphere tightened around the table, as I felt, even with averted eyes, Hugo's burning stare on my cheek, I knew, with a sudden inner peace, that I was capable now of going through with what I had started.

"Mother! What's all this about?"

"Your father's perfectly right. I *have* been picking up Denison-Adler stock. Quite a bit of it. I think it's time control returned to the family."

"But you never told me!"

"She never told me, either," Derrick intervened. "The only reason I found out was that Mark thought it his duty to warn me how deeply she was plunging."

"I particularly told him not to!" I exclaimed. "I shall know better than to use Mark as my broker again!"

"Look, Ma! Will you kindly tell me what this is all about? Why do you want to control the gallery?"

I turned to meet Hugo's eyes, which were fixed on me with a startled, glittering stare.

"Because I want you to run it," I answered in a level tone. "When I have all the stock I need, I shall turn it over to you. With no obligation on your part. You can do anything you want to with it. You can sell it or give it away or use it for wallpaper. That's entirely up to you."

"But, Ma!" he protested, with a groan of mingled despair and appreciation. "You should have asked me before you started! How do you know I even *want* the damn gallery?"

"That's your affair," I insisted. "Mine is that I've made up my mind to give you the stock. Don't worry. I have my reasons. They might not seem adequate to everybody, but they seem adequate to me."

"Suppose I refuse it?"

"The shares will be registered in your name and mailed to you. After that, I shall have nothing further to do with them."

There were several moments of uneasy silence at this. Hugo was actually flushed, and I had time to reflect that my calculations had been exact. He was deeply moved. All his irritation, even his anger, at my unwarranted intrusion had dissolved before the realization that I was doing something for him and for him alone, something even at the expense of Dorcas and Mark.

"You don't care, then," Derrick asked me angrily, "that you're giving all your stock in Denison-Adler to *one* of your children?"

"You can equalize it in your will. My estate hardly matters compared to yours."

"But that means you're *forcing* me to write a new will! You're dictating the terms."

"Look, Dad," Hugo intervened, "as long as you've got to do your will over, why not take me out altogether?"

"How do you know you're even in it?"

"I don't. But as long as Mother seems stuck on giving me this stock, let it be my share of both your estates. Let me sink or swim with it. Dorcas will never miss it. Everyone knows you have millions."

"Everyone knows no such thing!"

"Oh, come, Dad, don't play games with me. If Ma wants to give me the gallery, what do you care? Keep your money for Dorcas. I don't want it. I don't begrudge Mark a penny of it. Obviously, you have more confidence in him than you've ever had in your own son."

Derrick glowered down the table at Hugo. There was a mixture of sincerity and impudence in the latter's tone that must have been hard for him to bear. "Maybe I've found him more sympathetic than my own son," he grumbled. "More considerate. More affectionate!"

"Maybe he's polished the apple more brightly!"

"Hugo!" I protested.

"I'll have you know I resent that, young man!"

But there was no controlling Hugo now. "What right has he to go babbling to you what Mother does with her money?" he demanded. "What the hell business is that of his?"

"I think it's entirely natural for him to want to protect his wife's inheritance."

"His wife's inheritance!" Hugo sneered. "After all he's made out of your firm? After all you've given Dorcas? Mark Jesmond has one hell of a nerve objecting to anything Mother does for me. If I had a penny for every buck he's made out of both of you, I'd be a rich man. And on top of it all, he's angling for your job! Ask any of your sacred partners what he and Dorcas have been saying about *you!*"

"I think I can handle my own firm, thank you very much," Derrick retorted with massive dignity. "And if that's all the advice you have to give me for one evening, I hope you and your mother will excuse me while I retire to my study for coffee."

I waited until Derrick was out of the room and then turned in distress to Hugo. "You should *never* have said that about Mark wanting his job!"

"But it's true. I heard it at the Tysons'. The whole firm knows it."

"It doesn't make the slightest difference. You hurt your father's feelings. And what's the good of that?"

"Oh, shucks, he didn't believe it, anyway." Hugo put his elbows heavily on the table and rested his chin in his hands. "And why should I care if he does? Let him and Mark fight it out. He can cope with Mark."

"Are you so sure?"

"I'm so sure. But let's talk about you." He laughed, as if in despair of making sense of his subject. "Poor, dear, ridiculous, scheming old you. I know what you've been up to, mind you. I know all about your little ultimatum to Kitty. And your lunch at Minerva Denison's. And now this stock deal. Honestly, Ma, I don't know whether to laugh or cry. One resents interference in a mother. But interference on such a mammoth, such a gargantuan scale! There's something sublime about it. Something beyond resentment. My God, one can only gape before such a mother!"

"I'd do it all again," I said stubbornly.

"To have me marry Alfreda? To have me become head of an auction gallery and sell perforated wood to an idiot world as Louis XV? Is it so vital that I should do that? What's happened to you, Ma?" He gazed at me now in a speculative mood, slowly shaking his head. "When did you lose your doubts? Where on earth did you ever acquire this new serenity? Where did you learn to play God?"

"If you only *knew* how little it was that," I said with a shudder. "I'm nothing but a mass of frozen fears. But somewhere in that igloo there's one small candle of hope. No matter how much I tremble and chatter, it won't go out. Sometimes I think it's about all I have to live for."

"That I should marry Alfreda and live happily ever after?"

"Yes!" I stared at him gravely until the sarcasm faded from his eyes. "Yes," I repeated with a firmness that belied my desperation. "I may be an old fool, but I want the satisfaction of feeling that I've done one thing for one member of my family. I love you, my darling." When I saw the mist now in those hard eyes, I suddenly sobbed. We were to have a scene, he and I, for all his detestation of them. Well, why not? I covered my face with my hands as I sobbed again. "I love you more than anybody in the world. And if you marry Mrs. Tyson, I'll die, that's all. I'll simply die."

I looked up, after a considerable silence, and found him smiling.

"Well, I guess the least I can do, after that, is marry Alfreda!" he exclaimed. "Or at least try. In all good faith. I'm sure she won't have me."

"I'm sure she will!"

"Well, if she does, it's because you've sold me."

We both stood up, and I put my hands on his shoulders. "Hugo, dearest, you won't be doing it just for me?"

"Ah, now you're greedy." He took my hands and held them tightly in his. His old, cynical frown had returned. "If you really believe in a thing, why should it matter for whose sake it's being done?"

"Because it's for your happiness!"

"Yours and mine."

"Oh, no, darling, yours!"

"Can't I be allowed the pleasure of thinking that I'm doing something for my mother? After all, you care so much about doing something for *me*."

"Oh, Hugo!" I moaned. "Don't spoil it!" I saw with dread that his lips were tightening into the old look of suspicion. "You know in your heart that you love that girl!"

"Now who's spoiling it?" he demanded sharply. "Now who wants to have her cake and eat it? You've moved into my life like a bulldozer, and now you want to pretend that you haven't even been there. Or if you have, that your intrusion has been so subtle that I've never even been aware of your elfin feet! For what do you take me, a complete idiot? If you expect to maneuver men, do you think you can start at *your* age and with *me?*"

"Oh, Hugo, Hugo," I moaned again, but he was relentless.

"I want you to learn the courage of your convictions," he continued in the same bitter, deliberate tone. "I will go tonight to Kitty and break off with her. It will be a sticky business, but at least it will be brief." He smiled sourly, "I've done it once before, after all. And tomorrow I shall call on Alfreda and tell her that I'm turning over a new leaf. That I expect to become a great auctioneer and be appointed ambassador to Italy before I'm fifty. I shall then propose to her before the shock has worn off. And I will do it all for you."

"But will you be *happy*, darling?"

"Ah, now we want the moon!" He turned to the door and seemed about to depart without further word. But then he paused. For Hugo was merciful. Despite all his hardness he was the most merciful of my family. "Well, I'll tell you this," he said, turning back to me. "I'll tell you just this, and then bid you good night. I'll *probably* be happier than I would have been had you left me to my own devices. Probably. There. 'Probably' will have to content you. But what more, for the love of Mike, do you really want for your nickel? And since when have any of us spent more than that?"

17

DERRICK: 1950

Derrick sat moodily in his square grey office, late on a Friday afternoon, and contemplated the surface of a desk bare but for a spotless grey blotter, a clean crystal ash tray and two photographs in twin gold frames, of Dorcas gardening in a sloppy straw hat and of Derrick Granberry in football clothes. Everything was ready for Monday morning; even his secretary had gone.

But Mark, with whom he was to drive to Dorcas' that night, was keeping him waiting, Mark, who, a scant few years ago, would have dropped any job in the office so much as to light his father-in-law's cigar. Now, apparently, Mark found it more expedient to keep impressing him with the burden of his work and responsibilities that interfered with such minor accommodations. Derrick impatiently jerked a drawer open to get out the weekly market report and then slammed it shut again. Why should he have to give any color to his inactivity? Why should he pretend to Mark that he had *not* been kept waiting?

"I'll have to make him understand what a cocky little bastard he's getting to be," he exclaimed aloud. "And I'll have to make Dorcas understand it, too. If they think they can talk about *me* behind my back!" He fixed a wrathful eye on Dorcas' picture. The clumsy pose, the silly hat, that only a month ago had seemed so lovable, struck him now simply clumsy and simply silly. "At least I have Derrick," he muttered, shifting his glance to his grandson. "Whatever happens, I don't think they can shake my hold on *him*."

He thought with a faint discomfort of the last years of Linn Tremain and how it had been necessary to wrest the reins of leadership from his shaking hands. But they *had* been shaking; that was the point. Derrick stared now at his own clenched fists, held stiffly up before his face. There was no trembling there, and when there was, he would be the first to see it. The worst of aging was in the false assumptions of younger people. He had always cared about details, but now, undoubtedly, his care was stamped as fussiness. Now. . .

"Are you about ready, sir?"

Mark, a coat over his arm, stood in the doorway, as if Derrick would, of course, have been waiting for him, as if he could have nothing to keep him so late on a Friday afternoon but the fact that he had made an engagement to drive his busy son-in-law to the country. Even Mark's "sir," which he always alternated with "Derrick," sounded sarcastic.

"I'll be with you in a minute. Sit down."

"But you say you have to get back to town tonight. We won't have much time for dinner if we don't go now."

"Sit down. I want to ask you something."

Mark strolled in and sat in the chair by the desk, putting his leg promptly over the arm. He always made himself ostentatiously at home. It was his way of subtracting from any excess of deference that might otherwise have been read into his manner. Somewhere, in the curly hair, grey now, before his fiftieth year, in the diminutive stature, the round stomach, the bright, staring eyes and the eternally rumpled suits, lurked the legal boy wonder who had come out of the woods to astound his elders and who paused now, undecided, at the threshold of an age in life that compelled him to choose another role. Mark, Derrick surmised, would pass directly to the judicial. From a pompous cherub he would become a dimpled Nestor.

"Two of the new men have desks in the research library," Derrick began. "I asked them why, and they said you put them there."

"Nothing escapes you long, does it, sir? I think those desks went in last night. You know what our space problem is. The alternative was putting them in the reception hall. But don't worry, sir. I'm working on it. I'll get my space, if I have to go up to the roof and hire the water tank!"

"That's not the point," Derrick cut in. "The point is that we should not take on new men till we have the space for them. I have always made it clear that the research library is only for research. Why was the problem not referred to me?"

"Oh, come, Derrick, you don't want to be pestered by every detail in the office, do you? Besides, you've been taken up with Hugo's engagement. I hated to bother you."

Derrick glanced keenly at Mark, but his face revealed nothing. Perhaps it revealed too little, as if he were trying to hide something. Two things struck him disagreeably about Mark's answer, first, that Mark knew perfectly well that he was very much interested in just such details, and second, that Mark knew equally well that he was not in the least taken up with Hugo's engagement.

"The assignment of office space goes to the very guts of office morale," he retorted, getting up to pace the carpet. "I thought you knew my principles about that."

"But, Derrick, it's only temporary . . ."

"It shouldn't even be that!" He paused to stare Mark down, but when he saw the gleam of repressed exasperation in his son-in-law's eyes, he turned abruptly and walked to the window. How well he knew that look, the look of the junior who must suffer patiently the rantings of his tiresome but ultimately to be replaced superior! He felt the anger thickening in his throat. Of course he ought to drop the whole foolish matter, but he couldn't. "I know that people look on me as a hard taskmaster," he grumbled, "but I have to be, if I'm to look after my dependents. People judge these things so superficially. Everyone thought old Linn Tremain was the soul of benevolence because he used to fill up his car with young men when he left the office. I never have. I like to use my drive home as a time to think. But Tremain never gave a damn what those young men were paid or how many were herded into a room or whether they ever got a decent vacation. He thought they were privileged to help *him* make money!" His sudden awareness that he had told all this to Mark many times before intensified his irritation. "Nobody bothers to remember that it was I who arranged the highest salaries and the longest vacations of any brokerage house in New York! Oh, no, a cheap gesture of generosity is all they care about, a charming smile, a 'Get in, my dear fellow, get *in!*'" And he waved his arm jerkily in crude imitation of his late uncle-in-law's courteous gesture.

"Well, if the lecture is over," demanded Mark with the sudden impertinence that he felt to be part of his charm, "shall we go to the country?"

At once Derrick felt the relief of the explosion of his temper. He knew—oh, how *well* he knew—that it was not a time for it, that it was late in the day and that he was fretted. But one had, after all, to have *some* indulgences. "You will oblige me," he said gruffly, "by seeing that those desks are removed tonight."

Mark had been in the Navy during the war, a lieutenant in the office of the Judge Advocate General, and he had a uniform answer whenever he wished to indicate that Derrick had been arbitrary. He would jump to his feet, salute and cry "Aye, aye, sir!" But now he did not even do that. Instead, he rose, with a faint sigh and a curious shadow of a smile, and walked to the door.

"I'll see to it, sir," he said quietly as he left the room.

Derrick, alone, sat back in his armchair and stared out the window over the vast panorama of the harbor. He wondered, detached, to whom it would matter if he should die there and then. It struck him again that it was not growing old that mattered, but having people *think* one was growing old. The moment Mark began to suspect him of fussiness and repetitiousness, he *became* fussy and repetitious.

"All done, sir." It was Mark again on the threshold, cheerful and smiling. "Shall we go now?"

Derrick was silent on the drive to Glen Cove as he completed his strategy for the evening. He had to find out if there was any basis for Hugo's rumor of the Jesmonds' treachery, and his plan was to ask Dorcas what the other office wives were saying about him. He had picked the best and the worst of them to ask her about. Evie Lockhart was the troublemaker of Hartley and Dodge. She drove her husband's career from the back seat, convinced that she was helping him with little sniping attacks on the senior partners at cocktail parties. Everybody, including her husband, realized that she was his greatest obstacle. Sophie Besant, on the contrary, married to a man who might well have competed with Derrick himself had it not been for recurrent nervous trouble, had been a model of tack and loyalty to the firm and had even assisted Derrick in persuading her husband to accept a position of lesser responsibility. If Dorcas' answers to what these women were saying did not vary in some marked degree, she would have to be lying.

His plan made up, he could almost enjoy the drive. Most of the miseries of life lay in indecision. Looking at Mark, he lit a cigar.

"I can never understand why a man as busy as yourself lives in the country."

"You know your daughter."

"But Dorcas would do anything for you, Mark. We all know that."

"She's happier in the country. She has her garden."

Did he mean it? Did he care? Derrick reflected that he still did not understand Mark. The Mark of the long low small-windowed farmhouse that cost a fortune in maintenance, and which he had stuffed with Americana too good for its interior, did not seem to go with the urban Mark who lived for his work and whose idea of relaxation was a baseball game followed by a night of drinking in a smoky bar. Perhaps it was because farmhouses and Americana were now so fashionable. Perhaps it was a relic of Mark's rustic New England youth. Or perhaps he really loved the house and simply wanted Dorcas to be happy. It was a mistake, Derrick reflected, to assume that cold people had to be always cold. It was a mistake that many persons had made about himself.

"I bet Hugo and Alfreda never bury themselves in the country," he remarked.

"No, they're real city mice."

"They're taking an apartment in Fifty-fifth Street, only two blocks away.

Dorcas had better look to her laurels. A new daughter-in-law can be very attractive to an old man."

"Nobody's ever going to take Dorcas' place in your heart, Derrick, so don't kid yourself."

The assured ring of Mark's laugh brought back Derrick's darkest thoughts of the afternoon.

"I wouldn't count on that too much," he said dryly. He glanced at his son-in-law, but the latter appeared not to be listening. The big car was turning into his driveway, and they could see Dorcas on the lawn playing croquet with her children in the late spring twilight.

He had selected the moment when Mark was mixing cocktails which would give his son-in-law the opportunity, if he chose it, to dodge any questions and leave them to his wife. Derrick would know, of course, what to think if he did so. And Dorcas, who had a light head, always lost what little subtlety she had after the first drink. Seated in his accustomed chair by the fireplace under the serried rows of pewter pots and pans, he did not even pretend to listen as she talked about her girls.

"Dorcas, I want to ask you something," he inserted firmly in the first pause. "And I want you to be very frank. I don't relish talking about personal matters, but there are times when it has to be done. Your mother has never taken the smallest interest in the firm, and I have survived the few persons who used to advise me. I must depend more and more on you and Mark to keep me in touch, not with what's going on—I think I shall always know that—but with what people *say* is going on. Now that I'm in sight of seventy, I can't expect . . ."

"But, Daddy, no one would dream you were a day over sixty!" Dorcas broke in. "Mark and I never think of you as old, do we, Mark?"

"I didn't say I was old," Derrick replied testily, glancing at Mark's unturned back. "I never use that term. I said I was in sight of seventy. I am. I'm sixty-six. The digit is a fact. What others think about it is merely label. But labels have their importance in this world. I can't expect people to go on confiding in me the way they used to. I'm beginning to seem venerable to them. Therefore, I'm going to need you and Mark to tell me what people in the office are saying. Do they think I keep too much in my hands? Do they think I should accept a smaller share of the profits?" He paused significantly. "Or do they think I should retire altogether?"

He had been careful to break the question into three parts, which gave him time to study Dorcas' reaction. The first thing he noticed was that she was evidently collecting herself. She was sitting very still, and her cheeks had turned a mottled pink. Her first movement had been towards Mark, but the sudden silence at the bar table where he had been mixing the second drink seemed to act as a warning, for she looked back at her father and even managed a smile.

"Who in the world do you think would be talking like that?" she asked in her own peculiar version of a light tone. "And who do you think would have the impudence to say it to *me*?"

"Evie Lockhart," he replied promptly.

The relaxed slump of Dorcas' shoulders followed too quickly not to be relief. And her laugh was too loud. "Mark, shall we *tell* Daddy?"

Mark turned around for the first time, with his habitual grin. "You mean about the boarding school? Yes, I think your father's big enough to enjoy that."

"Evie asks everyone how long you're going to keep us in boarding school. She says all the partners are like little boys with stiff necks from smoking up the chimney."

"And a jag from drinking cider after lights," Mark added.

"Do people agree with her?" Derrick asked, unsmiling.

"Well, you know how people are, Daddy. They always laugh at things like that. No matter how much they basically admire you. They're afraid of seeming stuffy."

"But do they talk generally that way?"

"Oh, *generally*, I wouldn't know."

"What about Sophie Besant? Has *she* said anything?"

Once again Dorcas glanced at her husband, and Derrick thought he caught the faint, half-irritated shrug of his son-in-law's shoulders, as though Mark were counseling his wife that the handling of her father, was, after all, her responsibility.

"Well, Sophie is devoted to you, of course," Dorcas began more guardedly, "but she *is* rather a fuss-pot. She keeps taking me aside and murmuring how tired you look. And telling me how sorry she's always been that she didn't make Harold retire before the younger men started to laugh at him. Not, of course," she added lamely, "that anyone laughs at you, Daddy."

"They're still careful to hide it if they do," Derrick said dryly. He was convinced already that Hugo had spoken the truth. It faintly surprised him that where he had anticipated an almost unbearable spasm of pain, he should be feeling instead only the first tremors of what threatened to be a harmless, if nauseating anger. Dorcas with her mottled cheeks, her messy hair, her big, anxious eyes, had ceased in one searing flash to be his principal link with humanity. More simply, perhaps, she had ceased to be *he,* and what was not he had to be his enemy. Her worried eyes reminded him now of her mother's, and the wrath that mounted within him might have been only a bigger brother of the wrath which he had felt years before at Ida's clinging loyalty to the household gods of her childhood. But Ida, at least, had never preferred another man; Ida had never lied. Ida would never have twisted the innocent words of poor, loyal Sophie Besant, the one woman in the office family on whom Derrick could rely, into a warning that he should step down before he was senile. There was something horrible in Dorcas' crudity; it betrayed the violence of her eagerness to push her husband forward. She was too excited to concoct poisons; she could only reach for a club. She had even forgotten her initial position that nobody talked to her about her father!

"Such are the opinions of others." Derrick dismissed them in a hard, level tone. "Let us now get down to basics. What is yours? And what is Mark's?"

"You know mine, sir," Mark said in his easy drawl, coming across the room with the cocktail shaker. "I think you're as fit as you were the day I walked into your office and told you why you had to make me a partner!"

"Surely, Daddy, you can't think Mark and I would have any other opinion!" Dorcas grasped quickly at the cue so handed to her. "The only thing we worry about is that you're not having more of the good time you've earned."

"In what way?"

"Well, you never take a winter vacation, for example."

"I detest Florida, and I'm too old to ski."

"You've never taken one of those world cruises that all your friends go on now."

"To see Hong Kong from the deck of a steamer while I'm dummy? You know how I feel about *them*."

"You haven't even developed a hobby."

"My work is my hobby.

"But, Daddy, that's just the point. It *can't* be. Everyone should have a hobby *outside* his office."

"What's Mark's?"

Dorcas paused in momentary perplexity. "Well, if he doesn't have one, it's high time he did! Read any article about geriatrics. You have to *prepare* for retirement!"

"But suppose I don't mean to retire?"

"*Ever?*"

"Ever. Suppose I mean to die in harness like Uncle Linn Tremain?"

"Oh, but, Daddy, that's such a mistake!" She looked despairingly at Mark, but he had returned to the bar table to deposit the shaker. The very stolidity of that back seemed to warn her to drop the subject, but Dorcas was too excited to take his hint. Besides, she had taken a big sip of her second cocktail. "You should learn how to enjoy life while you still can. There's no point being obstinate about old age."

"But I do enjoy life."

"You can't expect to work forever!"

"I don't. One day, presumably, I shall die."

"You might think a little bit about Mummy," she said, almost crossly now. "Maybe *she'd* like to travel and see the world while she's still well enough to enjoy it."

"Your mother, like all her friends, may look forward to long, healthy widowhood in which to enjoy such things."

"I mean, enjoy them with *you*. She was saying only last week how she'd love to see India."

"What are you proposing, Dorcas?" Derrick demanded in a sharper tone. "That I retire from business and orbit the globe?"

"Oh, Daddy, you're so extreme. I never said a word about retiring, did I, Mark? Of course you shouldn't retire. I simply suggested that you take more time off and enjoy yourself. What's so wrong with that?"

"Mark will tell you what's wrong with that, won't you, Mark?" Derrick exclaimed, allowing the first note of sarcasm to slide into his tone. Mark picked it up immediately and turned around to direct at his father-in-law the fixed, small smile with which he always covered embarrassment. "Mark knows that there's no halfway about these things," Derrick continued, staring at him. "When you're the senior partner of a firm like ours, you don't journey to India to see temples, do you, Mark? And you don't take time off to spend the winter in Florida. You either stay here and do the job or you turn it over to somebody who can!"

"Well, what's so sacred about doing the job?" Dorcas demanded stridently. "It isn't as if anybody was suggesting that you shouldn't remain on as a limited partner. Or that you should take your name out of the firm. Why should you do all the work at your age? Haven't you earned some rest? And, as for the profits, what earthly difference would a cut make in *your* tax bracket?"

"Oh, you're suggesting I take a cut, too?"

"Dorcas!" Mark interposed warningly. "Why do we have to get into that?"

"Because I asked her, damn it!" Derrick suddenly thundered. In the awed silence that followed his outbreak Dorcas looked in bewilderment from her father to her husband. She might have been wondering how she had been maneuvered in so short a time into a passionate espousal of the very retirement that she had just said she was not proposing. But neither Goneril nor Regan had subtle natures, and Derrick had seen, before it was too late, what would happen to his hundred knights.

"All I was saying," she grumbled, like a fretful child, "was that it's time somebody relieved you of some of the load."

"Somebody like Mark, for example?"

"Well, why *not?*"

"So there we are at last!" Derrick cried, rising from his seat. "You might have had the candor to tell me at the beginning. You want to get rid of me to make room for Mark!"

Dorcas' mouth became a dark circle of open dismay. "Oh, Daddy," she breathed in a horrified half whisper. "How can you even *say* such a thing?"

"I must say, sir," her husband echoed, "you're going a bit far."

"Not as far as I intend to go!" Derrick answered wrathfully. "I had very good reasons, before I came down this weekend, to believe that you had both been deliberately undermining my position in the firm. With hints here and insinuations there. If you had owned up to it, I should have forgiven you both. After all, I know what ambition is. I, too, had to clear out an older generation. But what I don't think I'll ever be able to forgive is what happened here tonight. The way you lied to me, Dorcas! And your nauseating hypocrisy about your mother's happiness! As if you'd ever thought one moment in your life about your mother's happiness!" He turned now on Mark, whose fixed, foolish little smile had become hard and stale. "And the way you let her do it!" he snapped at him. "The way you stood there and let her do it, despising her all the time for making such a hash of it. But you wouldn't stop her because you thought me so besotted a father I wouldn't notice! Well, you've miscalculated, Mr. Jesmond. For once in your life, you've miscalculated!"

The most terrible aspect of the scene, as Derrick recalled it later, was the speed with which all three of them adjusted to their new relationship. He had read that human beings were infinitely adaptable, but perhaps their adaptability was simply the measure of their superficiality. They did not love as dogs loved, or even as eagles. Dorcas was thirty-eight years old; for more than half Derrick's life she had been the person for whom he had cared most in the world, and yet in the course of a handful of minutes he could accept a situation where his paramount feeling for her was contempt and hers for him hatred. Worse still, there was more than acceptance in that moment of crisis; there was a certain wry satisfaction. Derrick was experiencing a dizzy, but not wholly unpleasurable sensation in being swept along by the hissing, churning tide of his temper; it was a catharsis in which cleansing and destruction were indistinguishable. He knew that the evening would be followed by heartache and loneliness, but this very knowledge made him reach for heavier weapons, as if to merit his hanging at least for a sheep.

"How dare you speak to Mark that way?" Dorcas cried shrilly. "Hasn't he been your slave long enough? Hasn't he had to put up with you in his home as well as his office? Isn't it enough that he's had to defer to you twenty-four hours a day for the past fourteen years? Why shouldn't he expect to succeed you after all that? Isn't it human? Isn't it natural? *You're* the one who makes everybody seem mean and grasping by holding on forever!"

"Forever! At sixty-six? And in a firm that owes me everything? You ought to be ashamed to call yourself my daughter!"

"Your daughter!" she sneered bitterly, and Derrick would not have dreamed before that evening that her face could be so ugly to him. "What have I ever been to you but a possession? A convenience? Haven't I sacrificed my husband to you? My children?" Half hysterically she appealed to Mark. "Haven't I, darling? Haven't you told me so often enough?"

Mark, however, turned away abruptly, as though from an importunate child. "This is a private fight," he said peevishly, "between you and your father. Leave me out of it."

If anything could have made Derrick angrier, it was Mark's leaving Dorcas under fire. "There's nothing private about this fight, Mark!" he warned him. "You're in it, too. I want you to be quite clear that I have no intention of retiring while you're around to succeed me. And that I plan to remove you from the management committee tomorrow!" Derrick walked over to the table and struck it with his fist. "If I have to split the firm right down the middle, I'll split it! But I don't anticipate that will be necessary. I think I know, senile as you may consider me, on whose side most of the brotherhood will be!"

Mark gave a short, quick little sigh and then shook his head rapidly several times, as if to deplore his father-in-law's violence. He plunged his hands in his pockets and stared at the floor and finally whistled. It occurred to Derrick that it was the pose of a country boy who has just let a big fish get away. Yet surely this time it was genuine. What other fashion did Mark have of expressing so unprecedented a disappointment? He was simply facing the crash of the greatest hope of his life.

"Do you think we have to make all our decisions tonight?" Mark asked in a tone that was suddenly mild. "Over the stimulus of two rather potent cocktails?"

But Dorcas had been completely demoralized by Derrick's attack on her husband. She sank into a chair and buried her face in her hands. When she looked up at her father, the hate in her eyes was alarming. "You think you can get on without Mark?" she fairly screamed. "You don't know what you're about! All the customers, all the partners respect him far more than they respect you! You'll see!"

"Exactly," Derrick said grimly. "I'll see. We'll all see."

"He's done your job for years!" she went on in the same wild tone. "He's covered up for you, apologized for you, smoothed over matters that you've messed up! He's stood between your disgusting egotism and all the people who resent it. And now he's getting the gratitude from you that he might have expected. He's getting the treatment that Uncle Linn got, that Mummy got and that now I'm getting. What a fool I was ever to have expected anything more of you!"

"And what a fool Mark was," Derrick retorted brutally, "to have married *you* for the little he's going to get out of *me*."

Dorcas stared at her father in open horror and then again covered her face with her hands. She leaned over, and her big frame was shaken with dry sobs. Mark went over quickly to sit beside her; he put his arms around her and whispered something in her ear that Derrick could not catch. But she shook her head violently, and her sobs now burst out. Mark stroked her back clumsily; it was an odd sight. Suddenly he turned on Derrick, with more curiosity than dislike in his eyes.

"What a monster you are," he said in a soft, speculative tone. "What a real monster. Thank God in Heaven you've taught me not to care about the firm the way you care!"

He turned again to Dorcas and continued stroking her back, crooning low and indistinguishable sympathies in her ear. As Derrick watched dumbly, her sobs became louder and louder, and when she turned to fling her arms wildly round her husband's neck, he left the room. Hans, his chauffeur, was waiting in the front hall, and he wondered indifferently if Hans had heard. As the latter tucked his master warmly into the back seat of the Cadillac, fixing the rug securely about his knees with deft fingers, it occurred to Derrick that his servants cared for him more than any of his family did. At least he had always been happy in his relationships with underlings. They were simple relationships where each understood what the other expected. It seemed unreasonable to him now that family relationships could never be the same. Why, in a world that they themselves had complicated, did his children have to hurl his simplicity in his face? And confuse it with inhumanity? A monster? If he was a monster, the sea must be full of them. He closed his eyes to doze to the hum of the motor and the click of wheels on the parkway, but the sudden image of Dorcas' shaking shoulders made him start up.

"Hans!" he shouted.

Through the glass he could see his chauffeur's head turn in alarm, and the big car came to a quick stop by the side of the road. The sound of the traffic passing on their left increased to a roar. Hans was out of the car in a moment and had opened the back door.

"Sir? Are you ill?"

"Do I look ill?"

"Very pale, sir."

"It's nothing, but leave the glass down."

Hans rolled down the glass partition, and started the car. Back on the road Derrick felt better, knowing that he could now talk to Hans. He tried to doze, but once again he faced that vivid image. He clenched his fists.

"Hans!"

"Sir?"

"I had an argument with Mrs. Jesmond tonight. Did you hear us in the hall?"

"Oh, no, sir."

He was disappointed. He wanted to talk to Hans about it, but he could not bring himself to tell him. And certainly not to tell him how it had ended with every inch of poor Dorcas' big body quivering in anguished pain. Oh, no, no, he couldn't even tell himself! He couldn't! And then, like a relieving tide, came the sudden anguish in the chest, the stabbing, biting, clawing pain in which Dorcas' image was lost.

"Hans!" he gasped.

The car skidded as Hans looked back. But then he turned again to the wheel, and Derrick was jolted to one side as they swayed off the parkway onto a side road. "The hospital in Glen Cove is the nearest, sir," he shouted. "We can be there in six minutes!"

Before Derrick lost consciousness, he was able to reflect how astonishing it was that his untutored chauffeur should recognize so quickly the symptoms of a heart attack.

18

DERRICK: 1951

THE BALLROOM OF the Park Club, with its three huge, scarlet-draped French windows and its three narrow crystalball chandeliers, had always been the symbol to Derrick of Ida's idea of a party. There frivolity and enthusiasm could be policed by a staff selected by a council of wise women. There the very curtains, despite their misleading color, acted as chaperons. It had been the scene of celebration of the Hartleys' twenty-fifth wedding anniversary and of Dorcas' debutante party. And now, despite his son's protests that to have his wedding reception in the room where he had gone to dancing class would be to fox-trot into marriage over the parquet floor of a childhood preparation, there was Hugo, in grey and black, standing beside his bride before the center window and smiling, rather complacently, in his task of shaking four hundred hands.

Minerva had been responsible for it, Minerva, a recent member of the club, who had long visualized the Park ballroom as the setting for just such a scene. But, however appallingly magnificent she might have been in pink organdie and pink hair, holding up the long line as she shouted greetings and threw kisses and waved her brown arms, it was perfectly evident to Derrick, posted opposite the bridal couple in his wheelchair, that Ida was the central figure of the afternoon. For it was Ida's club; she had lunched there, almost daily for thirty years; she had served as secretary and treasurer and on every committee, and now a good tenth of the resident membership must have been numbered among the guests. And Ida, in the long gray which most became her, seemed slim and dignified beside Minerva, and serene in contrast to the white, gesticulating figure of a daughter-in-law already intoxicated with congratulation. Yes, it was Ida's day, and Derrick begrudged her none of it.

A wheelchair was the perfect vantage point from which to view the party. The gleam of its steel accessories and the presence of a nurse at his side—even more obviously a nurse in the flower print that she uneasily, if festively, wore—kept all but the closer friends and family away, and those who spoke to him did so briefly. Yet he felt well, better than he had in weeks. The damage to his arterial system might have been such that he would never be able to work or exercise again, but that blow, like hovering death, had been accepted. Now he would live, in a relaxed, cynical, observing twilight, as long as it was decreed. Instead of battling his way upstream, he would lie in a sunlit pool and be fed flies. It was all very boring, but it had come as little surprise. He had been warned by his doctor two years before, a warning which he had communicated to nobody and which, after due consideration, he had decided to ignore. He had gambled on a longer respite, but he had no regrets. They had been two good years. The alternative would have been something not too different from his present existence. What would it have gained him to have started earlier?

The room before him seemed full of Denisons. All of Ida's family had gathered for this wedding of cousins. Old Mrs. Willie Denison, the last surviving aunt and senior widow of Hartley and Dodge, now in her nineties, was making her slow progress past the receiving line, on Mark Jesmond's arm. Derrick smiled at the speed with which Mark had taken over the social duties of head of the firm. Behind the old lady were her son and grandson, also partners. Who could say that he had not repaid the Denisons for all they had given him? But of course they had known he would. They had known a good thing when they had seen it. They had made greater use of him, in truth, than he had ever made of them, and now that his use was over, they closed over him, like a softly flowing, remorseless river on whose gliding surface his washed rock had made its brief appearance. What else could a lone rock have expected?

But what fallacies, what nonsense! If he went on in this way he would end up as romantic as Ida and start borrowing historical novels from the addled medical female at his side. Who, after all, still owned the controlling shares of Hartley and Dodge? Whose voluntary act had it been to give that power of attorney to Ida? Could he not revoke it at will? Could he not pick up the dropped reins whenever he chose, even if the act of raising them should prove his last?

"Who is that wonderful old lady?" Miss Jonas exclaimed. "She must be what the newspapers call a grand dame."

"She's my wife's aunt, and she's going to live to be a hundred."

"Isn't that something!"

"It's something for a woman to do. They like such marathons. But not for a man. I thank the good Lord of bonds and shares and Wall Street panics that He has numbered my days."

"Oh, come now Mr. Hartley, you'll bury us all!"

"I may bury *you*, Miss Jonas, but only if I bore you to death first. Now please don't talk. I'm thinking."

Ida smiled at him across the room and he nodded back. He saw Alfreda nudge Hugo, and they both waved. It was wonderful how smoothly everybody got on now that Ida was in charge. In the hospital Dorcas and Mark had paid him brief but regular visits, and out of perfunctory conversation, seasoned with perfunctory smiles, they had managed to fling a slender but passable bridge over what had first seemed an unconnectible gap. Derrick had not had to be told that this was Ida's price. He had divined that the Jesmonds must have paid for Mark's senior partnership with their expressed good will to Mark's father-in-law. And would continue to pay. For Ida would never loosen the noose that her control of Derrick's interests had enabled her to cast over their necks. She had the tenacity of those who are late to act, the persistence of a benevolent Catherine de' Medici, called to power after years of neglect. There had been the matter of young Willie Denison's partnership and then the matter of pensioning certain old clerks whom she had considered insufficiently provided for. And there would be other matters, more and more, as time went on. Derrick chuckled at the thought of how slim a chance poor Mark would have of getting "Jesmond" into the firm name ahead of his own. He would be lucky if Ida did not oblige him to restore to the place of honor the "Tremain" which Derrick had deleted in 1924!

"Don't think too hard," Miss Jonas warned him. "It can be very tiring."

"How do you know?"

"Oh, Mr. Hartley, you're a scream! You really are!"

Mark, with a smile that was like a clean bandage on his wounded feelings, approached the wheelchair and began to talk in a loud voice of Hugo's gallery.

"My coronary has not affected my hearing, Mark. Please don't shout."

"I'm sorry, sir. I was just thinking, now that Hugo is president, why wouldn't it be a good thing to stake him to a new building? We might even reorganize his company and issue more stock. How would that be for a wedding present?"

"Is it your idea to give Hugo a wedding present or to make money out of the auction business?"

"Both, of course!"

"Well, it may be an excellent idea, but my doctor says I'm not to be troubled with decisions. You'll have to take it up with your mother-in-law."

Mark flushed and moved away, but Derrick was beyond caring. He had to have *some* fun in his wheelchair. Dorcas, the matron of honor, a stalwart pole of blue chiffon under a floppy hat, still clutching her bouquet, now walked across from the receiving line to take her husband's place. Was Ida sending them over, one by one, like sentries?

"How does Mark enjoy being senior partner?"

"It's too soon to tell. But I hope you haven't been asking *him* that."

"And why can't I ask my own son-in-law if he likes being head of my own firm?"

"Because he'll think you're being sarcastic. Which you would be."

Derrick was amused at her total predictability. "Suppose I happen to be in earnest?"

"Mark's *always* going to think you're sarcastic. The only thing you can do for him is leave him alone."

"Aren't those rather harsh words for an old father?"

"They might be. If the old father cared." Her pebbly tone suspended the brief truce that had started in the hospital, and Derrick reflected that it was the first time they had talked alone, without the presence of either Ida or Mark. "But what's the point of pretending now?"

He shrugged, smiling. "Because I'm an old wreck. A lonely old wreck."

"Pooh. I don't feel a bit sorry for you. You've done everything you've wanted in life. I'd settle for a fraction of what you've had."

"Oh, I've had a lot." He nodded. "I don't repine. But does that mean I can't have anything more? Suppose I'm greedy? Suppose I want to die surrounded by loving children and grandchildren?"

"Surely, Daddy, you're not going in for a spiritual rebirth, *too?*"

He followed her glance to the receiving line where Ida was being kissed by old Mr. Dodge. Ida was never gracious about being kissed. She was putting her hand now on the old man's shoulder as if to restrain the hidden beast in him. "If your mother can begin over again," he demanded, "why can't I?"

"Because she can't, really," Dorcas retorted fiercely. "She can't make a new woman of herself at her age, and it's ridiculous for her to try."

"That's your credo, isn't it, Dorcas? That we're all condemned to our initial positions. That we make our beds once and lie in them forever. But don't you see, that's exactly what your mother is challenging? She says it's never too late."

"But it is!"

"Is it?" Derrick was really enjoying himself now. "It seems to me that she's making vast strides. This wedding today is all her doing. And so is my beautiful state of resignation at my illness. She may even teach Mark how to relax. I wouldn't put it past her. But perhaps you wouldn't want him relaxed at the price of owing it to your mother?"

She looked at him angrily. "What a nasty thing to say!"

"Oh, come, Dorcas, let's not you and me pretend. You hug your bitterness, as I hug my selfishness. Your mother's the only one of the lot of us who has actually tried to step outside herself. What we are beholding is the rarest thing in the whole world—a naked exercise of will power."

"A naked exercise of domination! She's always wanted to rule the roost, and she jumped at the first opportunity. Which was your heart attack. She may have had to wait for years, but she was ready. God, was she ready!"

"If you're speaking of the firm, you forget it was I who gave her the proxies."

"Who else could you give them to? Who else could you trust? She saw it all coming, ages ago!"

"I wonder what her plans are for *you*, Dorcas. That will be amusing to watch."

"For me?"

"Yes. If your mother has decided to make us all happy, surely, she won't leave *you* out. Seeing how she goes about that job should almost compensate me for my enforced inactivity."

"I think Mummy will have the good sense to leave me alone."

"Why? You obviously think she's making a fool of herself. Don't people who do that always go on to make greater and greater fools of themselves? Oh, it should be glorious to watch!"

"You only say that, Daddy, to get my goat."

"And only because your goat is so easy to get." The incipient tears in her eyes provoked him. "Don't be so gullible, Dorcas. And *now* see what you've done! You've brought your mother to the rescue." Ida, indeed, was already headed in their direction. "Like a great general, she can spot dissension on her flank from the very heart of the fray."

Dorcas shook her head impatiently and walked off quickly as her mother came up.

"It's all right, my dear," Derrick said cheerfully, "we had only the briefest pass. I believe I pinked her."

Ida sat down in the chair beside him, her eyes watching Hugo and Alfreda who were being photographed. "It's very naughty of you. She's trying so hard to be good."

"I know. But you must remember how limited my diversions are."

"Alas, poor dear, I do."

"No, it's not poor dear. I really have no business being as happy as I am. I've been a shocking egotist for six and a half decades."

"We're all shocking egotists."

"That's what Dorcas thinks. She believes that you've taken my place, that's all. And that you've waited all your married life to do it."

Ida's smile was speculative. She turned her attention momentarily from the bride and groom. "What do *you* think?"

"Oh, I think differently. I think you're realizing the destiny that you elected as a child. I think you've become Aunt Dagmar at last."

"But I don't do things easily as Aunt Dagmar and Mother did. And the easiness is the whole point. Without that one is simply bossy and officious."

"Ah, but you see, their easiness was just your invention. The Denisons themselves were your invention. And you were very careful, being a guilt-ridden child, to invent an ideal that you could emulate but never approach. The Denisons, in your definition, were a crazy patchwork of inconsistencies. They had to be gay and lighthearted, even when they were being pure and dutiful. They had to be fearless, even when they were cautious. They had to be gallant and wear rubber boots in the house. They had to be endowed with all your terrors and yet never suffer from them. You made up the Denisons to prove to yourself that you were alone in the world!"

But Ida, apparently, could take anything now. Her smile deepened. "And why did I marry *you*?"

"To justify Geraldine's sacrifice."

"In giving you up? Was it so great?" She laughed cheerfully. "How little you still know of women! But, tell me, if all this was so, why have I changed? For I gather I *have* changed?"

"Because Geraldine's death exploded the myth of the Denisons. You saw the shabby reality."

"I saw Geraldine's shabby reality," she agreed quickly, "but then I always had. Geraldine was not typical of the family." For just a moment she brooded. "Oh, no, surely, she wasn't!"

He had gone too far, even in an invalid's game. "She had her share of the mythical qualities. Of the good ones, too, I mean. There's something I've never told you. It was she who broke off our affair. When she found I was never going to ask you for a divorce."

She looked at him in grave astonishment. "Is that a thing to discuss at Hugo's wedding?" But curiosity was too much for her, even then. "Do you imply it's a thing I should be *grateful* to Geraldine for?"

"No. But to her it was a matter of honor. She wouldn't be a kept woman. She was Denison enough for that."

Ida's laugh this time had a touch of the frantic. "Surely, our old Denison honor was something more than that!" Her eyes became softer, as she reflected. "Still, I see what you mean. Maybe it was something, after all. Poor, distracted Geraldine. Maybe she, too, tried. Or is that, too, my myth?"

"Your reality, my dear, is much finer than your myth ever was. If your mother and aunt could see you now, they would see that you had made something very beautiful out of the pieces and patches that they left you with."

"Beautiful pieces and beautiful patches," Ida replied, with tears now in her eyes. "And look at the crazy quilt I've made out of them! Oh, Derrick, you're a very good sport. Would Geraldine have made you happy?"

"Never! No woman could have done that. I sometimes think no woman could have lived with me but you."

She took his hand. "Can I build on that? Or would Mother have called that a 'sloppy' question?"

"You? You can build on anything!"

They looked up at the sound of many feet and saw Hugo and Alfreda coming across the ballroom to them followed by the wedding party. Alfreda, as they drew near, hurried ahead and threw her arms around her father-in-law.

"You poor, dear old darling, sitting there so patiently! We're going to cut the cake now, but I had to come over and give you a great big hug first!"

Derrick wondered, encompassed in white satin and lace, if the glaze of Alfreda's good manners would be the icing on Ida's cake. Why not? What was the harm of icing?

"Hugo," he heard Ida's voice, "wheel your father's chair into the other room so he can see!"

And as Hugo, his bride clinging to his arm, slowly wheeled the chair across the floor, the whole reception burst into applause. Derrick smiled to his left and right, like a sovereign in a carriage. It was the least he could do for the woman who was going to take care of him for the rest of his life. Even at the end, he was getting things cheap.